WHAT THE CAT SAW

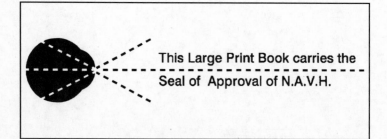

This Large Print Book carries the
Seal of Approval of N.A.V.H.

WHAT THE CAT SAW

CAROLYN HART

THORNDIKE PRESS
A part of Gale, Cengage Learning

Peabody Public Library
Columbia City, IN

Detroit • New York • San Francisco • New Haven, Conn • Waterville, Maine • London

GALE
CENGAGE Learning®

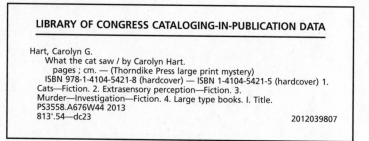

LIBRARY OF CONGRESS CATALOGING-IN-PUBLICATION DATA

Hart, Carolyn G.
  What the cat saw / by Carolyn Hart.
    pages ; cm. — (Thorndike Press large print mystery)
    ISBN 978-1-4104-5421-8 (hardcover) — ISBN 1-4104-5421-5 (hardcover) 1.
  Cats—Fiction. 2. Extrasensory perception—Fiction. 3.
  Murder—Investigation—Fiction. 4. Large type books. I. Title.
  PS3558.A676W44 2013
  813'.54—dc23   2012039807

Published in 2013 by arrangement with The Berkley Publishing Group, a member of Penguin Group (USA) Inc.

Printed in the United States of America
1 2 3 4 5 6 7 17 16 15 14 13

To Trent and Adrienne with love,
always.

1

On the upside, the airport was small. On the downside, a blustery wind took Nela Farley's breath away as she stepped out of the terminal, pulling her small wheeled bag. She shivered in her light coat. She'd expected cold temperatures, but she'd not expected a wind that buffeted her like a hurried shopper in a crowded mall. She'd also known she wouldn't be met. Still, arriving in a strange place without anyone to greet her was a reminder that she was alone.

Alone . . .

She walked faster, hurried across the double drive to a parking garage. Chloe's call this morning had been even more fragmented than usual. ". . . on the fourth level, slot A forty-two. Leland's car is an old VW, I mean really old. Pink stripes. You can't miss it."

In the parking garage elevator, Nela opened her purse and found the keys that

7

had arrived by overnight FedEx from her sister. They dangled from what seemed to be a rabbit's foot. Nela held it gingerly. In the dusky garage, she followed numbers, chilled by the wind whistling and moaning through the concrete interior.

She spotted Leland's VW with no difficulty. Why pink stripes? The decals in the rear window would have been distinctive enough. In turn, they featured a mustachioed cowboy in an orange cowboy hat and orange chaps with *OSU* down one leg, a huge openmouthed bass fish, a long-eared dog with the caption, *My Best Friend Is a Coonhound,* and a gleaming Harley with the caption, *Redneck at the Ready.*

Nela unlocked the driver's door. Soon she would be off on an Oklahoma adventure, all because Chloe had roared off one sunny California day on the back of her new boyfriend's Harley, destination the red dirt state. Plus, Nela had lost her job on a small SoCal daily and was free to answer Chloe's call that she come to Craddock, Oklahoma.

Nela was both irritated with her sister — one more call for a rescue, this time to protect her job — and grateful to have somewhere to go, something to fill leaden days. As for Chloe's job, she would have been pleased if she'd had an inkling of what

8

to expect, but in her usual fashion, Chloe had spoken of her job only peripherally.

Nela expected she'd manage. It definitely would be different to be in Oklahoma. Everything was going to be new, including subbing at Chloe's job, whatever it was. Knowing Chloe, the job could be raising guppies or painting plastic plates or transcribing medical records. Only Chloe could hold a job for several months and, despite hour-long sisterly confabs on their cells, always be vague about where she worked or what she did. Nela had a hazy idea she worked in an office of some kind. On the phone, Chloe was more interested in talking about what she and Leland had done or were going to do. *The wind blows all the time, but it's kind of fun . . . Hamburger Heaven really is . . . There's a farm with llamas . . . went to see the Heavener Runestone . . .* However, she'd promised to leave a packet full of "stuff" on the front passenger seat.

Nela popped her suitcase in the backseat. She breathed a sigh of relief as she slid behind the wheel. Indeed, there was a folder and on it she saw her sister's familiar scrawl: *Everything You Need to Know.* Nestled next to the folder was a golden box — oh, she shouldn't have spent that much money — of Godiva. A sticky note read: *Road treats.*

Confetti dangled from the rearview mirror. Taped to the wheel was a card. She pulled the card free, opened the envelope. The card showed an old-fashioned derrick spewing oil. She opened it. Chloe had written: *I gush for you. Nela, you're a life saver. Thanks and hugs and kisses — Love — Chloe*

Nela's brief irritation subsided. She smiled. She wished her little — though so much taller — sister was here and she could give her a hug, look into those cornflower blue eyes, and be sure everything was right in Chloe's world. So long as she could, Nela knew she would gladly come when her sister called.

She picked up the folder, opened it to find a garage parking ticket, a letter, and a map with directions to I-35.

. . . turn south. It's an hour and a half drive to Craddock. They say Hiram Craddock, a rail gang supervisor for the Santa Fe railroad, took a horseback ride one Sunday in 1887 and saw a cloud of butterflies stopped by the river. When the tracks were laid, he quit his job to stay and build the first shack in what later became Craddock. This fall when the monarchs came through, I loved thinking about him seeing them and saying, This is beautiful, I'll stay

here. He married a Chickasaw woman. That was real common for white men who wanted to be able to stay in the Chickasaw Nation. He opened a trading post. Anyway, I don't know if I explained about staying at Miss Grant's apartment after she died. I did it as a favor and I know you won't mind. It's because of Jugs. You'll love him. In case your plane's delayed, there's plenty of food and water, but the last I checked, your flights were on time. Anyway, it's sad about Miss Grant but I didn't mind helping out. Nobody knows you're coming in today and I didn't take time to explain but I left a note and said Jugs was taken care of. But they do expect you Monday morning and there are directions in the folder. The key with the pink ribbon is to Miss Grant's place. Oh, I left my car coat in the backseat. I won't need a coat in Tahiti! There's a pizza in the fridge. Anchovies, of course, for you. (Shudder.) When you get to Craddock . . .

Nela scanned the rest of the disjointed message, obviously written in haste. But Chloe could have a day or a week or a month at her disposal and her communications would still career from thought to fact to remembrance to irrelevance. Nela retrieved Chloe's map and the ribbon-tagged key. She placed the map on the passenger seat and dropped the key into her purse.

Nela drove out of the garage into a brilliant day. She squinted against a sun that was surely stronger than in LA. Whatever happened, she intended to have fun, leaving behind the grayness now that was LA, and the sadness.

Bill wouldn't want her to be sad.

Occasional winter-bare trees dotted softly rolling dun-colored countryside. Nela passed several horse farms. Cattle huddled with their backs to the north wind. The usual tacky billboards dotted the roadside. Nela felt more and more relaxed. The little VW chugged sturdily south despite its age. The traffic was fairly heavy and it was nearer two hours when she turned onto the exit to Craddock. After checking the map, she drove east into town, passing red-brick shops, several banks, and a library, and glancing at Chloe's directions, turned off again to the south on Cimarron. Ranch-style houses predominated. After a few blocks, the homes grew more substantial, the lots larger, the houses now two and three stories, including faux colonials, Mediterranean villas, and French mansards.

Nela noted house numbers. She was getting close. She came around a curve. Her eyes widened at a majestic home high on a ridge, a Georgian mansion built of limestone with no houses visible on either side, the grounds stretching to woods. Nela slowed. Surely not . . . Chloe had clearly written of a garage apartment.

Nela stopped at stone pillars that marked the entrance and scrabbled through Chloe's notes.

. . . so funny . . . I use the tradesman's entrance. Keep going past the main drive around a curve to a blacktop road into the woods. It dead ends behind the house. That's where the old garage is and Miss Grant's apartment. It's kind of prehistoric. You'll see the newer garages, much bigger, but they kept the old one. It isn't like Miss Grant rented it. People like Blythe Webster don't have renters. Miss Grant started living there when she first came to work for Harris Webster. He was Blythe's father and he made a fortune in oil. That's the money that funds everything. She went from being his personal assistant to helping run the whole deal. Now that she's gone, I imagine they'll close up the apartment, maybe use it for storage. Anyway,

it's a lot more comfortable than Leland's trailer so it's great that someone needs to be with Jugs. Be sure and park in the garage. Miss Webster had a fit about the VW, didn't want it visible from the terrace. No opener or anything, just pull up the door. It's kind of like being the crazy aunt in the attic, nobody's supposed to know the VW's there. It offends Miss Webster's "sensibilities." I'll bet she didn't tell Miss Grant where to park! Anyway the Bug fits in next to Miss Grant's Mercedes. Big contrast. The apartment's way cool. Like I said, nicer than a trailer, but I'd take a trailer with Leland anytime. So everything always works out for the best. I mean, except for Miss Grant.

Even with the disclaimer, the message reflected Chloe's unquenchable cheer.

Nela pressed the accelerator. Names bounced in her mind like errant Ping-Pong balls . . . Grant, Webster, Jugs . . . as she chugged onto the winding road. If delivery trucks actually came this way, their roofs would scrape low-hanging tree limbs. In the second decade of the twenty-first century, Nela felt sure that FedEx, UPS, and any other delivery service would swing through the stone pillars into the main drive. Trades-

14

men entrances had gone the way of horse-drawn buggies, milk bottles, and typewriters.

As the lane curved out of the woods, she gazed at the back of the magnificent house. A rose garden that would be spectacular in summer spread beneath steps leading up to a paved terrace. Lights blazed from huge windows, emphasizing the gathering winter darkness that leached light and color from the dormant garden. Lights also gleamed from lantern-topped stone pillars near the massive garages Chloe had described as new. Almost lost in the gloom was an old wooden two-door garage with a second-floor apartment. The windows were dark.

Nela coasted to a stop. She put the car in park but left the motor running while she pulled up the garage door. The Bug fit with room to spare next to the Mercedes coupe. She glanced at the elegant car as she retrieved her suitcase. Very sporty. It would be interesting to see Miss Grant's apartment. It would be odd to stay in the apartment of a woman whom she'd never met. But ten days would speed past.

And then?

Nela shook away any thought of the future. For now, she was hungry and looking forward to pizza with anchovies and taking sanctuary in a dead woman's home. *Miss Grant, wherever you are, thank you.*

She didn't take time to put on Chloe's coat, which surely would hang to her knees. She stepped out of the garage and lowered the overhead door. Pulling her suitcase, carrying Chloe's coat over one arm, she hurried to the wooden stairs, the sharp wind ruffling her hair, penetrating her thin cotton blouse and slacks.

On the landing, she fumbled in her purse until she found the ribbon-tagged key, unlocked the door. Stepping inside, she flicked a switch. She was pleasantly surprised. Despite January gloom beyond the windows, the room was crisp and bright, lemon-painted walls with an undertone of orange, vivid Rothko matted prints, blond Danish modern furniture, the sofa and chairs upholstered with peonies splashed against a pale purple background. A waist-high blond wood bookcase extended several feet into the room to the right of the door.

Her gaze stopped at car keys lying there next to a Coach bag. Had the purse belonged to Miss Grant? Certainly Chloe had never owned a Coach bag and, if she had, she wouldn't have left it carelessly in an empty apartment. Nela shrugged away the presence of the purse. The contents of the

16

apartment were none of her business.

As for Miss Grant, she wasn't the person Nela had imagined. When Chloe wrote, *Too bad about Miss Grant,* Nela knew she'd been guilty of stereotyping. Miss Grant was dead so she was old. Until she'd read Chloe's note, Nela had pictured a plump elderly woman, perhaps with white curls and a sweet smile. This apartment had not belonged to an old woman.

So much for preconceived ideas. Nela closed the door behind her. She set the suitcase down and turned to explore the rest of the apartment. She took two steps, then, breath gone, pulse pounding, stared across the room. She reached out to grip the back of a chair, willing herself to stay upright. She began to tremble, defenses gone, memory flooding, not hot, but cold and dark and drear.

The cat's huge round eyes seemed to grow larger and larger.

Lost in the intensity of the cat's gaze, she was no longer in a strange apartment half a continent from home. Instead, numb and aching, she was at Bill's house with Bill's mother, face etched in pain, eyes red-rimmed, and his sobbing sisters and all of his huge and happy family, which had gathered in sorrow. Bill's brother Mike spoke in a dull monotone: *He was on patrol . . . stepped on an IED . . .*

Unbearable images had burned inside. She had turned away, dropped into a chair in the corner of the room. Bill's cat was lying on the piano bench, looking at her. Splotches of white marked Big Man's round black face.

Big Man stared with mesmerizing green eyes. "*. . . He's gone . . . dead . . . yesterday . . . legs blown away . . . blood splashing . . .*"

Through the next frozen week, Big Man's thoughts recurred like the drumbeat of a dirge. But, of course, they were her thoughts, too hideous to face and so they came to her reflected from the cat Bill loved.

The next week an emaciated feral cat confronted her in the alley behind the apartment house. Gaunt, ribs showing, the cat whirled toward her, threat in every tense line. She looked into pale yellow eyes. "*. . . starving . . . That's my rat . . . Get out of my way . . .*"

Rat? She'd jerked around and seen a flash of gray fur near the Dumpster. Back in her apartment, she'd tried to quell her quick breaths. Her mind had been jumbled, that's all. She'd seen a desperate cat and known there was garbage and of course there might be rats. She had not read the cat's thoughts.

Of course she hadn't.

Like calendar dates circled in red, she remembered other episodes. At the beauty shop, a cuddly white cat turned sea blue eyes toward her. ". . . *The woman in the third chair's afraid . . . The redhead is mean . . . The skinny woman's smile is a lie . . .*" At a beach taco stand, a rangy black tom with a white-tipped tail and a cool, pale gaze. ". . . *rank beef . . . People want the baggies from the blue cooler . . . afraid of police . . .*" On a neighbor's front porch swing, an imperious Persian with a malevolent face. ". . . *I'm the queen . . . I saw the suitcase . . . If she boards me, she'll be sorry . . .*"

Now, a few feet away from her, a lean brown tabby with distinctive black stripes and oversize ears stood in a circle of light from an overhead spot — of course the cat chose that spot seeking warmth from the bulb — and gazed at Nela with mournful eyes. ". . . *Dead . . . Dead and gone . . . She loved me . . . board rolled on the second step . . .*"

Nela fought a prickle of hysteria. She was tired. Maybe she was crazy. Boards didn't roll . . . Unless he meant a skateboard. Skateboards were rolling boards. Was that how a cat would describe a skateboard? Was she losing her mind? Cats and a board that rolled and skateboards. How weird to think of a skateboard on a step. She hadn't thought of skateboards in years. Bill had done the best ollies in the neighborhood. His legs were stocky and strong. The IED . . . Oh God. Maybe it was because the cat had such distinctive black stripes. Bill's skateboard had been shiny orange with black stripes. She had to corral her mind, make her thoughts orderly. No one saw what was in a cat's mind. She was making it up. From a board that rolled to skateboards. Maybe she needed to see a doctor. No. This would pass.

The cat gave a sharp chirp, walked across the parquet flooring.

She backed away, came up hard with her back against the front door.

The cat looked up. *". . . Hungry . . . Feed me . . . We're both sad . . ."*

With the beauty of movement peculiar to cats, he moved swiftly past her toward the kitchen.

We're both sad . . .

Nela looked after him. Slowly her frantic breathing eased. The cat — he had to be Jugs with ears like those — was not a threat. She was fighting to keep away memories that hurt. It made sense that she'd ascribe sadness to a cat with a dead mistress. Cats needed attention. Maybe he'd let her pet him. As for imagining his thoughts, her mind was playing a trick. Maybe she wasn't quite crazy. She struggled to remember the professor's droning voice in Psych 1. What had he said? Then she remembered. Displacement. That's what she was doing. Displacement. She clung to the word.

It took every fiber of her will but she quieted her quick breaths, moved with deliberation toward the kitchen. Food would help and the welcome distraction of finding her way about in a strange place.

Next to the refrigerator, she spotted a sheet of paper taped to a cabinet door. Chloe had printed, neatly for her:

Feed Jugs a.m. and p.m., one-half can and one full scoop dry food. Fresh water. He's a sweetie. He adored Marian. Of course I called her Miss Grant at the office. You remember Marlene Dietrich in a black pillbox in No Highway in the Sky? *That was Marian Grant, a cool blonde, always efficient, knew everybody and everything and scared everyone to death.*

Jugs stood on his back paws, scratched at

the cabinet door.

Now she was able to look at the cat without a sense of dread. They were fellow creatures, both of them hungry, both of them grieving. "All right, Jugs." As Nela gently opened the door, Jugs dropped to the floor and moved toward his bowl. She emptied a half can into a blue ceramic bowl with *Jugs* painted in white on one side. Nela placed the bowl on newspaper already spread on the floor. She added a scoop of chicken-flavored dry pellets to a yellow bowl with his name in blue. She poured fresh water in a white bowl.

Nela found, as promised, pizza in the fridge. In only a moment, thanks to the microwave, she settled at the kitchen table with two slices of hot crisp anchovy pizza, a small Caesar salad, and a glass of iced tea.

Jugs thumped onto the other end of the table. He made no move to come toward the food. Instead, he settled on his stomach, front paws flat on the table.

Nela studied him gravely as she ate. "You are obviously a privileged character. But you have very good manners. Did Miss Grant allow you to sit on the table when she ate?"

The cat blinked. "*. . . She was worried . . . She didn't know what to do . . .*"

Determinedly, Nela looked away. That was

22

the human condition. Worry about the rain. Worry about cancer. Worry about war. Worry about money. Worry about . . . The list could go on and on, big worries and little, everyone had them. Whatever worries had plagued Marian Grant, she was now beyond their reach. Nela felt puzzled. Chloe spoke of Miss Grant as if she'd seen her recently at the office but she'd made no mention of illness. If Marian Grant hadn't been old or sick, how had she died? Why had she been worried?

Nela finished the second slice. She'd do the dishes and look through the rest of Chloe's notes. Surely, tucked in somewhere, she'd left directions to her job and explained what she did.

Nela carried Chloe's folder into the living room. She looked around the room at colorful Rothko prints. Nela's gaze stopped at a bright red cat bed near the desk. Jugs was curved into a ball, one paw across his face, taking an after-dinner snooze. She was, of course, wide awake. It was almost ten here and darkness pressed against the windows, but her body was still on California time. Oh well, she was in no hurry. No one expected her to do anything until Monday morning.

No one would call who really mattered to

her. Not since Bill died . . .

Nela hurried to the chintz sofa, sank onto one end, opened the folder, looked at a haphazard pile of loose sheets. She began to read the handwritten notes, glad to push away remembrance.

. . . different world. You know, the rich. They really are different. If I had Blythe Webster's money, I'd go around the world. But I guess she's been there, done that. She's pretty nice. She just started spending a lot of time at the foundation last fall. Blythe's around forty, kind of stiff and prim. Think Olivia de Havilland . . .

Nela's stiff shoulders relaxed. It was almost as comforting as pulling up one of her grandmother's afghans. She and Chloe had grown up on old movies, the free ones on Turner Classic Movies.

. . . in The Heiress, *dark hair, one of those cameo-smooth faces, neat features, but something about her makes you remember her. It's probably all that money. You think? She's looked washed-out since Miss Grant died. I don't know if she can handle things by herself. Miss Grant's the one that made the place go.*

Nela felt a spurt of exasperation. What place, Chloe? Nela scanned more tidbits about people.

. . . Abby's soooo serious. I mean, you'd think Indian baskets were like religious relics. Sure, the mess was a shame but a basket's a basket. If she'd use a little makeup, she has gorgeous eyes, but with those sandy brows you kind of don't notice them. Of course, Miss Grant took everything seriously, too. Maybe that's why she ran four miles every morning. You'd think handing out money would be easy as pie. I could hand out money and not act like I had boulders on my shoulders. Anyway, everything's been kind of nuts since the fire alarm and the sprinklers. I was afraid Louise was going to have a stroke. Usually she's pretty nice. The director's kind of like James Stewart in The Shop Around the Corner. *When he walks by women, it's boobs up, butts tucked. They don't even realize they're doing it!!!*

Nela smiled at the triple exclamation points though she'd chide Chloe for her language. Or maybe not. Chloe was Chloe.

. . . He's tall and angular and has this bony

25

appealing face. I'm pretty sure I glimpsed lust even in the eyes of the T. People call Miss Webster the T because she's the trustee. Not to her face, of course. I wonder if the job description for director of the Haklo Foundation stipulated: Only handsome dudes need apply.

Nela seized on the clue: Haklo Foundation. A few sentences later, she hit pay dirt.

. . . It's a five-minute drive. Kind of quaint after LA. Hills and trees and cows and stuff. The foundation's a yellow stucco building with a red-tile roof. When you leave the apartment, turn right on Cimarron and keep going. You can't miss it. Leland's dad — his mom's dead — had me over to dinner when we got to Craddock. His dad had some connection to the foundation. He tried to get me a job there but they didn't need anybody. Louise told him if anything opened up, they'd be glad to have me. When Louise's assistant quit, I got the job. Louise is the top dog secretary. I was lucky there was an opening. She probably wouldn't have left except for the car fire. She shouldn't have left her car unlocked. I didn't know there was any place in the world where people didn't lock their cars. Of course, she wasn't in the car

26

when it happened and I think the founda-
tion got her a new car. At least that's what
Rosalind told me and she always knows
everything and she loves to talk. She's a
sweetheart. Anyway, I'll bet it was just
somebody raising hell, though Rosalind
thinks the point was to screw things up for
the T. She's kind of under fire from some
of the old hands because she's the one
that brought in the new director and has
made a bunch of changes. But I mean,
that's a pretty roundabout way. Anyway, I
got the job and Leland drops me off and
picks me up. How about that! Chauffeur
service and . . . Oh well, you get the
picture.

Nela's lips curved. In a perfect world,
she'd like to see Chloe walking down the
aisle with a regular guy, not hopping on the
back of a vagabond's Harley. On a positive
note, Leland had brought her to his hometown and introduced her to his father. As
usual, Nela wasn't clear what Leland did —
if anything — but Chloe always sounded
happy when she called. Besides — one of
Chloe's favorite words — her sister's boyfriends might have their quirks, from a
vegetarian chef to a treasure hunter, but so
far they'd all turned out to be nice men.

Otherwise, Nela would have been worried about a faraway jaunt to Tahiti with a guy Chloe had known only since last summer.

Nela closed the folder. Tomorrow she'd scout around, spot the foundation, do some grocery shopping.

A creak startled her.

She looked up in time to see a cat door flap fall as lean hindquarters and a tall black tail disappeared into darkness through the front door. So Jugs was an indoor-outdoor fellow. He'd had his nap and was ready to roam.

An in and out cat. That meant he went down the garage apartment stairs. That's how he would see if a board rolled on the second step . . . Nonsense. Boards didn't roll and that's all there was to it.

Except for skateboards.

"That's enough, Nela." She spoke aloud. That was enough, more than enough, of her odd and silly imaginings about the thoughts of cats. She forced herself to focus on what she felt was an improvement. She and Jugs were sharing space. That was definitely a step in the right direction. Thankfully, he'd remained aloof. Maybe the next time she looked at him, she'd be able to discipline her mind. Maybe his presence would help prove she had nothing to fear from cats.

Maybe she'd finally be able to face what was in her mind, come to grips with grief.

Bill . . .

She pushed up from the couch, willing away memory. She walked swiftly to the bookcases that lined one wall, looked at titles to try to force other thoughts into her mind. It hurt too much to think of Bill and their plans that ended in blood and death. The phone rang.

Startled, Nela turned. After a moment's hesitation, she walked swiftly to the cream-colored phone on the desk near the book-shelves. "Hello." Her answer was tentative.

"Nela, you're there! How's everything? Did you find the pizza? Isn't Jugs a honey-bunch?"

Nela had felt so alone when she arrived. Hearing Chloe's husky voice was like a welcoming hug. "He's great. I'm great. How about you and Leland?"

"Oooooh." It was halfway between a squeal and a coo. "You can't believe how gorgeous everything is. We had to catch a red-eye to get to LA in time for our flight but we made it. We just checked in and we're leaving to ride an outrigger. Doesn't that sound like fun? He's already downstairs so I better scoot. Thanks, Nela. You're the best."

Nela shook her head as she replaced the receiver in the cradle. Talking to Chloe was like trying to catch a shooting star. None of her questions were answered: What was the job? Exactly where was it? What happened to Miss Grant? Perhaps she should follow Chloe's example and let the good times roll. In Chloe's world, everything seemed to work out. Nela smiled. *Have fun, sweetie. Be happy. Love him because . . .*

Again there were images to block, pain to forestall. She swung again to the bookshelves. She'd find a weighty tome, read until she felt sleepy. Midway through the first shelf, she pulled out a large picture book and carried it to the sofa. The cover photograph featured a marble statue of a tall, lean man. Even in cold stone, the hard-ridged face compelled attention. Deep-set eyes, a beaked nose, and jutting chin proclaimed power, strength, and ruthless determination. Behind the statue rose wide steps leading to a pale yellow stucco building. The title was in red Gothic letters: *The Haklo Foundation, the Story of Harris Webster and the Fortune He Shared.*

She thumbed through the beautifully crafted book. No expense had been spared in its production. She turned back to the introduction. Harris Webster was the descendant of an early Craddock family. Caleb Webster arrived in the Chickasaw Nation in 1885. After his marriage to Mary Castle, a member of the Chickasaw Nation, he began to prosper. He wrangled horses for her father, later opened an early dry goods store, apparently on very thin credit. He prospered, added a livery stable, and established a bank. His son, Lewis, increased the family's wealth with a cattle ranch. The Websters were one of Craddock's leading families, but the great wealth came from Caleb's grandson, Harris, a hugely successful wildcatter in the 1950s and '60s. He sold Webster Exploration to Exxon for one hundred million dollars in 1988. Harris Webster married Ellen White in 1970. Their first child died at birth. A daughter, Blythe, was born in 1973, and a second daughter, Grace, in 1985. Ellen died in 1987 from cancer.

Webster set up a trust, establishing the foundation in 1989 with an endowment of fifty million dollars. He served as the sole trustee until his death in 2007. His designated successor as sole trustee was his oldest daughter, Blythe.

The following facing pages featured portraits in oval frames. Caleb Webster's blunt, square-jawed face looked young and appealing, the black-and-white photo likely taken when he was in his late twenties. His hair was parted in the middle, his collar high and stiff. Mary Castle's dark hair was drawn back in a bun, emphasizing the severity of her features: the deep-set eyes, high-bridged nose and high cheekbones, thin lips pursed. She had looked gravely into the camera with a questioning gaze. The rest of the portraits were in color. Lewis Webster was dark-haired and narrow-faced with a strong chin. A merry smile curved the lips of his round-faced, blond wife, Lillian.

Harris Webster's color portrait, taken possibly when he was in his forties, exuded vigor and strength. Unlike the other photographs, he was pictured outdoors against a leafy background, a breeze ruffling thick black curls. Bronze skin suggested hours spent under the sun. His brown eyes stared confidently into the camera. His smile was that of a man who met any challenge with complete expectation of victory. His pale blond wife Ellen appeared fragile. Her expression was pensive, a woman turned inward.

The portraits of the Webster daughters hung side by side, affording an interesting contrast. Blythe Webster looked intelligent, imperious, and reserved. Ebony hair framed an oval face with a pleasant, though aloof, expression. The straight, unwavering stare of her dark brown eyes hinted at unknown depths. Her much younger sister Grace was blue-eyed with a fair complexion. Strawberry blond hair cascaded in thick curls. Her smile was amused, possibly wry, but there was something in the cast of her face which suggested a will that would not bend.

Nela bunched a pillow behind her and began to read.

2

Fasten seat belt sign . . . nattering shrill voices behind her . . . rain like tears . . . cat's eyes . . . alone, alone, alone . . .

Nela moved restlessly, swimming up from the depths of sleep. She'd tossed and turned for hours before drifting into fitful slumber. Her eyes opened. She stared at unfamiliar shadows, felt the strangeness of the bed. She blinked at the luminous dial of the bedside clock. Almost half past one. One in the morning. In a dead woman's apartment.

She'd chosen a guest room. There was no way she would use Miss Grant's bedroom where a red silk robe lay across the arm of the empire sofa. Had Miss Grant dropped the robe there with no thought that there would not be time ever again to straighten the room?

Nela had firmly shut the door to the guest bedroom in case Jugs was accustomed to sharing a bed, though surely when he came back inside he would seek out Miss Grant's room.

A splintering crash sounded from the living room.

Nela jerked upright, heart pounding. Had the cat knocked something over? But cats were agile, moving silently through time and space.

A heavy thud.

Nela swung her legs over the bedside. A line of light shone beneath the closed bedroom door. She had turned off the living room light before she came into the bedroom. Someone had turned on that light. Someone was in the apartment.

Fully awake now, adrenaline charged her mind and body. In one swift movement, she was on her feet and moving across the floor. An uncle who was an LA cop had drilled into his young nieces: React. Move. Don't freeze. Fight. Scream. Yell. Run.

Nela's mind closed in on the first necessity. Lock the door. Set up a barrier. Don't make it easy.

More crashes.

Nela reached the door. Her hands touched cold wood. The door panel was smooth. Guest rooms did not come equipped with dead-bolts. She slipped her hand down, found the knob, pushed the button lock.

Now for her cell . . . Her purse was on the dresser. She turned, moved through the velvety darkness, hands outstretched. She tried to judge where she'd left her suitcase. She veered a little, but one knee caught the case. Losing her balance, she tumbled forward. Scrambling up, she thudded into the chest, but her purse was there. She yanked out the cell phone, opened it. As the cell phone glowed, she punched 911.

Not a breath of sound came from beyond the closed door but she sensed menace. She felt threatened not only by the alien presence in the living room, but the darkness that surrounded her. She hurried to the wall and turned on the overhead light, welcoming the brightness.

A brisk voice. "Craddock nine-one-one. What is your emergency?"

"Someone's broken in." Her voice was shaky but forceful. "Send the police."

"Ma'am, please speak louder. Where are you?"

"Oh God, I don't know the address. I'm in a garage apartment behind a big mansion on Cimarron." She scrambled to remember. "The Webster house on Cimarron. Blythe Webster. Behind the house there's a garage apartment. Call the Craddock police. I need —"

The doorknob rattled.

Nela backed away. "I'm in a bedroom. Someone's trying to get inside. Send help." *Fight. Scream. Yell.* She lowered the cell, shouted, "The police are coming. They're on their way."

"Ma'am, try to be calm. We need the address."

"The garage apartment behind the Webster house on Cimarron." Again, she held the phone away, yelled, "The police are coming."

In the background behind the responder's calm tone, she heard a male voice. "Ten-sixty-seven. Ten-seventy. Possible four-fifty-nine."

"I have that, ma'am. Residence listed to Marian Grant." Her voice fainter, the responder spoke quickly, "Garage apartment One Willow Lane behind residence at Nine-thirteen Cimarron."

In the distance, a man's voice repeated her words. "Officers en route."

The woman's calm voice was loud and clear. "Help is on the way, ma'am. Can you describe the intruder?"

Beyond the door, there was a thud of running feet.

The responder continued to speak. "Officers will arrive in less than three minutes.

Tell the intruder help is on the way."

Nela's shouts hurt her throat. "The police are coming. They're coming."

She heard the slam of a door. She was breathless as she spoke to the responder. "I think he's leaving. Hurry. Please hurry."

The responder continued to speak calmly.

Nela held the phone but she scarcely listened. Finally, a siren wailed. Nela approached the bedroom door, leaned against the panel, drawing in deep gulps of air. More sirens shrieked.

A pounding on the front door. "Police. Open up. Police."

In the bedroom, Nela took time to grab a heavy silver-backed hand mirror from the dresser, then turned the knob. She plunged into the living room, makeshift weapon raised high, ready to dart and squirm.

She moved fast, focused on the door. She turned the lock, yanked open the front door.

Two policemen entered, guns in hand.

Nela backed up until she was hard against the wall. "He got away. I heard the door slam."

The older officer, eyes flicking around the room, spoke into a transmitter clipped to his collar. "Cars two and three. Search grounds for prowler." He nodded at his younger companion. "Cover me." He

38

glanced at Nela, his eyes cool. "Stay where you are, ma'am." With that warning, he moved warily across the room, alert, intent, ready for trouble.

Nela shivered, was suddenly aware of her cotton pj's. The night air was cold. As she turned to watch the officers, her eyes widened at the swath of destruction in the once cool and elegant room.

The officers moved fast. Doors banged against walls. They were in the kitchen. One of them muttered, "Nobody here. Window secure."

They moved back into the living room, oblivious to her. At the closed door to Miss Grant's bedroom, the lead officer shouted, "Police," flung back the door, stood to one side as he flipped on the light. There was silence in the bedroom. Cautiously, he edged inside, his backup advancing with him.

Outside, car doors slammed and men shouted. Cold night air swirled through the open front door.

Finally, the officers returned, guns put away. The tall man stopped in front of her, his face impassive, his hooded eyes moving around the room. "You hurt, ma'am?" His voice was gruff but kind. The younger officer closed the front door, but the room was already achingly cold.

"I'm fine." Maybe not fine. Maybe still a little breathless, pulse racing, but standing in the trashed room, she felt safe, safe and grateful for the quick response of the Craddock police.

"Check the living room windows, Pierce." The stocky officer began a circuit of the windows.

The officer in charge cleared his throat. "Ma'am, can you describe the intruder?" He looked into her face, his eyes probing.

Nela clasped her hands together. "I never saw him. I heard him. I was in the guest bedroom." She realized she was shaking with cold. "Please, let me get my jacket. It's right by the door." She moved fast and yanked Chloe's long car coat from a coat tree near the front door. She shrugged into it, knew she looked absurd in the big floppy coat, bare legs and feet sticking out below the hem.

When she turned back, the officer held a small electronic notepad in one hand. "Name?"

"Nela Farley. Actually, it's Cornelia, but I'm called Nela." With every moment that passed, she felt more assured.

"Cornelia Farley." He spelled the name as he swiped the keys. His questions came fast.

She answered, wishing she could be more help, knowing that all she had to report was noise.

Shouts and calls sounded outside. Officer Pierce made a slow circuit of the room, making notes.

The inquiring officer's nose wrinkled above a thin black mustache. "So you got here tonight. Anybody know you were here?"

"My sister."

He nodded. "I got it. You're in town to take her job. Anyone else know you're here?"

"They're expecting me at her office Monday."

"Do they know" — he was patient — "that you're staying here?" He jerked a thumb at the room.

"No." Chloe hadn't mentioned that Nela would be in Miss Grant's apartment.

The officer's gaze was intent. "You know anyone at the office?"

"Not a soul. I don't know anyone in Craddock."

"So, nobody came here because you're here." He surveyed the litter. The computer was lying on the floor. Drawers were pulled out and upended. Glass from a smashed mirror sparkled on the floor. The cracked mirror hung crookedly on a wall. "More than likely, somebody saw the death notice in the *Clarion* and thought the apartment was empty." He sounded satisfied. "Did the intruder make this mess?"

Nela nodded. "The noise woke me up."

"I'll bet it did. Wake anybody up." His tone was dry. "Looks like the perp got mad. Tossed that little statue and totaled the mirror. Maybe he didn't find cash. Or whatever he was looking for."

Nela, too, looked at the broken mirror. Lying on the floor was a crystal statuette of a horse that had been on the desk.

A woman's imperious voice rose above the hubbub outside. Footsteps rattled on the steps. "Of course I can go upstairs." The voice was rather high and thin and utterly confident. "The place belongs to me."

The front door opened.

Nela and her inquisitor — she noted his name tag: Officer T. B. Hansen — looked toward the open doorway.

A slender woman strode inside. Blue silk pajama legs were visible beneath a three-quarter-length mink coat. She wore running shoes.

She was followed by a middle-aged, red-headed patrol woman who gave Officer Hansen a worried look.

He made a slight hand gesture and the

42

officer looked relieved.

The newcomer held her fur coat folded over against her for warmth. Her black hair appeared disheveled from sleep, but her stare at the officer was wide awake and demanding. "What's going on here?"

Officer Hansen stood straighter. "Reports of a prowler, Miss Webster."

The woman's eyes widened in surprise. "Here?" She glanced around the room. "Who made this mess?"

The officer's tone was noncommittal. "The young lady said an intruder is responsible."

The woman stared at Nela with narrowed eyes. "Who are you?" Her tone was just this side of accusing.

Nela took a quick breath. "Nela Farley, Chloe's sister."

The woman raised one sleek dark eyebrow in inquiry. "You don't look like her."

"No." Nela glimpsed herself in the remnants of mirror. Not only did she not resemble her tall, willowy sister, she looked like a bedraggled waif, dark eyes huge in a pale face, slender bare legs poking from beneath the overlarge coat. "I'm five-four and dark haired. She's five-nine and blond."

Miss Webster asked sharply, "Did Chloe give you Marian's keys?"

Nela nodded. "She asked me to stay here and take care of Jugs. I flew in this afternoon and drove down. I arrived about six. I'm driving Chloe's boyfriend's VW. Chloe told me to park the VW in the garage."

"Oh." Miss Webster's tone was considering now, not hostile. "That car. God knows that monstrosity should be kept in a garage. Or driven into a lake." She sped a quick smile toward Nela. "Thanks for putting the VW in the garage. I didn't know you were staying here. I hadn't thought about it." Her tone was careless. Clearly, the habitation of employees was not her concern. "Louise told me the cat was taken care of. I didn't ask how." Also clearly, the care of a dead employee's animal was not her responsibility. These kinds of things were handled by others. "I suppose this is a convenient place to stay while you're visiting, and having you here puts off deciding what to do with the cat. We have to find him a home. Marian was crazy about that animal." She shook her head, looked abruptly sad. "I can't believe she's gone. And to have someone break in her home makes me furious. Did you see the burglar? I heard the sirens. By the time I reached a window, police were milling around with flashlights and yelling. I thought I was in the middle of a war zone."

44

Once again Nela told her story, climbing from the deep pit of sleep, bangs and crashes in the living room, hurrying to lock the bedroom door, calling for help, the turning of the knob, the arrival of the police.

Blythe Webster's eyes glinted with anger. "Someone must have read about Marian's death in the newspaper and come like a vulture to pick over her things. Look at this mess. I'm glad you were here. Who knows what might have happened to the rest of her things if you hadn't been here? It would be awful to think of a robber stealing from Marian. So everything's worked out for the best."

The echo of Chloe's favorite phrase was strangely disturbing to Nela. Was it all for the best that she'd known moments of dark fear?

Blythe must have sensed Nela's reaction. She turned over a hand in appeal. "Forgive me. It's dreadful that you have come to help us and run into something like this. Thank you for being here and calling for help. I don't know what we should do now." She looked at Officer Hansen in appeal. "What do you suggest?" Her gesture included the shattered mirror and the emptied drawers.

"Nothing for the moment. We'll send a tech tomorrow to see about prints. But I doubt we'll find anything helpful. Would you" — he directed his question to Blythe Webster — "know if anything is missing?"

"I have no idea about Marian's belongings. I guess they were looking for money." Her gaze settled on the Coach purse atop a bookcase near the front door. "That's Marian's purse. Why didn't a thief grab the purse?" She looked at Nela. "I guess he must have intended to take it but got scared when he heard you. He must have been shocked out of his pants when he realized someone was in the bedroom. Well, no harm done apparently, except for a bad introduction to Craddock for you." Her glance at Nela was sympathetic. "I'm sorry you've had such a rough welcome. We'll make it up to you. By the way, I'm Blythe Webster. I own all of this." She waved a casual hand. "Marian worked for me. I run the foundation. I'll be seeing you there." She turned toward the patrolman. "Send me a report." She moved to the door, looked back at the police officer, a faint frown on her face. "How did the thief get in?"

Hansen said carefully, "We haven't found evidence of a break-in." His hooded gaze settled on Nela. "When we arrived, the front door was locked. Ms. Farley opened the door for us."

Blythe Webster looked puzzled. "If nobody broke in and the door was locked, how did someone get in?"

Nela felt her face tighten. "I don't know." She didn't like the searching looks turned toward her. "Maybe someone had a key."

Blythe Webster's brown eyes narrowed. "I suppose somewhere up at the house we may have a key in case of an emergency. I'll ask my housekeeper. But I can't imagine that Marian passed out keys to her apartment. That would be very unlike her."

The officer turned to Nela. "Are you sure you locked the front door?"

"Positive."

He didn't appear impressed. He'd probably been told many things by many witnesses that turned out to be mistaken or false. "There was a real nice story in the *Clarion* about Miss Grant and a funeral notice. The intruder counted on the place being empty. Maybe he found the door unlocked."

Nela started to speak.

He forestalled her. "Or maybe he didn't. Maybe he jiggled a credit card, got lucky. It's an old door. Once inside, he locked the door to keep anyone from surprising him. When he heard you calling for help, he ran out and slammed the front door behind him." He glanced toward the door, gave a satisfied nod. "It's an old lock, one where the lock doesn't pop up when the inside handle is turned. Then it took only a minute to get down the stairs and disappear in the dark." He looked from Nela to Miss Webster. "Did either of you hear a car?"

Nela shook her head. Inside the apartment, she had been acutely aware of sounds from outside, waiting for the police to arrive. She hadn't heard anything until the sirens rose and fell.

Blythe Webster was dismissive. "I was asleep. The sirens woke me. But most cars don't make much noise these days."

Officer Pierce yanked a thumb toward the front door. "They haven't found any trace outside. It looks like he got clean away."

"Whoever came is long gone now." Blythe sounded relieved. She turned to Nela. "As soon as the police finish, you can lock up and feel quite safe. Can't she, Officer?"

Officer Hansen's face was studiously unexpressive. "You may be right, Miss Webster."

Officer Pierce, who had arrived with Hansen, spoke quickly. "Right. Once you scare 'em away, they won't come back."

The redheaded patrol woman, who had followed Blythe Webster inside, nodded in agreement.

"I locked the door." Nela was insistent.

Blythe Webster nodded. "You thought you did." Her tone was understanding. "Anyway, these things happen. I'm glad you're fine. I expect you're very tired. As for me, I'm ready for a nightcap . . . Oh, here's Jugs."

Nela distinctly remembered engaging the front-door lock. She would have objected again, continued to insist, but at the mention of the cat, she swung to look toward the doorway.

The big-eared brown tabby strolled past them, his gaze flicking around the room.

Nela looked into the cat's huge pupils, still dilated for night vision. *". . . Cars . . . strangers . . . like the day She died . . . lying on the concrete . . ."* The cat moved away, heading straight for the open door to Marian Grant's bedroom.

Blythe Webster's face abruptly tightened, cheekbones jutting. "Do you suppose he's hunting for Marian? I hate that." There was a quiver in her voice. "Anyway, now that everything's under control, I'll say good night." In a flurry, she was gone.

Nela scarcely heard the clatter as Blythe Webster hurried down the wooden steps. . . . *lying on the concrete . . .* There was a square of concrete to one side of the apartment stairs, possibly at one time intended for outdoor parking.

Officer Hansen adjusted his earpiece, spoke into the lapel transmitter. "Officer Hansen. Garage apartment behind Webster home. Possible intruder. No trace of perp. Search of living room apparent. Unknown if any valuables are missing. Alarm raised at one thirty-five a.m. by guest Cornelia Farley. She didn't see anyone but heard sounds in living room. Search of grounds yielded no suspects or witnesses." He stopped, listened. "Yes, sir. I'll do that, sir. Ten-four." He was brisk as he turned toward Nela.

She stood stiffly, watching as Jugs disappeared into Marian's bedroom.

"Ma'am —"

Nela felt a surge of irritation. Why did he call her ma'am? She wasn't an old lady. "I'm Nela."

His eyes flickered. "Ms. Farley" — his tone was bland — "a technician will arrive at nine a.m. tomorrow to fingerprint the desk and the front door and the materials on the floor. Sometimes we get lucky and pick up some prints. Usually, we don't. If you have any further trouble, call nine-one-one." He stared to turn away.

Nela spoke sharply. "I locked the door.

50

Someone had a key."

His pale brown eyes studied her. "The chances are the intruder knew Miss Grant was dead and thought the apartment was empty. Now it's obvious the place is occupied. I don't think you'll have any more trouble." He gestured toward the desk. "It looks like somebody was interested in the desk and not looking to bother you." He cleared his throat. "To be on the safe side, get a straight chair out of the kitchen, tilt it, and wedge the top rail under the knob. Anybody who pushes will force the back legs tight against the floor. Nobody will get in. Tomorrow you can pick up a chain lock at Walmart."

"That's good advice, ma'am." The red-headed policewoman was earnest. "I was in the first car the morning Miss Grant died. The housekeeper told me she ran up the steps to call from here because it was quicker. She didn't have a key. She used a playing card she always carries in her pocket. The seven of hearts. For luck." The officer raised her eyebrows, obviously amused at the superstition. "Anyway, she got inside. Like Officer Hansen said, it doesn't take much to jiggle these old locks. Not that it made any difference for Miss Grant that we got here quick."

"What happened to her?" Nela glimpsed Jugs in her peripheral vision.

The redheaded patrol woman was brisk. "She fell over the stair rail last Monday morning, straight down to the concrete. I was in the first car to arrive." The redheaded officer — Officer L. T. Baker — gestured toward the opening into darkness. "The housekeeper found her beside the stairs. It looked like Miss Grant tripped and went over the railing and pretty much landed on her head. Broken neck. Apparently she jogged early every morning. When we saw her, it was obvious she'd taken a header over the railing. Massive head wound. She must have laid there for a couple of hours."

Nela's eyes shifted to Jugs.

The cat's sea green eyes gazed at Nela. ". . . *They took Her away . . .*"

Paramedics came and found death and carried away a broken and bruised body. Nela didn't need to look at the woman's cat to know this.

"A header?" . . . *board rolled on the second step . . .* Nela felt a twist of foreboding. "Did you find what tripped her?"

Officer Baker shrugged. "Who knows? The stairs are steep. Accidents happen. She was wearing new running shoes. Maybe a toe of a shoe caught on a step."

No mention of a skateboard. "Did you find anything on the ground that could have caused her to fall?"

The policewoman waved a hand in dismissal. "These grounds are tidy. Not even a scrap of paper in a twenty-foot radius from the stairs."

"She probably started down the stairs too fast." Officer Hansen shook his head. "She was a hard charger. She always helped at the Kiwanis pancake suppers, made more pancakes than anybody. There were a bunch of stories in the paper. She was a big deal out at the foundation. Anybody looking for an easy way to make a buck would have known her place was empty." His look was earnest. "Craddock's a real nice place, Ms. Farley, but we got our no-goods like any other town. It seems pretty clear what we had here tonight was intent to rob. Now that the perp knows you're here, you should be fine." He gave a brief nod to officers Pierce and Baker and they moved through the doorway. He paused on the threshold long enough to gesture toward the kitchen. "Wedge that chair if you're nervous. I guarantee you'll be okay."

3

Jugs wrinkled his nose, cautiously sniffed the Walmart sack on the bookcase near the front door.

Nela inserted a nine-volt battery into a doorstop alarm. When shoved beneath the bottom of the door, the wedge prevented anyone from opening the door, with or without a key, plus any pressure activated an alarm. She didn't feel she could install a deadbolt in an apartment that, as Miss Webster had made clear, belonged to her.

Nela felt as though she'd been in the garage apartment for an eon with only the short foray to Walmart as a respite. She glanced around the living room, wished she found the decor as appealing as when she first arrived.

In her peripheral vision, she was aware of the shattered mirror. Slowly she turned her head to look at it fully. The crystal horse still lay among shards of glass. There was something wanton in that destruction. If she had the money, she'd move to a motel. But she didn't have enough cash to rent a room for a week. Besides, the cat needed to be cared for.

The blond desk held only a few traces of powder. The police technician, a talkative officer with bright brown eyes and a ready smile, had arrived punctually at nine a.m., fingerprinted the front doorknob inside and out, the desk, the scattered drawers, the tipped-over chair, the statuette. He cleaned up after himself. He'd kept up a nonstop chatter. He'd quickly identified Miss Grant's prints from a hairbrush in the master bath. "Lots of hers on the desk and some unidentified prints, but the drawer handles are smudged. Good old gloves. It takes a dumb perp to leave fingerprints. Usually we only find them at unpremed scenes." He'd departed still chatting. ". . . Not too many prowler calls . . . usually a bar fight on Saturday nights . . ."

Now she was left with the mess and her new defense against invasion.

Jugs batted at the sack. The plastic slid from the table and the muscular cat flowed to the floor. He used a twist of his paw to fling the bag in the air.

She ripped off the doorstop plastic cover

55

and threw it across the room, a better toy than a plastic sack.

Jugs crossed the floor in a flash, flicked the plastic, chased, jumped, rolled on his back to toss his play prey into the air, then gripped the plastic with both paws.

"Pity a mouse. Staying in shape until spring?"

Ignoring her, Jugs twisted to his feet and crouched, the tip of his tail flicking. After a final fling and pounce and flurry, Jugs strolled away, game done, honors his.

She stared after him as he moved toward the front door. Every time she saw him, she remembered that searing moment yesterday when their eyes had first met. She blurted out her thought while berating herself for what was rapidly becoming an obsession. "There wasn't a skateboard," she called after him. Her voice sounded loud in the quiet room. "They would have found a skateboard."

Her only answer was the clap of the flap as Jugs disappeared through the cat door.

Now she was talking out loud to a cat. Possibly he wondered what the weird-sounding syllables — skateboard — meant. More than likely his thoughts were now focused on a bird, a rustle in a bush, the scent of another cat.

Anyway, what difference did it make?

The difference between sanity and neuroses.

No matter what made her think of a skateboard, there was no connection between the vagrant thought, a pet cat, and the accidental death of a woman who moved fast.

Nela felt cheered. Monday she would go to the foundation, try to please Chloe's boss, and enjoy the not-exactly holiday but definite departure from her normal life. The normal life that an IED had transformed from quiet happiness to dull gray days that merged into each other without borders, without hope.

Nela looked down at the doorstop. There was no need to put the piece in place now. She shoved the doorstop into the corner between the door and the wall. So much for that. At least tonight she would feel safe.

She still felt unsettled by the knowledge that Marian Grant had fallen to her death. The police seemed competent. If there had been a skateboard in the vicinity of the body, the police would have found it. There hadn't been a skateboard — a board that rolled — on a step. Certainly not. But the image persisted.

She turned, walked restlessly across the

room, stopped and stared at the desk and the litter on the floor and the upended drawers. Why rifle a desk? Did people keep money in desks? Maybe.

However . . . She turned back toward the front door. Only two items lay atop the waist-high blond bookcase to the right as a visitor entered. A set of keys. A black leather Coach bag. Last night Blythe Webster said the purse belonged to Marian Grant.

When the intruder had turned on the living room's overhead light, he couldn't have missed seeing the expensive purse, especially if the purpose of entry was to steal. Wouldn't a petty thief grab the purse first? Maybe he had. Maybe he'd rifled the purse first, then searched the desk. They hadn't looked inside the purse last night. Wasn't that an oversight?

Nela stopped by the bookcase. She reached out for the purse, then drew her hand back. She hurried to the kitchen, fumbled beneath the sink, found a pair of orange rubber gloves, and yanked them on. She didn't stop to sort out her thoughts, but fingerprints loomed in her mind. She had no business looking in the purse, but she would feel reassured if there was no money, if a billfold and credit cards were gone.

Nela carried the purse to the kitchen table. She undid the catch. The interior of the purse was as austere and tidy as the apartment. She lifted out a quilted wallet in a bright red and orange pattern. It took only a moment to find a driver's license. She gazed at an unsmiling face, blond hair, piercing blue eyes: Marian Denise Grant. Birth date: November 16, 1965. Address: One Willow Lane. As Blythe had said, the purse belonged to Marian Grant, had likely rested atop the bookcase since she'd arrived home the night before she died.

Nela pulled apart the bill chamber. Two fifties, four twenties, a ten, three fives, seven ones. Four credit cards, one of them an American Express Platinum. She and Chloe always lived from paycheck to paycheck but, after she'd lost her writing job, she'd waited tables at an upscale restaurant in Beverly Hills and she remembered snatches of conversation over lunch at a producer's table, the advantages of this particular card, automatic hotel upgrades, delayed four p.m. checkout times, free access to all airline hospitality suites, and more.

An intruder could not have missed seeing the purse, but instead of rifling through the billfold, taking easy money, the intruder had walked on to the desk.

Nela placed the quilted billfold on the table. One by one, she lifted out the remaining contents: lip gloss, a silver compact, comb, small perfume atomizer, pill case, pencil flashlight, BlackBerry, Montblanc pen with the initials *MDG.*

Resting on the bottom of the purse was a neatly folded pair of women's red leather gloves. She almost returned the other contents, but, always thorough, she picked up the gloves. Her hand froze in the air. Lying in a heap at the bottom of the bag, hidden from view until now by the folded gloves, was a braided gold necklace inlaid with what looked like diamonds. Nela had a quick certainty that the stones were diamonds. They had a clarity and glitter that faux stones would lack.

Nela held up the necklace, felt its weight, admired the intricacies of the gold settings. A thief would have hit pay dirt if he'd grabbed the purse as he ran. She returned the objects to the interior compartments and carried the purse to the bookcase. She replaced the bag precisely where it had earlier rested.

And so?

There were lots of maybes. Maybe the thief planned to take the purse but her 911 call induced panic. Maybe the thief knew of something valuable in the desk. Maybe Marian Grant collected old stamps or coins. Maybe Marian Grant had a bundle of love letters the writer could not afford for anyone to see. Her mouth twisted. Maybe there was a formula for Kryptonite or a treasure map or nothing at all. Lots of maybes and none of them satisfactory.

The cat flap slapped.

Nela turned to face Jugs. He sauntered past her, beauty in motion, sinuous, graceful, silent.

"It's your fault that I'm worried." Her tone was accusing.

The cat flicked a glance over his shoulder. *". . . My territory . . . I showed him . . ."* He disappeared into the kitchen.

Nela wondered if he had vanquished a neighboring tom or if she was simply thinking what he might have done when outside. What difference did it make whether the thought was hers or Jugs?

A big difference.

Either the cat remembered a board that rolled on a step or she had dredged up a long-ago memory of a teenage Bill on a skateboard in happy, sunny days.

What if the cat was right? What if Marian Grant hadn't seen a skateboard on the step when she hurried out to jog early that January morning? The police surmised she'd caught a toe on a steep step, that she'd been going too fast. There had been no skateboard near the stairs when her body was discovered. But there could be reasons. Maybe some kid lived in that big house. Maybe the housekeeper saw the skateboard and either unthinkingly or perhaps quite deliberately removed it. Maybe the cat was thinking about some other skateboard on some other steps. Maybe the cat wasn't thinking a damn thing.

Moreover, a skateboard on the steps might explain why Marian Grant fell, but again so what? She fell because she caught her toe or slipped on a skateboard or simply took a misstep. Her death had been adjudged an accident. To think otherwise was absurd.

Then why did someone creep into the dead woman's apartment last night and search the desk?

This was the easiest answer of all. As Officer Henson said, every town had its no-goods and last night one of them had taken a chance on finding something valuable in a dead woman's apartment.

Still . . . Why the desk and not the purse?

The apartment was utterly quiet. She felt a light pressure on her leg. She looked down. Jugs twined around her leg, whisking the side of his face against her, staking claim to her. She reached down, paused to remove one rubber glove, and stroked his silky back.

His upright tail curved slightly forward. *". . . You're all right . . . I like you . . ."*

Nela felt a catch in her throat. "I like you, too."

The sound of her voice emphasized the silence surrounding them. There was no one to see them. With a decisive nod, she walked toward the door, retrieved the doorstop, pushed it beneath the door. Moving around the living room, she closed the blinds in the windows. She pulled back on the rubber glove and crossed to the desk.

She wasn't sure why she was wearing the gloves now. Maybe she had the instincts of a crook. After all, wasn't it reasonable for her to clean up the mess around the desk, make the room presentable again?

Although Nela was sure she was unobserved, she worked fast as she stacked papers. The cleanup turned out to be reasonably easy. In keeping with Chloe's judgment of Marian Grant as efficient, each folder had a neat tab and it soon became apparent that the drawers had been emptied but the papers had fallen not far from the appropriate folder and showed no signs of having been checked over.

Nela was looking for something to explain what drew an intruder past an expensive purse to this sleek desk. She started with the drawer emptied nearest the desk, turned it right side up. She restored Miss Grant's personal papers to the proper folder — insurance policies, a car title, medical records, bank and credit card statements, travel receipts, copies of tax submissions. Near the next drawer, she found clips of news stories about individuals, research programs, fellowships, and educational institutions. Each person or group featured had received a grant from the Haklo Foundation. She was getting good at her project and quickly placed clips in the correct folders. The second drawer slid into its place.

Doggedly, Nela continued until the floor was clear, the drawers replaced with the proper contents.

When she'd finished, she stared at the desk with a puzzled frown. She had a conviction that the searcher had emptied the drawers not to mess up the papers or even to check them, but to be sure there wasn't something hidden among the folders.

She looked across the room at the Coach bag. Instead of finding reassurance, she felt more uneasy. Had the searcher been hunting for that obviously expensive necklace? If so, why not look in the purse? Why the desk? But who knew what a thief thought or why?

Nela stripped off the rubber gloves, returned them to the kitchen. She found a broom closet, picked up a broom and dustpan. Soon the last of the broken mirror had been swept up and dumped into the trash container. Lips pressed firmly together, she carefully eased the frame with the remnants of the mirror from the hook on the wall. When she'd placed the frame inside Miss Grant's bedroom, she returned to the living room. She opened the blinds, welcoming bright shafts of winter sunlight.

Yet the apartment held no cheer. She had rarely felt so alone, so cut off from human contact. She wouldn't be around anyone until she went to Chloe's job Monday. The job . . . There probably wouldn't be anyone at the foundation on a Saturday but she could take a drive, find the way, make Monday morning easier. She grabbed her purse and Chloe's coat.

She was almost to the door when she paused. The Coach purse now seemed huge to her because she knew that it contained a large sum of cash and an obviously expensive necklace. She yanked wool gloves from Chloe's pockets. She put them on and picked up the Coach bag.

In the kitchen, she knelt by the cabinet that held Jugs's canned food. In only a moment, the purse rested snugly behind cans stacked four high. Maybe a thief would head unerringly for the cat food cabinet. But she felt better. Monday at work, she'd find out how to contact Marian Grant's sister and suggest that the purse, bank books, and other obvious valuables be removed from the apartment. She didn't have to admit she knew the purse's contents to suggest that it be put away for safekeeping.

She was considerably cheered as she stepped out on the high porch. The wind had died down. The day was cold, possibly in the thirties, but brilliant sunshine and a pale winter blue sky were exhilarating.

As she started down the steep steps, a streak of dark blue on the second baluster caught her gaze. She stopped and stared. An oblique line marred the white paint about sixteen inches above the step. The scrape on the wood indicated that something had struck the baluster, leaving an uneven mark on the paint.

Nela pictured early-morning darkness and a woman in a hurry, moving fast, not thinking about a familiar stairway. Likely her right foot would have come down on the first step, her left on the second. A skateboard could have flipped up to strike the baluster while flinging her sideways to tumble over the railing.

The police had searched the area and found nothing, certainly not a skateboard.

The streak looked new and fresh. Nela was abruptly irritated with herself. Since when was she an expert on a marred surface on a white post? Since never. The scrape might have been there for months.

She started down the steps. Carefully.

HAKLO FOUNDATION glittered in faux gold letters in an arch over stone pillars. Nela turned in. Leafless trees bordered well-kept grounds. Winter-bare branches seemed even more bleak in contrast to a green lawn of fescue. The velvety grass emphasized the Mediterranean glow of the two-story golden stucco building atop a ridge.

At the foundation entrance, an impressive portico covered shallow stone steps. The imposing statue of Harris Webster gazed into infinity at the base of the steps. The red tile roof made Nela feel homesick. There were so many Spanish colonial buildings in old LA. Even the ornate stonework on oversize windows seemed familiar, but there should have been palm trees, not leafless sycamores.

A discreet sign with an arrow pointed to the right: PARKING.

Obediently Nela turned right. She passed a line of evergreens. The short spur ended at a cross street. A sign to the right announced: GUEST PARKING. The guest parking lot was out of sight behind the evergreens. A sign to the left: STAFF ONLY.

She turned left. A wing extended the length of the drive. At the end of the building, she turned left again. A matching wing extended from the other side with a courtyard in between. Arched windows overlooked a courtyard garden with a tiled fountain, waterless in January. A cocktail reception could easily spill out into the courtyard in good weather. She glanced about but saw no parking areas. Once past the building, another discreet sign led to the staff parking lot, also screened by evergreens. Beyond the evergreens, a half dozen outbuildings likely provided either storage or housed maintenance. On the far side of sycamores that stood sentinel alongside the building, she glimpsed several rustic cabins.

She was a little surprised to see a car in the lot, a beige Camry. Nela turned into the parking area and chose the slot next to the

Camry. It would take only a minute to spot the entrance she should use Monday.

When she stepped out of the VW and closed the door, the sound seemed loud, the country silence oppressive. She wasn't accustomed to stillness. There was always noise in LA. She followed a covered walkway to the end of the near wing. The walk ended in a T. To her left was a doorway helpfully marked: STAFF ONLY. To the right, the sidewalk led past the sycamores to the cabins.

There were two keys on Chloe's key ring. One fit the VW. Nela assumed the other afforded entrance to the building. The key to Marian Grant's apartment had been separate, identifiable by a pink ribbon.

However, the foundation locks might be rigged so that any entrance outside of work hours triggered an alarm. As Nela hesitated, the heavy oak door opened.

A middle-aged woman with frizzy brown hair peered out. Pale brown eyes, magnified by wire-rim glasses perched on a bony nose, looked at her accusingly. "This is private property. The foundation is closed to the public until Monday. I heard a car and if you continue to trespass I will call the police."

Nela had no wish to deal further with law

69

enforcement personnel. She spoke quickly, embarrassed and uncomfortable. "I'm Chloe Farley's sister, Nela. Chloe gave me directions and I came by to be sure I knew the way on Monday."

"Oh." The brown eyes blinked rapidly. "I should have recognized you. Chloe has a picture on her bookcase. But so many things have happened and I'm here by myself. Oh dear. I hope you will forgive me. Please come in. I'm Louise Spear, the executive secretary. I'll show you around." She held the door wide. "That will make everything easier Monday. Do you have a key?"

As she stepped inside, Nela held up the key ring. "Is the bronze one the key to the staff entrance?"

Louise peered. "That's it. Did you intend to try it to be sure?"

Nela smiled. "No. I thought I could knock Monday morning if necessary. I was afraid to use the key after hours in case it triggered an alarm."

Louise shook her head. "Only broken windows sound an alarm. We can go in and out with a key at any time. The key works for all the outer doors." She closed the door.

Nela looked up a wide marbled hallway with office doors on one side and windowed alcoves overlooking the courtyard on the other. The marble flooring was a swirl of golden tones. Between the alcoves, paintings of Western scenes hung on the walls.

Louise reached out, touched a panel of lights. Recessed lighting glowed to illuminate the paintings. She was proud. "Isn't it beautiful? The paintings in this hall are from various places in Oklahoma. Our state has an amazingly varied terrain, everything from hills to prairies to mesas. There are beautiful paintings all through the foundation. I'm glad I can show you everything today when we don't have to hurry. Mondays get busy. There's a staff meeting at eleven. It's very responsible of you" — her tone was admiring and mildly surprised — "to make the extra effort to locate the foundation today. I will confess I wasn't sure what to expect from Chloe's sister. Chloe is" — a pause — "casual about things."

Nela well understood. Chloe was not only casual, but slapdash and last minute.

"Though," Louise added hurriedly, "she's a nice girl and somehow everything gets done."

Nela gave her a reassuring smile. There was no point in taking umbrage because truth was truth. "Chloe moves quickly." That was true, too.

Louise smiled in return. "Yes, she does.

I'll show you her office, but first" — she began to walk, gesturing to her right — "these small offices are for summer interns. We also have a new position this year." A faint frown touched her face. "For an assistant curator. The new director thought it would be good to put one person in charge of overseeing artifact donations. Haklo is unusual among foundations because we not only provide grants, we create our own programs to celebrate Oklahoma history. Thanks to Haklo, many schools around the state now have displays that we have provided, everything from memorabilia about Will Rogers to women's roles in early statehood to Indian relics." The frosted glass of the office door read:

ABBY ANDREWS
ASSISTANT CURATOR

Louise moved to the next door. "This is Chloe's office." She opened the door and flicked on the light.

Nela felt her sister's presence as they stepped inside. Chloe had put her personal stamp on a utilitarian room with a gray metal desk and a bank of filing cabinets. There on the bookcase was a picture of Nela and Chloe, arm in arm on a happy summer day at the Santa Monica pier. Four posters enlivened pale gray walls, an aerial view of Machu Picchu, a surfer catching a big one in Hawaii, a tousle-haired Amelia Earhart in a trench coat standing by a bright red Lockheed Vega, and the shining gold-domed ceiling of the Library of Congress.

Louise followed her gaze to the posters. "Has your sister been to all those places?"

"In her dreams." When Chloe was little, Nela had often read Dr. Seuss to her. She sometimes wondered if a little girl's spirit had responded to the lyrical call of places to go and things to see. If Chloe couldn't go there — yet — in person, she'd travel in her imagination.

"I suppose that's why she went to Tahiti." Louise's voice was almost admiring. "I don't think I'd ever have the courage, but she doesn't worry, does she?"

"Sometimes I wish she would," Nela confided. "She always thinks everything will work out and so far" — her usual quick prayer, plea, hope flickered in her mind — "they have. But I'll be glad when she and Leland get home."

Louise's glance was sympathetic. "I know. I always worried so about my son. I always wanted him safe at home and that's when he died, driving home from college in an ice

73

storm. Maybe Tahiti is safer." Her voice was thin. "Certainly nothing's seemed secure here lately. Chloe keeps telling me not to worry. But I can't help worrying."

Worry.

Nela pictured Marian's brown tabby looking up forlornly. . . . *She was worried . . . She didn't know what to do . . .*

"What's been wrong?"

It was as if Louise stepped back a pace though she didn't move. Her face was suddenly bland. "Oh, this and that. Things crop up. The foundation is involved in so many activities and sometimes people get angry."

Nela was abruptly alert. Someone had been angry last night in Marian Grant's apartment, angry enough to pick up a crystal statuette and fling it at a mirror. Nela wasn't reassured by Louise's smooth response. The intrusion in the dead woman's apartment last night had been wrong, and there seemed to be something wrong here at the foundation, but Chloe's boss obviously didn't intend to explain. Was the search last night related to things cropping up, whatever that meant, at the foundation? The secretary's threat to call the police because of Nela's unexpected arrival had to be based on some definite concern.

"Here is the connecting door to my office." Louise gestured toward an open door. "Unless I'm in conference, I leave the door open between the offices and that makes access easier. Chloe handles my correspondence and takes care of filing. We're having a meeting of the grants committee later this month and Chloe is about halfway through preparing one-page summaries of applications. Tomorrow, you can be sure the conference room is ready for the staff meeting, fresh legal pads and a pen at each place. There's a small galley off the main conference room. About ten minutes after everyone arrives, you can heat sweet rolls and bring them in with coffee. The foundation has the most wonderful cook."

She was now businesslike with no hint of her earlier distress. As they approached the front of the building, the size of the offices grew. Louise walked fast and talked fast. Names whirled in Nela's mind like buzzing gnats. ". . . These offices are provided as a courtesy to the members of the grants committee." She rattled off several names. They reached the front hall.

"The main hallway" — she made a sweeping gesture — "runs east and west. This is the west hall." She pointed across the spacious marble hallway. "The corner office belongs to Blythe Webster. She's the trustee of the foundation."

Louise flicked several switches, illuminating the magnificent main hallway. "There are only two front offices, one at each corner. Now for our beautiful rotunda." She looked eager as she led the way. "I love the fountain behind the reception desk."

Water gurgled merrily, splashing down over blue and gold tiles.

Louise stopped next to a horseshoe-shaped counter opposite the huge oak front door. She patted the shining wooden counter. "This is the reception desk. Rosalind McNeill takes care of the phones."

Nela was pleased to recognize another name. Chloe had mentioned Rosalind in her letter. Rosalind apparently had filled Chloe in on things that had happened at the foundation.

Louise pointed at the high ceiling. "Rosalind has the best view in the building."

Nela looked up at a series of huge frescoes, magnificent, fresh, and vivid.

Louise beamed. "The paintings reflect Haklo Foundation's encouragement of crop rotation. The first panel is wheat, the next is canola, and the third is sesame."

Nela felt swept into a new world as she admired the vivid frescoes, the three distinctly different crops, grazing cattle, a champion bull, an old field with ranks of wooden derricks.

"We're very proud of the frescoes. They were painted by one of our very own scholarship students, Miguel Rodriguez. The sculptures on either side of the fountain" — she pointed to alcoves in the stuccoed walls — "are members of the Webster family. That's Harris Webster's grandmother, Mary Castle, who was a Chickasaw. The Webster family goes way back to Indian Territory days when Caleb Webster married Mary Castle. Mr. Webster —"

There was reverence in her voice and Nela had no doubt she referred to the foundation's benefactor, Harris Webster.

"— honored his Chickasaw heritage when he named the foundation Haklo. That's Chickasaw for *to listen.* That's what we do. We listen to the requests from our community and respond. Our grants fund agricultural research, rancher certification programs, wildlife and fisheries management, biofuel studies with an emphasis on switchgrass, seminars of interest to farmers and ranchers, and, of course, we support the arts, including grants and scholarships to students, artists, musicians, a local nonprofit art gallery, and particular programs and faculty at Craddock College.

And we have our wonderful outreach with the historical exhibits that we create ourselves."

Pink tinged her cheeks. Her eyes glowed with enthusiasm. She gestured at the east wing. "That way is the director's office and conference rooms and the foundation library. The catering office and kitchen are at the far end. The other staff offices and an auditorium are upstairs. Aren't the stairs beautiful?"

Twin tiled stairways with wrought iron railings curved on either side of the fountain area.

They left the rotunda and walked toward the end of the main cross hall. "In the morning, I'll take you around early to meet —"

A rattle of footsteps clicked behind them on one of the curving stairways.

Louise stiffened. Her eyes flared in alarm.

Nela realized the executive secretary was afraid. Louise had said she was alone in the building.

A man spoke in a high tenor voice, the ample space of the rotunda magnifying the sound. ". . . don't know what the bitch will do next."

Louise exhaled in relief but again bright

pink touched her cheeks, this time from dismay.

A softer, more precise male voice replied. "Let it go, Robbie."

"I won't let it go. I won't ever let it go."

Louise gripped Nela's elbow, tugged, and began to speak, lifting her voice, as she hurried Nela back toward the reception desk. "I forgot to show you the sculpture of Mr. Webster."

Two men came around the curve of the stairwell. The older man's silver hair was a mane, matched by an equally dramatic silver handlebar mustache. A black cape swirled as he moved, accentuating the white of a pullover sweater and matching black flannel trousers and black boots.

Nela was reminded of a drama professor from summer school between her junior and senior years. When he quoted from a play, a character came alive, robust, individual, memorable. He had been fun and she'd enjoyed every moment of the class.

His companion was younger, with perfectly coiffed thick blond hair and a smoothly handsome face now soured by a scowl. He was more conventionally dressed in a black turtleneck and blue jeans.

Nela knew instantly that they were a couple. There was that sense of physical connection that imbued all unions, whether heterosexual or homosexual.

Louise bustled forward to meet them at the foot of the stairs. She smiled at the older man. "Erik, it's wonderful to see you." She gestured toward Nela. "I want you to meet Nela Farley. She's taking her sister's place this week while Chloe is on her great adventure. Nela, this is Erik Judd and Robbie Powell." There was the slightest hesitation and a flick of a glance at Erik, then Louise said hurriedly, "Robbie is our director of public relations." She looked at the younger man. "Robbie, you scared me. I didn't know anyone else was here. I didn't hear your car come into the lot."

"We're in Erik's Porsche. He insisted on parking in the visitors' lot." Robbie's tone was petulant.

Louise looked dismayed. "Oh, Erik, you are always welcome here."

Erik smoothed back a silver curl. "Since we're in my car, I thought it was more appropriate to park in the visitors' lot. I use the visitors' lot now when I do research here." But his smile was friendly. "It's good to see you, Louise, and to meet Nela." His nod was gracious.

Robbie managed a smile for Nela. "Thanks for filling in for Chloe. I hope you'll enjoy your time with us."

The two men walked toward the front doorway, Robbie leading. As Robbie opened the heavy door, a gust of cold air swirled inside. Erik Judd's cape billowed.

Louise turned back to Nela and picked up their conversation as if there had been no interruption. "Rosalind will buzz you about midmorning Monday to deliver the mail. She'll have everything sorted. Start with Miss Webster."

Clearly, Louise had no intention of discussing Erik and Robbie or explaining the odd emphasis on the visitors' lot.

"Now" — Louise sounded brighter — "let's look at the east wing."

Nela's grasp of who worked where was hazy. However, there was no doubt of the pecking order. Miss Webster had the big front office at the west end of the central hall. Whoever worked in the east front office must also be a major player.

Nela gestured at the door. "Is that the director's office?"

Louise drew in a sharp breath. "That was the office of our chief operating officer. She passed away last week. A dreadful accident."

Nela felt a moment of surprise that Marian Grant had outranked the foundation director in status. "Miss Grant's office?"

81

Louise stared at her, eyes wide.

Of course, Chloe hadn't bothered to explain where Nela would stay so Louise was startled by Nela's knowledge. "I spent the night at Miss Grant's apartment. Since Chloe e-mailed with Miss Grant's sister in Australia about arranging matters here, Chloe volunteered to stay in the apartment and take care of Miss Grant's cat until a home is found for him. I'm there while Chloe's gone." *Unless,* she qualified in her mind, *someone tries to break in again.* Nela almost told Louise about the entry in the night, but the secretary was staring at the office door in such obvious distress Nela didn't want to add to her unhappiness. Certainly if she grieved for her lost co-worker, it would upset her more to think the dead woman's home had been invaded. And it would be unkind to ask Louise to take care of the Coach bag. A woman's purse is very personal and Louise would have seen the bag many times.

"Her belongings" — Louise's voice shook a little — "need to be gathered up. Perhaps you can take care of that for us. I'll arrange for some cartons. I can't bear to think about it. Her personal trinkets . . ." She stopped and pressed her lips together. Louise cleared her throat. "We need to find out if Marian's sister wants to have everything stored or shipped to her or perhaps disposed of." She paused, said dully, "Disposed of . . . It's dreadful to talk of Marian's belongings that way. She was such a competent person. She knew everything. I don't know how the foundation will manage without her. Her death is a huge loss. And to think of Marian of all people falling from her stairs! Marian skied and jogged and climbed mountains. She wasn't the least bit clumsy." Her voice quivered with emotion, almost a touch of anger, as if Marian Grant had let them down. "But there's nothing we can do about it."

Steve Flynn slid into the last booth in a line of red leatherette booths at Hamburger Heaven. On a Sunday night, choice for dinner in Craddock was limited to the usual suspects: McDonald's, Sonic, Braum's, Applebee's, Olive Garden. The hometown restaurants closed after Sunday brunch except for Hamburger Heaven.

The crowd was sparse. Sunday was a family evening. Steve was getting used to eating out alone. He dipped a French fry in the side of ranch dressing that he always ordered with his cheeseburger. He felt a flicker of amusement. Living on the wild side, ranch dressing instead of Heinz. His hand froze midway to his mouth.

A dark-haired woman in her early twenties slipped onto a wooden seat at a nearby table. She was a stranger. Not that he could claim to know everyone in Craddock, but he knew most of her age and class. He had never seen her before, of that he was certain. He would not forget her. She wasn't conventionally pretty. Her face was too thin with deep-set eyes, narrow nose, high cheekbones, and a delicate but firm chin. There were smudges beneath her brilliantly dark eyes. She carried with her an air of melancholy.

She sat at a table close to him, but he had no doubt that though she was physically present, her thoughts were far away.

His image and hers were reflected in the long mirror behind the counter, two people sitting by themselves, a burly redheaded man in an old sweater, an aloof and memorable dark-haired woman in a thin, cotton blouse.

He didn't know if he'd ever felt more alone.

4

Nela used to love Monday mornings, especially a Monday when she was on her way to work. Since Bill died, the world had been gray. She did what she was supposed to do. Sometimes she was able to plunge into a task and forget grayness for a while. Maybe taking over Chloe's job, doing something different, would brighten her world. Sunday had been a long, sad day. She'd wandered about Craddock, ended up at Chloe's Hamburger Heaven. But sitting there, eating food that she knew was good but that had no savor, she'd accepted the truth. Old sayings didn't lie. Wherever you go, there you are. It didn't matter if she was in LA or a small wind-blown town half a continent away, there she was, carrying with her the pain and sadness. At least today she had a job waiting for her among people with tasks and accomplishments. She would concentrate on the people she met, think about the things they did, push sadness and pain deep inside. She turned into the Haklo grounds, following a short line of cars.

In the lot, she parked next to a sleek blue Thunderbird. At the same time, an old beige Dodge sputtered to a stop on the other side of the VW.

"Good morning." A plump sixtyish man with a mop of untidy white hair stepped out of the Dodge and bustled toward her, blue eyes shining.

Nela waited behind the Thunderbird. She noted the tag: ROBBIE.

Her welcomer's genial face reminded her of Edmund Gwenn in *The Trouble with Harry.* "You must be Nela, Chloe's sister. You look just like your picture."

Nela knew her dark curls were tangled by the wind. The day on the pier had been windy, too.

"Welcome to Haklo." He spoke as proudly as a man handing out keys to a city. "I'm Cole Hamilton." He spoke as if she would, of course, know his name.

Nela responded with equal warmth. "It's a pleasure to meet you, Mr. Hamilton."

"Oh, my dear, call me Cole. Everyone does."

Heavy steps sounded behind them. A deep voice rumbled, "Good morning, Cole."

Despite his size, well over six feet and two hundred plus pounds, the huge dark-haired man moved with muscular grace. "Francis Garth. Good morning, Miss Farley. I knew you immediately when you pulled up in that car. It's good of you to help us out while Chloe is gone."

They were moving toward the walkway to the building, an oddly assorted trio, Francis Garth towering above Nela and her bubbly new friend. Cole was chattering, ". . . Chloe told us you were a reporter. That must be an exciting life. But the pressure . . ."

Nela had thrived on deadlines. It was the only life she'd ever wanted, talking to people, finding out what mattered, getting the facts right. She'd written everything from light fluffy features to a series on embezzlement at the city treasurer's office. She'd learned how to dig for facts. More importantly, she'd learned how to read faces and body language. She wasn't a reporter now. She'd lost her job more than six months ago. Last hired, first fired. Print journalism jobs were as scarce as champagne-colored natural pearls. She'd once done a story about a woman who had spent a lifetime collecting pearls of many shades, white, black, green, purple, and greatest prize of all, the golden tone of champagne. After her last newspaper job, Nela had waited tables at a swell café on Melrose Place in Hollywood. That job, too, was gone. But someday she would find an editor who would give her a chance . . .

Immersed in her thoughts, she'd taken a good half-dozen steps before she realized that Cole's high tenor had broken off in midsentence.

Voices rose on the sidewalk from the cabins and around a curve came a very pretty girl and a lanky man in a light blue cashmere sweater and gray slacks. Nela knew him at once. Chloe's description had been right on. *The director's kind of like James Stewart in* The Shop Around the Corner . . . *He's tall and angular and has this bony appealing face.* His companion looked up at him with a happy face and her words came quickly. ". . . I haven't seen the Chihuly exhibit either. That would be such fun."

Perhaps it was the stillness of the trio standing by the building steps that caught their attention. Abruptly, light and cheer fled from her delicate features. The director's face reformed from boyish eagerness to defensive blandness. Nela wasn't personally attracted, but many women would find his cleft-chinned good looks irresistible.

Nela sensed antagonism in the men beside

her, though outwardly all was courtesy and good humor.

"Good morning." Francis Garth's deep voice was pleasant and impersonal. "Nela, here is our director, Hollis Blair, and" — his dark eyes moved without warmth to the blonde's delicate face — "our new assistant curator, Abby Andrews."

In the flurry of greetings, Cole Hamilton hurried up the steps, held the door. "Almost eight o'clock. We're all on time this morning." The dumpy little man with thick white hair suddenly looked as if his blue suit was too large for him.

As the door closed behind them, Hamilton veered toward a door marked STAIRS. "Have to see about some things." He was subdued with no echo of the pride that she'd heard when he'd greeted her in the parking lot.

"The new grant applications are in the first filing cabinet. The applications are made online but we print out copies for our records" — Louise gestured at the filing cabinet — "and we make copies for the members of the grants committee. Marian says they can look at them online but as a courtesy we also provide printed copies. The committee meets every fourth Thursday of the month. We have fifteen new applications to consider. Whenever a new application is received, Chloe prepares a one-page summary. I placed the remaining applications that need summaries in Chloe's in-box. The top folder holds one Chloe had already prepared and you can look it over for the format. You can —"

"Louise." The deep voice was gruff.

Francis Garth stood in Nela's doorway, making it look small. His heavy face was stern. He held up several stapled sheets. "There is an error in today's agenda."

Louise's face registered a series of revealing expressions: knowledge, discomfort, dismay, regret.

Francis raised a heavy dark eyebrow. There was a trace of humor in a sudden twisted smile, but only a trace. "I take it there was no mistake. Why was the proposal removed?"

Louise cleared her throat. "I understand the director felt that opposing the wind farms was at odds with the foundation's support of green energy."

"Wind farms can ruin the Tallgrass Prairie ecosystem. Isn't that a green" — it was almost an epithet — "concern? Hasn't Haklo always respected tribal values? The Tallgrass Prairie is the heart of the Osage

Nation."

"Oh, Francis, I know how you feel about the Tallgrass Prairie. But Hollis persuaded Blythe that it was important for Haklo to rise above parochial interests to fulfill its mission of nurturing the planet." Clearly Louise was repeating verbatim what she had been told.

"Nothing in this world should be permitted to defile the Tallgrass Prairie." He spoke slowly, the words distinct and separate. He didn't raise his voice but there was no mistaking his passion. He turned, moving swiftly for such a big man.

Louise stared at the empty doorway, her face troubled.

Nela had no idea what the Tallgrass Prairie meant. But whatever it was, wherever it was, Francis Garth was clearly furious.

Louise took a deep breath. "Let's make the rounds, Nela. I want to introduce you to everyone."

"I met several people coming in this morning, the director and the assistant curator and Mr. Hamilton and Mr. Garth. I met Miss Webster Friday night at the apartment." It wasn't necessary to explain the circumstances.

"Wonderful. We'll run by all the offices so you'll know where to take the mail and we can drop in and say hello to Peter and Grace."

As they reached the cross hall, Louise slowed. She looked puzzled. "Blythe's door is closed. Usually everyone keeps their doors open. Webster wanted everyone to feel free and easy at Haklo." She looked forlorn. "That's the way it used to be."

Nela doubted Louise realized how revealing her statement was. So Haklo was not a happy place. Not now. Was Louise's dismay because of the death of a colleague? Nela wished that Chloe had been more attuned to the place where she worked, but Chloe was Chloe, not self-absorbed in a selfish way but always focusing on fun. Nela knew her sister well enough to be sure that all kinds of emotions would have swirled around Chloe without leaving any impression.

"But we still" — and now she was walking faster — "make such a wonderful difference in so many lives."

They reached the horseshoe-shaped reception desk in the rotunda.

A plump woman with a round cheerful face beamed at them. "Hi, Louise. And you must be Nela. I'm Rosalind McNeill." She eyed Nela with interest. "You sure don't look like Chloe." There was no hint of disparagement in the soft drawl, simply a fact mentioned in passing.

Nela smiled at the receptionist. "That's what everyone says."

Rosalind's brown eyes sparkled. "Chloe's very nice. You look nice, too."

Nela imagined that Rosalind always found her glass half full and that her presence was as relaxing to those around her as a sunny day at the beach. In contrast, tightly coiled Louise exuded tension from the wrinkle of her brows to thin shoulders always slightly tensed.

"I'm taking Nela around to introduce her. If the mail's ready, we can deliver it."

Rosalind shook her head. "I'm about half done. Lots of calls for Miss Webster this morning. Something's got the members of the grants committee riled. They called, bang, bang, bang, one after the other. I've heard happier voices at wakes. I don't think Miss Webster was hearing love notes. If I had one, I'd toss in a bottle of bath salts with her letter delivery." She grinned. "I've been rereading Victorian fiction. Ah, the days when gentle ladies fainted at the drop of a handkerchief to be revived by smelling salts. Did you know they're really a mixture of ammonia and water? That would revive anybody. From the tone of the callers, I'm betting Miss Webster could use a sniff."

Louise looked ever more worried. "I'd better see what's happened. Rosalind, you can finish sorting the mail, then give Nela the room numbers." She turned to Nela. "I'm sorry you haven't met some of the staff yet."

"Meeting new people has always been what I enjoy most about working on a newspaper. I'll be fine."

Louise gave her a quick smile, which was replaced almost immediately by a furrow of worry as she turned and hurried toward the trustee's office.

Rosalind's glance was admiring. "Chloe said you were a reporter. That must be exciting."

"It can be. I'm looking for a job right now." She refused to be defensive. Everybody knew somebody who'd lost a job. She didn't mind waiting tables in the interim, but someday, somehow she would write again. Bill wouldn't want her to give up. The only happiness she'd known in this last dreary year was when she was writing. That became a world in itself, arranging facts, finding words, creating a story.

Nela came behind the counter. A vase of fresh daisies sat on the corner of Rosalind's desk. A foldout photo holder held pictures of three cats, a bright-eyed calico, a thoughtful brown tabby, and a silver gray with a

Persian face.

Rosalind saw her glance. "My gals, Charlotte, Emily, and Anne. They can't write, but they snuggle next to me when I read. Funny thing" — there was an odd tone in her voice — "and you probably won't believe me, but every time I sit down with *Jane Eyre,* Charlotte rubs her face against the book. Of course, she's making it hers, but it's only that particular book. Go figure." As she talked, she flicked envelopes with the ease of long practice into a long plastic tray. Dividers were marked with recipients' names. "I've added the mail for Miss Grant to Dr. Blair's stack. I guess Chloe told you about the accident. That was a shocker." She slapped the last of the letters in place. "The trustee's mail is always delivered first."

When Nela lifted the plastic tray, Rosalind gave a half salute. "If you need reinforcements, I'll be at The Office."

Clearly Rosalind's tone was wry, but Nela dutifully inquired, "The Office?"

"That's Craddock's home-away-from-home watering hole. Coldest beer, hottest wings." A grin. "When things get too hairy here at Haklo, we always kid around and say you can find us at The Office." A sigh. "In my dreams."

95

Blythe Webster's door was still closed.

Nela shifted the tray on her hip. She'd been instructed to deliver the mail. She would do so. She knocked lightly on the panel, turned the knob, and pushed the door open.

". . . have to investigate." The man's voice was loud, stressed.

The door made a sighing sound.

Nela immediately realized she'd intruded at a stressful moment. Blythe Webster stood behind her desk, face drawn down in an intense frown. Louise Spear stood a few feet away. Eyes huge in a shocked face, Louise twisted her hands around and around each other. The lanky director moved back and forth, a few steps one way, then back again, clearly distraught.

Nela obviously had interrupted a grim conversation. The sooner she departed, the better. "Excuse me. I have the morning mail for Miss Webster." She remained in the doorway, poised for a quick withdrawal.

Blythe lifted a hand to touch a double strand of pearls. Her face was set and pale. "Put the letters in the in-tray."

Nela quickly crossed to the desk, deposited several letters and mailers.

Blythe managed a strained smile. "Nela, this is Dr. Blair, director of the foundation.

Hollis, this is Nela Farley, Chloe's sister. Nela is taking Chloe's place while she's on her holiday."

"Thank you, Miss Webster. I met Dr. Blair earlier." She began to move toward the door.

"Wait a minute." Blythe's tone was sharp. She glanced at a diamond-encrusted watch. "It's almost ten. We must deal with this immediately. Nela, as you deliver the mail, inform each staff member that the meeting has been moved to ten o'clock. Attendance is mandatory."

5

Louise looked at the grandfather clock in the corner of the conference room. The minute hand stood at twelve minutes past ten. The golden oak of the clock matched the golden oak paneling. In the glow of recessed lights, the granite conference tabletop added more serene colors, streaks of yellow and tangerine against a wheat background.

A sense of unease pervaded a room where no expense had been spared to create a welcoming environment. In the mural on one wall, monarchs hovered over reddish orange blooms on waist-high grasses that wavered in a wind beneath a cloudless blue sky. On the other wall, a buffalo faced forward, dark eyes beneath a mat of wiry black curls in a huge head framed by curved horns, massive shoulders, short legs, and shaggy brown hair.

Nela sat to one side of the conference

table in a straight chair. Six black leather swivel chairs were occupied, leaving a half dozen or so empty at the far end of the table. The delivery of the mail had given her the chance to meet both Grace Webster, Blythe's sister, and Peter Owens, the director of publications. It had been interesting when she issued Blythe's summons to each staff member to be in the conference room at ten o'clock instead of eleven. She would have expected surprise. There had been wariness, but no surprise.

In what kind of workplace was a peremptory summons treated as if it were business as usual?

She looked with interest around the room. Cole Hamilton fiddled with a pen, making marks on the legal pad. Francis Garth sat with his arms folded. He reminded her of the buffalo in the far mural. All he lacked were horns and short legs.

Her gaze paused on Abby Andrews. Nela thought that Chloe's description of the new assistant curator didn't do her justice. Abby was a classically lovely blonde with perfect bone structure. Her brows could have used a bit of darkening, but her deep violet eyes were striking. At the moment, she sat in frozen stillness as if she might shatter if she moved.

Why was she so tense?

Nela had no doubt that Blythe's younger sister Grace was trouble waiting to happen. Grace tapped her pen on the tabletop. *Tap. Tap. Tap.* Her rounded face was not unpleasant, but she was clearly combative.

The quarter hour chimed.

Robbie Powell brushed back a lock of brightly blond hair.

Nela made a quick link. Tab Hunter in *Damn Yankees* but with longer hair. She knew Chloe would agree.

"I'm expecting a call from a Dallas newspaper. I may be able to place a feature story on that research into antibiotic overuse in stock. I had to change the time. And now we're sitting here, waiting." Robbie kept his tone light. "I assumed something important had occurred, but neither the trustee nor the director have shown up after the imperial summons." Robbie straightened a heavy gold cuff link in his blue oxford cloth shirt. His blue blazer was a perfect fit. He had the patina of a man at home in meetings, always sure to know everyone's name, quick with a smile and compliment.

Nela was good at reading moods, and beneath Robbie's surface charm, she sensed anger.

Louise was placating. "They'll be here

soon. There's been an upsetting development."

The faces around the table were abruptly alert. There was unmistakable tension.

Francis cleared his throat. "What development?"

Louise didn't meet his gaze. "It will be better for Blythe to explain."

Peter Owens shifted in his seat. "Ah, well, we're on company time." His comment was smooth, but he, too, looked uncomfortable. A lean man with black horn rims perched in wiry dark hair, he had wide-set brown eyes, a thin nose, and sharp chin. His good quality but well-worn tweed jacket with leather elbow patches made him look professorial. "How about some of Mama Kay's sweet rolls? A little sugar will lift your spirits, Robbie."

Louise looked at Nela. "Please serve the sweet rolls and coffee now. Except for Blythe and Hollis."

Nela warmed the sweet rolls and carried the serving plate to Louise. Nela poured coffee into Haklo Foundation mugs, gold letters on a dark green background, and served them.

Peter nodded his thanks, then lifted his mug. "Ladies and gentlemen, a toast to our newest addition. Welcome to Haklo Foundation, Nela. We enjoy your sister. She's definitely a breath of freshness in this fusty atmosphere. Have you heard a report from Tahiti?"

Nela responded to his genuine interest. "Just a call Friday night to say they arrived safely and everything was fantastic."

"Fantastic in all caps?" But his voice was kind.

Nela smiled. "Absolutely."

He nodded toward her chair. "Pour yourself some coffee, too. I highly recommend Mama Kay's raspberry Danish. The foundation is beyond good fortune to have her as our chef."

Nela glanced at Louise, who nodded.

Nela settled at her place with a plate. The sweet roll was indeed excellent, the flaky crust light, the raspberry filling tart and perfect.

Peter spoke in a mumble past a mouthful of pastry. "Speaking of travelers, I suggest we vote on a staff conference in Arizona. Surely there is something useful we could survey there. Or possibly Costa Rica. Francis, you're very good at sniffing out development prospects for Oklahoma beef. How about Costa Rica?"

Francis turned his heavy head. He looked sharply at Peter's smiling face, then said quietly, "In the past we've done good work gaining markets for Oklahoma beef. But the new budget doesn't support that kind of outreach."

Peter shrugged. "Your office has had a very good run." His face was still pleasant, but there might have been a slightly malicious curl to his crooked lips.

As he drank from his mug, Nela wondered if she had imagined that transformation.

Francis folded his arms. "Things change." His deep voice was ruminative. "I played golf with Larry Swift the other day. You know him, Swift Publications. He's pretty excited to be invited to submit a bid to handle the design of a pictorial history of Carter County."

Peter's face tightened. "I've been talking to Blythe. I think she understands that in-house design is cheaper and, of course, better quality."

"Does she?" Robbie's tone was ingenuous. "She asked me about Swift Publications the other day. I had to say they do swell work."

"Nela, please take the carafe around, see if anyone wants more coffee. My, I hope the weather doesn't turn bad . . ." Louise chattered about the awfully cold weather, and had they heard there was a possibility of an

103

ice storm?

Nela poured coffee and wondered at the background to the ostensibly pleasant but barbed exchanges.

The door swung open. Blythe Webster hurried inside. Her fine features looked etched in stone. Hollis Blair followed, his lips pressed together in a thin, hard line. He was Jimmy Stewart after he lost his job at the little shop around the corner.

Chairs creaked. There was a general shifting of position.

"My, my, my. What's happened?" Cole Hamilton's rather high voice quavered. Francis Garth's heavy bushy eyebrows drew down in a frown. Abby Andrews's lips trembled and she seemed even more fragile. Grace Webster's blue eyes narrowed as she studied her sister's face. Robbie Powell looked apprehensive. Peter Owens leaned back in his chair, gaze speculative, arms folded.

Nela half expected Louise to dismiss her from the meeting. This no longer seemed an occasion for her to serve pastries and coffee. But the secretary never glanced her way. In the stress of whatever prompted the earlier meeting, Louise wasn't thinking about Nela and her function. It wasn't Nela's job to remind her.

Blythe Webster stopped behind the end chair. "Sit down, Hollis."

Nela thought her tone was brusque.

Hollis Blair dropped into the empty seat to her right. He hunched his shoulders like a man preparing to fight.

Blythe remained standing, resting a green folder on the chair back. She made no apology for their late arrival and gave no greeting. "This morning I received calls from Alice Garcia, Kay Drummond, and Jane Carstairs. In today's mail, each informed me she had received a letter on Dr. Blair's letterhead which contained obscene material." She looked toward the director. "I immediately spoke with Hollis. He assures me he had no knowledge of the letter." The words were spoken evenly, suggesting neither acceptance nor denial of the director's involvement.

Hollis Blair's head jerked up. "Obviously I didn't send the letters. I know nothing about them. Someone obtained my letterhead and used it without permission."

Robbie Powell flapped his well-manicured hands. "We have to get those letters back. This could be a nightmare. Can't you see the headline in the *Oklahoman? Prurient Letter Linked to Haklo Director.*"

"It isn't his fault." Abby blurted out the

words angrily, a flush staining her pale cheeks.

Hollis looked toward her, his blue eyes suddenly soft. "It's all right, Abby. We'll find out who's responsible."

Peter Owens spoke quietly. "If there's no proof Dr. Blair sent the letters, the foundation can disclaim any responsibility. Since there have been other random acts of vandalism —"

It was like a picture that had been askew righting itself. Now Nela understood the reason why Louise spoke nostalgically about happy times at Haklo. Moreover, none of the staff had seemed surprised at a peremptory summons.

"Doesn't sound too damn random." Francis's voice was gruff. "Obscene letters sent to members of the grants committee suggests the recipients were chosen quite specifically. Of course" — he looked at Blythe — "you may soon be receiving other calls."

Blythe shook her head. "I don't think so. The calls came ping-ping-ping as soon as the morning business deliveries were made. I checked with Bart Hasting's secretary. He has a letter from the foundation from Dr. Blair. I asked her not to open it. Bart and his family are skiing at Vail. If anyone else in town had received a letter, I'd know by now. So, the damage can be contained. Since no one on the committee wishes harm to the foundation, they will keep this confidential." She glanced at the wall clock.

Cole Hamilton looked distressed. "This is a serious matter. A suggestion of immorality could taint the foundation forever."

"I'm afraid women with a juicy bit of gossip never keep it to themselves." Robbie shook his head in regret.

Nela wondered if there was a hint of malicious amusement in his light voice.

"Really?" Grace was dismissive. "I'm sure you never gossip, do you, sweetie?"

Robbie stared at her. For an instant, the handsome youngish man looked old and beaten. "I was misquoted, my words taken out of context."

"Grace, that matter is closed. Robbie apologized." Blythe's tone was sharp.

Grace laughed aloud. "Oh, my charitable sister. No matter if an employee is overheard describing her as Head Bitch at the foundation. But maybe truth is a defense."

For a long instant, the sisters stared at each other.

Cole Hamilton fluttered his hands. "Girls, girls. I know your father would move swiftly to correct the current dreadful situation here." His eyelids blinking rapidly, he spoke in a rush. "It is shocking how calamities have engulfed the foundation since Dr. Blair took over last fall."

Peter Owens cleared his throat. "Let me see, we had some road-kill out in front of the foundation last week. I guess that's Hollis's fault as well."

Cole's face creased in stubborn lines. "You can't pretend there aren't problems."

Blythe made an impatient gesture. "No one is pretending there aren't problems. Hollis has instituted inquiries into each incident."

Robbie raised a thick blond brow. "What has he found out? Who set that girl's car on fire? Who destroyed the Indian baskets? Who set off the indoor sprinklers and drenched my office? Who turned on the outdoor fountain and the pipes froze and it's going to cost thousands to fix it? Who took the skateboard from Abby's porch? Next thing you know, the vandal will strap a bomb to it and roll it up the main hall one night. Who stole your necklace? I find it puzzling" — his green eyes flicked toward Hollis — "that our director didn't call the police, and that necklace must be worth thousands of dollars with those heavy gold links and those diamonds. And now these letters . . ."

Nela remembered too clearly the heavy weight of the necklace, the glitter of the stones. Somehow she managed not to change expression. She had the same sense of unreality that an earthquake brought, jolted by one shock and then another. A missing skateboard. A stolen necklace. She pushed aside thoughts of a skateboard. That was her invention, extrapolating what a cat meant by a rolling board. But the gold necklace heavy with diamonds that rested at the bottom of Marian Grant's purse was real, not an invention. Up to this moment, she had been engaged as an observer. Now, with abrupt suddenness, she was as intensely involved as any of the Haklo staff.

"I" — Blythe's tone was imperious — "instructed Hollis to arrange for a private investigation about the necklace. I do not want the disappearance of the necklace to become a police matter. Inevitably, if there is a police report, there would be a story in the *Clarion.* We've had enough stories. I'm still getting questions about that car fire and the fountain. However" — she glanced at her watch — "if all of these incidents are connected, the person who wishes harm to the foundation may have been too clever. Within a few minutes, I expect to know whether one of our computers generated the message. Obviously the writer would have deleted the file but IT assures me that any deleted file can be found. At this moment, our IT staff is checking every computer. Penny Crawford will bring the results to me. As we wait, we will proceed with our regular meeting. Hollis."

Dr. Blair gave an abrupt nod. "I will be sending out a memo to staff today in regard to our annual . . ."

The words rolled over Nela without meaning. How many heavy gold-link necklaces studded with diamonds could be floating around Craddock? But if the jewelry had been stolen, why was it in Marian Grant's purse? From everything she'd heard about Marian Grant, the idea that she'd commit a theft was preposterous. But the necklace was in the purse.

Maybe that's what the intruder was looking for Friday night. Yet the person who entered had ignored Marian Grant's purse, instead slammed through her desk.

Whatever the reason for the search, Nela knew she had to do something about the purse that now rested behind a stack of cat food in Marian Grant's kitchen cabinet. Nela's situation was untenable. If she admitted she'd searched Miss Grant's purse and not mentioned to anyone what she'd found, it would be difficult to explain the fact that she'd hidden the purse. If she kept quiet, it would be devastating if anyone found the hidden purse.

A knock sounded on the door.

"Come in." Blythe spoke firmly.

The door opened and a dark-haired young woman stepped inside. She kept her gaze fastened on Blythe's face. "Miss Webster, I found the file."

Blythe's fingers curled around the double strand of pearls at her throat. "Which computer, Penny?"

The young IT tech looked uncomfortable. "The computer is in the office assigned to Abby Andrews."

Abby gave a choked cry. Her face flushed, then turned pale. She came to her feet, held out a trembling hand. "I never wrote anything like that. Never. I wouldn't hurt the foundation." She ignored Blythe, turned instead toward Hollis Blair, her gaze beseeching.

Hollis stood, too. His bony face flushed. "Of course you didn't. Someone else used your computer, Abby."

Blythe studied Abby. Her gaze was interested, neither supportive nor accusing. "Sit down, Abby, Hollis." She waited until both of them took their seats. Blythe's cameo-perfect face was composed.

Nela wondered if it was inherent in Blythe's nature to exercise control. She also wondered if the trustee knew that she was diminishing both Hollis and Abby with her cool instruction. *Sit down, children.*

Blythe continued in a measured voice. "Remain calm. There's no proof Abby created the file. There's no proof Abby didn't. Let's explore the possibilities." She nodded at the IT staffer. "When was the file created?"

"Thursday at eleven oh eight p.m." Penny Crawford carefully did not glance toward Abby.

"I was in my cabin." Abby's voice was defiant. "I was by myself. I had no reason to come here at night."

Cole Hamilton peered at the assistant curator. "It requires a password to access a computer." The question was implicit.

Robbie looked relieved, almost complacent. "They say you always leave an electronic footprint. This may explain all the trouble we've had this winter."

Abby swung toward him, her thin face stricken. "I didn't create that file. It's a lie. Why would I do something like that? If anyone had reason to cause trouble for Dr.

112

Blair, it's you. You and your boyfriend."

Nela realized that the usual office veneer had been stripped away. It was an unpleasant scene, but she watched each one, hoping that one of them might reveal something to explain the necklace in Marian's purse.

Robbie's smooth face turned to stone. "If Cole's worried about the taint of immorality, maybe we should start at the top. With our new director and his girlfriend."

"Let's all stop saying things we'll regret." Peter Owens's voice was calm.

"Don't be a bore, Peter." Grace was amused. "This is more fun than *The View.* What's wrong with some home truths? Everybody knows Robbie's as inflated with venom as a puff adder since Erik got canned. The psychology's a little twisted to tag Abby as the villainess but these days nothing surprises. She's the director's adoring slave even though the rest of us aren't sure he's up to the job. Of course, he responds. Maybe Abby caused the troubles so she could console him." She turned to Abby. "You are living in one of the foundation's guest cabins. I saw his car there very late one night. I told Blythe. But she didn't do anything about it. Of course" — she shot a questioning look at her sister — "you were hell-bent to hire Hollis and you never, ever make a mistake, do you, Sister?" Grace didn't wait for an answer. "It's too bad Dad isn't still around. Dad always had a rule about women in his office. He told everyone, 'Don't fool with the working stock,' and in case you want to know what that means, a man in charge doesn't screw the secretaries. They didn't have assistant curators in those days. But the rule should be the same."

Hollis's voice grated. "My private life and Abby's private life have nothing to do with you or with the foundation. The suggestion that she'd create any kind of situation that would harm the foundation is absurd. That's a nasty, twisted idea. If we're going to consider who might be angry with the foundation or" — his glance at Blythe was measuring — "with Blythe, we don't have far to look." He looked directly at Robbie Powell.

Robbie's boyish face hardened. "What's that supposed to mean?"

Grace laughed. "Come on, Robbie. Skip the hurt innocence. Be a big boy." Her tone was chiding. "You started the toe-to-toe with Hollis when you suggested Abby was vandal-in-chief. Our director may not be able to keep his pants zipped, but he's not a fool. If anybody wants to make a list of people pissed off at Blythe, you and your boyfriend clock in at one and two. Speaking of, how is our former director?"

Robbie's voice was clipped. "Erik's working diligently on a definitive history of the foundation."

Nela sorted out the players in her mind. It was Erik in the cape who had opted to park in the visitors' lot. Now she knew why.

Robbie looked at Blythe. "The foundation should be ready to sign a contract for its publication."

Grace gave a hoot. "Don't be a pushover, Blythe. Robbie's trying to make you feel guilty because you booted Erik."

"Grace, please." Blythe frowned at her sister. "It was time for the foundation to have younger leadership, a more forward-looking vision." The words were smooth, automatic, meaningless.

Robbie was strident. "Erik gave the best years of his life to the foundation. What thanks did he receive?"

Grace looked amused. "I rest my case. Who hates you the most, Blythe? Erik or Robbie? I'd say it was a tie. We know Robbie can get in and out of the building. You can bet Erik still has his keys. Or he could easily filch Robbie's."

"You have keys." Robbie's tone was hard.

"You've been furious ever since Blythe vetoed the grant to the Sutton Gallery. The vandalism began the very next week. I hear the gallery might have to close down."

Nela moved her gaze from one cold face to another.

"The gallery won't close." Grace spoke with icy precision. "I will make sure of that."

Blythe was impatient. "I insist we remain on topic. We have to deal with the file in Abby's computer." She turned toward the assistant curator. "An emotional response isn't helpful. We will deal with facts."

Abby sent a desperate glance toward Hollis. She looked helpless, persecuted, and appealingly lovely.

Nela didn't know these people but the idea seemed to be that Abby and Hollis were lovers. If ever anyone had the aura of a heroine adrift on an ice floe, it was Abby. Her need for support could be genuine or could be calculated to bring out the defending male response of chivalry. There was no doubt the handsome, lanky director was charging to Abby's defense. He gave her a reassuring smile. "We'll get to the bottom of this. It's unpleasant, but it has nothing to do with you, Abby."

Abby's eyes never left his face.

A skateboard disappeared from Abby's

porch. Whose skateboard? When did it disappear? Before Marian Grant fell to her death?

Blythe wasn't deflected. She tapped the folder. "Who knows your password?"

Abby's voice shook. "I don't know. Someone must have gotten it somehow."

Blythe's gaze sharpened. "Did you tell anyone your password?"

"Never. Someone got it somehow." Her violet eyes were dark with misery.

Blythe looked skeptical. "How?"

Francis Garth shifted his big body, rumbled, "Stop badgering her, Blythe."

Blythe massaged one temple. "My password's written on a slip of paper in my desk drawer. Maybe —"

Louise clapped her hands together. "Don't you remember, Blythe? Marian kept a list of current passwords in case a computer needed to be accessed." Louise looked excited. "We can check." She turned to Nela. "Go to Marian's office. She kept a small notebook with tabs in her right-hand desk drawer. Marian was always organized. Look under *p*s for password."

Nela closed the conference room door behind her. It was a relief to be outside that emotionally charged atmosphere. Maybe she would find an answer that would help

Abby. The assistant curator was upset for good reason. To be accused of sending out a sleazy message on the director's letterhead was bad enough, but obviously she and Hollis were more than employer and employee. All the dictums of good sense warned against an office romance, but dictums didn't matter to love. A casual friend had warned her against dating Bill, pointing out, for God's sake, he's in the army, and what kind of life is that? Good advice, but her heart didn't care. Bill hadn't planned to stay in the army. He was going to go back to school . . .

Nela jerked her thoughts back to Abby. Abby's wavering denials did nothing to prove her innocence. Nela walked faster. Abby couldn't prove her innocence and Nela couldn't prove she'd had good intentions when she found that necklace in Marian's purse.

In the main hall, Rosalind looked up from the reception desk. "Hey, is the meeting over? I've got a backlog of calls."

It wasn't Nela's place to say the meeting might go on forever and all hell was breaking loose. She forced a smile. "Still going. They sent me for something from Miss Grant's office."

She felt hopeful when she reached the office door. Maybe she would find the notebook and possibly offer at least a sliver of succor to Abby. If Marian had indeed recorded computer passwords, someone might have obtained Abby's password. The sooner Nela returned, the sooner the meeting would end. By then it would be nearing lunchtime. She'd go back to the apartment and do something about that damned necklace.

She opened the door to chaos. One word blazed in her mind. *Fury.*

6

"Why didn't you ask?" Blythe Webster flung out a hand. "I should have been consulted." Her face was tight with anger.

Rosalind McNeill looked upset and uncertain. "I'm sorry, Miss Webster. Nela stopped in the doorway and I knew something dreadful had happened. I hurried over there. When I saw the mess, I raced to my desk and called nine-one-one. Then I ran to tell you and now you're all here." She gestured toward the staff members, who milled about near Marian's office.

The sound of approaching sirens rose and fell.

Blythe pressed her lips together, finally said brusquely, "I understand, Rosalind. Of course you did the right thing." The words clearly came with an effort at civility. "It's just that we've had so much dreadful publicity. Now there will be more." She turned away, moved toward the front door.

Rosalind looked after her with a worried face.

"You did the right thing." Nela doubted her reassurance brought much comfort to Rosalind. "It's against the law to conceal a crime."

Nela stepped a little nearer to the open office door.

Hollis Blair stared into the trashed office with a tired, puzzled expression. Abby looked relieved. Perhaps she thought the violent destruction — drawers' contents flung on the floor, filing cabinets emptied, computer terminal smashed, art work broken or slashed, chairs overturned — benefitted her. Certainly the file on her computer was no longer the center of attention.

Nela caught snatches of conversation.

Cole Hamilton paced back and forth. ". . . grounds need to be patrolled . . ."

Francis Garth massaged his heavy chin. ". . . obviously dealing with an unbalanced mind . . ."

Grace Webster jangled silver bracelets on one arm. ". . . I heard last week that Erik still hadn't found a job . . ."

Peter Owens looked worried. ". . . suggest care in publicly discussing any grievances . . ."

Robbie Powell was businesslike. ". . . es-

121

sential to prepare a press release . . ."

Outside, the sirens shrilled, then cut off.

Hollis Blair braced his shoulders, moved to join Blythe.

The heavy main door opened. A fast-moving, dark-haired woman in street clothes was followed by two uniformed officers, a thin wiry blonde and a large man with a balding head.

Nela was glad it wasn't the same pair of officers who had been at Marian Grant's apartment. Even the most incurious of police might wonder that she had called for help Friday night and today she had found a vandalized office. Logic denied a link, but swift judgments often had little connection to logic. Happily, she'd never seen either the dark-haired woman or the uniformed officers before.

Blythe was gracious. "Thank you for responding to our call." She looked past the detective and the uniformed officers. Her face stiffened at the approach of a burly redheaded man in a worn pullover sweater and shabby gray corduroy slacks. The sweater looked very old, several threads pulled loose near one shoulder. The shirt beneath the sweater had a frayed collar. Blythe's tone was sharp. "The foundation is private —"

Robbie Powell moved past her to clap the redhead on the shoulder. "Hey, Steve. We don't have a statement yet. Apparently we've had some serious vandalism but let's see what the police can discover. Guess you picked up the call on the *Clarion* scanner?"

Wiry red hair flamed above a broad, pleasant, snub-nosed face spattered with freckles. His gaze stopped when he saw Nela.

Nela felt her lips begin to curve upward, then controlled her face. It was as if she'd looked into the blue eyes of an old friend, but her reaction to the redheaded man was nothing more than a funny link, half glad, half sad, to her past. It was as if Gram were beside her, describing happy summer nights watching first-run movies outside on a moonlit pier in Long Beach with the sound of the ocean as a backdrop. Gram's favorite movie star had been Van Johnson, a chunky, appealing redhead.

Nela put the pieces together. *The Clarion.* Statement. Police scanner. He was a reporter. A print reporter obviously, because he carried a laptop and no cameraman trailed him. Maybe her instinctive positive attitude toward him was as much a recognition of a mindset like hers as a legacy of long-ago movies.

She wondered if the stocky reporter, who

123

had given her one last searching glance before following a clutch of police officers, would ever have heard of the boy-next-door movie star so famous in the 1940s and '50s? Nela had managed to find DVRs of all of Van Johnson's films for Gram and they'd been a great pleasure to her those last few months.

"Nela, are you coming?"

She looked up, startled.

Louise gestured toward the hallway. "Detective Dugan will report on the progress of the investigation in half an hour. Then she will interview each of us individually. Blythe has arranged for lunch to be served in the conference room while we wait." .

Conversation was disjointed. No one spoke to Nela. The staff seemed oblivious to her presence and that suited her fine. She tried to maintain a grave but disinterested expression even though she was focused on a matter that each of them would find supremely interesting, the diamond-and-gold necklace in Marian Grant's purse. It was too late to explain that she'd found the necklace. Perhaps after work she'd pretend she'd been curious, wondered if the purse held a clue, and immediately call the police upon her "discovery" of the necklace. That seemed like a sensible course. But the weight of her knowledge wouldn't be lifted until she could finally hand the purse over to someone in charge.

The conference room door opened and the redheaded reporter stepped inside. He nodded at the large policeman who stood near the buffalo mural, then walked casually toward the far end of the table. If he was attempting to be inconspicuous, he didn't succeed. He was too burly, too vigorous, too intense to miss. His flaming red hair could have used a trim, curling over the rim of the collar that poked above his worn sweater.

"Excuse me." Clearly Blythe addressed him. "This is a private meeting, not open to the press."

"I'm covering the police investigation into a possible theft, possible breaking and entering, possible vandalism at the foundation." He nodded toward the policeman. "It's standard procedure for officers at the scene to sequester possible witnesses. The public portion of police investigations are open to the press."

"Hey, Steve, take a seat." Robbie Powell shot a quick warning look at Blythe. "The foundation always welcomes public scrutiny. From a quick survey, it appears the foundation has been subjected again to pointless vandalism. This probably won't be of much interest to you."

Blythe pressed her lips together. She said nothing further but her irritation was obvious.

The reporter's blue eyes checked out everyone around the table, lingering for a moment when they reached her.

Again she fought an urge to smile.

His gaze moved on. "Thanks, Robbie. You may be right." He strolled around the end of the table, dropped into the chair next to Nela. She noticed that he unobtrusively carried a laptop. When he was seated, he slid the laptop onto his knees, flipped up the lid. He did all of this without dropping his eyes to his lap. His fingers touched the keyboard as he made notes.

Without warning, he looked at her. Their gazes met.

Nela gazed at his familiar, unfamiliar face, broad forehead, snub nose, pugnacious chin. Once again, she fought a deep sense of recognition. She was the first to look away.

The foundation chef, a mountainous woman with blue-white hair and three chins that cascaded to an ample bosom, seemed unfazed by the request for an unexpected meal. Within twenty minutes, she had wheeled a cart into the conference room. Nela and Louise bustled to help and soon an attractive buffet was set on a side table. Louise looked pleased at the array of food: chilled shrimp with cocktail sauce, mixed green salad, crisply crusted ham and cheese quiches, steamed asparagus with a mustard and butter sauce, chocolate cake, coffee, iced tea.

The large police officer remained standing by the door, declining an offer of food. With a balding head but youthful face, Sergeant Fisher might have been an old thirty or a young fifty.

The staff members returned to the seats they'd taken that morning. The meal was eaten quickly and in almost complete silence.

Francis Garth pushed back his plate and glanced at the grandfather clock. "Sergeant" — he turned to the end of the table — "will we be seen in a particular order? I need to leave for Stillwater by one o'clock. I have a meeting with a researcher on switchgrass production."

Sergeant Fisher's voice was as unrevealing as his face. "I will inform Detective Dugan."

Cole Hamilton's face once again furrowed

in worry. He shot a sideways glance toward the policeman. "I'm sure all of us wish the police the very best, but why talk to us? What do we know that would be helpful? Someone broke in."

"Did someone break in?" Grace's tone was silky. "I suppose the police are checking all the ground-floor windows and doors. Of course, if any had been smashed, the alarm would sound." She flicked a glance toward the large square windows. "It would take a crowbar and maybe a sledgehammer to break in through these windows."

Nela's glance flicked to the swiftly moving fingers on the laptop.

Grace smoothed back a lock of strawberry blond hair. "It's the same in all the conference rooms and offices. Dad built this place like a fortress. The only windows that might be vulnerable are the French windows in the main rotunda. Funny thing, though. Nobody" — she looked from face to face — "noticed anything out of the ordinary when they came to work this morning. It's a little hard to believe Rosalind crunched through broken glass when she opened the French window blinds this morning and neglected to mention it."

Peter Owens poked his horn rims higher on his nose. "Your point?"

"If nobody broke in, how did the office trasher get inside?" Grace looked at each face in turn.

No one spoke.

Nela glanced around the room. Blythe looked grim, Hollis thoughtful. The reporter's freckled face was bland. His eyes never dropped beneath the rim of the table. The unobtrusive note-taking continued.

Grace's smile was sardonic. "My, what a silent class. It looks like teacher will have to explain. A key, my dears."

Beside Nela, those broad freckled hands moved silently over the electronic keypad.

Blythe's tone was cold. "It's better to let the authorities reach their own conclusions."

Hollis Blair rubbed knuckles on his bony chin. "We have to provide them with anything pertinent."

Blythe slowly turned toward Nela. There was a welter of conflicting expressions on her usually contained face: uncertainty, inquiry, and possibly suspicion.

Sergeant Fisher's curious gaze moved from Blythe to settle on Nela.

Nela's chest felt tight. She knew what was coming. These police officers hadn't connected Nela to Friday night's 911, but Blythe Webster had heard the sirens and hurried to see. Obviously Blythe was making a connection.

Nela lifted her head, spoke quickly. "Friday night someone broke into Miss Grant's apartment. The sounds of a search woke me up. I was staying there to take care of Miss Grant's cat." She heard the exclamations from around the table. Only Blythe was unaffected. Beside her, the reporter's face remained bland and interested and knowledgeable. He would have seen the police report about Friday night's break-in. Nela had herself looked at a lot of police reports. It had never occurred to her that one day her own name would be included in one.

Hollis Blair's frown was intense. "Why wasn't I told about this?"

Blythe made a dismissive gesture. "It didn't occur to me to mention it, Hollis. Friday night the investigating officers believed someone saw the obituary and thought the apartment would be empty. Marian's desk was searched."

"Searched for what?" Grace's tone was flat.

Nela shrugged. "I suppose for valuables of some kind. But I wonder if there is a connection to the search of her office." She tried to block from her mind the heavy gold necklace in the black Coach bag.

"That makes sense." Blythe suddenly sounded cheered. "Perhaps the thief went from the apartment to the foundation. This must be attempted robbery."

"I hate to throw darts at your trial balloon" — Grace was sardonic — "but there's still a pesky little question: How did a thief get into Marian's apartment and how did a thief get inside the foundation and what the hell was he trying to steal? Or she."

"That's for the police to determine." Blythe was impervious to her sister's attack. "Nela probably forgot to lock the apartment door. One officer said old door locks are easy to jiggle open and maybe someone opened it with a credit card."

Grace folded her arms. "Not even an American Express Platinum could budge a foundation door."

Francis Garth looked thoughtful. "As Grace points out, gaining access to the foundation would be challenging for someone without a key. Does anyone have any ideas?"

Louise shifted uneasily in her chair. Her hand trembled and she hastily placed her fork on her plate. "I don't see how any of us can have any information that would help the police."

Francis added a packet of sugar to his iced

tea. "It may be helpful to determine when the vandalism occurred. Marian's funeral was Thursday. Friday morning I went into her office. I was looking for a file on the Rumer Co-op. I found the file. At ten forty-five Friday morning, her office was fine. Who has been in her office since that time?" He looked inquiringly around the table.

Abby Andrews, violet eyes huge, looked terrified but spoke steadily. "Friday afternoon I returned some papers that I'd borrowed the week before. It was probably about two thirty. The office hadn't been disturbed."

Louise twined the red and gray scarf at her throat around one finger. "I was in her office a few minutes before five Friday. I checked to see if she'd finished the direct bank deposits before" — she swallowed — "before she died." Quick tears misted her eyes. "They were all done. Marian always took care of things on schedule."

Francis reached for the legal pad Nela had placed on the table that morning. The big head once again rose like a buffalo surveying the plain. "Anyone else?"

Silence.

He made quick notes. "How about this morning?"

Silence.

Francis tapped his pen on the legal pad. "Her office was entered after five p.m. Friday and before approximately eleven twenty this morning when Nela" — he nodded toward her — "was sent to look for password information." His face corrugated in thought. "Marian died a week ago today. Why did the searches occur this past weekend?"

Blythe was impatient. "You'd have to ask the thief."

Nela wasn't sure it was her place to speak out, but maybe this mattered. "Chloe exchanged e-mails with Miss Grant's sister. Her sister asked Chloe to stay in Miss Grant's apartment to take care of Jugs. Chloe was there until she left town Friday. I don't think anyone knew I was going to be there Friday night."

Cole Hamilton's round face was puzzled. "How would a thief know that your sister was there during the week or that she left on Friday?"

Grace clapped her long slender hands together. An emerald gleamed in the ornate setting of a ring on her right hand. "Cole" — her tone was a mixture of amusement and affection but her eyes moved around the room, steely and intent — "do you realize what you just said?"

He turned to Grace. "I fail to see anything odd. It seems to me that some thief reading the newspaper couldn't possibly know . . ." His words trailed away.

"Bull's-eye. But there's no bull about it." Grace's eyes were hard. "Only someone associated with the foundation would know that Chloe had been staying in Marian's apartment or that Chloe left Friday."

Nela quickly looked around the room.

Blythe's brows drew down in a sharp frown. Hollis Blair appeared startled. Eyes wide, Abby Andrews pressed fingers against parted lips. Robbie Powell's handsome face smoothed into blankness. Louise Spear shook her head, lips pressed together in negation. Peter Owens looked quizzical, his horn-rimmed glasses gently swinging from one hand. Cole sat with his mouth open, a picture of befuddlement. Francis Garth's heavy face closed into an unreadable mask.

Francis cleared his throat. "We're a long way from determining who might have known what and how either of these crimes occurred. I suggest we remain focused on timing."

"Anybody — with a key — could easily visit the foundation over the weekend. Nobody's here unless we have an event." Grace's tone was musing.

Louise looked uncomfortable. "I wish we'd gone inside Marian's office Saturday. Then we'd know if her office was entered Friday night."

Peter Owens raised an eyebrow. His glasses ceased to move. "You were here Saturday? With someone?"

Louise's thin face stiffened. "I don't have a computer at home. I was doing some genealogy research. It wasn't on foundation time. I'd already cleared it with Blythe."

Blythe waved a hand. "Of course you can use your computer on your free time. Who else was here?"

Louise nodded toward Nela. "Nela came to be sure she knew her way for Monday. I showed her around the building. And Robbie and Erik were here, too."

Robbie spoke quickly. "I can assure you that Erik and I had no occasion to enter Marian's office."

Nela saw a flurry of quick, covert glances. "I wanted to be sure I knew the way Monday." She was aware of a distancing by the staff members, as if each drew back a little, considering, thinking, wondering.

Francis's big chin poked forward. "Did you knock on the door? Or do you have Chloe's keys?"

"I have her keys." Nela lifted her chin,

tried not to sound defensive. "I didn't use them. Louise came to the door."

Grace's chair creaked as she leaned back, apparently completely at ease. "Nela, you look like somebody in the water with circling sharks. I fail to see why you'd stage a break-in at Marian's apartment or trash her office. Unless Chloe asked you to do more than sub for her, I'd say you're the original innocent bystander."

Heavy braided gold necklace with diamonds . . .

The door opened. Detective Dugan strode inside and the spotlight turned. She was perhaps in her early forties. Short dark hair faintly streaked with gray framed a broad face. She wore a wine-colored cable-knit turtleneck, moderate-length black wool skirt, and black penny loafers. She might have been a Realtor or a secretary or a shop owner except for an underlying toughness evident in the dominance of her gaze and the set of a strong chin. She carried an aura of competence, suggesting she could handle anything from gang members to a sexist cop in the break room.

Nela's tense shoulders relaxed. She gave a little sigh of relief. She was no longer the center of attention. Then she felt an intent gaze. She looked at the reporter.

His bright blue eyes watched her, not the police officer.

7

Nela was the last person to be summoned from the conference room to a small adjoining office.

Detective Dugan gestured toward a straight chair in front of the borrowed desk. "Thank you for your patience, Miss Farley." She spoke in a cool voice, rather deep for a woman. Sergeant Fisher sat to one side. He held an electronic notepad.

Nela took her seat and smiled. Her smile fled when the officer's face remained unresponsive.

Dugan glanced at a second electronic pad, read in silence. When she looked up, her gaze was sharp. "When the first responders arrived Friday night, you unlocked the front door. Investigating officers found no sign of a forced entry." She tilted her head. "With Miss Webster's permission, an officer visited the apartment a short while ago."

Nela's hands clenched. Had they found

the purse? She felt a pulse flutter in her throat.

"I have a report here." Dugan tapped the screen. "An officer made several attempts to engage the lock and open the door with a credit card. He didn't succeed. However" — her tone was judicious — "an intruder equipped with a plastic strip or a lock pick would likely gain entry."

"Friday night an officer told me that when the housekeeper found Marian Grant's body, she hurried upstairs and entered the apartment with a card from a playing deck." Nela felt triumphant.

There might have been a flicker of admiration in Dugan's eyes. "It isn't commonly known, but a laminated playing card is more supple than a credit card and more likely to succeed. Most people don't carry an extra playing card with them. Are you suggesting the housekeeper was the intruder Friday night?"

Nela's response was quick. "I have no idea who broke in."

"No one 'broke' in." Dugan spoke with finality. "If there was an intruder, the means of access hasn't been determined." She tilted her head to one side, like a cat watching a sparrow. "How do you think the intruder gained entry?"

"I don't know any thieves. I don't know what they carry or how they get in. I locked that door Friday night." Nela looked into Dugan's suspicious face. "Someone came in. I think they used a key."

"A key." Oddly, there was a note of satisfaction in Dugan's voice. "You have a key, both to the apartment and to the foundation."

Nela sensed a threat.

"You arrived Friday afternoon. You called nine-one-one at one thirty-five a.m. claiming the apartment of the late Marian Grant had been entered. Officers found much of the living room in disarray, suggesting an intense search. There was no sign of forced entry. Moreover, you had to unlock the front door to admit the officers. It is rare" — the detective's tone was dry — "for a fleeing intruder who has presumably jiggled a lock with a credit card or some other tool to carefully close and lock a door. That takes time. Fleeing criminals find time in short supply. Today police were summoned to find evidence of a search at Miss Grant's office." Dugan shifted forward in her chair, her brown eyes cold. "Let's say someone plans to search Miss Grant's office. There may be information in that office that someone cannot afford to be found."

Nela listened with increasing alarm. She didn't know where Dugan was going, but the detective's gaze was hard and searching.

The detective's eyes never left Nela's face. "The searcher might be aware that the foundation could not easily be broken into. In fact, the searcher must have known that no alarm was triggered by the use of a key after hours. Miss Spear reassured you about that when you came on Saturday."

Nela had thought Louise Spear liked her. But maybe she'd innocently told the detective about their conversation on Saturday.

The detective continued, her tone brusque. "It appears the searcher used a key to enter the foundation. There are a limited number of persons who have keys to Haklo Foundation. What steps could be taken by a possessor of a key to suggest innocence?" The question was as smooth as a knife sliding into butter. "Any ideas, Miss Farley?" Dugan's broad face looked heavy, formidable.

"I don't know anything about Marian Grant or her work at the foundation." But she knew Marian's purse held a stolen necklace. The necklace had to be the reason for the search. Maybe if she told the detective . . . Nela pictured Dugan's response — suspicion, disbelief, accusation.

Dugan spoke in a quick cadence. "Your sister, Chloe Farley, arrived in Craddock last September."

Nela was puzzled. What did Chloe's arrival have to do with a search of Marian Grant's apartment and office?

"The week after your sister arrived, a foundation employee's car was set on fire." Dugan leaned forward. "Gasoline was poured inside, ignited. The employee quit. The next week Chloe Farley was hired by the foundation."

Nela controlled a hot flash of anger. The interview with the detective had turned ugly. She had to think fast, try to reason with this woman. "Are you claiming that Chloe set fire to somebody's car on the chance that the woman would quit and Chloe would get her job? That's absurd. Chloe would never burn up someone's car. And how could she know the girl would quit or, if she did, that Chloe could get the job?"

The detective continued in the same clipped voice. "Your sister came to Craddock with Leland Buchholz. His father is a financial adviser who has worked with foundation investments. People get jobs because they know people. Jed Buchholz spoke to Miss Webster the week before" — she paused for emphasis — "the car fire.

Miss Webster told him if they had any openings, she'd be happy to hire your sister. Let's review what has happened since Chloe Farley started to work at the foundation." Her eyes dropped to the notepad. She brushed a finger on the screen. "Tuesday, November fifteen, Indian baskets being photographed for publication were found hacked to pieces. Monday night, December five, activated sprinklers in Mr. Powell's office flooded his desk and damaged a sofa and chair. The flooring and rug had to be replaced. Friday, December sixteen, outdoor fountains were turned on, allowed to run for some period of time, then turned off, causing the pipes to freeze and break. Up to this point, everything appears to be vandalism for the sake of destruction. Then what happens? Something entirely different." A flicker of irritation creased her face. "The police should have been immediately notified when Miss Webster's necklace — valued at two hundred and fifty thousand dollars — was stolen from her desk drawer. She discovered the theft Thursday morning, January five. However, now that we have been informed, it seems clear what happened."

Nela's voice was equally clipped. "What does any of this have to do with Chloe?"

"She's the only new employee." Dugan flung out the words like a knife thrower hitting a target.

Nela didn't try now to keep the hard edge of anger from her voice. "That's no reason to suspect her. Moreover, she isn't the only new employee. The foundation has a new director." She wasn't sure when Dr. Blair came to work but she didn't think he'd been there much longer than Chloe.

The detective was unimpressed. "This is Dr. Blair's first post as a foundation director. Should he someday seek to move to a larger foundation, his resume will have to include a description of these incidents and his inability to protect the foundation. Miss Andrews is also a new employee this fall. However, no one thinks" — her tone was bland — "that Miss Andrews would in any way jeopardize Dr. Blair's job. That leaves your sister."

"You're wrong. Besides, how could Chloe steal Miss Webster's necklace?"

"Miss Webster informed me today that it was common knowledge around the foundation that she kept the necklace in her desk drawer. The necklace was a gift from her father and a sentimental favorite. She made a point to wear it during the Monday-morning staff meetings." Dugan's face folded in disgust. "A quarter million dollars in an unlocked drawer. She might as well have hung up a sign with an arrow: Get rich here."

Nela couldn't imagine carelessly leaving a necklace worth — to her — a fortune in an unlocked desk. "She kept the necklace in her desk? That's crazy."

"Yeah. You got that right. But here's the point. That necklace rested safely in that drawer until your sister came to work here."

"Detective" — Nela's voice was icy — "you have no right to accuse Chloe. Where's your proof?"

"I don't have proof." Dugan's voice was dour. "I feel it in my gut. Your sister comes to town. She needs a job. Miss Webster says she can have the first opening. The next week, a fire scares off Louise Spear's assistant. There's a job available and your sister gets it. Nothing more happens until she's been here long enough to find out about a necklace worth big bucks. Now, if the necklace disappeared right after she came, there might be some suspicion. So she muddies up the water with vandalism. When the necklace is stolen, everybody chalks it up to just another crazy thing by somebody who has it in for the foundation. I don't buy that scenario. It stinks. Something's out of kilter here. All the vandalism accomplished was fouling up Dr. Blair's record and upsetting Miss Webster. The necklace is different. That's money. Lots of money. I checked out your sister. She's never had a regular job —"

Nela looked at Dugan. She would read the police office as steady, contained, purposeful. She had probably never had a flaky moment in her life. Would she understand that Chloe never lived for regular? Chloe frosted cupcakes, helped raise rabbits, parked cars at charity functions *(Nela, I got to drive a Jag today!),* was a magician's assistant, tracked island foxes on Catalina Island as part of an effort to protect the endangered species, worked as a kitchen hand in a gourmet restaurant.

"— and she doesn't have any money. We're checking everything out. I saw the feature in the *Clarion* about her boyfriend winning a free trip for two to Tahiti. Maybe that's phony. We'll find out. Maybe she's got a lot of money now."

"Chloe has no money. Neither do I. Does that make us thieves?" Nela's voice was tight with fury.

Dugan's jaw set in a stubborn line. "She comes to town. All of this follows."

"She wasn't here Friday night. She wasn't

here this weekend."

Dugan's hard stare was accusing. "You're here."

It was like coming around an outcrop on a mountain trail to find a sheer drop.

Dugan's stare didn't waver. "I understand you talked to her Friday night."

In high school, Nela had once gone to Tijuana with a bunch of kids. She'd not realized they were going to a bullfight. She'd hated watching the bull pricked by tiny barbs. She'd bolted from the stands, waited on a hot dusty street until the others joined her. Now she felt one sharp jab after another and, like the bull, there was no escape for her from the arena. The detective must have quizzed each of the staff members about Chloe and Nela. Louise had been kind and welcoming but it was she who must have told Dugan that Nela had a key and knew there was no burglar alarm. Even though the director of publications had seemed genuinely interested in Chloe, Peter Owens must have revealed that Chloe called Nela Friday evening. Dugan was taking innocent pieces of information and building a case against her and against Chloe.

"You know how I see it, Miss Farley? The necklace was stolen before Miss Grant's accident. What if Miss Grant knew Chloe took the necklace? What if she had some kind of proof? What if she told Chloe she was keeping that information in a safe place away from the foundation? But Miss Grant's unexpected death made things tricky."

. . . board rolled on the second step . . .

The detective's accusatory words jabbed at Nela as her thoughts raced. Nela heard them, understood them, but she grappled with a far more deadly understanding. Marian Grant either stole the necklace herself or she knew who took the necklace. It had to be the latter. That's why Marian Grant died. She must have told the thief that she had the necklace, that she'd put it in a safe place. She had not summoned the police. Perhaps she wanted to avoid more disturbing headlines about the foundation. Perhaps she wanted to use the possession of the necklace to block future attacks against the foundation. Perhaps she saw the necklace as a means of making the thief accede to her demands, whatever they might be. Perhaps she set a deadline for the thief to quit or confess. What if the deadline was Monday morning?

. . . board rolled on the second step . . .

Dugan threw words like rocks. "Maybe Chloe thought the information was in the apartment and that's why she volunteered

148

to take care of the cat. Maybe she looked and looked with no success. Maybe she worried all the way to Tahiti and called you and said you had to look for her. Once again we get the pattern. You dial nine-one-one and claim a break-in and that sets it up for the office search to look like someone else must have done it."

Nela wanted to shout that Dugan had everything wrong. She was looking for a vandal and a thief. She should be looking for a murderer.

Marian Grant had been murdered.

Nela opened her lips, closed them. What was she going to tell this hard-faced woman? That she'd looked into a cat's eyes and seen his thoughts? . . . *board rolled on the second step* . . . She could not claim to have special information. She could imagine Dugan's response to a claim that a cat had seen a skateboard. Yet now she felt certain that she knew the truth of that early-morning fall.

Nela wasn't ready to deal with the reality that she knew what was in a cat's mind, if reality it was. Not now. Maybe never. However the vivid thought had come to her — a psychic intimation, a reporter's intuition, a funny split instant of a memory of a teenage Bill and his skateboard tangling with her climb up steep steps to a dead

149

woman's apartment — she couldn't share that knowledge.

Yet she had to face the truth that a skateboard on the steps, removed after Marian's fall, inexorably meant that Marian Grant's death was no accident. But if Nela suggested murder, Dugan would likely add murder to the list of Chloe's supposed crimes.

Dugan was quick to attack. "You have something to say?"

"Yes, I do." Nela spoke with determination and confidence. "Chloe is innocent. I am innocent. I don't know what's behind the things that have happened at the foundation. Chloe never even mentioned the vandalism except for the girl's car. She seemed surprised that she quit."

Dugan raised a skeptical brow. "Your sister never mentioned the vandalism to you?"

Nela wondered how to explain a free spirit to the fact-grounded detective. "She talked about Leland and what they were doing. Chloe never thinks about bad things. She's always upbeat. You're right that something bad is going on at the foundation, but it doesn't have anything to do with Chloe or me. I agree" — her tone was grave — "there's something very wrong here. I think the theft of the necklace was part of the other things, not because it was worth a lot of money." And Marian Grant died because she knew the identity of the thief. But that she couldn't say, not without admitting she could, at this very minute, lead police to the necklace, which would likely result in her prompt arrest.

Dugan looked sardonic. "Nice try. Turning on a sprinkler system isn't in the same league as heisting jewelry worth a couple of hundred thou. Besides, if the necklace wasn't stolen for money, why take it? I've been a cop for a long time and, like a good coon dog, I know the real scent when I smell it."

Nela shook her head. "It isn't just the necklace. There was too much destruction in Miss Grant's office."

Dugan looked puzzled.

"There was fury. It wasn't just a search."

Dugan's smile was bleak. "Camouflage. Just like the baskets and the sprinkler and the fountains."

8

Steve Flynn's strong stubby fingers flew over the keypad. He was nudging the deadline, but he still had ten minutes. He'd fallen back into the routine as if he'd never been away, the early pages locked down around two, late-breaking news up to four. His six years on the *LA Times* until he was let go in one of the wholesale newsroom firings seemed like a mirage. Maybe they had been. Most of that life had been a mirage. Especially Gail. He felt the familiar twist, half anger, half disbelief. So much for 'til death us do part. Maybe that phrase ought to be dropped from modern weddings. Maybe the vows should read, *I'll stay until something better comes along.* Or, *been good to know you, but my way isn't your way.* When the call came about his dad's stroke, he had told her he needed to go back to Craddock to run the *Clarion.* Somebody had to do it unless they sold the newspaper that had been founded by his great-grandfather. His brother Sean was a surgeon in Dallas. Sean had never been drawn to the business while Steve had grown up nosing around the newsroom. He tried to explain to Gail about the paper and family and keeping a flame alight in the little town they loved. Gail stood there within his reach, close enough to touch, but she receded like the tide going out. Oh, she'd been kind. Or thought she had, her words smooth . . . *felt us growing apart for a while now . . . have such a great future here . . . got a callback today . . . The producer wants to see more of me . . . wish you the best of luck . . .*

He'd been back a little over a year and the divorce had been final for six months.

He returned to the screen, his fingers thumping a little too hard on the keyboard. He finished the story, glanced at the time. Four more minutes. He scrolled up.

A gold and diamond necklace valued at approximately $250,000 was stolen from the desk of Haklo Foundation Trustee Blythe Webster sometime between Jan. 4 and 5, according to Craddock Police Detective K. T. Dugan.

Detective Dugan said the necklace was an original work of art created by Tiffany &

Co. for Miss Webster's father, Harris Webster, who established the foundation.

The theft was revealed Monday when police were called to the foundation to investigate a possible break-in. Detective Dugan said the foundation had been entered, apparently over the weekend, and the office of late employee Marian Grant vandalized.

Detective Dugan said Miss Webster had not previously reported the theft of the necklace because she wished to avoid further negative publicity for the foundation, which has been attacked by vandals several times, beginning in September. Incidents include a car set afire in the foundation employees' parking lot; destruction of valuable Indian baskets; activated fire sprinklers in an office resulting in property damage; and water turned on, then off in an outdoor fountain, causing frozen pipes. The car fire occurred Sept. 19 during office hours. Other incidents occurred after hours.

According to the police report, the office vandalized this weekend had been occupied by Grant, who was chief operating officer at the time of her death, Jan. 9. Miss Grant, a jogger, was found dead at the foot of her apartment stairs, apparently the victim of a fall. Police said the fall may have been caused by new running shoes. Police said Miss Grant customarily jogged early every morning.

Police received a 911 call at 11:40 a.m. Monday from Rosalind McNeill, Haklo Foundation receptionist. In the call, Mrs. McNeill reported that an office was trashed, papers thrown everywhere, file cabinets emptied, the computer monitor cracked, and furniture overturned.

According to police, Mrs. McNeill said the office had not been emptied of Miss Grant's belongings and there was no way to determine if anything was missing.

Detective Dugan declined to suggest a motive for the invasion of the office.

The detective also declined to speculate on whether the damage to Miss Grant's office was connected to a reported break-in early Saturday morning at the dead woman's apartment at 1 Willow Lane. A 911 call was received at 1:35 a.m. According to the police report, the call was placed by Cornelia Farley, a temporary employee of the foundation who was staying at the apartment to care for the late resident's cat. Miss Farley told police she awoke to hear sounds of a search in the apartment living room. She called 911.

When police arrived, no trace of an intruder was found, but Detective Dugan said a desk had been searched and the living room was in disarray. Detective Dugan said it was unknown if anything had been removed from the apartment.

The Haklo Foundation issued a statement: "Operations at the Haklo Foundation remain unaffected by the series of unexplained incidents, which apparently are the work of vandals. Blythe Webster, foundation trustee, announced today a reward of $100,000 for information leading to the apprehension and conviction of the vandals. Miss Webster will personally fund the reward. No foundation monies will be used. Miss Webster emphasized that she and all the employees will not be deterred from the execution of their duties by this apparent vendetta against the foundation."

Detective Dugan said the investigation is continuing.

When he came home to the *Clarion,* Steve had insisted he was a reporter. There were five of them in the newsroom. He glanced around the room, gray metal desks, serviceable swivel chairs, maps of the county on one wall, a montage of early-day black-and-white photographs of Craddock on another.

At the far desk, Ace Busey looked older than Methuselah, with a lined face and drooping iron gray mustache. Ace still smoked, but he covered city and county politics like a burr on a horse's back, darting out of meetings long enough to catch a drag when he was certain nothing was going to pop. He'd never been wrong yet.

Freddi Frank nibbled on a cinnamon bun as she made notes. Freddi ran the Life section: houses, gardens, recipes, and women's groups, any spare inches allotted to wire coverage of the glitterati currently atop the celebrity leaderboard. Freddi was unabashedly plump and amiable, and her Aunt Bill's candy was the centerpiece of the staff Christmas party.

The sports desk was unoccupied. Joe Guyer could be anywhere: at a wrestling match, covering a high school basketball game, adding clips to his old-fashioned notebook. Joe worked on a laptop but he continued to distrust the electronic world. Balding, weedy, and always in a slouch, he had an encyclopedic memory of sports trivia, including facts large and small about the Sooners football team. He could at any time drop interesting tidbits: the first OU football game in September 1895 was played on a field of low prairie grass near what is now Holmberg Hall; the Sooners beat the Aggies seventy-five to zero on November 6, 1904 in their first contest; 1940 quarterback Jack Jacobs was known as Indian in a tribute to his Creek heritage; in 1952 halfback Billy Vessels was the first OU player to win the Heisman Trophy.

Jade Marlow rounded out the lot. Steve didn't glance toward her desk. He was aware of her. Very aware. The new features reporter, Jade was a recent J-school grad, good, quick, smart, glossily lovely, a tall slender blonde, curvy in all the right places, sure she was going big places. She'd been inviting, but he had simply given her a cool blue look and walked away and now she avoided him. That was good. He looked at her and he saw Gail — beautiful, confident, blond, smart, and a producer wanted to see more of her. How much more? Did she get the role? Or was she playing a different kind of role? He didn't give a damn. Not anymore. He wrenched his mind back to the newsroom.

Around the corner from the sports desk was the lair of the *Clarion* photographer, Alex Hill. Pudgy and always disheveled, Alex handled a Nikon D3S as delicately as a surgeon with a scalpel.

Steve felt pumped. It wasn't the *LA Times*

newsroom, but, in its own way, it was better. That's why he didn't mind spending part of every day in the publisher's office. Maybe Dad would come back. Right now he still had only a trace of movement on his right side and his speech was jerky and sometimes unintelligible. It was up to Steve to make sure the *Clarion* kept on keeping on. Ads were the paper's lifeblood. He went to all the service clubs meetings. He renewed old friendships, made new ones. He rode herd on ads and circulation and the aged heating system and the printing press that might need to be replaced. A memo from the business office recommended switching paper purchase to a mill in India. He'd worry about that tomorrow. Right now he was pleased with his afternoon. A good story, would probably run above the fold.

Steve clicked send and looked across the room at a trim, white-haired woman. As the file arrived, she half turned from her computer screen to give him a thumbs-up. Mim Barlow, the city editor, had worked at the *Clarion* since Steve was a little boy. She knew everyone in town, insisted on accuracy, and sensed news like a hawk spotting a rabbit. She was blunt, brusque, stonefaced, and scared the bejesus out of kid reporters. She was tough, but her toughness masked a crusader's heart. She'd helped break a story about abuse at a local nursing home that resulted in two criminal convictions and the closure of the home. The night Mim received the Oklahoma Press Association's Beachy Musselman Award for superior journalism, she'd walked back to the table carrying the plaque and taken her seat to thunderous applause. She'd bent closer to him. "If I'd sent the reporter out a month sooner — I'd heard some stuff at the beauty shop — maybe that frail little woman wouldn't have died. Good, Steve, but not good enough. I was busy with that series on the county commissioners and that road by the Hassenfelt farm. I let little get in the way of big."

Maybe it was being around Mim that made him look at people's faces and sometimes see more than anyone realized. He'd looked at a lot of faces today. One stood out, a face he wouldn't forget. He'd seen her last night at Hamburger Heaven. He'd watched her leave with regret, wishing that someday, somehow he would see her again, damning himself as a fool to be enchanted simply because a beautiful, remote woman sat at a nearby table and her loneliness spoke to his.

Today he had seen her again.

He reached for his laptop, checked his notes. Cornelia Farley, called Nela. Pronounced *Nee-la.* Pretty name. Glossy black hair that looked as if it would be soft to the touch, curl around his fingers. He'd known last night that he wouldn't forget her face and bewitching eyes that held depths of feeling.

She'd been the last to be interviewed by Dugan. As staff members exited the police interview, Steve queried them. All had "no comment" except Robbie Powell, who promised to provide an official statement. Powell refused to confirm or deny that Blythe Webster had declared a news blackout. Steve remained in the hall asking questions, though now he knew there would be no answers.

When Nela came out of the room, she'd walked fast, never noticed him standing nearby. Her cheeks were flushed, her eyes bright. She moved like a woman in a hurry.

Last night she'd been ice. This afternoon she was fire.

He wanted to know why.

She'd moved past him. He would have followed but he had a job to do. Brisk steps sounded and he'd turned to Dugan.

"Hey, Katie." He'd known Katie Dugan since he was a high school kid nosing after the city hall reporter and she was a new patrol officer. "Let's run through the various incidents here at the foundation."

The blockbuster was the revelation of the theft of Blythe Webster's two-hundred-fifty-thousand-dollar necklace. Katie had been grim about the fact that no report had been made at the time. She'd related the disparate incidents, including a somewhat vague reference to misuse of foundation stationery. She'd balked at explaining how the stationery had been used, but she'd provided a detailed description of the necklace: diamonds set in eighteen-karat gold acanthus leaves connected by gold links. He'd come back to the office knowing he had a front-page story.

Now he'd finished his story but he couldn't forget Nela Farley. He had seen her in profile as he left Haklo, sitting at her desk, working on a computer, but her face spoke of thoughts far afield. There was a determined set to her jaw. Now he looked across the room at the city desk, gave an abrupt nod, and came to his feet. As he passed Mim's desk, he jerked a thumb in the general direction of Main Street. "Think I'll drop by the cop shop."

Mim's sharp gray eyes brightened. "You got a hunch?"

"Maybe." Maybe he felt the tug of a story behind a story. Nela Farley's interview with Katie Dugan had transformed her. As a newcomer to town, her involvement at Haklo should have been peripheral. But he knew he cared about more than the story. He wanted to know Nela Farley. Maybe he was not going to let the little get in the way of the big.

At four thirty, Louise stepped through the connecting door. Her frizzy hair needed a comb. She'd not bothered to refresh her lipstick. Her eyes were dark with worry.

Nela watched her carefully. Had the detective told Louise that Nela and Chloe were her number-one suspects? Since the brutal interview with Dugan, Nela had made progress on the stack of grant applications while she considered how to combat the accusations against her and Chloe. It was essential that she continue to work at the foundation. It came down to a very clear imperative. She had to find out who was behind the vandalism, including the theft and likely the murder of Marian Grant, to save herself and Chloe. But first she had to get rid of the necklace.

Since Dugan hadn't returned with a warrant for her arrest, Nela felt sure that the purse still remained hidden behind the stacked cans of cat food. Would it occur to the detective that the search of the apartment and the office might be a search for the necklace? Right now, Dugan was convinced of Chloe's guilt and believed the necklace had already been sold and the proceeds pocketed. That's why Dugan questioned the expensive trip to Tahiti. An investigation would prove that there had been a contest and that Leland won. No doubt inquiries were being made into Chloe and Nela's finances as well. If poor equaled honest, she and Chloe had no worries. Unfortunately, the fact that Chloe's bank account and Nela's had lean balances didn't prove their innocence.

Louise gave a huge sigh. "What a dreadful day. That horrible letter . . . At least it wasn't sent to anyone other than members of the grants committee. That's a huge relief. But I don't know what to think about Marian's office. There doesn't seem to be any point other than making a mess. Of course there wasn't any point to any of the other vandalism. And you must have been very upset when someone broke into the apartment." Her glance at Nela was apologetic. "I'm afraid I've been so busy thinking about the foundation, I didn't even stop to think how you must be feeling." Louise came around the desk, gently patted Nela's shoulder. "A young girl like you isn't used to these sorts of incidents." Louise was earnest. "I don't want you to think things like this happen much in Craddock. I've been at the foundation for twenty-three years and we never had any vandalism before September. Poor Hollis. The car was set on fire only a month after he came. What a way to begin your first big job. He'd only been an assistant director at a foundation up in Kansas for two years, and it was quite a plum for him to become head of the Haklo Foundation. Of course, it was real hard on Erik, our former director. But anyone who works for a family foundation has to remember that the family runs everything. Blythe's the sole trustee and she has complete power over the staff."

"Why did she want a new director?" Nela knew the question might be awkward, but she was going to ask a lot of awkward questions.

"Oh." It was as if a curtain dropped over Louise's face. "She met Hollis at a big philanthropy meeting in St. Louis. We attend every year. Hollis made a good impression. Fresh blood. That kind of thing." She was suddenly brisk. "Here I am chattering away. You go home early and get some rest."

As Nela left, Louise was sitting at her desk, her face once again drawn with worry. Nela forced herself to walk to Leland's VW even though she felt like running. The sooner she reached the apartment, the sooner she could decide what to do about the damnable necklace.

Steve Flynn ignored his shabby leather jacket hanging on the newsroom coat tree. He rarely bothered with a coat. Oklahomans weren't much for coats even on bitter winter days. Hey, maybe it was in the twenties today. By the end of the week, it would be forty and that would seem balmy. He always moved too fast to feel the cold, thoughts churning, writing leads in his head, thinking of sources to tap, wondering what lay behind facades.

He took the stairs down two at a time to a small lobby with a reception counter. A gust of wind caught his breath as he stepped onto Main Street. Craddock's downtown was typical small-town Oklahoma. Main Street ran east and west. Traffic was picking up as five o'clock neared. Most buildings were two stories, with shops on the street and offices above. Craddock had shared in the prosperity fueling the southwest with the boom in natural gas production, especially locally from the Woodford Shale. New facades had replaced boarded-up windows. Some of the businesses had been there since he was a kid: Carson's Drugs at the corner of Main and Maple, Walker's Jewelry, Indian Nation Bank, Hamburger Heaven, and Beeson's Best Bargains. There were plenty of new businesses: Jill's Cupcakes, Happy Days Quilting Shop, Carole's Fashions, and Mexicali Rose Restaurant.

It was two blocks to city hall. He walked fast, hoping he'd catch Katie before she went off duty. Again he didn't use an elevator. The stairwells were dingy and had a musty smell. He came out in a back hallway and went through an unmarked frosted door to the detectives' room.

Mokie Morrison looked up from his desk. "Jesus, man, it's twenty-two degrees out there. That red thatch keep you warm?" Mokie wore a sweater thick enough for Nome.

Steve grinned at Mokie, who had three carefully arranged long black strands draped over an ever-expanding round bald spot. "Eat your heart out, baldie." He jerked his head. "Dugan still here?"

"She's got a hot date with her ex. Better hustle to catch her."

At Katie's office door, he hesitated before he knocked. Katie and Mark Dugan's on-off relationship evoked plenty of good-natured advice from her fellow officers. Katie blew off comments from soulful to ribald with a shrug. Steve was pretty sure Katie would never get over her ex. Mark was handsome, charming, lazy, always a day late and a dollar short. Like Mokie had told her one night as he and Steve and Katie shared beers, "Katie, he's not worth your time." Good advice but cold comfort in a lonely bed on a winter night. Just like he told himself that he was better off without Gail and then he'd remember her standing naked in their dusky bedroom, blond hair falling loose around her face, ivory white skin, perfect breasts, long slender legs.

He knocked.

Katie looked up as he stepped inside. "Yo, Steve." She glanced at a plain watch face on a small black leather band.

"Just a few questions." He turned a straight chair in front of her desk, straddled the seat. "I was out in the hall at Haklo when you talked to the staff. I timed the interviews."

She raised a strong black brow. "That's anal. Even for you."

"Sometimes I pick up a vibe in funny

ways. That's what happened today." His gaze was steady. "Some interviews lasted a few minutes, several ran about ten. You spent thirty-one minutes talking to Miss Farley."

Not a muscle moved in Katie's stolid face.

"Come on, Katie." His tone was easy. "I picked up some stuff at Haklo. Nela Farley's been in town since Friday afternoon. She's subbing for her sister, Chloe, Louise Spear's assistant. Why the inquisition?"

Katie massaged her chin with folded knuckles, an unconscious mannerism when she was thinking hard.

Steve kept his face bland.

Katie chose her words as carefully as a PGA player studying the slope of a green. "I thought it was proper to discuss her nine-one-one call from Miss Grant's apartment Friday night."

Not, Steve thought quickly, to talk about a break-in or even a *purported* break-in, but the placement of a 911 call. He kept his voice casual. "Yeah, the report said she awoke to find an intruder in the living room."

"She said" — slight emphasis — "she heard someone in the living room. She appeared to be upset." Kati's tone was even. "She unlocked the front door when the

169

investigating officers arrived. That's the only entrance to the apartment. No windows were broken. Officers found no sign of a forced entry."

He frowned. "How did an intruder get inside?"

Katie was firm. "Investigating officers found no evidence of an illegal entry at Miss Grant's apartment."

He raised an eyebrow. "Are you saying Miss Farley lied?"

"I am saying no evidence was found to suggest a forced entry." She glanced again at her watch. "If that's all —"

He was running out of time. Work was fine but other people's problems never beat out sex, and Katie was impatient to leave. He spoke quickly. "The apartment appeared to have been searched. Miss Grant's office was searched. Do you believe both incidents are part of the pattern of vandalism, including the missing necklace?"

"Yes." Clipped. Definite. One word. *Nada mas.*

"How can Miss Farley be involved since she arrived in Craddock Friday?"

"The investigation is following several leads." Katie came to a full stop, pushed back her chair.

Steve was exasperated. "That's no answer.

You talked to Miss Farley for thirty-one minutes. Is she a person of interest?"

Katie came to her feet. "At this point in the investigation, there is not a single suspect. No premature announcement will be made." She pulled out a lower drawer, retrieved a black shoulder bag, stood.

He rose and turned the chair to once again face the gray metal desk.

Katie was already out the door.

In the hall, he watched her stride toward the exit. Katie had been careful, circumspect, cautious, but when he connected the dots, he understood why ice had turned to fire. Nela Flynn was in big trouble.

Jugs followed Nela into the kitchen, chirped impatiently as she closed the blinds. She put the McDonald's sack on the counter. He jumped up and sniffed. "Not good for you, buddy. I'll get yours in a minute."

With the blinds closed, no one could see her. The front door was blocked by the safety wedge. She dropped to one knee by Jugs's cabinet, pushed aside the stacked cans of cat food, felt weak with relief. The black leather bag was there. She started to reach, quickly drew back her hand. If ordinary criminals were careful about prints, she wasn't going to be mutt enough to leave hers on Marian Grant's purse.

Once again attired in the orange rubber gloves, she edged out the purse, pulled the zipper, held the sides wide, moved the red leather gloves, saw the glitter of gold and diamonds. So far, so good. She took comfort that the police hadn't entered the apartment, found the stolen jewelry. But safety was illusory. She had to get rid of the necklace. ASAP.

Jugs stood on his back paws, patted at the shelf. "I know, buddy. It's suppertime and you think I'm nuts." She returned the purse to the cabinet, knowing any casual search would find it. But for now, that was the best she could do. She dished up Jugs's food, placed the bowls on the newspaper, provided fresh water.

Jugs crouched and ate, fast.

She found a paper plate for herself, opened and poured a Coke. By the time she settled at the kitchen table, Jugs was finished.

The lean cat padded to the table, jumped, once again settled politely just far enough to indicate he wasn't encroaching upon her meal. He gazed at her with luminous green eyes. ". . . *miss Her* . . ."

Nela stared into those beautiful eyes. For now, she would accept that whenever she looked at Jugs, she moved into his mind. She took some comfort from that rapport, whether real or imagined. "I'm sorry." And she was. Sorry for Jugs, grieving for lost love. Sorry for everyone lost and lonely and hurt in an uncaring world. Sorry for what might have been with Bill. Sorry for herself and Chloe, enmeshed in a mess not of their making. Sorry and, more than that, determined to do what she had to do to keep them both safe. It was, she realized, the first time since Bill died that she'd felt fully alive.

She looked into Jugs's gleaming eyes.

"*. . . You're mad . . .*"

She pulled her gaze away from his, unwrapped a double cheeseburger, began to eat. She felt a flicker of surprise. Yeah. Jugs had it right. She was mad as hell. So many paths were blocked. It was too late to report finding the necklace. She could claim it occurred to her to wonder if anything had been taken from the bag so she opened it . . . She shook her head. Nice try, but it wouldn't fly. The detective would never believe she'd found the necklace in the purse. Detective Dugan would see that claim as a lie and be convinced Chloe had stolen the necklace and left it in the apartment for Nela to keep safe. The necklace had to go.

Throw it away?

It would be her luck to toss the jewelry in a trash bin and be seen.

How about taking a drive, tossing the necklace into the woods? Two hundred and fifty thousand dollars flung into underbrush? Probably a birdwatcher would ring the police before she drove a hundred yards. If she parked and walked into the woods, maybe dug a hole, she'd leave footprints.

What did you do with something that didn't belong to you?

She ate, dipping the fries in pepper-dotted ketchup, drank the Coke, and made plans.

At Hamburger Heaven, Steve stirred onions and grated cheese into chili and beans. He spread margarine on a square of jalapeño-studded cornbread. He once again sat in his usual booth. Beyond the tables, every space was taken at the counter. A roar of conversation competed with Reba McEntire's newest country music hit. Steve shut out the lyrics about love gone wrong, picked through the nuances of his exchanges with Katie.

When he'd asked if Nela Farley was a person of interest, Katie could have made several replies. She was never shy about barking, "No comment." However, he could then have written a story saying that Detective K. T. Dugan declined to reveal whether Nela Farley was a person of interest. Any reader might reasonably assume, as he did, that Dugan's reply definitely indicated Farley was indeed a person of interest.

That wasn't the only red flag. Instead of discussing a break-in at Marian Grant's apartment, Katie talked about the 911 call and the fact that there was no proof anyone had broken in. If no one broke in, either Nela Farley had searched the room, then placed a fake 911 call — she had permitted someone to enter and leave, then ditto — or someone with a key to Marian Grant's apartment was the intruder.

If there wasn't an intruder . . .

Steve knew he wanted to believe Nela's story. But Katie was a good cop and she'd lined up Nela Farley in her sights. Why did he want to defend the girl with the intelligent, sensitive face? He knew better than most that beauty didn't count for much and a woman could look at you with love in her eyes one minute and it's-time-for-you-to-go the next. Women lied.

Why would a girl who'd never been to Craddock want to plow through the desk in a dead woman's apartment?

He always thought quickly and the answer

was waiting in his mind. Nela Farley had a connection to Craddock. Her sister, Chloe, worked at Haklo. In fact, Nela was in town to sub for her sister while Chloe and her boyfriend were on a two-week freebie to Tahiti. Freddi had written a fun feature for the Life section about Leland Buchholz's contest win and his and Chloe's plans for the Tahiti holiday. Alex took some great shots, capturing the couple's happy-go-lucky attitude.

Nela could be acting on behalf of her sister. However, her sister had been in the apartment for several days and surely had time for a thorough search. Even if Chloe asked Nela to search again, Nela had no need to create an intruder. She was staying in the place as a caretaker for a cat. She could search anything at any time she wished and no one would be the wiser.

Steve ate his chili without noticing the taste.

So he didn't get Katie's emphasis on the 911 call . . .

And then he did.

If it was absolutely essential to remove something from Marian Grant's office, a paper, a file, maybe a link to the theft of a two-hundred-fifty-thousand-dollar necklace, a previous search of the Grant apartment by an unknown intruder pointed away from Nela Farley.

But not if the police thought the 911 call was phony.

Steve pushed back the bowl. He lifted his Dr Pepper and drank.

Katie believed the apartment break-in was fake. She linked both searches to the vandalism and the theft of the necklace.

Steve gave a soundless whistle. Now he understood why Katie refused to name a person of interest. Clearly, following Katie's reasoning, the vandalism and theft had been committed by Chloe Farley and now Nela Farley was desperately trying to protect her sister.

He finished the Dr Pepper, but without his usual pleasure in the tingly burn of the pop. Katie Dugan always spoke carefully. Her final comment had been bland until he parsed the words: *At this point in the investigation, there is not a single suspect. No premature announcement will be made.*

He knew every word was true. There was no single suspect. There were two suspects, Chloe Farley and Nela Farley. There would be no premature announcement because Chloe Farley was in Tahiti, a nice place to hang out to avoid prosecution in the U.S.

Steve recalled the feature story written by

Freddi. Leland was part of a prominent Craddock family. Though Freddi wrote with humor and enthusiasm, Leland and his girlfriend came across as flakes. Nice flakes, but flakes. Had a quarter-million-dollar necklace been too big a temptation?

Steve realized he'd crushed the empty Dr Pepper can. *Ease up, man. You don't know her.* But she looked like a woman of courage touched by sadness. Her image haunted his mind.

She could be innocent . . .

Or guilty.

9

Nela, wearing the orange rubber dishwashing gloves, carefully positioned Marian Grant's purse on the bookcase by the door. A casual observer would never suspect the purse had been moved since Marian placed it there. Nela opened the purse and fished out the necklace. The diamonds glistened in the living room light. Nela dropped the necklace into a clear quart-size plastic bag and placed the bag also on the bookcase. The plastic bag, carefully eased by gloved fingers from the middle of its box, was fingerprint free. She felt a spurt of satisfaction as she returned the gloves to the kitchen. She was turning into an old pro at avoiding fingerprints. That was easy. Now came the challenge. She would be safe and so would Chloe if she could follow — sort of — in the footsteps of Raffles, one of Gram's favorite fictional characters. Nela doubted if Detective Dugan had ever heard of Raffles. Gram had loved the short stories as well as the movies, especially the 1939 film with David Niven as the gentleman thief. Tonight, Nela pinned her hopes on doing a reverse Raffles.

She ran through her plan in her mind. She'd leave about ten. She glanced at her watch. Almost two hours to go. She was impatient. There was so much she needed to do. She'd already tried to use Marian's home computer but there was no handy password in the desk drawer. Nela didn't have a laptop. If she did, she could seek information about the staff at Haklo. Still, she could use this time profitably.

She settled on the sofa with a notebook. Jugs settled beside her. She turned to a fresh page. She always traveled with a notebook. She might not be able to dig for facts and figures, but she could sum up her impressions of the people she'd met. She didn't doubt that the vandal/thief and possible murderer was among that group. Only someone with intimate knowledge of Chloe's schedule would have been aware of her departure Friday for Tahiti, leaving Marian Grant's apartment unoccupied for the first time since her death.

Nela wrote fast.

Blythe Webster —Imperious. Possibly spoiled. Accustomed to having her way. A woman with her emotions under tight control. Attractive in a contained, upper-class way, large intelligent eyes, a rather prim mouth. Seems on good terms with everyone at Haklo.

Louise Spear —Eager to please, thoughtful, a perfect assistant. Her eyes held uncertainty and worry, a woman who wanted someone else to lead. Distress about vandalism appears genuine. No discernible animus toward anyone.

Robbie Powell —Obviously resents the new director. Emotional. Angry enough at his partner's firing to vandalize Haklo?

Erik Judd —His flamboyant appearance said it all. He lived in bright colors. No pastels for him. How much did losing his post at Haklo matter? Probably quite a lot. He had swept out the door, cloak flaring, but there was a sense of a faded matinee idol. Did parking in the visitors' lot reveal festering anger? Vandalism on a grand scale might amuse him.

Cole Hamilton —She'd had only a glimpse of him in his office but he hadn't looked as though he was engaged in any work. His round face was not so much genial as lost and bewildered. He had an aura of defeat. What was his function at Haklo?

Francis Garth —Big, powerful, possibly overbearing. Not a man to cross. The thought was quick, instinctive. Though he'd remained calm about the agenda item, clearly the Tallgrass Prairie mattered more to him than a matter of business. Did he have other disagreements with the trustee and director?

Hollis Blair —Boatloads of aw-shucks, Jimmy Stewart charm but he had run into a situation where charm didn't matter. Was someone jealous of his apparent affair with Abby Andrews? Or was his assumption of the directorship offensive to more than just Robbie Powell and Erik Judd?

Abby Andrews —She would have looked at home in crinolines holding a parasol to protect her alabaster complexion from too much sun. Was she a clinging vine or a scheming woman who engineered problems for Hollis so that she could be there to offer support?

Grace Webster —To say there was an undercurrent between the sisters was to put it mildly. Grace was by turns combative, difficult, chiding, hostile. Grace struck Nela as reckless, daring, and impulsive. Several times she had been darkly amused. Maybe she thought vandalism was a joke, too.

Peter Owens —He'd seemed like a tweedy intellectual, but she didn't think she'd imagined his pleasure in tweaking Francis Garth. There —

Jugs lifted his head. He listened, came sinuously up on his paws, flowed to the floor. He moved toward the front door.

She spoke gently. "Ready for a big night?" Words didn't matter to a cat. Tone did.

Jugs stopped a few feet from the door, stood very still.

The staccato knock came with no warning.

Nela jumped up and bolted to the bookcase. She used the edge of her sweater to pick up the plastic bag. Heart thudding, she opened Marian's purse, using another edge of the sweater, and dropped the bag inside.

The quick, sharp knock sounded again.

Nela moved to the door, taking a deep breath. She turned on the porch light, but she couldn't look out to identify the visitor. The door lacked a peephole. She opened it a trace. "Who's there?"

"Steve Flynn. *Craddock Clarion.*" His voice was loud, clear, and businesslike.

183

Nela's tight stance relaxed. Steve Flynn, the redheaded reporter who could have been a double for Van Johnson. She'd almost smiled at him when their gazes first met. But he wasn't the boy next door.

Why had he come?

"Miss Farley, may I speak with you for a moment? About the break-in Friday night."

Nela's thoughts raced. The detective didn't believe there was a break-in. Would it be suspicious if she refused to talk to the reporter? She didn't need anyone else suspecting her of a crime. She glanced at the Coach bag, hesitated, then turned the knob.

The wind stirred his short red hair. The glare of the porch light emphasized the freckles on his fair skin. Steady blue eyes met hers. "I've been looking over the police report on the attempted burglary here. Can I visit with you for a minute?"

Cold air swirled inside. He stood hunched with his hands in his pockets, his only protection an old pullover sweater.

She held open the door.

As she closed it, his eyes noted the door wedge. He raised them to look at her.

Nela saw a flicker of interest. He didn't miss much.

She led the way into the living room, once

again saw him scan the surroundings, taking in the scrape on the back of the desk chair, the discoloration that marked where a mirror had once hung.

He declined coffee. "I don't want to interfere with your evening."

"I don't have anything planned." Other than transporting a stolen necklace as far away as possible.

"Then" — his smile was quick and charming — "if you don't mind, fill me in on what happened Friday night."

On closer view, his boy-next-door face was older, more appraising, less ingenuous than she'd first thought. There was depth in his blue eyes and a hard edge to his chin. She was also suddenly aware of being near him, of his stocky build, of his maleness.

Jugs padded toward him, raised his head.

The reporter nodded at the cat. "You have to have attention first, huh? No entrance without showing proper respect, right?" A broad hand swung down to stroke Jugs's fur. He straightened. "My mom's cat was a big tabby. He thought he was the man of the house along with my dad. What's his name?"

"Jugs."

He grinned. "Those are big ears, that's for sure. Now, about Friday night —"

Nela wondered if he was one of those reporters who always takes a cop's view. It was natural. She'd been there, too. Reporters understood the hard, tough, dangerous world cops face every day. Reporters admired courage masked by black humor. Good reporters never slanted a story, but they listened when a good cop spoke.

"— what happened?"

The cat moved toward her, looked up. *". . . wants to know you . . . not sure about you . . . doesn't trust women . . . women lie . . ."*

Nela jerked her gaze away from Jugs. "I was in the guest room. I'll show you." She turned to lead the way. Jugs padded alongside. Nela struggled for composure. What was wrong with her? Jugs couldn't know anything in the mind of this man who meant nothing to her — except that he might pose a danger.

As she opened the bedroom door and half turned toward him, their eyes met. "I was asleep."

He looked past her toward the bed.

She was intuitively aware of him, of his nearness, of the tensing of his body, of a sense of uncertainty, of a man who had been hurt and was still angry, of longing and wariness. She steeled herself. The emotions of the day had fogged her reason.

"Noise woke you?"

"Yes. Then I saw the line of light beneath the door." She shut the bedroom door, gestured toward the living room. "Come sit down and I'll tell you." She chose the easy chair, waited until he settled on the sofa opposite her. She spoke at a quick clip, wished her voice didn't sound breathless. ". . . bangs and crashes . . ." She described everything. "I yelled the police were coming. I heard someone leave. I didn't come out until the police knocked. Then I ran to open the door."

Those clear deep blue eyes never left her face. "The police said the door was locked when they arrived."

"The thief locked the door behind him. I think whoever came had a key."

He looked puzzled, his gaze flicking across the room toward the door. "How about the doorstop? A key doesn't do any good if that's in place."

"I bought the wedge Saturday morning. Somebody had a key Friday night. Somebody still has a key. I shove the wedge under the door now at night."

"What were they looking for?"

The necklace. She felt the answer deep in her gut. She stared at him and realized her peril. The quick sharp question had caught her unaware. Unless she knew more than she had revealed to the police, she should have quickly said she didn't know or suggested they must have been looking for money. She had remained quiet too long. When she spoke, she knew her answer was too little, too late. "I suppose whatever thieves look for. Money, valuables of some kind."

He didn't change expression, but he wasn't fooled. He was well aware that she had knowledge she had not revealed. He folded his arms, that classic posture of wariness. "Somebody with a key wouldn't be your run-of-the-mill thief."

"If you say so." She suddenly felt that they looked at each other across a divide. "I don't have any experience with thieves."

"A key makes everything different. Either someone knew her and had a key or someone knew her well enough to know, for example, that she tucked an extra key in a flowerpot."

"Flowerpot?"

For an instant, he was amused. "Metaphorically speaking. Somewhere. Under a flagstone. In the garage. People do things like that around here."

Nela considered the possibility. "If someone knew where Miss Grant kept an extra key, they must have known her pretty well. What do you know about her?"

"Smart, hardworking, type A, absolutely devoted to Haklo. She came to Craddock twenty years ago as Mr. Webster's executive secretary." He paused, gave a small shrug. "In any little town, the leading lights, and that's spelled *people with money,* are the focus of gossip. Everybody thought she was his mistress. Maybe she was, maybe she wasn't. Webster's wife was reclusive. Again it's all gossip but people said he and his wife didn't share a bedroom. In any event, Marian was a good-looking woman who never exhibited any interest in anybody else — man or woman — so the gossip may have been right. Haklo was definitely Webster's baby and pretty soon she was running it. All she cared about was Haklo, especially after Webster died. Maybe she saw Haklo as a monument to him. Maybe she felt closest to him out there. Anyway, Haklo was her life. Everybody knew better than to cross her, including the Webster daughters. Both of them were always charming to Marian but I don't think there was any love lost between them, which figures if she slept with their dad. Marian was always in charge. Anyone who opposed her ended up backed against a wall, one way or another. Marian maneuvered money and pressure from money to get the best deal possible for Haklo."

"If she found out who was behind the vandalism, she'd make them pay?"

"With a pound of flesh and smile while she was doing it." His eyes narrowed. "What are you suggesting?"

Her gaze fell. She hoped she hadn't looked toward the door. This man saw too much, understood too much. How would he feel if she blurted out that somebody put a skateboard on the second step and that's why Marian Grant died? He would demand that she tell him how she knew. She spoke hurriedly. "Nothing. I just think someone had a key to get in." Nela felt certain she had met the late-night intruder today at Haklo. "Maybe Miss Grant's office was wrecked before the thief came here. Maybe she kept a key lying in the front drawer of her desk. Maybe it had a tag on it: *Extra front-door key.*"

"That's possible. It certainly explains how someone got in here." He spoke in a considering tone. "Somebody has a key. They come in . . ." His gaze stopped at the purse on the bookcase. "Is that your purse?"

She should have put the hideous purse away. She deliberately kept her eyes away from the bookcase.

He waited for her answer.

"Miss Webster said the purse belonged to Miss Grant."

"Miss Webster?"

"She heard the sirens and came."

"Was the purse there Friday night?"

She tried to sound as if her answer didn't matter. "Yes."

"A thief walked right by the bookcase and ignored the purse?" He looked skeptical.

"I shouted that the police were coming." She had to convince him. "I heard running steps. He didn't take time to grab the purse."

"He took time to push the door lock."

"Maybe not, then. Maybe when he first came it, he locked the door so no one could surprise him." Nela figured that's what must have happened. "It's the kind of lock that has to be disengaged. It doesn't pop out automatically."

"That may be right."

"I think the thief went straight to the desk. It was a mess. Somebody was looking for something in her desk."

"Have you checked the purse? Maybe the answer to everything is there." He rose and took a step toward the bookcase.

Nela popped to her feet, caught up with

him, gripped his arm. "We can't do that. We have no right. Tomorrow I'll take the purse to the foundation and ask Miss Webster to take charge of it." She pulled her hand away from his arm, remembering the muscular feel of his forearm beneath the sweater.

He remained midway to the bookcase. "I suppose you have a point there." But he still gazed at the black leather bag.

She had to get rid of him.

"That's all I have to say, Mr. Flynn. If you don't mind, I'm rather tired. It's been a long day." She opened the door.

He stared at her for a long moment.

Nela felt an odd sadness. If she didn't know better, she would think she'd seen a flash of disappointment in his eyes, disappointment and regret.

"Yeah. I'll bet you are. Thanks." He turned away, crossed the small porch in a single step, started down the stairs.

She closed the door, leaned against the cold panel, and stared at the purse.

At the bottom of the stairs, Nela waited for her eyes to adjust to the darkness. She wore Chloe's big coat and her brown wool gloves. In one pocket she'd stuffed a pencil flashlight she'd found in a utility drawer in the kitchen. The plastic bag with the necklace

192

was in the other pocket. She'd tucked her driver's license in the pocket of her jeans along with a ten-dollar bill and Chloe's key to the employee entrance.

She gazed at the back of the Webster house. Light seeped from the edges of curtains, but there was no movement in the long sweep of gardens or on the terrace. Time to go. There could be no safety until she disposed of the necklace. She hurried down the steps. The wind was up. Knife-sharp air clawed at her face.

The garage door lifted smoothly. As she backed the VW from the garage, she clicked on the headlights. She made no effort at stealth. She had every right to run out to a 7-Eleven and pick up something. She left the car door open as she closed the garage door.

At the end of the drive, she turned left instead of right. She drove three blocks until she was out of the enclave of expensive homes. She entered a convenience store lot. As she locked the VW, one car pulled out from a line of pumps, another pulled in. She hurried inside, bought a six-pack of Cokes. In the car she placed them on the floor in front of the passenger seat.

She glanced at her watch in the splash of light from the storefront. Twenty after ten.

In her mind she traced her route. She'd studied the Craddock city map Chloe had included in the packet with one of her usual sticky notes. A thin squiggly line appeared to reach the main grounds of the foundation from a road on the west side. That would be safer than using the main entrance.

The drive didn't take long. Traffic was light. There was one set of headlights behind her when she turned onto the road that ran in front of the foundation.

Nela drove around a curve and jammed on her brakes. A doe bounded across the road, her fur a glossy tan in the wash from the headlights. In another bound, the deer cleared a fence and disappeared into a grove of trees. A car came around the curve behind her, slowed.

Nela started up again. She was aware of the headlights in her rearview mirror. The car pulled out to pass, roared around the VW, and now the road was dark behind her. She continued for about a hundred yards and turned right onto a narrow blacktop road with a thick mass of trees on one side and a fenced field on the other. The VW headlights seemed frail against the country darkness. She peered into the night. If the thin line on the map indicated a road into the Haklo property, it should soon come into view on her right. She saw a break in the woods. Slowing, she swung onto a rutted dirt road. The headlights seemed puny against the intense darkness, but she dimmed to fog lights, affording her just enough illumination to follow the ruts.

A hundred yards. Another. She reached an open expanse. Dark buildings loomed to her left. Light filtered through a grove of trees to her right. That would be light from the occupied Haklo guest cabin. Nela turned off the fog lights and coasted to a stop by a long low building. Her eyes adjusted to night. She rolled down the window. She was parked next to a galvanized steel structure, which probably housed equipment and supplies for the upkeep of the foundation and its grounds. Straight ahead was the line of evergreens that marked the staff parking lot. Quietly she slipped from the car. She looked again toward the cabin. Though light glowed from the windows, there was no movement or sound.

Except for the occasional *whoo* of an owl, reassuring silence lay over the dark landscape ahead of her. Once past the evergreens, she tried to walk quietly, but the crunch of gravel beneath her feet seemed startlingly loud. It was better on the sidewalk leading to the staff entrance. She took her time, using the pencil light to light her way. All the while, she listened for sound, movement, any hint that she had been observed. Surely if the police had left a guard, someone would have challenged her by now. Every minute that passed increased her confidence that only she moved in the stillness of the country night.

The building itself lay in total darkness.

At the staff entrance, Nela held the pencil flash in her gloved left hand, used Chloe's key. In an instant she was inside, safe in a black tunnel of silence. She ran lightly up the hallway, using the tiny beam to light her way. She was almost there, almost safe. In only a moment she'd be free of the incriminating necklace.

She opened the door to Blythe's office and dashed across the room. She pulled out the plastic bag, emptied the necklace onto the center of the desktop. The stones and precious metal clattered on the wooden surface. In the light of the flash, diamonds glittered and gold gleamed.

She whirled away from the desk. In the hall, she shut Blythe's office door behind her. The tiny beam of light bouncing before her, she again ran lightly down the hallway, not caring now at the sound of her sneakers on the marble. She felt exultant when she reached the exit. She and Chloe were safe. As soon as she reached the car and drove away, there was nothing to link her and Chloe to that damnable, gorgeous, incredibly expensive necklace.

She pulled open the heavy door at the end of the hall and stepped out into the night. The door began to close.

A quick bright light blinded her.

"The image also records the time. *Temporary Employee Exits Haklo After Hours.* Interesting headline, right?" His tenor voice was sardonic. "Care to comment?" He came quickly up the steps, used a broad hand to hold the door open. "Why don't we go inside?"

Once Nela had seen a bird trapped inside an enclosed mall, flying up, seeking, not finding. Sometimes there is no escape. Numbly, she turned and stepped inside.

He followed close behind her.

When the door closed, she lifted the pocket flashlight, held the beam where she could see his face.

He squinted against the light, his freckled face grim, his gaze accusing. He looked big, tough, and determined. He cupped a cell phone in his left hand. "What's your excuse? Forgot your hankie?"

His tone hurt almost as much as the realization that she had failed Chloe. She should have done something, anything, to be rid of the necklace. Instead, she'd tried to return the stolen jewelry to its owner and now she — and Chloe — were going to pay the price. She was cornered but she wouldn't go down without a fight. "Why are you here?" But she knew the answer. He was after a story and he couldn't have any idea just how big it was going to be. "Do you make it a practice to follow women you don't know?"

If she had no right to be here, certainly he didn't belong either. So he was a reporter. So he looked like Van Johnson, an older, tougher Van Johnson. Maybe Gram would have loved him, but his presence here was as unexplained as hers. Maybe he knew much more about what had happened at Haklo than she could ever imagine. "How did you know I was coming here?"

His mouth twisted in a wry half smile, half grimace. "Pirates used to fly the skull and crossbones to scare the hell out of ships. You sent plenty of signals tonight. You're as wary as an embezzler waiting for the bank examiner. You know more — a lot more — than you want to admit. You might as well have marked Marian's purse with a red X.

Once I got outside, I decided to hang around, see if anything popped. I didn't know what to expect, maybe someone arriving. Instead, you slipped down the steps like a Hitchcock heroine." There was an undertone of regret mingled with derision.

"You followed me? But I went to the Seven-Eleven . . ." Her voice trailed off.

His gaze was quizzical. "For a Hitchcock lady, you aren't very savvy about picking up a tail. Once you left the Seven-Eleven, you were easy meat. When you turned on Pumpjack Road, I knew you were going to Haklo. I was right behind you. I passed you, went around a curve, and pulled off on the shoulder. When you didn't come, I knew you'd taken the back entrance." His eyes were probing. "Not a well-known route. Clever for someone who's new to town. So, shall we take a tour? See if there are any other offices trashed?"

"Would you like to hear the truth?" She flung the words at him. "Or are you enjoying yourself too much?"

His face changed, disdain melding into combativeness. "Yeah. I'd like to hear some truth from you."

In his eyes, she saw disappointment and a flicker of wariness: *Fool me once, shame on you; fool me twice, shame on me.*

She met his gaze straight on. Maybe truth would help. Likely not. But truth he damn well was going to get. "Friday night somebody searched Marian's living room. Saturday I had the same thought you did. Why hadn't the thief taken the purse? I looked inside. I found an incredibly beautiful diamond-and-gold necklace in the bottom of the bag. I left it in the purse. I knew nothing about the theft of a necklace at Haklo. Chloe never mentioned the theft when we talked. All she cares about is Leland and fun and adventure. She told me about Turner Falls and Bricktown and the Heavener Runestone. I didn't know the necklace was stolen until the staff meeting this morning."

He listened with no change of expression.

"If you want more truth" — anger heated her voice — "I found out a stranger in town makes an easy target. The detective made it clear that Chloe is suspect number one as the thief, with me busy covering up for her. I knew Dugan wouldn't believe I found the necklace in the purse. Tonight I brought the necklace here and put it on Blythe Webster's desk."

"You put the necklace in Blythe's office?" His broad face reflected surprise, uncertainty, calculation, concentration. He stared at her for a long moment, then slid the phone into his pocket. "Show me."

The heavy silence of an empty building emphasized the sound of their footsteps on the marble floor. At Blythe's office, he opened the door and flicked on the lights. The necklace was starkly visible in the center of the desk, the diamonds glittering bright as stars.

Steve Flynn walked slowly to the desk. He stared down at the magnificent diamonds in the ornate gold settings. "I'll be double damned." He pulled his cell from his pocket. A tiny flash flared. He looked for a moment at the small screen. "You can tell the damn thing's worth a fortune even in a cell phone picture." He closed the phone, turned, and looked at Nela. Finally, he shook his head as if puzzled. "Why didn't you throw it away?"

"It would have been smarter." But nobody gets second chances.

"Why didn't you?" He was insistent.

"It wasn't mine." It was ironic that basic honesty was going to put her in jail. "The more fool I."

"Yeah. There's a small matter of property rights." He sounded sardonic. "All right, I may be a fool, too, but everything in here" — he waved his hand around the office — "appears to be in place. You came in, you dropped the necklace, you left. Come on."

"Aren't you going to call the police?"

"No. For some crazy reason, I believe you." He jerked a thumb at the door. "Let's get out of here. We need to talk."

10

Steve leaned back against the plumped pillow, legs outstretched, and listened. Pretty soon he had a sense of how Haklo appeared to her: Blythe Webster imperious but shaken, and staff members who weren't just names but individuals with passions. Louise Spear grieved over Marian and Haklo's troubles. Francis Garth was furious at a threat to his beloved Tallgrass Prairie. Francis was proud of his Osage Heritage — the preserve was the heart of the Osage Nation — and Francis was a formidable figure. Robbie Powell and his partner, Erik Judd, bitterly resented the new director. Hollis Blair was in a situation where aw-shucks charm didn't help. Abby Andrews was either a wilting maiden or a scheming opportunist. Cole Hamilton appeared subdued and defeated, but his comment that emphasized the necessity of a key to Haklo might be disingenuous. Grace Webster was at odds with her sister. Peter Owens was affable but possibly sly.

When Nela revealed the existence of the obscene letters sent out on the director's letterhead, he saw another link in the chain of ugly attacks on the foundation. But this one appeared tied directly to Abby Andrews, which might tilt the scale toward schemer instead of victim.

Steve liked Nela's voice. Not high. Not low. Kind of soft. A voice you could listen to for a long time. She looked small in an oversize chintz-covered chair, dark hair still tangled by the wind, face pale, dark shadows beneath her eyes. But she no longer seemed remote as she had in his first glimpse at Hamburger Heaven.

His eyes slid from her to a photograph on the table next to her chair. A dark-haired laughing man in a tee and shorts stood near an outcrop of black rocks on a beach, the wind stirring his hair. Across the bottom of the photograph was a simple inscription: *To Nela — Love, Bill.* A red, white, and blue ribbon was woven through the latticed frame.

Steve was accustomed to figuring from one fact to another. The picture had to belong to Nela. To carry the photograph with her as she traveled meant that the man and the place mattered very much to her. He was afraid he knew exactly why the ribbon was in place and that would account for the undertone of sadness that he'd observed.

But tonight, she was fully alive, quick intelligence in her eyes, resolve in her face, a woman engaged in a struggle to survive. The brown tabby nestled next to her. One slender hand rested on the cat's back. As she spoke, she looked at him with a direct stare that said she was in the fight for as long as it took.

When he'd caught her coming out of Haklo, he'd felt a bitter twist of disappointment, accepting that Katie had been right, that she was covering up for her light-fingered sister. At that point, he had a picture of her leaving Haklo, the time electronically recorded. She was cornered. All he had to do was tie up the loose ends. It was like ballast shifting in a hull. When the heavy load tipped to one end, the ship was sure to go down.

Now the ballast was back in place. He was pretty good at keeping score and she had two heavy hits in her favor: the return of the necklace and the door wedge. Sure, she could have found the necklace at the apartment, maybe not in the purse as she claimed, decided her sister was the thief, and returned the necklace to protect her. But the smart decision would have been to fling the necklace deep into woods on the other side of town. She could easily have found some woods and jettisoned the jewelry. She took a big chance bringing the necklace to Haklo tonight, which argued she not only wasn't a thief, she was too honest and responsible to throw away a quarter of a million dollars that didn't belong to her. That was one home run. The second hinged on one small fact: The morning after her 911 call, she went out and bought a wedge to shove under the door.

She turned her hands palms up, looked rueful. "I understand if you decide to call the detective. You're a reporter. You have to be honest with the cops you know. I was a reporter, too. Trust is a two-way street."

He wasn't surprised. She had the manner of someone who was used to asking questions, looking hard at facts, winnowing out nonsense. She'd showed she was tough when he confronted her at Haklo. She'd asked if he would listen to truth. Truth was all that mattered, all that should matter to a reporter. Maybe that was why he'd felt a connection to her right from that first look. They might have lots of differences in their

backgrounds, but they would always understand each other.

"If you call Dugan" — her voice was calm
— "I'll tell her what I've told you. Someone
came here hunting for the necklace and
that's the reason her office was searched.
Unfortunately, Dugan won't believe me."

He didn't refute her conclusion about
Katie Dugan. If Katie learned the necklace
had been in Nela's possession, she'd be sure
her judgment was right. As soon as Chloe
returned from Tahiti, they'd both be
booked.

"Let me be sure I get it." He watched her
carefully. "You arrived here Friday afternoon. Everything was fine. You went to bed,
somebody got inside, hunted in the desk.
You called nine-one-one. When the cops
came, you had to unlock the front door. You
believe someone entered with a key. That
likely comes down to a small list. Marian's
life was centered at Haklo. Either someone
knew where she kept an extra key or maybe
the intruder entered Haklo first and found
a key to the apartment in her office and
came here when the necklace didn't turn
up in the office. Saturday morning you
checked Marian's purse and found the
necklace. You didn't do anything about it
because you had no business snooping and

no reason to think she shouldn't have a necklace in her purse. You hid the purse to protect the necklace. You went to Haklo Saturday, Louise took you around. Monday you heard about the vandalism, including the obscene letters. But that receded into the background after you found Marian's office trashed. Then you learned that the necklace was stolen property. Katie Dugan believes your sister heisted the necklace after puffing up a smokescreen with the vandalism and you are covering up for her. Tonight you decided to put the necklace on Blythe's desk. That's everything?"

She hesitated, frowning. Her gaze dropped to the cat nestled close to her.

Why wasn't she looking at him? What else did she know? Steve came upright, leaned forward, his eyes insistent. "I've gone out on a limb for you. I know you went in Haklo after hours. I know where the necklace is. If this all came out, I could be charged as an accessory. I need to know what you know."

Slowly she looked up.

He stared into dark brilliant eyes that held both uncertainty and knowledge.

"I don't have proof." Her gaze was steady.

"Tell me, Nela." He liked the sound of her name, *Nee-la*. "I'll help you. All I ask is that you don't lie to me. I've heard too many lies from beautiful women." He stopped for a long moment, lips pressed together. "Okay. I want honesty. I'll be honest. I heard too many lies from one particular beautiful woman, my ex-wife. I'm telling you this because I want you to know where I'm coming from. I'll help you — if you don't lie to me. You have to make a choice. If you can't — or won't — be honest, tell me and I'll walk out of here and tonight never happened. I never came here, I never went to Haklo, I don't know anything about a piece of jewelry."

"I won't lie to you. I may not be able to tell you everything." She was solemn. "Whatever I tell you will be the truth. I think I do know something." She glanced again at the cat, then said, almost defiantly, "I can't tell you how I know."

He wanted to believe her, wanted it more than he'd wanted anything in a very long time. *Steve, you damn fool, women lie, don't let her suck you into something screwy. Why can't she tell how she knows whatever it is that she knows? Protecting somebody?* He almost pushed up from the chair. He could walk away, avoid entanglement. But he was already speaking. "All right. Keep your source."

As for how she obtained a piece of knowledge, the possibilities were pretty narrow. Either she or her sister had seen something that Nela now believed to be important in the saga of Haklo and its troubles. He'd bet the house she was protecting her sister. He was putting himself in a big hole if he didn't report her entry into Haklo and the necklace on Blythe Webster's desk. He needed every scrap of information to dig his way out. He would be home free — and so would Nela and Chloe — if the jewel thief was caught. "What do you know?"

"Marian Grant was murdered."

The words hung between them.

Steve had covered the story. Marian Grant was a prominent citizen of Craddock. Her death was front-page news. Marian's accident had been a surprise. She had been in her late forties, a runner, a good tennis player. However, accidents happen to the fit as well as the unfit. For an instant, Nela's claim shocked him into immobility. Then pieces slotted together in his mind — vandalism at Haklo, a missing necklace in Marian's purse, a thief fearing arrest, Marian's death — to form an ugly pattern, a quite possible pattern. Still . . .

"Are you claiming somebody was here and shoved her down the steps?"

"No. I have reason to believe" — she

spoke carefully — "that someone put a skateboard on the second step."

"A skateboard?" He pictured that moment, Marian hurrying out the door for her morning jog, taking quick steps, one foot landing on a skateboard. Hell yes, that could knock her over a railing. "If somebody knows that for a fact, the cops have to be told."

"They would want to know how I know. I can't identify the source."

He liked piecing together facts from a starting point. "You arrived here Friday, right? You can prove you were on a certain flight and that you were in LA until you took that flight?"

"Absolutely."

"You've never been to Craddock before?"

"No."

"Therefore, you couldn't know about a skateboard on the steps from your own knowledge. Who told you?" The list had to be short. Her sister, Chloe, had to be the only person Nela knew before she arrived.

Nela brushed back a tangle of dark hair. "I promised the truth. I'm telling you the truth. No one told me."

"If" — he tried to be patient — "no one told you and you weren't here, how do you know?"

"All I can say is that no one told me." She spoke with finality, looked at him with a faint half smile.

He understood. She wasn't going to budge. There had to be a strong reason for her silence. But she had nothing to gain from making a claim that Marian Grant had been murdered. If anything, turning the search for the necklace into a murder investigation might place her and Chloe in more peril. Once again Nela was making a moral choice: Return a quarter-million-dollar necklace. Expose murder.

"Steve —"

It was the first time she'd ever said his name. Someday would she speak to him, call him by name, and be thinking of him and not stolen jewels or murder?

"— you said I could keep my source. But we need to tell the police. Sometimes I got anonymous tips on stories. Will you tell the police you got a tip, an anonymous tip? Can't you say that somebody said" — she paused, then began again, this time in a scarcely audible wisp of sound — "Marian Grant was murdered. She knew who took the necklace. Someone put a skateboard on the second step of the garage apartment stairs . . ."

■ ■ ■ ■

Craddock had few public pay phones left. In the parking lot of a Valero filling station, Steve stood with his back to the street, his shoulders hunched against the cold. He not only didn't have his jacket, he didn't have gloves. In fact, he didn't own a pair of gloves. He'd found a shammy crammed in the glove compartment. He dropped in the coins, pushed the buttons. The phone was answered after five rings. He listened to the entire message, waited for his extension number, pushed the buttons. He heard his own voice, waited again, finally whispered, repeating Nela's words. He hung up and used the shammy to clean the receiver.

Nela looked down at the muscular cat stretched out with his front paws flat on the surface of the kitchen table. "You look like one of those stone lions that guard the New York Public Library."

Jugs regarded her equably. *". . . You're happier today . . ."*

Yes, she was happier today. Removing the necklace from the apartment was like kicking free of tangled seaweed just before a big wave hit. "That's just between you and me, buddy. Thank God cops don't read cat minds. I'd be in big trouble."

Jugs continued to stare at her. *". . . You're worried . . . She was worried . . ."*

As she sipped her morning coffee, a faint frown drew her eyebrows down. Although she felt almost giddy with relief every time she thought about the necklace now in Blythe's office, the removal of the jewelry didn't solve the main problem. Maybe that's why her subconscious, aka Jugs, was warning her.

She pushed away the quicksilver thought that her subconscious could not possibly have known if someone had rigged the step to make Marian Grant fall. But something had to account for that searing moment when she'd looked at Jugs and imagined his thoughts. . . . *board rolled on the second step* . . . When she thought of a rolling board, the image had come swiftly, a skateboard. Saturday morning when she'd looked at the banister, a streak of paint was just where a skateboard might have struck if tipped up. That was confirmation, wasn't it? Something had hit that banister. They said violence leaves a psychic mark. Who said? Her inner voice was quick with the challenge. All right. She'd read somewhere that there was some kind of lasting emanation after trauma. If Marian had been murdered, if someone left a skateboard on her steps, that certainly qualified as a violent act. When Marian plunged over the railing, did she have time to realize what had happened?

Nela shook her head. She might as well believe in voodoo. But some people did. Maybe she'd had a moment of ESP. But she'd never had any use for so-called psychics. The explanation had to be simple. There was that gash in the stair rail. Maybe subconsciously she'd noticed the scrape when she first arrived and the shock of confronting Jugs stirred some long-ago memory of a skateboard.

She looked at Jugs, but his eyes had closed. When he'd looked at her Friday night, other thoughts had come to her mind. . . . *She was worried . . . She didn't know what to do . . .*

About a stolen necklace?

Nela thought about the last few days in the life of a woman she'd never known, a smart, intense, hardworking woman who had devoted her life to Haklo.

A vandal struck Haklo again and again.

Blythe's necklace was stolen.

The necklace was in Marian Grant's purse that she placed atop the bookcase the last night of her life.

Did Marian steal the quarter-million-dollar adornment?

The violent searches of her office and apartment after her death appeared almost certainly to be a hunt for the necklace. Dumped drawers indicated a search for some physical object, not incriminating papers suggested by Detective Dugan. The destruction in her office reflected a wild and dangerous anger on the part of the searcher when the effort to find the necklace failed. From everything Nela had been told about Marian, there was nothing to support the idea that Marian could have been a thief. Instead, it was much more likely that Marian had discovered the identity of the thief and obtained the necklace. However, she didn't contact the police. She kept the necklace in her purse.

Why hadn't she called the police?

As Steve had made clear, Marian always protected the foundation. Her decision to handle the theft by herself meant that a public revelation would create a scandal. She was a confident, strong woman. Perhaps she insisted the thief had to confess or resign or make restitution. Perhaps she said, "I've put the necklace in a safe place and unless you do as I say, I will contact the police." Perhaps she set a deadline.

Had the thief killed her to keep her quiet?

She died early Monday morning. The funeral was Thursday. Chloe had stayed in the apartment since Monday night to take care of Jugs. Whether Marian's death was accident or murder, the presence of the necklace in her purse was fact. The thief's first opportunity to search the apartment had been Friday night after Chloe had left town.

Nela welcomed the hot, strong coffee but it didn't lessen the chill of another pointer to someone on the Haklo staff. All of them knew about Chloe's trip to Tahiti. Chloe hadn't mentioned that Nela would stay in the apartment until Chloe's return. As for access to Marian's apartment, perhaps a key was, as Steve suggested, secreted in some simple place known to the searcher. Or perhaps the office was searched before the apartment and a key found in that desk.

Whatever the order, the searches were fruitless because the necklace was in Marian's purse. The treasure wasn't hidden. The necklace had simply been dropped to the bottom of a Coach bag, a safe place in the eyes of its owner. A killer scrabbled through drawers, dumped files, and all the while the necklace was within reach.

Detective Dugan's instinct was good. The

necklace was the crux of everything. But Dugan was convinced that Chloe was the clever thief who'd created the vandalism as a diversion and that Nela was covering up for her. When Steve reported a tip about murder, Dugan might tab Chloe as a murderer as well as a thief.

Nela put down her mug. She couldn't count on the police investigation. But she wasn't blinded by hometown loyalties. If Dugan wasn't willing to look at the Haklo staff members as suspects, Nela was.

Detective Dugan stood with arms folded. "All right." Steve flicked on the speakerphone, punched for messages. He listened with a sense of relief. His whisper had been very well done, the faintly heard words sexless, unaccented wraiths that couldn't be grasped. "Message received at eleven forty-two p.m. Monday: . . . Marian Grant was murdered . . . A skateboard on the second step . . . threw her over the railing . . . She knew who took the necklace . . ."

Detective Dugan touched a number in her cell phone directory. "Mokie, get a trace on a call received at the *Clarion* last night at eleven forty-two. Send out a lab tech to One Willow Lane. Marian Grant died in a fall down the garage apartment stairs. Check for possible damage to the railing. Look for scratches, paint traces. If there is damage, get forensic evidence. Also measurements and photos. Thanks."

She turned to Steve. "Play the message again." She listened with eyes half closed. At its end, she shook her head. "Can't tell whether the caller was a man or a woman. Could have been anybody. No discernible accent." Her eyes opened, settled on Steve. "Why you?"

Steve was unruffled. "Goes with the territory. If you have a tip, call a reporter."

"Why last night?"

Steve kept his expression faintly quizzical. "A big story in yesterday afternoon's *Clarion*. It probably caught someone's attention."

Katie's face wrinkled in concentration. "I want to talk to that caller. Murder." Her tone was considering. She squeezed her eyes in thought. "I figured all along that the necklace was the key and that Grant knew who took it. That explains the search of her office. The searcher messed everything up to try and make it look like more vandalism. The point has to be the necklace. A quarter of a million dollars is serious money. Let's say Grant threatened to name the thief. People around her knew she jogged every morning. A skateboard on the steps couldn't guarantee she'd be killed but the probability was good. Okay, the thief puts a skateboard on the steps then shows up around six fifteen, taking care not to be seen. If she was still alive, pressure on the carotid would dispatch her pronto. If she's already dead, pick up the skateboard and melt away. Now, how could anyone except the murderer know about a skateboard on the steps? If someone did know, why keep quiet until now? Scared? Not sure? Maybe saw a skateboard in a weird place and decided Marian was too athletic to fall accidentally?" Her chin jutted. "I've got to find who made that call."

Steve felt uneasy. Murder made all kinds of sense, but he couldn't figure out how Nela knew. If her sister had stolen the necklace and committed murder, Nela would never in a million years have told him about the skateboard. That she had revealed the skateboard affirmed her and Chloe's innocence for him. But Nela had spent only one day at Haklo. Certainly no one would confide that kind of information to her. How the hell did Nela know?

"Maybe" — and he knew he was dealing with his own worries — "you should hunt for somebody who has a skateboard."

Katie looked sardonic. "Who on the Haklo

staff does wheelies? I'll ask around."

In the Haklo staff lot, Nela felt a tiny spurt of amusement as she parked once again between the snazzy Thunderbird and the old Dodge. The Thunderbird, psychedelic VW, and prim Dodge surely made some kind of statement. But grim worry returned when she reached the walkway to the staff entrance and saw a police officer waiting there. Even though she knew the police would be called when the necklace was found, her stomach tightened. She walked a little faster. Anyone would be curious, right? She came to a stop and looked up the shallow flight of steps.

Officer Baker's faded red hair curled becomingly under her cap. "Good morning, ma'am." She held the door open. "Please go directly to the conference room in the east wing."

Nela stopped and stared. Any innocent person would. "What's happened?"

Officer Baker was pleasant. "Miss Webster has asked that everyone report to the conference room. Detective Dugan wishes to speak with staff members."

In the conference room, Louise Spear stood at the head of the table, her brown eyes anxious. "Nela, please make coffee for us. I suppose the police know something now about Marian's office."

As Nela measured beans, placed them in the grinder of the coffeemaker, she heard low voices around the edge of the partition, several asking Louise about the purpose of the meeting. She listened, making out what words she could. So far, no one had mentioned the necklace. Nela was surprised that Blythe Webster hadn't told Louise of her discovery. Perhaps Louise knew and had been told not to mention the necklace.

While the coffee was brewing, Nela glanced around the partition. In addition to the staff members present yesterday, Rosalind McNeill, eyes bright with excitement, sat toward the end of the table next to the imposing white-haired chef. The receptionist was clearly delighted by the change in routine. The chef's brown eyes had the remote expression of someone in attendance but thinking of something else. A difficult recipe?

Nela added two more mugs. When the coffeemaker pinged, Nela filled mugs and carried the tray around the table. When she'd served those who accepted, she returned the tray and the carafe to the kitchenette, then settled on the straight chair a

222

little to one side of the long table.

Once again Haklo staff was in place. She had a quick memory of *Casablanca,* another of Gram's favorite movies, and Captain Renault's wry, "Major Strasser has been shot. Round up the usual suspects."

Blythe Webster looked like a woman who had received shocking news, her eyes wide and staring. The fingers of one hand plucked at the pearl necklace at her throat. Cole Hamilton's aging Kewpie doll face wavered between indignation, worry, and perplexity. Francis Garth looked immovable as a monolith, his gaze somber, his heavy shoulders hunched. Abby Andrews twined a strand of blond hair around one finger, her violet eyes uneasy as she looked from the detective to the director. Hollis Blair gave Abby a swift, warm look before his bony face once again settled into ridges of concern. Grace Webster noticed the exchange with cool disapproval. Robbie Powell wasn't as youthfully handsome this morning. His green eyes darted around the room. His face thoughtful, Peter Owens propped an elbow on the table, gently swung his horn rims back and forth. Rosalind McNeill had the air of a woman awaiting the start of a performance. The chef stared unseeingly toward the buffalo mural.

The door opened and Detective Dugan entered, trim in a stylish white wool blazer and black wool slacks. Detective Morrison followed, tape recorder in hand. In comparison with his fashionable superior, he looked down-at-the-heels in a baggy gray sweater and too large plaid wool slacks. He closed the hall door. Dugan stopped a few feet from the table and turned her gaze to Blythe.

Blythe looked at her with hollow eyes and nodded.

Dugan looked around the room, waited for silence. "Ladies and gentlemen." Her voice was smooth with no hint of threat. "We are continuing our investigation into a series of events at the foundation, including vandalism and theft. However, our investigation has taken a much more serious turn. We have received a report on good authority" — Dugan paused for emphasis — "that Marian Grant was murdered."

Louise Spear gave a cry. "That can't be." She touched her throat with a shaking hand.

"Murdered?" Grace Webster's round face was incredulous. "She fell down the stairs."

Dugan stared at the younger Webster sister. "It may be that a device placed on the stairs caused her to fall. Therefore, when I ask questions, I want each of you to understand that we are seeking information leading to a murderer. It is the duty of the innocent to answer truthfully and accurately. Detective Morrison will record this meeting. When you respond to a question, please preface your answer with your name."

If possible, Abby Andrews shrank even farther into her chair. Hollis Blair looked dazed. Cole Hamilton's face screwed up in dismay. Robbie Powell sat rigid in his chair. The horn rims in Peter Owens's hand came to a stop, remained unmoving. Rosalind's mouth curved in an astonished O. The chef remained imperturbable.

"Murder?" Cole's voice rose is disbelief. "That's impossible. How can you make such a claim? It was dark. Marian had on new running shoes. She fell."

"Forensic evidence supports the claim that her fall may have been caused by a foreign object placed on the second step." Dugan's gaze briefly touched each face.

Nela pictured that telltale scrape on the baluster. Dugan had wasted no time. Obviously, she had already received a report. Had a police officer viewed the scarred surface, possibly brought a skateboard, experimented to see if pressure on one end tilted the board enough for the tip to strike at that level?

Francis Garth cleared his throat. "Detective Dugan, I'd like to clarify our position. Is there a presumption by police that those present in this room are considered to be suspects in the as yet unproven murder of Marian Grant? If so, please explain how that conclusion has been reached."

Nela sensed both fear and indignation in the room.

"This investigation is focused" — Dugan's tone was firm — "on those who have keys to Haklo Foundation. Significant force would be required to break into Haklo. Yesterday when police arrived to investigate the search of Marian Grant's office, there was no evidence of forcible entry. We believe the search of her office was connected to the theft of Miss Webster's necklace. We believe Miss Grant had proof of the identity of the thief. This information may have led to murder. Miss Grant may have said the incident would be overlooked if the necklace was returned and the vandalism ceased. From what we understand, Miss Grant was always mindful of the Haklo Foundation's stature in the community. We think she was trying to protect the foundation. Possibly she told the thief that she had evidence hidden away and gave the thief a deadline. Since there is now evidence that her death was not an accident, we can reasonably assume a connection between her death and the search of her office."

Nela spoke out forcefully. "Someone also searched the living room of her apartment Friday night."

The detective's cold eyes paused at Nela.

Nela understood that Dugan still thought it was possible that the 911 call from Marian's apartment was phony. Dugan included Nela and Chloe among possible suspects. But if Nela and Chloe were the main suspects, what was the point of this inquiry? Did Dugan hope for some kind of damaging information about Chloe to surface? And why hadn't Dugan mentioned the return of the necklace? Nela clenched her hands, saw Dugan take note. She forced her hands to go limp, knew that movement had been cataloged as well.

Dugan continued smoothly. "We believe the person who took the necklace either searched Miss Grant's office or arranged for such a search." Again a quick glance at Nela. "That person had a key to the foundation." She glanced down at a note card. "I have here a list of every person who has a key. Three people with keys are known to have been out of town this past weekend and their absence has been confirmed.

Everyone in this room has a key. The final person who may have a key or access to a key" — she glanced at Robbie Powell — "is the former director, Erik Judd."

Robbie frowned. "Erik would never use his key to enter for any reason other than work."

"He has a key?"

Robbie was bland. "Yes. He's engaged in research here at Haklo for his history of the foundation."

"I understand Mr. Judd resented being fired."

Robbie shook his head. "Actually, he's welcomed the time to be able to concentrate on his writing."

"Why was he fired?" Dugan's tone was pleasant but her eyes sharp.

There was an uncomfortable pause.

Dugan's cool gaze moved to Blythe.

Blythe looked stubborn. "Erik was getting old and he wasn't very exciting. After all, he's in his fifties." She spoke as if it were a greatly distant age. "I wanted someone to lead Haklo to a new level, give us vision. I know Erik was disappointed, but he has a pension. And we'll publish his history."

Robbie said nothing.

Nela saw the twitch of one eyelid. Robbie was keeping anger over his lover's dismissal under wraps, but she had no doubt that beneath his smooth surface he harbored intense dislike for Hollis. She needed to find out more about both Erik and Robbie.

Cole brushed back a white curl. "Erik dealt with problems quickly. I think it's disappointing that Hollis hasn't made any progress on clearing up these matters." There was a flash of malice in his eyes.

"Erik could not have done more than Hollis has, Cole." There was an edge to Blythe's voice. "Hollis is in no way responsible for the dreadful things that have happened. His energy and enthusiasm have inspired us all." Blythe gave Hollis Blair a reassuring nod. "Anyway, vandalism doesn't matter now. If someone hurt Marian, we have to find out what happened. As for that necklace, I don't care if I ever see it again."

Nela was puzzled. The necklace was on Blythe's desk this morning. Had she turned the jewelry over to the police? Was that her meaning?

"I've told Detective Dugan that we will do everything we can to find out the truth of this" — she paused — "anonymous call that claims Marian was killed. I have to say it doesn't seem likely to me. But it is now a police matter." She was somber but there was no suggestion of personal distress.

Nela studied Blythe's composed face. Where was sorrow? Where was outrage? Blythe spoke like a woman directing a meeting and a troublesome issue had arisen. Marian Grant had been a part of Haklo since its inception. She had been important to Webster Harris . . .

Nela looked toward Grace Webster. She appeared shocked and uneasy, but again there wasn't the flare of sorrow and anger that would follow after learning of a cherished friend's murder.

Louise held tight to the gold chain at her neck. "This is dreadful. Nothing matters except Marian. Marian was part of our lives, the heart of Haklo. There's a picture in her office of Webster breaking a champagne bottle on the front pillar when the building was first opened and Marian clapping and laughing out loud. When I was with her, I almost felt that Webster would walk in the room any minute." Louise's face crumpled in misery. She looked up and down the table. "All of us have to answer the detective's questions. We have to tell the detective everything we know. For Marian."

"Of course we will," Francis responded.

Nela looked at the Webster sisters. Neither Blythe nor Grace spoke. Nela knew then that Steve had been right when he spoke of a small town's suspicion of an affair between Harris and Marian. It would be interesting to check the oil man's will. Nela had no doubt that Harris had made certain that Marian would remain as chief operating officer. Blythe and Grace had very likely long lived with hidden resentment.

Grace gave her sister a searching look, then said rapidly, "If anyone knows anything, speak up."

Blythe nodded. "Absolutely. We have a duty to aid the police."

A duty, but no impassioned call for justice from either Grace or Blythe.

The emotion came from Louise Spear. She pressed her fingertips against her cheeks. Her lips trembled. Hollis Blair's bony face looked haggard. Abby Andrews sent quick, panicked glances around the room. Francis Garth's heavy head moved until his dark eyes fastened on Peter Owens. Peter felt the glance and his professorial face hardened. Robbie Powell frowned, seemed to withdraw. Cole Hamilton was the picture of worried concern. Rosalind placed fingertips against her lips. The chef alone seemed unaffected, though her brown eyes were curious.

"We'll get started." Dugan glanced around the table. "Among those who work in this building, including any not present today, who —"

Nela sensed danger. Dugan wasn't confining her inquiry to this room. Was the expanded field — anyone with a connection to the foundation — a clever way to apply the question to Chloe?

"— possesses a skateboard or has ever been seen with a skateboard?"

Francis Garth's heavy head turned toward Abby Andrews. Peter Owens, too, stared at the assistant curator. Hollis Blair's bony face creased in dismay.

Abby pushed back her chair, came to her feet. She turned toward Hollis. "Someone's —"

"Name first." Dugan was forceful.

"Abby Andrews." She looked at the detective pleadingly. "Someone's trying to get me in trouble. They used my computer for those awful letters. And now a skateboard. Ask anyone. My little brother was here for a visit and he forgot his skateboard. It was on the porch of the cabin. It disappeared last week."

Dugan took a step nearer the table. "Describe the skateboard."

"It's black with orange stripes."

"When did you last see it?" The question came fast.

"The Saturday" — Abby looked frightened — "before Marian died."

"Where?" Curt, short, demanding.

"On the front porch of the cabin. It was propped up by the door."

"There are four cabins on the grounds west of the main building. You are the only person currently occupying a cabin."

Her violet eyes huge with fear, Abby nodded.

"When did he leave the board on the porch?"

"Craig was here the week before."

"Who would have occasion to see the skateboard on the porch?"

"Anybody. Everybody. Blythe had all the staff members out to the cabin next door to discuss redoing the interiors. They passed my cabin to go inside. The skateboard was right there in plain sight." Her voice wobbled but the challenge was clear.

Dugan turned to Blythe. "Is there anyone in addition to those present who were included in the survey of the cabin?"

Blythe's face creased in thought. "I think that's — oh, of course. Chloe Farley was with Louise."

Nela's glance locked with Dugan's. She hoped the detective read her loud and clear: *Look at these people. They're scared. I'm not.*

Chloe's innocent.

The detective's face didn't change. There might have been grudging respect in her dark brown eyes, but the brief silent exchange didn't deflect her from Abby. "When did you notice the skateboard was gone?"

"Sunday afternoon. I'd found a box in the basement and I was going to pack it up to mail to Craig."

Dugan gazed at each person in turn. "Does anyone have knowledge of the skateboard between Saturday and Sunday?"

No one answered.

11

Nela's fingers automatically worked the computer keyboard as she prepared a summary of a grant application. Below her surface attention to the task, her thoughts darted as she tried to make sense of the tense meeting with Detective Dugan. Of course murder mattered more than theft, but why hadn't Dugan even mentioned the return of the necklace, especially since she believed the necklace might be the reason for Marian Grant's murder? Why was Dugan keeping that information quiet?

All through the rest of the morning and during lunch and the afternoon, she'd waited for word of the necklace's return to reach her. She had waited for the sound of Dugan's firm steps and the level stare that accused.

It was shortly after three when Louise Spear stood in the doorway between her office and Chloe's. Louise's face was drawn with strain. "Nela, please come here for a moment."

Nela rose and walked into Louise's office. When she stepped through the connecting door, she expected to see Dugan. Instead, she was alone with Louise.

"Close the door. Sit down."

The door into the hallway was already shut. Louise's office was paneled in gleaming oak. Bookcases filled one wall. A print of a dramatic painting by the Baranovs hung behind her desk, the magnificent colors vibrant and life affirming. Nela loved the glorious colors favored by the Russian artists. The print commanded attention. Nela wondered if, consciously or subconsciously, plain and modest Louise chose the compelling print to make herself less noticeable.

Louise stood to one side of her light oak desk. A shaft of pale winter sunlight emphasized deep lines etched at the corners of her eyes and lips. She looked fatigued and worried.

Nela sat in the plain wooden chair that faced the desk. Had Louise been deputized to fire Nela? Why hadn't the police detective talked to her first? Had the redheaded reporter informed Dugan of her after-hours visit to Haklo?

Louise's brown eyes scarcely seemed to

acknowledge her presence. She was turned inward and her thoughts obviously weren't pleasant. Finally, she gazed at Nela. "Tell me about Friday night." She rubbed one thumb along the knuckles of her clenched right hand. "At Marian's apartment."

Nela described the sounds of a search and the light beneath the door and the arrival of the police.

Louise stared at Nela with wide worried eyes. "Did you see anyone when you opened the bedroom door?"

Nela knew abruptly that this was why Louise had called Nela into her office. Louise could have taken the necklace. But she could have taken the necklace many times in the last few years if she had wished. Why this fall? Did she need money? Did she resent Hollis Blair?

"Nela?" Louise appeared tense.

Nela felt suddenly that Louise was afraid of what Nela might say. "I didn't open the bedroom door until the police knocked. The thief was gone by then."

Louise's shoulders slumped. "I was hoping you might have some idea who was there. Well, I suppose if you knew anything you would have told the police."

"Yes. I would have told the police." But perhaps she'd been wiser than she knew

237

when she'd stayed safe in the bedroom waiting until the front door slammed behind the intruder, an intruder who looked everywhere for a hidden necklace and it wasn't hidden at all. "Have the police found out anything more about the necklace?" Why had no one discussed the return of the necklace? Surely its mysterious arrival was another pointer to someone with a key. That hadn't been Nela's intent when she brought it, but maybe underlining the connection to Haklo had been a very good idea.

"Unfortunately they haven't been able to trace it. The detective said they have queries out to pawnshops." She lifted thin fingers to touch one temple. "That will be all for now, Nela."

Nela managed to nod and get up and walk into Chloe's office without revealing her shock. She settled behind Chloe's desk and stared blankly at the computer screen. The necklace was still missing. But she'd left it on Blythe's desk. Nela opened the bottom drawer, pulled out her purse. She reached for her cell, then glanced at the open door to Louise's office. She couldn't afford to be overheard when she spoke to Steve. She had to wait until she left the foundation. She dropped the cell in the purse, closed the drawer.

It was one of those days. A tractor trailer overturned on the exit ramp into Craddock. One of Craddock's leading literary lights, a much-published Oklahoma historian, died unexpectedly. A black Lab saved his family by butting against a bedroom door to awaken sleeping parents in time to gather up their five children and escape a house fire caused by a frayed extension cord on a portable heater. Every winter when the frigid days came, the *Clarion* warned readers to be wary of the dangers of frayed cords and of carbon monoxide from faulty fireplaces and wood stoves and generators. Every winter there were blazes. This one had a happy ending. Some didn't.

Steve Flynn was in and out of the office. Lunch was a Big Mac on the run. It was almost three thirty before he had time to call Katie Dugan. He punched his speakerphone.

"Hey, Steve." Of course she had caller ID.

"Bring me up to date on Haklo."

"I suppose you plan a story on the anonymous call to the *Clarion*?"

He leaned back in his swivel chair, propped his feet on the desk, balanced a laptop on his lap. "We print the news as we get it." His tone was laconic.

"I can always dream, can't I? But probably our inquiries have tipped the murderer. If there is a murderer. Which isn't clear."

"And?"

"On the record, we are pursuing inquiries into the anonymous call to the *Clarion* that claimed the death of Marian Grant was murder."

Steve typed the quote, not that he wouldn't remember. It was stock Katie-speak when she didn't intend to elaborate. "And?"

Silence.

"Come on, Katie. Surely there's movement somewhere in this story. A little bird told me there was a bad" — he drew out the vowel but Katie didn't smile — "letter that went out to members of the grants committee."

She gave a quick little spurt of irritation. He knew she was wondering where he'd picked up that piece of information. "No comment."

"Do you have a lab report on damage to the apartment stairs?"

"No comment."

She hadn't said there was no report, which meant there was a report, but she was unwilling to reveal what had been learned. "Could a skateboard — if one is found — be tested for a match?"

"No comment."

"What's the status of the search for the necklace?" That should flush the fact of its return, although he was puzzled that Katie was playing coy about the jewelry's unaccountable arrival on the desk of its owner. The anonymous tip about murder was the lead of the story he would write, but the necklace would get big play, especially since once again a key had surely been used to enter Haklo. The noose would draw tighter around Haklo employees.

"At this point in the investigation, no trace of the necklace has been found."

Steve felt like he'd been sucker punched. The blow came from nowhere. His feet swung to the floor and he sat up straight. He listened blankly to the rest of Katie's response. "Inquiries have been made and will continue to be made at pawnshops and auction houses. Although Miss Webster has so far declined to request reimbursement from insurance, the insurance company with her permission has supplied photographs and a detailed description of the jewelry. If you ask pretty please, I'll send over a jpeg."

"Yeah." It was like staring at a billboard in

Czech. Nothing made sense.

"Hey, I thought you'd appreciate this puppy. Did a sexy broad just walk by your desk? I don't need a swami to tell me you've lost interest in our conversation. Ciao."

The connection ended.

He e-mailed the police department's Public Information office, requesting the jpeg. All the while, thoughts ran and nipped at each other's tails like hungry rats. . . . *She could have gone back to Haklo . . . intelligent eyes, quick on her feet . . . glossy black hair . . . promised not to lie . . . necklace gone . . . Someone took it . . . She could be telling the truth about the skateboard . . . If she didn't trust him, the smart thing was to remove the necklace . . . sure as hell must not have gotten a lot of sleep last night . . . Hurts, doesn't it, buddy? . . .*

He reached out to punch the speakerphone, slowly drew back his hand. What good would it do to call Katie Dugan? He had no proof. Yeah, he could pinpoint Nela in the doorway of Haklo after ten p.m. He had a picture of the necklace on Blythe Webster's desk. But still, it came down to his word against hers. She could swear she left with him and never returned, make it clear that he could as easily have returned for the necklace as she. Katie would believe him. Belief wasn't proof. He glanced at the clock. He had ten minutes to meet his deadline. The dog and the fire would run below the fold today. Murder trumped a feel-good story. Or was Nela's claim of a skateboard as phony as her promise not to lie? Of course, she hadn't lied yet. What would she say when he asked her about her return trip to Haklo? As for the skateboard, damned if there wasn't knowledge of one floating around Haklo. Could Nela have known about the skateboard missing from the cabin? He didn't know. As for now, he had a story to write. He typed fast, his face set in hard, angry lines. When done, he reread the piece.

An anonymous phone call to the *Clarion* Monday night claimed Haklo Foundation Chief Operating Officer Marian Grant was a murder victim. Grant died as a result of a fall down her apartment stairs early on the morning of Jan. 9.

The caller, who has not been identified, said Grant was thrown over the side of the stair rail when she stepped on a skateboard deliberately placed on the second step.

Police who investigated Grant's fall did not find a skateboard on or near the stairs.

Police Detective K. T. Dugan was informed of the call by *Clarion* staff. Detective Dugan refused to comment on the investigation into the call.

The anonymous caller said Grant was killed because she had discovered the identity of the thief responsible for the robbery of a $250,000 gold and diamond necklace from the desk of Haklo Trustee Blythe Webster.

Detective Dugan said police are continuing to contact pawnshops and auction houses in hopes of tracing the jewelry. Miss Webster has offered a $100,000 reward for the arrest and conviction of the thief.

The theft of the necklace is one in a series of unexplained incidents at the foundation.

Steve ended up with a summary of the vandalism, a description of Marian's career at Haklo, and the foundation's importance to Craddock.

He finished reading, zapped the article to Mim. He stared at the phone. He didn't like being played for a fool. Besides, he'd picked up a hand to play when he hadn't called the cops last night. Now he couldn't pretend to himself that he didn't know beans about a quarter-million-dollar piece of jewelry. His options were limited. Should he call Nela? Be waiting by the VW when she got off work?

To what purpose?

Ace Busey, his plaid wool shirt emanating waves of old cigarette smoke, settled one hip on the edge of Steve's desk. "Somebody's ticked you off big time. Must be a gal. Hasn't Papa told you that dames are deadly?"

Steve looked up into Ace's saggy, street-wise face. "Just concentrating."

Ace raised a shaggy eyebrow. "You look like a prune on a hot day. Lighten up. No dame is worth it."

Steve forced a humorless smile. "That's a given."

Ace slouched to his feet. "Got to catch a smoke." As he walked away, he said over his shoulder, "Don't say Papa didn't warn you."

Nela stepped into Louise's office with grant application folders. "I've attached one-page summaries to each application." Dry words for dreams and hopes and visions boiled down to a page. She wished that everything was different, that she could be excited about the foundation's outreach, make a difference for kids at summer camps, for libraries with budgets cut to the bone, for research to help drought-stricken farmers.

Louise looked up. Her thoughts seemed to come from a far distance. "Oh, yes." She gestured at her in-box. "I'll take care of them tomorrow."

Nela placed the folders in the lower receptacle. "Is there anything else I can do?"

Louise slowly shook her head. The movement seemed to take great effort.

Nela understood the burden of grief. "I'm sorry about Miss Grant. She must have been a wonderful person."

"Friday afternoon when I went in her office, I could tell she was upset. I asked if something was wrong. There was an odd look in her eyes. She said" — Louise's face crinkled in memory — " 'There's nothing wrong that can't be fixed. And I intend to fix it.' Of course, Marian believed she could handle anything." Louise massaged one temple. "Just a few days before she died, she told me she should have done something in St. Louis, that she'd known from the start it was a mistake to bring Hollis here. I knew what she meant. I was there, too. Hollis has too much charm. I know what happens when he walks into a room. Some women are more vulnerable than others." She shook her head. "And that girl chasing after him."

Her eyes were huge with distress. "If some-one put a skateboard on Marian's stairs and Abby's brother's skateboard is missing, there has to be a connection. Oh, I don't know what to think. I may be all wrong."

Nela looked at her sharply. "Do you have an idea who may have taken the skate-board?"

Louise drew herself up. Her voice was stiff. "I don't know anything about the skateboard." There was a ring of truth in her voice. But her eyes were still dark with worry. "It's just that I keep thinking about Marian. I can't bear to think what may have happened."

Nela knew, better than most, that outsid-ers couldn't lessen heartbreak. Nothing Nela did would ease Louise's sadness about Marian Grant or restore Haklo to happier days. But she knew, too, that kindness helps. "I'm sorry you're upset."

Louise's face softened. "You're a nice girl, Nela. Just like your sister. None of this has anything to do with you —"

Nela wished with all her heart that Louise was right.

"— and I'm sorry if I've troubled you. Don't worry. I know I'm tired. Things are always worse when you're tired." She glanced at the clock. "You can go home

247

now. Home . . ." For an instant, she pressed her lips together. "You're a long way from home. I don't think I could bear to go to Marian's apartment. Especially after someone coming inside Friday night." Once again lines of worry framed her eyes and lips. "Thank you for staying there. I know Jugs. He must miss Marian terribly. Go home early and pet Jugs for me. For Marian. Tell him he's a good cat." Louise turned away to look toward the windows.

By the time Nela reached the connecting doorway, Louise appeared lost in her thoughts, her thin face drawn and weary. In Chloe's office, Nela glanced at her watch. Only a few minutes after four. She shrugged into her coat. In the hallway, she walked fast, fumbling in her purse for her cell phone. Steve had to know about the necklace. As soon as she was safely alone in the VW, she'd call him.

Steve glanced at caller ID. He let the phone ring three times before he picked up the hand unit. "Flynn."

"Steve" — the connection was scratchy, obviously a call from a cell — "the necklace wasn't found."

"Yeah." The word was clipped.

She talked fast. "Someone took the neck-

248

lace from Blythe's desk. What can we do?"

"Someone took it?" His tone was taunting.

There was silence. Finally, she spoke. "What do you mean?"

"Two people knew the necklace was there. You. Me. I didn't take it. Do the math."

"You think —" She broke off. "I see." A pause. "That's a funny thing." Her tone was bleak. "It never occurred to me to think you went back and got the necklace."

The connection ended.

"Nela . . ." He spoke to emptiness.

Nela knew what it was to be alone, to feel separated from the world. There had been a moment with Steve — more than one — when warmth seemed near again. That brief connection was broken. There was no point in wasting time thinking about a stocky man with red hair. He'd been a stranger. He was a stranger again with no reason to share what he knew about people he knew.

It was up to her now to find the devious mind behind the troubles at Haklo and she might have very little time to act. She needed the perspective of someone who knew the staff. Louise not only might wonder if Nela came back inside, but, picturing faces in her mind, Nela had no idea which staff member to contact. What would she say? But she had to do something. She opened the car door, taking care not to let the wind butt the edge against the glossy blue Thunderbird with the personalized license plate: ROBBIE. The car was as slick as the PR director. Definitely he wouldn't be the right person to ask who might have a motive to cause trouble for Haklo. Although he kept his comments within bounds, his dislike of Hollis Blair was obvious. Vandalism might have appealed to Robbie as a way of attacking Hollis.

She'd liked Erik Judd. She had sensed beneath his drama that particular empathy that often belongs to creative people.

Nela stared at the Thunderbird, slowly shut the VW door. She used her iPhone, found an address and directions.

It was a five-minute drive to a quiet neighborhood with older homes, some of them brick duplexes, others 1950s vintage ranch-style houses. A green Porsche sat in the drive of the third house on the left, a one-story rambling brick house with bay windows. The house appeared well kept, no fading paint or cracks in the drive. The window glass glistened.

Nela walked swiftly to the front porch, lifted a shiny brass knocker.

The door opened almost at once. Erik Judd stared out at her, his face anxious. "Has something happened to Robbie?"

Obviously he knew who she was, that she had taken Chloe's place, and her unexpected arrival, certainly something beyond the norm, raised fear that something was wrong.

"He's fine." Nela understood the shock of unexpected arrivals. She still dreamed about the moment that Bill's brother walked in. "The police believe Marian Grant was murdered."

Erik's eyebrows folded into a frown. "Robbie called me. But" — his gaze was suspicious — "what does that have to do with you? Why are you here?"

"Everyone at the foundation is a suspect." She looked at him steadily. Sometimes truth wins the day. If he shut the door in her face, so be it. But he might not. She might have only a little time left to do her best for Chloe. He would do what he could to protect Robbie. "That's why I came. You and I both have someone we love who may be at risk from the police. The police are suspicious of Chloe because she's new to Haklo this fall. But Robbie may have publicly taken too much satisfaction from Hollis

Blair's difficulties because of the vandalism."

Erik raised a silver eyebrow. "From a bare acquaintance on Saturday, you seem to have learned a great deal about me and Robbie. But I fail to see why you are standing on our front porch."

"I'm an investigative reporter." She might not have a job right now, but that made no difference. She knew how to ask and probe and seek for a story. Now she would use her skills to save herself and Chloe.

Erik's pale blue eyes studied her. "Why do you want to talk to me?"

"You know everyone at Haklo." She saw a flicker of understanding in his watchful gaze. "I want you to tell me who could have committed the vandalism at Haklo and who would kill to avoid exposure as a vandal and a thief."

He smoothed one curling swoop of his mustache. "Aren't you a bit fearful of a private meeting with the 'disgruntled former director'?" His tone put the description in quote marks.

"Oh" — her tone was careless — "Steve Flynn knows where I am."

He was suddenly amused. "Quick thinking, my dear. But I don't believe that. However" — he held the door wide, made a sweeping bow — "enter my parlor if you desire."

She hesitated for only a moment, then stepped inside.

He led the way into a comfortable, manly den with leather furniture, a wide-screen TV, and Indian blankets hung on the paneled walls.

She skirted an easel with a half-finished watercolor of purple and gold wildflowers in a meadow, chose a cane chair.

Erik sat opposite in a red leather chair that was a dramatic setting for his curling white hair, black silk shirt, and white wide-cuffed wool trousers and black half boots. He listened, nodding occasionally as she marshaled her facts.

When she was done, he nodded approval. "Quite concise and complete. I'm aware of all the incidents. I should make it clear that I am not a recluse brooding over ill treatment. It was" — he paused, seeking the right word — "a shock when Blythe dismissed me, especially for a callow youth with no experience, except perhaps" — his mouth twisted in a wry smile — "in the useful art of charming ladies. I always assumed outstanding leadership was sufficient. I was wrong. However" — and now he sounded quite comfortable — "I have enjoyed thoroughly a return to the life of a writer. In fact, if you'd looked in the Haklo library a half hour ago, you would have found me there. I often spend the afternoon at Haklo with my research on the foundation. Robbie has remained angry even though I've assured him I am content. Now" — he leaned forward — "I want to be clear. Neither Robbie nor I have ever done anything that would be detrimental to Haklo. I devoted the best years of my life to making Haklo one of the finest charitable foundations in the country. I am sickened by the events that have occurred this fall. As for Robbie, I'm afraid he has enjoyed watching Hollis squirm, but Robbie knows that I would utterly oppose any kind of attack on Haklo. Haklo is bigger than Hollis or Blythe or me or Robbie."

"Someone there, someone with a key, must be behind the vandalism and the theft." Nela held his gaze. "If you care about Haklo, help me figure out who is guilty."

Erik frowned. One hand touched the crystal eagle that hung from a leather necklace. "From what you've told me, it does seem likely that the vandal is a staff member." His eyes narrowed. "Not Louise. Not Rosalind. I can't speak to the new director or his girlfriend or your sister." A stop. "Harris Webster used to worry about his daughters. Blythe has always been obsessive. Once she was obsessed with a young man who worked for Harris. Now she's obsessed with Haklo but the vandalism punishes Haklo. Grace is impulsive, a wild thing. She's furious that her father made Blythe the sole trustee. Francis is ruthless. Whatever is important to him is all that matters. Cole used to be a major force at Haklo, Webster's good friend. Now he's yesterday. I think it's broken his heart. Peter is fighting Blythe's ideas of outsourcing. He has a wife who likes money. But that tweedy, casual appearance is misleading. He's climbed Kilimanjaro."

As she drove away, Nela carried with her two impressions. Erik trusted Robbie, truly believed Robbie would never do anything to jeopardize the foundation that Erik loved. No doubt he would describe her visit and emphasize how he had made it clear that both he and Robbie had nothing to do with the attacks on Haklo. But if Robbie had been tempted to cause just enough trouble to harm the new director, exposure meant more than criminal action, it meant breaking the heart of the man he loved. Would Robbie be willing to kill to keep the vandalism from Erik?

12

"Have to eat, right?" Nela tried to sound upbeat. She spooned chicken-flavored food into a freshly washed cat bowl.

Jugs looked up. *". . . crying inside . . ."*

Nela put down the bowl. She'd pet Jugs after he ate, tell him Louise said he was a good cat. The words wouldn't matter. The tone would give him comfort. She knew she should eat as well, but her throat was tight and she wasn't hungry. She turned away, walked into the living room, dropped into the easy chair. How long would it take for the police to arrive? By this time, Steve Flynn would have contacted Dugan, showed her the photos in his iPhone.

Nela knew she had few options. Whatever she did, she wasn't going to lie. She would decline to comment and that would probably put her in jail. She glanced at her watch. Dugan was taking her own sweet time in coming. Would it do Nela any good to share Erik Judd's views? Or would Dugan have closed her mind to everyone but Chloe and Nela?

The hospital bed still looked odd in his parents' spacious bedroom. His dad was dozing. The home health aide looked at him eagerly. When Steve came for a visit in the evenings, she could slip out for a while, a walk in good weather, now a few minutes in her room, catching up on a favorite TV show. His dad loathed TV, said if he ever got bored enough to watch TV, he'd hold a funeral service for his brain.

Steve stood beside the bed. Sometimes it seemed they took a little step forward, then two steps back.

His father's eyelids fluttered open. His eyes were as blue as Steve's. His hair, too, had once been red, but was now white. His broad face sagged a little on one side, a visible reminder of the stroke that felled him.

"Hey, Dad." Steve spoke in a normal tone. His dad despised sickroom whispers. Though his speech was still somewhat garbled, he'd made it clear to a succession of helpers. ". . . Still hear . . . Up speak . . ."

Those bright blue eyes were as perceptive as always, reflecting a quick and facile mind trapped in an uncooperative body. ". . .

'Rubble . . ."

Yeah, there was trouble. Big-time trouble. Chances were he'd been a sap over a woman. One more time. But this time, he wanted to call her. He wanted to believe her. He admired the way her chin jutted when she faced opposition. He wanted to plumb the intelligence behind her gaze. He wanted to know about her. Did she like to go camping? Had she ever trout fished? He knew some things. She had guts. She loved words. Her face in repose suggested she knew sadness. A guy named Bill had loved her. But who else could have taken the damn necklace? Steve gave a shrug, tried to appear casual. "Hard day. Lots of stuff happening."

Maybe those blue eyes saw more because they'd had a glimpse of eternity. Maybe Daniel Flynn knew better than to waste time with niceties. His gaze was sharp, demanding. ". . . You . . ."

Steve pressed his lips together, knew his face was a road map of misery.

His dad lifted his head. ". . . heart . . . listen . . . promise . . ."

Listen to your heart. Maybe it wasn't a smart motto. Maybe he didn't give a damn about being smart. Steve reached out, touched a still muscular shoulder. "I will,

Dad. As soon as I think some things through."

Jugs lay at the end of the table in his lion pose, watching as she ate.

It wasn't much of a dinner. A bowl of tomato soup and some dry crackers from a box long past its fresh date. Chloe hadn't been in the apartment long enough to leave a half-empty box of crackers. Nela was eating saltines that had been purchased by Marian Grant. Odd. But Marian wouldn't begrudge crackers to someone taking care of Jugs. Nela looked into watching green eyes and felt certain of that. She wasn't certain of anything else. "Jugs, I don't know what to do."

". . . *She was worried . . .*"

"So am I, buddy." Oh hell yes, she was worried. She ate and listened for a knock at the door, for the questions she dared not answer. She cleaned up the kitchen in only a moment. In the living room, she dropped into the comfortable overstuffed chair and looked across the silent room at the sofa. Last night he'd sat there and given her a chance. When he'd walked into the main hall of Haklo late Monday morning, wiry red hair, broad open face, bright blue eyes, stocky and muscular, she'd instinctively started to smile. It wasn't until he looked at her late last night and gravely listened to her halting explanations that she'd realized he was a man with a hard edge, a man who had been hurt and was afraid to trust.

He'd trusted her. For a little while. She fought away sudden sharp sadness. What difference did it make? She scarcely knew him. Abruptly, she came to her feet, hurried into the living room. She picked up Bill's picture. She looked at his laughing face, young and strong, alive and loving her. Carrying the picture, she sank onto the sofa. The red, white, and blue ribbon she'd wound through the latticed wood of the frame brought no comfort.

Jugs jumped up beside her, pressed against her thigh.

She massaged behind big ears. "It's up to me, Jugs." She looked again at Bill's photograph and the familiar emptiness echoed inside. Bill wasn't here. Bill wasn't anywhere.

Jugs lifted his head, turned to stare at the front door. His ears flicked forward.

A sharp knock rattled the door.

Nela slowly came to her feet. She'd known this moment was coming. She walked to the door, turned on the porch light, twisted the knob. As cold air eddied around her, she stared, her lips parted.

Once again the wind stirred his short red hair. Once again he wore no coat. Tonight he carried a folder.

She looked past him.

"Just me. Maybe you'll tell me to take a hike. I thought it over. I didn't ask you. That wasn't fair." Now his blue eyes held hers. "Did you go back last night?"

"No."

The look between them was more than a question and answer.

His face softened. "Sorry. Sometimes now" — the words came slowly — "I expect bad outcomes. I shouldn't have jumped to a stupid conclusion."

"It wasn't stupid. You don't know me. I found the necklace in Marian's purse, but I can never prove that it was there. I tried to see it safely back to Blythe. I feel like I've done everything I can do. But thank you for coming. It was very kind." She started to close the door.

He held up the folder. "Can I come in? I've got some stuff that may help."

Nela hesitated. "You've already done more for me than you should." He hadn't called the police when he found her coming out of Haklo. She was sure they'd broken some laws leaving the necklace on Blythe's desk, but he didn't deserve to be in trouble because of her. "I'm afraid it's dangerous to hang around with me."

"That's a chance I'll take."

Nela wanted to let him inside. She wanted him to leave. She didn't know what she wanted, but she was acutely aware of his nearness. He was alive and strong and vital. Bill —

"I don't know." She knew she must sound like a fool. "I'm sorry. I don't want to have anything else to do with what's happened at Haklo. I'm going to be here for Chloe until she returns. But she and I have nothing to do with the problems there. Let's leave it at that." She closed the door.

Now she had lied to him. She'd promised him she wouldn't lie and now she had. She couldn't walk away from the turmoil at the foundation. She was going to find out more, much more, seek the truth. For her and for Chloe.

But she didn't have to involve Steve Flynn.

She leaned against the cold wooden panel and listened to the sound of diminishing steps.

Slanting beams from passing headlights created a silhouette of leafless limbs on the bedroom ceiling, jumbled dark splotches that made no sense, formed no coherent pattern. Steve always sought a pattern. This time he was out of luck. His thoughts shifted from her rebuff to his damn fool determination to help someone who didn't want help, swung from certainty to uncertainty. Was she honest? Did he care? People did what they thought they had to do. She'd help her sister at all costs. Was that why she sent him away? Or was she running from him because she, too, felt the attraction between them when they stood close together? She carried sadness with her. He thought he knew why. Someday he would ask her about the dark-haired guy standing on a beach and the red, white, and blue ribbon that wreathed the brown wooden frame. Someday. Not now.

His mouth twisted in a wry grin. Big talk on his part. Her good night had been a pretty definite good-bye. One thing was for sure. He'd wanted for months to be free of memories of Gail. Maybe he should have remembered to be careful what he wished for. Was the god of hilarity laughing aloud? Gail was fading. Her name no longer conjured images that excited desire or bitterness. Instead, he saw Nela's intelligent, vulnerable face with lips that he wanted to kiss.

The grin slipped away. She was in trouble. She — and her sister — would be safe only if he discovered the truth behind the vandalism and the theft of the necklace. He'd made a start last evening on figuring out who could have taken the necklace from Blythe Webster's desk. Tomorrow he'd narrow the field. He might not have a white horse to ride to Nela's rescue, but he knew Craddock maybe even better than Katie Dugan.

Though Nela was weary to the bone, sleep was elusive. She kept hearing the sound of Steve's footsteps fading into silence. She pushed away thoughts of Steve. She heard Bill's voice . . . *If I don't come back* . . . Bill had wanted to tell her that if he died, she must live. She had placed her fingers on his lips, warm living lips, to stop the words she didn't want to hear. She had read the message in Bill's eyes just as tonight she'd looked into blue eyes and seen another message: *I want to know you. Give me a chance.*

She turned restlessly, tried to get comfortable. She knew what Bill had wanted for her. But not yet. Not while emptiness filled her heart.

She'd sent Steve away. She wanted him to be safe. As a reporter, he was jeopardizing his job to keep information about a crime from the police. She had involved him in a crime when he learned that she'd returned the necklace to Haklo. Detective K. T. Dugan could charge him with obstruction of justice and possibly conspiracy in regard to transportation of stolen property. Right now there was no reason Dugan should ever learn that Steve had been at Haklo last night. Nela would never tell anyone.

She began to sink into the oblivion of exhausted sleep. Faintly, Nela heard a *click-click-click* on the bedroom door. Her eyelids fluttered open as she turned her head on the pillow. Jugs . . . wanted in . . . good cat . . . lonely . . . Groggily she rolled on an elbow, sat up. *Click-click-click*. She came to her feet, crossed the cold hardwood floor. She'd learned a lesson Friday night. The door would always be locked while she slept. She turned the knob, held the panel open. A dark shape flowed past. When she settled again on the bed, Jugs snuggled beside her, soft and warm. A faint purr signaled his happiness.

13

Steve took another bite of a glazed dough-nut, washed away the sweetness with strong coffee. Not much of a breakfast, but enough. He wrote fast, his printing big and legible on a legal pad. He could have made notes on his laptop. For quick jottings, he still liked real paper. He had been in kindergarten when the *Clarion* installed computers. He remembered thick yellow copy and the clack of Remingtons and an ever-present smoky haze. Now the newsroom was silent, the walls had long ago been repainted to remove years of nicotine scum, and the copy spike on Mim Barlow's desk was a memento. He was finishing his third cup of coffee when Mim's brisk steps sounded in the newsroom.

She stopped beside his desk. "Something big?" She sounded hopeful.

"Background."

Her glance was sharp. "Let me know if I

should hold space."

"Not today."

"Right. Do a follow-up on the missing necklace."

"Already sent it over."

"If everyone was as efficient . . ." She turned toward her desk.

Steve put the legal pad to one side of the screen, ready now for a summation that he could print out. He wanted to have a copy for Nela. Stubby fingers flew over the keys.

HAKLO TIMETABLE

1. *September 19.* Car set afire in employee parking lot. 1995 Camaro destroyed. Unsolved. No suspects. Anne Nesbitt, 23, owner of car, relocated to Norman, now works at the Sam Noble Museum of Natural History. No record of troubled relationships in her personal life. Police investigation concluded the fire was randomly set and not directed at Nesbitt personally.
2. *November 15.* Nine Chickasaw baskets found hacked to pieces in exhibit room.
3. *December 5.* Sprinklers activated in Robbie Powell's office.

4. *December 16.* Courtyard fountain turned on, frozen pipes.
5. *January 5.* Necklace missing from desk of Blythe Webster.
6. *January 9.* Marian Grant died from a fall down garage apartment stairs.
7. *January 14.* Nela Farley called 911 to report intruder in Marian Grant's apartment.
8. *January 14.* Nela Farley found expensive necklace in Marian Grant's purse.
9. *January 16.* According to Nela, members of Haklo grants committee received obscene material on Haklo Director Hollis Blair's letterhead.
10. *January 16.* Ditto, letter traced to file in computer of Assistant Curator Abby Andrews. Andrews denied creating file.
11. *January 16.* Search of Marian Grant's office discovered by Nela Farley. Office searched sometime after 5 p.m. Friday and before late Monday morning.
12. *January 16.* Nela Farley learned about necklace stolen from Blythe Webster and realized the necklace was in Marian Grant's purse.

13. *January 16.* Nela Farley entered Haklo after hours and placed necklace on Blythe Webster's desk.
14. *January 16.* Unidentified caller to *Clarion* claimed Marian Grant was murdered, her fall caused by a skateboard placed deliberately on the second step.
15. *January 17.* Detective Dugan informed Haklo staff of the anonymous message. Theft (or claimed theft) of skateboard from the porch of Abby's cabin revealed.
16. *January 17.* Necklace once again missing.

Steve didn't need a reminder of the incidents. He'd written too many stories to forget a single one. Instead, he focused on dates. The car was set afire in September. After a lapse of two months, several acts of vandalism occurred. Was the car fire an anomaly, independent of the other incidents? Maybe the car fire gave someone an idea.

The fire caused no harm to the foundation. The later vandalism was clearly intended to cause problems for Haklo. The fire could have been set by anyone. The destruction of the Indian baskets, water damage in Robbie's office, theft of Blythe's necklace, and use of Blair's letterhead could have been done only by someone familiar with the foundation.

The vandalism could have had any of several objectives: To harass either Haklo or its trustee, Blythe Webster, to mar the stewardship of the new director, to make the theft of the necklace appear simply to be another in a series of unlawful acts, or as an act of revenge by a disgruntled current or former employee.

Katie Dugan settled on the fact that no vandals had ever struck at Haklo until this fall. Katie believed newcomer Chloe Farley committed the vandalism but that her goal was to take the necklace. The lapse of time between the car fire and the destruction of the Indian baskets supported Katie's theory. Chloe likely would not have known until she'd worked at Haklo for several weeks that Blythe Webster kept a quarter-million-dollar necklace lying in a desk drawer in her unlocked office.

However, Chloe was not the only new employee at Haklo since summer. He thumbed through notes. Hollis Blair arrived August first. Abby Andrews was hired August fifteenth.

Steve stared at the list. Why was there a

two-month lag between the car fire and the hacked baskets? Maybe when he knew the answer to that, he'd know the truth behind vandalism, theft, and murder.

He clicked several times on his computer. The burned car had been front-page news. Who had handled that investigation?

Nela turned into the main Haklo drive. She was alert as she passed the main building and turned left to drive to the employee lot, but she didn't see any police cars. Nela parked again between the Thunderbird and the Dodge. Louise's car was also in the lot. Nela looked in every direction as she walked to the staff entrance. When she stepped inside and the door sighed shut behind her, she scanned the hallway. No trace of police. It seemed strange to be wary of the police. Her uncle Bob had been a sergeant in the LAPD, a big, ebullient, loud man. Her aunt always worried. A cop never knew when a stopped car might harbor danger, yet every day cops walked toward cars, some with tinted windows. They carried a gun in a holster, but they approached empty-handed, keeping streets safe for ordinary people.

Lights spilled from Louise's open door. In Chloe's office, Nela dropped her purse into a desk drawer. Despite the lack of a police presence, she continued to feel apprehensive. What was Detective Dugan doing now? Driving to Haklo to interrogate Nela again? But the detective had no reason to inquire into Nela's activities Monday night. Surely she was focused on a search for the missing skateboard.

Nela hung Chloe's large jacket on the coatrack, checked the clock. She stepped to the open door between the offices.

Louise's office was brightly lit. She looked up. "Good morning, Nela." Although her face was wan, she made an effort to smile. "That's a pretty skirt."

"Thank you, Louise." Nela's wardrobe was limited by what she'd managed to put in one suitcase. The long swirling skirt was silk with a pattern of blue and black circles. She added a crisp white blouse and black pumps. It was one of her best outfits, one she'd often worn when working as a reporter. If she saw Steve . . . But she wouldn't see him. She'd turned him away, listened to the fading sound of his footsteps. The thought brought a quick stab of unhappiness. She wanted to see him. She didn't want to see him.

". . . put some more application folders on your desk. After you finish the summaries and deliver the morning mail, please pick up the proofs of a new scholarship brochure from Peter." She looked a little defiant. "He sent me the brochure online but I still like to look at paper." She gave a decided nod and turned back toward her computer.

Nela settled at Chloe's computer. It was important for her to act as if Haklo's troubles didn't affect her personally. As she read and typed, willing herself not to think of Steve, she listened, alert and wary, for the brisk sound of official steps in the hallway. She felt like a fish in a barrel, easy prey. As soon as possible, she had to figure a way to discover the truth behind the tangled relationships at Haklo, what mattered and what didn't matter, who had stolen a necklace and committed murder to prevent exposure.

She'd started her investigation with Erik Judd. He'd been willing to talk to her, but would any of the rest of the staff be willing to respond?

Her fingers hung in the air above the keyboard.

Maybe there was a way to take advantage of her reporter background. She glanced up at the clock. In a few minutes, she was scheduled to deliver the mail to Haklo staff, starting, of course, with Blythe Webster.

Monday morning, as soon as Blythe heard from members of the grants committee about the obscene letters with the Haklo director's letterhead, she had set in motion a thorough search. She hadn't been passive, hadn't waited for anyone else to take charge. Tuesday the police dropped the bombshell of the anonymous call claiming Marian Grant's death was instead murder. Blythe made it clear at that meeting that all staff members were to cooperate with the authorities. Yes, the police were investigating, but Blythe might see a role for Haklo itself to seek truth. And maybe Nela could help.

Steve dropped into the straight chair next to Mokie Morrison's desk. "Glad I caught you." Most of the other desks in the detectives' room were unoccupied.

Mokie was cheerful. "Katie believes in old-fashioned shoe leather. At least she didn't send me out to check with the sanitation guys to see if anybody noticed a skateboard disappearing into the jaws of death last week. In case you're wondering, the jaws of death are those big choppers that grind up garbage when the guys throw stuff in. The choppers can turn metal pylons into mincemeat, damn near. The garbage guys need to watch their elbows and hands.

That's just one hazard. Do you know anybody who works harder than garbage guys? Hang on and freeze their butts in winter. Hang on and bake in summer. And, man, the smell. And they're supposed to check out the trash before it splinters? I don't think so. Anyway, Katie's frustrated. Plus too many places in this case — the apartment behind the Webster mansion and the assistant curator's cottage on the Haklo grounds — don't have any convenient nosy parker neighbors. So I got no complaints about my assignment, but Marian Grant's banker and lawyer aren't ready to chummy up with the cops. Lots of mutters about court orders, sanctity of client information. Me, I think the whole idea that Marian Grant was murdered is just another poke by the Haklo Vandal, one more way to make things awkward for the T. It's kind of a blot on Haklo's shiny bright rep if somebody bumped off the COO. The hell of it is, nobody can prove murder or accident, but once the story's out there, some people will believe in murder and think there's a big cover-up."

Steve was casual. "Maybe, but it's funny that the tip was specific, a skateboard on the second step, and then it turns out one of the Haklo people is missing a skateboard.

That gives the story some legs."

Mokie leaned back in his chair. "Nah. The Haklo Vandal used a skateboard in that call you got because the Vandal spotted a skateboard on the cabin porch and then, to muddy things up even more, filched the skateboard."

"The skateboard disappeared before the call was made."

"So? Can't say the Haklo Vandal doesn't plan ahead. Anyway, what can I do for you." Mokie smothered a yawn. "Got to be more interesting than listening to lawyers and bankers talk in great big circles."

Steve pulled some folded copy paper out of his pocket. "You covered the Camaro fire out at Haklo. I know it's been a while, but I'd like to run through what you remember."

"Oh, man." Mokie's eyes gleamed and he sat up straight. "Hot stuff."

"The fire?" Weren't fires always hot?

Mokie's eyes squinted in remembrance. "Nah. The babe. Stacked." He moved his hands in a modified figure eight. "Boobs with a life of their own. Hips . . ." He sighed. "Inquiring officer couldn't touch but he could dream. At least I got to sit in the back of the patrol car with her. Inches away." He wriggled his nose. "Gardenia perfume. Like a summer night in the bushes

276

with a babe."

Steve shook his head. "If you can get past primal appeal, tell me about the fire."

Mokie grinned. "Man, you got to remember, first things first. Wow. Drop-dead gorgeous. As for the fire" — his tone was suddenly matter-of-fact — "let me take a look." He swung around to his computer, clicked a couple of times. "Yeah. Here it is. Call came in at three fifteen, car on fire in Haklo staff lot. Arrived at three twenty-two. Bystanders wringing hands. Fire truck arrived at three twenty-four. Flames shooting from Camaro windows. Fire out by three thirty-eight." Mokie's nose wrinkled. "Pretty bad stink. Plastic seats melted by heat, interior destroyed, car turned out to be totaled. A gardener called in the alarm, tried to douse the blaze with a watering hose. The sirens brought people outside and somebody alerted the Camaro owner, who came running outside. One Anne Nesbitt." A deep breath. "Man, I wish I'd been there to see her run. Daffodil yellow cotton top, molded, tight cream skirt. Very short."

"The fire," Steve reminded gently.

"Somebody splashed the interior with gasoline, stood back, and lobbed a wad of burning rags." He raised a crooked black brow. "That was pretty clever. The arsonist was smart enough to know there could be a flash explosion so the perp used a kid's bow and arrow. The bow was in a plastic trash barrel at the edge of the parking lot. No fingerprints. A piece of a plastic shaft, all that didn't melt, was found inside the car. Arson investigators can figure out a lot from residue. Anyway, that's the theory." He raised a crooked black brow. "I always figured it was some dame who was jealous of the victim. A bow and arrow sounds girlie."

"Did you trace it?"

Mokie raised both eyebrows. "Like we can trace the sale of a Walmart toy. You know how many Walmarts there are in a fifty-mile radius? You can bet the perp didn't get the bow and arrow in Craddock. No luck there. Actually, no luck anywhere. I dug hard and didn't find a whiff of anybody who had a grudge against the babe."

"How about hard feelings on the staff?"

"Why? Because she's gorgeous?" A slight frown tugged at his brows. "Have to admit there didn't seem to be any loiterers out there that afternoon. The gardeners didn't see anybody walking around. One guy claimed nobody came in by the service road. The only other access was to park in front and either come through the main door or walk down the east road. The east road was closed off for some repair work that afternoon. The crew didn't see anybody. I asked her every which way I knew and she couldn't tell me anybody that was mad at her. I checked out which staff members were there that afternoon. You want the list?"

Steve nodded.

Mokie clicked twice. "Easier to say who wasn't there. Hollis Blair was in Kansas City at a meeting. Everybody else was on site. You can't say I didn't give it my all." His mouth slid into a suggestive smile. "I talked to her a half-dozen times. Finally" — a regretful sigh — "I had to give up. There was no rhyme, no reason." He pulled his cell phone from his pocket, slid his thumb several times over the small screen. "Take a gander."

Steve looked at the image. Mokie hadn't exaggerated. Anne Nesbitt was a babe, shining thick golden hair, delicate intriguing classic features, and, not to be missed by any male between ten and ninety, a voluptuous body.

Nela was midway through the stack of folders when Chloe's phone buzzed. "Nela Far—"

"Come to my office at once." Blythe Webster's voice was sharp with a tense undertone. The connection ended.

Nela took a steadying breath as she replaced the receiver. Obviously, Detective Dugan had shared her suspicions of Chloe and Nela with Blythe. Was Blythe going to fire Chloe and her substitute on the spot? Nela walked up the hallway with her shoulders squared.

She stepped through the open door to Blythe's office. Each time she'd been in this elegant office, there had been a background of tension. The first time she'd overheard the worried exchange between Blythe and Hollis occasioned by the arrival of obscene letters on Haklo stationery. The second time she had slipped inside with the stolen necklace, eager to leave the jewelry behind and escape. The third time Steve Flynn marched her inside, but the glitter of gold and diamonds had persuaded him that Nela — and Chloe — were innocent of wrongdoing.

Now the office was once again a backdrop to drama.

Blythe Webster stood rigid next to her desk. She wore her luxuriant dark mink coat and held a sheet of paper in one hand. On the desktop lay a white envelope that had been opened. "Shut the door. Where did this letter come from?"

Nela stared at the trustee's haggard face and realized in a welling of relief that Blythe had not called Nela into the office to accuse her or to fire her.

"The letter, where did it come from?" Blythe's voice wobbled. "Answer me."

"I didn't bring the letter. I haven't made deliveries yet this morning. I was summarizing —" She broke off. Blythe didn't care about Nela's work. She cared only about how the envelope had reached her desk.

In a jerky movement, Blythe reached toward the envelope, stopped inches away. She stared for a moment, pulled open the center drawer, picked up a pen, used the end to tip the envelope address side up. "There's no stamp. If the letter didn't come through the mail" — Blythe's words were reluctant — "someone must have put it on my desk." Her lips compressed, she turned and picked up the telephone receiver. "Rosalind, have there been any visitors in the building this morning?" She listened. "No visitors?" Her expression was grim when she replaced the receiver.

She looked at Nela. "Go to your office. Remain there. Do not discuss the letter with anyone."

■ ■ ■ ■

Steve Flynn set a full mug of coffee on his desk. Arson of the Haklo employee's car seemed more and more like an outlier to the subsequent vandalism. His mouth twisted in an almost-smile. Mokie might be an old dog, but he hadn't forgotten the hunt. Maybe his instinct was right, some woman had set sexy Anne Nesbitt's car on fire in a jealous rage.

Steve laid out his notes on his desk, scanned them. Mokie had been thorough.

. . . boyfriend in Norman, doctoral student. No hanky-panky there. Known each other since college, never dated anyone else. Nesbitt had no known enemies . . . Acquaintances insist Nesbitt was on good terms with everyone. . . . Gardeners working on west side of grounds claim no strange cars in or out within half an hour either side of fire . . . East-entrance road under repair that day, closed, no cars entered from that direction . . . Perp could have parked somewhere else, walked on foot, but no strangers noted . . .

Maybe no stranger did arrive that afternoon. Maybe the perp was already present, a member of the Haklo staff, the crime carefully planned, the bow and arrow, gas tin, and wad of cloth hidden near the employee lot. Yeah, there was an odd lag in time between the fire and the destruction of the Indian baskets, but he'd try to reconcile that puzzle later. For now . . . He pulled out a fresh legal pad, picked up his pen.

KNOWN TO HAVE KEY TO HAKLO
Blythe Webster, Haklo trustee; Grace Webster, honorary trustee; Hollis Blair, director; Louise Spear, executive secretary; Cole Hamilton, advisory vice president; Francis Garth, business development research fellow; Robbie Powell, director of public relations; Peter Owens, director of publications; Abby Andrews, assistant curator; Chloe Farley (and thereby Nela Farley), administrative assistant; Rosalind McNeill, receptionist; Kay Hoover, chef; Erik Judd, former director.

He'd known Rosalind since kindergarten. Some people could be badasses. Some couldn't. Rosalind couldn't. He drew a line through her name. Kay Hoover was the grandmother of his best buddy in high school. She made pralines to die for. Mama Kay thought about food. And family. And food. And family. He marked out her name. Two more quick strokes went through Chloe and Nela's names. He couldn't vouch for Chloe, but he believed Nela. If she was innocent, Chloe was innocent.

Now for a closer look at those with easy access to Haklo.

In the chair behind Chloe's desk, Nela had a good view of the portion of hall revealed by the open door. She waited and watched. The sound she had expected was not long in coming. Not more than ten minutes later, brisk steps clipped in the hallway.

Nela had only a brief glimpse, but the glimpse was telling. Detective Dugan strode purposefully past, accompanied by a somber Blythe Webster. Dugan was in all black today, turtleneck, skirt, and boots. The cheerful color of Blythe's crimson suit looked at odds with her resolute expression, a woman engaged in an unwanted task. Two uniformed officers followed, balding, moon-faced Sergeant Fisher with his ever-ready electronic tablet and a chunky woman officer in her late twenties.

Nela eased from the chair and moved to the open door. She didn't step into the hall.

Instead, unseen, she listened.

"The light is on, but the office is empty." Dugan had a clear, carrying voice.

The squeak of a chair pushed back. Rapid steps sounded. Louise Spear hurried past Chloe's doorway, didn't even glance toward Nela. "What's wrong?" Her voice was anxious, held definite foreboding.

"Where is Miss Andrews?" Dugan sounded pleasant, but firm.

"Usually at this time she's upstairs in the artifact room." Louise sounded puzzled.

"Sergeant, ask Miss Andrews to join us."

"Blythe, what's going on? Why are the police here?"

Blythe sounded remote, as if she were trying to remain calm. "The police have to make an investigation. I don't have anything to say right now. Let's see what happens."

Nela slid closer to the door. No one spoke until the officer returned with Abby.

Abby's face was fearful and pinched. She stared with wide, frightened eyes at the cluster of people outside her office. "What's wrong? Why do you want to talk to me?"

Blythe Webster spoke in a tight, contained voice. "Abby, it's necessary for the police to search your office. I have granted them permission to do so."

"Why?" Abby's breathing was uneven.

"What are they looking for?"

Hurrying steps came down the hall. Hollis Blair strode forward, brows drawn in a tight frown. He looked from Blythe to Dugan to Abby. "I saw police cars. What's happening?"

Abby's voice shook. "They want to search my office."

Nela stepped into the hallway. She might be sent away, but surely it was only natural to respond to the arrival of the police.

Abby's delicate face twisted in fear. "I don't think they have any right. I haven't done anything." She lifted a trembling hand to push back a tangle of blond hair.

Hollis appeared both shocked and angry. "I'll take care of everything." He swung toward the police detective, who stood in the doorway. "Detective, I want an explanation."

Dugan was brief. "Information received necessitates a search of the office. The search will proceed."

"On whose authority?" The director bit off the words.

"Mine." Blythe Webster spoke quietly.

Abby turned toward Blythe. "I haven't done anything. Why are you —"

Dugan interrupted, "The search of the office is not directed at you personally, Miss

Andrews." But Dugan's brown eyes never moved from Abby's lovely, anxious face. "Please step into the doorway and see if you notice any disarray in your office."

Arms folded, a gold link bracelet glittering on one wrist, Blythe listened, eyes narrowed, lips compressed.

Two more uniformed police came from the main hallway along with Detective Morrison.

"Disarray?" Abby repeated uncertainly.

"Anything out of place? A drawer open that you left shut? Any suggestion that an unauthorized person had been in your office?" Dugan's questions came quick and fast.

"Oh my God." Abby hurried to the doorway. In a moment, she faced her tormentors. "I don't know. I don't think so. I don't know." Her voice rose in distress. "Why? What are you looking for?"

Dugan nodded toward Detective Morrison and the two newly arrived uniformed officers, a lean, wiry man with bushy eyebrows in a pasty face and the redheaded policewoman who had come to the garage apartment when Nela called for help.

Hollis Blair glared at Blythe, his handsome features strained, his jaw rigid. "Why wasn't I notified? There better be a damn good reason for this." He jerked a thumb toward Dugan.

The trustee's shoulders stiffened. She gave him a level stare, her brown eyes cool. Her expression was not hostile, but the distance seemed to increase between them.

By now, the hallway around Nela was crowded. Louise Spear stood a little to one side, eyes huge, staring at Abby's office, her face puckered in a worried frown. Other staff members hurried toward the clump of people, likely drawn by the arrival of the police and the hubbub in the west hallway. Rosalind McNeill tried to appear grave but she almost bounced in excitement. Cole Hamilton moved back and forth uneasily, darting quick looks past Dugan. Occasionally one eyelid jerked in a nervous tic. Peter Owens, his gaze intent, looked from Blythe to Abby to Hollis. Francis Garth stood with folded arms, heavy head jutting forward, thick black brows lowered, massive legs planted solidly. Robbie Powell muttered, "Police again. This can't be good for Haklo."

Heels clicked on marble as Grace Webster arrived. She clapped her hands. "Never a dull moment."

Hollis moved nearer Blythe. "I'm the director. I should know if the police are called. And why."

288

"I'm the trustee." That was all Blythe said.

Hollis Blair stiffened. His angular face flushed. After a tense pause, he took two steps to stand beside Abby.

"Whoop-de-do, Blythe's in her dowager queen mode. Sis, I hate to break it to you" — Grace Webster's tone was saccharine — "but what are sisters for? That frozen face makes you look fifty, not a happy number for somebody who's barreling up on the big Four-O."

"I didn't know you were coming in today." Blythe's voice was cold.

"Can't stay away. Haklo used to be boring. Not anymore." Grace yanked a thumb over her shoulder. "What's the cavalry here for?"

Blythe ignored the question, her face smooth, her eyes focused on the doorway.

Grace's look of amusement faded, replaced with anger.

The public relations director took a few steps toward Blythe. "The *Clarion* will pick up the call. We need to be prepared —"

Sergeant Fisher came to the doorway. "Detective."

The silence among the onlookers was sudden and absolute. Abby Andrews clutched Hollis Blair's arm.

Detective Dugan stepped into Abby's of-

289

fice. A muttered murmur, no words intelligible to those in the hall. The office door closed.

Blythe stood with a hand at her throat. Louise shivered. Abby wavered on her feet. Hollis slid a strengthening arm around her shoulders. Cole Hamilton's face drew down in disapproval. Francis Garth gazed at the assistant curator speculatively. Robbie Powell was impassive, but his eyes locked on the office door. Grace's look of defiant amusement fled.

14

Steve Flynn picked up a folder. He'd gathered up odds and ends of information about those with Haklo keys. Nothing had jumped out at him. No bright red arrow pointed to a vandal, thief, and murderer. Somewhere there had to be a fact that mattered. He settled down to reread the dossiers.

Blythe Webster, 39. BA in English, OU. After graduation returned to Craddock and lived at home. Younger sister still in middle school. Served as a hostess for her father. Unmarried. Craddock gossip in 2005 linked her to a handsome young land-man who worked for Webster Exploration. Rumor had it that Harris Webster offered the landman a hundred thousand dollars to relocate — by himself — to Argentina. Harris told Blythe he knew a skunk when he saw one and he was saving her from an unhappy marriage. Blythe spent a year in Italy. She returned to Craddock when her father's health worsened. At his death, she became the sole trustee of Haklo Foundation. She traveled extensively and left the running of Haklo to Marian Grant, COO. However, as trustee, she always attended the annual conference of small charitable foundations. Following the conference this past summer in St. Louis, she took a renewed interest in the foundation. In short order, she instituted a number of changes. From corporate luncheons to the bar at the country club, the locals delighted in totting up the casualties both inside and outside the foundation. Erik Judd was fired. A grant to a local art gallery wasn't renewed. Haklo ended support of a scholarship program for Native Americans at Craddock College.

Steve glanced at a photograph. Shining black hair framed an olive-skinned face. Her eyes, large and expressive, were her most compelling feature. Her lips were perhaps a little too reminiscent of her father's thin mouth. Her composed expression suggested a woman with power. He'd often dealt with Blythe Webster. She expected to be treated with deference. She could be abrupt and was reputedly wary in personal relationships. That he could understand. How did you get over knowing a man preferred cash on hand to your company? He knew odds and ends about her. She collected Roman coins and had a take-no-prisoner mentality in her dealings. She once drove a coin dealer into bankruptcy when he sold a coin she wanted to a rival collector. She played scratch golf. She was generous in her praise for employees and gave substantial bonuses at Christmas.

Grace Webster, honorary trustee, 27. A strawberry blonde who liked to have fun. Usually ebullient, though she was often caustic with her sister. Her contemporaries dubbed her the wild one. Five colleges. Never graduated. Backpacked across Europe. A succession of boyfriends. Harris Webster was amused by her escapades. He told a friend that he never worried about Grace and men, saying she always had the upper hand, enchanting men but never enchanted. When her father died, she was angry that Blythe became the sole trustee. Everyone thought that Harris saw Grace as too young and carefree for the responsibility. Perhaps out of spite, she comes to Haklo daily when she is in Craddock and keeps up a running critique of

293

Blythe's decisions. Their relationship is frosty. Her latest lover was a local artist, Maurice Crown, who delighted in satiric paintings. A recent painting juxtaposed the Haklo Foundation crest with gallons of crude oil gushing from a Gulf platform. Blythe promptly cancelled a grant to the gallery that featured Crown's paintings. Grace was furious, insisting foundation bylaws prohibited cancellation of grants except on the basis of criminal malfeasance. However, the trustee had all the power. Grace is markedly different from her sister, adventurous, enthusiastic, always ready to take a dare, impulsive, careless, optimistic. Perhaps the trait they hold in common is bedrock stubbornness. Each is always determined to do exactly as she chooses.

Steve had clear memories of summers at the lake and Grace's daredevil boat races. She appeared supremely pleased in her photograph, strawberry blond hair cascading to her shoulders, an exuberant smile, seductive off-the-shoulder white blouse. Her chin had the same decided firmness as her sister's.

Hollis Blair, director, 32. BBS in business,

OSU. MA in art history with an emphasis on the American West, SMU. PhD in education, University of Texas. At 28, he joined the staff of a medium-size charitable foundation in Kansas City. Blythe Webster heard Blair speak at a foundation workshop in St. Louis last summer. After the session, she invited him to join her for dinner. She met with him several times during the weeklong workshop. Within three days after her return to Craddock, Erik Judd had been fired and Hollis Blair hired. He arrived August 1. He is affable, charming, outgoing, eager to please.

The photo had accompanied the press release put out by Haklo when Hollis became director. Chestnut hair, deep-set blue eyes, a bony nose, high cheekbones, full lips spread in a friendly smile. Steve had played golf with Hollis several times and found him good-humored and intelligent with perceptive questions about Craddock. The last time they'd met had been at a reception in early December for the new director of the chamber of commerce. Steve recalled a man who looked tired and worried. Hollis had brightened when he was joined by the Haklo assistant curator, Abby Andrews. At the time, Steve had thought it generous of Hollis to bring an assistant curator to a function. Apparently, he was interested in more than Abby Andrews's work advancement.

Louise Spear, executive secretary, 58. Widow. A grown daughter in Corpus Christi, three grandchildren. Louise started as a secretary at Webster Exploration in 1974, moved to the foundation when it was created. Louise is precise, careful, responsible, and follows instructions. She considered Harris Webster a great man. Haklo was second only to her family in her affections. She has taught Sunday School at the Craddock Methodist Church for 34 years. Kind, gentle, thoughtful, always ready to help.

Steve didn't bother to look at Louise's photo. He knew Louise. Casting her as a vandal, much less a murderer, was ludicrous.

Cole Hamilton, advisory vice president, 64. BBA 1969, OU. Widower. No children. Longtime crony of Harris Webster. When Haklo was formed, he left Webster Exploration to serve as senior vice president. Active in local charities, he served as a sounding board for Harris. A former member of the grants committee once said caustically, "Cole always loses at poker to Harris. That seems to be his primary qualification for his title. But he's sure he's indispensable, second only in importance to Harris." His advice always began, "Harris agrees that Haklo should . . ." A man who took great pride in being a part of Haklo. But Harris was dead and Blythe was now the trustee.

Steve turned to the screen, brought up several photos of Cole Hamilton. One had been taken with Harris Webster on the deck of a cruiser. Each man held up a string of fish. Harris's string was longer. The oilman's predatory face was relaxed. Cole beamed, basking in the moment. In a more recent picture at a November open house at Haklo, Cole's round face was morose as he stood by himself at the edge of a group.

Cole was no longer at the side of Harris Webster, the center of Haklo. After Harris's death, Marian Grant ran the foundation. Very likely Marian treated Cole kindly. Marian had been part of that close-knit group, Harris, Cole, herself, and Louise. But this summer Blythe Webster took over and soon there was a new director and

Cole's title changed from vice president to advisory vice president.

Steve reached for the phone. "Louise? Steve Flynn."

"Yes." Her tone was tense.

He spoke easily. "I hear Cole Hamilton is being pushed out of his job."

"Steve, don't print that." A tiny sigh traveled over the connection. "I don't know what's going to happen about Cole. Just between you and me, Blythe has asked him to step down, but he won't turn in a resignation. I don't think Blythe wants to terminate him. In any event, he is the current advisory vice president. Let's leave it at that."

"Right. I'll wait until there's an announcement. Thanks, Louise."

The call ended. Steve looked again at Cole's pictures, such an affable, comfortable man, especially in the early photos. How much did his job, not just the work, but the prestige of being a part of Haklo, matter to a man who had no family and who had spent his life working for Harris Webster? Wasn't vandalism the kind of revenge a somewhat effete, deeply angry, and hurt man might take? Stealing the necklace was part of that pattern, striking out at the woman who was treating him badly. Cole

Hamilton, soft-spoken and genial, scarcely seemed likely to kill. But murder might have been the only way to prevent exposure.

Steve looked at the next name on his list.

Francis Garth, business development research fellow, 47. BA, MA, University of Tulsa. PhD in economics, University of Chicago. Native of Pawhuska. Active as a member of the Osage Tribe. Prominent family, longtime civic supporters. Divorced some years ago, no children. Long-distance runner. Mountain climber. Taught in Chicago, a think tank in Austin, joined Haklo in 1994. A proponent of encouraging Oklahoma exports to foreign countries, especially Costa Rica. Knowledgeable about beef industry and exportable non-food crops. Instrumental in arranging grants for factory expansion. Passionate in his support of the Tallgrass Prairie.

Steve scanned the index in the annual report of the Haklo Foundation issued shortly after the end of the fiscal year in October. He flipped to the business development section. A figure jumped out at him. The business development budget last year had been two hundred and eighty thousand dollars. The current budget had been cut to one hundred and fifty thousand. Just as in Washington, money meant power. Francis Garth was an impressive man at the peak of his career, whose priorities weren't those of a new director.

Steve turned back to the computer. Burly, muscular Francis stared into the camera with a heavy, determined face. Not a man to welcome a downgrade. Would a bull of a man be likely to resort to vandalism? It didn't seem in character. But Francis Garth was highly intelligent, able to think and plan a campaign. A series of unfortunate incidents would damage Hollis Blair's resume. As for murder, Francis had the air of a man who would, without a qualm, do what he had to do.

A very different man from Robbie Powell. And Erik Judd. Steve didn't hesitate to combine their resumes.

Robbie Powell, director of public relations, 44. BA in public relations, University of Missouri. Worked at PR agencies in Kansas City and later Dallas. Joined staff at a medium-size Dallas charitable foundation, became the protégé of the foundation director, Erik Judd. Judd, 55, was a University of Cincinnati graduate in social work. Worked in social service agency in Ohio, earned his PhD in finance, joined the Dallas foundation, within ten years named director. When Judd was hired by Harris Webster as director, he brought Robbie with him. They shared a home in the older part of Craddock, a rambling ranch-style house. When an anti-gay city councilman berated Harris for their lifestyle, the philanthropist's response was forcible and pungent. "I hired Erik to run my foundation and he's doing a damn fine job. Robbie's dandy at PR. When I need a stud for breeding, I buy the best bull out there. For the foundation, I bought the best PR man available. I know the difference between the foundation and my ranch." The Webster clout made it clear that no hostility to its staff would be tolerated. That power and changing mores assured acceptance by Craddock society. Erik was highly respected for his accomplishments as was Robbie. But past success didn't matter to Blythe when she decided she wanted new ideas and younger leadership.

There were plenty of file photos taken over the years, individually and together, of Robbie Powell and Erik Judd: Robbie making a presentation at a Rotary luncheon, Erik shaking hands with a visiting congressman,

Robbie handing out prizes at a livestock show, Erik in earnest conversation with Harris Webster. Robbie's young blond good looks had aged into well-preserved smoothness, hair always perfectly cut, face tanned, expensive clothes well fitted. Erik's dramatic personality might amuse some, but he always got the job done and he was known for kindness and thoughtfulness. He was also a scholar and in his free time wrote highly acclaimed essays on early Oklahoma history. Under his direction, Haklo had maintained a reputation as a conservative, well-run foundation, nothing flashy but year after year of steady growth.

Steve was thoughtful. Robbie and Erik were highly respected for their abilities. On a personal level, they were committed to each other. Until this past summer, they had very likely never imagined a cataclysmic change in their lives. Steve had seen too many men who had lost jobs in the last few years to dismiss the effect of that loss. He'd heard that Erik had withdrawn from many activities, presumably to concentrate on writing a history of Haklo. Was he depressed or was he genuinely enjoying time to be a scholar? How angry was Robbie at the injury to Erik? Erik was polished, civilized, erudite, and now diminished. Robbie was quick to react to slights and never missed an opportunity for a dig at the new director. Did the acts of vandalism cause more injury to Hollis or to Blythe?

Steve picked up the next dossier.

Peter Owens, director of publications, 38. BA, MA in media relations, University of Maryland. Wife, Denise. Owens and wife met in college, married shortly after graduation. He worked at publications in various cities, moving to accompany his wife, Denise, from one teaching post to another. She was named an assistant professor of English at Craddock College six years ago. He worked for a local horse publication and met Marian Grant when he wrote a series of articles about breeding seminars hosted by Haklo. He became director of Haklo publications three years ago. Owens and his wife have twin nine-year-old daughters who are stellar swimmers.

Steve had met both Owens and his wife. Peter was casual, understated. Denise was intense, vocal, and self-assured. There were two photos, the official photo online at the Haklo website and a picture at the college last spring with his wife and a visiting poet. The official photo was bland and unreveal-

303 Peabody Public Library
Columbia City, IN

ing. At the university event, he stood with his hands in his trouser pockets, smiling pleasantly. He was perhaps six-two, shaggy dark hair, horn-rimmed glasses, relaxed demeanor. He stood a pace behind his petite, dark-haired wife, who was engaged in intense conversation with a heavyset, white-haired woman.

Abby Andrews was the last entry, but definitely not least, thanks to a file in her computer and a missing skateboard. However, this dossier contained very little information.

Abby Andrews, assistant curator, 23. BA in anthropology, University of Kansas. 3.7 grade point average. Active in her sorority and several campus activities, including yearbook staff and student council. Met Hollis Blair when he spoke to the anthropology club. Blair hired Abby to be his assistant in Kansas City one month later. He arrived in Craddock August 1. Abby came to Haklo August 15.

In Abby's Haklo staff photo, she stared gravely into the camera, her lovely features composed. She wore a string of pearls with a pale blue cashmere sweater. The *Clarion* always carried photos of new Haklo staff.

Abby appeared very young with a smooth, unlined face.

Steve tapped impatient fingers on his desk. There was nothing odd or peculiar in her background. A nice recent college grad. Yet, an obscene letter was found in her computer and a skateboard went missing from the front porch of her cabin.

Steve's face crinkled. Why was she living in a Haklo cabin?

He speed-dialed Louise. "Just rounding up a few points. Tell me about the Haklo cabins. Their history and function."

Louise's tone was bland. "Harris thought it would be appropriate for visiting scholars and scientists to be able to stay on the foundation grounds. Eventually, it was decided the cabins would be ideal for summer interns." Full stop.

"And?" Steve prodded.

"The cabins have always been useful for guests."

"Abby Andrews isn't a guest."

"I think Hollis offered her a cabin since she is paying off student loans."

"Right. Thanks, Louise." He wasn't sure that the knowledge mattered, but it was one more out-of-the-ordinary fact about Abby Andrews. Except it wasn't out of the ordinary once her relationship with Hollis Blair was evident.

He felt great uncertainty about the importance of Abby Andrews. Surely the idea that she engineered the vandalism, which hurt Hollis, didn't make sense. But on another level, it made all kinds of sense in Katie Dugan's initial premise that the point of the vandalism was to make the theft of the necklace possible. Student debt was a crippling factor for a lot of college graduates, and a quarter-million-dollar necklace could pay off loans and then some.

As for the missing skateboard, it became important because of his whispered message. He'd based that message on Nela's insistence that there had been a skateboard on Marian's steps. How and when had Nela learned — or guessed — that Marian Grant stepped down on a skateboard and fell to her death? Nela said she could not tell him how she knew. He felt a ripple of uneasiness.

"Hey, buddy." He spoke aloud. "Don't get spooked." But his Irish grandmother would have looked at him and said softly, " 'There are more things in heaven and earth, Horatio, Than are dreamt of in your philosophy.' "

Maybe so, but he wanted to know the basis for Nela's claim. He didn't think Nela was protecting Chloe. Chloe might have known that Abby's skateboard was missing. However, it seemed unlikely that Chloe would link a missing skateboard to Marian's fall. Why would she? Was it possible that Chloe was suspicious about Marian's fall and for some reason saw Abby as a threat to Marian? It seemed very unlikely. But, as he had also learned long ago, if you want to know, ask.

He picked up his phone.

The office door opened. Her face impassive, Detective Dugan looked at Blythe. "Miss Webster, we can use your assistance."

The trustee's eyes widened. She gave a tiny sigh. Her demeanor was that of a woman whose fears have been confirmed. She pressed her lips together and moved purposefully into the office.

As Blythe stepped inside Abby's office, Dugan firmly closed the door after them.

Grace turned toward Abby. "What have you got in there?"

"I don't have anything —"

The door opened. Dugan walked out. "Miss Andrews, come this way."

Tears brimmed in Abby's violet eyes. She clung to Hollis's arm. "Why? I haven't done anything wrong."

"I have a few questions."

Hollis Blair stepped forward. He was combative. "Abby doesn't have to answer your questions."

Dugan nodded. Her voice was mild. "In the search of Miss Andrews's office, a diamond-and-gold necklace was discovered in a filing cabinet. Miss Webster has identified the necklace as the one taken from her desk. If Miss Andrews prefers, we can take her into custody for questioning in regard to grand theft." She turned to Blythe. "Now my officers need to search the cabin where Miss Andrews resides. Do we have your permission to do so?"

"Yes." Blythe's voice was thin. She didn't look toward Abby. She turned to Louise. "Get a key. Take them there." Her words were clipped, brooked no disagreement. She didn't wait for an answer, but swung away, headed for her office.

Louise Spear stared after Blythe. Louise's face was pale and apprehensive. She was obviously upset. But she had her orders and she had taken orders for many years.

Dugan nodded at Sergeant Fisher and the plump woman officer. "You know what to look for. Call me if anything is found."

The police officers followed Louise into her office.

Abby took a step toward Dugan. "I didn't steal that awful necklace. Someone put it in the cabinet." She looked at Hollis in appeal. "I didn't take it."

Hollis Blair was grim. "Of course you didn't take it. I'll get a lawyer for you."

"I shouldn't need a lawyer." Abby's thin face, twisted in despair, was no longer pretty, but desperate and frightened. "It's all a lie."

Dugan was brisk. "We will take your statement at the station. If you wish to have counsel present, that is your prerogative. We'll go out the front entrance. This way." She gestured toward the main hallway.

Abby shot a panicked look at Hollis.

He gave her a reassuring nod.

Dugan and Abby walked together toward the main hall, Hollis a step behind. Dugan was purposeful, striding fast. Abby's shoulders hunched as she hurried to keep pace.

Grace looked puzzled. Her expression was distant, as if her thoughts were far away and not pleasant. She moved swiftly toward the main hall. Peter Owens glanced toward Louise's office. "I guess the show's over for now." He moved toward the rear stairs.

Cole Hamilton spoke in a soft aside to Robbie. "All these new people were a mistake. I told Marian it didn't look right for a man to bring a pretty girl in as soon as he gets a new job. It wasn't like there wasn't a pretty young thing in the office. Why, Anne Nesbitt was pretty enough to please anyone. He noticed her. What man wouldn't? But a nice girl. Now I wonder if Abby set her car on fire so there wouldn't be another young girl around."

He intended his comment for Robbie, but Nela was near enough to overhear.

Robbie's eyes gleamed in his old-young, pleased face. "A lust for diamonds. They say some women can't resist them. But vandalism to serve as a smoke screen was clever. I wouldn't have thought Abby was that clever."

Francis Garth's heavy voice was stolid. "She's nice. Pleasant. Pretty if you like them young and callow. But not clever. She doesn't have the nerve to be a vandal — or a murderer."

Francis's words thrummed in Nela's mind as she returned to Chloe's office, sank into the chair behind the desk. She agreed with Francis. And that put the question squarely to her. What was she going to do now?

From down the hall, Grace's strident voice carried clearly. "What's the deal? You gave the cops carte blanche to search. First Abby's office, now the cabin. How'd you know

—" A faraway door slam cut off Grace's voice in midsentence. Nela wondered how forthcoming Blythe would be with her sister.

Nela knew the answer to Grace's question. Someone had placed a letter on Blythe's desk. Obviously, the message suggested a search of Abby's office for the missing necklace.

But Nela knew more than Blythe or any of the others. Nela had put the necklace on Blythe's desk Monday night. Some time after Nela's foray into the building Monday night, the necklace was removed. Today an anonymous letter on Blythe's desk indicated the necklace could be found in Abby's office.

The sound of voices and footsteps faded in the hallway. Finally, there was silence. Abby Andrews was in a police cruiser, on her way to the police station.

Nela retrieved her purse. She slipped the strap over one shoulder. She walked down the hall to the staff exit, car keys in one hand, cell phone in the other.

15

The connection was surprisingly clear. ". . . don't know if you remember me, Chloe. This is Steve Flynn for the *Clarion.*"

Chloe's husky voice burbled with delight. "How sweet! I love the *Clarion.* You know that feature you do every Sunday, the Craddock Connection? That's the nicest thing, stories about everyday people like firemen and teachers and bricklayers. I loved the one about the lady at the nursing home who was turning a hundred and nobody knew she'd been a nurse on Corregidor during WWII. It just makes you think," Chloe Farley said solemnly. A pause and she rushed ahead, "I'm from LA and you can live in an apartment house and never know anybody. Nela always told me everybody has a story. Instead, most newspapers just write about politics. Of course, Craddock has a few drawbacks. I get tired of roosters crowing. I never heard a rooster 'til I came to Craddock but there's one in the field next to Leland's trailer. I'll bet you want to do a story about Leland and me and our trip. Oh, you can't believe the water here in Tahiti. It's like looking through blue glass and the shells —"

Steve tried to divert the flood. "When you get back, we'll do a big story. Right now I want to ask about Marian Grant's fall down her apartment steps."

"Marian's fall?" There was no hint of uneasiness or wariness in Chloe's froggy tone. "That came as such a surprise. Why, she was so graceful —"

Nela turned the heater up full blast, but the VW was icy cold. Yet there was a deeper chill in her thoughts as she called the *Clarion,* gave Steve's extension number. Once she spoke, there was no turning back. She wasn't surprised when the message came on: *I am either away from my desk or engaged in another call . . .*

She waited until the ping. "Steve, it's Nela." She was brisk. "Blythe got an anonymous letter this morning, saying the necklace was hidden in Abby's office. Blythe called the police and they found the necklace in a filing cabinet. Dugan's taken Abby to the police station. I'm on my way there now. I'll tell Dugan how I found the necklace in Marian's purse and that I brought the necklace to Haklo Monday night and left it on Blythe's desk. I won't mention you." She clicked off the phone, put the VW in gear.

Steve ignored the call-waiting beep.

". . . hard to imagine Marian falling. She had an air, you know. Why, it would be easier to imagine Tallulah Bankhead in a pinafore." A throaty gurgle. "My gram thought Tallulah Bankhead was hilarious. Gram loved to quote her and Bette Davis. People would be surprised if they knew how women told it how they saw it even then." It was as if she spoke of a time far distant. "Of course, Marian never talked like that. Marian was serious." Chloe drawled the word. "But that's all right." Her husky voice was generous. "Marian was *somebody.* You knew that the minute you met her. I even had that feeling staying in her apartment. And Jugs is a sweetheart, which shows she had a soft side. If you need a quote, I'd call Louise Spear or Cole Hamilton. They'd known her forever. Anyway, got to go, the catamaran's ready . . ."

Steve replaced the phone. If there was any guile involved in Chloe Farley's discursiveness, he'd find a pinafore to wear. So how and where did Nela come up with a skateboard on Marian's steps? He didn't want to ask her again. Her refusal to explain had been definite. Why?

He tussled with the question as he punched listen to retrieve the message from the call he'd missed.

"You can sit there." The policeman — or maybe he was a detective because he didn't wear a uniform — slouched to a seat on the other side of a utilitarian metal desk. There were nine or ten similar desks across the room, some with occupants, most empty.

Nela remained standing. "I'm sorry." She was polite but firm. "I have to talk to Detective Dugan."

"She's busy. I'll take down the information. I'm Detective Morrison." He gave her a swift, admiring glance, then his narrow face smoothed into polite expectation. "Whatever it is, I can handle it."

A door rattled open behind her. Quick steps thudded on the wooden floor.

Morrison looked past her. "Yo, Steve. Haven't seen you move this fast since they handed out free gumdrops at the county extension office."

"Mokie." But Steve's voice was abstracted

and he was looking at Nela.

She half turned to see the now familiar freckled face and bright blue eyes.

He stopped beside her. "I came as soon as I got your message."

She was glad and sad. Glad to know he would be with her. Sad to know she was going to cause him trouble. "You don't have to stay. You don't have anything to do with any of it." The words were quick.

He gave her a swift, lopsided grin. "I signed on Monday night. I did what I did — and I'm damn glad I did. But you're right. Katie has to know."

Mokie Morrison was looking from one to the other, his brown eyes curious and intent. "Sounds like an episode in a soap. Not that I watch soaps." The disclaimer was hasty. "My ex loved *As the World Turns,* still in mourning for it."

"I can't get in to see her." Nela's voice was anxious.

Steve turned to Mokie. "Tell Katie we've got stuff she needs to know now."

The office was small. Thin winter sunlight slanted through open blinds. Katie Dugan's sturdy frame was replicated by the shadow that fell across the legal pad and folders open on her desk. The office was impersonal, no mementos on the desktop, a map of Craddock on one wall, a map of Oklahoma and a bulletin board with wanted circulars, notes, and department directives on the other. Two metal filing cases. The detective's face was impassive as she listened and took notes.

There was tight silence when they finished.

Nela was intensely aware of Steve's nearness. They sat side by side, separated by only a few inches, on worn wooden chairs that faced Dugan's desk.

Dugan's cool gaze settled on Steve. "Why should I believe you" — a flicker toward Nela — "or her?"

Steve was affable. "How does it help either one of us to lie?" He retrieved his cell phone, touched, pushed it across Dugan's desk. "Note the date and time. Ditto the next pic. Maybe enhanced details will prove one was taken at the Haklo staff entrance, the other in Blythe Webster's office. Nela was your main suspect until the necklace was found in Abby's office. If Nela had kept quiet, she and her sister would be off your radar. Right?"

There was a touch of frost in Dugan's voice. "I'm not smart enough to see the possibility Abby Andrews was picked to be a fall guy?"

Nela felt a sickening swoop of disappointment even though she'd expected Dugan to be hostile.

Steve's face looked suddenly tough. "You know me better than that. I know you look at everything. Always. We're trying to help, Katie. Give us a chance."

"Maybe it would have been a help if you people had told me the truth from the start." Dugan's broad face was equally tough. "I got news for you, and not the kind to put in the *Clarion.* Everybody's on my radar. Including your girlfriend." Her cold gaze moved to Nela. "Maybe you found the necklace in the purse. Or maybe your sister asked you to take care of it, but you got cold feet. Maybe —"

Her phone rang. She glanced at caller ID, picked up the receiver. "Dugan . . . So anybody who took a close look would find it?" She raised a dark eyebrow, looked sardonic. "Yeah. Check for prints. Want to bet nothing doing except for the owner's? Test for a match on the stair rail. Right. Thanks." She replaced the receiver. She turned to Nela, went back to her attack. "Or maybe you decided the necklace was too damn hot to keep. I learned a long time ago that a pretty face doesn't mean squat.

You could be lying your head off. Or you could be telling the truth down the line. If you are, then something strange is going on out at Haklo and that necklace is at the heart of it. If you left the necklace on Blythe Webster's desk, the water gets muddy. We found the necklace in a filing cabinet in Abby Andrews's office. The tip came in an anonymous note left on Blythe Webster's desk. Traffic has been pretty busy in and out of her office, apparently. The upshot? Anybody could be the perp." She looked steadily at Nela. "Including you."

But Nela was thinking. Paint flecks . . . "They found the skateboard, didn't they? You told Louise to take the officers to Abby's cabin and they found the skateboard there."

Dugan stiffened, like a hunter on point. "Lady, you seem to know everything. You know too much."

"You said to check for a match on the stair rail. What else could it be but the skateboard?" Nela tried to speak naturally, as if she didn't see Jugs's glowing eyes. "I read in the *Clarion* that there was a call claiming there was a skateboard on Marian Grant's stairs. Abby claimed someone took her skateboard. Now it's back. Doesn't it figure after the necklace was planted in Abby's of-

319

fice that the skateboard would be back?"

"Next thing I know" — Dugan's voice was sardonic — "you'll be filling out an application to be a cop. Thanks, but I can figure out what may or may not have happened. If you're telling the truth, I appreciate the fact that you came forward. If you're lying to me, I won't be fooled. Now" — and she looked from Nela to Steve and back again — "nothing said in this room is to be repeated, revealed, discussed — or printed. Go out the back way. I don't want anybody seeing you two leaving here. If either one of you gets loose lips, you'll be my guest at the county jail." She stared hard at Nela. "Ask Steve about the county jail. It makes the city jail seem like a resort."

They stood in an alleyway behind city hall, a few feet from a row of trash cans.

Nela hugged Chloe's coat tight, warding off not only the cold but the chill of fear. "Somebody put that necklace in Abby's office and the skateboard at her cabin. It has to be the killer. How else could the skateboard show up again? It's diabolical. Abby said the skateboard was missing and now they've found it in her cabin. You heard what Dugan said. It was some place where it wasn't hard to find."

Steve looked thoughtful. "Maybe the murderer got a little too cute. Katie will give a fish eye at how nice and easy the evidence is falling in her lap. But she won't cross Abby off her list. There's been a lot at this point, the obscene letter file in her computer, the necklace, the skateboard." He hunched his shoulders against a cold gust.

The wind was frosty on Nela's face, tugged at Chloe's big coat. "Your ears are red from the cold. You need a coat."

He grinned. "Last I heard they didn't have an ear coat in my size."

Nela laughed and felt a surge of gratitude. Steve had made her laugh when she was half scared, half mad. But the laugh died away. She reached out, gripped his arm. "I'm sorry about everything, Steve. Katie Dugan was your friend. Now she doesn't trust you."

"Katie's got a big bark. She'll figure things out. But we have to play it her way. You'd better get back to Haklo. I'll drop by the station later in the day, see what the official line is. I'll be over to see you tonight." It was a statement. He paused. "Okay?" The tone was light, but his eyes were serious.

"If you were smart" — her voice caught in her throat — "you'd stay away from me."

"Not," he said quietly, "in this lifetime."

He reached out, gently framed her shoulders with big strong hands, turned her around. "Walk straight and you come out on Alcott. You can take it to Main."

She walked away without looking back, still feeling the strength of his grip on her shoulders, and knew he stood, red hair stirred by the wind, ears red with cold, hands jammed in his pockets, and watched until she reached the end of the alley.

Nela put the McDonald's sack with a cheeseburger and fries on Chloe's desk. She glanced at the clock. It was a few minutes after one. She stepped to the connecting door to Louise's office, ready to apologize for her lateness.

Louise sat at her desk, but she wasn't working. She stared out the window, her pale face lined and unhappy, unaware of Nela's presence. Indeed, she seemed to be very far away, sunk in a somber reverie. One hand fingered the collar of her pink blouse. The pink added a note of cheer to her gray jacket and skirt.

Nela said quietly, "Excuse me, Louise. I'm sorry I'm late getting back from lunch." She could eat while she worked if Louise had some tasks for her.

"It doesn't matter. I won't need you now.

I'm" — she appeared to make an effort to be matter-of-fact — "going to look over some materials this afternoon. I'll need to concentrate. Please shut the door."

Nela was dismissed. She nodded and closed the door. She settled at Chloe's desk, ate without tasting the food.

Her phone buzzed. "Nela Farley."

Rosalind McNeill's words tumbled. "Everything's off schedule." Her voice dropped to a conspiratorial whisper. "After somebody dropped that anonymous letter on the T's desk, she quizzed me like she was a private eye. But she didn't waste any time calling the cops. First thing I know, they're trooping in the front door and the T's waiting for them like she's a commissar. When they found the necklace in Abby's office, I thought I was in a Brad Pitt movie. You know how the cops whisked Abby off in a cruiser? I thought they'd lock her up and throw away the key. Not so. Abby and Hollis just got back. They came in the front door, which is crazy, too, but everything's jigsaw today. Maybe if the cops take you away, the cops bring you back. I'll bet the director was right behind them in his snazzy Cadillac sports car. The T bought the Caddy for him, said it was more appropriate than the old Ford he used to drive. Anyway, they came in the front, Hollis looking like Sir Galahad and Abby clinging to his arm, pretty much in a Victorian swoon. She hung back, kept saying she couldn't bear to be here, and he was all manly and stiff upper lip that she was innocent and the innocent don't have anything to fear. So she sucked it up and they went down the hall and she turned to go to her office —"

Nela heard steps in the hall and looked up in time to see Abby Andrews walk past. Abby stared straight ahead. Porcelain-perfect face pale, shoulders tight, she looked young, vulnerable, and scared.

"— and Hollis marched into the T's office and closed the door. A closed door at Haklo means something pretty stiff. Anyway, I guess we have to keep on keepin' on. Neither hail nor sleet nor cops nor damsel in distress can stay the appointed rounds, so if you've got a minute you might drop around and get the mail. I've got everything sorted."

Nela hadn't given the morning mail delivery a thought after Blythe summoned her. "I'm sorry. I'll be right there."

The long blue plastic tray, almost three-fourths full of envelopes, rested on top of the horseshoe-shaped reception counter. Rosalind looked up with a smile and bounced to her feet, her brown eyes excited. The soft splash of water in the tiled fountain between the reception desk and the French windows to the courtyard was cheerful, a restful counterpoint to Rosalind's vitality. Before Nela could pick up the tray, Rosalind leaned on the counter, looking eager. "Did Louise fill you in on the cabin?"

"The cabin?" Everyone standing in the hallway outside Abby's office this morning heard Dugan ask for permission to search Abby's cabin, but Nela maintained a look of polite inquiry. "She didn't say anything about it."

"Well" — Rosalind looked around to be sure no one was near — "when the officers came through here, one of them — the tall, skinny one — was carrying something in a big billowy plastic sleeve and I'll bet I know what it was." She looked triumphant. She didn't wait for Nela's response. "Abby's skateboard was supposed to be missing. Well, they found it — I guess in her cabin — and I'd like to know the story behind that."

"Someone could have taken the skateboard and put it back."

Rosalind squeezed her face in thought. "Someone else here at Haklo?"

"Who wrote the anonymous letter? You

can bet it wasn't Abby."

Rosalind's eyes were huge. She looked uneasy. "I guess somebody doesn't like Abby very much."

As Nela walked down the hall, the plastic tray balanced on one hip, she wondered, was there bitter enmity toward Abby? There had certainly been an effort to focus blame on her, the file in her computer, the use of her brother's skateboard to commit murder, the discovery of the necklace in her office, the reappearance of the missing skateboard. Was Abby a target simply because she made a good scapegoat? Or was she a vandal, thief, and murderer? Did she really care for Hollis Blair or was she willing to see his career jeopardized so that she could steal a quarter-million-dollar necklace? However, there was the clear fact that Abby's latest problems had been caused by an anonymous letter. Did Abby have a gambler's instinct and the guts to do a double bluff, write a note that accused her, then use the fact of the note to assert innocence? Had she decided the necklace was too dangerous to keep and well worth sacrificing to escape an accusation of murder?

Nela pictured the strained face of the girl walking toward her office. Abby had been oblivious to Nela sitting at Chloe's desk so Abby's expression wasn't formed with the expectation of presenting an air of innocence. But she had good reason to be fearful, whether innocent or guilty.

Nela stopped at Blythe's closed door. She knocked, then turned the knob. She felt an instant of déjà vu. Monday morning she'd stepped inside with the mail, interrupting a tense conversation between the trustee and the director. This afternoon, she walked in on the two of them again.

There was a decided difference today. Blythe was nodding, her expression reassuring. Hollis had the air of a man unexpectedly encountering good fortune. His bony, appealing face was grateful. ". . . appreciate your understanding. Like I told Abby, we'll get to the bottom of everything."

"Excuse me, may I leave the mail?" Nela hesitated in the doorway.

Blythe nodded and waved at the in-box. A ruby ring flashed as red as her crimson suit.

Hollis unfolded from the chair. Despite his lanky height, he looked very young as he gazed down at Blythe. "I'll tell Abby. I told her to rest for a while, then go up to the lab. She'll feel better if she keeps busy, and there are a bunch of donations to catalog.

Knowing you're behind her will be a huge relief."

"Hollis, I think you may be right that Abby is innocent." Blythe was thoughtful. "Things certainly look black against her but it's silly to think she'd hide the necklace, then put a note on my desk saying the necklace was hidden in her office. And if she did hide the necklace, who could possibly have known about it?"

Just for an instant, his jaw was rigid. "The whole idea that she'd do anything dishonest is outrageous. As for the police, I think even that hard-faced woman detective is having second thoughts. We were waiting for her. Then, when she came in, she hadn't really started when someone buzzed her and she left. When she came back, she didn't say a word about Abby being a person of interest or give a warning. If she had, I would have said nothing doing 'til we got a lawyer. I still think maybe I should see about a lawyer. Instead, she said she just had a few factual questions. I thought" — he was earnest — "that it was all right for Abby to answer those. Dugan asked a few questions, then said we could go." He was like a man who receives an unexpected bonus check in the mail and wonders if it's for real. "I know you expected the worst." His lopsided smile was rueful. "I wish you could have seen your face when I walked in and said we were back. You looked like you'd seen a ghost. So, now we have to hope the cops turn up the truth." He turned away from the desk and moved past Nela with a brief nod.

Blythe's smile faded as he stepped into the hall. She looked tired and grim.

Nela placed a half-dozen letters and several mailers in the upper box, but she didn't turn away. "Miss Webster, may I speak to you?"

Blythe looked at Nela in surprise. Until this moment, Nela knew her presence had scarcely registered with the trustee. Nela might have been a robot carrying out assigned duties. "Yes?" Her response was clipped. Clearly she was impatient, in no mood to waste time with Nela.

Nela knew she was taking a gamble, but as Gram always pointed out, "Sure, the answer can be no, but it will never be yes if you don't ask." Nela was glad she'd chosen her best blouse and the skirt that swirled as she walked. If nothing else, she felt more confident and professional. She placed the tray on the corner of Blythe's desk, noted the slight thinning of the trustee's lips. She also shed, just a little, the deference of a minimum wage employee. "Miss Webster, I was between assignments at home and I was glad to be able to come to Craddock and take Chloe's place while she's gone. I'm an investigative reporter —"

There was a flare of alarm in Blythe's eyes. Certainly Nela now had her full attention.

"— which makes me skilled at asking questions and discovering facts. I can help you protect the foundation."

Blythe frowned, her thin dark brows drawn down. Her brown eyes had a hard stare. "How?" The demand was sharp. "There have been too many stories already. I'm sick of stories about Haklo." There was a distinct chill in her tone.

Nela realized Blythe thought Nela was threatening to write an exposé revealing that only a member of the Haklo staff could have committed some, if not all, the acts of vandalism, including the destruction in Marian Grant's office.

"I'm not talking about writing a story. Here's what we" — she placed a slight emphasis on the noun — "can do."

As Blythe listened, her rigid body relaxed and she no longer looked wary.

Steve Flynn's freckled face was thoughtful. As far as Katie Dugan was concerned, he and Nela hadn't been in her office, certainly had not heard her conversation with the officers searching Abby's cabin. But she'd tipped her hand when she'd dryly commented that there likely wouldn't be any prints but to check with the paint flecks on the stair rail. Nela had instantly made the connection. Katie had neither confirmed nor denied Nela's guess that the missing skateboard had been found. To get the quotes he wanted from Katie for a story, he had to have some outside ammunition.

Steve punched his speakerphone.

"Hey, Steve. How's everything?" Robbie Powell's voice was smooth and bland.

"Doing a roundup on the latest at Haklo." Steve was equally smooth. "What's the statement about this morning?"

Robbie was too much of a pro to stammer and stutter. Instead, he was silent for an appreciable moment. Finally, he cleared his throat. "Haklo Trustee Blythe Webster this morning received an anonymous letter suggesting that her missing necklace was hidden in a staff office. Police were summoned. The necklace was found and is currently being held by police as evidence."

"Whose office?"

"That information has not been released."

"And the further search?" Robbie might assume Steve's information came from the police. But if the point ever arose, Steve certainly hadn't made that claim.

Robbie didn't question the fact that Steve knew about the second search. "I have not spoken with a police officer. Haklo Foundation remains confident that the police investigation will be successful." A pause. "If you have further questions, please contact Detective Dugan." The connection ended.

The delivery of mail afforded Nela quick glimpses of staff members, to whom, after a perfunctory nod, she became invisible, cloaked in the comfortable anonymity of a cog in the well-oiled Haklo machine.

Louise Spear, sunk in apathy, held a folder at which she gazed with empty eyes. The brightness of the Baranovs' print seemed almost shocking in contrast to the paleness of her face.

Abby Andrews hunched at a desk covered with a welter of papers in her small, spare, utilitarian office. Her young face was pale, her eyes red-rimmed.

In the east hallway, Hollis Blair's office was not as large as either Blythe Webster's or Marian Grant's, but still imposing, with red velvet drapes, oak-paneled walls, a broad oak desk, a sofa and several easy chairs grouped on either side of a shiny aluminum coffee table. Filled bookcases lined one wall. Seated at his desk, he spoke into the speakerphone, his face grim. "I don't want a criminal lawyer. That looks bad, like she might be guilty. You've represented the foundation for years —"

A woman's brisk voice interrupted. "As you've explained the circumstances, it wouldn't be appropriate for me to represent her. Of the names I suggested, Perry Womack is one of the best. And he's welcome" — the tone was wry — "in polite society. Now if you'll excuse me, I have another call waiting."

The remaining staff offices were on the second floor. Grace Webster occupied the corner front office to the west, directly above her sister's office. The difference in decor was interesting. Blond Danish modern furniture, jagged slaps of oil on unframed canvases, swirls of orange, black, crimson. A sculpture of partially crushed Coke cans, coils of rusted barbed wire, and withered sunflower stalks stood stark and — to Nela — ugly in the center of the room. A casually dressed Grace lounged on an oversize puffy pink sofa, eyes half closed as she held her cell to one ear. ". . . missed you too. Two weeks is too long. Way too long . . ."

The large second-floor east office, the same size as Marian Grant's on the first floor, had a shabby, lived-in, fusty, musty air with stacks of books, framed photographs tucked on curio stands. The desk held more pictures, but no computer monitor. There was an aura of yesterday, pictures of a young, vigorous Webster Harris and an eager Cole Hamilton with a bush of curly brown hair. There was no evidence of work in progress. He looked up from a worn book with a frayed cover, then his eyes dropped back to the page.

Robbie Powell's office was light and airy with calico plaid drapes that matched the sofa, splashes of color in photographs of outdoor scenes, and a sleek modern desk with three computers. He reclined in a blue leather swivel chair. His smooth voice was as schmoozy as a maître d' escorting high rollers to their usual table. ". . . hope you and Lorraine will mark the donor dinner on your calendars if you're not in Nice or Sydney. We'll definitely have lamb fries in honor of the Lazy Q. You know —"

The interruption over the speakerphone was brusque. "What's this I hear about somebody pushing Marian down some damned stairs?"

Robbie's face tightened, but his tone remained soft as butter. "Now, Buck, you know gossip runs wild sometimes. That's absolutely false. Now the dinner —"

"The dinner be damned. There's no getting around the fact that a bunch of strange things have been happening out at Haklo, and I don't give money if it's going to be wasted cleaning up after vandals. Or, for God's sake, killers."

Francis Garth barely glanced up from the keyboard as Nela deposited the incoming mail. His massive hands dwarfed the keys. His heavy face was somber beneath the thatch of thick brown hair. He looked like a man thinking hard and darkly. His office was bare bones, uncarpeted floor, obviously worn wooden desk, wooden filing cabinets. The only decoration was a representation of the Seal of the Osage Nation depicting a blue arrowhead against a brilliant circle of yellow. A peace pipe crossed an eagle feather in the center of the arrowhead.

Pride of place in Peter Owens's office was a low broad wooden coffee table covered with brochures, flyers, and pamphlets. Deeply absorbed with a sketch pad and a stack of photographs, he scarcely noticed the arrival of the mail. Working, he had an air of contentment, a man enjoying thinking and planning.

As Nela hurried down the stairs to the rotunda, carrying the empty tray, she hoped that she would be smart and lucky. At some time between the disappearance of the necklace and Marian Grant's fall, Marian had gained knowledge of the whereabouts of the necklace and the identity of the thief. When had she found the necklace? Surely there had been some act, some word by Marian that revealed how or when she came into possession of the stolen necklace.

Thanks to Blythe Webster, Nela could now ask questions as she wished. Nela accepted the fact that no matter how carefully she phrased her questions, she might alert a murderer. One of the persons with a key to Haklo hid ruthlessness and danger beneath a facade of civility. Nela understood the risk, but she had a chance to make a difference and she was going to take it.

She hurried across the rotunda to the reception desk. There was no better place to start than with Rosalind McNeill, who saw staff members come and go as they moved about the foundation.

At the slap of the tray on the counter, Rosalind whirled around on her desk chair. Her eyes lighted and she popped to her feet. "I saw you go in the T's office and Hollis come out. He looked like a man who just got sprung from death row. Is Abby in the clear? I figure since she and Hollis came back, the cops must have learned something to clear her. What's going on?"

"The investigation is continuing, but the detective is looking at everyone at Haklo, not just Abby." Nela thought it might cheer Abby if that word trickled back to her. "I talked to Blythe Webster and offered to help since I have a background in investigative reporting. She agreed that it would be a good thing for me to gather information from staff members." Speaking with Rosalind was the next best thing to putting up a public placard. How better to establish herself as the new eyes and ears of Haklo?

Rosalind's eyes widened. "That's cool. Gee, I wish I could perch on your shoulder." Her gaze was admiring.

"Miss Webster authorized me to speak to everyone on her behalf. Rosalind, I want you to think back to Marian Grant's last week here. Start with Thursday . . ." The day the theft of the necklace was discovered.

16

Mokie Morrison brushed back his one strand of black hair, slanted his eyes toward Dugan's closed door. "I've seen feral hogs in a better mood."

Steve grinned. "When was the last time you were in the woods?"

"Boy Scouts. I went on a campout. Once and done. We met up with two copperheads, a cave with bats, and a feral hog. I haven't been outside the city limits since. But today" — and he was almost not kidding — "I'd pick the snakes, bats, and hog over Katie."

"Yeah. Well, I got a deadline." He gave Mokie a mock salute. His smile slid away as he knocked lightly on Katie's door, turned the knob.

She looked up from the papers spread on the desktop. "Yeah?" Her broad face was as inviting as a slab of granite.

"Clarion," he said gently, making his visit

official. He stepped inside, closed the door, pulled folded paper from his pocket, turned it lengthwise. He already had a soft-leaded pencil in his other hand. Without an invitation, he dropped into the wooden chair. "I talked to Robbie Powell out at Haklo. He said Blythe Webster received an anonymous letter saying the stolen necklace was hidden in a staff member's office. Robbie said to check with you about the necklace and the second search."

Katie briefly compressed her lips, obviously not pleased by Steve's questions. "The necklace was found." Full stop.

"Where?"

The reply was grudging. "In a filing cabinet. Miss Webster identified the necklace, which is now in police custody."

Steve's glance was chiding. "Where was the filing cabinet located?"

"The discovery was prompted by an anonymous letter. At present, there is no proof that the occupant of the office knew of the presence of the stolen property. Therefore, the identity of the office occupant is not necessarily relevant."

"What prompted a search elsewhere on the grounds?"

"Information received in the anonymous letter."

"Where did the search take place?"

"No comment."

"Was anything found that appears to be linked to Marian Grant's fall?"

Her eyes narrowed. She knew he knew about the skateboard. "No comment."

"Is there a person of interest?"

Katie shook her head. "Not at this time."

Steve felt like high-fiving Katie. She hadn't succumbed to the lure of evidence against Abby that had been so nicely and neatly wrapped up and delivered to her. "How did the anonymous letter arrive?"

"That has not been determined."

"Did the letter come through the mail?"

"No."

"Did the contents or envelope contain fingerprints?"

"The only fingerprints belonged to Miss Webster, who opened the envelope and read the letter. She immediately notified police."

"Was the letter handwritten?"

"No."

"Was the message printed?" Should there be another search of files in Haklo computers?

"No."

Steve figured that out in a flash. Words, maybe even pictures, pasted on a blank sheet. That took time. Last night or this morning, someone from Haklo had worn gloves, patiently clipped needed words from newspapers or magazines.

"Did you send somebody through the wastebaskets out at Haklo?"

"You're quick." That's all she said.

"Katie" — Steve's voice was quiet — "you want to figure out what happened out there and whether somebody killed Marian Grant. I do, too. I want to clear up the mess. I don't want Nela Farley hurt."

Katie's eyes narrowed. "But you just met the woman. What's with the white knight to the rescue?"

Steve looked at Katie. They'd known each other for a long time. They had a careful relationship because he was a reporter and she was a cop. But they were — deep down, where it counted — friends. "You know how it works, Katie. You look at someone. Your eyes meet and there's more there than you can ever explain or describe. You and Mark. Me and Nela. Maybe everything will be good for us. Maybe not. But for now, it's me and Nela. I think she's honest. I want to help her. The best way to help is to figure out what the hell happened at Haklo. Can you and I talk it out for a minute?" He put down the sheet with notes on her desk, placed the pencil beside the paper. "Off the record."

"Marian had an air. Everybody always kept on their toes around her. She was her usual self that week except" — a little frown creased Rosalind's round face — "she was really mad about the necklace. The necklace disappearing upset her even more than the vandalism. That was Thursday. Friday morning she looked distracted, as if she was thinking hard. But she looked really upset again Friday afternoon."

"Friday afternoon?" Nela prompted.

Rosalind gestured toward the French windows to the courtyard. "It's been cold since you came to town, but that week — Marian's last week — we had a couple of beautiful days. It was in the sixties that Friday. Marian loved the courtyard. Sometimes she'd take a cup of coffee and go out and sit in the sun with a book of poetry. She said poetry helped her think better. Oh, golly." Rosalind's eyes widened. "She was reading *Spoon River Anthology*. She didn't know she was going to have her own epitaph the next week." Rosalind's voice was a little shaky. She paused for an instant, then continued, talking fast, "I was on the phone with a teacher calling about a school tour group. I looked up as Marian came inside.

She looked odd. I worried maybe she didn't feel well. Of course, it may just have been being out in the courtyard and seeing the fountain still messed up. Like I said, the vandalism really made her mad. But she had a weird look when she came in. She walked past me and turned to her right. She was heading for the west wing. I didn't see her again."

Hollis Blair's face crinkled in thought. He looked bemused, interested, finally eager. "Blythe's got a good idea. And she's smart to send you around to ask. You know, she's a nice person but even people who have known her for years find her a little daunting. She's been swell to me. And like she said to me, just because the necklace was in Abby's office, it doesn't mean Abby had anything to do with any of it. I know that Blythe had to call the police when she got that letter."

He gave Nela an appealing smile and his eyes were warm and appreciative. His lopsided grin had aw-shucks charm. He was a big, handsome, rawboned guy. Consciously or unconsciously, he made any woman aware that she was a woman. Nela suspected he had been charming women since the day he went to kindergarten and he had probably discovered that intense looks and an air of total focus paid huge dividends.

"At least Blythe hasn't blamed me for everything that's happened." His relief was obvious, then he looked discouraged. "Everything started so well here at Haklo, then things began to fall apart. But let me think about that last Friday." His brows drew down. He shook his head. "I talked to Marian that morning. She was quite pleasant. I didn't see her that afternoon. But I can tell you one thing." He was forceful. "The idea that Abby would hurt anyone is crazy. Absolutely crazy. As for that damned necklace, somebody put it in her desk."

"Why?"

Hollis stared at her. "How would I know? To get rid of it? Abby spends a lot of time up in the artifact room. Her office is often empty. Just like those letters. It was easy to use her computer."

"You don't think someone chose Abby's desk for a particular reason?"

"I don't know why anyone would be ugly to Abby." But there was an uneasy look in his eyes.

Louise Spear's eyes widened in surprise. "Blythe said you could ask questions?"

Nela stood a few feet from Louise's desk. "When I explained my background, she agreed that I might be able to find out something useful about Marian's last week. The police now know that Marian had possession of the necklace when she died. The police believe she threatened the thief and that's why she was killed." As she spoke, she sensed the same change in perception that she'd felt in Blythe's office. To Louise, Nela was no longer simply a pleasant replacement for a flighty young assistant. It was a reminder of how easily people made assumptions about worth based on a level of employment. Nela hoped that she'd never simply relegate people to the guy who parks the car or the girl who does nails or the frail inhabitant of a nursing home. It didn't matter what people did or where they came from or their accent. Either everyone was important or no one was important. Steve would agree. The quick thought surprised her, pleased her.

"That's the week the necklace disappeared." Louise looked sick. "And then Marian died. That awful necklace."

"Do you have any idea when she might have discovered the thief?"

Louise slowly shook her head. "She was upset when the necklace was stolen. But

Friday morning, she seemed more her usual self. She was busy making plans for the donor dinner. That was very special to her. She was looking ahead . . ." Louise shivered. Her face drooped with sadness.

Nela knew every word was painful for Louise. She hated to make her remember, but Marian was dead and beyond help, Abby was alive and needed help, and she and Chloe were still on the cold-eyed detective's list. "Did you see her Friday afternoon?"

Louise sighed. "The last time I saw Marian was Friday morning. She was cheerful, making lists, thinking of a speaker. She loved planning the dinner. Tables are set up in the rotunda. She always had the portrait of Webster that hangs in her office placed on an easel between the twin stairways. She never said so, but I think to her it was as if he were there. She always opened the evening with a recording from one of his last speeches. It's a very big event. It won't be the same without Marian."

Louise's description of Marian's last week tallied with Rosalind's. Nela felt convinced that she was on the right track. Marian had been upset by the theft of the necklace, but the next day she was her usual, competent, businesslike self until that afternoon. Nela knew without question that Marian had been in possession of the stolen necklace when she died. Had she found the necklace Friday afternoon?

Louise fingered the ruffled collar of her pink blouse. "What did Blythe say about Abby?"

"We didn't talk about her. I think Blythe agreed that it was important to try and discover how Marian knew who took the necklace."

"The necklace . . . I've tried and tried to understand." Louise's expression was drawn and weary. "Sometimes things aren't what they seem and it's easy" — her voice dragged — "to think you know something. But we can't get around the fact that the necklace was found in Abby's office. Abby either hid it there or someone put it there to get her in trouble." She looked away from Nela, her face tight. "She shouldn't have been there. But I saw her . . ." She sat up straighter, looked at Nela with a suddenly focused gaze. "It's good that Blythe asked you to help. That makes me feel much better. Maybe things will get sorted out after all."

Nela looked at her sharply. "Who did you see? Who shouldn't have been where?"

Louise looked uncomfortable. "That

347

doesn't matter. It's easy to be wrong about things, isn't it? Besides, having you talk to everyone makes everything better. I'm not as worried now." She reached for the phone. "I must make some calls about the dinner."

Nela had been dismissed. She stood in the hall for a moment, heard Louise's voice. "Father Edmonds, I was wondering if you would do the invocation . . ."

As Nela walked away, she puzzled over Louise's disjointed comments. They'd been talking about Abby. Had Louise seen Abby somewhere that surprised her? Why was Louise relieved that Nela was asking questions? That fact had lifted Louise's spirits, which seemed odd and inexplicable.

Abby's office was empty. Nela took the back stairs to the second-floor west wing. As she'd expected, she found Abby in the long room with trestle tables where donations and artifacts were sorted and examined and exhibits prepared to be sent to schools around the state.

At the sound of Nela's steps, Abby looked up from a back table that held an assortment of Indian war clubs. Abby held a club with an elongated stone head. Some of the clubs were topped with ball-shaped polished stones, others with sharp metal blades, one with sharp-tipped buffalo horns. Propped against the wall behind Abby was a long board upon which she was mounting the clubs along with short printed annotations denoting the origin and tribe.

Abby watched, eyes wide, body stiff, as Nela crossed the room. As soon as Nela mentioned that Friday afternoon, Abby relaxed.

"I was working up here that day." She sounded relieved. "I don't think I ever saw Marian on Friday. Why does that matter?"

"She was upset Friday afternoon. I think she discovered the identity of the thief. She came to the west wing."

Abby spoke sharply. "She didn't come up here. I don't know what she did."

"Friday afternoon?" There was a curious tone in Grace Webster's throaty voice. Even in a plaid wool shirt and jeans and boots, she reflected high gloss, Western casual at an exorbitant price. "You're here at Blythe's direction? That's interesting." She looked past Nela, seemed to focus her gaze on the jarring sculpture with its strange components. Grace's face had the hooded look of a woman studying her cards and not liking the hand she held.

The silence between them seemed to

stretch and expand.

Nela said quietly, "If you saw Marian —"

"I didn't." Her gaze moved from the sculpture to Nela. "I don't think we will ever know what happened with the necklace. In any event, it's now back. Sometimes" — and Nela wasn't sure whether there was warning or threat in Grace's eyes — "it's safer not to know."

Pink stained Cole Hamilton's cheeks. "Things have come to a sad state when Blythe sends an outsider to ask questions. I don't believe any of this is true about Marian. Whoever took that necklace was just trying to make trouble for the foundation. It's been one thing after another ever since that girl's car was set on fire. I know what's behind that." His tone was sage. "She was too pretty." He was emphatic. "Too many pretty girls always causes trouble. I knew when Louise hired that girl that there would be trouble. Not that she didn't behave herself. But every man here, except those of us who know how to be gentlemen, couldn't take their eyes off of her. And before we turn around, there's another pretty girl and this one's obviously an old friend" — there was more than a hint of innuendo in his tone — "of Hollis's. Erik knew better than to hire pretty girls. But nothing's been the same, not since that bumptious young man took over. Why, he's barely thirty. As for that necklace, no one took it to sell or it wouldn't still be around. And that pretty young woman may have the brains of a feather but even she wouldn't be foolish enough to keep the thing in her office. It was just more troublemaking. How would Marian know anything about that? The whole idea's nonsense. Mark my words, someone took the necklace and put it in Abby's office to stir up more trouble. And it has, hasn't it?" He didn't wait for a reply. "Marian's fall was an accident and that's all there is to it."

Robbie's young-old face congealed into a hard, tight mask. "If anyone's asking questions, it should be me."

"Miss Webster said she was sure everyone would cooperate." Nela stared at him. "Do you object to telling me if you saw Marian that Friday afternoon?"

His green eyes shifted away, fastened on the penholder on his desk, a red ceramic frog with bulging eyes. "I caught a glimpse of her in the main rotunda that afternoon." He frowned. "I'd been down in the library. Erik was doing some research. He often comes in the afternoons. I was on my way to the stairs. Back upstairs. Marian came in from the courtyard. She didn't look as though her thoughts were pleasant. So I walked faster. I didn't want to talk to her when she was in that kind of mood."

"Mood?"

"I'd seen Marian in her destroyer mode before when something threatened her precious Haklo. I didn't know what had raised her hackles, but I knew it was a good time to keep my distance."

Nela thought he was telling the truth. But was he describing Marian's demeanor because he was well aware that Rosalind, too, would have seen Marian's obvious displeasure? Maybe he was telling the truth because he felt he had no choice.

Nela walked swiftly from Robbie's office to the stairway. She still needed to speak with Francis Garth and Peter Owens, but she wanted to see the library first. In the library, Nela stopped in the doorway.

Erik Judd sat at one of the writing tables, papers spread out around him. He had the look of a man whose mind is deeply engaged.

She glanced from him to a French window opposite the doorway that opened into the courtyard. If he lifted his head, he would have a view of the central portion of the courtyard.

"Excuse me."

He looked up at her, blinked, nodded in recognition. "Miss Farley. How can I help you?"

"I'm sorry to interrupt you, but may I ask you a question?" Since he no longer worked for the foundation, he was under no compulsion to answer simply because Blythe had authorized Nela to speak to staff. "I'm trying to find out more about Marian's last afternoon here. I will report what I learn to Blythe Webster."

He squinted from beneath his thick silver brows. "I see. Blythe is hoping someone might have information that will be useful to the police. Certainly, I will help if I can."

Erik didn't sound worried. But the mind behind the darkness at Haklo would always keep emotion in check.

"Mr. Judd, did you see Marian in the courtyard?"

There was a thoughtful pause. Finally, he spoke. "I had a brief glimpse. I'd been shelving books. When I turned to go back to the table, I saw her."

Nela knew one question had been answered. The library door had been open and

Erik had glanced outside.

"She was hurrying up the center path toward the main hall. That's all I saw. I'm sorry I can't be of more help."

"Hurrying?"

"Moving with a purpose, I'd say." He frowned. "I thought something had happened to upset her."

Francis Garth's size made everything in his office seem smaller, he desk, the chairs, even the framed replica of the Seal of the Osage Nation on the wall to his right. Now he stared at Nela, elbows on the bare desktop, heavy chin resting on massive interlaced fingers. He was silent after she finished, his gaze thoughtful. He slowly eased back and the chair squeaked as he shifted his weight. "I don't think it is wise" — his voice was as heavy as his body — "to draw too many conclusions from a single glimpse of Marian on that Friday."

Nela persisted. "Marian Grant came inside the rotunda from the courtyard Friday afternoon and she was visibly upset."

Francis stared from beneath thick black brows. "Why?"

Nela shook her head. "I don't know. But everyone who saw her after that moment describes her as grim or upset."

Francis bent his big head forward. Finally, he lifted his chin. "I don't lie. But remember that truth can be misleading. I was checking on a matter with Louise, I think it was shortly after three o'clock. When I stepped out into the hall, Marian was coming out of Abby Andrews's office. She was" — he chose his words carefully — "deeply in thought. She moved past me without speaking." A pause. "I don't think she saw me."

Peter pushed his horn-rimmed glasses higher on his nose. As Nela finished, he shook his head. "I didn't see Marian Friday afternoon." He spoke absently, his thoughts clearly elsewhere.

Nela had done enough interviews to know when some nugget of information was almost within reach. Peter might not know about Friday afternoon. He knew something and was debating whether to speak.

"If you know anything that could help, please tell me."

He took off his glasses. He dangled the frames from one bony hand. "Ever since we found out that somebody killed Marian, I've been thinking about everything that's happened. I don't know anything about Marian that last Friday, but this fall she did something out of character."

355

Nela scarcely breathed as she listened.

"It was about a week after the car fire. She knew I was a good friend of a curator at Sam Noble." He glanced at Nela, almost smiled. "That's the natural history museum at the University of Oklahoma. You'll have to drive up and take a look at it one day. Anyway, Marian came in my office and closed the door. She stood in front of my desk and" — he squinted in remembrance — "as clearly as I can remember, she said, 'Peter, I need a favor.' I said sure. She said, 'See if you can get Anne Nesbitt a job offer from Sam Noble. Do it. Don't ask me why. Don't ever tell anyone.' She turned and walked out." His smile was half wry, half sad. "When Marian said salute" — he slipped on the horn rims, lifted his right hand to his forehead — "I saluted."

Katie Dugan looked at Steve Flynn quizzically. "If the circumstances were different, I'd say Nela Farley's a nice woman. She has a nice face. Of course, nice faces don't mean much when it comes to protecting family."

Steve grinned, almost felt carefree. "Katie, that dog won't hunt. I talked to Nela's sister. I've interviewed everybody from narcissistic, guilt-ridden, emaciated movie stars to nuns who tend to lepers. I won't say I can't be fooled, but Chloe Farley is about as likely to be involved in a jewel heist as a kid running a Kool-Aid stand. Ditzy, happy, doesn't give a damn about appearances or money or status. If you knock out protecting her sister, Nela doesn't have a ghost of a motive. Right?"

A small smile touched Dugan's broad face. "Yeah. And she's got a cloud of soft black curls and a sensitive face. Man, she's pulled your string. Quite a change from that elegant blonde you married."

"Yeah." Steve had a funny squeeze in his chest. He couldn't even picture Gail's face. All he saw was a finely sculpted face that reflected intelligence and character and a shadow of sadness. He met her two days ago and he'd known her forever.

Katie reached for the thermos next to her in-box, rustled in a drawer for foam cups. When they each held a cup of strong black coffee, she raised hers in a semitoast. "Okay. Just for the sake of supposing, let's say your girl's home free along with ditzy sis. Where do you go from there?"

"Haklo. What the hell's wrong out there, Katie? I think there's been a lot of misdirection." He spoke slowly, thoughtfully. He had the ability to recall printed material as if he were looking at it, and this morning he'd outlined the start of trouble at the foundation. "Let's look at what happened in order: the girl's car set on fire, Indian baskets destroyed, office sprinklers activated, frozen pipes from water running in the courtyard fountain, stolen necklace —"

Katie interrupted. "Everything besides the necklace is window dressing."

Steve spoke carefully. "Just for now, let's keep it in the line of events, not make it the centerpiece."

Katie shrugged. "I get your point. I don't think I agree, but finish your list."

"The necklace is stolen. Then Marian Grant dies in a fall apparently caused by a skateboard, Nela Farley disrupts a search of Marian's apartment, Nela finds the necklace in Marian's purse, Marian's office is trashed, obscene letters on a Haklo letterhead are traced to Abby Andrews's computer, Nela leaves the necklace on Blythe Webster's desk, the necklace is missing Tuesday morning, an anonymous call" — he refused to worry now about Nela's source and his complicity — "links Grant's fall to a skateboard, Abby Andrews is missing a skateboard, another anonymous letter leads to the necklace hidden in Abby's office, skateboard used on Marian's stairs found in Abby's cabin." He paused to give

Katie time to object but she remained silent, which he took as a tacit admission that the skateboard found in the second search at Haklo had matched the scrape on the rail of Marian's steps.

Katie sipped her coffee. "Hate to say been there, done that. I know all of this."

"What's the constant?"

She raised an inquiring eyebrow.

"Trouble at Haklo." At her impatient look, he barreled ahead. "All along, Katie, you've pitched on the necklace as the only thing that matters and, yeah, a quarter million dollars barks pretty loud. But think about the scenario. A lot of things happened before the necklace disappeared. You pitched on the idea that Chloe Farley set the girl's car on fire to scare her away and, after she got the job and had been there long enough to know about Blythe's carelessness with the necklace, Chloe decided to steal it and committed vandalism to make it appear that the necklace wasn't the objective. But if we wash out Chloe —"

Katie moved restively. "I've been a cop in this town for a long time. Haklo never had any problems 'til these new people came to town. Maybe Chloe Farley's not the perp. Maybe Abby Andrews planned everything. Sure, she's supposed to be sappy about the new director, but maybe she's sappier about a quarter million dollars. Plus every time we look, we find a link to her. But maybe she's not a dumb blonde. Maybe she figured she might be suspected so she set it up to look like she might be behind everything but there's always an out, somebody else could have used her computer, somebody took her skateboard, somebody sent an anonymous letter tagging her with the necklace. A double game."

"And she's lucky enough to go in Blythe's office and find the necklace lying on top of the desk?"

Katie wasn't fazed. "Somebody found it. Somebody moved it. Top of the list, Nela Farley and Blythe Webster. Probably Louise Spear. I'll bet she's in and out of the trustee's office a dozen times a day. As for Abby Andrews, if she's behind everything that's happened at Haklo, she'd be nervous about anybody showing up there after hours, like your girlfriend coming in the back way Monday night. Abby lives in a Haklo cabin. Maybe she saw headlights. Maybe she came out to take a look. Maybe she saw you waiting by the staff entrance and stayed to watch. She would have overheard every word. When you and Nela went inside, she followed. If she stayed out of the way, you two would never have seen her. But if she wasn't there, didn't take the necklace, it could have been anybody the next morning. People pop in and out of offices all the time. Somebody came to ask a question, do a tap dance, announce the end of the world. Hell, I don't know. But it all comes back to the fact that nothing like this ever happened until these new people came to town."

A quicksilver thought threaded through Steve's mind, was there for an instant, then gone . . . Not until the new people came to town . . .

Nela wished she'd taken time to pluck Chloe's coat from the rack in her office, but once outside in the courtyard, she shivered and kept going, looking from side to side. In spring, the courtyard would be magnificent. Flower beds bordered the walks. Benches surrounded a fountain. Even in winter it might have had an austere charm except for the back hoe and stacked copper pipe near the damaged fountain.

Nela reached the center of the courtyard, made a slow survey. Windows in the west and east halls overlooked the yard. Marian Grant could have chosen a place anywhere here for her moment of peace and poetry.

However, when she came back into the rotunda, she had turned, her face set, and moved decisively toward the west wing.

Nela walked past the west wing windows, noting Louise's office, then Chloe's. Francis Garth saw Marian leaving Abby's office. She continued another ten steps. Bare yellow fronds of a weeping willow wavered in the wind that swirled around Nela, scudded withered leaves across the paved walk. Nela reached out to touch the back of a wrought iron bench, yanked back her fingers from the cold metal. The bench was turned at a bit of an angle. Someone sitting there had a clear view into the west hallway and, through the open door, into the interior of a small office. Abby's office. The desk faced the doorway.

Nela shivered again, both from cold and from a touch of horror. She knew as surely as if she'd sat beside Marian Grant that she'd lifted her eyes from her book and watched as someone stepped inside Abby's office.

Nela took a half-dozen quick steps, peered inside the window. Her gaze fastened on Abby's desk.

She looked and knew what had happened. Someone known to Marian had walked into Abby's office. Perhaps Marian had been surprised enough by the identity of the visitor to continue to watch. It seemed obvious that the visitor pulled the necklace from a pocket and placed it either in the desk or a filing cabinet. Wherever the necklace was put, Nela didn't doubt that a shaken Marian understood what was happening. She knew the theft was intended to implicate Abby and she knew the identity of the thief. She now had it in her power to protect her beloved Haklo.

Katie Dugan raised an eyebrow at caller ID. She lifted the receiver. "Dugan . . . Yeah? . . . Hold on." She covered the mouthpiece. "Blythe Webster's on speakerphone with Nela Farley. Apparently your girlfriend's been busy. Blythe wants me to hear what she found out. Since Nela will give you the lowdown anyway, I'm going to turn on my speakerphone. But you aren't here." With that, she punched. "Okay, Miss Farley, what have you got?"

Steve heard more than the sound of Nela's voice. It was as if she were in Katie's impersonal, businesslike office, looking at him with those bright, dark eyes that held depths of feeling that he wanted to understand and share. As she recounted her passage through Haklo, he gave a mental fist pump. Good going, good reporting. He made quick, cogent notes:

Rosalind McNeil pinpointed a change in Marian Grant's demeanor to her sojourn in the courtyard Friday afternoon. When Marian came back inside, she walked toward the west wing.

Louise Spear, worried and upset, focused on the necklace's iscovery in Abby's filing cabinet.

Abby Andrews claimed she was upstairs in the laboratory and didn't see Marian.

Grace Webster said it might be safer not to pursue the truth about the necklace.

Cole Hamilton dismissed the idea of murder and linked the car fire and incidents around Abby to the presence of pretty young women. He said too many pretty girls always causes trouble.

Robbie Powell confirmed Marian's distraught demeanor as she walked toward the west hall.

Erik Judd claimed he caught only a glimpse of Marian.

Francis Garth saw Marian coming out of Abby Andrews's office.

Peter Owens claimed he didn't see

Marian Friday. He revealed that, after the car fire, Marian asked him to arrange a job offer for Anne Nesbitt in Norman.

He and Katie listened intently as Nela continued, "I went into the courtyard. It was a pretty day that Friday and Marian went outside with her book of poetry. Not like today."

Steve knew the bricked area must have been cold and deserted this afternoon. There was a memory of that cold in Nela's voice.

"A bench on the west side has a good view of Abby's office. I think Marian saw someone walk into the office and hide the necklace. And then" — Nela's voice was thin — "I think Marian came inside and went to the office and got the necklace."

Blythe's words were fast and clipped. "Marian should have called the police." A short silence. "But she didn't. Instead, she obviously decided to handle everything herself. She should have come to me." Anger rippled in Blythe's voice. "I" — a decided emphasis — "am the trustee. I should have been informed. Oh." There was a sudden catch in her voice. "It's terrible. If she'd come to me, I would have insisted we contact the police. If we had, she would be alive now. Why didn't she realize that Haklo didn't matter that much, that Haklo wasn't worth her life? But she was Marian and so damnably sure of herself." There was an undertone of old rancor. "I suppose she accused the thief but promised she'd keep quiet if the thief left Haklo. I can see why Marian thought that was the best solution. Everyone would forget in time about the vandalism if it stopped. Instead . . ." Blythe trailed off.

Steve knew all of them pictured a dark figure edging up Marian's stairs and placing a skateboard on the second step, returning unseen in the early-morning darkness to watch a woman fall to her death, then pick up a skateboard with gloved hands and slip silently away.

"Anyway" — Blythe sounded weary — "perhaps this information will be helpful to you. Do you have any questions?"

Katie's face quirked in a sardonic smile. "That all seems clear, Miss Webster. Thank you for your call. And thank you, Miss Farley, for your report. I'll be in touch." As she clicked off the speakerphone, she raised an eyebrow at Steve. "Notice anything?"

"Yeah. Kind of interesting about the necklace. First, it's put in Abby's office. Second, Marian retrieves it. Third, the necklace is in Marian's purse. Fourth, the necklace is on Blythe's desk. Fifth, the necklace is found in Abby's office."

Katie flicked him an approving glance. "You got it. Starts with Abby, ends with Abby. What are the odds, Steve?"

Steve sat at his desk and tried to ignore the undercurrent of worry that had tugged at him ever since he'd heard Nela's report over Katie's speakerphone. Yes, she'd done good work. But there could be no doubt that she was now on the murderer's watch list. He forced himself to concentrate and maintain the coldly analytical, unemotional attitude that made him a good reporter. Figuring out what to accept and what to discard came down to more than the five *w*s and an *h*. There had to be innate skepticism that questioned motives and discounted conventional wisdom.

In the case of Haklo, there were facts. New staff members had been added, including the director. Six incidents of vandalism and a theft occurred between mid-September and this week, beginning with a car fire. Marian Grant died in a fall. There were suppositions.

The vandalism was committed to detract attention from the theft of a quarter-million-dollar necklace. Marian Grant threatened the thief. Marian Grant was murdered.

Steve accepted the facts, but there were two pieces of information, one that came to him, the other picked up by Nela in her talks today with staff, that entirely recast his ideas about what happened at Haklo and why.

He glanced at the clock. Just after seven. He reached for his cell, shook his head. He'd told her he was coming. As he slammed out of the office, a couple of folders and a legal pad under one arm, the worry he'd fought to contain made his throat feel tight. He had lots to say to Nela. He hoped she would listen.

17

Jugs's ears tilted forward. He stared toward the front door, luminous green eyes unwavering.

Nela's heart lifted. He'd said he would come. She shouldn't feel this way. She hadn't felt this way in a long time. Not since . . . Her gaze shifted to Bill's photograph. But it was only a picture and there was, always, the desolate feeling of nothing there, nothing, nothing.

She was on her feet before the sound of a rapid knock. She'd left the porch light on. When she pulled the door back, Steve looked down at her. In the bright glare, his wiry red hair looked like a patch of flame and his blue eyes were commanding and insistent. His broad freckled face again surprised her because he wasn't now a mirror image of a smooth, always-young celluloid figure. His face was not only the face of a man who could be kind and pleasant

369

and thoughtful, but the face of a man with a hardened worldview and a memory of loss and betrayal. He was a man who had to be reckoned with and who'd taken up space in her life in a brief span of hours. But that was how life happened. Things changed, not just in hours but in minutes. Bill had walked up a dusty road in a distant land and the world turned gray and cold for her.

Cold . . . Steve's ragged diamond-patterned sweater was familiar now. Before she thought, she blurted, "Don't you ever wear a coat?"

"Too much bother. You okay?"

The query surprised her. There was worry in his eyes, worry and concern. She felt a flicker of happiness. She'd been so alone and now she didn't feel alone anymore, not as long as he was here.

He looked into her eyes, saw her response. His smile was as warm as an embrace.

With a quick breath, Nela stepped back, knew she talked too fast. "I'm fine. Come in. Let me get you some coffee."

She felt steadied as she served fresh hot coffee in thick white pottery mugs. They sat on the sofa, Nela taking care to provide space between them, disconcertingly but gloriously aware of his nearness.

Jugs jumped to the coffee table, sliding a

little on Steve's papers.

Steve grinned. "Hey, boy, you're in the way."

Jugs gazed at him for a moment, then flowed to the couch, settled between Steve and Nela.

As Nela reached down to stroke the black-and-tan striped back, Steve moved to smooth Jugs's bristly ticked coat. Her hand brushed Steve's. There was an instant's pause, the two of them still, then Steve reached for the mug, spoke rapidly.

Nela listened, trying to corral her thoughts and her feelings. Steve was so near, so big, the remembered warmth of his touch, Bill, emptiness, Chloe, Haklo . . .

". . . and here's some stuff I put together about the people who have keys, plus I was in Katie's office when you called this afternoon." He handed her several sheets of paper.

Nela read swiftly. Steve's bios added substance to her personal encounters with the staff members. She stopped reading when she turned to the sheet with the italicized head: *Nela Farley's Report to Katie Dugan.* She started to hand back the sheets.

He gently massaged behind Jugs's prominent ears, prompting a throaty purr. "Read all of it."

Everything was as expected except for one surprising twist. In Nela's report on Cole Hamilton, Steve had marked *too many pretty girls always causes trouble* with a canary yellow highlighter.

Nela repeated the sentence, looked at him inquiringly.

"That could have been an outlier. Nobody else has talked about pretty girls. But I picked up a vibe from Mokie Morrison this morning. He's the cop who tried to deflect you from Katie. Mokie is a man with an eye for good-looking women. When he talked about Anne Nesbitt" — Steve's grin was wry — "if he'd melted in a puddle right there in the squad room, I wouldn't have been surprised. Apparently she was hot." Another wry smile. "Presumably she still is. But here's what I wonder." He leaned back against the cushion. "Maybe we've been off on the wrong track, right from the start. The conventional wisdom dismissed the car fire in September, like it wasn't a part of the stuff that started happening in November. What if the car fire was part of everything? What if somebody was angry about pretty girls?"

Nela stared. "Why?"

His gaze was serious when he answered. "Short answer, sex. Long answer, people can get twisted up in knots about love or lust or whatever you want to call it. Now" — his eyes narrowed — "I'm thinking something off the wall. Not the usual triangle stuff. But how about this. Anne Nesbitt apparently packed a potent punch. There are women" — there was an undertone of grimness in his voice — "who are like pots of honey to bears. Bears can't help themselves. They have to nose around. Cole Hamilton may be old but he isn't dead and he all but said in his gentlemanly way that testosterone bubbled. Maybe one of the bears thought he had a chance with her and then Hollis Blair arrives."

"He really cares about Abby." Nela shook her head. "He wouldn't go after someone else."

"Maybe not. But he has an aura around women. Right?"

Nela understood what Steve meant. "Yes." She didn't have to say more.

"In fact . . ." He broke off, pulled out his cell, found a number. "Hey, Robbie. I got a question. You're a canny guy about people. You notice things. Think back to late last summer. I understand Anne Nesbitt was a pretty gal. Did Hollis Blair notice?" Steve listened, looked satisfied. "Pretty blatant, huh? . . . No, nothing to do with much of anything. Just a bet with a friend. We got to talking about Anne Nesbitt and I swore she was a magnet for males. Right . . . Thanks."

"Robbie doesn't like Hollis."

Steve laughed. "Despises him, actually." He was abruptly serious. "But Robbie notices things. He said every man up there but him found one reason or another for a nice chat with Anne every day. That included the director. With Hollis, I think it's pretty much automatic pilot. Hollis learned a long time ago that ladies like him and he's ready to soak up a little sun when he can. But maybe somebody thought the handsome young director had cut him out."

Nela felt a wash of horror. "And he set her car on fire? That's unbalanced."

Steve's gaze was somber. "Someone is desperately unbalanced. Step back and look at the vandalism. There's a fury in everything that's happened."

Nela wasn't convinced. "Anne Nesbitt left. Why the other things?"

"Hollis Blair is still there."

Nela slowly shook her head. "I can't imagine anyone at Haklo being that" — she looked at Steve, used his word — "twisted." If Steve was right, someone she'd met, spoken with, perhaps shared a smile with, had a monstrous ego willing to destroy, steal, and ultimately kill because of jealousy. Or was the viciousness not even prompted by jealousy? Perhaps the motive was uglier, darker. Perhaps a perceived affront would not, could not be tolerated.

"There's something bad out at Haklo." He looked uneasy. "Like a nest of rattle-snakes. That's why" — he reached out, took her hand — "I want you to back off. I've already told Katie what I think. She listened. She'll be looking at them."

Them . . .

Nela knew the list was short. If Steve was right, the vandal, thief, and killer was either Cole Hamilton, Francis Garth, or Peter Owens.

"Nela, stay in your office. Stay out of it. Leave everything to Katie."

After Steve left, Nela poured another cup of coffee, carried it to the sofa, settled by Jugs.

The cat turned his wedge-shaped face toward her.

She stared into Jugs's brilliant green eyes. "*. . . You wanted him to stay . . . He likes me . . . I like him . . .*" Slowly, Jugs's eyelids closed.

Nela petted his winter-thick coat. "Sure he likes you. Who wouldn't? Cats rule, right?" She would be very alone now if it weren't for Jugs. He was alive and warm, his presence comforting. Maybe some evening somewhere, she and Steve would sit with Jugs between them and they could talk of books and people and places, not of death and murder and anger.

Did everything hinge on the theft of the necklace? If not, the entire picture changed. If Steve was right, if the car fire was central, the first act in an unfolding drama of passion, then it mattered very much why the fire was set.

Had one of the men felt scorned by Anne Nesbitt and been determined to punish her? Perhaps there had been momentary pleasure after Anne left. Nothing else happened until the attraction between Hollis and Abby became obvious. The next vandalism destroyed the Indian baskets precious to Abby. The rest of the incidents caused difficulties for Hollis, his first directorship marred by the unsolved crimes, for Blythe as the foundation trustee, and for Abby.

As for the necklace, the intent might never have been money but a hope of implicating Abby. Marian Grant found the necklace in Abby's office. Marian knew who had taken it. That knowledge cost Marian her life. But when the stolen jewelry — thanks to Nela — appeared on Blythe's desk, the necklace ended up in Abby's office. It had never mattered that the necklace was worth a quarter million dollars. Moreover, once again placing the necklace in Abby's office indicated a depth of obsession. The thief should have been worried about the return of the necklace, wondering if someone was going to be a danger. Instead, the vendetta against Abby continued.

Nela shivered.

Jugs stirred, looked up. "*. . . Afraid . . .*"

Nela felt a catch in her throat. Yes, she was afraid. She saw faces, Cole Hamilton almost cherubic with his fringe of white curls, heavy, bull-like, massive Francis Garth with a dark commanding stare, lanky, professorial Peter Owens with his genial smile.

Which one?

Jugs gave an irritated chirp as Nela moved restlessly deep in the night. She was aware of him but only dimly. Distorted dreamlike images jostled in her sleep-drugged mind. But once, with sharp clarity, came the lucid thought: Grace warned me. Or were her words a threat? *Sometimes it's safer not to know.*

Nela carried with her a sense of danger

Thursday morning. The hallway seemed cold and remote with no hint of life or movement. She walked faster, but the quick clip of her shoes emphasized the silence. She pushed open Chloe's door, turned on the light. The connecting door between Chloe's office and Louise's was open as usual, and a cheerful shaft of light spilled across the floor.

Nela crossed to the doorway.

"Good morning —" She spoke to emptiness. Louise's coat hung from the coat tree. There were papers on her desk, but Louise wasn't there.

Nela turned away. She checked her in-box. It was empty. Nela had completed the stack of applications Louise had given her yesterday. She glanced at the clock. A quarter after eight. Nela would have been glad to have tasks to do. It would be nice to be absorbed, pushing away worries about Haklo and the investigation. But surely Katie Dugan had realized that Nela wasn't covering up for Chloe, that the necklace was only a part of a whole, and that none of the peculiar events at Haklo had anything to do with Nela or with Chloe.

Nela settled at the desk, waited. Time seemed to crawl. The minute hand moved with stately slowness. Another quarter hour passed. It was too early to make the morning round of mail deliveries. Finally, restless, Nela opened a side drawer, fished out a legal pad. She wrote a half-dozen statements in no particular order, fast. She liked, when writing a story, to pluck out the most interesting facts. Then with a quick scan, she'd rank them in order of importance and that's how she'd structure the story.

In the adjoining office, Louise's phone rang. And rang. Finally, it clicked off. Nela almost rose to go answer but she'd not been instructed to take Louise's calls and she might well prefer to later pick up messages.

Nela returned to her fast-draw observations:

Blythe Webster's active role as trustee began this summer.

Grace Webster resented her sister's appointment as sole trustee yet she made it a habit to be present at Haklo when she was in Craddock.

The vandalism began after Erik Judd was fired.

Hollis Blair seemed to effortlessly charm women.

Francis Garth was a huge man with a strong personality. Whatever course he followed, he would be formidable, either as friend or adversary.

Nela tapped the pad with her pen. Did any of these observations point to the figure behind the events at Haklo?

Chloe's phone rang.

Nela looked at caller ID: Craddock Police Department. Nela lifted the receiver. "Nela Farley."

"Miss Farley, Detective Dugan. Do you have time to talk?"

"Yes." She felt a twist of amusement. Nice of Dugan to ask. If she had questions, she could insist they be answered.

"I have a question I can't ask Steve Flynn. Wrong gender." Katie Dugan was brisk. "I know a bit more about you now. You're a reporter, used to sizing people up. I want you to consider three men: Francis Garth, Cole Hamilton, Peter Owens. You're an outsider at Haklo. Your impressions will be fresh."

Nela realized that she was being treated as an equal although she should always remember that Katie Dugan was a woman who could play many roles. "How can I help?"

"Francis Garth. Cole Hamilton. Peter Owens. Think sex."

Nela got it at once. There is office decorum and there is the rest of life, from an encounter on a beach to a glance across a crowded room. Men are men and women are women and there are glances and smiles and eye contact that say more than words ever could. Not that the lines often didn't blur. Hollis Blair could no more be around a woman without sending out a primal signal than he could forego using his diffident charm in any setting.

Katie nudged. "You're sitting in a bar and Francis Garth's on the next stool."

Removing the men from Haklo, placing them in a dusky, crowded bar with music and movement and the splash of whisky over ice cubes, she saw them without the veneer of work. "Francis Garth." Nela's tone reflected her shift in perception. "Magnetic. Powerful. Definitely a man who notices women." She felt a flicker of surprise as she continued. "Cole Hamilton may have the aura of a kindly older man, but he's very aware of women." As Steve had observed, Cole Hamilton was old, but he wasn't dead. "Peter Owens has that tweedy, professorial aura, but he's very masculine. Any one of them could be sexually on the prowl."

Mim looked up from the page layout on her monitor, gray eyes inquiring. She was to

Steve unchanged and unchanging, a rock in his life, her short-cut white hair making her thin, intelligent face look young and vibrant. She had the air of a sprinter ready for the gun, poised, ready to go. She never wasted words, suffered fools impatiently, incompetence never.

Steve propped against the edge of her desk. "You know everybody in town." He grinned. "If I were a cub, you'd snap, 'Don't tell me something I already know.' "

She raised an eyebrow, waited.

"I want the backstairs gossip on Francis Garth, Cole Hamilton, Peter Owens. Bed playmates. If any." There was no playfulness in his voice. The request was serious.

Mim was always self-possessed. The only indication of surprise was a brief flicker in her eyes. Then, she gave an abrupt nod. She didn't take the time to say *not for publication,* to warn that she couldn't vouch for gossip, that of course she picked up scurrilous comments about Craddock movers and shakers that she never shared. She wasn't going to tell Steve something he already knew. "Francis reportedly has been sleeping with the mayor's wife, but lost out this summer to Mack Harris." Mack Harris was a tall, rangy rodeo champion who'd bought a ranch near Craddock. "Cole Hamilton spends a lot of time at the Cowboy Club and he likes 'em young." The Cowboy Club was a gentlemen's retreat with gambling, music, and dancing women dressed as briefly as Dallas Cowboys cheerleaders. "Denise Owens and the twins spent the summer at her parents' lake home in Minnesota. My granddaughter's on the same swim team as the Owens girls and there was a lot of surprise that they stayed away all summer. Press of 'work' kept Peter in Craddock."

With one ear cocked for the sound of Louise's brisk steps in the hall, Nela tidied and straightened the office, finally began to rearrange the contents of the center drawer in Chloe's desk. As she worked, she ignored the ringing of Louise's telephone. Trinkets and odds and ends brought her sister near, as if Chloe were smiling at her with laughing eyes: two ticket stubs from the Oklahoma City Civic Center production of *Peter Pan,* keepsake menus from a half-dozen Oklahoma City and Norman restaurants (on the menu from Legend's in Norman, Chloe had written in huge letters with a half-dozen exclamation points: *Better Than the Best!!!!!!*), a map of Turner Falls, a dog-eared copy of *Far Side* cartoons, jacks and a rubber ball in a plastic bag, a Rubik's cube, a deck of cards. The motley collection was typical of her quirky sister.

Finally, Nela picked up a much creased and folded sheet of ruled paper. She sensed something that was not meant for other eyes, not even those of a loving sister. She gently laid the folded strip in the back center of the drawer, returned each item. She had just closed the drawer when the staccato tap of heels sounded, coming fast, coming near. They stopped just short of Chloe's office. "Louise?" Blythe Webster's tone was sharp, just this side of angry. "Louise . . ." There was an exasperated sigh.

Nela knew that Blythe had realized Louise's office was empty. A flurry of steps and Blythe stood in Chloe's doorway. Blythe was trim in a soft gray cashmere sweater and black slacks. Impatience was evident in every line of her tense body. Her face was tight with irritation. "Where's Louise? I keep calling and I get her answering machine."

"I haven't seen her this morning." Nela glanced at the clock. Almost ten. She'd been at work for two hours. "She wasn't in her office when I arrived."

"Not here?" Blythe's voice was odd. "She's always here. She would have told me if she were going out."

"Her coat's in her office." Nela meant to be reassuring but realized that her voice held a question.

"Well." Blythe seemed at a loss, uncertain what to do. Then she looked relieved. She pulled a cell phone from a pocket, touched a number.

In only an instant, there was a faint musical ring, a ghostly faraway repetition of the first few bars of "Oklahoma."

Nela pushed up from her desk. Blythe was right behind her. The musical ring continued twice again, louder now as they reached Louise's desk. Nela pulled out the bottom-right drawer. The last ring was ending. A black leather shoulder bag nestled in the drawer.

"Well, she's here if her purse is here." Blythe sounded relieved. "She's somewhere in the building. Find her for me." She swung on her heel and surged out of the office.

Nela was glad to have a task. The directive hadn't been delivered with grace or charm, but if you ran the ship, you could navigate any damn way you pleased. Anyway, she had her orders, she'd carry them out.

■ ■ ■ ■

Steve wasn't a lazy reporter. He had one more call to make. In fact, it took five calls to track down Anne Nesbitt. The connection crackled.

". . . almost time for the next presentation. I'm at an elementary school in Bartlesville. It's such fun. I have a slide show of our dinosaur exhibits. Kids love it." She sounded sunny and happy. "How can I help you?"

"This is Steve Flynn, *The Craddock Clarion.* The police haven't given up on the arson of your car."

A pause. "Oh" — a small sigh — "I appreciate the police continuing to try but I think it had to be some kind of nut. Not anybody I knew. Like" — she paused — "how do they put it when the criminal is a stranger? A casual crime. That's what happened."

Steve picked his words. "There have been other problems since you left Haklo. It's important, in fact it may be a matter of life and death, to know if the destruction of your car is linked to later vandalism. I want to ask a serious question. Was a male staffer at Haklo hitting on you? If so, did you rebuff him?"

She didn't rush to answer. "Men are" — now it was she who spoke with care — "often very nice to me. Some men always see women in a certain way. Hollis Blair was very friendly, but he was never over the line. Hollis" — there was good humor in her tone — "is a guy who automatically sends out signals to women. The other men were interested, but I made it clear that I'm in a committed relationship. I've been fortunate in both school and jobs that I've dealt with nice men who recognize boundaries. No one bothered me at Haklo."

Steve ended the call with a feeling of bewilderment. He'd been so certain . . .

Rosalind waggled a hand in greeting. She was speaking brightly into the phone. ". . . some unexpected repairs have to be made and the foundation won't be available for tours this Saturday. If you would like to reschedule, please call." She gave the number. "We're very sorry for the cancellation. Again, this is Rosalind McNeill at Haklo Foundation." She hung up and heaved a sigh. "The T is definitely out of sorts. But I kind of get her point. She cancelled the Saturday tours. She said there's not a good feeling here." Rosalind's round face suddenly looked half scared, half uneasy. "She's got that right. Anyway" — she managed a smile almost as bright as her usual — "I have the mail tray ready." She nodded at the blue plastic tray on the counter.

Nela started to explain she was looking for Louise, then realized she would be visiting each office with the mail and she could combine the tasks. She would, however, change her route and end up at Blythe's office. Hopefully, she would be able to report Louise's whereabouts when she delivered Blythe's mail. And, in fact, her answer might be right here at hand. Rosalind knew who came and who went.

"Is Louise in Hollis's office?" Louise handled correspondence and projects for both the director and the trustee.

"The director isn't here this morning. He called in and said he would be in around noon." Rosalind's face took on a conspiratorial glow. "Abby called in, too. She said she had an appointment and would come in around noon." Rosalind raised both eyebrows.

Nela had not paid particular attention, but remembered that Abby's office had been dark. Nela had assumed Abby was upstairs in the artifact room. She didn't care about the twin absences of Hollis and Abby. "I guess Louise is upstairs." She gestured toward the broad steps of the curving twin stairways to the second floor. "What time did she go up?"

Rosalind was too good-natured to be offended by Nela's lack of interest in the activities of the director and assistant curator. Her smile was cheerful. "I've been here since eight. I haven't seen Louise this morning. She must have taken the back stairs."

Nela received the same answer everywhere she delivered mail. No one had seen Louise. Nela deposited mail in the in-box on Grace Webster's desk. There was no jacket on her coat tree, no evidence she had been to Haklo this morning. Nela very much doubted that Grace had bothered to inform Rosalind of her presence or absence.

There was no one left to ask.

As she stepped out of Grace's office, the plastic tray held only the mail for Louise and for the trustee. Nela headed for the back stairs that led down to the first floor of the west wing. She would leave Louise's mail, and if Louise had since returned to her office, all would be well.

Light spilled into the hallway from the open door to the artifact room. Abby had called in, said she wasn't coming until late morning. There was no reason for the light to be on if Abby wasn't working. Possibly Louise was there.

Nela walked faster. She reached the doorway and stopped. She glanced across the room. Her breath caught in her throat as she stared at death.

Louise's body lay facedown in a crumpled heap near the back table where Abby cataloged and mounted Indian war clubs. Yesterday Louise's pink blouse had been soft and pretty with the gray wool suit. Harsh light from overhead fluorescent panels threw splotched dark stains on the back of Louise's gray suit into stark relief.

18

Muttered voices and heavy footsteps sounded from the far end of the hallway near the staff entrance and the back stairway to the second floor. Nela assumed more police were arriving as well as the medical examiner and a forensic unit and all the various people involved in a homicide investigation. This time there was no question as to the cause of death. Homicide by person or persons unknown. Louise Spear had walked into the artifact room sometime late yesterday afternoon and someone, someone she knew, someone with a key to Haklo, struck her down, crushing the back of her head.

Nela sat numbly at Chloe's desk and waited. Dugan had taken only a moment to talk to Nela — how did she find the body? — then directed Nela and the other shaken and shocked Haklo staff members, who'd gathered in the upper-west hallway, to

391

remain in their offices until further notice. Rosalind, eyes red-rimmed, brought lunch, ham sandwiches, chips, coffee. Nela forced herself to eat. The day was going to be long and hard. She needed energy to recall and tell Katie Dugan what she knew. Louise Spear had been worried and upset yesterday, but it had never occurred to Nela that Louise was in danger. Her distress had seemed natural, the care of a woman who had served Haklo for so many years. If only she had asked Louise what troubled her . . . *If only . . .*

Nela was painfully aware of the spread of light through the connecting doorway. This morning she'd assumed that any moment Louise would return to her office.

More steps, these coming from the other direction. "Yeah, yeah, yeah, I'm not going to talk to her. I'm on my way upstairs, but I want to see her, Mokie."

Nela came to her feet. Steve was coming down the hall.

"Katie'll have my head on a platter if any of the witnesses talk to anybody." Mokie's gravelly voice was steely.

Nela realized with a chill that there must be officers stationed in every hall to prevent conversation and ensure staff members stayed sequestered.

"That includes you, Steve." It was an order.

"Not to worry." Steve's voice was nearer, loud, determined. He came through the open door in a rush.

She moved to meet him.

He reached her, gripped her shoulders. His broad freckled face was grim, but his blue eyes looked deep into hers, saying, *It's bad, I'm here, I'll help.*

She drew strength from his reassuring gaze and from his touch, the warmth and certainty of his hands.

"I know it's rotten." His voice held a recognition of the grisly scene she'd found and taut anger at the death of a woman who had been good and kind and generous.

"I kept hunting for her." Nela hated thinking how long Louise's body had lain there. "And all the while —"

Mokie stood in the doorway. "Save it for Dugan." Mokie's voice was gruff.

Nela glanced at Mokie, nodded. "Right." She looked back at Steve.

He tightened his grip on her shoulders. "I've got to cover the story. I'll see you tonight. I'll bring dinner."

The afternoon dragged, one slow hour after another. Nothing to do. No one to talk to.

Only the sounds of people coming and going. She tried not to remember what she had seen, tried to figure who might have committed murder, knew the list was long. All the staff members had been present late yesterday afternoon. Erik Judd had been in the library. Any of them could have killed Louise.

It was a quarter to five when footsteps came near, purposeful, quick steps. Detective Dugan came through the open door, followed by Mokie Morrison. He was much taller, but Dugan carried with her an air of command.

Dugan flicked a thumb at Mokie. He settled in a chair a little to one side, pulled out a small recorder, turned it on. "Office of Nela Farley, temporary assistant to murder victim. Time: four forty-six p.m. Investigating officers Detective Flynn, Detective Mokie Morrison. Investigation into homicide of Louise Spear."

Dugan didn't draw up a second chair. She stood in front of Chloe's desk, arms folded, and stared down at Nela. Although her white blouse, gray cardigan, and gray wool skirt would have been proper attire in any office, she looked every inch a cop, eyes sharp and questioning, face hard. "When did you last see Louise Spear?"

"Just before I left yesterday. A few minutes before five." When had Louise died? Why had she gone upstairs to the artifact room? That was where Abby worked. Once again, always, there was a link to Abby.

"Where did you see her?"

Nela gestured toward the connecting doorway. "In her office. I stood in the doorway, said good night."

"Did you talk to her?"

"Not then. I talked to her earlier in the day. She was very upset after the necklace was found in Abby's office. When I came back from lunch, she was sitting in her office and she looked dreadful. She wasn't doing any work. And later, I talked to everyone, asking about Marian Grant's last day —"

"We'll get to that in a minute." Dugan was impatient. "Tell me about Louise Spear."

Nela's eyes narrowed as she tried to remember Louise's words. "Louise said she didn't see Marian in the afternoon, that the last time she saw her, Marian seemed fine. Then Louise started talking about the necklace. Louise said that things sometimes weren't what they seemed to be, but we couldn't get away from the fact that the police found the necklace in Abby's office. It was all a little confused. She said either

Abby put it in the cabinet or someone put it there to get Abby in trouble. And then she said" — Nela hesitated because the words seemed so damning now — "that 'she shouldn't have been there. But I saw her.' "

Dugan's expression was thoughtful. " 'She shouldn't have been there. But I saw her.' "

When Nela opened the apartment door, Steve wished he could wipe away the pain and distress in her face. She carried too many burdens. He wanted to see her smile. He wanted her eyes to light up with happiness. He wanted her to know laughter and carefree days. And nights. Preferably with him. He held up a carryout bag. "Greek food. And" — he paused for emphasis, waggling a red can of coffee mixed with chicory — "I brought the Flynn special, coffee that will stiffen your spine."

Nela had already set the table.

He put the coffee on to brew while she emptied the sacks. "Dinner first, then I'll bring you up to date. But nothing about Haklo while we eat."

They feasted on chicken kabobs and Greek salad, finishing with baklava and steaming mugs of chicory coffee. "Can't end a meal at the Flynn house in the winter without coffee that barks." He looked toward Jugs, in his usual place at the end of the table. "Sorry for the language."

Resisting a second piece of baklava, Steve raised his mug in a salute to Jugs. "I don't usually like to share a girl with another guy, but I'll make an exception for you, buddy."

Jugs looked regal, front paws outstretched.

"Jugs is a gentleman." Nela smiled. "He has definite ideas on the proper place for a cat during meals, but he minds his manners."

Soon enough the dishes were done and they were in the living room.

Jugs settled between them on the sofa.

Nela smoothed Jugs's bristly coat, welcomed the warmth. "Tell me, Steve." The brightness from their cheerful interlude fled her eyes.

He didn't have to look at notes. He'd covered the investigation all through the afternoon, written the lead story with five minutes to spare on deadline. "You are the last person to admit seeing Louise, so she was alive at a few minutes before five. Her death occurred sometime between five and nine p.m. They can figure that from the state of rigor mortis. The autopsy will likely be more definitive. Katie thinks she was killed shortly after five p.m. For some reason, she went to the artifact room. There's no indication from the position of the body that she fought her attacker. Instead, she was apparently struck from behind, a blow that crushed the base of her skull. She fell and was hit at least three more times. Death from massive trauma. The weapon was a Plains Indian war club, a rounded polished ball of stone fastened by a strip of leather to a handle. The stone has a circumference of seven inches. The handle is eighteen inches long, partially wrapped in hide. On the length of the handle, there are several prints belonging to Abby Andrews along with some unidentified prints. Katie doubts the murderer was thoughtful enough to leave prints, and likely the unidentified prints belong to a previous collector or shop owner."

"Abby was cataloging the clubs. Of course her prints are on them." Nela had a quick picture of Abby yesterday as Nela crossed the room.

Steve shrugged. "Yeah. A point in her favor. Or a point against her. Everybody knew she was handling the war clubs. If she killed Louise, she didn't have to worry about gloves. Like you said, her prints are all over the clubs. Some of the prints are smudged either by Abby or by gloves worn by the murderer. If somebody else hefted the weapon, they must have worn gloves. But why not? If it was after five o'clock, maybe the murderer was already in a coat, ready to leave. Louise wouldn't be surprised at gloves in this weather."

"I don't see why Louise went to the artifact room."

"That's easy, whether the killer's Abby or someone else." Steve felt confident. "Abby could ask Louise to come up, say she needed to check out something with her. If it's someone else, it's even easier. Abby had the tail pinned on her a half-dozen times Wednesday. The murderer says, 'Louise, I may have found something in the artifact room that implicates Abby but I don't want to take it to the police unless you agree.' "

"Why did the murderer leave on the light?" Nela shivered. "That bothers me. I keep thinking about the light on all night and Louise lying there dead."

Steve didn't believe the light mattered one way or the other. "Maybe the idea was that the light would attract attention and Louise would be found sooner rather than later."

"She would have been found early today by Abby, except Abby and Hollis were gone this morning. I don't think Grace ever came in today, although she wouldn't pay any attention if she had."

"Why do you say that?"

Nela gave him a quirked smile. He noticed for the first time that she had a hint of a dimple in her right cheek. "Grace wouldn't consider it necessary to personally check on anything. She and Blythe are accustomed to having others take care of details for them. When Blythe came here Friday night, she hadn't given a thought to who would take care of Jugs. She'd assumed it was taken care of. Minions can always be dispatched."

"You aren't a big fan of the Webster sisters?"

Nela considered the question. "Neither for nor against. As Fitzgerald said, 'the rich are different.' But" — and she looked a little shamefaced — "to be fair —"

Steve was touched by her rush to be generous. She had a kind heart. And that, he realized with an odd sense of sadness, was nothing he would ever have said about Gail.

"— Blythe is doing her best to find out what happened, even though I don't think either she or Grace were fond of Marian. Too much history there because of their father and mother. As for Grace" — and now she again felt the prickle of unease that she'd experienced when she spoke with Grace Webster about Marian's last day —

"I don't know if she was warning me or threatening me when we talked about the necklace and she said that 'sometimes it's safer not to know.' "

"It could have been either?"

Once again Nela gave a question grave consideration. "It could have been either."

"We have to look at everything again." He hated the sense of uncertainty that enveloped him, but they had to face facts. "I was positive the car fire meant a lot, that one of the men was hot for Anne Nesbitt, that she'd brushed him off. I talked to her. If one of them was interested, she didn't pick up on it. I think she was telling me the truth. She would have known, right?" He wondered if she knew how he felt, sitting so near her.

Nela looked at him. Her eyes widened, then her gaze slipped away. Her voice was soft when she answered. "She would know."

He felt a quickening of his breath and then her eyes moved to the photograph of the dark-haired man in the latticed frame with its carefully worked border of red, white, and blue ribbons. Steve willed his voice to be businesslike. "So, scratch the idea that one of the men was getting back at her. That means we still have to figure out whether the vandalism started with the car fire or whether the fire gave someone a clever way of setting up camouflage to steal a necklace or whether the necklace was just one more way of attacking Haklo and making life miserable for the director and the trustee." His lips compressed for a moment. "It's like trying to catch minnows with your bare hands, too many of them and too slippery and fast."

Nela smoothed Jugs's fur.

Steve gazed at her long fingers, a lovely hand, smooth, graceful, gentle.

She look at him with quick intelligence. "If the objective was to steal the necklace, would there have been so much destruction? The Indian baskets were slashed. A crystal statuette was thrown at a mirror in Marian's apartment. The mess in her office was more than just the aftermath of a search. I think" — she spoke slowly — "someone is frighteningly angry."

"And scared." He tried to sort out his confusion. "Scared as hell, now. That's why Marian and Louise died. I don't think there was ever a plan to murder anyone. It was a campaign to cause trouble. Maybe Abby Andrews really did see a way to snatch a quarter million dollars worth of jewelry. If so, her heroine-tied-to-the-tracks posture is an act. But there are other reasons Haklo could be the target. Blythe decided to get really involved at Haklo this summer. Grace not only resents her sister's status as sole trustee, she's mad because Blythe squashed support for her lover's art exhibition. Erik Judd lost his job and Robbie Powell's been furious ever since. Cole's miserable about being pushed out as a vice president. Francis's budget has been whacked. Peter may be looking at the end of in-house publications if Blythe decides to use a local agency and that might ease him out of his job. Or maybe my first instinct was right and Anne Nesbitt's wrong. Maybe one of the overtures at the workplace wasn't gracefully deflected and somebody was infuriated by Hollis's usual approach to a good-looking woman."

Nela looked discouraged. "What troubles me is that when I think of everyone at Haklo, I see nice faces."

"I do, too. We have to hope Katie gets a break somewhere. She's smart. If anyone can ever figure out the truth, it will be Katie. She'll put on pressure. Somebody will crack. The murderer has to be in a panic now. Everything's spiraled out of control." He reached out, gently touched her shoulder. "Tomorrow will be better." He gathered up his papers. He wished he believed his words.

He stood and Nela came to her feet.

He looked down at her. She seemed small and vulnerable to him. He wished he could take her in his arms, reassure her, lift her face . . . "Yeah. Well. I better let you get some rest." He needed to leave before he said things he knew she didn't want to hear from him now. The best he could manage sounded lame and awkward. "We'll get through this."

Jugs twined around his ankles. He looked down, managed a grin. "Hey, Jugs, you'll look after the lady, right? Promise?"

"I'll count on Jugs." She managed a smile, said swiftly, "We'll talk tomorrow."

As the door closed behind him, he carried with him a memory of her smile.

As Nela picked up the coffee mugs, she heard a clatter behind her. She knew the sound now, Jugs pushing through the cat flap. She turned and glimpsed the end of a black tail as the flap dropped. It would be interesting to know what Jugs did when he was outside, what he saw, the thoughts in his mind. Was he watching Steve climb into his car and leave? Or was he immersed in stalking a mouse? Were mice frisking about on cold January nights? Surely a sensible mouse was ensconced behind a wall or nestled in a corner of the garage.

She knew Jugs's evening pattern now. He would return in a little while. She would be glad of his company tonight. They'd already established a routine, Jugs padding into the guest bedroom just before she shut and locked the door.

Nela rinsed out the mugs and the coffeepot. The apartment seemed empty without Steve. He brought strength and calmness and she wished that he were still here.

A knock sounded at the front door.

Nela dried her hands and stepped out into the living room. Had he left something behind? But the coffee table by the sofa was clear. As she walked toward the door, she felt eager. Perhaps he had something more to say. Perhaps they could talk for a while yet and she could feel safe and content. He hadn't left anything behind, except a vivid memory of his presence. She smiled. Not a coat certainly. She would have to encourage him to wear a coat.

She had left the porch light on for him to see his way to his car. She opened the door and felt an instant of déjà vu. Blythe Webster had worn her elegant mink coat over pajamas on Friday night. She again wore her mink, but tonight the coat was open to reveal a black sweater and slacks and ankle-

405

high black leather boots, not pajamas and sneakers.

She appeared haggard, worried. "I couldn't relax and I decided to walk on the terrace. I saw Steve Flynn come down the stairs. I suppose he wanted more information about Louise since your office was next to hers. Anyway, I thought maybe he'd told you more about what's happened. I can wait and see what's in the paper in the morning, but I'm so upset about Louise. Do you mind telling me what he said?"

Nela understood. When something horrible happens, facts don't ease the pain, but there is a desperate hunger to know what there is to know.

Blythe's tone was almost beseeching. "If it isn't too late . . ."

Blythe's unexpected diffidence surprised Nela. Here was a woman who was accustomed always to having her way, accustomed to ordering, not asking.

"Of course." Nela held the door wide. "Please come in." She stood aside for Blythe to enter, then closed the door and led the way to the living room. Nela sank into the easy chair.

Blythe sat on the edge of the sofa, facing Nela. Behind her stretched a shining expanse of flooring. The bookcase next to the front door was bare tonight. Nela never saw it without remembering Marian's Coach bag and the secret it had held.

Light from a lamp beside the sofa emphasized Blythe's haggard appearance. One eyelid flickered. Lines were grooved deep beside her lips. Perched there, she looked small in the long luxurious coat.

Nela abhorred fur coats, sad that small living creatures were killed when cloth would serve as well. But tonight she found the huddled figure on the sofa pitiable. Blythe looked as if she would never be warm.

"I'm afraid none of us know very much." Nela marshaled her thoughts, made an effort to repeat all that Steve had said.

Blythe hunched in the big coat, absorbing every word. Her features remained tight and stiff. She looked much older than her late thirties.

A clatter.

Blythe's eyes flared. She jerked to look behind her. "Oh, it's the cat."

Jugs stood just inside the front door, the pupils of his eyes huge from his foray into darkness. He sat down just past the bookcase.

Nela smiled. "It's too cold out tonight even for Jugs."

Blythe let out a sigh. Her tense posture relaxed as she once again faced Nela.

Nela knew nothing she could share would ease the core of Blythe's distress, but she laid out the possibilities, one by one. ". . . and everything may hinge on why Anne Nesbitt's car was set on fire." Nela leaned forward. "Perhaps you can help. You were there every day. You know these men. Did one of them make a play for Anne Nesbitt?"

Not a muscle moved in Blythe's face. "Anne Nesbitt." Blythe's tone was cold.

Jugs paced silently across the floor, stood a few feet behind the sofa. He looked at Nela with his huge green eyes. *". . . angry . . . angry . . . danger . . ."*

Nela stared at Jugs.

Anger.

Abruptly, Nela felt the presence of anger, hot as flickering flame. When she mentioned Anne Nesbitt . . .

Bill once told her that you could never fool a cat. A cat always knew exactly what someone thought and felt. There might be a smile, a face ostensibly expressing sympathy or welcome, but a cat knew the truth. A cat knew if there was sadness or heartbreak or fear or horror or love or hatred.

Or anger.

Slowly Nela turned her gaze to Blythe.

The older woman's posture hadn't changed, but naked now, unmistakable in that hard tight face, were eyes that glittered with fury.

Nela's recoil was instinctive. She reached to push up from the chair.

"Don't move." Blythe's right hand darted into the capacious pocket of the fur coat. In an instant, she held a black pistol aimed at Nela.

Nela sat rigid in the pretty chintz-covered chair, her hand gripping the arm. Was the feel of chintz beneath her fingers the last sensation she would ever know? Nela's chest ached. The hole in the barrel of the big gun seemed to expand. The gun never wavered in the grip of the small hand with brightly painted, perfect nails.

Nela looked into the eyes of death. "You hated Anne Nesbitt. Because of Hollis."

Blythe went to Kansas City and met Hollis, a handsome, lanky man who made women feel admired, attractive, desirable. It was in his nature. The woman across from her responded, but she didn't see that the admiring glances, the soft touch of a hand were meaningless. She'd once lost love, her father buying off a man she thought cared for her. She was lonely, hungry for a man. Marian Grant and Louise Spear saw the danger. Hollis's easy charm was automatic, any woman, anytime. Blythe thought he was hers for the taking and Hollis turned interested eyes on Anne Nesbitt.

Blythe's lips quivered. "We danced at the hotel. I thought . . . Oh, it doesn't matter what I thought. He was a lie. He made a fool of me. I brought Hollis here. I made him the director, introduced him to everyone, bought him a car, and then he went after that sluttish girl, had the nerve to tell me how beautiful she was. I thought when she left . . . but that's when I realized he'd been involved all along with Abby. She's a simpering, stupid, irritating fool. A nobody. I could have fired her, but I knew a better way." There was a flicker of malicious delight across her face. "No one ever suspected me." She was pleased with herself.

Nela's thoughts whirled. She was cornered. There was no one to help her, no one to save her. But she would fight. At the end, she would lunge to her feet, slam the coffee table hard against Blythe's legs, jump to one side. That's when the gun would roar. Perhaps if she kept Blythe talking long enough, she could take her by surprise. She'd keep her talking . . . "You're very clever, Blythe. You planned everything well. You must have felt confident that Abby would be blamed for the vandalism, but Marian saw you put the necklace in her office."

"Marian threatened me." Blythe's voice trembled with outrage. "She said I had to 'find' the necklace, say it had never been stolen. She said I had to step away from Haklo, leave the running of it to Hollis, move to the house in La Jolla."

A clatter at the door.

Blythe heard the sound behind her. This time she didn't look around. "I always hated Marian. She stole Dad from Mother. I had to be nice to her, but I hated her. She thought I would do whatever she asked. She said she had hidden the necklace."

This time it was not Jugs entering through the cat flap. Jugs crouched a few feet behind the sofa, tail flicking. His head turned to watch the figure coming inside.

Nela forced herself to look at Blythe, not at the figure that stepped inside, face somber. But there might not be hope there for Nela, either. "You took Abby's skateboard and put it on Marian's steps. You knew when she jogged and you were there to get the skateboard after she fell."

Blythe looked satisfied for an instant, then anger again distorted her features. "Marian told me the necklace was in a safe place. I was wild all week. I was afraid to go in the apartment during the daytime. There's always someone around, the housekeeper or one of the maids. I couldn't take a chance someone would see me. They knew I didn't like Marian. I hadn't been to Marian's apartment in years. At night your stupid sister was here and then I thought I had my chance Friday night. I had to find the necklace. No one told me you were in Marian's apartment."

How ironic that Blythe had desperately searched the apartment and Marian's office only to find the necklace, courtesy of Nela, lying a few days later in the center of her desk.

Near the front door, Grace Webster listened, too, her rounded face drawn and sad.

"I found the necklace in Marian's purse." Nela nodded toward the bookcase by the door, felt a lurch inside, prayed that Blythe didn't turn around.

Blythe's gaze never wavered, nor the gun in her hand. Another spasm of anger twisted her face. "Her purse?" There was a sudden blinking of Blythe's eyes. "Oh. A safe place. I thought she meant she'd hidden it away. I should have taken her purse but I didn't know anyone was here and I couldn't afford to be seen. I thought about taking the purse as I ran across the room. If only I had."

Grace Webster, slim and athletic in a rose turtleneck and gray slacks, walked nearer on the thick soles of running shoes.

Nela continued with only a flicker of a glance at Grace. "I put the necklace on your desk Monday night. You found it there Tuesday morning and thought you had another chance to destroy Abby, but Louise saw you, didn't she?" Now Louise's troubled words were clear. *She shouldn't have been there. But I saw her . . .* Louise wouldn't have been surprised if Abby had come down to her office from upstairs, but the trustee didn't visit the offices of employees. Not usually. Not except the day Blythe came because she knew Louise lay dead upstairs and she wanted her found. Staff came to the trustee's office. Blythe shouldn't have been there . . . but she was.

Blythe sagged inside the big fur coat. Tears trickled down her cheeks. "Louise came to my office Wednesday and said she was glad I'd asked you to find out more about Marian's last day. Then she asked if I'd seen anything when I came to Abby's office. I couldn't have her tell anyone I'd gone to Abby's office. I told her I'd been worried and had dropped by to talk to Abby but she wasn't there. I told Louise I'd see if Abby

413

would meet with us upstairs a few minutes after five. Just before five, I slipped upstairs and put one of the clubs just inside the door. I left the light on. I waited until I thought everyone had left. I put on my coat and gloves and stopped at Louise's office and said we could run upstairs and talk to Abby. We went inside and I said that Abby must have just stepped out and we'd wait for her. Louise walked over to look at the exhibit of clubs. I came up behind her . . ."

Grace Webster briefly closed her eyes, opened them. She looked at the woman huddled on the couch, the woman who was her sister. There were memories in Grace's haunted gaze, perhaps of an older sister pushing her on a swing, of family dinners, of sunny days and laughter, of a special link between an older and younger sister that quarrels might fray but never quite destroy.

Grace came around the end of the sofa. Her eyes dropped to the gun, rose to her sister's face. "You didn't know what you were doing, did you, Blythe?"

Nela looked into Grace's stricken blue eyes, saw a warning, a command.

"Gracie." Blythe still aimed the gun at Nela, but she looked up at her sister in dismay. "Gracie, why are you here? You have to go away. I can't let her tell the police."

"Everything's all right, Blythe. There won't be anything for her to tell."

Nela felt a rush of terror.

"You won't remember anything about your conversation with Nela. We'll go home now and call Dr. Wallis. You've simply been confused. Sometimes you get confused." Grace spoke with emphasis. She stared into her sister's eyes. Slowly she edged between Nela and the pistol in Blythe's hand.

Nela understood. Grace was telling her sister that she could pretend confusion, perhaps mental illness.

"Dr. Wallis will explain to the police that you are so upset you didn't know what you were saying." Grace was soothing, calm. "Everything will work out. Come home now."

Blythe shook her head. "Oh, no. I have to make sure she never tells anyone."

"Hush now. Don't talk anymore. I'll take care of everything."

Blythe bent to look beyond Grace at Nela. "She'll tell the police."

"That's all right. People can say anything, but there's no proof." Grace's voice was reassuring. "People don't know about your blackouts —"

Nela saw the surprise in Blythe's face and knew there were no blackouts.

"— and how sometimes you do things and don't even remember."

Nela watched the sisters. Blythe didn't have blackouts. But Grace was trying to save both Nela and her sister. The Webster money would probably protect Blythe from the death penalty, but no matter what happened, Blythe was burdened by guilt, would always be burdened.

Grace held out her hand. "I'll take the gun now."

"Why are you here?" Blythe was querulous.

"I saw you leave the house. When you didn't come back, I thought I'd better see. I couldn't find you anywhere, but your car was in the garage. I looked everywhere and finally I knew there was only one more place you could be. Now" — she was firm — "give me the gun. I'll put it back in the safe."

Slowly Blythe handed the gun to Grace.

"Thank you. The safe's a better place for it, don't you think?"

Grace held the gun in one hand, gripped Blythe's elbow with the other. It seemed to take forever for them to cross the space between the sofa and the door, Blythe talking faster and faster, words spewing, "Louise would have told someone . . . I had to keep her from talking . . . I didn't have any choice . . . Gracie, you see that I didn't have any —"

The front door closed.

Shaking, Nela came to her feet, struggling to breathe. She ran to the door, shoved the wedge into place, then raced across the room to the telephone. She yanked up the receiver, punched 911. "Help, please come. Blythe Webster has a gun. Her sister took the gun, but please come. One Willow Lane, behind the Webster mansion. Blythe Webster killed Marian Grant and Louise Spear. Please hurry. Get Detective Dugan. Grace Webster took the gun —"

Muffled by distance, Nela heard shouts. She strained to listen over the calming voice on the telephone. "Detective Dugan is off duty. Please explain . . ."

Jugs stopped a few feet from the door, shoulders hunched, ears flicked forward. His acute hearing picked up movement and sound long before anyone in the apartment would know someone was coming up the stairs.

Nela now heard thudding on the steps.

The doorknob rattled. "Open up." Blythe's shout was angry.

Nela gripped the phone. "Hurry, please hurry." Where was Grace? Why had Blythe returned?

"Ma'am, remain calm. A car is en route. The car will be there quickly. If you can —"

Nela broke in. "There's a murderer trying to get inside."

Blythe's voice was hoarse and desperate. "Let me in. I have to come in. This place belongs to me. Open the door." The pounding on the door was loud, sounded like the hard butt of a gun against wood. Had Blythe managed to wrest the gun away from Grace?

"Blythe, stop." Grace's voice rose above the banging on the door.

The pounding stopped. "Go away, Grace. I can't talk to you now. You mustn't interfere. I have to be safe. Don't you see? Go away."

A shot and a panel of the door splintered.

Nela ducked down behind the desk.

Sirens wailed.

Nela's head swung back and forth. She needed a weapon. Her only chance was to find something to use as a club. When Blythe shot away the doorknob, Nela would strike. Stumbling to her feet, she ran to the small table beside the sofa, grabbed the brass table lamp, yanking its cord from the socket.

She was midway to the door when a deep voice shouted, the sound magnified by a

megaphone, "Police. Drop that weapon. Police."

Nela stopped and listened.

"Drop that gun."

A final shot exploded.

19

The wind ruffled Steve's hair, tugged at his old gray sweatshirt. The day was beautiful, the temperature nudging sixty. "We'll stop in Norman, have lunch. There's a great new Mexican restaurant downtown. We'll have plenty of time to meet Chloe and Leland's plane."

Nela liked the way Steve sounded, as if they were going to a fun place and there would be fun things to do. Each day that passed eased some of the horror of the night that Blythe held a gun and planned for Nela to die. Grace had done her best, but Blythe was wily. She'd grabbed the gun from Grace, struck her sister and stunned her, then whirled to run back to the garage apartment stairs.

When the police came, when voices shouted out of the night and lights flooded the stairway, Blythe had lifted the gun to her own head. When they gathered around her on the concrete patch below, her body lay quite near where Marian Grant had been found.

Nela pushed away the memories. She didn't have to think about Blythe now or about Haklo and its future or whether Chloe would want to return there to work. She did have to make plans, for her and for Jugs. Ever since that dreadful night when she'd called Steve, she and Jugs had stayed at Mim Barlow's house. But Nela had to decide soon where to go, what to do.

On the highway, Steve turned those bright blue eyes on her. "You won't go back to California."

Was he asking? Or telling?

Or hoping?

The employees of Thorndike Press hope you have enjoyed this Large Print book. All our Thorndike, Wheeler, and Kennebec Large Print titles are designed for easy reading, and all our books are made to last. Other Thorndike Press Large Print books are available at your library, through selected bookstores, or directly from us.

For information about titles, please call:
(800) 223-1244

or visit our Web site at:
http://gale.cengage.com/thorndike

To share your comments, please write:
Publisher
Thorndike Press
10 Water St., Suite 310
Waterville, ME 04901

IT SEEMS LIKE ONLY YESTERDAY

IT
SEEMS
LIKE ONLY
YESTERDAY

*Memoirs of Writing,
Presidential Politics,
and the Diplomatic Life*

JOHN BARTLOW MARTIN

William Morrow and Company, Inc.
New York

Copyright © 1986 by John Bartlow Martin

Library of Congress Cataloging-in-Publication Data

Martin, John Bartlow, 1915–
  It seems like only yesterday.

  1. Martin, John Bartlow, 1915–   —Biography.
2. Authors, American—20th century—Biography. 3. United
States—Politics and government—1945–   . I. Title.
PS3525.A7525Z465 1986   818′.5409 [B]   86-12417
ISBN 0-688-06209-1

Printed in the United States of America

First Edition

1 2 3 4 5 6 7 8 9 10

BOOK DESIGN BY RICHARD ORIOLO

TO OUR CHILDREN, CINDY, DAN, AND FRED

CONTENTS

PART ONE

FAREWELL
TO INDIANAPOLIS

ONE

BACK HOME IN INDIANA

1.

On a warm spring morning in 1938, I was sitting on the sand at Fort Myers Beach, Florida, with my then wife, Barbara. We had been married a little more than a year; I was only twenty-two, less than a year out of college. The sand at Fort Myers Beach is white and powdery, and when trod by many feet it compacts until it is like concrete, as nowadays, when thousands of people jam Fort Myers Beach; but at that time we were almost the only ones there. A couple who looked a little older than we, maybe thirty, came along and sat down to talk. The man's name was Jack DeWitt and it turned out he was a writer. All my life I had wanted to be a writer, but I had never even met one. I asked what he wrote and how he did it. He wrote for the fact detective magazines, which I had never heard of. They were not the pulps—not, that is, fiction magazines containing mystery and western fiction printed on rough pulp paper—nor the big slicks like *The Saturday Evening Post*. Instead, the fact detective magazines published true accounts of criminal cases (or so they claimed). DeWitt gave me the name of an editor of two fact detective magazines in Chicago who was open to suggestions from unknown writers, Harry Keller. I had been covering police for the

Indianapolis Times; I'd try Keller. I told DeWitt we were on our way home after spending several months in the Dominican Republic and I had thought I'd try to write a piece about Generalissimo Trujillo, the Dominican dictator. I told him Trujillo was running a true totalitarian state—secret police, torture chambers, prisons full of political prisoners. Recently Trujillo's troops had massacred some twelve thousand Haitians.

DeWitt thought this sounded like something that would interest *Ken,* then a magazine published by *Esquire,* a magazine of liberal bent, opposed to all dictators, and given to exposés. DeWitt asked what I meant when I said the soldiers under Trujillo were all-powerful. They could, I said, do anything; and I related how one night at a dance in a small town in the interior I had seen a soldier take a teen-age girl by the hand and disappear with her into the darkness. (Actually I had no way of knowing whether she was afraid of him or enamored of him.) DeWitt told me to embellish that story and use it to personify the military's power.

He went on to tell me how to organize the piece—start with the Haitian massacre or the girl episode, give a few paragraphs on the republic's history, relate Trujillo's origins and how he came to power, describe his regime, and end by explaining the United States' policy toward him.

Soon Barbara and I took a bus back to Indianapolis. I don't believe I ever saw Jack DeWitt again. But that was for me the start of a lifelong career of writing.

2.

I had been raised in Indiana and gone to DePauw University, a small Methodist college in Greencastle, Indiana. Barbara and I had met there when she was a freshman and I a junior. I had attended a big public high school in Indianapolis that was mostly vocational, for the children of workingmen; she had attended what was then called a small exclusive girls' school in Evanston, Illinois. She was the only freshman girl at DePauw who wore a full-length mink coat. She lived with her wealthy parents in Evanston, the first suburb on the North Shore north of Chicago, then fashionable. Her house seemed to me a mansion; her father was a wealthy manufacturer who drove a big Packard, her mother was formal and distant, nei-

ther of them drank. Barbara's older sister had made her debut at the Stevens Hotel, later the Conrad Hilton, and Benny Goodman had played for it, and she had married a rich young man, all according to her parents' plan. Barbara and I broke up her parents' well-ordered world. Barbara took me to the Blackhawk Restaurant in the Chicago Loop, where one of the big swing bands of that period, Bing Crosby's brother's band, was playing and where the waiters spoke with Italian and East European accents I had never heard in Indiana; an exotic place. Chicago, so big, so gorgeous, so powerful, so exciting, so glistening by the shore of the inland sea—Barbara undertook to show me Chicago. I discovered later that she knew little about the real Chicago—only the nightclubs and the shops like Saks on upper Michigan Avenue. But at the time she seemed to be ushering me into a wonderland, and I fell in love with Chicago, a love affair that never ended.

Barbara was not beautiful but she was a gorgeous lascivious blonde. We became engaged. We were wildly in love—or so we thought: How we knew at that age I cannot now imagine. She was vulnerable, easily hurt, and she had an almost childlike manner. She came from what was called polite society; I did not; she taught me manners and how gentlefolk talk—when asked a question, for example, you respond, "No, I don't," not with the flat twangy boorish Indiana "Nah." She was no intellectual and she dropped out of college after one year. She feared her father was trying to prevent our marriage so she came to Greencastle and wanted to get married at once, and we did—were married on a bitter February night in 1937 by a justice of the peace in his shabby quarters upstairs over a saloon on the deserted town square. I went to Chicago and told her father we were married. He said only, "You married her, now support her." My own parents obtained a divorce at about that same time.

As editor of the DePauw newspaper and string correspondent for the *Indianapolis Times,* I was earning enough money to rent a small furnished room for us off the campus. In May the *Times* offered me a full-time job as a reporter; I arranged to complete my courses in absentia and Barbara and I moved to Indianapolis. I was making $22.50 a week at the *Times.* Barbara's father relented and gave us money to buy furniture for a one-room apartment.

My first assignment at the *Times* was to cover police. The city

editor said only, "Report to Heze Clark at the police station at 4
A.M. tomorrow. He'll tell you what to do." Clark had been the
Times's police reporter for as long as anyone could remember, a
gruff, squat man who couldn't write an English sentence but was
probably the most thorough collector of facts on police cases I ever
knew. He was switching to the afternoon shift; I would replace him
on the 4-A.M.-to-noon shift. In a few days he taught me all I needed
to cover police. Years later, when I was teaching at Northwestern
University's Medill School of Journalism, I marveled how a student
could spend ten thousand dollars and a full year learning less than
Heze Clark taught me in a few days free. And I am sure the same
could be said of any other journalism school.

The *Times*, a Scripps-Howard paper, was the third paper in town.
The other two, Republican and stodgy, were bigger and more profitable; the *Times* was lively, aggressive, liberal, and leaning Democratic, more fun to read and to work on. The *Times* hired you young,
paid you little, and promoted you fast. At twenty-three I was covering the Indianapolis City Hall.

That fall I fell ill with pneumonia, and the doctor advised me to
spend the winter in a warm climate. Barbara's father gave us money
and her uncle, a travel agent, booked us for a thirty-day Caribbean
cruise on a freighter that carried about eight passengers. I was feeling so expansive that I bought a copy of *Harper's* magazine, at fifty
cents; a luxury I could not ordinarily afford, and we took a train to
Louisiana. I had never been so far from home. Our ship called at
several ports in Puerto Rico, then headed homeward, but we didn't
want to go back to the Indianapolis winter that soon, so when the
boat stopped at Ciudad Trujillo—as Santo Domingo, the capital of
the Dominican Republic, was then called—we got off. We knew
nothing whatever about the Dominican Republic; we picked it only
because the other passengers on our boat were Texans getting off
there to drill for oil. All this was pure chance, and it led us to Jack
DeWitt, the writer in Florida, and to writing an article on Trujillo
for *Ken*.

3.

When we returned to Indianapolis early that spring, I went back to
the *Times*, reporting and also doing rewrite, that is, working on the

city desk, taking telephone calls from reporters, making notes on what they reported, and writing the stories for the paper. I wrote fast and apparently satisfactorily, and Norman Isaacs, the managing editor, later a well-known editor and educator, told me I should be writing magazine, not newspaper, pieces.

I was trying, writing weekends and nights, not an easy task with a full-time job. I wanted to write a novel and a Caribbean travelogue but I needed money. Using Jack DeWitt's name, I wrote to Harry Keller, the editor in Chicago of *Official Detective Stories* and *Actual Detective Stories of Women in Crime,* and he invited me to submit outlines of criminal cases I might write for him. I wrote to the editor of *Ken*—Arnold Gingrich, founder of *Esquire*—and outlined the piece on Trujillo. He said he'd been looking for a piece on Trujillo. I did the piece fast and sent it in. He sent it back for rewrite. This time I took my time, and I elicited the aid of my *Times* city editor, Vern Boxell, who taught me something about tightening up writing. I did as DeWitt had suggested: invented a girl who was raped by a soldier. I never again invented an episode in a serious magazine piece, for it is a shabby trick, a counterfeit substitute for solid reporting. This time *Ken* bought the piece for $150. I carried the voucher from that first story check in my wallet until it wore out. As the years pass, patterns emerge in one's life. Here was one in mine: writing, and traveling to the Dominican Republic. That doomed beautiful island republic played a crucial role for me lifelong.

Late that summer Barbara's mother died, and her father asked us to come and live with him in Evanston. The *Times* refused me a leave of absence so I resigned, and moved with Barbara into her father's house. A mistake.

Her father was a self-made conservative Republican businessman. He was fond of saying, "I went to the college of hard knocks," and capable of singing a jingle to the tune from *Snow White and the Seven Dwarfs:*

> *Heigh ho, heigh ho,*
> *We're in the CIO,*
> *We pay our dues*
> *To the goddamned Jews,*
> *Heigh ho.*

I was trying to write but finding it hard going in that house. I had several ideas for stories for *Ken;* I went down to Chicago to the towering lakefront Palmolive Building at the head of Michigan Avenue and talked to the editors of *Ken.* They were not enthusiastic—the ideas were not really worked out, were only glimmerings of ideas. I went also to see Harry Keller of *Official Detective.* By contrast to the glistening tower of *Esquire-Ken,* Keller's office was in a dingy warehouse district on Plymouth Court near the Dearborn Street railroad station. Keller was a tall bald man who looked to be in his forties. He encouraged me to write for him—at present he had no reliable contributor in the Chicago area. I told him about an old murder case in Indianapolis, and he thought it sounded promising. He introduced me to his two associate editors, Mickey Maloney and Phil Weck, and after work I went across the street with them to drink beer in a dark little saloon.

I wanted to write for Keller but did not know how to get started. I had no sources in Chicago, knew no detectives or lawyers. And I didn't know Chicago itself at all except for the Loop and that glittery strip on Michigan Avenue that Barbara knew. Occasionally she and I went down to the Loop to drink and dine and dance. But it wasn't much fun, perhaps because we were spending her father's money, not mine.

One morning when I woke up, Barbara was not in her bed beside mine. I dressed and went downstairs and after the maid brought coffee, I asked Barbara's father where she was. "She's gone," he said. I asked where. "To Columbus." That was the hometown of the young man she had intended to marry before she met me.

When she came home a couple of days later, she told me she no longer loved me and had gone to Columbus to see if she could marry her old flame but had found him married to somebody else. She didn't know what she was going to do. But she thought I should leave and she and I should get a divorce. That night in our bedroom I pleaded with her to change her mind. She would not. Then she laughed at me and said I was being silly, she didn't love me anymore. I did not understand it but accepted it as though I did. Again, I wonder how we thought we knew—she was then, I believe, not quite twenty-one, I twenty-three. I have since come to someone else's definition of love—love is what you've been through together

—and we had been through little then. (And yet for a long time I could not shake the memory of her lying naked with me in an apartment fold-down bed in the hot Indianapolis summer night.) In any case, next day I packed and she drove me down to Chicago, to the office of Harry Keller. We said goodbye, she in the car, I standing in the cobblestone gutter, and she drove off.

I went into Keller's office and told him I was leaving my wife. He thought it might be hasty. I told him it wasn't my idea and I had no choice. I told him I wanted to go to Indianapolis, do legwork on the old murder case there, then come back to Chicago, and he indicated that if I did the story well he'd buy it. I thought I could—by this time, from reading his magazines and talking at length with Mickey Maloney and Phil Weck, I had learned a good deal about how stories for these magazines were put together. Then Keller said he could see I was taking this pretty hard and he told Maloney to take the rest of the afternoon off and go across the street and drink beer with me until train time. I never forgave Barbara's defection but never ceased being grateful to her for introducing me to a wider world than Indianapolis.

4.

Most people who write their memoirs seem to have had happy childhoods. I hated mine. Many seem to regard the years of their youth as the easiest years of their lives. Mine were the hardest. Therefore, of both childhood and youth, I will say only what is necessary. My parents' forebears had come from the rural part of the crucial pioneer triangle where Indiana, Ohio, and Kentucky come together, and I was born on August 4, 1915, in a house in Hamilton, Ohio, but we moved to Indianapolis when I was three or four. My father was a contractor. I did not like him much when I was young, and he was disappointed in me, for I read all the time. Although he himself read nothing but the *Engineering News-Record,* he nonetheless bought me books for Christmas. He was a tall angular man just over six feet, a willful stubborn man, a bluff loud man in a noisy and rough industry from which I shrank. One afternoon he came home early, his face scratched, his nose and mouth bleeding, his eye puffed up, his suit torn and dirty. "I got whupped," he said and told my mother and me how: An ironworkers' union boss had come to

his job to organize the workers, my father had "run him off the job," the union boss had refused to go, they had fought, and the union boss had knocked my father down and beaten him up and stomped him.

He had not finished high school; the eldest of three sons, he had had to quit school and go to work at thirteen when his father died. He began as a carpenter, became a carpenter contractor, became a general contractor, and in the 1920's became well-to-do. Even more to his credit, he refused to join the Ku Klux Klan, not easy in Indiana in the 1920's, for the Klan controlled Indiana, some of my early boyhood memories are of watching a seemingly endless parade of robed and hooded Klansmen marching around Monument Circle in Indianapolis in dead silence. The grand dragon of Indiana proclaimed, "I am the law in Indiana," and he was. Nearly every businessman belonged to the Klan. My father disliked everything about it, just why he never explained. He was a lifelong Democrat, as his father had been. Some Saturday nights my father, accompanied by my mother and me, would drive down to Indiana Avenue, the heart of Indianapolis's segregated Negro district, and pull up grandly in his long blue Buick touring car in front of a crowd of Negroes hanging around outside a pool hall and call out, "Which ones of you niggers wants to go to work on Monday?" There was no malice in it; it was his way of hiring labor. One of his regular workers asked him for a loan on Monday; my father said, "But you just got paid on Saturday—what'd you do with it?" The Negro said, "Mr. Martin, you ain't never been a nigger on Saturday night."

The buzz of insects, the whir of the lawnmower, the swish of the garden hose in the long summer evening, the fireflies over the dew-wet grass—this was my Indiana boyhood. This, and "niggers." Because of segregated housing, few Negroes went to grade school where I did; as a boy I feared the few, they could fight too well. My mother taught me that Catholics always build their churches on the tops of hills; she had been taught they were preparing to take over the country and the churches would be their military strongpoints. We lived in a small house on Brookside Avenue. Brookside Avenue—a mean street in a mean city. It was a wide brick street with streetcar tracks and trolley wires, the houses small and wooden, a tumbledown wreck of some stucco "flats," scattered neighborhood

stores. When I was growing up there, our neighbors were a brick-layer, a railroad freight conductor, a minor-league baseball umpire, a painter. Across the street lived a family of Negroes but they did not show themselves on Brookside Avenue; they knew they were not welcome there. Later I brought my college friends to our house by a roundabout route so they would not see the meanness of Brookside Avenue; I was ashamed. My father planned to build for my mother a new house of stone in a "good"neighborhood on the North Side far from Brookside Avenue, but he lost everything in the Depression.

I suppose my childhood was not all bad—my father took me fishing in the spring and summer, and in the fall we went to the country to gather walnuts and hickory nuts, and every Thanksgiving we drove to Anderson, Indiana, to have dinner with my grandmother Bartlow and my mother's sister, Aunt Verl. But most of my childhood memories are dark. My mother was small, quiet, soft, sweet, and always sad. She was a romantic but romantic about her children, life, God, not about her husband—the few times I saw him try to demonstrate affection toward her, she fended him off. For nine years I was an only child. Then my brother Billy was born. Not long after that another brother, Dickie, was born. One Sunday morning when Dickie was about six months old, I found him dead in his crib. My mother dressed his body in his best white dress and a lacy bonnet and brought it downstairs to the front porch, where I was sitting in the wicker swing shaded by the awning, and put his body in my lap and told me to hold it. At least this is what she wrote in the "baby book" she was keeping; my present wife has read it, I have not.

My father doted on my brother Billy, perhaps because there was something wrong with him. I think now he was retarded, but I never heard the word until many years later. He was late learning to walk, he scarcely talked at six and did not enter first grade then. We rarely spoke of his condition except when he learned something like how to clean his hands by wiping them on his overalls—I taught him that playing with him in our sandpile in the backyard, and proudly showed my mother, who said, "See, he's getting better. He's healing." She was a devout Christian Scientist. That was why we never knew what was wrong with Billy—she refused to let a doctor see

him. She would say, "He's God's child," as people called the afflicted in the Dark Ages, and add a Christian Science homily, "God is love."*

In 1931, when I was fifteen, I fell ill with scarlet fever, then a dread disease. I was deathly sick but my mother refused to have a doctor, instead she called her Christian Scientist practitioner and asked him "to work on it." I recovered, but before I did Billy caught it from me. He became even sicker than I, delirious, his body burning red. Again she refused to call a doctor and prayed and she took the streetcar downtown to see the practitioner. Finally, past midnight at the climax, when Billy seemed about to die, my father, unable to stand by doing nothing any longer, burst out, "I'm going to get some medicine," and though my mother protested, he went—alone. When he returned my mother met him at the top of the stairs and said to him, "He's gone, John." I always thought she spoke almost in triumph but surely I was wrong. I was huddled in my bed in my room behind her. Never before had I seen my father, that big strong man, cry. I thought I had killed Billy.

I think it was Billy's death that broke my parents' marriage. It had been in trouble for several years. In the 1920's, my father had had several big construction jobs in Cincinnati and he had taken up with a woman there, he had taken her to the opera at the Cincinnati Zoo and to the Latonia racetrack and to the Hotel Gibson roof garden, where Jan Garber played and where they danced and drank bootleg whiskey, all things my mother abjured, things alien to Brookside Avenue, they had taken me with them. But I do not think it was his woman friend that broke his marriage; it was, rather, losing his business and his son. He had to get away—away from my brother's death, away from Christian Science and my mother, away from failure and no job, away from Brookside Avenue. Though he wanted a divorce he could not afford to keep two households so we three lived together a year and a half with almost the only dialogue among us being carried on by my mother, who was trying to convince me that it was all my father's fault. They quarreled often, "fighting," they called it, and seemed to enjoy it, sometimes she tried to hit him with

* Many years later, my present wife and I discovered that we have what is called Rh factor incompatibility—a blood incompatibility that sometimes results in the birth of deformed or defective children. (First children escape, I believe; subsequent ones do not.) She thinks my brother's condition may have resulted from the same Rh factor incompatibility in my parents, at that time unknown.

her fists, and I have memories of violent scenes, though I may have invented them—I was aways making things up. It is of course possible I have this all wrong, all this about Billy's death and its effect upon my father and upon me.

When Billy died, I was in my third year of high school, and an English teacher had opened a new world for me—modern literature. Throughout high school, and even in grade school, I wanted to write. I tried to write poetry and I sent it to my aunt Verl, who I imagined, wrongly, knew more about poetry than my parents. I had always read a lot but now I put aside Zane Grey and James Oliver Curwood for the authors my teacher sent me to—Hemingway, Dos Passos, Dreiser, O'Neill, Sherwood Anderson, Sinclair Lewis, Faulkner, Mencken, and more. I read them all, some several times, especially Dos Passos' *42nd Parallel* and Thomas Wolfe's *Look Homeward, Angel,* for in the first I found a world I aspired to know and in the second I thought I could see myself. (And also especially *The Sun Also Rises* and *A Farewell to Arms*—later when I met Barbara I thought she resembled the nymphomaniac heroine of *The Sun Also Rises,* Lady Brett Ashley, and perhaps I was right.) I read *The American Mercury* every month. My father called me, derisively, the bookworm. I began writing short stories and a novel and even a play, all imitative of those authors, no doubt, all unpublished and forgotten till now. I studied *Writer's Digest.* It must have been along in here that I knew I wanted to spend my life writing.

Something else happened too. A boy I knew in high school who lived in a working-class neighborhood was the son of a German immigrant ironworker, the first authentic proletarian I had ever known. Wolfgang, as I shall call him here, introduced me to Marx and Spengler, Kant and Nietzsche and Schopenhauer. I could not manage the *Critique of Pure Reason* or *Das Kapital* but I read the others. Wolfgang could roll his own cigarettes with one hand while walking down a railroad track, explaining to me what a gandy dancer was (one was mentioned in a Dos Passos novel). He liked to recite the life histories of Big Bill Haywood and Joe Hill. On many nights he and I sat up late at his house, drinking his father's home brew and talking about the Depression, the union movement, and the Communist party. He tried to convert me to communism. Wolfgang was a member of the Young Communists' League and wanted

me to join. Once he urged me to accompany him to a Communist march in another Indiana town, a "Red Parade," and I intended to go but for some reason did not; the marchers were beaten and jailed. I used to say I didn't go because I had a date with a girl, but to be honest I don't remember why. Actually Wolfgang was more mature than I in many ways and used to explain things to me that I hadn't understood when my girl and I were fumbling around. He was, I now suppose, brilliant. He used to take me walking through the slums of Indianapolis, on the South Side and the West Side, among the unemployed and derelicts, talking about "when the revolution comes." He thought it not far off if the Depression continued. Many people agreed. I had always heard my father talking politics, but Democratic-Republican politics. This was a new political awakening.

I lost track of Wolfgang for many years. One Sunday after World War II he came to see me in my house in a Chicago suburb. He had gone to college, became a nuclear physicist, and during the war worked on the Manhattan Project, developing the atomic bomb. I don't know whether he was still a Communist. He was full of awe at the bomb, "the most important development since the discovery of fire"; but he must have been repelled by our quiet Sunday suburban life, for I never saw him again.

5.

I graduated from high school at sixteen—I had skipped two grades in elementary school. My father had always wanted me to go to an engineering school and go into his business. I had always refused—I wanted to be a writer. He doubted—sensibly—that anything much could come of a career so odd as writing. Now we had to decide. It was not really his decision—he could not afford to send me to college at all, my grandmother Bartlow would have to send me. I applied for admission to Indiana University, but one day shortly before school started a high school friend's older brother, Tom Ochiltree, an upperclassman at DePauw University, told me that if I would go to DePauw instead of Indiana he would get me into his fraternity. So I did. College admission was neither so difficult nor so carefully considered as later, when my own chidren went to school. (Cheaper too—I believe tuition at DePauw was $125 per semester.)

So far as I know, no other member of my family on either side had ever graduated from college.

That first year in college I behaved like a fool—went drinking and whoring in Terre Haute on Saturday nights, played poker and drank in the Delta Chi house and speakeasies on week nights, cut chapel and cut classes. I think now that I had come of age intellectually the last two years in high school but not emotionally and that I simply couldn't handle being away from home, happy as I was to escape Brookside Avenue. In any case, one morning near the end of the year I got drunk alone in my room and made a fool of myself; a fraternity brother who was studying to be a minister reported me to the dean of men, and he expelled me from school.

I went home and told my parents. My father said nothing. My mother said we mustn't tell my grandmother, it would kill her. My father was at home all the time. He had no work. In the 1920's he had plowed his large earnings back into his business and invested them in common stocks. He lost everything in the stock market crash and ultimately he had to put his business through receivership. He refused to declare bankruptcy, considering it dishonorable; eventually he paid off his creditors. That summer he was looking for work, any kind of work. Sometimes he took me with him—they might hire a young fellow where they wouldn't an older man. Once we went at dawn to the Real Silk Hosiery mill not far from Brookside Avenue to be first in line at the employment gate, only to see at opening time the foreman put up a sign on the gate, NO HELP WANTED. In the past, when I have told this story, I have said we went out together at dawn every morning to stand in line at factory gates, but the truth is that we only did it once, it was useless. The lines were long that summer. My father thought things would get better now that Franklin Roosevelt was president, and every time the president gave one of his "fireside chats" my father sat in front of the old Atwater-Kent radio, listening to every word, agreeing vehemently. My father was right. Roosevelt—*there* was a leader! All he did was save our house—the mortgage banker would have foreclosed if Roosevelt's HOLC (Home Owner's Loan Corporation) had not stepped in. All he did was give my father a job—my father, who had bossed so many men on big construction projects, got a job on WPA (the federal Works Progress Administration) as foreman of a

small crew that was making a topographical map of Marion County (Indianapolis). (How you make a topographic map of anything as flat as central Indiana is beyond me, but the WPA worked many wonders.) Roosevelt saved us all.

I was looking desultorily for work myself that summer and a miracle happened: I found it. The father of my school friends was Sam Ochiltree; he was chief of the Indianapolis bureau of the Associated Press and he gave me a job as a stock gummer. My task was to take stock market quotations off a ticker tape and gum, or paste, them onto sheets of paper containing the names of stocks. I was paid nine dollars a week. For several months that was the only money coming into our household. My father bore it silently.

When the NRA—the National Recovery Act—was enacted it set a national minimum wage of $14.50 a week, as I recall, and so I got a raise. I also got promoted to night copyboy. I worked from 3 P.M. till 11 P.M. in the stark bare office filled with chattering Teletype machines. My job was to tear the copy from the machines and distribute it, one copy to the telegraph editor of the *Indianapolis Star,* one to the head of the night AP office who edited it for the Indiana state wire, one to the pony editor who edited it for small newspapers, and so on. If the story was hot I delivered it at a dead run. I loved it. I was working with editors and reporters. Indoors I wore my hat on the back of my head, as had Hildy Johnson in the Hecht-MacArthur play *The Front Page.* I learned to punch a Teletype machine, and they let me punch relief on the state wire when the regular puncher took a coffee break. Once in a while they let me edit copy for the pony editor. I even went to a state political convention with the AP political writer; my job was to run his copy back to the office, but sitting at a press table down front in the big convention hall, I felt as though I were covering the convention. I have seldom been happier than at this time. I hoped it would last forever. But when I asked Sam Ochiltree to make me an editor or a reporter, he said he would not until I had gone back to DePauw and graduated.

So in January or February of 1935, at the start of the spring term, I went back to DePauw. I was glad to leave Brookside Avenue again—my mother and father were both living there but it was hardly a marriage, they slept in separate bedrooms and seldom spoke to each other, often eating dinner with each other in silence;

they were only waiting for him to make enough money to afford a divorce. But though glad to get away, I disdained college. I had been out of school a year and a half and had held a job. I put a good deal of energy into becoming editor of the school paper and working as a string correspondent for the *Indianapolis Times* but I also bore down hard on my studies. I took no more English than was required, concentrated instead on political science, history, and economics. I learned some history and a little economics. But I think I learned less in my entire three and a half years of college than in my last two in high school. And I did graduate (being by then married to Barbara). At about the time we were married, my parents were divorced. Barbara and I were married in 1937. This, I now realize, was only six years after my brother Billy had died. A good deal had happened to me.

6.

So now in the fall of 1938, having left Barbara in Evanston, I was back at my mother's house on Brookside Avenue. I did the legwork on the old Indianapolis murder case I had described to Keller and wrote it and sent it to him, and while awaiting reply I did preliminary legwork on two story ideas I had for *Ken*—a piece on Paul V. McNutt, formerly governor of Indiana, then high commissioner to the Philippines, and an exposé of the Indianapolis 500 race. I visited my father and his new wife in their apartment on the North Side. I liked her, so much jollier than my poor sad mother, now left alone on Brookside Avenue, the scene for us of so much conflict and woe. My father was dubious about my going to Chicago to write; his wife said, "Let him go, John." At about that time the issue of *Ken* that carried my Trujillo piece came out. My father said nothing to me about it, but I learned later that he took a copy downtown and showed it off to his lawyer and his banker and the construction cronies with whom he ate lunch, and years later I found his copy— the Trujillo page number written on the cover in his longhand— among his things when he died. He did not like me much in my teens and my early twenties, nor I him, but long before he died I realized he'd been right at that time, I'd been a fool, and I regained my love and even my respect for my father.

Keller bought the murder story and sent me a check for $175,

about $25 over the going rate. I took the money and went to Chicago alone to become a freelance writer.

The end of a marriage, the start of a career—I thought at the time I simply wanted to get away from Indianapolis and go to the big town, but I think now that I went to Chicago because I wanted to show my divorcing wife that I could succeed in the big town at my chosen work and without her—as though she'd care—and perhaps too because for a time I wanted to be near her and hoped she would change her mind about having fallen out of love. She did not, probably best for both of us; I never saw her again, and a year later I married Fran—and in the forty-six years since, *we* have been through quite a bit together, and I think I can say with more confidence than when we were twenty-two and twenty-four that we're in love.

TWO

CHICAGO: A LONG WAY FROM BROOKSIDE AVENUE

1.

In Chicago, I moved into the Hotel Milner, a sooty old brick hulk at the foot of Rush Street down by the river, a hotel that advertised, "$1 a day, laundry free, we pay cab fare from the railroad station, $5 a week on a monthly basis." It suited me fine. I had nothing but one suitcase and a portable typewriter. I had a room with a bed and through the dirty window a view of the fire escape. For a brief time I again acted like a fool as I had my first year in college—slept most of the day, wrote at night, and drank beer while I wrote. I soon leaned I couldn't make a living that way, and for the next forty-odd years of writing I worked from 9 A.M. to 5 P.M. and never drank between those hours.

I was writing everything—a book-length Caribbean travelogue that I never sold, the two Indiana pieces for *Ken,* a piece on the Black Hand, precursor of the Mafia, for *Esquire.* Those sold. But fact detective stories—Keller's magazines, *Official Detective* and *Actual Detective* (*OD* and *AD,* as we called them)—were the meal ticket. At first, a little timid about going out on the street to do legwork among the forbidding police in the big city, I wrote older cases that I could research in the library. Gradually, I began to work on current stories. Many were byliners for *AD*—stories ghostwritten for

women involved in crimes. For example, a young Polish stickup man shot a man during a robbery; I persuaded his wife to tell me her life story and wrote it under her name. Keller paid her $50, paid me $150. I did a good many of these.

In such pieces, I had to check the facts of the crime with the police and at the criminal court. Doing so I built up a small network of sources who would talk to me—detectives, court clerks, assistant state's attorneys, the coroner. And I began to write fewer byliners and more straight crime stories. Chicago detectives were under standing orders not to talk to reporters without authorization by the police commissioner. They talked to reporters from Chicago papers anyway but not to me. I began hanging around outlying district police stations, then, when I had met some officers, hanging around the Detective Bureau at downtown headquarters. They got used to me, people are always hanging around police stations; Jack Ruby, who killed Lee Harvey Oswald, did. Sometimes I took a bottle of good brandy to a detective or promised to "buy you a hat"—give him a twenty dollar bill. I soon learned that some of my best sources were assistant state's attorneys, who would let me see police reports when detectives wouldn't, and the coroner, since his questioning elicited testimony from detectives that they otherwise would reserve for the trial. Newspaper reporters, naturally, tend to neglect such sources; I cultivated them assiduously, and through them met detectives in the Robbery Detail at headquarters, the "heavy men"—they went after armed robbers who held up banks and currency exchanges at gunpoint.

In all these fact-detective-magazine stories the bare facts were true—So-and-So really had killed someone on x date, and on y date he was convicted and sentenced to z number of years in the penitentiary. Plus the names of the detectives and the state's attorney. All this I checked most meticulously, mindful of libel. The two nightmares in this business were libel and what we called "post office." Post office: At that time the U.S. postal authorities had the power to decide what was obscene and to deny second-class mailing privileges to its publisher. The post office could put a magazine out of business. The trick was to write right up to the edge of the obscene and stop.

Except for the descriptions and a few bare facts of the case, the rest of a seventy-five-hundred-word story was almost pure fic-

tion—invented dialogue, invented or embellished episodes, invented clues, rhetoric. None of this is to say that I could do it with my left hand. Not at all. I worked as hard at this writing as at any I ever did and, given the constrictions of the genre, made it as good as I could. And I thought of what I was writing not as articles but as stories. Thus I learned the uses of description, dialogue, characterization, and perhaps above all narrative pull—that mysterious invisible force that pulls the reader onward. (I still think of my pieces as stories.)

This work was almost perfect training for someone who aspired to write serious fact pieces. After all, I was learning to do legwork, how to interview people. I was learning the real Chicago—the vast checkerboard wards spreading for miles back westward from the lakeshore where dwell both the millions of workingmen in "two-flats"—two-family dwellings—who built Chicago and the thousands of criminals in slums who have given Chicago its reputation. And probably most important of all, I was writing. And slanting stories straight at a market. I have always believed, even later while teaching at journalism school, that writing cannot be taught. It can, however, be learned, by reading and writing. I was learning. And I had the added advantage of talking evenings with Mickey Maloney and Phil Weck; they could tell me why they had rejected a story.

Soon I no longer needed to read *OD* and *AD* but could read what I pleased. What I was reading was almost as important for my future as what I was writing. New books by Steinbeck and Hemingway and Faulkner, old ones by Forster and Huxley. I tried to adapt fictional devices to my crime writing and I began hanging around bookstores, especially Ben Abramson's Argus Bookshop. I was reading *Harper's* and *Life* and dreaming of the day when they would lie on my desk not because I enjoyed them but because I was working for them.

After a time I arranged for an experienced Chicago police reporter to do some of the legwork for me. When I hit my stride, I was writing a million words a year and at first selling a third of them at two cents a word, then selling half, which brought me ten thousand dollars a year, a good income at that prewar time. The two-cents-a-word market, as we called it, wasn't bad. Often, under assumed names, I had three or even four stories in one issue of Keller's maga-

zine. Toward the end Keller was taking just about everything I could write. But by then I was spending more and more time on serious writing. None of this seemed extraordinary to me. I had set out to be a freelance writer and I was one. Looking back, I wonder at my temerity in moving to Chicago to write. Groucho Marx used to tell a relevant story. He related how his father had taught him to swim by throwing him off a dock into deep water. His straight man asked, of course, "Wasn't that hard?" Groucho: "Nothing to it once I got out of that burlap bag." All I needed was to get out of the burlap bag called Brookside Avenue.

2.

OD and *AD* were owned by M. L. Annenberg. Moe Annenberg also owned the *Daily Racing Form,* and it was published in the same place on Plymouth Court as *OD* and *AD,* the only authentic record of the past performances of racehorses in America. At that time, about 1940, there were in Chicago some five hundred illegal handbooks—gambling joints that accepted bets on horses—and they were owned by Al Capone's heirs, called by criminals the Mob or simply the Outfit, by outsiders the Syndicate and today the Mafia. The Syndicate's handbooks were dependent on Annenberg's *Daily Racing Form* and on a telephone and telegraph network that hooked up every handbook in the country with every racetrack in the country. The Syndicate killed the man who had run that network.

During my time at *OD* and *AD,* Annenberg was expanding his publishing enterprises. He started two new magazines—a third crime magazine, *Intimate Detective,* and a "true confession" magazine, *Living Romances.* I now wrote confession stories as well as crime, and for a time I wrote a monthly advice-to-the-lovelorn column for *Living Romances.* Annenberg was also starting *TV Guide;* it became one of the most successful of all magazines. And he bought the *Philadelphia Inquirer.* Keller used to play poker with his son Walter Annenberg and other Annenberg corporate executives. (Walter later became President Nixon's ambassador to the Court of St. James's and frequent host to President Reagan.) I played with them once, but the stakes were far too high for me.

Moe Annenberg became interested in the history of the Molly Maguires, a post–Civil War organization in the Pennsylvania coal fields that has been variously described as a secret fraternal order, a

nascent labor union, and a terrorist and murder gang. Annenberg suggested that Keller send a writer to do a series of stories on the Mollies for *OD,* and Keller sent me. Keller and I had intended perhaps three pieces. But Annenberg became so engrossed in them that he could not get enough, and I believe I strung it out for eleven months. At about this same time Annenberg was convicted of income tax evasion. Before he went to the penitentiary, he asked for advance *OD* galleys to see how the Mollies story came out.

3.

Rush Street, where I lived on the Near North Side, was jammed with little bars, expensive nightclubs, jazz clubs, and gambling joints. Many stayed open all night. Gambling was wide open, protected by the police and politicians and controlled by the Syndicate. Living there you felt the Syndicate was never far away. Harry Keller's wife had been a nightclub singer there, and one night while she was sitting out a number a customer had asked her to dance. The dance ended, and as she walked back alone to her table, gunfire broke out behind her. The man she had just danced with lay dead on the dance floor. When the police came, she told them she never had seen him in her life. In the expensive nightclubs you could see not only well-to-do suburbanites but big-shot Syndicate men with their show girls. Ever since Capone's time, Chicagoans have enjoyed gangster watching. To me it was all new and all exciting, a long way from Brookside Avenue. I am afraid at times I was a little foolish about it. I took up briefly with a man in my hotel who said he was a police reporter. He drove a Cadillac and carried a huge roll of bills and loved to drive close to traffic policemen on rainy nights and splash them and curse them, then speed away. When I discovered he carried a gun, I stopped seeing him.

The rest of the Near North Side lay along Michigan Avenue and up the Outer Drive along the lake to Lincoln Park—the famous Gold Coast. At that time I knew nobody who lived there. West of the Rush Street strip and the Gold Coast, the night plunged into the criminal slums that had spawned the bootleg gangs and the Mafia: Little Italy, hard by the scene of the St. Valentine's Day Massacre, then only ten years into history. These were not the little slums of Wolfgang's and my Indianapolis. These were big, the real thing, mile after splotchy mile of them scattered over the enormous city.

At that time, Chicago was Mecca for all the yearning young men in all the mean little towns all over the Midwest, as it once had been Mecca for their mothers and fathers, now back in the little towns, defeated; the young men didn't know what they were yearning for, standing in the evening by the garden gate, but they felt it every time they heard the evening train go whistling by—somewhere there must be something more than the town they lived in. Chicago? Sherwood Anderson must have felt it too. And now I'd made it to Chicago. I used to walk up Michigan Avenue alone at night, across the river on the drawbridge, past the white-spotlighted Wrigley Building and the Tribune Tower and up the glistening avenue with its lofty spires and serrated skyline under the black night over the lake, traffic flowing, a great dynamo; and I used to think about Chicago: There's a lot of power and money here, a lot going on. I ached to write about it all for serious magazines. I couldn't do it for *OD-AD-ID*. But someday, somehow.

I must be careful here. I am not sure how consciously I was thinking all this. Perhaps it was more of an inchoate longing.

At that time I was consorting with two entirely different sets of friends. One consisted of the *OD-AD-ID* editors, married, with children and suburban houses or outlying apartments. Often on Saturday nights we ate supper in one of their homes and played nickel-and-dime poker and talked about our work. Sometimes Keller and his wife joined us. Keller was a difficult man. He was moody and he often drank too much. Imperious, highly opinionated, he ran his employee's lives to the extent he could. He himself had been married several times. He took his work very seriously and demanded that we do too. When he was not there, we make jokes about it. Keller always chose the titles of stories, and one of his favorites was "The Clew's in the Barrel with Julia"—he insisted on spelling it "clew"—and one of the staff invented a limerick:

> *This murder is mighty peculia,*
> *The Motive in it would foolya;*
> *Hate past endurance?*
> *Or simply insurance?*
> *The Clew's in the Barrel with Julia.*

Mickey Maloney and Phil Weck wanted to write. Weck was a natural writer, with a creative bent, and Maloney had worked several years for United Press. But they were afraid to attempt what I was doing, freelancing—they had mortgages, wives, children; they could not gamble. Eventually Maloney did try it but it didn't work out and he went back to United Press. He and I spent many evenings together, drinking beer and talking about writing. And about politics and the war—when Hitler sent his panzers into Poland, I heard his speech on the radio in my hotel lobby. In the summer Maloney rented a cottage on a lake in far northern Wisconsin and took his family there, and I visited them. All my life I had loved fishing and in Indiana as a boy had dreamed of someday fishing in the northwoods.

My other group of friends at that time consisted of several young married couples, childless, living on the Near North Side or the far South Side. They were jazz enthusiasts but seldom went to nightclubs, being unable to afford it and anyway preferring to sit on the floor in each others' dim-lit living rooms, drinking and playing jazz recordings. They were gay and frivolous. The jobs they held had little to do with their lives, were only ways to earn enough money to pay the rent and buy the beer and the recordings. I enjoyed my frivolous friends but I felt intuitively that my own direction lay more in that of the *OD-AD-ID* editors.

At that time too, usually alone, I was listening to jazz in nightclubs. In high school in Indianapolis I had gone often to what were then called black-and-tans—dance halls that were predominantly Negro but that welcomed white people—in order to listen to big Negro bands playing one-night stands, Louis Armstrong and Fletcher Henderson; and in college late at night we would gather around the radio in the fraternity house to listen to broadcasts of big-name bands from Chicago. And now here I was on the Near North Side of Chicago right in the middle of it. Jimmy McPartland and Wingy Manone and Muggsy Spanier were succeeding each other at the Three Deuces, and Cab Calloway was at a black-and-tan on the South Side, and Benny Goodman at the Stevens or Congress. Anita O'Day was singing at the Three Deuces, my favorite place, and she usually sat with me between sets and several times I took her out before or after her night's work. She was the only girl vocalist I ever

saw who sang more to the band than to the audience. Billie Holiday came to the Three Deuces for a guest appearance, and when she heard Anita sing, she said to me, "Give that lady my purse." I wrote the lyrics of two songs for Anita and I told her if she didn't make it to the big time by the time she was thirty, she was finished. The last I heard she was still going strong in the big time past sixty.

4.

On the rebound from Barbara, I suppose, I was having a string of brief affairs. Some of the girls I met in the jazz clubs, more in the little Rush Street bars, a few in northern Wisconsin. About none was I serious nor, I am sure, were they about me. But on an October Sunday night that year, 1939, something different occurred. I was in The Pub, a little bar across Rush Street from my hotel with sawdust on the floor, frequented by students and young professional people. I was drinking scotch at the end of the bar with Grant Robbins, who in college had introduced me to Barbara. He went over to two couples at the bar. Presently he returned and told me they were trying to remember the Ernest Dowson poem "Cynara"—they had the first line or two but couldn't remember the rest, and he'd told them I'd know it. It happened that I did, and he and I joined the others. Thus, he introduced me to the second of my two wives—the one trying to remember the poem, a pretty little girl called Fran. She was with her date and her brother and his wife. I recited the poem and we stayed for a drink and I got Fran aside and got her telephone number. Next day I called her and on Tuesday took her to dinner at a Near North Side restaurant. That day my divorce from Barbara became final. Fran remembers the date clearly as October 10 because exactly ten years before, James Oliver Curwood had lectured at her grade school and adjured the students to go home and write in their Bibles, "What will I be doing ten years from today?" Fran was conventional enough to do it. She was still growing up, was twenty-one, two years younger than I, but in some ways more mature—and stable—than I. She was slight, not quite five feet tall and one hundred pounds, with brown hair and brown eyes and a strong jaw which, on occasion, she set. Her name was Frances Rose Smethurst, and her parents called her Frances Rose but I called her Fran. She had gone to Lawrence College in Appleton, Wisconsin, for two

years. We began to see each other regularly that winter. She lived with her parents in an old ramshackle but attractive house on a shady street in Elmhurst, a middle-class suburb west of Chicago. Her father was old and stooped, with a white mustache—he had been fifty-one when Fran was born and he was a Spanish-American War veteran—and her mother seventeen years younger. Her father was traffic manager for a can manufacturer. He had had a heart attack many years earlier and his family had regarded him as a semi-invalid ever since. He did not drink and smoked only a few cigars; Fran's mother neither smoked nor drank and strongly disapproved of both. They never raised their voices.

Fran introduced me to her friends from high school and college in Chicago and Elmhurst; I thought them conventional and dull. I introduced her to my friends; she did not like the hard-drinking frivolous set and thought the editors lower middle class. Her family had little money but traced its lineage straight to London. (Her mother teased her father about being descended from the infamous English mass murderer Dr. Smethurst; he teased her about being descended from John Wilkes Booth; neither was true.) Fran liked to sing and dance; I did neither well; she taught me. I taught her to listen to jazz that winter, to play poker that spring, to fish that summer in northern Wisconsin. I took her to Indianapolis to meet my parents—separately—and my aunt Verl in Anderson, and when she returned she told her own mother that my parents were divorced, my aunt was divorced, and so of course was I. It must have been quite a shock. Her mother did not think much of me at the outset.

Having been burned by Barbara, I held something of myself in reserve, I had determined never to fall in love again, in our foolish idiom then, which seemed strange to Fran, though she said little about it, just looked knowing. One night, while I was taking her home, I said to her, "Why don't we get married?" She agreed. I said we'd have to do it this week; I wanted to go north, fishing. She agreed. I took her to her house in Elmhurst, and we wakened her mother and told her the wedding would be Saturday—this was Tuesday—and her mother said she'd have to paint the porch. We were married in the Congregational church in Elmhurst. Today, forty-six years later, we are still married, an idea that would have astonished me at that time (but not Fran). My own

mother and father came to our wedding together. My father had rebuilt his business, made a second start after fifty; whatever it was that had hurt him had healed, and he had come back to my mother, and about the time Fran's and my first child was born, he remarried my mother and took her away from Brookside Avenue and built for her the stone ranchhouse on the North Side on Kessler Boulevard she had always wanted.

The morning after our wedding, Fran and I started driving north. I didn't want to go to Wisconsin, too many tourists; I wanted to go farther north to more remote country, the Upper Peninsula of Michigan, and we picked out an isolated town on the map with a name we liked, Michigamme. The day was cold and rainy. Passing through Wisconsin, Fran fell asleep beside me, covered with a topcoat. Near the town of Pembine the road crossed a narrow bridge at the bottom of a little rise of land, and as we hit the bridge the car skidded. I righted it, nothing happened. I looked at Fran. She was sleeping peacefully. Suddenly I felt a terrifying sense of responsibility. Now I really *was* responsible for her. I had never felt that way about Barbara. As I have said, Barbara had, when I first knew her, reminded me of Lady Brett Ashley in *The Sun Also Rises.* Later, when I read Somerset Maugham's *Of Human Bondage,* she reminded me of that novel's principal female character, Mildred, dumb, unreliable, cruel. And obsessive. Men write novels about the Lady Ashleys and the Mildreds of the world. But, if they are lucky, they marry the Frans. And live happily ever after.

We rented a camp, as cottages and cabins are called in Upper Michigan, at Three Lakes, five miles west of Michigamme. The camp was not much—no electricity, kerosene lamps, no running water, a hand pump, an outhouse. Some honeymoon! But it was on the shore of a beautiful lake and it shared the shore with only a few other camps, and the fishing was excellent, and we met people who remained our friends until they died. We were, without knowing it, setting another lifelong pattern—summers in Upper Michigan.

5.

Two months after Pearl Harbor, our daughter Cindy was born and we rented a little house on a secluded street in Winnetka, Illinois. Something happened: I doubt that Winnetka itself had anything to

do with it, except that it was our first house and we were happier there than before; but the fact remains that it was during these years in Winnetka, 1942–1944, that I began to write my way out of the fact detective field. We began seeing a man I had known in high school, Francis S. Nipp. He had come to Chicago to teach English and work on his Ph.D. at the University of Chicago. In high school he had given me lists of modern American writers and their novels and, like Wolfgang, had spent long evenings with me talking about books. Now he became important to my writing and he stayed important for many years. He and his wife Mary Ellen spent long weekends with us in Winnetka, listening to music and talking about writing. He set me to reading *The New Yorker* regularly—"the best-written and best-edited magazine of all." Francis himself had when younger tried to write but he was no writer (whatever that means). He was, however, a natural editor. More than anyone else at this stage he encouraged me to write serious nonfiction for *Harper's*.

Eight German agents landed on the east coast from submarines with the intention of sabotaging the American light metals industry. They were captured and convicted. One of them, Herbert Haupt, had been raised in Chicago. I proposed to the *Harper's* editors a piece on Haupt's Chicago background. They responded as any magazine would to an unknown writer: They would not make an assignment but they would be interested in reading the piece if I wanted to do it on speculation. I did. And they bought it, my first piece for *Harper's*, published in April 1943.

I am mortified to admit that I didn't do much legwork on that story. I cannot remember that I so much as interviewed Haupt's parents and friends. I fear I wrote the piece mainly from newspaper clippings or from trial transcripts, plus legwork in the Chicago neighborhood where Haupt grew up. At that time I did not really understand what a serious "heavy fact" piece is. It is not a rehash of material taken from newspaper clippings and other magazine pieces, nor a piece based on telephone interviews. Instead, it is an original work and it is based on documents—trial transcripts, congressional hearings, other official papers, correspondence—and above all on personal interviews—long face-to-face interviews with everybody involved, often, in the case of key figures such as Haupt's parents, several interviews each lasting two hours or more. But I didn't know that then.

Soon I did another piece for *Harper's,* this time with more leg-work. A gang of young men and a woman called the Polkadot Gang held up several Chicago taverns and in one robbery shot an off-duty policeman dead. In doing a story on the case for Keller, I had found in court records a probation officer's report on the criminals. Back-ground on their lives for *Harper's*—I pursued its leads. They had lived in a Near West Side slum; it happened I knew a detective there from my fact detective legwork; he supplied more details, took me on a tour of the neighborhood, and taught me about police work and criminal life. All this found its way into the *Harper's* piece, which sold. Still I did not myself interview the robbers themselves, as I did in later years.

At about this time I went to New York and met Frederick Lewis Allen, the editor of *Harper's,* and his associate editors, Russell Lynes, George Leighton, John Kouwenhoven, Jack Fischer, and Eric Larrabee. George Leighton had been handling my pieces. He was an excellent writer and reporter himself and had written a won-derful book about America, *Five Cities.* He had started out to the left of Roosevelt but during the isolationist debate had switched to the side of Senator Robert Taft, and he ended up leaving *Harper's* and working for the Republican Policy Committee in the Senate. (He was the first of several far-left liberals I came to know who over the years switched 180 degrees to far-right conservative. I've never really understood the switch but have wondered if it did not result from some personality instability as well as ideological conversion.) In connection with the Polkadot Gang piece, Leighton suggested I start writing what he called "crime in its social context"—take one of my fact detective cases and flesh it out with heavy fact, throw away the phony detective work, and develop the lives and social backgrounds of the criminals and their victims. Eventually George Leighton's idea of "crime in context" became an important base for my writing career—crime became, for me, simply a way of writing about human beings and our society, a matrix, a prism through which one viewed life.

But at that time, I was still writing a little of this, a little of that—occasional pieces for *Outdoor Life* and *Esquire,* minor pieces for *Harper's.* And always I wrote for the money market—Keller's *OD-AD-ID.* It therefore came as a shock when Keller announced one

night at our house that he and the magazines were moving to Philadelphia permanently. He asked me to go with them. I asked for time to think it over.

I believed we should go. I didn't know how I was to make a living cut off from Keller's *OD-AD-ID*. True, I could stay in Chicago and write crime stories for his magazines. But the market would shrink. I couldn't make a living in other magazines—*Harper's* was paying $250 or $350 for a piece, and while that was more than Keller's 2 cents a word, it took far longer to do a *Harper's* piece. *Outdoor Life* was paying $100 or $150, *Esquire* $150, the same as Keller. Living in Winnetka, we were spending more money than ever before. And we had a child. I didn't see how we could risk it.

Fran disagreed. She had never liked or trusted Keller—it turned out she was right—and now she saw a chance to get free of him. She had confidence that I could make a living by writing, either writing for him at long distance or not writing for him at all, which is what she really preferred. Fran is small but she can be tenacious. She won—I reluctantly agreed to stay. Keller didn't like it. I wondered if I had made the mistake of my life.

6.

Ben Abramson, the Chicago bookseller, not only sold books but also read them and he liked to encourage young writers. At that time some booksellers used to call themselves bookmen, as booksellers no longer do or can. Ben gave me a book I'd never heard of, H. W. Fowler's *Modern English Usage,* and told me to read the article on rhythm. I had never read anything about writing so exciting. I use it yet. I was beginning to take writing seriously, under the guidance of Ben Abramson and Francis Nipp in Chicago, of Frederick Lewis Allen and George Leighton in New York. I had begun to think vaguely of writing a book about the Upper Peninsula of Michigan. Ben Abramson said it might fit into a series of regional books that Alfred A. Knopf was publishing. He would write to Knopf.

When I had been in high school, Alfred Knopf had been one of my idols—Knopf, colleague of H. L. Mencken, publisher of Mencken's *American Mercury* and of European novelists, probably the most distinguished publisher in America. Never had I dreamed I might write for him, might even meet him. I sent him an outline for

a book on Upper Michigan; he sent me a contract, itself as beautifully printed as Knopf's books, and that summer Fran and I went to
Upper Michigan to do the research.

I did a lot of it in bars in the mining and logging towns, talking to
miners and lumberjacks and trappers and union men. Often Cal
Olson, an old man who stayed with us at Three Lakes, took me, introducing me to men who remembered the old days. We concentrated on the Marquette Iron Range and the copper range and the
forestland between. Fran and I did research in the Marquette
County Historical Library. The Marquette County district attorney,
John D. Voelker, had just published, under his pen name Robert
Traver, *Troubleshooter,* a book about some of his cases, and I went
to see him in his hometown, Ishpeming. There was not much law to
practice in Ishpeming unless you worked for Cleveland Cliffs, the
big iron-mining company, or the Northwestern Railroad; and
Voelker, a liberal Democrat, was intuitively on the other side of the
table, on the side of the workingmen and their unions. So he ran for
district attorney and was reelected several times. Voelker was the
only *natural* writer I ever knew. He published rough drafts. His
writing was, basically, yarn spinning. He wrote many books, none in
my opinion, so good as his first, *Troubleshooter.* When he finally was
defeated for reelection, Governor G. Mennen Williams, urged by
labor, appointed him to the Michigan Supreme Court, where he did
a liberal's work in workmen's compensation cases. While there he
published his first novel, *Anatomy of a Murder;* the Book-of-the-
Month Club took it, Otto Preminger made a film of it, and Voelker,
rolling in dough for the first time in his life, resigned from the court
to devote himself full-time to fishing. I felt he had betrayed labor
but who am I to say what he or anyone else should do with his only
life? We remained close friends, and this led by chance to a chain of
events that had an important effect on my life, as we shall see.

Knopf responded promptly and briefly to my manuscript (he was
always prompt and brief)—it was satisfactory and he was putting it
into production. I was disappointed; I'd hoped he would be enthusiastic. Francis Nipp said, "He's published books before." The first
time I met Alfred Knopf he seemed forbidding, even intimidating,
with his memorable head, his dark distinguished face, his Continen-
tal manner, his carefully chosen clothes. But as I came to know him,

I learned there was nothing artificial about him; he was extremely down to earth, with good common sense, not unlike Frederick Lewis Allen. When, not long after I had first met him, Knopf invited Fran and me to his country estate for Thanksgiving dinner, it was as though we were summoned to Valhalla. The turkey was tough, Knopf had to brace himself with one foot on a bench to carve it, and after dinner he played Shostakovich recordings so loudly that he drove us and his other guests outdoors (Paul Gallico and his wife, Thomas Mann unable to come); but Knopf himself seemed wise, approachable, yet still Olympian, and his editor who was cutting the manuscript of *Call It North Country* tossed off a remark about writing I never forgot: "Remember, one beaver trapper is like a hundred." (At least, I hope I haven't forgotten; readers of this book will know.) Knopf was kind to us, two youngsters starting out. I was so overwhelmed by being where I was that I can remember little more about it. But I did get the impression that the money in books was not in writing them but in publishing them—Knopf's estate seemed to me almost baronial.

Call It North Country was published in 1944, the first of sixteen books. I have not reread it—nor, until now, anything of mine after it was published—but I have the impression that it contained the bare bones of Upper Michigan's history, with emphasis on how people lived, heavy on atmosphere and flavor, less a serious work than popular history. But it received good reviews and, for a regional book, sold well, around ten thousand copies, as I recall. It was at this time I decided to use my full name as author on serious writing. Always before, I had been simply "John Martin." But there were at least two other John Martins writing then so I used "John Bartlow Martin." I have since found it too long to print or pronounce, like a pompous Christian divine's, but once I did it I was stuck with it.

7.

In those days you went to New York by train, either the *Twentieth Century Limited* or the *Broadway Limited*. You went down to the railroad station and waited at the gate with the crowd and, when the gate opened, walked through clouds of steam alongside the long train, all Pullman cars, and found your numbered car, and the Negro Pullman porter in white uniform asked your space and, hear-

ing it, called you by name and took your bag and led the way to your roomette, the tiny antiseptic room with its grey steel walls, its gleaming chrome washbowl that popped out of the wall, the heavy windows with their rounded corners, the spongy upholstery, the rust-colored blankets lettered PULLMAN, the little shoebox with a door in the aisle so the porter could get your shoes and shine them during the night and replace them gleaming in the morning. I used to go to the bar car and sit with a drink, watching flames belching from the Gary steel mills, watching industry disappear as the train slid across the flat plain of northern Indiana. Dinner in the diner while crossing Ohio where I was born, white tablecloths and shining silver and smiling waiters, a rose in a bud vase on each table. Then to my room to work awhile at my portable typewriter on a table the porter put in place. Usually I was writing a memo or a story outline for an editor. I would go to the bar car for a nightcap then back to my room, pull the bed down feeling it brush my pajamas, then squeeze into bed and snap off the lights and lie in bed watching the night, listening to the soft clickety-clack of the steel wheels on the steel rails in the night, sleeping. Sometimes I wakened in the middle of the night when the *Broadway* stopped alongside the silent black river flowing past snowy railroad yards, the river formed here at Pittsburgh, the great Ohio, which drained the Midwest, my Midwest. In New York, I always stayed at the Algonquin, at first because of its writers' tradition but later because I came to love its Edwardian elegance and came to know its staff and its owner and manager. At first I took only a room but before long a suite (twenty-five dollars in those days). As years passed, I kept getting increasingly good tables in the dining room until eventually I was seated at Table No. 1, no doubt because of my distinguished literary reputation, though it may have had something to do with large tips. One Saturday I took George Roy Hill there for lunch. He was a well-known theatrical and television director, later a film producer. The maître d', Raoul, saw Hill was without a necktie and said he was sorry. I laughed and told Raoul that a play Hill directed had just won a Pulitzer Prize. Raoul loaned Hill a tie and seated us—and swiftly brought to Hill a copy of the current *Time* magazine, which by chance had a short piece about me as a successful freelance writer, saying, "So there." I knew it was all foolishness but I loved it.

I liked the Algonquin for a more practical reason: It was within walking distance of almost everywhere I had to go. Virtually the whole United States communications system was crammed into a postage-stamp-sized patch of midtown Manhattan, roughly from *Harper's* down on Thirty-third Street up to Knopf in the Fifties, with most of the magazines and, later, television networks, in between. I'm afraid I've come to think that New York is not a good place to be unless you are either young—young enough not to mind the tense jostling crowds, the hopeless traffic jams, the harum-scarum taxi rides—or unless you are rich—rich enough to keep a car and driver. At that time I was not rich but I was young and I loved it.

Sometimes I went to lunch with Frederick Lewis Allen. In high school or college, I had read Allen's *Only Yesterday,* the best book till then on the 1920s in America, and, like Knopf, he had long represented to me something unattainable. But here I was having a drink with him and his wife in their home, an old narrow three-story brownstown on Murray Hill. Allen was a slight man, so slight he looked almost frail, with sparkling eyes and a ready laugh, a wise man with an endlessly inquiring mind. He taught me much, most of it by the editing he did on my stories, cutting, tightening, endlessly tightening, and pointing up. Now and then he pronounced a dictum, such as: Never be afraid to address the reader directly, to write, "As we shall see," or "Let us first study the slum itself."

I was learning something else. New York editors, at least the good ones, felt cooped up in New York, isolated from the rest of the country. Time and again they asked me, "What's the mood of the Midwest these days?" Or "What's going on out there?" Just as farm boys yearn to go to New York, so do New York editors yearn to know what's on the farm boy's mind. Sometimes they sounded almost anxious. I myself had a strong sense of place, a sense that I belonged to the Midwest. I have always done a lot of place writing, that is, descriptions of places, setting of scenes, using place as a character in the story. I began to see that living in the Midwest, not in the East, was, for me as a freelance writer, a tremendous advantage. The Midwest was where things happened, it was, almost, the locomotive of America. And I as a writer almost had it all to myself, while in New York little happened and writers were scrambling all over each

other. I was receiving an unanticipated bonus for staying in Chicago instead of going east with Keller.

And something else was happening. Just as New York editors got a new perspective on the Midwest from me, so was I, in New York, getting from them a sense of the nation that was new to me. Having grown up and worked only in the Midwest, my view of the nation had been parochial. Suddenly, as I talked to New York editors about their concerns, I began to develop a new and more spacious view of the nation—its problems, its politics, its concerns. From editors I got something more valuable than editing—insight and perspective.

8.

It is therefore not surprising that my next *Harper's* piece was on Muncie, Indiana, which, in the 1920s, had been studied by two sociologists as "Middletown," a typical small Midwest city. Now in wartime I went there to see what was going on. I found Muncie a three-shift war-plant boomtown, with all its irritations and wrenching change, all its crowded raw rough living, all the influx of hillbillies from Kentucky, all the misgivings about the future. This was my quintessential American heartland. For the first time, on this story I did true heavy-fact legwork. I interviewed at length all sorts of people—local United Autoworkers union leaders, rank-and-file workers, businessmen, farmers in their fields, the county agricultural agent, courthouse politicians, soldiers on furlough, people in cafeterias, the editor of a local newspaper, a professor at the local college, a banker. From several I drew their life stories. And repeatedly I asked: "What do you hear people talking about these days?" This was the heart of my story—what Midwesterners were thinking in wartime. I was working on such issues as labor, wartime strikes, national politics, postwar international relations. I thought then and I still think that you can get a more accurate sample of public opinion by that kind of lengthy interviewing than by the so-called scientific public-opinion polling so pervasive today. Certainly you can get nothing reliable whatsoever by a telephone poll. The *Literary Digest* went under because its telephone poll predicted FDR's defeat. Time and again today's polls are wrong—they missed the Reagan landslide—and yet ordinary people and even politicians who should

know better continue to rely on them. Even face-to-face polling is unreliable—all too often it is done not by trained reporters but by inexperienced young people and housewives spitting out questions from a questionnaire fastened to a clipboard; nobody talks to a clipboard. But the greatest problem with polling is that if you ask a man directly to state his opinion on specific issues, he may or may not give you a straight answer. And he may even say he doesn't know because, privately, he thinks it's none of your business—many "undecideds" or "don't knows" are really so firmly decided that they don't want you to know it. On the other hand, if in a careful, probing, hour-long interview you ask him not what he thinks but, rather, what he hears his neighbors and friends saying, he will tell you what he himself is really talking and thinking about. Often at the end of an interview, I would ask about issues he had omitted. Highest on that list was postwar international affairs; almost nobody was thinking about that.

I was beginning to think about writing another regional book, one on Indiana. Alfred Knopf was interested. But in November of 1944 I was drafted into the Army.

THREE

UP FROM SLAVERY–
MAYBE

1.

At the time, the Army seemed to me a total waste of time. Looking back, I don't quite think so, and I only wish I had given a little more of myself to it. I couldn't; I hated it; it was the force that was tearing me apart from Fran and Cindy and tearing up my writing career just as it seemed to be getting started. (Too bad about me!) I was sent to a camp near Little Rock, Arkansas, for infantry basic training. In my memory it rained or sleeted every day down there that winter, and Arkansas was nothing but an ocean of freezing mud. In Europe the Battle of the Bulge began, and the training cycle just ahead of mine was cut short and the troops flown directly into the Bulge only about twelve weeks from civilian life. We expected the same. I declined an opportunity to apply for Officer Candidate School—I had the romantic notion or an underdog's instinct that I preferred to remain an ordinary soldier, and I had acquired the enlisted man's dislike of officers, a dislike not diminished by a young second lieutenant who kicked me while I was lying prone firing a rifle. I shed no tears when, later, a grenade blew off his hand.

Fran and Cindy came down to Little Rock and lived in a rooming house run by a woman who drank paregoric and turned their gas

heater down when she thought they were asleep. After basic training, I was sent not to the Bulge but to a school for military police and then to CID School—the Criminal Investigation Division. It made sense; criminal investigation differs little from reporting. Spring came, the war in Europe ended, and the Army formed its first CID platoon; I was assigned to it and we were shipped to Camp Boerne, Texas, a tent camp outside San Antonio in hilly desert country. Fran and Cindy lived in a tourist cabin. The manager gouged them on the rent. People in Texas and Arkansas resented the influx of Yankee soldiers and profiteered on them. Nevertheless, to me, after the winter mud of Arkansas, the CID in Texas seemed like paradise. The others in the platoon were about my age, thirty, professional men, a New York lawyer, several FBI men, a Border Patrol officer, several detectives. I had more in common with them than with the eighteen-year-olds in basic training. Mostly we played poker and drank whiskey and went on "jeep training marches"— actually long trips to resort hotels in the Texas hills or along the Mexican border. Every one of us was made a noncommissioned officer. The lieutenant in command explained to me that he gave me the lowest grade, T-5, technician fifth grade, because he knew I was writing pieces for Keller and for *Harper's* to supplement my Army pay and, if I didn't have heavy duties, as a staff sergeant would, I would have more time to write. It was fine with me. Fran too—I had been in the Army only a few months and was already almost a full corporal.

We were transferred to Houston and assigned to work with various Houston detective squads, I with homicide. Soon we were ordered overseas but first given a short furlough. Fran and I went to New York and stayed at the Algonquin and went to the theater, a last fling. We went to the Stork Club or "21," I forget which, and when we entered the maître d' greeted me coolly, "Good evening, Corporal," but I gave him a large tip, ten or twenty (my Army pay was about thirty dollars a month); and when we departed, he bowed and said, "Good night, sir." I wrote another *Harper's* piece, the only piece of pure rhetoric I ever wrote, called "Anything Bothering You, Soldier?" It is the question that an examining officer periodically asks each enlisted man. Nearly always the answer is "No, sir," for the soldier knows the taunting rejoinder of comrades if he

complains: "Your story is very touching. Would you like to see the chaplain? Or use the crying room?" My piece voiced all the enlisted man's complaints about the Army and about civilians profiting from war. Frederick Lewis Allen thought it bespoke the bewilderment and discontent so many Americans felt. Fran and I were having lunch with him and his wife the day President Truman announced we had dropped the bomb on Hiroshima, and Fran said she thought that, to secure peace, we should share the bomb secrets with the Soviets, and Fred Allen looked at her as though he thought she'd lost her mind.

I went to a shipping depot in California, prepared to go to the Pacific, but almost at the last minute I was taken off the shipping order and in February of 1946 discharged. I came out resolved never again to write for fact detective magazines, a form of slavery. Reality soon overcame that resolve. But only briefly.

2.

The editors at *Life* had read my *Harper's* stuff and asked me to travel the Midwest and do a long piece about its postwar mood. I spent six weeks crisscrossing the territory between Columbus, Ohio, and Smith Center, Kansas, between Louisville and Bismarck, North Dakota. I did several trick things, like taking a train from Chicago to Waterloo, Iowa, called *The Land of Corn*, but I also did a lot of serious reporting—the life story of a young combat veteran who was marrying a girl and buying a farm in Nebraska; the economics and politics of farmers' cooperatives in Minnesota; an assembly line in Kansas City; race relations in Lousiville and Indianapolis; conversion from tank building to auto building in Michigan; anti-Semitism in Indianapolis; the small-town clubrooms of beer-drinking legionnaires; strikes and lockouts in Ohio and Indiana. Everywhere I asked, "What are people talking about?" and "Who runs this town anyway?" and "How'd it change during the war—will it go back to the way it was?" It was an extension of what I'd done on Muncie for *Harper's*. Finished, I sent some five hundred pages of notes to *Life* and asked what they wanted me to carve out of them. Nothing, it turned out—*Life* simply did not know what to do with this flood of facts and paid me five-hundred dollars and kept but never published the manuscript. But I never considered the work wasted.

I learned a lot about the Midwest. So did *Life*—years later a friend on *Time,* John Steele, told me *Time* and *Life* were still consulting my Midwest notes. And some of that legwork came to inform other things I wrote. I was getting my Midwest into national perspective.

I went back to Muncie and did a piece for *Harper's* called "Middletown Revisited"—Muncie in transition from war to peace. In Muncie too I found a man, Court Asher, who had been a kleagle of the Ku Klux Klan and was the publisher of a hate newspaper containing anti-Negro and anti-Semitic articles; and I did a separate piece for *Harper's* about him. And I went back to my second regional book for Knopf, *Indiana: An Interpretation.* It became quite a different book from the Michigan book. Instead of the earlier book's picturesque explorers and lumberjacks and miners, the leading characters of *Indiana* were politicians, union leaders, industrialists, writers. Instead of the wilderness, the atmosphere was that of farm revolt, strikes, violence, industrialization, and bored farm-town life. Since I had hated my childhood, one would have assumed I would hate Indiana and I was therefore surprised to find a certain affection suffusing parts of the book; and when I quoted the old saw "Many good men come from Indiana, and the better they are the quicker they come," it was more in jest than in bitterness. I wrote about Theodore Dreiser and Hoagy Carmichael and Cole Porter, who had come from Indiana, and James Whitcomb Riley and Booth Tarkington, who had stayed there. I tried to re-create the down-to-earth hard-to-beat Hoosier, a shrewd salesman at heart, who emerged in this century. I resurrected several Indiana politicians from the Civil War period, for it was the Civil War that had put Indiana into business—made the Indiana Republican party one of the most powerful in the nation, while native American capitalism flourished. The longest single chapter in the book was on Eugene V. Debs, the Indiana railroader turned Socialist; indeed, Debs almost ran away with the book (and that may explain why the conservative booksellers of Indianapolis did little to sell the book). But though *Indiana* sold poorly, for me it was not wasted. Just as the *Harper's* pieces on Muncie and the Klan and Asher and the *Life* legwork had helped prepare me to do *Indiana,* so did *Indiana* prepare me for my future work and for politics.

3.

Fran and I bought a house on Sunset Road in Highland Park, Illinois. This changed our lives. We had hoped to find a house in Winnetka but couldn't. Although both Highland Park and Winnetka were North Shore suburbs of Chicago, they differed vastly. Winnetka was inhabited mainly by well-to-do Anglo-Saxon Republican Protestants. Highland Park was equally well-to-do but, although normally Republican, in recent years it had been casting a surprising number of Democratic votes. Moreover, it was far more heterogeneous than Winnetka, and it had a large Jewish population. Indeed, although the population was less than a third Jewish, many people thought Highland Park overwhelmingly Jewish, I suppose because the Jews were highly visible, being successful and influential—prominent doctors and lawyers and businessmen. The town's bookstore was owned, as a hobby, by the wives of two successful Jewish lawyers and two successful Jewish businessmen; the husband of one was a leader in national Jewish affairs, especially the Anti-Defamation League of B'nai B'rith. We initially became acquainted because of the bookstore, to which I naturally gravitated, and when the ladies who owned it learned I was a writer, they and their husbands welcomed us and they became our close friends and many of their friends became ours. All these people and many more whom we met were readers; all were better educated and better traveled than I; all were thoughtful people interested in ideas. Many years later, one of them paid us the ultimate compliment: Chatting with Fran on the phone, she caught herself short and said, "Oh, I forgot—you're not Jewish." If Fran and I had settled among the conservative Protestants of Winnetka, I do not know how our lifeiight have turned out but I am sure it would have been far different from what it became under the liberating influence of our new Jewish friends.

The house on Sunset Road had the look of a low cottage snuggled into the side of a slight rise of land. White clapboard, it had two closed-in porches, a thirty-foot low-ceilinged living room with a fireplace. Across the street was a big park, and Cindy walked through it to school. I have always worked at home—one of the principal attractions of freelancing is that you don't have to go to an office. I appropriated the big downstairs bedroom—Fran says I al-

ways get the best room in the house—and installed my fifteen-dollar oak desk, which Fran had bought secondhand, and my secondhand typewriter, and my father built bookcases to line the walls. A good place to work. I always referred to it simply as "my room," not "my study," just as I referred to "my work," not "my writing." And Sunset Road was a good place to live, the first home Fran and I had had for our marriage. Always before it had been a string of hotels and apartments, motels and parents' houses, one rented house, all temporary, transient. Now we had a solid base. E. M. Forster wrote in *Howard's End:* "London was but a foretaste of this nomadic civilization which is altering human nature so profoundly, and throws upon personal relations a stress greater than they have ever borne before. Under cosmopolitanism, if it comes, we shall receive no help from the earth. Trees and meadows and mountains will only be a spectacle, and the binding force that they once exercised on character must be entrusted to Love alone. May Love be equal to the task!"

When I proposed marriage to Fran, I had told her not to expect a little white house in the suburbs with a picket fence. (No doubt I was playing Jake Barnes in *The Sun Also Rises*—trying to protect myself against too deep a commitment because of Barbara's betrayal.) Now our little white house in Highland Park had a picket fence. I took care of the yard myself, mowing the grass, planting a garden, raking leaves, doing all the things that a conventional young father in the suburbs does. One Saturday while I was atop a ladder putting up storm windows, wearing my old Army fatigue shirt, an Army captain from the nearby fort came by and called up to me, "You own this house, soldier?" I replied, "Yes, Captain" (not "Yes, sir"). He said, "My wife and I want to rent a room in it." "No, Captain," I said and went back to putting up storm windows, avenged at last on the officer corps.

I was buying and reading a lot of books, especially modern European fiction—Camus and Sartre, Dostoevsky and Kafka, Forster and Celine, Koestler and Malraux. I read F. Scott Fitzgerald and Mark Twain and Ring Lardner, *The Scarlet Letter* and *Moby Dick*. And *Madam Bovary* and *Of Human Bondage*. Why I had not read them sooner I do not know. They seemed to speak to me directly, especially Camus and Kafka.

In these years, however, I was too careerist, and too preoccupied with getting my private life organized at last, to integrate all this

closely into my work and my life. Twice married, now with a permanent wife and child, with mortgage payments and car payments, I was almost obsessively concerned with the precarious existence of a freelance writer. Whether I might have as a young man written serious fiction, I'll never know, though I doubt it. By the time many years later that I could afford to risk attempting a novel, I had written heavy fact so long that the novel I wrote was highly topical—I had a vision, but it was a vision not of life but of a particular political situation. Similarly, I now think it was careerism that prevented me from becoming seriously interested in politics until I was thirty-seven years old. Even in college in the 1930s, I had been so preoccupied with getting a diploma and a job that I took no part in the peace marches and other campus protests of the time. World War II largely passed me by. I was aware that I was living through great events but even though I was in the Army, I was not really engaged with those great events—was intent on getting out of the Army and getting on with my writing and my private life. After the war, even writing for serious magazines about public events and public officials did not engage me in politics—they were stories to be written, not events to be myself involved with. Not until Adlai Stevenson first ran for president in 1952 did I really become engaged in politics and public life. I have remained so ever since.

Often Francis and Mary Ellen Nipp came out to our house on Sunset Road from Chicago for long weekends, and again we talked about writing and listened to recordings. I was buying and savoring old jazz—Bix Beiderbecke and Benny Goodman, Mezz Mezzerow and Sidney Bechet, Jack Teagarden, Duke Ellington and Fletcher Henderson and Jelly Roll Morton and above all Louis Armstrong. As a bachelor in Chicago, I had scorned jazz vocalists, except for Anita O'Day, had liked only instrumental jazz. But now on Sunset Road after Fran and I were married, I also came to enjoy Bing Crosby and Russ Colombo and Frank Sinatra (his songs, not the man). Fran had taught me to sing and when our children came along we taught them to sing, family singing.

And Francis Nipp brought me now to serious music—Beethoven and Mahler, Stravinsky and Moussorgsky, Debussy and Ravel and Sibelius. I took to it immediately. Why this should be so is mysterious. I remember as a child on Brookside Avenue listening to Caruso records my father brought home and played on the old Vic-

trola. I hated it. Why my father, uneducated, a carpenter and contractor in a rough business, the son of a rural man, loved music I have never known; but he did. Where he got it I do not know. Perhaps from his parents. But I never knew his father—he died before I was born—and I remember his mother only when, in her dotage and incontinent, she came to live with us briefly before she died. Her daughter Ethel played the piano in a neighborhood theater near Brookside Avenue and she played beautifully, another aunt tells me, especially, for her own enjoyment, serious music. In any case, I had nothing to do with serious music from childhood till I was about thirty-two, living on Sunset Road. (Francis Nipp even brought me to chamber music, which I would not have thought possible.) Great music moves me deeply, as does good writing, and to this day, listening to certain passages of Beethoven, I find myself weeping for human aspiration.

Late too I came to looking at paintings. I think it was not long after Fran and I were married that I took to going to the Chicago Art Institute, with its marvelous collection of French Impressionism, and to the Museum of Modern Art in New York. Why I went, I have no idea. Nothing in my childhood or youth presaged it. But I found I responded to Picasso and Matisse and Cezanne somewhat as I did to Kafka and Camus and Beethoven, and after I became a collaborator and friend of Ben Shahn, I spent more and more time in museums and galleries.

All this, I now see—literature, politics, music, art—was a late education and late coming of age. I have no idea why it took so long—nor why it happened. But I have often wondered whether Fran is not the key to it. When I met her, she read no serious literature, she knew nothing about politics, she liked only popular music and even that only if she could sing or dance to it. She knew nothing of art. Yet it is possible that, by giving me an emotional base to build a stable private life on, and by attending to my writing, she set free something in me that had up till then been locked up.

4.

In Peoria, a tough railroad and industrial town in downstate Illinois, two powerful homegrown Midwestern forces collided as they had throughout the bitter strikes of the 1930s and '40s, management and labor, in this case a stubborn, Roosevelt-hating railroad president

with his anti-union fervor and his armed strikebreakers ranged against quiet determined hometown strikers; a union man was shot dead on the picket line and the railroad president was later ambushed and killed near his home. I did a piece about it for *Harper's* that went further in the direction of George Leighton's crime-in-context than anything I had yet done. *Reader's Digest* picked it up, and then the *Digest* editor who handled it, Paul Palmer, suggested I look into the recent Centralia mine disaster; he had heard that none of the people involved, including the union officials and the governor of Illinois, seemed to have done anything to prevent it. I had been dimly aware that a coal mine at Centralia, Illinois, had exploded and killed more than one hundred men earlier that year, in March of 1947. I checked clippings. I would do the Centralia piece; the *Digest* would pay me twenty-five hundred dollars plus expenses. The *Digest*, with a big circulation and plenty of money, often planted stories in smaller magazines, including *Harper's*, then picked them up; with the *Digest's* encouragement, I told Fred Allen of *Harper's* about Centralia. He was dubious but agreed to read it. I set forth, driving away alone from our house on Sunset Road and heading downstate, thinking, "I've got a hell of a nerve, starting out single-handed, with nothing but my typewriter, to overthrow the political machine of the governor of Illinois." It turned out that the Centralia story changed the course of my career.

FOUR

A MINE DISASTER

1.

Whenever I started out to do the legwork on a story, I was afraid. I knew so little about the story; the people I would interview knew so much. Moreover, far from the brash reporter of *The Front Page*, I was diffident, at times almost shy. And when working for a newspaper, I had felt I had a right to ask questions, since a newspaper has an inherent right to keep the public record; but as a magazine writer, I did not feel equally privileged, I was after all writing a story which I hoped to sell at a profit to a magazine, whose publisher hoped it would entertain his readers and thus attract advertisers. Had I the right to question a coal miner's widow?

The only way to cure my hesitancy was to master the facts—to study the public record until I knew more about the case than anybody directly involved. (Some years later, when I had to make public speeches, the only way I could make my knees stop trembling was to remind myself, "You know more about this subject than anybody else in the room.") A law school maxim says, "On cross-examination, never ask a question that you don't already know the answer to." Interviewing a person reluctant to talk is like that. You already know the answer, the facts; what you want from him is

how he sees those facts, and you want it in his own words. From this flow not only flavor and atmosphere but also character. (The lawyer wants only the answer that he already knows to come out; I want everything to come out, especially the human details that make the bald facts real.) And another interviewing rule on a difficult story like Centralia: First you study the printed public record before you interview anybody, then you interview the people involved who are likely to want the story told, and finally you interview those who are likely not to want it told, the hostile witnesses. I was learning that the success of an interview depends upon your advance preparation—on how well you know the facts before starting the interview, on whether you know when you arrive what questions you want to ask and in what order (if you ask the hardest first, that may end the interview).

Over the years I developed certain interviewing techniques. I learned it's best to interview a person in his home, since he will be at ease there and the objects that surround him will suggest questions to you and remind him of details. If this is not possible, see him at his office, or at a restaurant he knows, but almost never in your own home. If you want to interview a man of high position, such as a governor or the president of General Motors, you will have to arrange an interview formally through a secretary, but if you telephone the secretary and cannot reach him, never leave word for him to call you back—he won't. Just keep calling him. If you want to interview an ordinary private citizen, such as a miner's widow, it is best to do nothing by telephone—simply knock on the door. (It is hard to say no to someone face to face, easy on the telephone.) I always used a notebook and pen or pencil, not a tape recorder. A recorder tends to put a person on stage, as a TV camera does, and you want him to speak to you in his own idiom, not a stagy idiom. Nonetheless, never walk in on him with notebook and pen in hand; you may frighten him. Instead, keep them in your pocket when you start the interview. How to get them out? Simple—ask a first question that requires a numeral for an answer, such as "When were you born?" Nobody would expect you to remember his birth date; you take out your notebook and write it down, and from then on the notebook is out. I write down everything he says. If I don't, he will notice what I'm making note of and what I'm skipping; he will then

start talking to the notebook, not to me, and there again we introduce a stagy note. Of course, I have encountered people who absolutely forbade any note-taking; I developed a memory trick for
dealing with them. Another device: If you want someone's life story
and he is reluctant, tell him your own life story; he may find threads
in your life that match his own, and soon he is telling his. You
should always try to establish an understanding, a sympathy even,
with everyone you interview, even the villains; they're not totally
evil, only human, and what you want to discover if you can is why
they behaved the way they did.

2.

In the case of Centralia I went first to St. Louis since the *St. Louis
Post-Dispatch,* being nearer, had covered the mine disaster better
than the Chicago papers. The *Post-Dispatch* had taken the lead in
exposing the failure of Governor Dwight Green to do anything to
prevent the disaster though he had had ample warning that the mine
was dangerous. It also had exposed how Illinois mine safety inspectors collected political contributions to the Green machine from coal
mine operators (but not at Centralia). The *Post-Dispatch* editors
gave me access to their files. They were proud of what they had done
and well they should have been; they helped me, for they wanted the
story told.

What had happened at Centralia was, briefly, this: The coal dust
raised by cutting coal in a soft-coal mine is explosive. If it is allowed
to accumulate on the floor and walls of an underground tunnel, any
spark, such as one from an electric motor, can ignite it; the first
small explosion throws more dust into the air, and that dust ex-
plodes, and so on—a self-propagating chain reaction of explosions
that can reach throughout the mine. To minimize the danger, federal and state safety regulations require rock-dusting—sprinkling
pulverized rock on top of the coal dust, thus damping it down.
Rock-dusting will not prevent but it will limit an explosion. For
years, the miners who worked in the mine called Centralia No. 5
had known that it was dangerously dusty, and that the company was
rock-dusting inadequately. The state mine inspector, Driscoll O.
Scanlan, agreed and repeatedly reported that the company was vio-
lating the state mining regulations, but his superior, Robert M.

Medill, director of the Department of Mines and Minerals in Springfield, handled his reports as routine. Medill told Scanlan to ask the miners to be patient. They refused. The union, Local 52 of the United Mine Workers of America, instructed William E. Rowekamp, a miner and the local's recording secretary, to write direct to Medill and finally to Governor Green himself. The letter to the governor said Inspector Scanlan had tried to get the mine cleaned up, but his superiors had done nothing and the mine was still dangerous—"In fact, Governor Green, this is a plea to you, to please save our lives." Nothing resulted. Less than a year later, on March 25, 1947, the mine blew up, killing 111 men.

I could not document all this in St. Louis but I saw enough to prepare me for interviewing in Centralia and to tell me that I must nail down each document in Springfield—if I could.

Centralia, a town of sixteen thousand, was no coal camp like the dismal company towns of West Virginia. It looked like any Midwest farm town—wide main street lined with low flat-faced stores, sprawling railroad shops and the ungainly black coal-mine tipple on the edge of town. I began by doing background legwork on the town itself—talked, as I had in Muncie, to farmers, businessmen, housewives. Only after that did I interview the people directly involved. And I began with the miners and miners' widows, for they were the victims, the aggrieved, and would want the world to know. I did not want the story to turn into debate among the powerful—Governor Green, and John L. Lewis of the UMWA, and the coal company. I wanted it to be the miners' story, the story of helpless ordinary people, what Spaniards call *los de abajo*, "those from below."

I went to see William Rowekamp, the miner, a tall lanky man in overalls, in his little house on a small plot of ground where he kept a garden. I told him what I was doing and said I'd like to talk to him. He said something like "Go ahead." He was by nature taciturn but soon he was talking freely, explaining mining to me, talking about his life, about the town, the mine, the union. He told me* how he, as recording secretary of Local 52, had written the "save our lives" letter, as it came to be known, to Governor Green, written it at his

---

* I am uncomfortable writing "he told me." In writing my stories, I kept myself entirely out of them and never used the first person unless it was unavoidable. In these memoirs, however, I feel I must, for here I need to show how I did the legwork and wrote the stories. My purpose then was to tell stories about other people; now it is to reveal myself. Which is why writing memoirs is harder.

cluttered little desk in the living room, typing it carefully and affixing the union seal—"I dassen't use the seal without it's official." When we finished, I asked him whom else I should talk to, as I always do, and he gave me the names of other miners. For the next few days, I went from one to another and I took to hanging around the bare upstairs union hall and they became so used to seeing me that they paid little heed, always what a reporter wants. I came to understand that the miners considered themselves a breed apart, superior to men who toiled on assembly lines or farms. The danger they were always in was part of the fascination. They were fierce fighters for their rights. They had a strong sense of being the underdog; talking about the hearse that had taken the body of a man killed in the disaster away from the scene, another told me, "I'll bet it's the only time he ever rode in a Cadillac." I felt as he did. Whence came my own underdog feeling I don't know. Perhaps from my size—as a kid I'd been small. Perhaps from seeing what the Depression did to my father and hearing Roosevelt talk about "the forgotten man." Perhaps from Wolfgang the Communist and his ironworker father. Perhaps from starting my own work at the bottom—stock gummer and copyboy for the Associated Press, cub reporter for the *Times,* and early member of the first newspaperman's union. Perhaps from my legwork in the Chicago slums on criminals and their victims. Wherever it came from, it remained a powerful force in my life and my writing.

To bring the disaster home to the reader, I needed to talk to the miners' widows, and several miners suggested I talk to Joe Bryant's widow: She had lost both her husband and her son. I found her four-room house near the railroad tracks in a cluster of houses around another mine shaft. She was a big woman, forty-four years old, sitting on a sofa in her parlor. She had borne eleven children. Two had died in infancy. Her husband, Joe, had gone to work in the mine at fourteen. When their oldest son, Harold, got out of the Army, Joe had helped him get a job in the mine, and Harold married a girl of fifteen named Ruth. Twice Harold was hurt in the mine. It frightened Ruth. She told me, "He always said if he was going to die he might as well die in the mine." (I interviewed her separately from Mrs. Bryant. I tried never to interview two people together.)

I asked Mrs. Bryant to tell me everything she had done the day of

the explosion. Her second son had heard about it soon after he got off work at 3:30. He picked up his wife and went to his mother's house. She had heard nothing, was frying potatoes and sausage for supper. He went to Harold's house and told Ruth there'd been an accident in the mine and took her to Mrs. Bryant's house. They all sat down to wait for news.

As word of the disaster spread through town, some of the miners' wives went out to the mine. Cold rain turned to sleet toward dark; for warmth they went into the washhouse, a dim-lit barnlike structure where each morning their husbands took off their street clothing and put on their miners' clothing and each afternoon showered and changed again. Each of the wives, many of them already widows though they didn't know it, found her husband's clothing hanging from high racks and each sat down under her husband's clothing to wait. Mrs. Bryant and Ruth stayed at Mrs. Bryant's house. Throughout the long evening, neighbors kept coming in to see if she'd heard anything, and her son kept driving back and forth to the mine, but there was no news. They waited all night. At 9 A.M. Ruth's sister came to the house. She took Mrs. Bryant's oldest daughter into the kitchen and whispered to her, then she took Mrs. Bryant to the kitchen. "It was Harold," Mrs. Bryant told me. "They'd found him, they'd talked to a man who had seen him. I just said, well, I guess that's true." Nobody knew how to tell Ruth, so nobody did tell her, and when she came into the kitchen the whispering stopped, until "two merchant men" from town came to the house and told her. Mrs. Bryant waited all week and heard nothing. Past midnight on Saturday the two businessmen returned and asked how Joe had been dressed. Overalls and a white sweatshirt, she said—she knew because she'd just mended them. It made her cry, remembering for me. She told them he'd been carrying a pocket-knife, a white cigarette case, and a whistle with a chain on it. They left. Not until nine o'clock the next morning did they return. They had Joe's cigarette case and his whistle. And they also brought some notes he had written. Harold had been right at the heart of the explosion, he had died instantly and violently. But Joe and thirteen other men had been some distance away, and they ran into the maze of tunnels, looking for a way out, deadly fumes pursuing them, till they came to a dead end, trapped. Here they lay down on the

floor—breathable air would last longest down low. Waiting, they wrote notes to their wives. It must have taken Joe Bryant a long time to die; his notes were carefully lettered, not scribbled. Mrs. Bryant showed them to me. In one, on a page torn from a time book, he wrote: "Dear Wife fro Give [forgive] me Please all love you Be shure and don't sign any Paper see Vic Ostero [a warning against signing away her compensation rights] My Dear wife good By. Name Baby Joe so you will have a Joe love all dad." The baby was born three months later, a girl, and Mrs. Bryant named her Joedy.

While Mrs. Bryant was talking to me, several small children were playing around her legs, pulling her dress to distract her. On the wall hung two new pictures tinted in color and gilt-framed, one of her husband and one of Harold, and to each was affixed a little plaque: "Know Ye These Presents Certify That This is an Heirroom [sic] Portrait of Joe Bryant made from a photograph taken in the year 1935 and faithfully portrayed by the artist in a manner and quality befitting a work to be passed on to future generations as a priceless heirloom." She told me "a man from Chicago came round selling them." She paid $18 for each frame and $18.75 for Joe's picture; the man from Chicago "threw the boy's picture in." She received $1,000 from the union's welfare fund and nearly $1,000 from other welfare sources; the funeral took most all of this. For five years she would also receive $44 a week from state industrial compensation and Social Security combined. After five years the industrial compensation would stop, and after her children reached eighteen the Social Security would stop too until she herself reached sixty-five.

I asked her whom she blamed. She said, "I don't know nothin' about the mine, I wouldn't blame no one, them accidents happen, seems like it just has to be." And she said, "There ain't much to say. It don't pay to say much." But her young daughter-in-law Ruth said, "Everybody says it was just one of those things, it was their time to go, but I don't believe it. If that mine'd been safe they'd still be here."

When I left her and drove away down the black dusty road, I thought that from her and Rowekamp I'd gotten half the story. The other half I would get in Springfield—politics and the government bureaucracy.

The sources there would be unfriendly but by now I knew so much that I was prepared. What I needed most was access to the files of the Department of Mines and Minerals and an interview with its director, Robert Medill. When I went to his office in the cavernous statehouse, he was not there but his deputy told me I could go through the files—they'd all been published anyway during various investigations, he said. But it turned out they hadn't. I found a mountain of paper accumulated over five years. Piled up, the evidence was devastating. Every three months for three years, Inspector Scanlan had visited the Centralia mine and written a report listing many violations of the mining laws and regulations and sent it to the Department of Mines and Minerals in Springfield. His constant finding was that the mine was dangerously dusty and should be rock-dusted. I was able to trace the progress of his reports almost hour by hour as they wound their way through the bureaucracy. The department director, Medill, a genial politician, had not seen Scanlan's first thirteen reports (1942 through 1944); his deputy handled them. When a report arrived in the department's high-ceilinged old office, Medill's secretary stamped it "Received" with a time and date and put it on the deputy's desk. He read some but not all the reports and gave them to a girl in the typing pool; she corrected them for grammar and spelling and compressed their recommendations into a form letter addressed to the mining company, beginning, "The Department endorses" Scanlan's recommendations, and hoping the company would comply with them and let the department know. Medill's deputy signed the forms and they were mailed to the company's Chicago office. Not only did the company not comply with Scanlan's recommendations, it did not even bother to reply. In 1942 federal mine inspections started, and the federal inspector found the same violations and made the same recommendations as Scanlan. The company ignored them too.

In November of 1944 the union local instructed its recording secretary, Rowekamp, to complain directly to Medill that the tunnels were "very dusty and dirty. . . . They are getting dangerous." Medill's deputy sent Scanlan to investigate; he reported as he had all along. This time the company did sprinkle some of the tunnels, and in early December Rowekamp thanked Medill, but by the end of December the mine was as dusty as ever—the company's mine man-

ager explained that in the winter "you can sell all the coal you can get out. So you want top production, you don't want to stop to rock-dust." Early in 1945 Scanlan telephoned Medill, who told him to write to him, and Scanlan did, saying that the mine should be shut down long enough to dust because "the coal dust in this mine is highly explosive." (This letter too was duly stamped "Received" with the time.) This time Medill acted—himself wrote a letter to his friend William P. Young of Chicago, the operating vice-president of the Centralia mine's parent company, Bell and Zoller, one of the big Illinois coal companies. "Dear Bill," Medill's letter began, and he recited Scanlan's and the miners' complaints and closed, "Please let me have any comments you wish to make. . . .Very kindest personal regards." Young replied to "Dear Bob," pleading the wartime demand for coal and a shortage of manpower and hoping things would improve so they could do what Scanlan wanted—"With kindest personal regards." Medill sent the correspondence to Scanlan and told him to ask the miners to be patient. They told Scanlan they'd wait till April, a hint of a wildcat strike.

In mid-March Scanlan took the unusual step of seeking Medill out at a statewide mine-safety meeting. Scanlan said to me, "I told him that the mine was in such condition if the dust became ignited that it would sweep from one end of the mine to another and probably kill every miner in the mine." Medill replied, according to Scanlan (Medill later denied it), "We will just have to take that chance."

The union local brought charges against the mine manager and asked the state Mining Board to revoke his certificate. Medill's deputy investigated and the board rejected the charge. Then the local voted to prefer charges against both the mine manager and mine superintendent. This paper too was stamped "Received." Medill convened the Mining Board and told Scanlan to come to Springfield. But there he shunted Scanlan aside to a coal operator, who tried to persuade Scanlan to withdraw one of his recommendations. Scanlan refused. Scanlan had been told he could go before the board, but though he waited all day in the outer office, the board never called him and it dismissed the union's charges.

Next the miners turned to their own union, to district headquarters in Springfield. Its bureaucracy proved as impenetrable as the state's, and its ties to management equally as close as the state's. It

did nothing, contending it could do nothing. Actually the union could have called Medill and told him to get the mine cleaned up within *x* number of days or they'd strike every mine in the state. The Centralia miners made one further try—they voted to authorize their local's recording secretary, Bill Rowekamp, to write directly to Governor Green, and he did, the "save our lives" letter. The four officers of the local union signed the letter in the mine washhouse. Of the four, only one, Rowekamp, lived through the explosion. It is doubtful that Governor Green ever saw the letter until after the disaster; one of his aides sent it to Medill with a memo asking for a careful investigation—in effect, Medill should investigate himself. It is only sixty yards from the governor's office in the statehouse to the Department of Mines and Minerals office but this journey took the memo and the miners' letter two days. (By now I knew the importance of what is called telling detail and I knew you get it only by looking for it so I paced off that sixty yards.) Medill's reply cited the war effort and the Mining Board's actions and said conditions were no different from what they had been for the last ten or fifteen years. Medill suggested the governor tell the miners that he was calling their letter to the attention of the Mining Board. This apparently satisfied Governor Green's aid, for he dictated, over the governor's signature, such a letter. Medill summoned Scanlan to Springfield and "severely reprimanded" him, as Scanlan remembered it, and he also told Scanlan's political sponsor, a state representative, that he was going to fire Scanlan, Scanlan was convinced that only his sponsor saved his job.

In an unrelated action, the coal miners struck nationwide, and President Truman ordered the mines operated by the federal government under an enforceable safety code. This generated another mountain of paperwork, and federal authorities wrote to the company, requesting compliance with the inspector's recommendations, and the company said that "a substantial" number of the reported violations had been corrected and more would be when possible. The federal officials renewed their request, the company promised fuller details soon—but, as I wrote in the *Harper's* piece, "before any other correspondence arrived to enrich file CMA81-swr, the mine blew up." Copies of Scanlan's last report and the federal inspector's were still thumbtacked to the bulletin board outside the washhouse.

I spent days in the department's office, making notes on scores of federal and state inspection reports, correspondence, transcripts of the six hearings and investigations into the Centralia disaster. When I finished, I went to see Medill in his home on Lake Springfield. He was a large jovial man with a loud blustering voice. He offered me a drink—"I know you reporters"—but I declined. To bring him alive in the piece, I led him through his life story—how he started as a miner but switched to management, his gay life in the 1920s, his entrance into Republican politics. He had worked in 1940 for the election of Governor Green, and Green had rewarded him by appointing him director of the department.

When I left him, I thought that his interview, plus the heavy documentation, gave me the other half of my story. I stayed on in Springfield, interviewing legislators, union men, lobbyists, coal operators. All seemed to agree that coal mining could never be made safe until we stopped sending miners underground and instead developed the process of converting coal into gas in place—"underground gasification." I tried to see Governor Green but could not get an appointment. I went up to Chicago and interviewed an executive at Bell and Zoller, operator of the Centralia mine. I sent a telegram to John L. Lewis in Washington asking for an interview; I received no answer. So I started to write.

It was not that simple. The story was big and complex, jumbled up in my head, all disorganized and out of order. Once a writer had told me, "We always send our stories in too soon," before we've made them the best we can. (The temptation is almost overpowering: The minute a writer finishes a draft he can hardly wait to have someone read it.) Not only that—we also begin to write them too soon, before we have really digested the materials. I took a few days off, drove alone to Upper Michigan, and went fishing, trying not to think about Centralia, letting it marinate. This succeeded. Driving home I began to see the story. The principal elements were the town of Centralia, the miners, their union, the mine operators, and state and federal authorities. The story's impact would depend on two things: bringing the characters alive, and piling up the evidence of the history of the disaster. I dumped my notes and documents on my desk in the house on Sunset Road. In writing *Indiana,* I had organized research material on three-by-five cards but now I was developing a new organizing system. I went through my notes and docu-

ments, giving each a code number and numbering the pages, and when I came across something I wanted to use, I typed it out, triple-spaced, keying it to code and page numbers. I then cut up the typing line by line into slips of paper. I moved the slips around, arranging and rearranging them. Thus I was able to fit a striking quotation or telling detail into its proper place in the main narrative line. When I had the slips all arranged as I wanted, I pasted them together. The result was a long scroll. I rolled it up and put it on my typing table and began writing, letting it unroll and fall to the floor as I used it, and when I came to the end of the scroll, the rough draft was done. A few years later, when one of these scrolls became more than 150 feet long, running out of my room and out the front door and across the lawn, I abandoned the system and used 5-by-8 cards.

Francis Nipp had once remarked that he didn't see why a factual article couldn't be constructed as a work of fiction is constructed—according to the three Cs: Conflict, Characters tightly related to conflict, and Controlling idea. (By the last he meant that you must absorb the material well enough to be able to say what the story is about in a single sentence. If you can't do that, you haven't sufficiently conceptualized the story.) On Centralia, as I shuffled the bits of paper into the scroll, the complicated parts of the story began to fall into place. I decided to structure the piece like Beethoven's Fifth. The first movement should strike all the principal themes, with the explosion itself dominant; each succeeding movement should develop the themes one by one, until at the climax we return to the explosion. If the story worked, you should get narrative pull and even suspense—not the suspense of surprise, as in a mystery novel, but what Francis Nipp called the suspense of fine inevitability, as when you see a boxer get hit hard just once during the first round and you watch him in successive rounds knowing that though he tries to stay on his feet he is surely going down—and he does, about the sixth round.

I write a rough draft on the typewriter, never in longhand, never dictating. I do my thinking at the typewriter. I write a very long, very awkward, very loose rough draft and I write it fast—probably fifty pages a day on the average (triple-spaced). In rough draft, I am mainly trying to string the material together in an organized way, sometimes doing little more than eliding a document or an interview. Over the years I taught myself to cut about one for six. That

is, if I want to end with a final draft of 20 pages, I write about 120 pages of rough draft. I put most pieces through six rewrites. Just before I do the final rewrite, I ask Fran to read the draft to me aloud, for by then I've marked it up so heavily that it is hard to read, and I have become too close to it—I can no longer see an awkward sentence or a dull passage but I can hear one. To me, writing is more like carpentry than art.

I get to my desk between 9 and 9:30 A.M. and work till 5 or 5:30 P.M.; I do not work evenings; I take Saturday off, and on Sunday deal with correspondence and other accumulated afflictions and plan the next week's work. I never end a day written out, with nothing more to say; instead I stop at quitting time by the clock and type out a quarter or half page of notes about what exactly is coming next; thus in the morning I can readily take up where I left off—getting started, on a story or on a day's work, is hardest. I make a carbon of everything, especially the rough draft, and at the end of each day I get the carbon to a safe place out of the house, for fire is the nightmare—I once knew a writer who worked two years on a novel in a cabin in the Minnesota woods, and the cabin burned down and, with it, the only copy of his novel.

Although in the rewrite I move sentences and paragraphs around and do heavy rewrite, trying to allow no rough-draft sentence to survive to the final draft, cutting every line that I am especially pleased with, doing the real polished writing on rewrite, not rough—in spite of all this the basic organization remains about the same because the basic conception remains the same. It takes me about as long to rewrite as to write the rough. Talking to Arthur Schlesinger and Dick Rovere, I found that they wrote entirely differently, only a few pages a day, slow writing, tight writing, and their rough drafts resembled final drafts far more closely than mine. But it took all of us about the same overall length of time to do a story from start to finish; I spent my time on rewriting, they on rough drafting. There is no "right" way to write; there is only *your* way.

Francis and Mary Ellen Nipp chanced to come out for the weekend just as I finished the Centralia rough draft. He read it and said, "If *Harper's* publishes this in anything like its present form, it'll make your reputation." It was the longest piece I had yet written,

some eighteen thousand five hundred words in final draft. What made it so long and what made it so powerful was the relentless documentation—I kept piling it up and piling it up and piling it up—showing that for years everybody had known the mine was going to blow up but nobody had stopped it. After it was published, another editor told me, "As I started to read it I thought it was going on and on, but then I realized you knew exactly what you were doing." When Frederick Lewis Allen read it, he wrote me an extraordinarily (for him) long letter, which ended, "This office is rocking with cheers." He paid me five hundred dollars for it and made it the lead story in his March 1948 issue, the longest story *Harper's* had ever published in its hundred-odd years. *Reader's Digest* paid me twenty-five hundred dollars and published it at unusual length in its April issue. Allen tried to nominate it for a Pulitzer Prize but the Pulitzer Committee had no magazine category. Russell Lynes of *Harper's* got Ben Shahn to do some drawings to illustrate it. They published twenty-four of his drawings but he kept making more and in the end developed the material into several major paintings. Later Fran and I bought his collection of thirty-two Centralia drawings.

3.

Years later a Hollywood agent who had become interested in my work asked, "Don't you ever write any happy stories?" I'm afraid not, or almost never. It bothered me, however, that it is the fate of the writer of heavy fact to thrive on other people's troubles. This can be justified if one argues that serious heavy fact is intended not only to entertain the reader but to educate him, to alert him to something amiss in our society, even to bring about reform. And I was bursting to tell the world the awful truth about the mine disaster. But such efforts rarely bring about real reform. The Centralia story may have helped Adlai Stevenson defeat Governor Green, who was up for re-election that year, and it helped bring about a new federal safety code with teeth in it. But today, more than thirty years later, coal mines are still blowing up for roughly the same reason that Centralia blew up, and gentlemen in executive suites are still talking about underground gasification of coal. It is true that a later piece of mine in *The Saturday Evening Post* helped defeat a venal politician and still another got a man out of prison, where he had been sent

wrongfully. But such things are rare. I have always interviewed and sympathized with *los de abajo,* as I have said, but I have no illusions about being the Sir Galahad of the downtrodden. No doubt Joe Bryant's widow got not one cent more in compensation for her husband's death than she would have had I never written the Centralia story.

What, then, can be the justification of heavy fact writing that, in effect, exploits misery? I am afraid it has to be literary. Only rarely did I work as an "investigative reporter," that recently overused and misunderstood term—produce evidence of a crime before the authorities knew there's anything wrong. Rather, I came along after the event; I studied all the available evidence and interviewed everybody I could find and I put the whole thing together. This is what a magazine writer can do that a newspaper reporter cannot— put a story in perspective, conceptualize it. Thus what began as a story about a mine disaster became a study of heedless immovable government bureaucracy, politics, profit-seeking business, indifferent unions, indifferent public officials, and a general breakdown in the machinery that runs our lives. I conceived the story in a sense that a hard news story cannot be conceived. It is a literary notion. I do not mean to compare the sublime with the ordinary, but Napoleon's retreat from Moscow existed as a fact but did not exist as an epic event until Tolstoy created it in *War and Peace.* Nor did the retreat from Caporetto exist until Hemingway wrote *Farewell to Arms.* Nor, if I may say so, did the Centralia mine disaster exist in that sense until I conceived and wrote my piece.

PART TWO

FREELANCE WRITER

FIVE

THE BIG SLICKS

1.

The 1940s and 1950s were in the United States the great days of magazine journalism. *Life* and *Look, The Saturday Evening Post* and *Collier's, Harper's* and *The Atlantic, Reader's Digest,* yes and the women's magazines, *McCall's* and *Cosmopolitan* and *Redbook*—each stood for something, each had its own character, and all published serious nonfiction—what was called heavy fact. They influenced our lives until the 1960s, when television drove them from the temple.

It was my good luck to come along when the "big slicks," as mass circulation magazines printed on glossy paper were called, were at the peak of their circulation and their profits, their prestige, and their power. I wrote for all of them.*

Francis Nipp had been right—publication of the Centralia story in *Harper's* did make my reputation, not with the reading public at large but with what counted more to a writer: with editors of other magazines. *Harper's* was one of the high-quality, low-circulation (and low-pay) magazines that the editors of the big slicks read seeking new writers. Editors' doors theretofore closed suddenly opened;

---

* Some of these magazines folded; some were later revived; some are still being published but they are vastly different from what they were then.

indeed, editors began coming to me. And in working this miracle, the Centralia story had considerable help. Frederick Lewis Allen told me that *Harper's* could not publish all the pieces I could write (one year I had pieces in eight of its twelve issues) and, furthermore, *Harper's* could not pay as much as I would need if I intended to make a living as a freelance writer of heavy fact. The big slicks, Fred Allen thought, were the answer. I needed to spread my work among them. To do this, he said, I needed an agent, and he offered to help me find one, though he hoped that in the future I would continue to write for *Harper's* as well as the big slicks. He spoke to Harold Ober, the agent, on my behalf.

At that time there were, I suppose, several hundred men in the United States who called themselves literary agents. Most were of utterly no use to a writer and the reputation of some with editors was so bad that they were actually a hindrance. Many advertised for clients, charged fees to read manuscripts, and prated about "helping" unknown writers, whereas what they did in fact was exploit them. Only a handful of agents was effective and professional. They never took on unknown writers, would not even read their work unless an editor or another client introduced them. The literary business in New York is a small, tightly knit world. No figure in it commanded more respect than Harold Ober. He had formed his own agency in 1929; by the time I came along he had two associates, Ivan von Auw and Dorothy Olding. Ivan handled books, and nobody paid much heed, since in those days books made no money, the big money was in the magazine market. Dorothy Olding handled magazines but so did Harold Ober himself. (Today the situation is reversed—the money is in books, not magazines.) Harold Ober had been F. Scott Fitzgerald's agent (and had helped raise his daughter). He was agent for William Faulkner, Philip Wylie, Catherine Drinker Bowen, J. D. Salinger, James M. Cain, John Gunther, Paul Gallico, and a long list of other well-known writers. He handled the best-selling novels of Agathie Christie; he also handled the poetry of Langston Hughes.

As I moved along, I developed associations with editors, particularly with Ben Hibbs and Stuart Rose of *The Saturday Evening Post,* that closely resembled a staff writer's relationship, and frequently I dealt directly with them on a piece, with little intervention by

Harold Ober.* But I always kept him informed, I always submitted the completed manuscript first to him and asked him to pass it along to the editor if it seemed all right, and I always paid his 10 % commission. Some writers in similar situations, like Richard Rovere, could see no reason to employ an agent, and once when an editor asked Rovere to come in and discuss a piece she wanted written and she offered him, let us say, a thousand dollars, he replied, "Let's pretend I have an agent. He would get ten percent. Why don't you pay me eleven hundred?" But my situation was different from his. For me, an agent can do many things. He can talk money to an editor, which I am not good at. When he thinks I am due for a rise in rates, he can ask the editor for it (and he knows what the market rates are). He can handle subsidiary rights—paperback rights to a book, foreign rights, film and dramatic rights. He can handle important administrative matters such as obtaining copyrights and renewing them. He can read a contract expertly, and film contracts are extremely complicated. He is in the market—and I am in Highland Park. He is talking to editors all the time; he goes to them with manuscripts and they come to him with ideas for pieces they want written. He knows what editor will want which piece. A good agent can introduce you to editors who would not otherwise see you. Soon I was going to New York about five times a year to have lunch with editors or visit them in their offices, discussing story ideas; Harold arranged it.

But above all, an agent gives an author support. Freelance writing is at best a risky, lonely business. The writer is all alone at his typewriter or in the editor's office. He needs support. He needs someone to turn to in difficult times. An agent like Harold Ober can be a rock to cling to in a stormy sea. The Ober agency became my agent in 1948 and it is still my agent, though we never had so much as a handshake agreement.

When people hear the term "literary agent," they probably think, if at all, of a flashy figure who talks glibly and rapidly, wears checkered vests, and commutes between Hollywood and New York. Harold Ober looked more like a banker than an agent. He had a modest suite of offices on Forty-ninth Street just off Madison Ave-

---

* Hibbs was the editor in chief of the *Post*. Rose was a senior editor.

nue, but he himself was a million miles removed from Madison Avenue and all it stands for. A white-haired New Hampshire man, with a dour manner but wide-open sparkling blue eyes, he was courteous almost to the point of seeming deferential—but not quite. He said little but listened to everything. I sometimes met editors in his office, and while we talked, Harold sat silent, looking down at his desk and doodling with a delicate letter opener, only rarely looking up at us from under his bushy eyebrows to make a comment in a low monotone (or more likely answer a question). After Harold's death and von Auw's retirement, Dorothy Olding became head of the agency.

Sometimes my pieces were my ideas, sometimes an editor's. When I submitted an outline showing the bare bones of a story and telling the editor how I would handle it, he would either decline it or tell me to go ahead. *The Saturday Evening Post* never made an assignment. But if the *Post* liked the proposal, it was almost certain to buy the final manuscript unless you blew it, for the *Post* editors, unlike many, knew what they wanted. And they not only bought pieces; they also published them—and the point of anybody's writing is, of course, to publish. I would always rather have a *Post* expression of interest than a firm assignment from several other magazines. Over the years, *Life* gave me a number of assignments but not until 1965 did they actually pay the full price for and publish anything I wrote. (*Life* and other magazines, if they made an assignment but decided not to publish the story, would pay a "kill fee" for it, usually about 15 % of the agreed full price.) Full price was between fifteen hundred and twenty-five hundred dollars plus travel expenses, and Harold Ober persuaded the *Post* editors to raise my rate and they also began paying me a generous bonus on nearly every piece. Moreover, the *Post* would give you a decision in a week and pay you in another, important to a freelance.

Advice to would-be writers usually includes advice to "slant" your story at a particular magazine. I would put it a little differently. I have always written with a reader over my shoulder—an editor who, while I was writing, in my mind was peering over my shoulder, watching; and if I was tempted to overwrite a sentence, or leave one loose, or collapse upon a cliché, or otherwise write something idiotic, the imaginary reader would frown; I would fix it. Early he was Frederick Lewis Allen of *Harper's* or Alfred Knopf, and then Stuart

Rose of *The Saturday Evening Post,* and there have been others. A generation of *New Yorker* writers must have written with the painfully gentle face of William Shawn peering over their shoulders. I wonder if editors really know how all-pervasive they are.

Many readers who remember *The Saturday Evening Post* at all remember it as a magazine that published pleasant stories by Clarence Budington Kelland and about the super tractor salesman Alexander Botts, articles about motion picture stars, cartoons, and color photographs. It did. But it also published fiction by William Faulkner and F. Scott Fitzgerald and serious nonfiction by Jack Alexander and Alva Johnson, two of the best journalists of our generation, and the rather somber pieces that I wrote. The *Post* was, in a few words, not unlike the network television that took away its audience—both frothy and serious.

In Harold's office I would meet Stuart Rose of the *Post* on his regular Tuesday trip to New York from the *Post* offices in Philadelphia in search of manuscripts. Stuart Rose remained my editor at the *Post* throughout my career there, and we became good friends. Yet he was in many ways a rather unlikely collaborator for me. He had begun his own career by writing a column on men's clothing for *The New Yorker.* He himself was a fancy dresser—derby hat, tightly furled umbrella, splendid neckties. He looked the classic man-about-town. In New York he stayed at the St. Regis and he lunched at Voisin and other then fashionable and expensive East Side restaurants. He was primarily a fiction editor. The *Post* had editors who were themselves expert nonfiction reporters and writers, like Jack Alexander; Stuart chanced to handle me because he was the man the *Post* sent to New York to see writers and agents. He lived in the country outside Philadelphia and kept a stable, went riding early every morning, and every weekend went fox hunting. He had been a U.S. Army cavalry officer and had never lost his love for the military life. And he was a Republican. Stuart Rose and I had little in common except a love of writing and a confidence that, as he put it, a good reporter could report anything. This was the way he handled me: not restricting me to a single narrow category of stories, such as crime, but rather giving me leeway to report and write what I wanted to or what he was interested in. It was, really, an ideal editor-author relationship.

Not only did he know what he wanted; he knew how it ought to

be put together. Twice he returned manuscripts to me with memos telling me how to reorganize them, almost paragraph by paragraph, and I did his bidding without understanding it at all, and only when I saw the stories in proof did I realize how right he had been. Stuart Rose and Ben Hibbs and their associates at the *Post*, Fred Allen and George Leighton and their associates at *Harper's*—Rose and Hibbs and Allen and Leighton are all dead now, and it may be that other great editors like that are still alive, but I know of none. (Of course, it may be possible that in those days I myself was more open to editors' suggestions than later, after hardening of the writing arteries set in.)

2.

During the next fourteen years, I wrote for the big slicks. Many of the stories were the sort of thing I'd begun doing for *Harper's*—George Leighton's crime-in-context. But now I was really doing it—doing the hard interviewing it requires, collecting all the evidence I could about the crime, its actors, and their world. Many of these stories could as well have appeared in *Harper's* as in the *Post* or *Cosmopolitan.* Indeed, several of them did.

A few examples:

I did a story about a Chicago boy of twelve who killed his seven-year-old playmate. His mother had been married several times and was often absent. The story somewhat resembled the Centralia story—I found a thick file of correspondence between her and the school, where her boy had gotten in trouble time after time. Repeatedly she had appealed to Chicago's ponderous legal and educational machinery to take him and raise him; nothing resulted; the street raised him. Now what to do with him? The jury found him guilty of murder, and the judge sentenced him to twenty-two years in the penitentiary—the state of Illinois had no reformatory, no proper place to put him. As at Centralia, the state had failed.*

For some time I had wanted to do a story about capital punishment. I found a recent Ohio case, and Dorothy Olding took the idea to Herbert Mayes, editor of *Cosmopolitan.* Murl Daniels was

*I lost track of him but I have the impression that efforts were made to find a place for him in other institutions. I don't know what finally became of him.

twenty-four, the son of poor, unlettered hill people in a Columbus, Ohio, slum. He had suffered brain damage at thirteen when a truck hit him and soon he began getting in trouble—sexual delinquency, petty thievery, stealing cars. He was bounced around by the courts and by doctors and social workers and put in a reform school. Though not psychotic, he was diagnosed as a psychopathic personality, that wastebasket of psychiatry which contains so many dangerous men, men whom the psychiatrists cannot label psychotic or mentally defective but who have some inexplicable emotional and mental problem that drives them to make war on society. When at twenty he held up a storekeeper, the court sentenced him to an institution at Mansfield that was called a reformatory but was really a harsh maximum-security prison. Paroled after three and a half years, he teamed up with a violent moron he had met there, and they began holding up taverns. In one they killed the owner. They decided to get even with a prison guard who had, they thought, mistreated them at Mansfield. They couldn't find him but found his superior, one of the head guards, and they executed him and his wife and daughter. On the run, they killed a young man to get his car. At a roadblock, police captured Daniels and killed his partner. Daniels was sentenced to death by electrocution.

I wrote the Daniels story largely from interviews—interviews with everybody I could find who survived the crimes. His father told me, "Society raised him and now they'll kill him." He was right. Society knew of nothing to do with him but to execute him. I went to the Ohio State Penitentiary and witnessed the electrocution, lined up in the death chamber with the prison warden and other witnesses about eight feet in front of the electric chair while the chaplain and two guards half dragged him in, praying with the chaplain, mumbling while he was strapped into the chair, "Our Father who art . . ."; then a little blue light over his head went off and a red one on and a dynamo hummed, and his body jerked once, hard, and he strained forward against the heavy straps, a little wisp of blue smoke curling up from the electrode on his bare white leg. I never witnessed another electrocution.

"The Chair" was a grim story. In publishing it, Herbert Mayes of *Cosmopolitan* showed considerable courage. I doubt that anybody who has witnessed an execution favors capital punishment. I never

knew a prison warden who did. No one, of course, can condone what Murl Daniels did; the world lost little when it lost him. Nonetheless, the idea of the state's closing in to take the life of a man it helped to raise is difficult to support.

Killers do not always come from the slums. Teen-age children of the middle class kill too. And sometimes, writing about them, I was struck by the parallels between their lives and my own. Milton Babich was nineteen, the son of respectable parents in a suburb of Milwaukee. The Babich and Birmingham families lived only a few blocks apart; their children went to high school together. Kathleen Birmingham was not quite eighteen. She fell in love with Milton Babich. They planned to get married. Kathleen became pregnant. They could not bear to tell their parents. They decided to elope. But Kathleen had a kid sister, Pat, who was a great tease. Kathleen and Milton came to believe that Pat knew Kathleen was pregnant. They thought she was teasing them about it. They feared she would tell their parents. Milt told her that she must stop talking about Kathleen's pregnancy because the neighbors would talk and embarrass their parents. She just giggled. He killed her. He was sentenced to life imprisonment.

My piece consisted almost entirely in the texture of the lives of these youngsters and their families—hardworking father, mother with few interests outside her children, the honor roll, a long dress for the senior prom, college plans, strict parental rules. After Kathleen became pregnant she and Milton Babich talked about little else. "The more we thought about it," Kathleen told me, "the more we dreaded telling our folks. We'd disgrace them." Nothing in Milt Babich's life showed criminal tendencies. If ever a crime had a social context, this one did—and the context was the rigid morality of the middle class in 1949. Such a crime is almost unimaginable today. One has to reread the Babich story to realize fully what is meant by the phrase "the revolution in morals" of the 1960s and 1970s.

In some such cases, I began concentrating not only on the social context of the crime but also on the mysteries of human behavior. On the night of September 15, 1951, in Ann Arbor, Michigan, a quiet college town, a nurse was walking home alone on a tree-lined street from the hospital where she worked. Three teen-age boys

came along in their car and one of them, Bill Morey, got out, stalked her with a heavy rubber mallet in his hand, and, coming up behind her, smashed her skull for no apparent reason. They did not even know her. Two of them were eighteen, and the other seventeen. They had no felony records. They came from respectable families. They were nice-looking boys, well spoken, neat, mannerly. The town was shocked. More than one parent thought, as one told me, "There but for the grace of God goes my own son." Why? Why did they kill? I went to Ann Arbor to try to find out.

Ordinarily I would have talked to the parents of the boys last, but in this case I realized that if the parents, especially the parents of Bill Morey, would not talk to me freely, I had no story; so I went to see Mr. and Mrs. Morey—I might as well find out now.

The Moreys lived in Ypsilanti, Ann Arbor's neighboring town. I went there by bus and walked to their house. Bill Morey lived all his life in the same house on a quiet street shaded by fine old trees. His house was a low rambling cottage, comfortable and lived in, Bill Morey's father had been born in this house.

Mr. and Mrs. Morey were reluctant to talk to me. The whole thing was over, Bill was in prison, they did not want to relive it—but they actually relived it every day, they dated everything in their lives as "before *this* happened" or "after *this* happened," this terrible shattering event, the murder. I told them I was trying to write not a sensational story but a thoroughgoing study for a serious magazine that would try to discover *why* it had happened. They said they themselves did not know why. I talked awhile about my own life, saying that in high school I had done many of the same things Bill Morey had done—drinking, driving fast and recklessly—and I talked about Fran's and my own daughter, approaching adolescence with all its perils.

At length they began responding, Mrs. Morey nodding her head at things I said, volunteering something about Bill—they both still called him that. I said I wanted to find out what kind of boy he really was, not what the newspapers said, and they began to tell me. For an hour and a half. I did not press them on anything and, leaving, I said I'd like to come back tomorrow. I did, and we talked for two hours, and the day after that for four hours, and the following week for more.

But although I spent weeks talking to them, to the families of the

other boys, to their schoolteachers, to their friends, and to everybody else I could find who knew them, to their lawyer, to a psychiatrist who thought Bill a psychopathic personality, and to the boys themselves in prison,* I never really answered the question of why—why they had killed. Why?—to a reporter, it is the only question that matters and it is the only question he can never really answer.

An important part of the boys' lives was the world they lived in— Ann Arbor, the quiet, somewhat stuffy college town, and its rowdy neighbor, Ypsilanti, where they themselves lived, a blue-collar town turned upside down by the war, which drew thousands of hillbilly workers to the Ford Motor Company's huge Willow Run bomber plant, hillbillies who after the war went on relief and turned Willow Run into a slum and whose children ran wild and smoked marijuana and drank; Ypsilanti and the automobile with its roaring exhaust became characters in the story. So the Morey story combined crime in its social context and inquiry into the roots of human behavior, an ambitious undertaking. I made a book of a longer version of the Morey story and there I had room to expand the material on the boys' society. It was well reviewed. But it didn't answer "why?"

I did a piece about racial segregation—the web of legal and traditional barriers that kept Negroes† jammed into a Chicago ghetto. This was 1947, before the civil rights movement, long before the Negro revolution; it was not only before the Supreme Court struck down school desegregation but even before it struck down the restrictive real-estate convenant that helped keep housing racially segregated. I wanted to do not an article, crammed with demographers' statistics, but, rather, a story about a man. James Hickman had been a sharecropper in Mississippi. He was deeply religious and deeply devoted to his children. In 1945 Hickman came to Chicago seeking to better his lot. He found a job in a steel mill and began looking for an apartment so he could bring his wife and eight children up from

---

* Morey and one of his confederates were sentenced to life in prison—in Michigan life is not parolable; the third boy was sentenced to twenty-two years to life.
† Instead of "blacks," the word in current usage. I write "Negro" for historical reasons, as does Ralph Ellison.

Mississippi. He looked for months—apartments open to Negroes were desperately scarce. Finally he found a place, an attic room atop a four-story tenement owned by a Negro. The three youngest children slept with Mr. and Mrs. Hickman; the others slept in the other bed. The attic had no electricity, no gas, no heat, no water. But it was shelter. Soon, however, the landlord decided to cut the building up into smaller apartments in order to produce more rent. To do this, he wanted to evict all the present tenants. He and Hickman quarreled, and the landlord said if he couldn't get the tenants out any other way he'd burn the building down. On January 16, 1947, the fire occurred. Four of Hickman's children were killed in the fire. The coroner's jury could find no innocent origin for the fire but no hard evidence of arson.

Hickman was convinced that the landlord had burned the building. He sat alone and spoke to the dead children. He bought a .32-caliber automatic pistol. He shot the landlord dead. He was indicted for murder. An organizer for the Socialist Workers party, two Chicago labor leaders, and two civil liberties lawyers formed the Hickman Defense Committee. After the first trial ended in a hung jury, the defense committee brought pressure to bear on the Chicago political machinery and reached an agreement with the state's attorney, and the judge found Hickman guilty of manslaughter and sentenced him to two years on probation.

In preparing to do the piece, I read Gunnar Myrdal's *An American Dilemma* and other books, but only for my own background information—I wrote the piece almost entirely from interviews, especially interviews with Hickman and his wife and with the landlord's relatives. I simply told the story of Hickman's and the landlord's lives and their world—the world below.

I fear that in describing all these stories here so briefly and so baldly, I have robbed them of their humanity. And that I may have seemed to reduce human suffering to journalistic techniques. If this is so, I am sorry. While I was doing the work, while I was listening to these people and writing about them, I felt quite otherwise, and I like to think I helped the reader feel some of what they felt.

Russell Lynes of *Harper's* asked Ben Shahn, the artist, to do some drawings to illustrate the Hickman story. Ben and I talked in the

quiet paneled library at *Harper's*. He was a big burly man with the kindest eyes I ever saw. He asked what Hickman and his family looked like and I described them; he asked about the tenement and I drew a sketch for him. (*I*, drawing sketches for Ben Shahn!) We became friends and collaborators. Soon I did another piece for *Harper's,* one about the Mecca Building in Chicago, once a fancy apartment house on the South Side, now a vast slum, and about the lives of some of the two thousand–odd Negroes who lived there in misery, and Ben came to Chicago to see it and illustrate the story, wonderful drawings. He and his wife and Fran and I took to spending weekends in each other's homes. When I visited New York, Ben would take me on walking tours of the Lower East Side slums where he had grown up; and when he came to Chicago I would take him on walking tours of the Negro ghetto and the white criminal slums, where dwelt the people I wrote about. He believed that the human eye can really see nothing unless it is traveling slower than five miles per hour. I had known this intuitively all along—I never made notes on the appearance and atmosphere of a neighborhood from a car but always on foot. I like to think I saw things as he did.

I had known little about Ben's work but now I went to see all his pictures I could find. I came to love his slab-faced men, his savage portrayals of the persecutors of Sacco and Vanzetti, his passionate pictures suffused with liberal idealism. He had what most of us lack—a vision of life. His was a tragic vision. Yet he was a very funny man. He was fond of saying that Michelangelo, up on a scaffold painting the Sistine Chapel, hollered down to the pope, "What color you want the ceiling, boss?" Once at the height of the Senator Joe McCarthy madness an FBI agent came to see him, for he was considered by the McCarthyites a radical. The FBI man tendered his identification. Ben, instead of glancing at it perfunctorily and handing it back as most of us do, held on to it and gazed at it long and carefully, several times glancing up from it to stare at the agent's face. Finally he shook his head and said, "That ain't you." The agent protested. Ben just kept repeating it and also saying, "A nice-looking fella like you, you shouldn't let them make you carry a picture like that around. That ain't you." The agent retreated in disarray. Ben told me that once as a child he had come home from

school late, and when he knocked on his apartment door, his mother had called, "Who's there?" and he had said, "It's me," and she had called, "That ain't you." He had been terrified. Later, on a day when Ben had received word that he had won some high international honor, his small son asked him to tie his shoe, and Ben said, "Not today, son, not today." Ben thought the most romantic experience of his life was a visit to the villa of a wealthy South American friend where, when he went to bed, he found that his hostess had sprinkled perfume on his pillow. During the years of America's prosperity in the 1950s, he and I thought to collaborate on a book about poverty in Appalachia; one of the regrets of my career is that we never did it. He once told me that I should write only about things I deeply loved or hated; it was, he said, the way he painted.

The Hickman story affected Ben powerfully and it influenced his work. Later, in a book, *The Shape of Content,* he traced the origins of one of his most powerful paintings, *Allegory,* to the Hickman story. It was a picture of a great red beast, part lion, part wolf, standing over the huddled figures of its child victims. Ben wrote that when Russell Lynes of *Harper's* first asked him to make the Hickman drawings, he had assembled visual material, then discarded it, for he felt the universal implications of the event transcended the immediate crime. He tried an abstract approach and discarded that too. He finally returned to "the small family contacts, to the familiar experiences of all of us, to the furniture, the clothes, the look of ordinary people." This had been my own approach. (I always made notes on the things in a man's apartment while interviewing him.) Of all the symbols he developed in his preliminary Hickman drawings, Ben used only one—a highly stylized wreath of the tongues of flame with which he crowned the Hickman house. When he finished his *Harper's* drawings, he could not get the story out of his mind. It had awakened memories—the tenement where he lived as a child had burned. The lionlike head, its mane derived from the tongues of flame over the Hickman house, became the painting *Allegory.* He tried to imbue that great red beast with all the terror he had ever felt about fire, and under its body he placed the figures of the four dead children, "which, to me, hold the sense of all the helpless and the innocent." Thenceforward, Ben repeatedly used the beast's fire-ringed head in his work. He gave Fran and me a rendering of it;

under it he lettered in Aramaic, "Where there is a pen there is no sword; where there is a sword there is no pen."

3.

The *Post*'s normal length for a piece was eighteen and a half pages, about five thousand words. So was most magazines'. This was good discipline for a writer—it forced you to write tightly, without an unneeded word. But some stories simply could not be forced into that straitjacket. Stuart Rose and Ben Hibbs knew it and occasionally would give me eight thousand or ten thousand words and print the piece as a "special double-length feature," or give me even more space and print it as a series of articles. (The Morey story ran as a four-part.) A few other magazines did the same.

As I have said, today there may be editors like that but I don't know them. Like television "news," printed articles have gotten shorter and shorter. Instant info. Recently I proposed an op-ed page newspaper piece comparing U.S. policy after the fall of Somoza with our policy in the Dominican Republic after the fall of Trujillo. (I had been U.S. ambassador there then.) *The New York Times* editor said it absolutely must not exceed 1,000 words. I asked for a double-part space. No. I wrote about 5,000 in rough draft, cut it radically down to 1,120, and submitted it; he turned it down—too long and not very good. He was right that it was no good—it couldn't be done in 1,000 words or anything like it. I sent it, rewritten at 4,500 words and pretty good, to *The Washington Post*. The editor liked it but regretfully turned it down: His absolute limit was 3,000. I do not blame these editors; they are following publishers' dictates. But under their rules they never would have published my Centralia story, at 18,000 words. They never would have published John Hersey's "Hiroshima"—to make room for *it*, the editor of *The New Yorker* threw everything else out of that issue. I am not arguing that my little piece on the Dominican Republic and Nicaragua was worth as much space as Centralia or Hiroshima. I am only arguing that an editor is supposed to have the freedom, and the judgment, to edit. His present course may make him extinct—if one has a computer to count words, who needs an editor?

Each of the stories I have presented so far dealt with a particular criminal case. Gradually, under the guidance of Stuart Rose, I

began writing for the *Post* long series of pieces not on criminal cases as such but about subject areas—a series on abortion, another on divorce, another on school desegregation, a series on Joliet-Stateville Penitentiary in Illinois and one on the riot at the maximum-security prison in Jackson, Michigan, as well as a long series on Columbus State Hospital in Ohio and the care of the mentally ill, another long series on television, and another on criminal justice and why it sometimes goes wrong. These stories ran as serials in the *Post*, sometimes as many as seven installments. These were not midwestern stories, they were national stories. On abortion, I did most of my legwork in Los Angeles. On divorce, I did the legwork in Las Vegas and New York, in Los Angeles and Beverly Hills and Long Beach, California, as well as in Chicago, Toledo, and Brownstown, Indiana, attending court, talking to divorce lawyers, divorce judges, marriage counselors, law professors, and couples that were going through divorce.

My writing was changing in another way. Earlier, in the pieces about crimes, almost my entire effort had gone into packing into the story every single fact I had space for and, to a great extent, letting the facts speak for themselves. Now, in the desegregation and divorce stories, not only was I permitting myself to draw conclusions, but also my pieces were more consciously *written*, were not simply agglutinations of facts. In the divorce piece, for example, I wrote, "But he moved out and she sued him for divorce; and indeed the story is repeated so often that after a few days in divorce court you would think that every little ranch house in the suburbs is a little nest of hate." I even quoted the wonderful passage from E. M. Forster that ends, "May Love be equal to the task." I don't know why my work was changing. Perhaps it was the confidence that comes with experience—I'd been writing for a good many years by now. And perhaps I was now able to spend enough time on each story to feel, when I started writing, that I had become an expert on the subject, enough time too to allow me to reflect upon the facts—and to shape the language.

In publishing some of these stories, the *Post* showed considerable courage. At the time I wrote the abortion story, abortion was a far different issue from what it is today. Abortion was entirely secret and illegal, a crime in every state except to save the mother's life. Moreover, it was something never mentioned in polite society; the

newspapers still called it "illegal surgery," not abortion. Once again I was proud that the *Post*, a family magazine, dared publish anything about it at all. (I saw other examples of editorial courage—in a story for *McCall's* I wrote a picture of the bloody butchering inside the Chicago stockyards; a major meat-packer threatened to pull his advertising out of *McCall's* if the magazine published it; Otis Wiese, the editor, defied him and published it as I had written it.) On abortion, I concluded that support was growing for medically therapeutic abortion, that it was growing less rapidly for abortions for socioeconomic reasons, but that in general the trend seemed to be toward more permissive laws. Neither I nor anybody else had any idea the trend would move so fast as to bring us to where we are today.

When the *Post* editors asked me to do a story on what had happened since the Supreme Court school desegregation decision two years earlier in 1954, they did not know exactly what they wanted but felt sure there was a story in it for them. I spent about two weeks floating around the Deep South looking for the story. South Carolina, Georgia, Alabama, Mississippi—it was all new territory to me, and eventually the South itself became the central character in my story. Like many northerners, I had tended to think of the South as monolithic, had not realized how much state differed from state, South Carolina from Mississippi, how great were differences even within one state—raw Birmingham had little in common with graceful Montgomery. But in the region as a whole, what struck me most forcibly was that I, a northern liberal, had never fully comprehended the breadth and depth of southern resistance to desegregation. The resistance's principal instrument was the Citizens' Councils, called White Citizens' Councils in the northern press. This, I thought, was the story—the councils, their leaders, and the South itself. Whether I could get the story was a different question. Southern segregationists were at that time suspicious of, if not downright hostile to, northern reporters, who, they thought, had used them ill. I managed. In the end I cast up accounts on the Citizens' Councils. I thought that at that time the councils were losing momentum and the Ku Klux Klan gaining. I thought anti-Semitism was on the rise and free speech on the decline. Labor unions were being hurt, for while their national organizations supported desegre-

gation, most of their southern members opposed it. Negroes were leaving the Deep South. I thought violence might replace peaceable resistance and Birmingham was the most dangerous city. (Both opinions later proved correct.) I raised the question whether the Supreme Court's Fabian approach to desegregation had been a mistake, allowing resistance time to organize. Three revolutions, I thought, might in time, by altering the situation of Negroes, swallow up the whole issue—urbanization, industrialization, and farm mechanization. (I also thought that in the long run the only solution to the problem was miscegenation but I did not say so.)

The *Post* editors liked the series but thought it left the impression that desegregation could never be accomplished anywhere, so I did a fifth installment on successful desegregation in the border states and failure in Chicago (still, in the 1980s, probably the most segregated city in the nation). This was a national, not a regional, problem.

After the series was published, J. J. Simmons, a moderate council leader, called me up from Mississippi and told me, "They're tearin' down all the statues of Robert E. Lee down here and erectin' statues to John Bartlow Martin." I told him that had not been my purpose but I was glad he thought the piece fair. He came up to visit Fran and me and spent a night with us. (Fran had some American Civil Liberties Union literature lying on her desk in the kitchen; she quickly hid it.) We got along fine with Simmons, and both he and I thought it important, in those difficult days, to maintain some sort of North-South dialogue, even if only between him and me. Later the *Post* series was published as a book, *The Deep South Says Never,* and Arthur Schlesinger, Jr., contributed a generous foreword to it. Still later, at the 1960 Democratic national convention, southern delegates arrived wearing lapel buttons reading simply NEVER.

A series I did for the *Post* on the Jackson prison riot, as well as other pieces about other prisons, convinced me that big maximum-security prisons—still the heart of the American prison system—make no sense. Jackson Prison in Michigan blew up in riot in 1952, one of a wave of riots that swept the country like a contagion, as prison riots do. In a certain way, the Jackson prison riot resembled the Centralia mine disaster. Over the years, investigation after in-

vestigation had been warning that Jackson was some day going to explode. But nobody had done anything about it. The investigations had warned that all the ingredients of trouble were there—it was too big, too overcrowded, and its convicts were too diverse. Big—it was the biggest prison in America, with 6,569 inmates. Overcrowded— because Michigan's state mental hospital and its reformatory and its only other prison were overcrowded, Michigan had for years been using Jackson as a dumping ground, until by the time of the riot no cells could be found for more than 100 inmates, and they were sleeping on cots in the halls; and overcrowding means idle convicts with no prison jobs, and that means trouble. Diverse population— young first offenders thrown in with hardened criminals and psychotic killers: Jackson had everything, including 547 lifers (*Michigan* lifers, nonparolable), but also 307 men who could just as well have gone to the county jail, including 35 convicted of nonsupport, and it had 859 sex offenders and 126 sexual psychopaths. Jackson had no psychiatrist. But it had between 1,000 and 2,000 prisoners who should have been in mental institutions, not prison. Jackson was almost totally unmanageable—and everybody had known it for years.

I concluded that Jackson had not worked under the old system of iron discipline in the 1930s, not when discipline relaxed and the convicts ran it, nor when prison industry expanded, nor when "individual treatment" became fashionable. Perhaps it was time to conclude that Jackson wouldn't work under any dispensation. And the same could be said of most other American prisons.

This suggested, I thought, that prison itself is at fault. Its purpose is to protect society. But it doesn't. The most remarkable fact about the Jackson riot and the others in 1952 was that none of the inmates tried to escape. They simply wanted to vent their fury against their condition. Just so, the Negro rioters in the city streets of America in the 1960s did not attack whites; they wrecked their own slums. A riot never occurs in a prison honor camp. A few men walk away from one. But they never show the terrible tension and hatred they showed at Jackson. The pressures built up by prisons themselves cause prison riots. Parole boards know that a prisoner who adjusts well to prison life will not necessarily behave himself in free society. Did not this suggest that we were really teaching men to adjust to

prison, not to the free world? That we were prisonizing them, not rehabilitating them? And 95 % of them return to live among us. Most of those go back to prison for new crimes. Prison controversy tends to polarize around whether convicts should be "coddled" or "cuffed." This, I thought, missed the point. We had known for years that we should separate the prisoners who could be rehabilitated from those who could not, should help those "curable" find their way back. But we didn't do it. We were manufacturing habitual criminals then turning them loose on ourselves.

One afternoon at Jackson a middle-aged inmate told me, "I got what I deserve. But the punishment never ends. This abnormal life, this regulated life, the dull, deadly, corroding monotony—you can't expect anything good to accrue from such a life. Of course we know this is no hotel, it's a prison. . . . [But] here there is no hope, nothing. Without hope you're a zombie, a living dead man. They come to life when there is a riot somewhere else. Then there is feverish excitement. I never saw such an outpouring of hatred as I saw in the riot. The hate in here would sicken a pig. Hate begets hate, violence begets violence. Here all you hear is lock up, lock up, lock up, day after day, year after year in this cold gray world, you lose touch with the decent men, no one ever says 'please' or 'thank you'—" He broke off, a red-faced Irishman, a devout Catholic, and looked upward, saying, "If God spares me I'll never come back."

"But," I wrote, "they do."

I expanded the Jackson series into a book on prison reform, *Break Down the Walls,* visiting other prisons and studying what we know about the roots of criminality, especially the "psychopathic personality." I became convinced that prisons were being run according to a myth, the myth of rehabilitation. Rehabilitation, I thought, was all but impossible inside a maximum-security prison. I concluded further that prisons as we know them should be abolished. That was a long-term aim. We could not rehabilitate a man until we knew what made him a criminal. To find out we needed research into the roots of criminality. When we knew how to rehabilitate him we would not put him into prison to do it. In the meantime, until that distant day, we should institute certain reforms, including separating hardened criminals from the others, razing or breaking up such monstrosities as Jackson, building numerous prison camps and farms and a few

medium-security prisons plus institutions for the criminally insane, letting about half of all inmates out of prison (to prison farms and camps, parole), putting the few truly dangerous ones into a few small maximum-security institutions, revising the inequitable criminal code, and abolishing the death penalty. Ballantine published the book and *Harper's* published a brief summary of it under the apt title "Prison: The Enemy of Society."

But all this noble crusading had little effect. Nearly thirty years later, Attica prison in New York and a number of other prisons blew up in riot for roughly the same reasons that Jackson had blown up. So, in 1981, did Jackson itself. And we are still building big new maximum-security prisons.

Having used Jackson Prison as a way to write about convicts and prison reform, I wanted to use a state hospital to write about the mentally ill and their care. Looking for a hospital that was neither snakepit nor showplace, I visited several and fastened on Columbus State Hospital and did a six-part *Post* series. For five weeks I lived there day and night.* (One night Fran tried to call me and the switchboard operator told her, "He's on a locked ward.")

There were in the United States some 750,000 persons in mental hospitals. One of every 12 children born today would spend some part of his life there. Mental illness was America's number one health problem.

Columbus State was in many ways like all the other state hospitals in America—big, overcrowded, short of doctors and attendants. And full of human suffering. There were only 10 doctors who were actually seeing to the day-to-day psychiatric care of the 2,700 patients—and not one of them was a full-fledged certified psychiatrist. Attendants, mostly farmers and laborers, were so scarce that frequently at night one attendant had to try to handle three wards alone, a block-long labyrinth of rooms and corridors and locked doors with 250 patients. Day after day after day, I prowled the cav-

---

* I should make it clear that I did not, here or ever, masquerade as an inmate, as some reporters do. I consider that melodramatic, phony, and useless. A reporter masquerading as a convict, for example, does not really feel like one, because, unlike the real thing, he knows he can leave anytime he wants to. All he gains is a melodramatic line in his story that he "lived like a convict." He did not. I simply lived at Columbus State to get the feel of the place and because it was convenient.

vernous old high-ceilinged wards, usually with a doctor, sometimes alone. Psychotic patients wandered about aimlessly, dim figures moving silently in dim passageways, some fixed rigid in grotesque trance, some screaming in terror. Some of us think, "It's OK— they're crazy, they're happy, they don't know anything's wrong with them." But this is simply not so. They are most assuredly not happy—they live in agony, in a private hell; and they *do* know that something is terribly wrong with them. At first, the wards seemed forbidding to me, chilling, unfathomable. Later, after I had come to know the doctors and understand what they were trying to do, after I had talked to the patients and studied the histories of their broken lives, the lives for them unbearable, I realized that this place, far from frightening, was for the patients a place of peace. Sometimes the old words are best—we no longer call such a hospital an asylum but that is, really, what it is: an asylum, a refuge.

I presented cases to illustrate each of the major diagnoses of psychoses and patients to illustrate the treatments they received. Only a handful were receiving psychotherapy, 117 were on electroshock. The tranquilizing drugs such as Thorazine and Serpasil were new at that time, and on them patients became more manageable and less violent, the drugs were eliminating psychosurgery and reducing electroshock. They had originally been called miracle drugs, but by the time I was there some of the early enthusiasm had abated, and the medical director told me, "The new drugs are not a cure-all." And, speaking of one schizophrenic patient, "We know darn well a pill isn't going to change her into a normal girl. We'll hope to get her out someday, but we'll never make her well."

Later, after visiting other hospitals and doctors, I made a book of all this, a book about the care of the mentally ill in America in the mid-twentieth century. Dr. Daniel Blain, medical director of the American Psychiatric Association, wrote a generous introduction for it. Ben Shahn made a marvelous dust jacket, and Harper published it under my title, *The Pane of Glass*. (A schizophrenic once said to a psychiatrist, "There is a pane of glass between me and mankind.") Though it was flawed, I thought it the best book I'd yet written. What surprises me upon rereading is the sympathy it evokes not for the patients but for the doctors, whereas in writing about prisons, I had evoked sympathy for the prisoners, not their keepers.

In the book, I wrote of the need for more support for both public and private mental institutions—some patients at Columbus who might have benefited from the new drugs were denied them because the state did not provide enough money—and above all the need for more money for research—we simply didn't know enough about schizophrenia. While I was still editing the book, a stranger telephoned me long distance early one Sunday morning and said she had read my stories in the *Post* and wondered if I knew of any worthwhile psychiatric research projects she might support financially—she was, I believe, the wife or widow of a wealthy Texan. I told her about two projects, and she contributed a good deal of money to them. I dedicated *The Pane of Glass* to her.

The *Post* editors asked me to do a series on television but, as with the Deep South, didn't know exactly what they wanted. As before, I floated around in the field for a while, then proposed a series that would raise these questions: Why is so much of television so bad? Why is some so good? How do programs get on the air? Why do they go off? Who is responsible—who decides what comes into your living room? Can television be improved? How?

I knew almost nothing about television. I began my work by arising one day at 5:30 A.M., breakfasting hastily, and, sitting down in front of our television set, turned it to Channel 5, stared at the screen with its ellipse containing a figure 5 and the words "NBC WNBQ Chicago," watched the screen blink, and heard a voice say, "Good morning, we welcome you to another day of outstanding television programs." Outside it was barely light. I had chosen the day and the channel wholly at random. I stayed seated in front of the set, watching unremittingly, commercials and all, until Channel 5 went off the air twenty hours later. Like many of my friends, I myself seldom watched television, considering it uninteresting, tasteless, and a waste of time. Until that day, however, I had not fully realized how uninteresting, how tasteless, and what a waste of time television was. No one, of course, watches twenty hours of television straight. Nonetheless, this was what one television station, affiliated with a leading network in a big city, sent out over the airwaves, which were owned by the people, that day.

I did legwork in Hollywood, Chicago, Washington, and New

York—spoke to local broadcasters, network executives, advertising agencies, news broadcasters, film producers and directors, members of Congress, Newt Minow (the Federal Communications Commission's new reform-minded chairman), and people who operated the life-or-death oracle called the Nielsen ratings. I was with Walter Cronkite in the CBS news room in New York—the real one, not the one you see on the evening news—when the Bay of Pigs invasion story broke. I was having breakfast with Frank Stanton, president of CBS, in his private dining room atop the CBS building in New York the morning the United States was shooting a man into the air in a missile, an early preparation for later space shots, live on all networks, and Stanton, watching intently, said, "We'll do more and more of this. . . . All entertainment goes in cycles. Fatigue sets in—audience fatigue. But there's no fatigue for this," nodding toward the screen.

I concentrated my study of a network on CBS, reporting on its economics and its bureaucracy, on what kind of people its executives were, on why *Playhouse 90*, one of the highest-quality series of television drama ever, went off the air. (Stanton told me, "Because the audience turned its back on it. The fatigue factor. Television wears out ideas and men faster than anything." Because, said some of the people who had made *Playhouse 90*, CBS decided it was easier, cheaper, safer, more popular, and more profitable to present junk.) What all networks and stations and what all advertisers were interested in was "cost per thou"—how many dollars it cost an advertiser to reach one-thousand viewers. The bigger the audience, the lower the cost. Network TV was first of all a business. It was a tough business, like the auto-making business. Theater people sometimes did uneconomic things because they wanted to or thought they ought to. Publishers still published poetry. There was little room for such sentiments in television.

I reached several conclusions. Television people seemed vaguely uneasy. They had always deeply feared—and held in contempt—the viewing public. Now they had begun to fear that people would simply quit watching. They wished that programs were better but felt there was little they could do about it—they must make profits. Anyway, nobody knew in what ways people wanted television improved. The people themselves could not know. If one hundred

years ago you had asked people how they wanted lighting improved, they would have asked for a longer wick or better kerosene. Nobody would have asked for an incandescent bulb. How could TV be improved? Some people looked hopefully to pay television, to public television, to UHF stations, hoping their high-quality presentations would force the commercial networks to upgrade their programming. Some people thought the government ought to establish its own network much as the Tennessee Valley Authority had been established as a yardstick by which to measure utility rates. But not much of this has come to pass in the quarter century since I wrote this series. To date, nobody has invented that incandescent bulb.

Over the years I had seen criminal justice go wrong many times—innocent men convicted, guilty men convicted but convicted wrongfully, guilty men set free. I decided to do a series on why and how criminal justice sometimes goes wrong, and the *Post* approved.

For a long time I had been interested in civil liberties, the citizens' defenses embodied in the Bill of Rights in the Constitution. I suppose I was drawn to this by my sympathy for the guy who never had a chance. By now Fran had gone on the Illinois board of the American Civil Liberties Union, and I became somewhat involved. In doing preliminary legwork for my *Post* series, I saw that justice sometimes went wrong because of an overzealous prosecutor, incompetent defense counsel, misidentification by eyewitnesses. Sometimes it went wrong because of procedural matters: illegal detention, coerced confession, no right to counsel, self-incrimination, illegal search and seizure—things that laymen term "mere technicalities" but things that lie at the heart of the Bill of Rights and so at the heart of freedom in our democratic system. I wanted to find criminal cases illustrating each of those problems. And cases scattered around the country, for injustice knew no geography.

In San Antonio, Texas, I found the case of Álvaro Alcorta, who, while a Mexican migrant farm worker of twenty-seven, had married a beautiful girl of fifteen. She neglected their children, became a B-girl in a bar, and taxi drivers told Alcorta she was prostituting herself. She took a young Mexican as her lover. Alcorta, crazed with jealousy, came upon them together one night by chance and stabbed her to death. At his murder trial he had a fumbling elderly lawyer

who presented a weak defense. The overzealous young prosecutor, eager to run up a record of death penalties, suppressed all evidence of her love affair, and her lover testified falsely—with the prosecutor's knowledge. Alcorta was sentenced to electrocution. But another lawyer intervened, and the U.S. Supreme Court overturned the conviction—during the arguments the justices took the hide off the prosecutor—and in the end Alcorta was sentenced not to death but to a term of years that would make him eligible for parole in one more year. The lawyer who saved his life, Fred Semaan, told me, "It was hard. I was groping. And all for a 'Meskin.' That's what they call 'em. Everybody said, 'Why the hell do that for a damn Meskin?' Everybody's attitude—that was the damndest thing about the case." And "They damn near got away with it. And if they can do that to a poor Mexican like Alcorta, and someday they decide to get you or me, they can do it."*

An expensive Chicago criminal lawyer in another case told me the night his client was aquitted of murdering his former wife, though many Chicagoans still considered him guilty, "He might have been convicted, but he was lucky—he had money. The terrible thing about it is, what do you do if you don't have money?"

In my series, I used another half-dozen cases to show why justice went wrong. In Georgia, a happy-go-lucky ne'er-do-well with a minor criminal record was accused of murdering a small-town grocer in a stickup; the grocer's wife identified him positively, and he was sentenced to the electric chair; the Georgia Supreme Court affirmed the verdict and the U.S. Supreme Court refused review. But before he could be executed another man confessed the murder and was sentenced to life, and the man on death row was set free. Lay-

---

* One night Semaan's investigator took me down into the West Side Mexican slums and parked, and we sat watching the young men and women promenading along the shadowy sidewalk in front of the bars. Presently he signaled to the leader of a little band of street musicians, and they played for us a new song that was on all the jukeboxes, a sad song, *El Corrido de Alcorta:*

> *Alavaro Alcorta mató,*
> *Y es necesario un castigo;*
> *Pero hay que ser de razón*
> *Y comprender los motivos*

> (Alavro Alcorta killed,
> and a punishment is necessary;
> But one must be reasonable
> And understand the motives)

I bought a recording and took it home to Highland Park.

men tend to consider "circumstantial" evidence—physical evidence—less reliable than eyewitness testimony, but actually criminal justice probably goes astray more often because of mistaken eyewitness identification than for any other single reason. (At a murder inquest while I was working on this series, a witness, asked to point out the man who was suspected of the murder and whom the witness said he had seen near the scene of the crime, pointed straight at me. A funny feeling.)

Two cases, one in North Dakota and one in Chicago, illustrated the issue of coerced confession. In Chicago, a young man, Emil Reck, was beaten mercilessly by the police for several days until, vomiting blood, he confessed a murder, and he was sentenced to 199 years in prison. An ACLU lawyer (and friend of ours) appealed the case to the U.S. Supreme Court, which reversed the conviction because the confession had been coerced, and he was freed. In North Dakota, the sheriff took two Indians suspected of murdering a girl out to the countryside, where a hostile crowd gathered, and somebody brought a wrecking truck and they chained one prisoner's arm to a fence post and his other arm to the wrecking truck winch—"They were going to stretch him," a witness said. Not surprisingly he confessed, pleaded guilty, and was sentenced to thirty years. The Supreme Court of North Dakota upset the conviction—"The acts that took place at the Big Flat schoolhouse are a reversion to mediaeval methods condemned ages ago." The rack was used in medieval times to torture prisoners. On it almost anybody would confess to almost anything. No confession obtained by torture can be trusted. In sixteenth-century England, men protesting the inquisitorial methods of the Star Chamber and the ecclesiastical courts advanced the idea that "no man is bound to accuse himself." From this derives the clause embedded in the Fifth Amendment of the U.S. Constitution—"No person . . . shall be compelled in any criminal case to be a witness against himself." Only the Fifth Amendment saved the Indian in North Dakota—that and the fact that his ordeal took place in front of witnesses, whereas most police torture is done in secret.

In this series, the case that meant the most to me was the case of John Simon, I suppose because I myself became involved.

I received a fan letter from a *Post* reader in Pittsburgh, an almost

illiterate letter saying that her son John Simon had been imprisoned eighteen years ago even though he was innocent. They all say that, of course, but one thing in her letter caught my attention: She said he had had no lawyer. Through Fran and her Illinois ACLU board, I asked the ACLU in Pittsburgh to look into the case. It refused, but a young lawyer there, Martin Lubow, was interested. I went to Pittsburgh, and Lubow and I investigated the case together.

Eighteen years earlier, between April 30 and May 28, 1942, in the wooded hills overlooking the West End of Pittsburgh, a series of five women and two little girls were assaulted by a robber usually wearing a blue hood over his face. He grappled with them; sometimes he used a club; he took most of the women's purses and raped or tried to rape the two little girls. All these crimes were fumbling, clumsy. The newspaper outcry was enormous. Mothers escorted their children home from school armed with clubs, citizens held a mass meeting and threatened to "take the law into their own hands," as newspapers say. The police superintendent promised the mothers that the man would be caught. Sure enough, a man was caught, and quickly, on June 2—John Simon. Just seventeen days later he began serving a prison sentence of twenty to forty years.

Lubow and I began by checking court papers, talking to John Simon in prison, and talking to his mother. Even that preliminary check convinced me we had a story. The court papers showed Simon had not had a lawyer. They showed that one of the crimes of which he was convicted had never occurred, statutory rape: A police inspector testified that the child's own doctor said she had not been raped. John Simon was feebleminded. He had been eighteen or nineteen years old at the time. He had no father, his mother was a scrubwoman and she had not been present at his trial. (So disorganized had his life been that it was not even certain when he was born.) He had little schooling. His IQ tested between 55 and 61. He had been in juvenile court several times.

He had been convicted almost entirely on the eyewitness testimony of the victims (though the attacker usually had worn a hood) and on the report of a court-appointed psychiatrist or psychologist. We would have to try to find and interview those long-ago eyewitnesses and get the doctor's report. I asked the *Post* editors if they would pay expenses and pay Lubow for his time. They would.

To find the eyewitnesses, we hired a skip-trace agency, a private

detective agency. Awaiting their report, I interviewed the policemen I could find who had been involved. Simon had told us the police had beaten him and had planted a hood in his pocket, an unlikely story, and had told him he could see his mother, as he begged, if he would sign a confession, so he did. The police, of course, denied beating him, and indeed they probably had not needed to, but they did hold him four days. During that time nobody told him he had a right to remain silent, to have a lawyer, to telephone his mother, to be arraigned before a magistrate. The police brought the seven victims in and asked them if, as eyewitnesses, they could identify him. Only one did positively, so far as we could learn, though the impression at the time was that all did.

The skip-trace agency found most of the eyewitnesses. One told me, when I asked about the lineup at which Simon was identified, "I said I wasn't too sure. The other woman said, "Yes, that's him exactly." and I was pretty young—seventeen or eighteen—and when the others pointed to him, I guess I did too." In court she testified that when the attacker tried to force her over backward, he failed because she was "a lot taller" than he. She was five feet two or three; John Simon was five feet six. She told me, however, she did not doubt his guilt.

Another of the victims did. She told me she was certain he was not the man. "He was by himself in a room, and all the women came." (Standard police procedure is, of course, to put the suspect in a lineup with other men and oblige the witness to pick him out, not to put him in a room alone.) "They said, 'This is the man.' I said, 'No it isn't. The man who grabbed me was bigger, older, taller, sharp-featured.' One of the others said at first she was not sure, but then she went along with the others. They were out to get somebody." The charge against Simon was dropped in her case. The skip-trace agency also located a man who had grappled with the attacker unmasked and he told me he had not been taken to the lineup—a fact that had always puzzled him.

Mrs. Simon told me that she had tried to hire a lawyer, John J. McGrath. When he asked if she had any money, she said she would cash a one-thousand-dollar life insurance policy. She took the policy to him, she said. To me, McGrath denied that he had been John Simon's lawyer at the time of the trial and insisted that he had not

talked to John Simon or Mrs. Simon before the trial, though oddly he said he had been in the courtroom at the trial "as a spectator . . . out of curiosity." He did, however, later represent Simon at a clemency hearing. Who, then, I asked, got the insurance money? He said he didn't know. I pursued it, however, and found that the Monumental Life Insurance Company of Baltimore had in its files a check made out to the order of McGrath for $108.76, the cash surrender value of the policy. The check was endorsed by John J. McGrath and was dated July 7, 1942—shortly after Simon was sentenced. Apparently it came too late. (At a legal proceeding ten years later, both Mrs. Simon and John Simon testified they had not tried to get a lawyer before the trial, and Mrs. Simon testified she had not employed McGrath until after John was in prison. But of course they were then trying to get John out on the ground that he had had no lawyer.)

Awaiting trial, Simon had been examined by a psychologist or psychiatrist from the Behavior Clinic of the Allegheny County Criminal Court. The clinic's report was confidential, to be seen only by the judge and prosecutor, but we got a copy. It said that Simon was "potentially dangerous," would repeat his crimes, and should be locked up for a "prolonged or indefinite" period in a place like the Huntington School for Defective Delinquents. In jail, Simon had waived arraignment and presentment to the grand jury, though he told me he did not know he had, and when they took him to court only twelve days after he was put in jail, he did not know, he told me, that it was his trial. The judge, William H. McNaugher, was by the time I got into the case president judge of the court of common pleas, one of the most respected judges in western Pennsylvania, a Republican and a Presbyterian elder; he had been serving his twelfth year on the bench when John Simon came before him. The courtroom had been crowded that day with witnesses and victims, spectators and press. The trial lasted perhaps a half hour. Somebody asked Simon if he pleaded guilty and he said yes and the man said, "Sign right here," and Simon did. The transcript showed that no attorney for Simon was present nor was Simon advised that he had a right to one. The prosecutor told him he had signed pleas of guilty to six charges and asked if he understood. He said, "Yes, but I only had five," and denied guilt in one case. A police inspector thought it

must be a certain case and the prosecutor said, "Well then, we will leave that out," but it turned out that the one Simon denied was another, and so the prosecutor dismissed that one, though its victim was the only one who had positively identified Simon in the police lineup. From first to last the case was shot through with the incomprehension of a feebleminded youth, with the haste and sloppiness of the machinery of criminal justice. No victim identified John Simon in court. The judge pronounced sentences including a sentence for the statutory rape that had not occurred. No single sentence was longer than five to ten years but the judge made the sentences consecutive; they added up to twenty to forty years in prison. At a later hearing, Judge McNaugher said Simon was "entitled to a correction" of the sentence for the rape that never had occurred—he changed the conviction from rape to attempted rape, thus cutting six months to a year off Simon's long sentence.

I interviewed Judge McNaugher. He told me he had made the sentence so severe because of the Behavior Clinic report. "I was left with nothing else but to give him a life sentence for the protection of society—of course, subject to change, as all sentences are. And I'd do the same today." He said he could not have sentenced Simon to the Huntington School. The penitentiary where he sent him had no program for reeducation of mental defectives.

There matters stood when Martin Lubow and I got into the case eighteen years later, in 1959, eighteen years that John Simon had spent in prison. That Simon was guilty of at least some of the crimes seems pretty sure. But even assuming guilt, the way he was convicted raised serious questions about the process of criminal justice. Even a guilty American is not to be imprisoned except through the just processes of the law. How we convict matters more than whether we convict. Due process is society's fundamental protection because it is the individual's only protection. Due process is more important than the incarceration of individuals, however dangerous.

John Simon was held by the police for four days. During that time he confessed, thus providing virtually the only evidence against him. The police may not have beaten him, but a confession seems dubious when it is obtained from a suggestible feebleminded youth during four days of questioning. The eyewitness identification too seems questionable. The other damning evidence came from the Be-

havior Clinic examination. There Simon was induced to incriminate himself. No one else was present. No one may know what happened at the proceeding. The psychiatrist or psychologist—not the victims or the police—became Simon's chief accuser. Yet he did not confront Simon in open court, was not under oath, and Simon had no chance to cross-examine him. It was this opinion—and it was only an opinion—that sent Simon to the penitentiary. All this smacks of the Star Chamber—gives too much power to one who works in secret, when the accused is surrounded by no safeguards at all. Nor was John Simon surrounded in open court by the safeguards offered by a lawyer. Several defenses were possible. Nobody made one on his behalf. And the proceedings were, to say the least, lacking in exactitude.

Eventually, however, we got John Simon out of prison. Lubow filed a petition for a writ of habeas corpus on the ground that Simon had had no lawyer. Judge McNaugher denied the petition. The constitutional right to counsel had not yet been established by the U.S. Supreme Court. We decided to try to establish it. Lubow appealed to the Superior and then to the Supreme Court of Pennsylvania. Both courts upheld Judge McNaugher, though both split. Meanwhile, a similar case was going up to the U.S. Supreme Court from Florida, *Gideon* v. *Wainwright,* and in 1963 the Court decided it for the defendant, establishing the right to counsel. The U.S. Supreme Court had refused to take the Simon case direct from the Pennsylvania courts, though Justice William O. Douglas had been of the opinion that it should, so Lubow started over, moving into the federal chain of courts. A federal district judge, following the landmark *Gideon* ruling, granted the petition for habeas corpus but kept Simon in prison until the Pittsburgh district attorney could try him again. After negotiation with Lubow, the DA recommended to the judge that at his new trial Simon be placed on probation. He was set free June 22, 1964, almost exactly twenty-two years after he went to prison.

The Supreme Court has held that the police may not obtain a confession while holding a man illegally, even though they did not mistreat him—what is called illegal detention. The landmark case is *Mallory* v. *United States.*

Andrew Mallory was charged with rape in Washington, D.C. He had been arrested the day after the crime betweeen 2 and 2:30 P.M. At police headquarters, he at first denied guilt. At 4 P.M. he agreed to take a lie detector test. During it he confessed. At 10 P.M. the police tried to reach a U.S. commissioner—a magistrate—to arraign him. They failed. Next morning they brought him before a commissioner. At the trial, the confession was introduced as evidence. He was sentenced to death. He appealed.

The U.S. circuit court of appeals affirmed the conviction but Judge David Bazelon wrote a dissent that soon became, in effect, the Supreme Court decision overturning the conviction. The Supreme Court applied one of the Federal Rules of Criminal Procedure, which provided that a federal officer making an arrest must arraign the prisoner before a commissioner "without unnecessary delay."* Andrew Mallory, the Court held, had not been arraigned "without unnecessary delay," nor while being questioned had he been advised of his rights to counsel, to preliminary examination, and to stand mute. The Court unanimously reversed the conviction and ordered Mallory tried again. But the district attorney dropped the case because the only evidence was the confession. Mallory was set free.

After making his mark on legal history, Andrew Mallory was arrested in Philadelphia and convicted on charges of burglary and aggravated assault. More than once civil libertarians have been chagrined when defendants for whom they won freedom have committed new crimes. I myself had misgivings about whether John Simon was still dangerous when we got him out of prison. None of that, of course, invalidates the constitutional rights of the accused.

---

*The purpose of the rule had been spelled out in 1948 by the Supreme Court in the famous *McNabb* case—"The awful instruments of the criminal law cannot be entrusted to a single functionary. The complicated process of criminal justice is therefore divided into different parts." Now the Court wrote in the *Mallory* decision: "The scheme for initiating a Federal prosecution is plainly defined. The police may not arrest upon mere suspicion but only on 'probable cause.' The next step in the proceeding is to arraign the arrested person before a judicial officer as quickly as possible so that he may be advised of his rights and so that the issue of probable cause may be properly determined. The arrested person may, of course, be 'booked' by the police. But he is not to be taken to police headquarters in order to carry out a process of inquiry that lends itself, even if not so designed, to eliciting damaging statements to support the arrest and ultimately his guilt."

The *Mallory* case blew up a storm—police, prosecutors, and conservative legislators cried that courts were "handcuffing the police," and civil libertarians replied equally shrilly. Congress investigated, and support arose for the notion that hoodlums and subversives "should be made to talk." In my conclusions I wrote:

> The fundamental importance of the Bill of Rights must not be lost sight of in fleeting uproar over subversives and Teamsters. To deny a hoodlum the right to "take the Fifth" is to start down the road that leads to Emil Reck's vomiting blood on the stationhouse floor. To hoot at "Fifth Amendment Communists" is to start down the road that leads to the prisoner on the wrecker's rack on the North Dakota plain. Undeniably the police today are impaled cruelly on the horns of a dilemma by courts that say they may not interrogate and by a public that cries for a solution of crimes by any means. But it is no remedy to permit the police to enforce the law by breaking it.

Today, what is astonishing about that series on criminal justice is that it was published at all. It was published, remember, not in *The New Republic* but *The Saturday Evening Post,* a journal not noted for liberal crusading. Yet the overarching idea of the series was to uphold the rights of the accused. As I write today, in the 1980s, the climate in the country being what it is, with cries of "law and order" abroad in the land, and with the Congress and the attorney general and the president and sometimes even members of the Supreme Court itself climbing aboard, it is almost inconceivable that such a series of articles could be published anywhere. Yet they were published during the Eisenhower years, with Senator Joe McCarthy barely behind us and his poison still infecting the body politic. Apparently there were antibodies against it. Today, in the 1980s, liberal antibodies seem absent or at least scarce.

4.

Out of these stories and many more, almost without my willing it, a theme was developing—our society does not always work as well as it ought. The Centralia mine disaster; the boy who killed his playmate; Murl Daniels, who was electrocuted; James Hickman, who

killed his slum landlord; prisons; criminal justice—through all those pieces ran the theme of society's stresses, its failures, its downright wrongdoing.

And in some, such as the Daniels and Morey stories, another theme: What are the roots of human behavior, especially human misbehavior? Indeed, all this could be subsumed under the heading "The Psychopathy of People and Their Society." I don't think I ever stated these themes explicitly, but they were there. Crime-in-context had expanded into a rather dark vision of society.

5.

Writing about politics was more cheerful. Those years, the years when I was working the Chicago streets and slums, its courts and city hall, for the big slicks, were the great years of the Chicago Democratic political machine, the machine lush and wicked, smooth and powerful. In the 1920s, the Republican machine had run Chicago, but at the bottom of the Depression, the Democrats elected one of their own, Anton Cermak, mayor in 1931, the 1932 Roosevelt earthquake destroyed the Republicans, and by 1936 most of their good precinct captains had switched to the Democratic party, and the Democratic machine, led by Mayor Ed Kelly, was on its way to becoming in the 1940s and 1950s, my time, the most powerful political organization in America.*

The machine covered every one of Chicago's fifty wards but its greatest strength lay in the river wards, the slums across the Chicago River from the city's shining false lakefront. On various stories I spent a good deal of time there, especially in the Hull House district centered on Halsted Street and Blue Island Avenue across the river—a region of garbage-strewn alleys and sagging tenements, truck docks and cheap saloons. The first waves of immigrants to wash over the Hull House district had been Germans and Irish. Then the Italians poured in, and the Germans and Irish moved westward. Then came the Negroes, and now the Mexicans. As each

---

*Mayor Cermak was assassinated in Miami at the side of Franklin D. Roosevelt. Officials believed the assassin, a crazed anarchist, had intended to shoot Roosevelt and had hit Cermak by mistake. But the Chicago whisper I heard when I reached Chicago a few years later was that the Syndicate had sent a gunman to kill Cermak because of some obscure short circuit in Chicago's notorious crime-politics switchboard.

of these peoples came here, their children went wrong, but when they moved west their later children did not, leading one sociologist to suggest that the neighborhood itself was delinquent, that it taught its children crime as other children are taught to eat with a spoon. (The trouble with this theory is that all children learn to eat with a spoon but not all the children raised here went wrong— Supreme Court Justice Arthur Goldberg, Admiral Hyman G. Rickover, William S. Paley of CBS, and Benny Goodman, among others, didn't.)

The Democratic machine controlled the election machinery, of course, and in the old days of paper ballots its poll watchers and judges could tie the pencil in the voting booth on a string too short to reach the Republican column; counting ballots, they could spoil a ballot by marking it wrongly with a bit of pencil lead concealed under a fingernail. When voting machines appeared, they could set the counting dial on the back of the machine to arrange the needed Democratic majority before the machine ever reached the polling place from storage. When computer punch-cards came in, they could while counting alter a ballot by punching a nail-hole in it. Tales abounded of ballots dumped in the river, of votes cast by dead men or by voters registered from vacant lots. No doubt mostly true. The Republicans, of course, were equally perfidious years earlier when they were in control. This is Chicago. I enjoyed it hugely. And as a matter of fact, the Democratic machine, with all its money and with more than enough city and county jobs to put a precinct captain and at least one assistant on the public payroll for every one of the city's precincts—such a machine had little need of chicanery to win. On election day the precinct captains delivered the vote. A vote—this was the payoff their constituents made to the captains, who had been doing favors for them yearlong. The rest of us forget that politicians, from precinct captains to presidents, think of nothing else, all their waking hours every day for 365 days a year, but politics.

Becoming a precinct captain was one of the few ladders a slum boy could climb up from the depths. A politician was respected. He had power. He was a white-collar man. Indoor work. He might get rich. And the entire party machine—the mayor, the ward committeemen, the aldermen—rested at bottom on the precinct captain. He was likely to be an intelligent if uneducated man, industrious, a

longtime resident of his ward. One whom I knew wore a sports shirt and slacks and spoke in breezy, side-of-the-mouth tones. His leader was the ward committeeman, who wore a diamond ring and expensive suit and drove a Cadillac, a powerhouse, member of the Cook County Democratic Central Committee, which decided who would run not only for mayor but for governor, senator, and president. Ward headquarters was only a dingy abandoned storefront with a single naked light bulb dangling over the ward secretary's desk, but it was not only a hangout for the precinct captains but also a power center where at least once a week the committeeman held court and received the supplications of the citizens whom the captains brought in. A friend of mine, an idealistic young man fresh out of law school, thought to do his bit for the democratic system by entering ward politics, despite its noxious reputation, and he walked into his ward headquarters and so announced. The ward secretary, head bent over a voters' list, looked up at him suspiciously and asked, "Who sent ya?" "What do you mean, who sent me?" "Your precinct captain send ya?" "Nobody sent me." The ward secretary said, "We don't want nobody nobody sent," and went back to his list. (The young man, Abner Mikva, later became a congressman and is now a judge on the U.S. court of appeals for the District of Columbia.) Most good precinct captains did nothing but politics lifelong, for they were rewarded with good jobs on the city or county payroll. The chief bailiff of the Cook County municipal court, for example, Al Horan, a ward committeeman, the second most powerful man in the Democratic machine, had four hundred deputy bailiffs—four hundred patronage jobs. He gave them to his precinct captains. To hold so good a job a captain had to bring in about three hundred fifty votes. How did he do it? One of them once told me, "You have to canvass the precinct. When new people move in, you make sure they change their address so they're qualified to vote. You call on them, leave your card; if we can be of any service in the future, don't hesitate. You help them renew their driver's license, pay their real estate taxes, pay their parking and speeding tickets. They're working men, they got no time to go to court. You take them to different hospitals. Who wants a letter to a state institution? There's so many things you can do personally." Trivial? Of course. But votes won that way can help decide who is president of the United States.

A precinct captain could do other favors for his relatives or close friends. He could get a man a job driving a city garbage truck, or fixing street lights. He could intercede quietly with the Parole Board on behalf of a convict in Stateville Penitentiary. He could get a man on the Chicago police force. This was supposed to be a civil-service appointment but if no civil-service examination had been held recently and the eligibility list was exhausted, anybody could be appointed temporarily. Some "temps" held their jobs for years, political patronage.

"And of course," a politician told me, "the West Side wards are your crime centers. So the most important thing the precinct captain does there is help out when someone gets in trouble with the police. Here you get into the twilight zone. The precinct captain tries first to induce the police not to file charges or to file a lesser charge. If that doesn't work, he goes to the courts, talks to the deputy bailiff and has him talk to the judge. A deputy bailiff is merely supposed to keep order in the court. But he can be the fixer."

Sometimes the fix can go pretty far. I did a piece about a Chicago policeman who, off duty, went on a drunken spree and killed two lads, one Mexican and one Italian, and wounded another Mexican in the Hull House slum. One of the policeman's brothers, a precinct captain and a deputy bailiff, had put him on the police force and then got him a choice assignment to the state's attorney's police. (The brother was a precinct captain in the ward of Al Horan, who was a close ally of the state's attorney.) The Chicago Crime Commission got a tip the case would be fixed, and sure enough, the grand jury refused to indict. But the commission and the *Sun-Times* got the case reopened and a special prosecutor appointed, and despite efforts to intimidate or bribe the key state witness, the policeman was sentenced to life imprisonment.

All this was Chicago politics. But there was more.

In years to come, Mayor Richard J. Daley of Chicago became a national figure. The election that set him on that road took place in 1955, when he was first elected mayor, and I did a series on it for the *Post*. In the state senate, Dick Daley had been Governor Adlai Stevenson's floor leader. Ward committeeman of the Eleventh Ward, a South Side Irish and East European ward near the Stockyards, he

had become the powerful Democratic county chairman when Jacob M. Arvey moved up to national committeeman. Now in 1955 the Democratic Central Committee slated him for mayor. Thus they were trying to dump the incumbent Democrat, Mayor Martin H. Kennelly. Kennelly, however, declared he would run for reelection. So there would be a Democratic primary fight, a rarity.

Martin Kennelly was an honest businessman, not a machine politician. The Democratic machine was nothing if not flexible, and a few years earlier when outcry had arisen about bossism, its leader, Jack Arvey, had persuaded Mayor Ed Kelly to step down and had slated Martin Kennelly for mayor. Jack Arvey had been a founder of the machine and was at that time its mastermind. A lawyer, a small bald man with a quick grin but a viselike mind, a man of great courtesy who could suddenly become hard as steel when crossed, Arvey had grown up in the Twenty-fourth Ward on the West Side, where Jews had moved a generation earlier to escape the Hull House ghetto. Arvey had made the Twenty-fourth Ward the most powerful Democratic ward in Chicago—Adlai Stevenson carried it by 25,000 against Eisenhower (and so could have any other Democrat, something I understood if Stevenson did not.) It surprised many people to learn, as I did when I came to know him well, that Arvey himself was far more than a machine politician; he was, by conviction, a fiercely partisan fighting liberal. As mayor, Martin Kennelly had run neither the machine nor the city but had made himself a ceremonial figure. His predecessor, Ed Kelly, the machine boss, had said, "If you don't run the machine, it'll run you." Since Kennelly chose to reign but not rule, he created a power vacuum, and in Chicago what fills a power vacuum is the criminal Syndicate; during Kennelly's reign the Syndicate took over six of the city's fifty wards, I've been told, and it drove the Democratic state chairman out of office and into hiding by sending him in the mail a little black coffin. By 1955, the machine had had enough of Mayor Kennelly and so slated Daley. And it faced more trouble that year. A young Alderman, Robert Merriam, intellectual, liberal, son of a well-known university professor, wanted to run for mayor. He had led the little bloc of reform aldermen in the city council who opposed the Democratic machine. He himself was a Democrat but he had told me if the Democrats would not slate him for mayor, he would run as a Republican. This he now did.

All this was the most formidable challenge to the Chicago Democratic machine in its twenty-four years. For weeks, starting in the slush and snow of February, I spent my days interviewing candidates and their workers in their headquarters, in city hall and the county building, in law offices and hotels, spent my evenings at their little ward meetings.

Mayor Kennelly's strategists rented a large Loop office, filled it with publicity men, a speakers' bureau, all the paraphernalia of campaigning. They attacked "the bosses." They used television as never before—"Television is our precinct captain." Every newspaper supported Kennelly. Their attacks on Daley and the machine were merciless. On television and in the papers, Kennelly was doing fine. But not in the wards, I knew.

Dick Daley, being a machine politician, inspired precinct captains. Yet good-government groups could hardly object to him—he had never been touched by scandal. (Nor was he ever.) Labor liked him. He already had twenty-eight years' experience in politics and government. He was an Irish Catholic and he was running in the largest Catholic archdiocese in the country. He never stopped campaigning. He was a thoroughgoing professional politician and looked the part—chunky body, ruddy complexion, wide-set blue eyes, dark hard-finished suits, black polished shoes. He was almost overpoweringly Irish. He was affable, smart, quick thinking. He too was by conviction a strong liberal. Around reporters, he seemed on guard. He had a wide-eyed way of talking in public about the sanctity of the American home; cynical politicians were surprised to learn that he truly believed such homilies.

The goods of Daley's political trade were his humble boyhood, his wide personal acquaintance, his loyalty to his friends. Campaigning, he lost no opportunity to proclaim that he had seven children and still lived at 3536 South Lowe Avenue, where he was born. He used the English language cruelly. Once in a speech when he meant to say "St. Lawrence Seaway," he said "St. Lawrence seaweed." Introducing an a cappella choir, he called it the "Acapulco Choir." (He is reported to have said, "We look forward to the future with nostalgia," but I never heard that.)

Daley denied it to me but his basic strategy against Kennelly seemed to be to lie low. Instead of making high-visibility appearances, he was working on the ward organization, the committeemen

and precinct captains—taking care of the good ones, getting rid of the weak ones. The machine was closing ranks. It invited back to the fold a traitorous Negro leader. It asked a liberal congressman, Sid Yates, who had never been close to its bosom, to help Daley. It asked Senator Paul Douglas and former governor Stevenson to come out for Daley. The machine showed its might the last week of the campaign—filled the downtown Opera House with four thousand party workers, and Jack Arvey warmed up the crowd, and when Daley came down the aisle surrounded by aides and bodyguards, the crowd arose and cheered, and the men close to the aisle stretched out their arms to him and screamed, "Dick! Dick!" and the pit band struck up "Chicago, Chicago, that toddlin' town" and "Happy Days Are Here Again." Happy days! They were ready for it, after the limp years of Martin Kennelly. Daley in his speech defended the machine, said, "Good politics is good government," and, scarcely mentioning issues, drew around him the mantle of the party and the common man and his beloved city. (He really did love it.) One night that week I went with him to a ward meeting, and in a bar across the street a precinct captain in a yellow shirt told me in the detached way of a surgeon facing a minor operation, "I run a precinct here, and Kennelly's going to get killed." He did, citywide—on election day, Daley got 369,362 votes to Kennelly's 266,946—a plurality of 102,416.

Next, in the general election, Daley had to run against Bob Merriam, whom the Republicans nominated and whom all the newspapers endorsed. Merriam campaigned hard. His attacks became increasingly shrill. I thought he had fallen into the hands of bad advisers. His advertising agency prepared television commercials showing not only traffic jams and uncollected garbage but also the bodies of hoodlums in the trunks of cars, which seemed to have little to do with Daley. Merriam referred often to "the Morrison Hotel politburo," which seemed to me a rather McCarthyesque attempt to attack both the machine's Morrison Hotel headquarters and the national Democratic party's supposed softness on communism.

One of Daley's aldermen said on television that Daley had seven children and they were all his own. (Merriam had been married twice, so had his wife, and two of their three children were his wife's by her first marriage.) In Catholic neighborhoods, Daley's workers

said, "You don't want a divorced Protestant for mayor, do you?" A leaflet distributed in Negro wards in Merriam's behalf said that Daley was anti-Negro. In Jewish neighborhoods, Daley workers passed the word that Merriam was anti-Semitic; in other neighborhoods they said he was a Jew.

I spent the last Sunday of the campaign in the famous Twenty-fourth Ward, riding around with the ward committeeman in his big red convertible, watching him check on his precinct captains making their final canvass. Election day, Daley won—708,222 votes, to Merriam's 581,555. Claiming victory, Daley said, "As mayor of Chicago, I shall embrace charity, love, mercy, and walk humbly with my God." He was reelected mayor every four years until he died twenty-one years later, in 1976. Though he became a national figure, he never changed, remained the same man I knew in that 1955 campaign. He was, almost surely, the best mayor Chicago ever had (but he had two flaws—he had an ineradicable blind spot for Negroes and, like most authoritarians, when he died, he left no successor). That 1955 election convinced me that reformers may turn out no better than what they seek to reform and that politics is best left to the professional politicians, and this piece and others on Chicago politics and on the state legislature in Springfield reminded me—by then I was a liberal partisan Democrat—that all virtue did not reside in the Democratic party nor all wickedness in the Republican party, that all probity did not reside downstate nor all villainy in Chicago, and that many legislators and other public officials were better than their constituents thought, that they were at least as good as their constituents deserved, that the best got too little credit, and that not enough of the worst ones got caught.

SIX

PROFESSIONAL

1.

What I have said thus far about my writing probably makes it sound a good deal more orderly and carefully planned than it was. I was doing legwork and writing all the time without any plan at all, simply taking up whatever subjects I could find or came to hand. To make a living, a freelance writer must above all keep busy. While working on a story, I always tried to look ahead to what story I would do next. Often I started on a new story the day after I finished one. Thus from time to time I took targets of opportunity—a story that presented itself in the papers, one that I ran across, or one that I had had in mind for some time.

I did a couple of *Post* stories about cases my detective friend from the fact detective days, Emil Smicklas, and his squad were working on, stories that illuminated the jungle that Chicago criminals and detectives alike inhabit. Night after night I rode the squad car with Smicklas and his two partners, cruising the West Side criminal slums, watching them stop a man on the street, search him, and put him in the squad car and take him to the dingy downtown police headquarters. I listened while Emil talked to his stool pigeons on the street. I spent days with Emil in his home. He thought of himself as

a "professional policeman." His hobbies were policeman's paraphernalia, especially wiretaps—he had his whole house wired. He loved tape recorders, invisible ink, fingerprints. But he knew that most cases are solved through information from stool pigeons. Over the years, Emil and I became friends, and he helped me with my legwork and, as I became involved in Chicago Democratic politics, I was able to help him with promotions, and he ended up a captain, the highest operating rank in the department. Once, when in her teens our daughter decided to run away to New York, I called Emil, and he and his squad intercepted her at the airport.

I put together a collection of six crime pieces from *Harper's* and the slicks for a book, *Butcher's Dozen*. I first took it to Alfred Knopf but he was in the hospital with an ankle broken from skiing and referred me to his wife, Blanche, who, the publisher of Camus and Sartre and Brazilian novelists, could not make head or tail of my project. I then took it to the Harper book publishing house, where Simon Michael Bessie and Joan Kahn accepted it. *Butcher's Dozen* was the first of several books of mine that Harper published. Ours was a good publisher-author relationship. Nevertheless, I have often thought that if I had it to do over, I would never have left Knopf. Knopf always said, "We publish authors, not books," but that sometimes makes trouble too. Ivan von Auw of the Ober agency never thought it was necessarily in an author's interest to stay with one publisher; each particular book should find its best publisher. This, too, has disadvantages. I have had several publishers, and our relationship was always good at first, but inevitably trouble came, and I about concluded that although an author and his publisher are bound together, they are, in a sense, natural enemies.

At that time, most people in the United States probably would have dimly recognized the name of Nathan Leopold. Thirty years earlier, Leopold, together with Richard Loeb, had been convicted of senselessly kidnapping and murdering a child in Chicago they chose at random—a "thrill murder," the newspapers called it—and they had been sentenced to life for murder plus ninety-nine years for kidnapping. But few Americans probably thought of Leopold as someone still alive. He was, however. I wanted to do a piece about

what happens to an intelligent man during thirty years in prison. I drove down to Stateville Penitentiary, with its high massive wall, and told him so. He listened to me without expression. Then in his precise pedantic voice, he said he wanted to consult his lawyers, his brother, other advisers. He did, and we reached agreement—the story would concentrate on his life in prison, not his crime, and he would have manuscript approval. Agreement wasn't easy—his advisers were men of substance in Chicago. And I had a special problem—some of them were friends of ours who belonged to the Jewish community in Highland Park. We saw them at dinner parties, some were involved in Fran's ACLU or in liberal Democratic affairs (as by then was I), some had grown up with Leopold himself, and their parents had been friends of his parents. At the time of this crime, the 1920s, the wealthy Jewish community of Chicago, leading merchants and philanthropists, had lived near the University of Chicago on Chicago's South Side. They belonged to the same clubs, supported the same charities, and contributed largely to the city's cultural and intellectual life. Their homes were mansions. Later most of these families had moved to Highland Park and Glencoe, where we knew them. I'm sure none welcomed my news that I was doing the piece—those memories were painful. But not one objected or tried to dissuade me. Indeed, they helped me re-create that long-ago milieu. And after the *Post* published the series, an elderly neighbor of ours who had known Leopold's parents told me it was the first fair and understanding story she had ever read about him.

Born to wealth, small and sickly as a boy, precocious, with a phenomenal IQ, Leopold had entered the University of Chicago at fifteen and by the time he was arrested at nineteen he had studied fourteen different languages, including Vulgar Latin, Sanskrit, and two Italic languages called Oscan and Umbrian that have not been used since the destruction of Pompeii.

Most of my story was an account of Leopold's thirty years in prison. As I piled up the details, it became a story of human endeavor and human endurance, in places moving; for whatever one thinks of Nathan Leopold's rather cold, forbidding character or of his terrible crime, he was a human being, and he had to survive in prison, not an easy thing—brutal guards, dehumanized convicts, deadly deadly *deadly* monotony. And always the struggle to sub-

merge himself in the vast mass of inmates, something he, being the famous Nathan Leopold, could never do. Over the years he went through several periods, some lasting months, some years, when he strove to accomplish something—studied semantics and languages, rebuilt the prison library after it was wrecked in a riot, helped other convicts get paroles by helping them find jobs on the outside, even establishing, with Richard Loeb, a correspondence school for other inmates both here and in other prisons. But when Loeb was killed in prison by another convict, Leopold lost interest in everything. He was just doing time. He was becoming an old con.

Finally in 1944 he was assigned to the prison X-ray laboratory. The war was on, and the United States was losing more men in the Pacific to malaria than to the Japanese, and Army doctors wanted to test new drugs on human volunteers. Leopold took the lead in getting inmate volunteers. He told me candidly, "I wanted to do my part [in the war]. And here was a chance to do myself some good; I knew nobody was going to hate cons for this, and there might be a reward." Sure enough, in 1947 Governor Green directed the Parole Board to review the cases of all the malaria volunteers. Some were paroled immediately; others, including Leopold, ineligible for parole, were told to petition for executive clemency. Finally in 1949, Governor Stevenson commuted Leopold's ninety-nine-year sentence to eighty-five years, making him eligible for parole in January 1953—three and a half more years.

The Stevenson Parole Board might well have paroled Leopold. But Stevenson ran for president, and Governor William G. Stratton was elected to replace him, and Stratton appointed a highly political board. It postponed the Leopold case until May, 1965—he would not even see the board again for twelve more years. Many people believed that the decision was a political one, though to me the governor denied it.*

Leopold applied for a rehearing again and again. He thought he'd be dead in twelve years. That was where things stood when, in 1954, I wrote my story. Finally the board granted a rehearing on February 5, 1958. At his request, I went down to Stateville and testified for him. I emphasized that neither the coroner nor the trial judge had

*No wonder convicts follow politics more closely than most of us—their freedom, indeed their lives, many hang on an election result.

found evidence that the murdered boy had been sexually molested, as was widely believed, and that Leopold himself during all those years in prison had received not a single guard's citation for any sort of homosexual activity. I recommended parole. The board paroled him. Later a newspaperman told me that it was my testimony that had won the parole—it got the board off the hook of paroling a "sex criminal." Leopold went to Puerto Rico to work in an X-ray clinic run by a religious order. Soon he married. Then he died. Few men have lived lives like his.

2.

A freelance has to go where the story is that some editor wants. Otis Wiese of *McCall's* sent me to Washington to cover the treason trial of Axis Sally, an American woman who had spent World War II in Germany making radio broadcasts for Hitler beamed at American troops. *Harper's* sent me to Labrador to do a piece about the opening of the iron ore field there. Herbert Mayes, a creative editor who liked to think of stories he wanted in *Cosmopolitan* and then match them to unlikely authors, called me to New York to do a piece about *South Pacific,* the most successful musical play till then produced. I asked Mayes what kind of piece he wanted. He said, "I want *your* piece." I knew next to nothing about the theater.

I read *Tales of the South Pacific,* by James A. Michener, and *South Pacific,* the musical play that Oscar Hammerstein II had adapted from it for the stage, then I went to see the show. I took notes all the way through it. Later I saw the show several more times, but what I used in my *Cosmopolitan* piece came from that first look. I have always believed in the technique of "the first look." A reporter can see a thing, anything, for the first time but once. A young newspaper reporter will for the first time race to follow a fire truck to a neighborhood alley, watch while the firemen raise a ladder to the top of a telephone pole and rescue a cat. This first look of his will be vivid, clear, all-inclusive, brilliantly lit as on the morning of creation, and he can write that kind of piece about it. But forever after, when the same thing occurs, he will simply write, "Firemen today rescued a cat on a telephone pole in the alley behind the 3000 block of Westover Street." Or he will write nothing at all. I myself could never repeat my description of the first electrocution I wit-

nessed. I have never visited a steel mill; I wanted to save my first look for the time I needed it.

In any event I loved the first *South Pacific* performance I ever saw, thought it dramatic, exciting, even in places magical. I must have communicated some of this in the Ober office, for Dorothy Olding said, "We're going to have a very stagestruck young author on our hands."

The play's central plot deals with the romance between a wholesome young American girl who is a naval ensign in World War II, played by Mary Martin, and a worldly French planter in the South Pacific twice her age, played by Ezio Pinza. (You see? Firemen rescued cat. Period.)

Oscar Hammerstein II, the author, and Richard Rodgers, the composer, were trying out a new play in Boston, and I spent several days with them there, learning how they had done *South Pacific*. Among American theatrical producers at that time, Rodgers and Hammerstein ranked at the top, and their earlier show *Oklahoma* had helped transform the American musical play. In their hotel rooms in Boston they discoursed to me on this as well as on *South Pacific*, and by going with them to see their new show and afterward listening to them criticize it I learned a good deal about casting and guiding a play to Broadway. I found them both careful, hardworking craftsmen. Back in New York I interviewed almost everybody connected with *South Pacific*, from Ezio Pinza and Mary Martin down to stagehands. In talking to them, I was struck again by their no-nonsense professionalism. Pinza was the premier basso of the Metropolitan Opera. When Rodgers first offered the female lead to Miss Martin, he told me, "She was scared to death. She didn't want to get out there and be made a fool of by a Metropolitan Opera star. She has no illusions about her singing." She had never met Pinza and had heard him only on the radio. They took her to one of Pinza's concerts. She told me, "I'd never been to a concert before. The thing I couldn't get over was, here was just this man and a piano and a bare stage. The audience was still coming in. To watch this man wait and wait and wait until you could hear a pin drop, then just start to sing—I was floored." When I saw her, she still seemed as astonished as a schoolgirl and this similarity between the leads' roles in *South Pacific* and their offstage personalities may have contrib-

uted to the believability of *South Pacific.* One night, having removed her makeup and changed into street clothes, she emerged from her dressing room with her husband, Richard Halliday, and walked down the quiet, dimly lighted corridor. As she passed Pinza's dressing room, she called out, "Good night, Ezio," and he called, "Good night, beautiful." My own silliest behavior occurred the first night I went backstage. I encountered Miss Martin's husband and, recognizing him, I introduced myself as I was accustomed to doing: "My name is Martin, M-a-r-t-i-n," spelling it for him, who was married to a Miss M-a-r-t-i-n. When I had finished the legwork on *South Pacific* and the time had come to go home and write the piece, I was sorry, an unusual circumstance; I had become involved with the story and with the people. I suppose I was indeed stagestruck. It was not that I was bedazzled by glamour but that the people involved made so much sense. They were just workmen, as I was myself. Yet down to earth as they were, what they made was magic. I found this fascinating. I even wondered if some day I myself might not make that magic. It was no longer mysterious.

Herbert Mayes of *Cosmopolitan* sent me next to Norway to do a story on Kirsten Flagstad, the Metropolitan Opera's Wagnerian soprano who was being picketed in America by people who believed she had been a Nazi or a Nazi collaborator during the German occupation of Norway in World War II. Mayes wanted me to find out if it was true. Fran and Cindy and I went to Europe aboard the *Nieuw Amsterdam*—what a marvelous way to travel!—and came back aboard the *Queen Elizabeth,* a stuffy bore. I spent several weeks on the life of Madame Flagstad, studying court documents and talking not so much to her musical associates as to her personal friends and neighbors and to business associates of her husband. I concluded that Madame Flagstad's husband had indeed collaborated with the Nazis, that he had made a great deal of wartime money from it, and that, a rabid anti-Communist himself, he had to some extent sympathized with them, but that Madame Flagstad herself had not been directly involved. She was never charged in Norway with collaboration with the Nazis. She seemed to have remained almost indifferent to wartime events, even when the Germans sent the young man next door to a concentration camp. She

was almost completely apolitical, her whole world was her music (and herself and money).

3.

I wrote a few—and only a few—fragile off-trail pieces that, unlike criminal cases or big subject areas, were not "given," did not exist until I concocted them. A few and only a few—they were too risky for a freelance. But they were pieces I wanted to do. A self-indulgence.

Up in Michigan one summer, the teen-age son of our friends Earl and Hilma Numinen got lost in the big woods, and I joined the sheriff's posse that searched for him for three days before he found his way out. When I proposed a piece on it, Fred Allen of *Harper's* was dubious and advised me not to try it unless I could make it a work of art. I wrote it anyway, and Fred liked it and published it.

One year at spring vacation time when Cindy was in fourth grade, Fran and I took her on a trip by car to follow the trail Abraham Lincoln's family followed in coming to Illinois. We started at the Cumberland Gap and headed northwest across Kentucky to Springfield, Illinois, stopping at Lincoln's birthplace and at other quiet places where his family had lived. We rummaged through ancient courthouse records, finding a land title written in blood on a sheepskin. Fran's maternal forebears had come from Kentucky and we were doing research into their lives too. This was indeed a high-risk piece, one that had to be lyric, almost poetic; it was successful, Jack Alexander of the *Post* thought, because it was so evocative of Midwest history and rural life.

One of the last pieces I did for the *Post* was a sort of valedictory on Chicago (though I did not think of it that way at the time). It was quite unlike any other story I had ever done. It was a lighthearted, nostalgic piece about my experience of Chicago and the history of its reputation. The idea for it came when Ben and Bernarda Shahn came to town and Fran and I took them to lunch at Henrici's, an old ornate Loop restaurant near city hall favored by politicians and, in earlier times, celebrated gangsters. I found the Shahns immensely cheered. For in recent years they had heard that Chicago had mended its roaring, wicked ways and assumed a dull respectability,

but the previous night Roger Touhy, an important gangster in the beer wars of the 1920s, had been shot dead on the steps of his sister's home. The noon editions were filled with gory photographs of Touhy's body, expert opinions on the prospects for a renewal of gang warfare, and fond reminiscences of the good old days when bodies had been dropping all over town. A newspaperman had asked the police commissioner if he thought hoodlums had killed Touhy for something he had done in the 1920s, and the commissioner had responded as he always did, "There are no hoodlums in Chicago." (A friend of mine wondered if Touhy had been done in by a committee of bank presidents.) Bernarda Shahn thought "There are no hoodlums in Chicago" ought to be set to music. Somehow Touhy's demise rejuvenated her and Ben, and Bernarda, a gentle little lady, said, "Thank heavens, there'll always be a Chicago." So I did my piece about what kind of place I had found it and I called it "To Chicago with Love."

As I had grown up in Indiana and become a reporter, I wrote, Chicago had come to be for me the place where the Big Story happened. Even Indiana's John Dillinger made it to Chicago to get assassinated. In my piece now, I recounted how I had come to Chicago in 1938 to write and how foolishly I had loved it—with my passion for the poor, I had even loved its slums, acres and acres of them, all mine; with my yearning for excitement, I had loved the speeding traffic on the Outer Drive and the roaring elevated trains on the El, Randolph Street in the theatrical district with blazing lights, the French restaurants and Syndicate gambling joints on the Near North Side. Each person in a saloon eyed everybody else warily, each wondering if all the others were gangsters, and it seemed to be part of the code not to touch or talk to strangers, though you might drink beside one for hours, lest a false move, as in a grade-B movie, trigger violence. I took to carrying my money loose in my pocket; no wallets for me any longer. (In Indiana, men squeezed pennies from tightly zippered wallets, called pocketbooks.) And always there was the wondrous lake, the limitless inland sea.

It was all rather innocent foolishness, I acknowledged in my piece. By now the El no longer seemed romantic to me, just an obsolete nuisance; the slums were not picturesque, just appalling; Randolph Street and Rush Street were not glamorous, just tinsel

cheap; gangsterism not exciting, just dreary and dangerous. But this change was in me, not the city.

By now I had developed a tour of Chicago that I took visiting eastern friends on. Most Chicagoans took visitors to lovely upper Michigan Avenue, yacht harbors, the Art Institute. But those were places where Chicagoans spent holidays. I took visitors on a different tour, to places where the millions lived and worked and where over the years I had done my legwork, and in the piece I described the tour—down clangorous Western Avenue thick with trucks and lined with the two-flats of workingmen, the Twenty-fourth Ward birthplace of the Democratic machine, the factories on the southwest side, the house of my detective friend Emil Smicklas up Blue Island Avenue to Halsted Street, the Hull House district, where old Greeks wearing hats sat drinking coffee in the windows of little coffee shops, where Mexicans drank liquor and fought in tough saloons, where Gypsies encamped in tenements; to Maxwell Street close by, with open-air stalls selling used clothing and kosher hot dogs, little doorways leading into tiny hole-in-the-wall shops that years later I remembered when I visited the *medina* in Fez, in Morocco. I took Ben Shahn on a walking tour near Hull House, and he showed me the Star of David carved in stone over a doorway, now so eroded I had missed it, a relic of the poor Jews. I then took my visitors south to the Negro ghetto—and I told them I thought that in not many years Chicago would be an all-Negro city ringed by sullen white suburbs.

Chicago's boosters, I wrote, would probably think I did Chicago's reputation no good by my tour. Chicago's defenders had always been numerous and sensitive. Rudyard Kipling once wrote after visiting Chicago, "It is inhabited by savages." Chicago was outraged, as it was at A. J. Liebling's *New Yorker* pieces on Chicago entitled "Second City." When Billy Graham said that Chicago's reputation was "the worst in the world," Mayor Daley was deeply wounded, and he invited the Reverend Dr. Graham to accompany him on a tour of the city to view its glories.

Chicago's defenders usually made two points: that Chicago's reputation for wickedness was born during Prohibition, and that it was a reputation undeserved today. They were, I thought, wrong on both points. I adduced historical evidence: When Father Marquette ar-

rived on the site of Chicago, he found a bootlegger selling liquor to the Indians, and the writer Lloyd Lewis discovered that the census that admitted Illinois to the Union was crooked, and time and again in the nineteenth century preachers and other reformers led crusades to cleanse Chicago (in one parade through the tenderloin a float was emblazoned somewhat enigmatically, THE CUBS MUST CUT OUT CIGARETTES, MURPHY SAYS). I went on to relate twentieth-century history, including the St. Valentine's Day Massacre and press conferences held by Al Capone. Then I presented evidence that Chicago in recent years, during the benign reign of Mayor Kennelly, still had been run by a corrupt alliance of politicians, police, Syndicate big shots, union leaders, and businessmen. I added a few private anecdotes of my own: Recently the wife of a wealthy friend of ours, attempting to organize a mothers' committee at her child's private school, had insisted to another mother that she participate, until the woman told her gently it would be inappropriate—her true name was not the one she was known by at school, for her husband was one of the most feared leaders of the Syndicate. And when the daughter of another Syndicate leader planned a birthday party and the mothers of some of the invited guests expressed misgivings, they were assured by the hostess that the children would be perfectly safe, for they would be picked up in a bulletproof car.

Nonetheless, during the dozen years before 1959, Chicago's leaders, throughout Mayor Kennelly's reign and Mayor Daley's rule, pretended that crime and corruption and the Syndicate did not exist. The city seemed to be rebuilding—superhighways sliced through slums, the St. Lawrence Seaway opened, new industries arose, high new apartment buildings sprang up along the lakefront, high new office buildings sprang up in the Loop, planners and editorialists proclaimed the rebirth of the central city. Mayor Daley hailed it. He toured it. He announced that suburbanites were returning. Did minor scandal erupt in city government? Mayor Daley moved on it swiftly. Thus, I wrote, for a dozen dreary years Chicago dwelt in an atmosphere of virtue, and prosperity, and progress.

Then in 1959 the roof fell in. It began in the fall. A Chicago police lieutenant was found touring Europe with Tony Accardo, the head of the Syndicate. Hearts lifted a little, faith was renewed. But the police commissioner announced there was no Syndicate in Chicago,

and the lieutenant was suspended for associating with a gangster. (It was reported that the Syndicate suspended Accardo for associating with a policeman.) Then Roger Touhy was assassinated, the historic occasion that so delighted Ben and Bernarda Shahn. And a few weeks later a young burglar said that he had stolen merchandise to the order of policemen and that while he was at work they had acted as his lookouts, helped him carry the merchandise out of stores, and hauled it away in squad cars. (The policemen were indicted, but the indictments were dismissed.) The police scandals spread. The press was in full cry. Civic leaders held emergency meetings. The mayor returned from Florida. The police commissioner became the goat and resigned. The state legislature met in emergency session. It was all like old times.

The mayor appointed a new police commissioner, a California criminologist, and he went on television and appealed to the people to support him tangibly by desisting from carrying five- or ten-dollar bills clipped to their drivers' licenses, an old Chicago custom to ensure against arrest if stopped for speeding. Chicagoans enjoyed it all immensely. I heard a joke: The Outer Drive was "the last outpost of collective bargaining." Another: A speeding motorist, stopped by a cop, asked, "What is it—a pinch or a stickup?" The new superintendent said he didn't want his police-men working as part-time bartenders; the bartenders' union passed a resolution barring members from working as part-time police-men. Policemen in district stations, mindful of the merchandise their brethren had stolen, took to answering the stationhouse phone, "Good morning, Polk Brothers." Polk Brothers was a big discount house.

Why, I wondered, was Chicago's spirit so indestructible? I thought it best epitomized a few years earlier when, during a scandal over horsemeat—gangsters and others had conspired to sell horse-meat for hamburger—Fran's butcher asked her, "How do you want your hamburger—win, place, or show?"

Chicago, I wrote, was a friendly town. During World War II, it had been every serviceman's favorite. It was a tolerant town. People approved aldermen's wearing three-hundred-dollar suits (an outra-geous price then). Congressional investigators said sixty-four Chi-cago disc jockeys accepted bribes, a claim that no other city could make (Los Angeles had only twenty-three). Chicago, remember,

housed the only major-league baseball team that ever threw a World Series (so far as is known, a true Chicagoan would add darkly). Crime was played up heavily in all Chicago papers. A visitor told me, "This is your sport. This is your baseball."

Chicago was an openhanded, openhearted, young, and foolish town, I thought. Chicagoans believed that everything was fixed. And many things were—a man I knew who opened an office in Chicago encountered one frustration after another in getting routine services connected until friends told him whom to get in touch with. "It is universal," he said in awe. "You have to be able to say 'Joe sent me' everywhere." This society ran on clout, on influence. Europeans called Chicago the most American city, perhaps for the very reason that it ran on clout, and so indeed did America. But Chicago did it best. A word to a judge's bailiff that the accused is a ward leader's friend, a phone call to an alderman if you want an alley vacated, the five-dollar bill clipped to the driver's license— this is clout. If Chicago hadn't existed, America would have had to invent it.

What kind of place was it to live in? Terrible, I thought—cruel winters, stifling summer heat, broken streets in spring, hopeless rush-hour traffic jams, and at times small dead fish came out of kitchen faucets. The Stock Yards stank, the streets were filthy, restaurants were overcrowded, many people were afraid to go on the streets at night. On Lake Shore Drive, life in Chicago was lovely— for the few. For the millions, life in Chicago was toil and ugliness, if not squalor and privation.

As for me, I wrote, I lived in a suburb and wouldn't have Chicago if you gave it to me—but always, away from home, said if asked, "I'm from Chicago." I shared Fran's feelings. She was born there, and she often said, "I never think of Chicago any more till I drive down the Outer Drive and see all those tall buildings and see how pretty the lake is, and then I feel excited and wonder why I stayed away so long. I don't ever feel strange there; I always feel at home. I think it's the people. The people of Chicago are wonderful."

"They are," I wrote. "These big cities are, really, monuments to human endurance. People will put up with anything; they can survive anything. Chicago is quite possibly the worst place to live in the United States—except maybe New York."

4.

The 1950s were not only the golden years of the big slick magazines, they were also the golden years of serious television, the years of *Studio One* and *Playhouse 90,* and I began to get involved. (I wrote my *Post* series on TV later, in the 1960s. By then, television was destroying the magazines and was somehow managing almost to destroy itself.) John Houseman, then a theater and film producer, later an actor, had wanted to make a movie of my Centralia mine disaster story ever since it was published. Now he saw his chance to do it for television: He would produce it as one show in his series for CBS-TV, *The Seven Lively Arts,* calling journalism one of the arts. Fran and I spent a long weekend with John and Joan Houseman at their spectacular house at High Tor up the Hudson from New York, John and I planning the Centralia show. John looked the part of and indeed was one of America's most distinguished theater people, a remarkably talented man who had produced the Negro *Macbeth* and other plays for the Federal Theater during the New Deal's efforts through WPA to help the theater in the Depression, the original Martian star-wars fantasy on radio (with Orson Welles) that scared everybody in America to death, *Lute Song* for the commercial theater, Gertrude Stein's *Four Saints in Three Acts,* a number of big films including *Julius Caesar, Lust for Life,* and *The Bad and the Beautiful*; and he had made both a reputation for taste among serious critics as well as a good deal of money (though never so much money as later when, after himself starring in *The Paper Chase,* he made TV commercials selling cooking oil and a stock brokerage's services, a development of his career in his seventies and eighties that pleased and amused [and profited] him vastly.)

For the Centralia TV show, he was getting Loring Mandel to write the television play and George Roy Hill to direct it. Off and on in coming months I worked on the script with John and George Roy Hill. Hill was a kinetic, creative man who laughed easily and was fun to work with. I had never before worked on a dramatic script, and thought it fascinating. Loring Mandel had written a good one; I think Hill and I improved it. The script was extremely faithful to my original story. One particularly effective sequence showed the bureaucracy endlessly shuffling and stamping and filing and ignoring

the mine inspectors' reports warning that the mine was dangerous. The show went into rehearsal in January of 1958, as I recall it, and the cast included two of the finest actors of our time, Maureen Stapleton and Jason Robards. Miss Stapleton played the widow of the coal miner, Joe Bryant. Jason Robards, who can do anything, from *The Night They Raided Minsky's* to *Long Day's Journey into Night*, did not appear on camera in Centralia—the script employed a device, a voice-over or narrator who represented me, the journalist, explaining the story, and Robards did the voice-over. I attended rehearsals, first in a big bare rehearsal hall at CBS, then, shortly before air time, in a small uptown movie house converted into a television studio. Here the set had been built—our underground mine tunnel, the living room of the miner's widow with the "heir-room" photographs of her dead husband and son, the office of the state Department of Mines and Minerals. During rehearsals, I made a number of suggestions to George Roy Hill, one, for example, that when the newspaper reporters try to interview Governor Green they not behave, as they were, like a bunch of raucous characters out of *The Front Page* but that, rather, they be serious and subdued—after all, 111 men had just died. Only the day before air time, I believe, a high executive at CBS, watching a rehearsal on a monitor at CBS headquarters, telephoned Houseman and told him he would have to make a change. In the script, among my own conclusions that Jason Robards was reading as voice-over, was a sentence saying that the system that runs our lives does not always work well. The CBS executive thought "system" sounded vaguely "communistic"; it would have to go. John told me to try to find a substitute. I came up with "the machinery that runs our lives," which was, I think, an improvement. And it satisfied the CBS man.

In the studio during rehearsals, I sat in the darkened little control booth with Hill and John Houseman, and I was fascinated as I saw how a TV show was directed, Hill watching a monitor for each camera and ordering "take one" or "take two," and his assistant flipping a switch to put camera one or camera two on the air. Hill wanted me to play myself on camera, interviewing Maureen Stapleton, the miner's widow, and so I too rehearsed, pretending to be a reporter making notes while she talked. She told me she was afraid she'd forget her lines, and so I copied them onto my reporter's notebook,

placed so she could read them. John Houseman smiled; he knew she wouldn't forget. The show went on the air live on Sunday afternoon, January 26, 1958. I nearly blew the whole thing. During rehearsals, as Hill took breaks between scenes, I had grown accustomed to taking my time strolling from the control booth to the stage and onto the set to "interview" Miss Stapleton. When the show actually went on the air, I left the control booth on cue but I had forgotten that Hill would cut immediately to my scene, and I had to race downstairs and onto the set, barely getting into a chair facing Miss Stapleton before the camera took us. During rehearsals, like many fine actors, Miss Stapleton had held herself back, not giving all she had; but now on air live, she did, and it was the emotional climax of the show. Needless to say, she did not forget her lines.

The show went beautifully. After it, John and Joan Houseman took Fran and me to a party at the home of the actress Viveca Lindfors, a big party filled with show people, and Marilyn Monroe was expected but didn't show up (as usual, I'm told). The Housemans and we had a fine time, congratulating each other and being congratulated by the others. Late that night Fran and I took a plane to Chicago. We arrived in a blizzard but it didn't matter, I had parked our Jeep at the airport, and we drove home in the blizzard, and I remember shouting to her, "This is the greatest night of my life." Not publishing a book, not publishing a magazine piece, not winning a prize is nearly so exciting as seeing something you wrote come alive on a screen (or I suppose on a stage), and I still cherish that night.

Another television adaptation of a piece of mine turned out less happily. CBS had decided to do a dramatization of my book about the care of the mentally ill, *The Pane of Glass,* and I went to New York to advise during rehearsals. Elaine May was the star, one of the patients, and she wanted to throw a schizophrenic fit and tear up the set; she walked out on rehearsal, and one of my assignments was to seek her out and take her to dinner and persuade her to come back and not tear up the set. I did not think the television play very good nor did I find the people involved so congenial as those in the Centralia TV show. It was shown on the network on April 21, 1960. Almost at the last minute the producer tried to take my name off the screen credits, which he could not do under my contract. At the time

I didn't understand why. Later I did: He developed the script into a stage play, though he didn't own the stage rights to my work, and it appeared in an off-Broadway house. Ivan von Auw and I went to see it, and Ivan put the producer and the author of the stage play on notice, but the show folded anyway. During those years several television plays appeared on my home screen that seemed to contain material lifted from *Post* stories of mine without permission or pay, but I never did anything about it, I was too busy writing to clutter up my life with litigation.

Having produced *Executive Suite* for Metro-Goldwyn-Mayer, a movie about the power struggles in the board of directors of a big corporation, John Houseman wanted to make a movie for MGM about big labor and he wanted me to write it with him. I told him I knew nothing about writing a movie; he said it didn't matter, I wouldn't have to write the screenplay, only research and write a "screen treatment," and he would work with me on that. MGM would pay me. First, research: I started with my own writings that touched on labor—Centralia, stories about the Pennsylvania coal miners and the Upper Michigan copper miners, the Muncie autoworkers. I was surprised to find I already knew a fair amount about labor. I read books on it and in Chicago did fresh legwork—interviewed labor lawyers, politicians with labor support, and local labor leaders like Carl Shier, a friend of mine and a left-wing activist shop steward in the UAW. I began to see glimmerings of a story line and characters. After six weeks' work, Fran and I went to California.

We stayed with John Houseman and his wife Joan in their beach house at Malibu, only a few yards from the glorious ocean's edge. Early every morning—everybody in the motion picture industry went to work early, and most worked late—John and I would drive to the MGM lot and in his office talk out the story. I had the union background in mind and the main character too—a young iron miner from the Upper Peninsula of Michigan who goes to Chicago to organize production line workers for one of the big new CIO unions. John devised the plot, brought the hero into conflict with an elderly labor leader named Bannon, introduced female characters, invented scenes. We named the movie *Bannon*. We usually ate lunch

at the MGM commissary. Once Fran came down and was taken on a tour of MGM's famous back lot, with its fake villages and castles and rivers. John and Joan took us to a cocktail party or two at Malibu and once to the Garden of Allah, the sad hotel on Sunset Boulevard where F. Scott Fitzgerald had lived toward the end.

Back home, I set to work to write the screen treatment. A treatment is simply a narrative—it might be only twenty-five pages, it might be five hundred; I think mine was some five hundred—that contains background, develops characters, describes scenes, and moves plot. I was, for the first time, doing something like writing a novel. To feel comfortable doing it, I made it as much like my regular magazine writing as possible—made a card outline of all my research and of the sizable manuscript that John and I and his young associate Judd Kinberg had produced, then made a writing outline, then wrote and rewrote the rough draft. John Houseman liked the treatment and so did Dore Schary, production head at MGM, and John began planning how to cast it. But when the project reached the high corporate officers of MGM in New York, they vetoed it: They were afraid it would get MGM into trouble with the unions MGM itself dealt with. Years later John Houseman told me that the abandonment of *Bannon* was one of the greatest regrets of his life.

5.

As time passed, it is probably clear by now, I came to write almost exclusively for the *Post*. And increasingly long series on big national issues, sometimes spending a year on one. Stuart Rose and Harold Ober once estimated that no more than fifty people in the country were successfully doing what I was doing for a living—full-time freelance heavy fact writing. What I was writing ended up, without my intending it, as a panorama of our times in America and our problems.

Nevertheless, to me they were always "stories," never "articles." The distinction was important. To my somewhat fuzzy way of thinking, an article was a collection of facts about a given subject, likely to be abstract, and almost certain to be pontifical. But a story was about people, some people in a time and place and what happened to them. Even when I did a long series about a subject for the *Post,* it was always in my mind "the divorce story" or the "criminal

justice story," as it had been "the Centralia story," not "the mine safety article"; "the Daniels story," not "the capital punishment story." The individual man, the woman, the child—that was what mattered to a storyteller.

Everything I worked on was potentially libelous, and I was acutely aware that I was writing for the biggest magazines; I could not afford even a nonlibelous mistake. Increasingly I submitted my manuscripts to my sources, asking them to point out factual errors (but reserving my right to my conclusions), and took to rechecking every fact in a piece after I had finished it. Only once in my writing career did I make a factual mistake—at least one that was called to my attention. In my series on the Deep South, I quoted Senator Herman Talmadge of Georgia as saying in a public speech that the "Supreme Court refuses to recognize that it cannot by a mandate shrink the size of a Negro's skull, which is one-eighth of an inch thicker than a white man's." Senator Talmadge protested that he had not said it, the Citizens' Councils' theoretician had. I asked that man; he acknowledged it. I had found the quotation in a Birmingham newspaper. In rechecking my manuscript, I had sent the quote to the newspaper, as I sent other quotes to their sources. I received no reply to this query. That should have made me suspicious but I let it pass and published the quote. I was wrong. The *Post* apologized to Senator Talmadge. It was one of the few times I ever printed a newspaper quotation without corroboration.

The *Post* began emblazoning the titles of my stories on the cover and promoting them heavily with newspaper ads proclaiming me "One of America's Great Reporters." Heady stuff. The association of American magazine publishers established a group of prestigious awards, the Benjamin Franklin Awards, for magazine nonfiction, and I won one in each of four years until, as magazines declined, the awards ceased. They were presented at an annual dinner in New York attended by all the magazine editors and publishers, and Fran and I went, together with Ben Hibbs and the other *Post* editors, a gala occasion. Once when Theodore H. White and Robert Bendiner (one of the most underrated writers of our times) and I were all receiving awards, White remarked that he never saw three more unlikely-looking winners—everybody else at the dinner looked more distinguished than we. Once during these years, Ben Hibbs sent me

a proof of a new masthead. Without consulting me, he had added Stewart Alsop and me to the list of contributing editors. I declined, preferring to remain freelance, and with help from Harold Ober succeeded in extricating myself without offending Ben Hibbs.

My friends in Highland Park, most of whom took the daily 8:10 to Chicago, considered my work risky, writing about crime. A few times I thought to be careful. I did not consider one *Post* story entirely safe, a story about a Chicago murderer and politicians who were trying to intimidate state witnesses; some of the fixers were dangerous, and I took care to interview one of them only in his lawyer's Loop office and to interview the state's key witness in my parked car on a street with his police bodyguard watching. The only time in my career that I was actually threatened was while I was doing legwork on the Centralia story; two mining officials waited on me at my hotel in a coal town and told me to drop the story and get out of town. One of them had a reputation as a bad man with a knife. Later that day I tried to continue my interviewing, but my sources had dried up. I got out of town. But I did not drop the story.

Whenever I met a criminal to get information, I made sure a detective knew I was meeting him. I got a good deal of fan mail from readers of the *Post;* I usually answered it on stationery without my home address. For years we kept our telephone number unlisted. Once a man called me up from St. Louis, said he'd read a crime story of mine, and said he had some information I'd be interested in. Ordinarily I would not respond to such a call, but I thought that if he already knew my telephone number, he knew a good deal about me and I'd better find out who he was. I told him I'd meet him in the Loop, in a bar off the main lobby of the Palmer House, a conspicuous place. I took Fran with me and found a chair for her in the lobby near the bar and told her that if I came out and turned right she would know everything was all right, but if I turned left she should call my detective friend, Emil Smicklas, at headquarters. The man arrived, we talked, he had some information that he thought might lead him to a lot of money and wanted my help in using it, I turned him down and walked out alone and turned right, and Fran followed me out. One night, while doing a *Post* series on the Illinois

legislature, I accompanied a representative who was also a Chicago ward committeeman to his ward headquarters in the Hull House slum to watch him doing favors for his constituents, as he did every Thursday night. When he took me to the railroad station to go home, I was surprised to see he was wearing a revolver. I made a date to meet him again the following Thursday at his headquarters. But something came up that morning, I had to break the date. That night when he left his headquarters and drove to his home, three men kidnapped him. He was never seen again, presumed murdered. I did a *Post* story on an infamous gang of gunmen led by the Shelton brothers who for years had controlled gambling and other rackets all over downstate Illinois and had been involved in the violent deaths of at least thirty-five people; the Chicago Syndicate had recently moved in on them, killing two of the Shelton brothers and breaking the power of the sole survivor. I went to see the survivor, Earl, at his farm. When I rang the bell, he came to the door with a shotgun. I told him what I was doing. He said nothing. I asked if I could come in and talk to him. He said, "I've got to go slop the hogs." I said I'd go with him and we went to the barnyard. He was a big hulk of a man. Finished, he picked up his shotgun and walked back to the house. I went along. He let me follow him inside. He showed me around his house; he was proud of it, so new and so neat. He said, "Let's go downstairs," and led the way to the basement bar, got a couple of cold beers out of the cooler, and sat down. He looked at me and said, "I'd do anything I could to stop you from writing that story." "Do anything"—one did not take that lightly when it came from a Shelton, especially, perhaps, a Shelton with a shotgun. I told him there was no way to stop it, I was not alone, other *Post* reporters and writers were also working on the story, I was just covering this end of it, and whether I wrote it or not, there was going to be a story in the *Post*. I couldn't tell whether he believed me. But I got him started talking about his house, his farm, his brothers, his mother who lived down the road. I got the story. A local guitar player had composed a country ballad about the murder of his brother Carl and made a recording of it, and Earl played it for me to show me in what high esteem Carl had been held by folks around there and he gave me the record. I have it yet, a prized possession.

Doing legwork on the Sheltons, I had asked Emil Smicklas what

he knew about them, and he said he knew only that the Chicago Syndicate had offered a reward of ten thousand dollars for any of the Sheltons dead or alive and he knew a gunman who had tried to collect it. He had been Smicklas's stool pigeon on a case I'd written about, and Smicklas arranged for me to meet him alone on a certain street corner on the Near North Side. I drove there at the appointed time and saw a man who seemed to fit the description. He was reading a newspaper. He didn't look up, or at least I didn't think he did. Puzzled, I drove around the block and came back. He was gone. I paused. In that moment, he was at the front door of my car, getting in. I never saw him approach. I asked where he wanted to go to talk. He said, "Just drive around." So I drove around, all afternoon, and he talked about the Sheltons and about the Syndicate. And about his own trade—he was a lifelong professional criminal. Explaining this, he pointed to a young woman walking down the sidewalk and said, "What do *you* see? A pretty girl. But *I* see she's got an envelope under her arm and I recognize the envelope—it's her boss's money, and she's taking it to the bank. See what I mean?"

He was a loner, would have nothing to do with organized crime. Indeed, he preyed on organized crime—with a submachine gun, he led several other gunmen in holding up Syndicate handbooks, about as dangerous a trade as is imaginable, and when I was with him, both the police and the Syndicate were looking for him. His viewpoint was that of the professional criminal. The world simply did not look the same to him as it looks to the rest of us. I decided to do a piece about him for the *Post* and then a book—the autobiography of a professional criminal. And he became a friend of sorts. Fran and I had him out to our house for Sunday dinner several times, sometimes for the weekend. He was about forty-five though he looked younger and he was always neatly dressed in sport jacket and slacks. Women, I suppose, would have considered him just short of handsome. He laughed easily, squinting as he did so. He was soft spoken and well spoken, well mannered, clean-cut, and extremely funny. Fran enjoyed him, and he was nice to Cindy. He had one drink with us before dinner, no more. After Sunday dinner, he would sit all afternoon in the living room talking of his criminal career. For a time he had been a confidence man—though his principal trades were burglary and armed robbery—and he enjoyed

explaining how his confidence games relied on the foolish sentimentality or the secret dishonesty of "straight" people. He seemed lonely and glad for a chance to spend a weekend in a suburb with us. I trusted him and he came to trust me. (Most people did.) Once Fran's mother came to visit while he was there and she took Fran out into the kitchen and asked if this was somebody Fran herself "found attractive." (It was her Victorian way of asking if Fran was having an affair.) Fran explained. Her mother disapproved vehemently—a criminal in the house wasn't safe! (Actually, the only conceivable danger was if somebody who wanted to hurt him did so while I was with him. I was the last person that he himself would have harmed.) Once he told Fran he wanted to buy a Christmas present for his nine-year-old niece and asked if a heart-shaped ring would be appropriate—"Would she like it?" Fran said, "She'd love it." His story that she liked best was how he'd held up a roadhouse that kept a fierce watchdog: He tossed it a frankfurter loaded with strychnine.

Though I probably came to know him as well as anybody on earth knew him, I was sure I did not understand him completely. When he was in our house, we felt he was one of us. But as he left to go back to his own world, we realized that instead of having pulled him into our orbit, he had pulled us into his.

I was impressed by what he had accomplished in his chosen field, crime, and by what he might have accomplished in another. He possessed charm, intelligence, physical courage, human warmth, a quick intuitive insight into people—and none of the qualities most people associate with lifelong criminality. Why did he choose crime? I do not know. In his background were none of the usual elements of criminality—slum life, broken home, poverty, truancy, bad luck, bad heredity. Even the label of psychopath did not fit him.

For two weeks straight, he and I sat together at my desk while he talked and I took down on my typewriter verbatim his life story, occasionally asking questions to clear things up. We ended with a rough draft of about five hundred pages. I edited it, arranging the material on chronological lines, breaking it into chapters, eliminating repetition, tightening, inserting footnotes and bracketed explanations. But it was not an "as told to" book; it was his own story in his own language, a picaresque tale of his wanderings, his girls, his crimes.

Harper thought the book a potential best-seller, but it sold only about ten thousand copies, I believe. It suffered from a bad title, *My Life in Crime*, as did other books of mine. The Ober agency sold the paperback and foreign rights. Before publication, on the day I received galley proofs, I telephoned him to invite him out to the house to read proof with me. Somebody in his rooming house answered and said somewhat hesitantly, "Oh, that fella. He's dead. They found him dead in bed last week." I called Emil Smicklas. He knew nothing about it. I could not believe he had died a natural death and so I looked up the coroner's inquest. Sure enough, he had died in his sleep of a heart attack. Since his was an old Chicago family, it owned a grave site in one of the most respectable cemeteries in Chicago, and he was buried there.

Today as I go through my appointment books of those years, I am astonished at my energy and single-minded, almost relentless devotion to my work. I was out of town more than I was home. Often I would return home on a Saturday from a trip doing legwork, repack my suitcase, and leave on Sunday on another trip. I carried a briefcase stuffed with railroad and airline timetables. In New York, I scheduled appointments every hour (except for two hours for lunch). At home, writing, I kept regular office hours and I often ate lunch at my desk. Sometimes I would finish writing one story in the morning and begin another in the afternoon. I have always thought I managed to make a success of freelance writing not because of any talent but because I worked hard. I almost never took a day off, except in the summer in Upper Michigan—we bought a camp at Three Lakes but even there I took work with me. It is perhaps a measure of my later tendency to relax this discipline—or perhaps grow a little more sure of myself—that when I was in my room working, our first child, Cindy, was not allowed there; when our second, Dan, came along, he was allowed to come in and crawl under my desk and sit there so long as he remained quiet; and the third, Fred, was allowed to climb up on my lap and pretend to help me write.

In the midst of all of this writing, something happened that changed the direction of my life: I met Governor Adlai E. Stevenson.

PRESIDENTIAL POLITICS

SEVEN

CAMPAIGNING WITH ADLAI STEVENSON

1.

Adlai Stevenson did not win the 1952 presidential election, he lost it to General Dwight D. Eisenhower, but in losing he won the admiration of millions of people who responded to graceful speeches and to ideas and he aroused an excitement and a fervor that no presidential candidate save the Kennedy brothers (and, God help us, Reagan) has aroused since. I became involved in Stevenson's 1952 campaign by chance alone.

As I have said, in Upper Michigan I had met John Voelker, the writer and district attorney; he had suggested I look up a friend in his old Chicago law firm, Raymond Friend; Raymond in turn had introduced me to one of his partners, Louis A. Kohn. That had been four or five years ago; since then, Lou Kohn and I, and our wives, had become close friends. In 1948, Lou Kohn had helped get Adlai Stevenson nominated for governor. In his campaign, Stevenson had used my Centralia story, denouncing Governor Green for failing to save the coal miners' lives, but I never had met Stevenson. Now early in 1952, Lou Kohn wanted me to edit a book of the speeches Stevenson had been making as governor, which, he said, were extraordinarily thoughtful and eloquent. I presumed he hoped to use

the book in Stevenson's forthcoming campaign for reelection as governor. But suddenly that winter people began talking about Stevenson's running for president—they wondered if President Truman could be reelected (and soon he declared he would not run). I interested Jack Fischer of Harper in the book—a collection of speeches with a long biographical introduction by me. Our daughter Cindy's birthday was February 5, a Tuesday, and on the preceding Sunday Fran and I took her down to the Chicago Loop for dinner and afterward to Lou Kohn's apartment—Governor Stevenson's birthday was the same day as Cindy's, and Cindy and he cut the cake together. After that Stevenson and I talked about the book of speeches. Stevenson was more interested in a different book. He said it was a shame that so few people were interested in state government and he proposed that after he was reelected governor I come to Springfield and spend six months or a year sitting inside his administration and finding out how things worked then write a book about it. This sounded interesting, and I told him it might also make a series for the *Post*. Meanwhile I'd go through his speech texts with both books in mind.

My first impression of Stevenson was one of a thoroughly engaging man. His forehead ran almost to the back of his head, his features were uneven—a big irregularly shaped nose, high unruly eyebrows that gave him a quizzical expression, eyes of the bluest blue and large, staring out at the world perpetually perplexed. His was an intelligent and a striking face. He laughed easily, smoked often. He continually made self-deprecating remarks, often funny. He grumbled about the burdens of office and his own weariness. Always he pretended not to be a politician but, rather, an amateur good-government man surrounded by politicians who probably wanted to do him in. He pretended astonishment and bewilderment at the presidential boom. In his presence, at that time, friends and advisers did not mention the presidential boom—like anxious relatives hovering at the bedside of a patient they know is stricken with a fatal disease but who doesn't know it himself.

I consulted Francis Nipp. He was dubious about the book—feared that if I became too closely identified with Stevenson, I would compromise my position as an independent freelance. I wanted to go ahead anyway. The Stevenson speech file was huge;

Francis agreed to help research it. In New York, I found my friends in the publishing world agog about Stevenson. They thought him a liberal in the Roosevelt-Truman tradition. Actually, he was not so liberal, was a man who favored balanced budgets, feared federal executive power, looked with favor on business, deplored what he considered labor's excesses. Elected governor, he had simply gone down to Springfield as a buttoned-down-collar reformer from Lake Forest out to cleanse the cesspool of Illinois politics. His reputation for liberalism rested on his veto of the Broyles bill, a McCarthyesque bill designed to ferret out Communist sympathies, on his deposition in behalf of Alger Hiss's reputation, and on his support for Truman's Korean policy. Nevertheless he was emerging as the champion of liberals and intellectuals in the Democratic party. That week in New York, at lunch at the Algonquin and in editors' homes, everyone wanted to know about Stevenson, and something like a holiday mood prevailed. Even Fred Allen had two drinks before lunch, and Fran told him she'd rather have him, Allen, for president than anybody; he stood up straight, bowed, and asked her to dinner. Fran and I went to see Ethel Merman in *Call Me Madam,* a musical play about a Washington society leader and politician, a play that spawned what became one of the most effective campaign songs in American political history, "I Like Ike." Another of its songs contained the line "If you're feeling presidential." We all were. Eric Larrabee made a cardboard button six inches across on which he lettered, MADLY FOR ADLAI, and Fran wore it going home on the *Twentieth Century.* It was an exciting time. I don't think any of us, I least of all, fully realized how serious a commitment we were making.

As the Stevenson boom grew, Harper bade me hasten—another publisher had commissioned a book on Stevenson. I went to Springfield and spent a week with Stevenson and his young staff and cabinet. Francis Nipp had researched Stevenson's speeches, and he and I made an outline of the book. By then Harper and I had decided to expand my "biographical introduction" and to print the speech texts as an appendix. (Eventually we dropped the speech texts entirely and the book became simply a brief biography rather like a *New Yorker* profile.) Hastened by the rival biography, I wrote the rough draft in about two weeks. As I finished it, Stevenson is-

sued a statement on April 16 that most people thought took him out of contention for nomination. I didn't believe it. During the rest of the spring I tried to get definitive word from his staff or the Democratic party that he would be drafted and would accept, as I believed. Nobody could give it. So Harper stalled on my book manuscript.

I gave my manuscript to Stevenson to check for factual errors but he had no time and asked his sister, Elizabeth Ives, called Buffie, to read it, and I went over it with her. Later I came to know Mrs. Ives well. She was a strange woman, at times outgoing and charming, at times as difficult as one can be. She was not a well-educated woman nor one with wide political experience. To this reading she brought principally an almost single-minded adoration toward her mother and father and brother, plus a temperament that saw no blemishes but only joy and success in their lives. Our meeting was not easy but we got through it without too many scars. Scars were things Buffie Ives bore well anyway, if indeed she suffered them.

2.

Ever since Dan was born, Fran and I had been thinking of buying a bigger house, preferably on the northeast side of Highland Park, a "better" section and closer to the schools. Fran had found one she wanted to show me; I took one look at it and knew I wanted it. It was an old, high, narrow, Victorian white frame house with eleven-foot ceilings and a marble fireplace and ornate gingerbread on the roof line, set on a wooded ravine lot nearly an acre in extent. It had been built a year after the Chicago fire in 1871 by a contractor who was burned out and bought a big farm out here in the country; this was his version of a Chicago townhouse. His granddaughter still owned it and, a spinster, lived in it alone. We bought it. We live in it yet, more than thirty years later.

We moved into it on June 26, 1952. The trouble with a big old house is that, if you don't maintain it, it looks like a rooming house. Ours did. It was what was then called "an old clunk," today "a charming historic Victorian." We began rejuvenating and restoring it.* And in the midst of this, our house guests arrived to attend the

---

*State and federal government agencies have recently asked us to consider letting them declare it a historic landmark; we have declined.

Democratic National Convention in Chicago—Eric Larrabee of *Harper's* and his wife Eleanor, Ben Shahn and his wife Bernarda and two of their children. And during the week other New York writers and artists came out from the convention for drinks and dinner. Fran kept cooking turkeys, and we ate at a long roughhewn table we found in the basement. Bernarda Shahn said she loved old houses—"They're so solidly built,"—and Ben said, "Yes, Bernarda, that's why they're putting a new foundation in." Ben said he saw no need to build a new kitchen—he would simply paint a mural on the walls depicting kitchen cupboards, new sink, automatic dishwasher, even a Negro maid, then we could all go to a restaurant for dinner.

We went down to the convention every day. The first day, I was on the floor just below the podium when the chairman introduced Governor Stevenson for what is ordinarily a perfunctory governor's welcoming speech; the delegates broke into applause so long and loud—"WE WANT STEVENSON!"—that he had difficulty getting started. His speech was incandescent; in the supercharged atmosphere of this convention and in the national atmosphere of foreboding as Senator Joe McCarthy stalked the land and clouds of bigotry descended, this speech bespoke freedom of thought and belief: "Here [in Illinois] there are no barriers, no defenses, to ideas and to aspiration. We want none; we want no shackles on the mind or the spirit, no rigid patterns of thought, and no iron conformity. . . . As a Democrat perhaps you will permit me to remind you that until four years ago the people of Illinois had chosen but three Democratic governors in a hundred years. One was John Peter Altgeld, whom the great Illinois poet Vachel Lindsay called the Eagle Forgotten—he was an immigrant; one was Edward F. Dunne, whose parents came here from the old sod of Ireland; and the last was Henry Horner, but one generation removed from Germany. John Peter Altgeld, my friends, was a Protestant, Governor Dunne was a Catholic, Henry Horner was a Jew. And that, my friends, is the American story, written by the Democratic party here on the prairies of Illinois." His speech broke up the convention. It was one of the most thrilling political moments of my life.

What was happening was that the diverse old Democratic coalition held together by Roosevelt and Truman was rearranging itself, and it could rearrange itself only around Stevenson. This was one of

the last of the old-fashioned conventions, with power brokers and bitter floor fights. It was also the first television convention, and some evenings we watched it at the dining room table on television. We did when, past midnight, Stevenson was nominated, Ben Shahn keeping a tally of votes on a sheet of typing paper, and while Stevenson delivered his acceptance speech—which I did not much like though it became famous—Ben turned his tally sheet over and sketched a caricature of Stevenson. It, along with other sketches he made that week, hangs now on our wall.

Stevenson's press secretary called and asked me to go to Springfield and help him. I went on August 21.* I had been there only a few days when I discovered I was less interested in the press operation than in what was going on at the Elks Club.

The campaign had rented space in the local Elks Club building for the writers who had come to Springfield to write Stevenson's speeches. Stevenson wanted them out of sight—he liked to think he wrote all his speeches himself, and they were obliged to call themselves speech researchers. Only once or twice all fall did "the Elks" see Stevenson himself. Now and then Carl McGowan, his trusted chief of staff, would visit the Elks and tell them what Stevenson was thinking about and wanted to say. Sometimes they themselves decided the themes, even the policies. Carl usually edited the speeches before giving them to Stevenson. Some Stevenson delivered almost as he received them, some he himself edited. Carl McGowan always accompanied Stevenson on his road trips. One or two Elks went along on each one. I joined the Elks Club writers.

The principal Elks, those who stayed throughout and wrote most of the speeches, were David Bell, thirty-three, tall, blond, affable, who had been a member of President Truman's White House staff for five years and who assigned speeches to us; W. Willard Wirtz, about forty, a member of Governor Stevenson's administration, a man in whom Stevenson had great confidence and who usually encouraged Stevenson to do what Stevenson wanted to do, a man who later became Stevenson's law partner and still later secretary of labor in the Kennedy and Johnson cabinets; Robert Tufts, thirty-

*A full account of Stevenson's 1952 presidential campaign appears in the first volume of the biography I wrote, *The Life of Adlai E. Stevenson.* The first volume is titled *Adlai Stevenson of Illinois.*

six, tough-minded and clear-minded, a profes.or of economics at Oberlin College who, as a former member of George F. Kennan's policy planning staff, wrote Stevenson's foreign policy speeches; and Arthur M. Schlesinger, Jr., gay, funny, articulate, brilliant, an Americans for Democratic Action leader, professor of history at Harvard, biographer of Andrew Jackson and Franklin D. Roosevelt, Pulitzer Prize winner, rapidly becoming at thirty-four a leading American intellectual. Other writers contributed drafts to the Elks, including John Kenneth Galbraith, the towering—in physique and reputation—Harvard economist, Jack Fischer and Bernard De Voto of *Harper's,* and Archibald MacLeish, the poet. Stevenson was an extraordinary candidate who burst like a meteor across the political firmament and galvanized such writers. Thus, suddenly, a whole new cast of characters came into my life. And many of them stayed there: Thirty years later some are among my closest friends. It was for me a new world.

Never before had I written a speech. From my work on the Stevenson book that spring, I knew something about Adlai Stevenson's speaking style, I could tell when something sounded Stevensonian or didn't. But I knew nothing whatsoever about speech structure. And I knew little about the issues of this campaign. In my writing, I simply had not handled issues as such—had written stories about people that raised such issues as segregated housing and prison reform, but I had rarely handled the issues frontally.*

Nor did I know the politics of the issues. Furthermore, as a writer I had never collaborated with another writer, for freelance writing is the loneliest trade; but speechwriting is more often than not collegial.

Some of the Elks were mainly interested in the quality of the prose in a speech draft. Others, like Arthur Schlesinger and Dave Bell, possessed highly developed political instincts and were interested in a speech's political effectiveness. I began by worrying about the prose and soon learned to worry more about the politics. I had never before thought of politics this way. I had, of course, never before allied myself with any politician. Indeed, I had always shared most reporters' skepticism or even suspicion of all politicians. At

---

* Later I did write articles that attacked these issues frontally, not simply through a set of characters. Indeed, it may have been my experience in the 1952 Stevenson campaign that impelled me to change my approach.

first I was almost shocked to hear Arthur Schlesinger and Dave Bell talking about people as voting blocs—Jews, Catholics, Negroes, farmers; I had thought that was the language of political hacks in ward headquarters. I came to see that in a diverse pluralistic democracy like ours, a politician can approach his electorate in no other way. (Stevenson himself intensely disliked doing it, and two of his worst speeches of the campaign were to union labor in Detroit and to Negroes in Harlem.)

But for me, the biggest wrench of all in joining the Elks was the complete reversal of my own situation. All my life, I had been a reporter, on the outside looking in. Now suddenly I was on the inside looking out. I was not reporting what the public man said; I was putting the words in his mouth. I was not reporting policy nuances; I was making them. All my life, reporters had been my colleagues and friends; now of a sudden they were the enemy, to be avoided.

Arthur Schlesinger considered Stevenson far too conservative, even antilabor and anti-Truman, and most of the other Elks agreed. I soon found myself joining their efforts to make Stevenson sound more liberal than he was. Liberalism seemed to come almost automatically to me. I've often wondered about the sources of it. An underdog feeling in childhood perhaps; and certainly the authors I read in high school, such as Dos Passos, must have had an influence, and so did my high school Communist friend. And surely important was what President Roosevelt did for my family, and my own standing in line at a factory gate during the Depression. Later, when I covered a strike for the *Times,* I was instinctively on the strikers' side. Not long after Fran and I were married, we visited her uncle Lowell Lathrop on his farm in Wisconsin. When younger he had been an active leader of the Progressive party, and he had been the head of the local Rural Electrification Administration office in FDR's time, and one evening he stood with me on a hill beside his barn and pointed down to the Kickapoo Valley, the farmhouses a string of lights up and down the valley, and he said, *"That's* what Roosevelt and the REA did for us." His wife told Fran, "If it hadn't been for President Roosevelt, people would be driving past today and say, 'That's the old Lathrop place.' " When Lowell Lathrop died, florists in the county ran out of flowers, and a hundred mourners couldn't get into the church, and REA provided loudspeakers for

them. Things like these go into forming liberalism; it is not a program but a state of mind. In my own serious magazine writing, I wrote almost instinctively about life's losers—men in prison, the Centralia coal miners, James Hickman whose children were burned to death.

The underdog, *los de abajo,* those from below—the purest I ever heard it given voice was about this time when I was doing a piece for the *Post* on copper mining in the Upper Peninsula of Michigan, not far from where we spend summers. This had been Michigan's first boom country. But now only a half-dozen copper mines were still operating, deep underground mines, far deeper and hotter than the iron mines. I spent an evening in a workingmen's bar with a union organizer, Gene Saari, and two of his friends. Drinking beer at a round table, Saari and a younger man were complaining loudly about working conditions in the mine and saying that young men were refusing to go underground, preferred safer, cleaner, better-paying jobs in city factories. An older man, Finnish like Saari, spoke up. He had been sitting without saying much, smiling a little, picking at the label on his beer bottle. Facing me, he began slowly: "You asked why we do this kind of work if we don't like it. Well, I'll tell you why. You can work awhile and sit down awhile. You don't punch a clock. You're all by yourself all day. You're your own boss in a way. I started in the mine in 1922. Two dollars and seventy cents a day. I worked one year, and I decided to go to the city to improve my status. So I went to Detroit; an auto company paid me five dollars a day. I operated what they call a reamer on connecting rods. Standing up all day. That assembly line moving. Wearisome toil. My quitting time was four o'clock. One day I shut down two minutes before four. The foreman came running over. 'What's the trouble?' he said. 'Trouble? No trouble, quitting time.' He looked at his watch. 'Well, I don't mind half a minute, but two minutes is too much.' Well, it was September, and I started thinking of bird season, and I thought, 'Detroit, the hell with you and your five dollars a day.' I quit and came back in the mine."

He took a drink of his beer. Both Saari and the young man were listening with respect. He went on, "You want to hear some more of this life history? I was twenty years old. I stayed here till 1926, working in lumber camps and mines on and off. Then I decided to see

what Butte, Montana, was like. So I grabbed up a armload of freight cars and I landed in Butte, Montana, with fifteen cents. That same night I saw a white man running down the street with a Chinaman shooting at him with a forty-five. And I thought, 'This is the town for me.' I went to work in the Belmont Mine about which the only thing they could brag about was that they had just installed a big electric hoist. It was the hottest mine on The Hill. I hired out as a miner. They paid four seventy-five then. But in the fall of the year I'd heard about the Coeur d'Alene district of Idaho and so I went down to Idaho and I hired on as a miner there at the Sunshine Mine. And at the Sunshine Mine I learned something more about mining. I learned to work the glory hole. The bottom. Going straight down. And I also learned about the IWW [Industrial Workers of the World]. I carried a red [IWW] card. Which you had to do. There was no choice. I had signed up in Butte." He laughed. "In Butte also I got my rustler's card. Do you know what a rustler's card was? In order to apply for a job in Butte, Montana, in 1927 you had to have what is known as a rustler's card. You went to the Anaconda offices on Main Street to apply for one and they put you through a third degree—your political opinions and affiliations, background, and if they found that you met their requirements they issued you a rustler's card. It entitled you to apply in any mine in Butte, Montana, for a job as a mucker or a miner. One of the prime questions I remember—and I'll remember till I die—was: What is your opinion of unions and organized labor? And I told him that my experience with unions and organized labor was a sad one. What did I mean by that? I meant by that I wanted to get that rustler's card," he said, grinning sardonically. "Also, in Butte, Montana, I decided to become a Democrat because the cheapest place to eat was a little beanery and they had a big sign in their window that said: IF YOU DON'T EAT HERE I'LL VOTE FOR HOOVER. And he did a land-office business. I'll be back in a minute." And he got up, a long-waisted man in a T-shirt, with powerful arms, and walked around the bar to the men's room. While he was gone, Saari said, "He doesn't hold any office in the union now but he could have about any office he wants. He doesn't want one. Thinks it might hurt the union. Because of his background. The name I introduced him by isn't his real name. When he gets up to talk in the union meeting, they all listen. They've got more respect for him than for anybody else."

He came back and sat down and continued: "Do you know Coeur d'Alene? Wallace, Mullen, Bunker, and Kellogg sets down between two mountain ranges, down at the bottom of a V, you might say. Well, after a while I wanted to see what was on the other side of that western mountain range. So I went to Spokane, Washington, and I got off at the union depot and went across to skid row. And do you know what paid my fare? That red card. The IWW card. Without it you couldn't travel." Saari looked at him in surprise. He said, "That's right, Gene. West of Minnesota you couldn't ride a freight train without it. They asked you, 'What are you ridin' on?' and if you didn't have it you got off. That was the way I was inducted into democracy," he added. "Well, on skid row I looked around out there in Spokane, Washington. They were all strikes on, 1927, '28. Wheatfields and all over. Wheatfields was burning." Saari looked perplexed. "Burning, Gene. They set 'em afire. The big struggle was on. There was a big battle down in San Francisco. I didn't look for a job. I was looking for a fight. I was a soldier and I was on the front line. I went to Bellingham, Washington, where the coal mines are and—well, we wound up in a lot of trouble." He paused. "Well, anyhow, I came back here. Why? I was born and raised in the Copper Country. And I thought the fight should be extended this way. I started thinking of '12 and '13." (In 1913, the miners, led by the head of the Western Federation of Miners, an affiliate of the IWW, struck. It was Upper Michigan's bloodiest strike. It lasted nearly a year. The strike leader was mobbed. Riots began; the militia came. People went hungry. On Christmas Eve, strikers' families were gathered in a hall for a children's party, and somebody falsely cried, "Fire!" and in the crush to escape more than seventy people were killed, most of them children.) "I knew what my aim was going to be here—the struggle. Suppose your old man left home and didn't come home for three days. Like mine did during the 1913 strike. He left our house to go to the store and the vigilantes got after him and he skied across country and holed up in Quincy. He was from Finland, came here before 1900 and worked for Copper Range. I was born in 1904. I was nine years old at the time of the strike. The first day of the strike a big Austrian came up to me in Painesdale and said, 'What are you?' I said, 'I'm a union.' I had on a Western Federation of Miners button. Nine years old." He laughed. "Well, anyhow, I came back here late in 1928 and I was broke. I went to work

for the Copper Range. Mining. I stuck it out. Speaking unions. In 1928 I got fired. They didn't want me anymore. You see, after the 1912 and 1913 strike my old man was on the blacklist. He had to work at the White Pine, forty-two miles from where we lived, came home every two weeks to see the family. My old man died in 1941. He was seventy-one, seventy-two. He pooped out in 1921. He was played out, couldn't make it anymore. There were five of us kids—two sisters and three brothers. I'm the baby. Only two of the brothers are living. The sisters died of polio. One of my brothers is a clerk in the post office in Detroit. I'll explain that too. In 1924 he was held up and robbed of the U.S. mail and his skull was fractured and he was left blind on the side of the road. One of the brothers also is a polio victim, crippled. He's at home in Painesdale."

He drank his beer slowly. Others had gathered around. Nobody else said anything except Saari, who said, "Jesus." The older man said, "Where was I? Oh yes, I was working for Copper Range in the Champion Mine about 1928. I'd been on the blacklist anyway because my old man was. I got fired. What happened next? Well, I don't know if I should tell you."

Saari said quickly, "Don't tell him. It's better not. Just leave a gap." He turned to me. "There's a gap from 1930 to 1943. I know about it. Just leave a gap."

He said, "I'd just as soon tell him."

I said it was up to him. Saari said it was better to keep still.

He shrugged. "I came back here in 1943 to the Copper Range. Mining. I was more or less restricted; I was confined to the boundaries of the county," he said sardonically. "I was injured a few months ago, a rock burst. Ruptured the sciatic nerve. You want see my scars again?" His face was seamed and leathery. He wore gold-rimmed glasses and a little baseball player's cap. "And in conclusion, gentlemen, all I can do is quote Joe Hill just before the firing squad executed him in prison: 'Don't mourn for me, you're the guy.'"

Saari waved for more beer. He said, "I never heard your story before. It's some story. Now listen. I'm going to get you into a discussion right here and now. I'm—"

"It's hard to do," the older man said. "I had to learn to keep my mouth shut."

"—when I came to this country in 1939—"

"I was still day shift," grinning at a secret joke.

"—the problem has not changed fundamentally from then. Failure to put through the subsidy and conservation program will be the most costly error ever made. During the war"—the Korean War was on—"America is consuming more copper than she is producing. I've got all the figures. I love these people in the Michigan copper district. But I'm concerned about the basic problem. It's a problem greater than these goddamn trade unions and companies. Every pound of copper in the United States of America must be extracted. And if we don't put in a subsidy for our own marginal mines and stop paying a subsidy to Chilean mines, we're going to become dependent on Chile and Rhodesia for our copper. But Calumet and Hecla"—the big mining company here—"will have copper for eighty years—if the government does what it ought to do. If not, we'll lose it for the economy of our nation and the prosperity of our people. The Korean War—"

Saari was pounding the table and shouting. The young miner was saying to him intensely, "We know where the copper is and we can get it out of there if they give us the kind of living we ought to have." But the older man had stopped listening and was trying to talk to me about the novels of John Dos Passos, which he admired. Saari, noticing he wasn't listening, said directly to him, "This isn't an ordinary trade union problem. This is a problem in the unorthodox economies of this area. What are we going to do about it?"

The older man said, as though reciting a lesson, "Through education and consolidation of our forces, progressively through the increasing understanding of trade union problems, we will win through to our goal."

Saari said, "Quit it."

He said quietly, "My interests lie with the downtrodden people. I'm a Finlander. But my interests lie just as deeply with the Austrian or the Croatian. I know what happened here in '12 and '13. You see a man riding a horse and slapping a miner across the face with a billy club that long, you know. I'm here for a cause."

Saari, distracted in spite of himself, asked, "What is the cause?"

"Humanity."

"What is the answer to humanity?"

"I don't know."

"What is the answer?"

He said, smiling a little lopsidedly, "I haven't quite put my finger on it."

Adlai Stevenson of Lake Forest, Illinois—surely a strange spokesman for revolutionaries like that. And yet, in my confused head at the Elks Club in 1952, he was. Liberalism, the labor union cause, racial segregation, injustice, the underdog—at the Elks Club, all this was unsystematic, was emotion, instinct, feeling for people. In college I had not learned to think rigorously or systematically. I had never worked out a liberal credo, had never needed to. Now suddenly I had to. What I brought to liberalism and to the Elks Club was, in addition to writing, a life's experience and instincts. With the tutelage of Arthur Schlesinger and Dave Bell and the others, I managed to translate this into a system of liberalism that could be applied to political campaign speeches. One cannot be the biographer of Jackson and Roosevelt as Schlesinger was, one cannot work in the Truman White House as Dave Bell had, without working out a rational system of liberalism. No more could I spend that fall in the Elks Club without doing it.

Preparing to write a speech, I read the speeches written by the other Elks. From Bob Tufts I learned a good deal about foreign policy, which I had never thought much about. And I had a memorable lunch alone with Senator Hubert Humphrey. We Elks were struggling with a speech about foreign trade and aid, and I knew little about it, and I mentioned it to Hubert Humphrey; at the lunch table he delivered for me a speech he himself often gave on his idea of exporting surplus food to other countries. This was the principal origin, in Hubert Humphrey's head, of what later became the Food-for-Peace Act, PL 480, which began as a way of getting rid of U.S. farmers' surplus crops and ended as a U.S. foreign policy instrument and a way to feed the hungry world. I conceived an admiration and affection for Hubert Humphrey that I never lost, and in later years, we became collaborators in politics. Indeed, that fall nearly all the Democratic heroes became my heroes. Two or three years later, I was in New York, walking up Forty-fourth Street from the Algonquin Hotel, when a car double-parked and a woman got out and

walked across the sidewalk to the Harvard Club. It was Eleanor
Roosevelt. Without thinking, I stopped and stood at attention and
took off my hat and held it over my heart, something I have done
only that one time. Seeing her drew together so many threads for
me—Brookside Avenue in the Depression, Franklin Roosevelt, my
own mother and father, unions and liberalism, my writing about the
disadvantaged, Adlai Stevenson's doomed 1952 campaign.

That September at the Elks Club, the Stevenson candidacy
seemed anything but doomed. We thought we had the best of it on
all the issues. Eisenhower was not turning out to be, as the song had
it, "good on a mike." A scandal almost blew Richard Nixon, running with him, off the ticket. We Elks worked and ate and slept together. We talked of almost nothing but the campaign. Few things
are so all-consuming as a presidential campaign. Now and then we
telephoned our wives at home to ask not only about the children but
about how the campaign was going in our home states.

We put nearly all major speeches through at least six drafts.
Sometimes we would sit around the big worktable and mark up a
draft together; sometimes Dave Bell would assign rewrite to one of
us alone. Arthur Schlesinger and I developed a way of writing a
rough draft together—he would write the substantive center of the
speech while I would write the pleasantries and setup at the beginning and the rising rhetoric at the end; then we would trade drafts
and mark them up, then put them together. In talking, we Elks
poked fun at Eisenhower, and at Stevenson too, for we were having
a good time. But underneath we were deadly serious about the campaign. We regarded Senator Joe McCarthy as a sinister force in
American life. We came to despise Eisenhower because he refused
to renounce McCarthy's support. We came to think his election
would be a national disaster. We hated Nixon and his hatchetwork.
The other side of all this was that we became fiercely loyal to Stevenson even though he sometimes disappointed us. We were more
partisan than he. Before long I ceased to wonder even privately how
I, an "objective reporter," could feel so partisan.

Where Truman was able to ad-lib at whistlestops, where FDR
was able simply to go out to the rear platform and wave to the crowd
with his cigarette holder—where others could win crowds that way,
Stevenson insisted on a full text and a different one for each whistle-

stop speech. He was ill at ease without one, and he grew bored repeating the same speech. But this made endless trouble—he rarely had time to familiarize himself with each text, newspapermen riding the train, being lazy, didn't like it for they had to write their stories several times a day, and we Elks were obliged to produce ten or eleven different speeches for a single day of campaigning instead of concentrating on the big speeches that, being nationally televised, reached millions of voters, not a few hundred.

The first trip Dave Bell sent me on with Stevenson was to Indiana and Kentucky. I had written the speeches since I knew the area, and on the trip I worked with Stevenson rewriting them and went with him while he delivered them. In Indianapolis I took my mother and father aboard his plane and introduced them to him. At Paducah our motorcade took us to Vice-President Alben Barkley's country home and we ate a leisurely picnic lunch on the lawn. Eight years later, in the fiery furnace of John F. Kennedy's nonstop campaign for the presidency, such a leisurely lunch would have been unthinkable.

Back in Springfield, I reported on the trip to the other Elks. I thought we were on the wrong track with our courthouse speeches. A courthouse speech could not be the lyrical graceful speech Stevenson liked, nor a serious substantive speech, nor a rousing rally speech to a partisan audience (a courthouse crowd contains people passing by, at least half Republicans). Rather, it should be partisan enough to arouse Democrats but not so partisan as to offend Republicans; it must be an "image" speech, creating an impression of the candidate, not an "issue" speech, and if it must contain an issue that issue must be presented bluntly, in black and white; above all it must be simple. Furthermore, I thought we needed to know more in advance about the occasions we were writing speeches for. Too often our speeches were inappropriate. And I wished we could become involved in scheduling. This appeared impossible—the schedulers decided where Stevenson would go on an almost purely political basis, with little regard to what he might say when he got there. As I traveled increasingly with Stevenson, I became convinced that scheduling is the heart of any campaign. Only scheduling brings together the candidate, the issues, and the audience. It involves, or should involve, the highest political strategy. Is it wise

to maximize your Democratic vote or should you fight for the Republican and independent vote (with the risk of stirring people up to vote against you when they might stay home)? What kind of audience is your candidate best with and whom does he need most—students, labor, businessman, suburbanites? And if the writers decide he needs to deliver a foreign policy speech the day after tomorrow, the schedulers should change his schedule to give him a thoughtful indoor sitdown audience, not a state fair grandstand; and if the writers decide he should switch to the attack, the schedulers should provide hot partisan crowds. Television was a major problem. Stevenson used it poorly, and so did our schedulers, sometimes buying TV time to broadcast a partisan speech to a rally of screaming machine Democrats—when at least half the people watching in their homes were Republicans. We never solved these problems. I resolved that if I ever again became involved in a campaign I was going to try to bring scheduling and speechwriting together.

I wrote a speech for a Democratic-Farmer-Labor party rally in St. Paul, putting into it material from my long-ago memo on the Midwest for *Life* about the terrible times on upper Midwest farms during the Depression—"When FDR took office in 1933, the farmers of the Northwest were burning their wheat in their stoves because they couldn't sell it for the price of coal. The land lay barren, just gray-black dirt, and thistles blew across it, and farm wives canned the green thistles to have something to eat." That came almost verbatim out of my *Life* memo. It became something of a model for later rollicking rally speeches. I enjoyed writing them more than any others, and Stevenson seemed to enjoy delivering them, but afterward he seemed apologetic about them—no doubt some of his personal friends in Republican Lake Forest chided him. I went with him on a long southern trip and a long west-coast trip, and virtually all the Elks and I went with him on his train on a final grand eastern tour. Whistlestopping homeward from New York to Chicago, I stayed up all Friday night working on the next night's Chicago Stadium speech, the last of the campaign. So did others. Carl McGowan put the drafts together.

That Saturday night, Fran met me at the Conrad Hilton, and after dinner, the motorcade led by a torchlight parade headed slowly west on Madison Street. No crowds—I was worried. We were riding with

Lou and Mary Jane Kohn. A crowd was massed around the stadium, and Democratic ward committeemen were trying to drive the precinct captains up to the topmost gallery but their feet hurt. The stadium was vast and it was packed. The Chicago machine had done its job. Fran and I found standing room with the working press just below the platform. The speech was broadcast on nationwide television. The crowd was hot, it had come to laugh and boo and cheer, and Stevenson was delivering the speech well. But he had started slowly, as he often did, and as he approached the ending, he was running out of TV time. He reached the ending I had written:

I see an America where no man fears to think as he pleases or say what he thinks.

I see an America where slums and tenements have vanished and children are raised in decency and self-respect.

I see an America where men and women have leisure from toil—leisure to cultivate the resources of the spirit.

I see an America where no man is another's master—where no man's mind is dark with fear.

I see an America at peace with the world.

I see an America as the horizon of human hopes.

This is our design for the American cathedral, and we shall build it brick by brick and stone by stone, patiently, bravely, and prayerfully....

He had reached that litany almost at the end of his TV time, and he knew it, and when the audience tried to break in with applause at every line, he held up his hand to stop them. At the end the crowd took the roof off. Some had tears in their eyes. And when he finished, the press arose and applauded him, something rare. Next morning's *New York Times* carried his "I see an America" litany on page 1. I liked to think that the opening welcoming speech to the convention, with its Altgeld-Dunne-Horner litany, and the closing stadium speech, with its America litany, framed the lofty elegance and idealism of the campaign.

Fran and I took Dave and Mary Bell and Arthur Schlesinger and Bob Tufts home with us. One the way I asked Fran how we were doing. She said, "I think you're doing fine most places. Of course, you're not going to carry Illinois." Dave said, "If we lose Illinois, we lose the election." Arthur called his wife in Cambridge, and she said

Stevenson was doing find although of course he would lose Massachusetts. Arthur went home next day and at the airport in New York encountered Max Lerner, who said that everything looked great for Stevenson except of course he would lose New York.

We spent the weekend at our house in Highland Park then on Tuesday, election day, aboard Stevenson's plane in Springfield, devised a pool among those aboard, including Stevenson himself, each of us contributing five dollars and writing down the number of electoral votes he thought Stevenson would get. He needed 266 votes to win. Arthur Schlesinger's guess had been 325, Bob Tufts's about 450, Stevenson's own 325 or 350, mine about 400. Fran did her own figuring and came up with Stevenson losing. I told her she couldn't put down a losing figure, so she put down the bare minimum he needed to win. All the rest of us thought he was going to win. Nonetheless, on the plane we were quiet and subdued. In Springfield as the polls were closing, we Elks at dinner listened to early returns. They did not sound good. When industrial Democratic Bridgeport, Connecticut, came in wrong, Dave Bell said, "That's bad—we'd better go," and we went to the ballroom of the Leland Hotel where an election headquarters had been set up, crowded but quiet as state after state came in for Eisenhower. Here and there we saw glimmerings of hope, as when a flurry of Stevenson votes came in from Minnesota, and we told each other, "Just wait till we hear from Ohio," or "Michigan and Illinois"; before the night was over we were saying, "Just wait till we hear from California." John L. Lewis stalked around the ballroom, scowling and alone.

About 10 P.M. we went to the Governor's Mansion. Stevenson was working in his ground-floor office, working I suppose, on his concession speech. About fifty of his friends and close staff were upstairs in the living rooms, sitting quietly. Fran and I sat at a little end table that had a radio on it. Stevenson's sister, Buffie Ives, asked me how it looked. I told her very bad. By 10:30 the Republican national chairman claimed victory. Stevenson wanted to concede at once but the Democratic national chairman dissuaded him—premature concession might imperil Democratic senatorial and congressional candidates. By midnight, however, the Eisenhower sweep was clear, and at 12:40 A.M. Stevenson went to the Leland ballroom and before TV cameras delivered his concession speech.

We Elks, thinking he would want to be alone with his family and

personal friends, started to leave, but as we did, he came back from the Leland and asked, "Where's everybody going?" And "Come on upstairs and have a drink; let's celebrate my defeat." We went, and he told a butler to bring in the champagne. His Lake Forest friends were there. Most of them had voted for Eisenhower, and one woman was wearing a big diamond Eisenhower pin. One told him, "Governor, you educated the country with your great campaign," and he said, "But a lot of people flunked the course." The champagne came, and Stevenson offered Fran the first glass. She had won the electoral vote pool; drinking the champagne, she gave the pool money to Stevenson and told him it was an early contribution for the 1956 campaign fund. "I take it shamelessly," he said, putting it in his pocket. After a time we left.

Fran and I went home to Maple Avenue. A carpenter was working in our house and when we arrived he said, "Yah, yah, we beatcha." I should have told him to leave immediately (and in a few days did—he was not only a rude Republican carpenter but an incompetent one). For a week Fran and I moped around the house, lost. The campaign was over; suddenly there was nothing to talk about. The newspapers and television were full of Eisenhower's landslide. I felt a stranger in my own country. You put so much of yourself into such a campaign. I could not help it—I did not want to stay in this country. On the Tuesday after the election, Fran and I went to Cuba and spent two weeks in the sun on the beach at Varadero, healing. What do to? Well, I would go back to writing for the magazines. But after this campaign, nothing would ever be the same again.

EIGHT

THE LONGEST CAMPAIGN

1.

Reentering the world of magazine writing was not so easy as I had imagined. I had an assignment for *McCall's,* and I went to Cleveland to do the legwork, but after a few days I realized I couldn't do it, couldn't stop thinking about the campaign, had no heart for this story, and I went home. It was the only time I ever did that. I felt ill. I had not realized fully how emotionally involved I'd been in the Stevenson campaign. My doctor, Sylvan Robertson, an internist but one psychoanalytically oriented, suggested that my malaise might be due to guilty feelings that I was to blame for Stevenson's defeat and suggested I write something about the campaign to get it out of my system. I was not conscious of such feelings and anyway knew enough about politics to know that the results would have been the same had I never been involved. I also knew enough about magazines to know they would not be interested in such a piece. But I took his advice and wrote a five-hundred-page memorandum on the campaign. I added to it my files along with all the speech drafts, itineraries, and research matter from the Elks Club, a Stevenson archive. Years later, when I came to write Stevenson's biography, I was glad I had it, and I did feel better after writing it.

Many serious newspapers and magazines will not take back a writer who takes a leave of absence to work for a political candidate; they fear he has lost his objectivity. Stuart Rose and the others at the *Post*, though most of them were Republicans, welcomed me back after the Stevenson campaign. So did other editors. And I found that I could understand some stories the better for having been in the Stevenson campaign. It was the *Post's* confidence in me—and Harold Ober's—that helped me forget the Stevenson loss and restored my confidence in myself as a writer.

2.

But I kept in touch with Adlai Stevenson and I did some work for him. Hundreds of organizations wanted him to speak to them or, if he could not, to send them a message of encouragement, and he paid me to write the messages. I worked closely with Bill Blair, who was his partner in his small new law firm, along with Bill Wirtz and Newt Minow. Fran helped him too—she went down to the Loop every Thursday for the American Civil Liberties Union board meeting at lunch in the YMCA cafeteria and after it she worked in Stevenson's law office as a volunteer, drafting answers to some of his mail. In drafting messages and letters, Fran and I learned to imitate Stevenson's eloquent and rather arch style, and he once told Fran, "You sound more like me than I do." Sometimes at the end of the day on Thursday, she drove him home, occasionally bringing him to our house for a drink en route. On the ACLU board, Fran usually voted with the moderates, with neither the purist constitutionalists nor the leftists who saw a civil liberties issue in every liberal cause. When she tells people now that she was at the ACLU in the 1950s, the time when Senator Joe McCarthy was riding high, they are greatly impressed, but actually at the time we thought little about it.* Once when the ACLU held a fund-raiser in Chicago, it wanted Stevenson to speak; Fran asked him, and he said he would if I'd write the speech. I did. I also drafted other speeches for him, especially during the 1954 congressional campaign, and that election

---

* I proposed a series to the *Post* that would show McCarthy in action at some of his famous hearings. Stuart Rose and Ben Hibbs approved, but someone in higher authority, no doubt at the corporate level, vetoed it, the only time the *Post* refused to let me do a political piece on what I have to believe were political grounds.

night we watched election returns with him in his house in Liberty-ville, Illinois. It was a happy occasion, for the election was a triumph for Democrats—and for Stevenson too. Since 1952 he had made a reputation as a world statesman and he was the acknowledged leader of the Democratic party. When in 1955 it became clear, at least to me, that he was going to run for president again in 1956, I did a piece about him for the *Post*—how he lived in his country house at Libertyville, what he'd been doing since 1952, his prospects for 1956. It was a nice affectionate piece yet a highly political one, and I was greatly pleased when the *Post* published it as I wrote it.

That fall, 1955, Fran's father died at eighty-nine. For Fran, his death was hard. He was a patriarchal figure. Fran's mother and brother brought his body back from Colorado, where her parents had retired, and we buried him in Elmhurst, Illinois. He actually had three funeral services—a religious one, a Masonic one, and a military one, which seemed a little excessive. He had risen to the rank of lieutenant in the Spanish-American War and during World War I, I believe, he was elevated to captain, although he was not in that war, and so when he died he held the rank of captain. Many years later Fran was checking on something about his grave site, and the man at the cemetery said, "Oh yes, Colonel Smethurst." He was the only man I ever knew who was promoted posthumously, a triple promotion at that.

That year I quit smoking cigarettes. The cigarette–lung cancer linkage was just surfacing. I had smoked since high school; quitting was no fun. After seven months Sylvan Robertson told me, "There are some things worse than lung cancer, and one of them is your disposition when you're not smoking." He was an excellent doctor. I have always thought quitting smoking gave me ulcers. Perhaps, however, it was the stress of the work I'd been doing, or some sort of midlife crisis—I was forty. Dr. Robertson diagnosed gastric ulcer and put me in Highland Park Hospital early in 1956. It was the beginning of an ulcerated existence I led, off and on, for some fifteen years—restricted diet, in and out of bed, in and out of hospitals. It did not, however, seriously interfere with my work. During the 1956 Stevenson campaign, traveling almost constantly, I carried a thermos of milk, which airline stewardesses suspected contained martinis. How I wished it had.

3.

In earlier presidential election years, preconvention maneuvering had been largely behind the scenes and indeed the actual nominee was usually chosen at the convention behind the scenes. This year, 1956, was the beginning of the system of primary election contests that increasingly, at each four-year interval, have so overwhelmed our political system. In 1956 it was clear that if Stevenson wanted the nomination again, he would have to fight for it in the primaries —Senator Estes Kefauver of Tennessee was running against him.

While I was still in the hospital, Bill Wirtz, Stevenson's law partner, had come to see me and said that when I got out they wanted me to go to work writing Stevenson's speeches. I agreed. I joined the staff on March 20 and I stayed until the election in November, with only, as I recall it, a single two-day holiday. For me, as for Stevenson, it was the longest campaign.

Stevenson was running in four contested primaries that spring and his name was on the ballot in a number of others, but as things turned out the most important were the contests with Kefauver in Minnesota, Florida, and California.* He had assembled a small staff. This time for a campaign manager he picked not an amateur, as in 1952, but a thoroughgoing professional, Jim Finnegan, leader of the Democratic organization in Philadelphia, a congenial funny man whom I liked enormously. When Stevenson was not present, Finnegan called him "my tiger." But face to face with Stevenson, Finnegan was so in awe of him that he hesitated to give him the advice he needed.

To do research Stevenson brought in John Brademas, who had been a Rhodes Scholar and who was running for Congress in Indiana (he didn't win that year but eventually he did and became Democratic whip in the House, one of the ablest men in Congress). Helping him was Ken Hechler, a scholarly young man also later elected to Congress. The writers were three—Bill Wirtz and I and Harry Ashmore, a southern editor of great charm who loved to tell yarns, and who later went to the Center for the Study of Democratic

---

* A full account of the 1956 campaign appears in the biography I wrote, *The Life of Adlai E. Stevenson*, Volume 2: *Adlai Stevenson and the World.*

Institutions in California. From time to time Arthur Schlesinger or Ken Galbraith or someone else sent in a draft for a major speech.

The day I joined the staff, Stevenson lost the Minnesota primary. He had been supposed to win Minnesota big, for he had the support of Senator Hubert Humphrey and Governor Orville Freeman, the leaders of the Democratic-Farmer-Labor party, then at the peak of its power. But Kefauver fooled everybody. Seizing the underdog position, he made "the bosses" the issue, and he won big.

For Stevenson, Minnesota was a disaster, and that night Finnegan and the rest of us discussed whether Stevenson should withdraw from the entire campaign. What was most dangerous to him was that Minnesota might start an unstoppable Kefauver bandwagon in California. And already Stevenson was not doing well in California—he had gotten in trouble on civil rights. Following the U.S. Supreme court decision ordering school desegregation, Stevenson recently had been making statements on civil rights that sounded to Negroes like "gradualism"—they could have their rights, but gradually. This hurt him badly with California Negroes and liberals, his strongest supporters there.

We decided that Stevenson must go to California at once and "put out the Kefauver fire" with a television speech from Los Angeles and San Francisco. Stevenson agreed. He wanted the speech to avoid substantive issues, to attack Kefauver, and to be angry and aggressive in tone. I wondered if this could be "the new Stevenson" some people had been clamoring for. Wirtz, Ashmore, and I each wrote a draft. We spent most of one day working together on the passage on civil rights. Stevenson would have to move left on civil rights in California. At the same time, he could not forget that what he said there would be read in segregationist Florida, where he was also running in the primary. It was the most dangerous issue of all, the one that could derail Stevenson's candidacy. But it also could rescue him if he could convince the Democrats that he alone could unite the party. We went over our civil rights passage with Stevenson word by word. He took our full drafts and put them together. He asked me to go to California with him. He, Finnegan, Bill Blair (his law partner and right-hand man), Roger Tubby, (his press secretary), and I went the next day, March 28. Aloft, Blair told me to sit beside

Stevenson. Stevenson spent an interminable time going through his briefcase, reading memoranda, handing some to me. I became impatient. Finally he asked what he should talk about at a rally and a labor meeting that night in Los Angeles after his television speech. I said, the same thing—attack Kefauver. He asked what he should say when he arrived at Los Angeles airport. The same thing, I said. What should he talk about on TV from San Francisco tomorrow night? Repeat the Los Angeles speech, I said. He balked. I suggested labor, Social Security, or foreign policy. The minute I mentioned foreign policy he seized it and talked about it the rest of the way to Los Angeles, but in the end decided he would not have time to do it justice, he would have to resign himself to repeating the Los Angeles speech.

That speech went well. So did his other meetings afterward. To me, before going to bed, he balked again at repeating the TV speech in San Francisco and, in the morning, I rewrote it, strengthening a passage on labor because I'd been told that San Francisco labor leaders were lukewarm. When I gave it to Stevenson on the plane to San Francisco, he demanded, "Why do I have to give them all this crap about labor?" and irritably hacked up the labor passage. He kept saying he'd never finish before reaching San Francisco and he didn't. He was angry with himself for having spent so much time on the speech and at the rest of us for not having it ready in final form. At the San Francisco airport he was mobbed, and, during a wild motorcade into town, started trying to rewrite the speech's desegregation passage; I begged him not to in these circumstances, and he finally desisted. But at the hotel he closed his bedroom door to work on the speech. He was running late, and the speech was getting long, and Blair and I were marking optional cuts that would keep him within his TV time. Two Negro leaders were waiting for him in the parlor. Stevenson finished only five minutes before time to leave for the TV studio and the Negroes barely had a chance to shake his hand as he brushed past them. And he was in trouble with Negroes here. So often I saw him seclude himself to work on a speech when he should have been talking to local leaders. The speech turned out to be one of his best TV performances ever.

Next morning on the plane back to Chicago he talked to me for two hours about what he ought to do and say and about an all-

purpose whistlestop speech that he had been demanding, it seemed, forever. He never got it, it can't be written. And he showed me a memo from an eastern friend who asked hard questions about foreign policy—admission of Peking China to the UN, arms for Israel, the impossibility of reunifying Germany. Looking out the window at the barefaced Rockies, he mused that perhaps he should tell the people the truth about these questions—"I'm sure it would be the end of me as a politician, but I think it would make my reputation as a prophet."

Nonetheless, when we had been home a while, it seemed to us that, if Stevenson had not entirely put out the Kefauver fire in California, he had certainly damped it down. And some of us thought the Minnesota defeat might have been the best thing that happened to Stevenson. He had been the front runner for so long, and had been so widely acclaimed as a world statesman after 1952, and had so immersed himself in lofty issues, that it had seemed impossible that a lanky man in a coonskin cap like Kefauver could beat him. Now during his two-day trip to California he had suddenly seemed not the visionary philosopher-statesman but a hard-hitting candidate in a primary fighting for life. Not since his 1948 campaign for governor against Green had he sounded that way. Some of his Lake Forest friends didn't like it and thought he was demeaning himself. But after Minnesota he had no choice—Kefauver had pulled him off the pedestal and he had to fight on the ground.

The campaign was disorganized. We writers were putting too much energy into polishing the big prestigious speeches in the East, where Stevenson was entered in no contested primaries, and not enough into the day-to-day political stuff for Florida and Oregon and California, where he was. We had not even divided up the states. Now we did. I took California. Nobody from our headquarters was out there. I went there alone on April 26 and I stayed till the primary on June 5. California, everybody agreed, was the key to the nomination.

I began by meeting with Stevenson's California supporters, including state attorney general Pat Brown,* Fred Dutton, Don Bradley, and Alan Cranston. Then I did the kind of legwork I'd always

* Edmund G. Brown, soon elected governor, as, later, with his son, Edmund G. (Jerry) Brown, Jr.

done—interviewed people of all sorts to find out what was on their minds. I worked especially closely with Don Bradley, Democratic organization man in San Francisco, and Jack Abbott, his friend who knew issues. Together we worked out Stevenson's schedule and decided what issues he should discuss at each stop. Thus, for the first time in a campaign, I was able to bring scheduling and issues together.

And I did something else. Since I alone was writing nearly all of Stevenson's California speeches, as many as sixteen whistlestops a day, I obviously could not provide a full text for each one. He would have to speak extemporaneously. But I knew he'd balk if he had no paper in front of him. So I developed a technique of preparing briefing sheets for him on each stop—a page or two on the nature of the occasion, the setting, the size of the expected crowd, its composition (whether farmers, laborers, Negroes, aircraft industry workers, Democrats, general public), indoors or outdoors, who would introduce him, where he would be standing, which issues he should raise and which avoid, which local candidates or local leaders he should mention and which avoid, and a few lines on the locale so he could identify with the audience. If the issue to be discussed was a new one or a dangerous one in California, I provided language designed to handle it. If it was an old issue, I simply copied out enough material from earlier speeches to remind him. To gather material for this, I talked not only with Bradley and Abbott in San Francisco and Fred Dutton in Los Angeles but also with local people of all sorts. All this required hard political decisions; by now I had learned not always to trust local advice, to keep in mind not other people's interests but only the interests of my own candidate.

When Stevenson came to California the night of May 1, I met him and told him what was up. At first, he was dubious about the briefing sheet system but agreed to try it. (Like many of us, he was dubious about anything when it was first proposed.) Next day in San Francisco he had twelve stops between 9:45 A.M. and midnight. We handed him my briefing sheets one by one, just before each stop, and Stevenson took them and read them then scribbled notes on the back of them, making the pages his own, and he used them, speaking, in effect, extemporaneously from notes. The crowds loved it. The newspapers wrote of "the new Stevenson" who enjoyed hand-

shaking and whistlestopping. It was one of the best days of whistle-stopping of his life.

He was all over California for nearly two weeks. My editorial advance, as the briefing sheets came to be called, helped keep him on the track; he never arrived at a speech without knowing what to expect and what was expected of him. In years to come, I used this system with other candidates, and I believe others adopted it.

One of Stevenson's most difficult appearances was before the Ministerial Alliance in Oakland, a Negro group where Stevenson was in trouble. It had originally been planned as a closed meeting, with Stevenson submitting to questioning. I opposed that. I didn't like the question-and-answer formula, if the meeting was closed the press would try all the harder to find out what was said, and an unfriendly minister might leak a distorted paraphrase. Bradley and the others finally agreed to open the meeting but insisted that Stevenson make a brief statement, then take questions. As I saw it, my job was to write a statement that would anticipate all questions so none would be asked. By doing legwork, I ascertained what questions were likely then I drafted a statement to answer them. Stevenson resisted the project strongly—didn't see why he had to say all over again what he thought about civil rights. We persuaded him he must. The meeting started badly—the room was small and dark and crowded and no lectern had been provided, and Stevenson, near-sighted, could not read his text and had to speak sitting down. Manfully, he read my draft word for word. When he finished, the chairman asked, "Any questions?" No one spoke up, Stevenson left. It had worked.

Until then, national Democrats had been afraid to attack President Eisenhower. For a major speech in San Francisco, I wrote for Stevenson what I think was the first speech attacking the president frontally, attacking him both for his policies and for playing golf at times of national crisis, picturing him as an amiable man but not a serious president. I did not take up the issue of Eisenhower's health, though it was on everybody's mind—he had suffered a heart attack and a serious intestinal disorder. Later I came to the conclusion that we should have raised the health issue from the start. But we did not.

The rest of the primary campaign was frantic. Stevenson won eas-

ily in Oregon. He squeaked through in Florida. And he won California big, overwhelming Kefauver with 1,139,964 votes to 680,722—he got 62 percent of the vote, far more than anybody on his own staff had expected.

After the convention nominated Stevenson, I moved to Washington with him and his expanded staff. The writers were Wirtz, Arthur Schlesinger, and I full-time, Bob Tufts and others part-time. Jim Finnegan remained campaign manager. It was odd. When we met with Stevenson, often Finnegan, the professional politician, took the lofty idealistic position, while Arthur Schlesinger and I found ourselves urging a hard-nosed political view. But early on we all agreed that the only way Stevenson could beat Eisenhower was by campaigning as he had in the California primary—whistle-stopping hard in pockets of discontent in a largely complacent country, maximizing his support among workingmen, Negroes, coal miners, and others. California had, however, made Stevenson overconfident. He wanted to make foreign policy his major issue—we told him there were no votes in it—and to make eloquent speeches on grand themes, as in 1952. The conflict was never really resolved.

The 1952 campaign had been exciting fun but 1956 was just hard work. I traveled with Stevenson some, especially in the Midwest and California, but I spent more time in Washington. When President Eisenhower began to campaign about mid-September, I realized we were going to lose. Nevertheless, we ran a good campaign. Indeed, I have always thought it a better campaign than 1952, though most of Stevenson's friends and idolaters thought not. It was, really, two campaigns. It was, inevitably, an attack campaign—Eisenhower was the incumbent. And it was a programmatic affirmative campaign. In sober specific speeches, and in long position papers, we set forth affirmative programs that went far beyond the New Deal–Fair Deal, that dealt not just with food and clothing and shelter but with issues affecting the quality of American life—better education, better medical care, the defense of civil rights and civil liberties, the problems of children and of the elderly. In doing this Stevenson laid the groundwork, really, for President Kennedy's New Frontier and President Johnson's Great Society. And he made two national security proposals that the Republicans loudly denounced but that soon

became Republican policy—stopping nuclear testing and ending the military draft.

Toward the end, Polish Communist leaders defied the Kremlin, and the Hungarian revolt began, and Israel invaded the Sinai Peninsula. Some of us regretted having persuaded Stevenson to avoid foreign policy—he had laid no groundwork to attack this collapse of the administration's foreign policy. At the very end, on election eve, he made his worst mistake—predicted, on national television from Boston, that Eisenhower would not live out his next term if reelected.

Back in Chicago, Fran and I listened to the returns in the Blackstone Hotel with Stevenson and the others. It became clear early that Stevenson was losing badly. Scotty Reston of *The New York Times* telephoned Jim Finnegan and asked if Stevenson wouldn't concede now. Jim said, "I'll have to ask my advisers," and turned to Fran and asked her opinion. She shook her head, and Jim told Reston, "The answer is no." I set to work on a concession statement. Ben Hibbs of the *Post* told me later he hoped Stevenson would run every four years because he so enjoyed his graceful concession statements. It turned out that Stevenson lost by a bigger margin than in 1952, carrying only seven states, every one but Missouri from the old Confederacy. Eisenhower received 57.7 percent of the votes. I think that Suez and Hungary turned an Eisenhower victory into a landslide—when the country gets in trouble, the people rally round the president, even though he may be the one that got it in trouble. Afterward, Arthur Schlesinger, Seymour Harris, and I edited a book of Stevenson's 1956 speeches and position papers, published under the title *The New America,* which had been his campaign slogan.

NINE

THE KENNEDY BROTHERS
AND JIMMY HOFFA

1.

I had had much more influence on the 1956 campaign than on the 1952. Now, I thought, I was through with politics. I went back to full-time magazine writing. As things turned out, I was by no means through with politics, but my way back into it was quite by chance. This is how it was charted:

Stuart Rose had an idea. The Senate Rackets Committee had been investigating Jimmy Hoffa and his Teamsters union for more than two years. When it held a public hearing, the newspapers carried scrappy reports. But, Stuart said, nobody had ever put the whole story together, and he suggested I do. It took nearly a year and ended as a seven-part series, the longest yet.

Robert F. Kennedy was chief counsel of the Senate Rackets Committee. I knew him—he had been aboard Stevenson's 1956 campaign plane for a time, seeking, with his brother Jack in mind as a candidate in 1960, to learn how to run a presidential campaign. (He told me later he had learned how *not* to run one.) I went to Washington. I was there off and on during the next six or eight months, for as the Rackets Committee investigation dragged on so did my legwork, and I came to know something of Washington—the

cluttered frantic offices of the Rackets Committee in the Old Senate Office Building, the splendid gilded Senate Caucus Room where the Army-McCarthy hearings had been held, the shabby little Carroll Arms Hotel across the street where senators' staff aides ate lunch and where I usually stayed; dinner at the Metropolitan Club and at a French restaurant in Georgetown, parties in narrow three-story brick houses crowded close together on Georgetown's old narrow streets; Bobby Kennedy's opulent estate, Hickory Hill, out in McLean, Virginia, rolling hill country dotted with white rail fences and old trees, a gracious antebellum house with high ceilings, crystal chandeliers, white woodwork, marble fireplace, candlelit dining room.

I liked Bobby Kennedy from the start. Though born to wealth and power, he had about him not a trace of superiority or affectation. He was young, only thirty-two. He was handsome, slender, standing five feet ten and weighing about 150 pounds. He had a boyish grin. His trademark was a lock of dark-blond hair falling over his forehead; it blew in the wind as he drove his big convertible. He drove fast and skillfully. He had hard, direct blue eyes. His white, even teeth protruded slightly. He was tanned. He had a high-pitched, nasal voice. He spoke with a flat Boston accent. His expression in repose was sober; his quick flashing smile was infectious. He thought fast, his memory was remarkable. He wore narrow-shouldered dark blue suits, button-down collars, narrow neckties. At his desk he worked in his shirt sleeves, sleeves rolled up. Often, discussing committee strategy in his office, he and his administrative assistant, Kenneth O'Donnell, passed a football back and forth—both had played football at Harvard. He moved fast, handling his body well, like an athlete. He ran upstairs and downstairs. He scheduled himself remorselessly, and he drove his staff just as hard. Staffers conversed with him freely, as equals, but when he wanted something done he could be curt.

On this story, I probably spent more time with Bobby Kennedy than with any one else. Sometimes I spent all day talking to him in his office, with a sandwich sent in at noon. I watched him at the hearings. Many times he took me home for dinner with his wife Ethel and their six children, and on weekends I played touch football with them (not very well) and went swimming with Bobby in

his pool (not very well). A number of times when he came to Chicago on an investigation, sometimes accompanied by one or two of his investigators, they stayed at our house with Fran and me, and one night there he, before setting out with his men to try to dig up an ex-convict's body in a cornfield near Joliet, had dinner with us in Highland Park and he played cops and robbers all over the house with Dan and Fred. At that time Fran was betting on horses, and once while Bobby was at our house, the laundryman came to collect her two-dollar bet and she had to ask me for the money in front of Bobby, and, knowing he was investigating Syndicate gambling, she said "I owe the laundryman two dollars." Understanding, I gave it to her and said nothing. Bobby never knew.

When at the end of a day at his office on Capitol Hill he went home to Hickory Hill, his children and dogs swarmed all over him; he loved it. Watching, I thought that this was a Bobby Kennedy nobody knew who only saw him boring in on hostile gangsters at the hearings. It was during these years as counsel for the Rackets Committee that he acquired a reputation for being "ruthless." I did not think him ruthless—thought him hard driving, tenacious, aggressive, competitive, suspicious, abstemious, a man with a single-minded purpose, for his struggle to get Hoffa had become for Bobby Kennedy a holy crusade. He considered Hoffa the most dangerous man in the United States; something had to be done about him. In later years, I came to know another side of him—compassion, a deep concern for the disadvantaged, the poor, and especially Negroes, an abiding devotion to justice, a passionate interest in young people, a spontaneous warmth and affection, a brooding, almost tragic sense of life. Perhaps, in later years, after the Rackets Committee had ended its investigations and he had gone on to other things, just as in those years I discovered these qualities in him, so did he discover them in himself.

I had no way of knowing it at the time, of course, but meeting Bobby Kennedy on this story changed my life (and Fran's and our children's), just as had my first meeting with Adlai Stevenson. It was the beginning of my long association with Bobby Kennedy and his brothers, Jack and Ted. I wrote speeches for them and advised them throughout two of their presidential campaigns, advised them during other campaigns, and became a member of President Kennedy's

administration. It all began with the Bobby Kennedy–Jimmy Hoffa story for the *Post* in 1958–1959.

I talked to some of the senators on the committee—John F. Kennedy, John L. McClellan (the chairman), and the leading Republican, Barry M. Goldwater, whom I approached with some trepidation because of his conservative reputation but whom I found to be an amusing, engaging man. I spent more time with Senator Kennedy than any of the others, seeing him alone in his office, at breakfast in a New York hotel, at dinner in Washington with his wife Jacqueline. When alone, he and I talked politics almost entirely. He was getting ready to run for president in 1960. The primaries would start in a little more than a year. He knew I had worked for Stevenson in two campaigns, and he wanted to know what kind of campaign staff he would need, what I thought of various issues such as the worldwide population explosion (I thought it important but voteless; he disagreed), and, though himself a Harvard overseer, he wanted to know how he could get "wired into" the academic world of policy ideas and position papers, as Stevenson was. Jack Kennedy struck me as an extremely attractive and extremely intelligent young man. He presented a lighthearted funny exterior, sometimes almost frivolous, but inwardly he was deadly serious and he had an astonishing fund of information about all manner of subjects, such as France's problems in Algeria and the number of Nigerian exchange students in the United States. He was tall and strikingly handsome, his mind was lightning fast and compelling, and he seemed much more tightly focused, both on issues and on his own ambitions, than Stevenson ever had. And he seemed to welcome challenges, not be burdened by them. Many people whom I ran into in Washington that winter and spring were already committed to Kennedy and were proselytizing for him, including some, like Hy Raskin, who had served Stevenson. I myself did not quite put Kennedy down in my mind the way Walter Lippmann had once described Roosevelt—a very nice young man who would very much like to be president—but I was not sure at first that he was presidential material. He was so young.

I spent a good deal of time with several members of Bobby Kennedy's staff. O'Donnell, Bobby's administrative assistant, was a tough, small, wiry young Boston Irishman who later became chief execu-

tive officer on Senator Kennedy's campaign plane in 1960 and still later President Kennedy's appointments secretary in the White House. Walt Sheridan was a former FBI man and one of Bobby's best investigators, another slight, taut young man. Nearly all of Bobby's investigators were in their late twenties and early thirties, and they lacked the tolerance of human weakness that big-city detectives like Emil Smicklas acquire. They condemned wrongdoing unequivocally, they had the moral certitude, the fervor, and the lust for a better world that go with youth, and sometimes I thought there was something a little chilling about their certitude and zeal. Pierre Salinger was somewhat different. A tolerant, self-indulgent, cheerful, cigar-smoking fat man, he had been a newspaperman and magazine writer. I had known Pierre ever since the 1956 Democratic primary in California. While I was resident there, alone and swamped with too many speeches to write, Salinger had sought me out and offered to help. I welcomed him. At that time he was the San Francisco correspondent of *Collier's* magazine. The editor of *Collier's* came to San Francisco, and Pierre brought him around to see me, and he wanted me to do a series of articles for *Collier's* on the Teamsters union. (At that time the investigation of the Teamsters had not yet begun.) I told him I couldn't undertake it till after the presidential election; he said he couldn't wait; I suggested he get Pierre Salinger to do it, and he did. At about the time Pierre finished his story, *Collier's* folded. The Rackets Committee was just beginning. Pierre took his material to Bobby Kennedy, and Bobby hired him as an investigator. By the time I went to work on the story, Pierre was acting, really, as the committee's—and Bobby's—press secretary, not only putting out press releases but also drafting the committee's reports, summarizing the testimony and stating its conclusions. Later, of course, Pierre became Senator Kennedy's press secretary in the 1960 presidential campaign and, still later, President Kennedy's press secretary in the White House. The Rackets Committee investigation changed quite a few lives.

It was one of the biggest investigations in recent American history, perhaps the biggest since those of Teapot Dome in the 1920s and banking and securities in the 1930s. Those investigations exposed wrongdoing by big business. The McClellan Committee alone went after big labor, especially the Teamsters. It also investigated

eleven other unions as well as the Mafia and the Chicago Syndicate, but it concentrated on the Teamsters because the Teamsters, the biggest union in America, with more than a million and a half members, controlled truck transportation and so possessed the awesome power to stop the United States in its tracks. And its president, Jimmy Hoffa, in Bobby Kennedy's view, was evil and was in league with the worst criminal elements of the United States.

If Bobby Kennedy and his committee were half of my story, obviously the second half was Jimmy Hoffa and his union. I had first brushed up against the ponderous bulk of the Teamsters union as a kid reporter on the Indianapolis *Times*. During a truck strike, I was sent to interview the president of the Teamsters, whose national headquarters was then in Indianapolis. Dan Tobin, an old man who had been president since 1907, had an office with a door that was locked and steel-barred, like a prison cell, and I had to stand in the corridor outside it and shout my questions at him, and, sitting at a little desk, he yelled the answers at me, usually "No" or "No comment" or "Go to hell." I got nothing out of him. No reporter ever got much out of the Teamsters. Jimmy Hoffa was no exception. When I set to work on my story for the *Post*, he was seeing no reporters. He sat in the Teamsters headquarters in Washington facing the Capitol across the park, surrounded by secretaries and aides and assorted characters, and simply refused to see anybody except his own people. After several weeks talking to Bobby Kennedy and his staff and studying committee documents, I was ready to talk to Hoffa. While Hoffa would not talk to other reporters, I thought he might talk to a reporter from *The Saturday Evening Post,* with its prestige, particularly if I could convince him that I offered him a chance to tell his side and would write an unbiased story. But how could I get to him to convince him of that?

I adopted a stratagem. I went home and every day went down to the Chicago advertising office of the *Post* and put in a call for him. This had two advantages. The switchboard operator placed the call and announced that it was the *The Saturday Evening Post* calling and left the *Post* number in Chicago for him to call back. Moreover, this kept my home telephone number, and hence my address, out of Teamsters headquarters, which seemed only prudent in view of the

reputation of some of Hoffa's associates. Every morning for a week I placed the call then sat all day in a little cubicle in the *Post* offices, waiting. Finally he called back and agreed to see me in Washington the following Thursday.

I interviewed him for two hours. We were alone (except that I thought, from the way he guided me to a particular chair, that our conversation was probably taped). He looked oddly out of place alone in his sumptuous office. It was so big, he so small. Yet he dominated it by force of personality and by his sense of his own power. He was built like a truck, low to the ground, burly, boxy, hard to knock over. He stood only five feet five and a half inches tall but he weighed 180 pounds. He was muscular, with thick legs, thick wrists, broad heavy shoulders, big feet. He ran up and down stairs. His shoes were scuffed and his pants baggy. His features were rugged and somewhat Indian in cast—straight black hair, high cheekbones. A hint of a sardonic smile often played around his mouth. His eyes were small, bright, green, hard. He had big, hard, calloused hands, stubby fingers. He could flash a quick grin but it was not a boyish grin, it was somewhat lopsided as though he didn't really mean it. He sometimes talked out of the side of his mouth, as Chicagoans do.

I no longer remember what we talked about at that first interview—I probably asked him what he thought of Bobby Kennedy and the committee and how the union worked, anything to convince him I wanted his point of view. And this was easy for me, because I really wanted his point of view. I told him I would need to see him several times again and needed to talk to other Teamster officers, but that even more I needed to talk to the guys on the trucks, men in the locals, and not just heads of locals but organizers and plain truck drivers. I told him I'd go anywhere and visit any locals he wanted me to. For I wanted to understand the union (and again, I really did).

Somewhat to my surprise, he would cooperate. He said he himself tried to stay close to the union membership. "It's a pretty elaborate building here, and you get pretty prominent visitors; you're staying in good hotels—but I think you got to get back where you belong. Back where you come from." He arranged for me to talk to other Teamsters officials in the Washington headquarters and he tele-

phoned the head of a big Chicago local and told him to see me. He would telephone others.

I saw Jimmy Hoffa next in Chicago—spent a week with him at a lakefront hotel while he negotiated a new contract with Midwest truckers. From Chicago he was going to Miami for the annual meeting of the Teamsters executive board. I asked if I could go with him, and he said I could. I met him at Midway Airport at midnight. He arrived accompanied by Joey Glimco, a Chicago man whom newspapers usually identified as an associate of the highest leaders of the Chicago Syndicate. Hoffa and Glimco had been taking a steam bath; Glimco was just there to see him off. Hoffa had an airline ticket for me. I had anticipated this and bought my own. We flew to Florida together, and I spent a week with him at the Eden Roc, one of the gaudy seaside hotels on Miami Beach, and Hoffa introduced me to members of the executive board and told them to talk to me, and they did in bars and hotel rooms. They in no way resembled the caricature of lazy pot-bellied unionists; they were hardheaded, hard-driving men who knew what they wanted and how to get it.

I did other legwork on the Teamsters but I made the story that night I flew from Chicago to Miami with Jimmy Hoffa. On the plane, I sat beside him all the way. He could not escape. We talked all night. there was no telephone, no interruptions (though a stewardess recognized him, which secretly pleased him). I did not ask questions about the various cases the committee had brought against him, for I knew I would simply get the unresponsive answers the committee got. Rather, I was interested in his own life and character and his views on unionism, and by the time the long flight ended at dawn at Miami Airport, I had it. I liked him. He was first and last an underdog—born in Brazil, Indiana, son of a coal prospector who died when Jimmy was seven, taken to Detroit with his brother and two sisters by his mother "looking for some way to keep us alive," seventh-grade school dropout, street boy, grocery warehouse worker—and at the warehouse, because of bad working conditions, he organized a union, took it out on strike, won, and took it into a Teamsters local. The Depression was on. He told me, "The Depression in Detroit—it was knock down, drag out, starving people; it was murder, murder." He went to work for the union full-

time, organizing, day and night. "We'd go out, hit the docks, talk to drivers, put up picket lines, conduct strikes, hold meetings day and night, convince people to join the union." They moved in on over-the-road drivers; they followed trucks to terminals and told dock workers there not to unload hot cargoes. "In the early days every strike was a fight. We used to sleep out in cars on the picket line. Detroit was the open-shop capital of America. Every time you'd go near a place to organize it you'd get picked up and put in jail. The police beat you on the head with night clubs. It was a mess. We fought everybody on the streets, mounted police, tear gas, I got in a lot of fights, got my head broke, got banged around. My brother got shot. We had a business agent killed by a strikebreaker." Once Hoffa was arrested eighteen times in one day. His police record did not show his picket line arrests; it showed only that between 1937 and 1946 he was arrested sixteen times, not counting traffic charges. Not one of his arrests was for an offense unconnected with his union activities. He had three convictions, none serious. He became president of Local 299 in Detroit. That became and it remained his power base. From there he clawed his way upward to the Teamsters presidency, using along the way rough tactics and men who did not scruple about force.

He was a far different man from Dave Beck, his predecessor. Beck was remote, cold, lofty, a "labor statesman"; Hoffa called hundreds of truck drivers by their first names. Beck had traveled with a retinue; Hoffa traveled alone. "His great delight," Hoffa said scornfully, "was to travel to Europe and come back, make a speech about it." Beck took the Fifth before the Rackets Committee; Hoffa did not, he defied it. Hoffa had no interest in sports, had no hobbies. Ideas did not interest him. Neither did political issues that did not directly affect labor. "I got no time," He deeply distrusted politicians. He disliked lawyers and public relations men. He was difficult to work for, demanding, curt, impatient of stupid men and old fogies. He ran the union out of his hat. He made snap decisions. He was explosive and unpredictable. What little he said seemed emotion charged. He probably trusted no one. He was a "more and better" unionist—more pay and better working conditions. I asked what labor leader he admired most, and he said without hesitation, "John L. Lewis." What historical figure? "Henry Ford. Then Truman," another underdog. He did not smoke or drink. He was an oddly moralistic

man. In the lobby of the Eden Roc in Miami Beach, he and I were watching bellhops and elevator girls parade past in military style as they changed shifts, and Hoffa said, "If I had a hotel union, the first thing I'd do is stop parading people like cattle." He once walked out on a nightclub striptease act. He once forced nightclubs to stop requiring their hatcheck girls to wear uplift brassieres. Hoffa had married a girl he met on a picket line; he showed up for their first date wearing a bloody bandage on his head. By the time I was working on the story, she was forty, a shy tense disturbed woman, perhaps because of her age, perhaps because of the continuing pressures of the investigation. Hoffa treated her gently, with real affection. He was protective of her, and once when Bobby Kennedy considered Hoffa's answers on the witness stand evasive and threatened to call Hoffa's wife as a witness, Hoffa quickly said it wasn't necessary, he'd answer, and he did.

He and his wife had a modest house in Detroit. They rarely went out. Weekends they visited her sister or went to the house of one of his organizers or went to a lake where they owned a cottage. Saturday nights they watched television. Hoffa was interested in nothing but work—the union. And, in Bobby Kennedy's view, enriching himself. Kennedy, of course, suspected that Hoffa was not nearly so devoted to the welfare of the rank-and-file truck drivers as Hoffa claimed. He suspected Hoffa of making sweetheart contracts—contracts with employers, in return for kickbacks, that gave the drivers less than their due. This enraged Hoffa. Kennedy also suspected that Hoffa was anti-Negro, another lie, Hoffa said.

Although the backgrounds of Bobby Kennedy and Jimmy Hoffa could hardly have been more different, I was struck by certain similarities between them. Both were aggressive, competitive, hard driving, somewhat authoritarian, suspicious, temperate, at times congenial and at other times curt. Both were physical men who wanted to keep their bodies in shape—both did push-ups. Both spent their leisure time with their business associates; despite their wealth and power, both eschewed frivolity or indulgence and both seemed oblivious of their surroundings. Both were serious men and, in their own ways, dedicated.

The committee ended its work after three years. I drew some conclusions. It had produced a strong demand for reform labor legisla-

tion, and a bill eventually passed. The new law did little to shift the fundamental balance of power between big business and big labor, restricted picketing somewhat, probably drove a few crooks out of unions and made it harder for them to loot union treasuries (though that is still going on), and tried to improve union democracy but accomplished little. As a result of the committee's investigations, the AFL-CIO expelled the Teamsters and another union and put three more on probation. On the whole, I felt that the committee staff had performed an investigation task of greater difficulty with great skill. Bobby Kennedy and the senators conducted the hearings in a responsible way and with a high regard for accuracy. On the other hand, the committee did browbeat some Fifth Amendment witnesses mercilessly, forcing them to take the Fifth over and over again. Some lawyers felt the committee strayed far from legislative purposes. It produced damaging evidence against Hoffa and showed that his financial deals were, to say the least, odd. It never proved in the legal sense that he took a dime of union money or that he accepted an employer's payoff to sell out the workers—but it came close to proving both. The committee was unable to find the hoard of cash it believed he possessed. And it proved his affinity not only for ex-convicts but also for important Syndicate leaders. But it did not get him—he was acquitted in two criminal trials growing out of the investigation.

When I finished the story I offered to show it to both Bobby Kennedy and Jimmy Hoffa. Hoffa didn't want to see it, he didn't care what I wrote, they never do. Bobby and I spent the better part of a day going over it, not an easy negotiation—he was as tenacious with me as with the witnesses. He kept saying, "But you know he's a crook—why don't you just say so?" Fran, who was present, told him—a lawyer—"But Bobby, you know there are libel laws in this country." What bothered him most, I think, was my view that there were similarities between him and Hoffa. He never had thought of it and he simply refused to believe it.

My series was published as a paperback book by Fawcett under the execrable title *Jimmy Hoffa's Hot.* (I disliked the title so much that I never listed it along with my other books till now.) Bobby Kennedy went on to prepare for his brother Jack's run for president. Eventually Jimmy Hoffa went to a federal prison, though not on a

charge directly connected with the committee's investigation. Released, he was no longer president of the Teamsters, and after a time he disappeared, apparently kidnapped and killed.

2.

The campaign for president began that spring of 1960. Senators John F. Kennedy and Hubert H. Humphrey were contesting the primaries. I considered this unfortunate, since I liked and admired both. Stevenson had not entered. But he would not declare himself out. Kennedy had made overtures to him to take himself out (and once may have offered to name him Secretary of State if he would). I myself advised Stevenson to do so, and so did Bill Blair and Newt Minow. I told Stevenson I did not think he could be nominated, and even if he were, he might lose to Richard Nixon, who seemed certain of the Republican nomination, and losing to Nixon would break his heart. But Eleanor Roosevelt and Agnes Meyer, wife of the owner of *The Washington Post,* and various other Stevenson idolators kept urging him to keep himself available, and that was what he was doing, right into the Los Angeles convention.

Bobby Kennedy asked me to join his brother's campaign staff. He said he had not wanted to mention it until after the Hoffa story was done but now he could, would I write speeches for and advise Jack? I told him I couldn't—I was for his brother's nomination, I thought Stevenson should take himself out and thus get out of Jack's way, but I had been with Stevenson a long time and I could not support another candidate so long as Stevenson remained obdurate. Bobby understood; all the Kennedys understood loyalty. I told him I would go to work for his brother the day after the convention nominated him, which I predicted would happen. In June, I saw Bobby again, and after that did a draft of an acceptance speech for his brother and also a memorandum proposing that I do editorial advance for him as I had during Stevenson's 1956 California primary race.

3.

During those years, the 1950s, my ulcers had not responded to medication and diet, and in 1956 Dr. Robertson, thinking they might be of psychosomatic origin, had referred me to Dr. Maxwell Gitelson, a Chicago psychoanalyst, and I had entered into analysis with him

that lasted an hour a day three days a week for four years. Some people who have gone through analysis have found it the most rewarding experience of their lives. I found it painful and, as a way of getting through a midlife crisis, extremely helpful. But one's analysis is, really, of no more interest to anybody else than one's surgery.

Several years earlier, Fran's mother had come to us from Colorado. We took her to a Chicago hospital, but nothing could be done for her, so we put her in a nursing home in Highland Park, and it may have been analysis that enabled me to pick her up and carry her into the nursing home and put her in bed. She, who had not wanted Fran to marry me because I drank and had been divorced, looked up at me from her bed and said, "I wish you were my son." After three years she died. Fran was in Europe with Cindy at the time. I was home, however, and took care of things. Dan and Fred helped me, marching into the front row of the funeral home in their best suits like soldiers. Fran's brother, John, Jr., came from Colorado, and the boys and I helped him as best we could. I needed pallbearers—all her own friends were dead—and called our next-door neighbor, Jerry Goldwach, and he mustered out his company executives and they carried her casket to the grave beside her husband in an Elmhurst cemetery. It was a restricted cemetery. Jerry Goldwach and his pallbearers were Jewish. Only after the funeral did I call Fran in Paris. John, Jr., was not supposed to drink but after the funeral, taking him to the airport to go back to Colorado, I gave him a couple of whiskey miniatures, and he was grateful.

Fran and I were at an age when our friends were dying—Frederick Lewis Allen, Harold Ober, Lou Kohn, Dr. Robertson, and, a little later, my analyst Dr. Gitelson. Aside from that, however, those years, the 1950s, were among the best years of our lives. We were doing a little traveling—Cuba, Mexico, Central America, especially Nicaragua, which reminded me of the Dominican Republic; but for the most part we were living the suburban good life in our old Victorian house on Maple Avenue in Highland Park. (We had bought it in 1952, as I have said, and we live in it yet, and love it.) We saw our Highland Park friends at dinner parties and garden parties. Francis and Mary Ellen Nipp often came out for weekends. We had become

close friends of several people we had met in the Stevenson campaigns, especially Marshall and Doris Holleb of Chicago. So many people you meet in a campaign become your permanent friends. A campaign is a watershed in your life and later you tend to date everything by whether it happened before or after a certain campaign. In the summer we sat on the screened back porch I had built low to the ground overlooking the lawn sloping down to the ravine, drinking martinis and cooking steaks on a charcoal grill. If you rode the Northwestern Railroad train to Chicago on a Sunday afternoon, you would see a little plume of smoke arising from every backyard along the tracks, and I fear we were no exception to the convention. Sometimes we had a lobster race—put a big kettle of water to boil on the charcoal grill and set live lobsters on the porch floor and prodded them to scramble toward the grill, and the first to get there was privileged to be the first boiled. Dan and Fred loved it and soon were big enough to pull the wooden plugs out of the lobsters' claws. And big enough to play softball in our backyard. Fred was big enough too to argue with me—"That's not three strikes, it's only two." Fred was our risk-taker. As a little boy he got into more scary adventures than anybody. Most of them were not funny, though he thought they were. One fall day he lay down in the gutter of the street in front of our house and covered himself with leaves, and a man who drove around the corner and almost ran over him got trembling out of his car and told Fred over and over, "Don't you ever do that again." Even when he had been tiny and still in a crib, trouble: One night Fran was wakened by a peculiar grinding sound and went into his room and found that he had broken his baby bottle and was chewing the broken glass. A constant joy. But he was. So was Dan. Fred, the youngest of our three, was highly competitive, pedaling his tricycle furiously to try to keep up with Dan on a bicycle on their way to school. Dan was not competitive, was quieter, gentler. Cindy was bright but she was not doing well in Highland Park High School, a big public school, and we feared she soon would sink without a trace. And so I called on my friends in politics and publishing to write letters recommending her to private boarding schools—in those days, admission to boarding school and college was difficult, and a father would do anything short of murder to get his child in—and I took her to visit several schools in New

England. She wore a long drab coat with a fake-fur collar, and at her interviews with the school people, she somehow managed to look like a drowned mouse. And to mumble. None of the sparkling Cindy that Fran and I knew and loved came through. She was admitted nowhere. So she went back to Highland Park High, and only after many rescue operations did she graduate in 1960. And again I went with her through the whole miserable business of taking her to visit schools, and she was finally admitted to Sarah Lawrence College.

During those years, Fran and I played nickel-dime-quarter poker with the neighbors and we went to the track, to the horse races at Arlington Park. My greatest day at the races came when I, after diligent study of Moe Annenberg's *Daily Racing Form,* picked a long shot named A Dragon Killer, bet him five dollars across the board, sat down to watch, decided he was sure to win, went back and bet him again across the board and also to win, bet also two dollars our maid had given me to bet for her, then went down to the rail to watch; and as they came down the stretch A Dragon Killer was far back, but I yelled, "Wake up, A Dragon Killer," and he woke up and ran around all the other horses and won going away. I never kept accounts but I'm sure I lost far more at the races than I won. Fran did rather well, both at the track and betting through a bookie in Highwood, the next town north of Highland Park, filled with taverns and handbooks controlled by the Syndicates. Fran had a system. She bet on horses whose names she liked. She bet on Painted Porch because she had just painted our porch (as her mother had painted hers for our marriage). She bet on Yukon Jake because Yukon Jake is the hero of a takeoff on a Robert W. Service poem about the Arctic that we recite at camp in Upper Michigan. And others—all were long shots; all won. Word got out around Highwood that Mrs. Martin must have an inside pipeline to the mysterious "they" who fixed the races, and the laundryman and others respectfully solicited her picks.

Summers Fran and I often took the boys to the Lake Michigan beach a block and a half from our house, in front of the house of Lawrence and Viola Stein. This friendship went back to the time we first moved to Highland Park and I published my book on Indiana. Mrs. Stein's daughter was Ruth Nath, one of the owners of the

Chestnut Court bookshop in Highland Park. Mrs. Stein's other daughter, Louise Steele, was about our age and married to John Steele, chief of the Washington bureau of *Time,* and they became good friends. Louise visited her parents, the Steins, for part of every summer, and with her, Fran and I took our boys and her children down to the beach to cook hot dogs and drink martinis and watch the kids swim, long golden afternoons, usually ending with dinner at the Steins' house or ours. John Steele would come out from Washington and at neighborhood parties he and I would talk national politics. We sometimes stayed with the Steeles in Washington; I was staying with them when President Kennedy was assassinated. In 1956 John Steele had wanted to go to work as Adlai Stevenson's press secretary, for he was an admirer of Stevenson, and I had brought them together, and Stevenson wanted him, but *Time* would not guarantee to give him back his job after the campaign, so he had been obliged to turn it down.

Every summer we spent a month or six weeks at the camp we had bought at Three Lakes in the Upper Peninsula of Michigan. I taught the boys to fish, as I had Cindy, and took them to other lakes to sleep in a tent for a night or two. When they were small, I put them in a pack on my back and carried them up to a high rock bluff from which we could see all three of the lakes and the woods and highway spread out below. In 1956 we bought a Jeep, enabling us to go farther into the woods to remote lakes, and we took the boys on day-long Jeep rides, looking for animals and stopping alongside a logging road in the woods to cook lunch. But Three Lakes was changing. The highline came in, and while electricity made life easier, it also changed the camp's atmosphere from the kerosene lamp days. We put in gas space heaters, and that destroyed the fireplace, made it purely ornamental, not essential. We even put in a telephone. But there was worse. When we first had come here to Three Lakes, there had been few camps on our lake, you seldom saw another boat, and it was quiet. Now a nightclub opened up, traffic on the highway became terrible, a cluster of trailers sprang up behind our place, the shoreline was almost completely ringed by camps, and water-skiers despoiled the lake. Fran and I began looking for a piece of land farther out in the woods. We studied maps and the platbook, checked titles at the courthouse, and went by Jeep into the woods to

look at property. We started out looking for only a 40-acre tract on a lake. We came close to buying several. But there was something wrong with all. I knew, however, of a lake far out in the woods north of the highway, Smith Lake, extremely remote, no road to it, only a wretched logging road reaching within a mile of it, virgin land in the wilderness. I checked the title and found that there were three owners on Smith Lake, all loggers. I felt pretty sure two of them wouldn't sell—I knew them—and even if the third one would, his was a big piece of property, a quarter section—160 acres plus a narrow strip along the far shore, too much for us. It looked discouraging. But one day I took Fran to Smith Lake, parking the Jeep and walking through the woods the rough last mile to the lake by compass, took her up on a high granite bluff with a mighty hemlock grove sixty feet above the glistening water, and I told her, "Someday we're going to have a camp here." She thought I was crazy. But, as we shall see, one day we did.

Several times during those years my mother and father came to visit us up at Three Lakes, he with great enthusiasm. Anything he did, he did with great, even boisterous, enthusiasm. These last years of theirs had been good years. He had sold the old house on Brookside Avenue and built her the lannon stone house on Kessler Boulevard up on the North Side she'd always wanted. His health was good, he took her on auto trips, they traveled abroad, they visited us more often than ever before, he and I came to terms as I came to like and understand him, and he took pride in articles and books I published and in my association with Stevenson and Kennedy. My father loved to fish and had taught me to fish as a boy. He had never before fished north of Indiana, I think, until he came to us in Upper Michigan. His first fishing rule was, as we began, to put one finger to his lips, and whisper loudly, *"Shhh—don't say anything—you'll scare the fish,"* meanwhile himself stomping on the boat bottom heedless. He was essentially a live-bait fisherman but in the 1920s he had taken up casting artificial baits for bass. It was new in Indiana, it was the latest, and he, the quintessential consumer, always had to have the latest. His method of casting was to stand up in the boat— which is unsafe—to draw back his arm full-length, and then, spinning his whole body half around, to heave the bait, a wooden plug

with three wicked treble-hooks, toward shore not overhead but side-arm, which is not only inaccurate but downright dangerous to any-body else in the boat—I always had to duck. I don't think he had any idea where the bait was going. Hunting, he was not a very good shot, and fishing, he was not a very good fisherman, but he was a good sportsman if only because he loved it. By this time I had grad-uated to split bamboo casting rods but he still used his old, long, bent steel rod, tubular steel at that. The reel was tied to it with a string, the reel-seat being broken. The reel—that was his pride. I believe when he originally acquired it he was under the impression that it was a fly reel, but it was not, was only a bizarre casting reel. It was six or eight inches in diameter and its spool was less than an inch wide. On a rod, it looked as ungainly as a windmill, and it worked not nearly so smoothly. It was called a Winona reel, after Winona Lake in Indiana. In the 1920s my father used to take my mother and me up to Winona Lake for a week or two in a rented house. The Winona Lake colony was led by an evangelist, I forget whether Billy Sunday or E. Howard Cadle. My father took a con-tract to build sewers for it. But when the work was done, the De-pression came on, and the reverend evangelist's flock could not pay my father, so under Indiana law, he took instead a number of vacant lots. I believe he let them go for taxes in the Depression. About all he salvaged as a souvenir was the Winona reel. By the 1950s it had broken down time and again, but he had fixed it up with wire and an assortment of wing nuts, square nuts, bolts, and string. He was proud of it. It was special. And proud of how he'd fixed it. No one else had a reel quite like it. Indeed, I never saw another Winona. One day up in Michigan I took him fishing, as he had taken me as a boy, and we went to a lake out in the woods that was full of bass and walleye pike. I rowed him to a cove I knew was good and told him to go ahead. He stood up, rocking the boat, drew back, stretched his arm, let fly with a mightly whoosh, I ducked, and the Winona reel flew apart, it showered us with wing nuts, square nuts, bolts, wire, pieces of reel. He stood there, astounded. I could not help it: I laughed. He turned to me. He was grinning sheepishly. He said, "I'll be demmed." He never really swore unless he was angry. He couldn't believe the Winona had failed him. I asked if he wanted to go home. "No," he said, "you go ahead and fish. I'll see what I can

do," and he laid down his old rod and began poking around in the bottom of the boat looking for parts, though some of them had flown into the water. That night at camp he sat up late at the kitchen table, poking through little boxes of nuts and bolts to find something that would save the Winona, a single long white hair floating above the bald top of his head. I watched him and loved him.

That June of 1960, my father and mother and my aunt Verl visited us in Highland Park for Cindy's graduation from high school. He had not been feeling well, most unusual for him, and when he reluctantly told me his symptoms, I thought he might have a heart condition. With difficulty, I persuaded him to see Dr. Sunoll Blumenthal, who had taken over Sylvan Robertson's practice and was now my doctor, and Dr. Blumenthal told him he had had a heart episode and strongly urged him to go into the hospital for further tests and treatment. He refused. I tried to persuade him. He was adamant. I knew what was in his mind—prolonged hospitalization, perhaps even a nursing home. Can you imagine that big strong man in a nursing home? Next morning he got up early as usual, dressed, ate a big breakfast, and in that big booming voice of his called upstairs, "Anybody going to Indianapolis?" My mother and Aunt Verl came down and away they went, he no doubt driving seventy as always. They made it.

Fran and I went up to our camp at Three Lakes the Fourth of July weekend. At dawn four days later somebody knocked on our screen door, an unheard-of thing. Our best friend, Earl Numinen, was standing at the door, his face as gray as the presunrise dawn, and he said, "John, your dad died last night."

Several times in recent years I had brought my father up to Michigan in October partridge hunting, and he and Earl had become good friends. Why not—not only was Earl a construction engineer and my father a contractor but they were both great human beings. Several times my father told me, "I like that Earl Numinen." It was about as high a compliment as he ever paid anyone. We took my father hunting on the terrible logging roads, and when in the Jeep we would come to a mudhole, he could not believe we were going to try to go through it, no vehicle could, and when we had ground our way through successfully he would look back at it, still in disbelief.

He became enthusiastic about partridge hunting and discarded his old double-barreled shotgun and bought a new automatic. An automatic is really not the best gun for partridge but it was the latest so my father bought it. After he died I gave it to Earl.

That dawn I wakened the children and told them their grandfather had died—they had loved him—and I went to town with Earl and from his house called my mother, who had called Earl, and asked her what had happened. She said that in the middle of the night he had half-raised himself on the bed and had looked at her and had said, "Poor dearie." He always called her dearie. Then he had lain down dead of a heart attack. In the bed they always slept in and that I was born in. I told her we'd be down. We drove the six hundred miles that day, I mindful all the way of something my father once had said: "More demmed fools get killed goin' to funerals"—grief stricken, they become heedless. My uncle Paul, my father's brother and my favorite relative, was there. As a young man Uncle Paul had played semipro baseball and now he had retired to Arizona. He told us how one day he had gone out to watch the Chicago Cubs in spring training in Arizona and how, after watching awhile, being then past seventy, he had gotten up and strolled to home plate, picked up a bat, gestured to the pitcher to throw, and hit a home run, then strolled over to the bleachers on the other side. Everybody thought he was a big-league scout and from then on he didn't have to pay to get into spring training. That story, and others he told, were about all that made that week bearable.

After the funeral, Fran and I stayed on a bit, helping Mother with the estate, and although she wanted to move into an apartment at once, I insisted that she stay in the house on Kessler Boulevard for at least one year, and I did some figuring to show her she could afford it and told her we'd help her if she couldn't. She stayed in her house on Kessler until she died ten years later.*

The day in 1960 my father was buried, the Democratic National Convention began in Los Angeles, and three days later it nominated John F. Kennedy for president. The Kennedys sent Richard N. Goodwin, a young writer and issues man on Kennedy's staff, to

---

* Her sister, my aunt Verl, to whom I had always been close—I was her only living relative—died ten years after that, in 1980. During their last years, Fran and I had helped take care of her parents and my mother and my aunt. A melancholy task.

Highland Park to talk to me. (Goodwin had made his reputation as counsel to a congressional committee investigating TV game-show shenanigans.) We went over the issues and positions Kennedy intended to stress. Kennedy wanted to try my editorial advance system on his whistlestop trip down the Central Valley of California, coming up in ten days. I would go at once.

TEN

JFK

1.

So, though it was not clear then, a period of my life ended, the period that encompassed Chicago crime and Adlai Stevenson.

I went immediately to Philadelphia, told Ben Hibbs and Stuart Rose I was going to work for Kennedy, and went to California. I spent a week there, doing legwork and writing briefing sheets for Kennedy's whistlestop tour, and went to Detroit and did the same thing for his swing through Michigan the next week. On Labor Day, I stood in the crowd in Cadillac Square, watching Kennedy speak, as I had watched Stevenson speak, and I was struck by how much more forceful, even aggressive, Kennedy was. He seemed to assume this labor crowd was with him, and if it wasn't he would convert it, and he did, to cheers.

I went with him through the Michigan whistlestops and stayed with him aboard his plane the next two days through the Northwest then on to California and the whistlestops down the Central Valley, five-minute speeches delivered from the back platform of a train, and before each one I gave him my briefing sheet. He liked it and wanted me to continue throughout the campaign. I couldn't do the sheets all myself, so I taught a young journalist, Joseph Kraft, and another man to do them.

* * *

I had joined John F. Kennedy with some misgivings. After all, he was a totally different man from Stevenson, and I had admired Stevenson so long. Transferring political loyalty is not easy. And Stevenson had seemed a statesman. Kennedy was so young. I had never followed a leader younger than I. At the start of the campaign, Theodore Sorensen once wrote, people thought of Kennedy as wealthy, inexperienced, young, and Catholic; while his Catholicism did not bother me, the other things did. By the end of the California trip, however, I knew I had my candidate, a candidate for president I believed in.

He never wavered, never took his eye off the ball. He was out to win. And he was out to convince a complacent nation that its peace was precarious and its prosperity false. He stuffed even his whistle-stops with facts—the average wage of female laundry workers in the five biggest cities, how many more classrooms and how many more jobs the country would need in the next ten years, per capita income figures in Libya. He began such recitations by saying, "I am not satisfied when . . ." He ended each by saying, "I think we can do better." And over and over and always he declared, "It's time to get this country moving again."

Sometimes watching Kennedy speak, I felt a twinge of nostalgia for Stevenson's graceful prose, his choked uncertain utterance, his convoluted, almost tortured sentences that sought out the truth, all the qualities that endeared him to his followers. It takes nothing away from Stevenson to say that Kennedy was being far more effective in rallying the country to him. Kennedy differed from Stevenson, not only in his youth and personality, but in his approach to issues, a hard pragmatic decisive approach quite unlike Stevenson's thoughtful discursive expositions. Kennedy spent far less time preparing speeches and far more time talking to local politicians. He repeated the same speech over and over and over. He gestured forcefully, almost seemed to seize the audience physically, and threw himself wholly into every speech and upon every audience. His speeches did not soar and capture the imagination as had Stevenson's 1952 speeches, but they got his message across—that he was young, vigorous, and could get this country moving again.

In writing a Stevenson speech, as I have suggested, you put your

emphasis on good writing. For Kennedy, you put it on political effect. Nevertheless, when I first went aboard the Kennedy plane, Ted Sorensen, telling me how to write a Kennedy speech, said, "A Kennedy speech has to have class," and he was right, it did, and some of the most eloquent campaign prose in our time came from Kennedy, particularly in some of the endings that were almost parables, in what he said about his Catholicism, in the parallelisms he devised. But when he spoke on foreign affairs, he did not seem burdened or tentative, as Stevenson sometimes had; rather, he seemed to know exactly where we should go and how we could get there. Clearly he cared little whether people admired his speeches as oratory, cared a great deal about whether his speeches made people want to follow him, to vote for him. Once that fall, introducing Kennedy at a rally, Stevenson said, "Do you remember that in classical times when Cicero had finished speaking, the people said, 'How well he spoke'—but when Demosthenes had finished speaking, the people said, 'Let us march.' " It was so apt it stung.

The campaign raised no single big decisive issue. It set forth no new proposal except the Peace Corps. Kennedy's religion dominated until he squelched it at Houston. Such issues as Castro and the missile gap rose and fell. (I became involved in working on the Castro issue since I knew something about the Caribbean area, especially Cuba and the Dominican Republic.) He had almost unbelievable appeal to young people, and when he motorcaded at a college campus, they stopped his car, yelling and screaming and jumping up and down, beside themselves. But he appealed too to others less demonstrative—workingmen, suburbanites, Negroes, even farmers. People began saying, "That young fella's got something." He had a regional strategy—concentrated on the seven biggest states, especially doubtful ones, plus most of New England and the South. But he was above all, as few are, a national politician. His great causes—America's future, America's prestige, America's peril—these were national causes. He spoke thus even at the whistle-stops, a candidate for the whole nation swooping down on some little farm town for a brief bright moment.

I was the only one aboard the plane who had also been with Stevenson. The Kennedy people played with a hard ball. Ted Sorensen, sitting right outside the door to Senator Kennedy's private cabin,

was the keeper of the portals—nobody got in to see Kennedy unless Sorensen approved. Just so, Kenny O'Donnell, with his jutting Irish jaw, stood at the foot of the stairs while the plane was boarding, and nobody went aboard unless O'Donnell approved. It was a no-nonsense campaign, work to be done, no time wasted on people's feelings. Arthur Schlesinger wanted to come aboard and help, and called me, and I spoke to Ted Sorensen, but Sorensen said no— Arthur was a good writer but he was identified with the liberal ADA and why should Kennedy take on the burden of being criticized as the captive of the ADA, as Stevenson had been? It was a hardboiled political decision. Sorensen was a quiet, solid, abstemious man. He had been with Kennedy so long that they communicated almost by shorthand. When the plane came to a stop for a brief airport speech, Kennedy, on his way out to speak, would pause beside Sorensen, and Sorensen would look up at him and utter a sentence or two, suggesting a speech theme, and Kennedy would think, nod, remember, and go out and deliver it. Dick Goodwin was brilliant and he became my friend but at that time he was terribly young, only twenty-eight, and he was somewhat abrasive and heedless of others; once sitting beside me in the window seat, he sprang up to go talk to Kennedy and in his haste actually stepped on my stomach. Ted Sorensen wrote, rewrote, or reviewed every speech. In delivering a speech, Kennedy almost never followed the prepared text. Stevenson's texts always had read better than they sounded. Kennedy's always sounded better than they read—reading some of them later, I wondered why the applause. It was, of course, Kennedy's own personality, his conviction, his purposefulness, his mastery, the confidence and enthusiasm he inspired, inspired as few candidates if any since Roosevelt have. When the campaign began, Kennedy was an underdog. His opponent, Nixon, was better known, was considered more experienced in government, was certainly more experienced in national campaigns and national television, while the Democrats were divided, Kennedy's nomination had soured the South, his choice of Lyndon Johnson for vice-president had soured the North, Stevenson diehards were unreconciled, and the nation's newspaper editors and publishers were against Kennedy (but the reporters covering the campaign were for him). And this underdog, by the sheer force of his campaigning, did turn it around.

* * *

It would be tedious to relate my travels across the country during that 1960 fall campaign. About half the time I was out ahead of Kennedy doing editorial advance, about half with him aboard his plane. He was far easier to work with than Stevenson—he never complained, never lost patience, never became short-tempered, was far more accessible. He took advice more readily, made decisions faster. He wasted no time. He used his staff well. He did not hold large staff meetings, believing that nothing ever gets decided by a committee, only by two men talking to each other—or by one man alone.

As time passes, all campaigns tend to blur into one another, but I retain a few scattered impressions of the 1960 campaign. Early one morning in Kennedy's hotel suite in St. Louis, while his aide Dave Powers was rousing him as usual by asking him, "What do you suppose Nixon's doing while you're lying there in bed?" I waited in the living room with Jacqueline Kennedy. When Kennedy came out, he greeted us briefly, and she started to say something, but he went into another room, where a delegation of men—I have the impression they were from India—was waiting, and the door closed behind him. She stood staring at it. She looked absolutely alone and lost. I never felt sorrier for anyone. She was terrified by campaigning, helpless in its inexorable pull. Several years later, at Bobby's house in McLean, after both he and her husband had been assassinated, I saw her again like that, that same vulnerable look on her face. To millions of Americans, she was in those years a great lady, a glamorous creature; to me she was a frightened child.

Once in Kennedy's hotel in Baltimore I needed to see him about a coming speech, and Kenny O'Donnell told me to go ahead, but when I went into his bedroom I found him stretched out flat on his bed, his face grimacing in pain from his back, his eyes glazed, even a Kennedy utterly exhausted by the cruelties of campaigning, and I left him alone.

One day near the end of the campaign, on the plane as we were approaching Chicago, Kennedy called me into his cabin. He showed me a copy of the current *Saturday Evening Post* and it contained my piece "To Chicago with Love," and he said, "What are you trying to do—lose Illinois?" He was kidding—he had read the story and en-

joyed it. But of course it did contain material on Chicago's corrupt crime-politics alliance, and the Chicago newspapers were making a brief uproar over it, and Mayor Daley had told a press conference, "I think John must have come through Chicago with blinders on." He knew I was with Kennedy. I sent Mayor Daley a letter saying, as I recall it, that I was sorry if the piece had discomfited him, I had written it in fun out of my great affection for his great city of Chicago, and, furthermore, in this campaign we had the candidates and the issues and we were going to win. The mayor had his floor leader in the City Council read the letter into the record. On that trip Otto Kerner, running for governor, came aboard and wanted to advise Kennedy on his Illinois speeches, and Kennedy told him to talk to me. When he had finished, I went into Kennedy's cabin, told him what Kerner had advised, and told him I thought it all wrong. He said, "OK, then forget it." On that trip we made a swing across the far southern counties of Illinois, and at the first main stop, Southern Illinois University, Kenndy was introduced by state representative Paul Powell, an old boodler whom I had known in the legislature, and Powell outdid himself. He told at great length the famous story of Kennedy's heroism when, in the Pacific during World War II, the torpedo boat he commanded, PT-109, had been cut in half by a Japanese destroyer, and Kennedy had heroically rescued his men. Powell, embellishing the tale, described how Kennedy the young hero had tied a rope not around only one of his injured seamen and towed him to safety, as the story usually related, but had tied the rope to half of the shattered hulk of the torpedo boat itself, containing his entire crew, and, putting the other end of the rope in his teeth, had dragged all hands to safety on an island through mile after mile of mountainous seas—"and he swum and he swum and he swum," Powell cried hoarsely, chopping the air with his arms in swimming motions. His introduction was far longer than Kennedy's speech. And to a college audience. After the speech, as we got back in the motorcade, Kennedy called me over and told me to persuade Powell to soft-pedal it the rest of the day. A delicate mission—Paul Powell was a formidable figure; but I managed, and we survived the day.

On election night, Fran and I were in Hyannis Port, up all night—it was one of the closest elections in history. Kennedy won by less than 120,000 out of nearly 69 million votes cast. He carried

Illinois by only 8,858. He lost California, lost Indiana, Wisconsin, and Ohio; he barely won Michigan. He was a minority president—had got less than half the total votes cast.

In a sense, I grew up politically in Kennedy's 1960 campaign. Stevenson in 1952, as he had while governor, had maintained a certain amateur attitude toward politics. Kennedy never had it at all. From him and his staff and his campaign strategy, I learned hard politics. And this was backed up by what I had learned writing about politics. For almost the first time I began thinking of myself as, if not a professional politician, at least no longer an amateur.

2.

That winter, while I was going back to write for the *Post*, the Kennedy administration was being formed. Arthur Schlesinger went on the White House Staff as a sort of cultural attaché, with the title special assistant to the president. Other friends of mine were going on the president's staff, Ted Sorenson to head it and Kenny O'Donnell, Pierre Salinger, Fred Dutton, Dick Goodwin. Bobby Kennedy was attorney general. Stevenson's entire law firm joined the new administration, Stevenson as ambassador to the UN, Bill Wirtz as undersecretary of labor (later secretary), Bill Blair as ambassador to Denmark, Newt Minow as chairman of the Federal Communications Commission. And so many more people I knew were ambassadors, aides to Bobby at Justice, officials at State and other places (Dave Bell was budget director, Ken Galbraith ambassador to India). Never before had I known so many important people in an administration. It was an aspect of political campaigning to which I had given no thought.

Fran and I were invited to the Kennedy inauguration. Numerous parties preceded it; we watched amused as others played the game of the "A Party" and "B Party"—a man will sacrifice his closest friend in order to himself get to the "A Party," the one behind guarded doors, where will be found all the political figures that count. We were staying with John and Louise Steele. They and we had been invited to the party at the house of Kay Graham, daughter of Agnes Meyer and now the wife of *The Washington Post*'s publisher, the most prestigious party of all, held the night before the inaugural.

That night a blizzard paralyzed Washington and, since John had to meet his boss, Henry Luce, at the airport, Louise essayed to drive Fran and me to the Kay Graham party. For what seemed hours we struggled through blinding driving snow and mounting drifts, traffic askew all over the streets, cars abandoned; and at last we drew up in front of what looked like an abandoned library. Not a track crossed the snow. The house was dark. "My God," Louise gasped, "I've brought you to her mother's house. Agnes Meyer's." We spent the rest of the evening in our finery getting back to Louise's house, where we had several drinks.

Inauguration day was clear but bitter cold, with an icy wind, and rather than sit out in the open at the Capitol to witness the swearing-in and hear the president's speech, Fran and I went to the chambers of Judge Bazelon* in the Federal Courthouse not far from the Capitol and, with a party of his friends, watched President Kennedy's inaugural speech on television: "Let every nation know, whether it wishes us well or ill, that we shall pay any price, bear any burden, meet any hardship, support any friend, oppose any foe to assure the survival and the success of liberty," and, after setting forth in soaring prose the tasks ahead, "All this will not be finished in the first one hundred days. Nor will it be finished in the first one thousand days, nor in the life of this administration, nor even perhaps in our lifetime on this planet. But let us begin."

That night we went to the Inaugural Ball at the Washington Armory and next day to a brunch at the home of Phil Stern, a Democratic publicist whom we had known in the two Stevenson campaigns. All the old Stevenson people who were going into the Kennedy administration were there, a gala time. George Ball shocked me a little by saying, "Well, I always thought if Stevenson won, I'd be undersecretary of state for economic affairs, and now I am anyway." He and Stevenson and others left to go to the White House to be sworn in. In a day or two Fran and I went home. How I wished my father, a lifelong Democrat, could have lived a few months longer to see John F. Kennedy elected president.

---

* David Bazelon, originally from Chicago, a judge on the U.S. court of appeals for the District of Columbia, was one of America's most distinguished jurists, a champion of the rights of the accused, often mentioned for appointment to the Supreme Court. We had become friends while I was writing my series on criminal justice.

3.

The firm that handled public relations for Puerto Rico invited Fran and me to visit Puerto Rico for a week or ten days, expenses paid, in the hope that I would find something to write about but placing me under no obligation to do so. I checked with the *Post* then went. I found no story for the *Post* but this did not seem to bother our hosts—they were playing for the long haul, and indeed in years to come I did do some writing about Puerto Rico.

We were about to leave when I suggested to Fran that on our way home we visit the Dominican Republic. I had never been back since Barbara and I had been there the winter of 1937–1938 (twenty-three years ago—was it possible?). I had always wanted to go, for I had liked the Dominican Republic and its people better than any other in the Caribbean, but, since I had published my anti-Trujillo piece, I had not thought it entirely safe. Trujillo had had the author of an anti-Trujillo book kidnapped in New York and murdered in the Dominican Republic. Now, however, I thought it might be safe because of my connections with the Kennedy administration.

Knowing that, since I entered the republic as a journalist, our hotel room would probably be searched, I wrote letters to Ted Sorensen and Arthur Schlesinger in the White House, giving them our detailed itinerary and telling them when to expect us back, and I left carbons in my briefcase in the hotel room. Trujillo's secret police and their informers were everywhere. And now that events seemed to be closing in on him, his iron rule tightened. Last August the United States had joined the other members of the Organization of American States in imposing economic and diplomatic sanctions on Trujillo; we had no ambassador there now, and our economic sanctions were hurting Trujillo.

Fran and I spent a week there, ostentatiously visiting tourist sites and, more quietly, talking to a wide scattering of Dominicans about the dictatorship. The country, especially the capital, seemed unnaturally tense. When we got home, I wrote a memo on Trujillo, the republic, the effects of the sanctions, and the likelihood of subversion directed, organized, or inspired by Castro, and I sent it to Arthur Schlesinger in the White House.

* * *

Several times that spring while in Washington doing legwork for the *Post,* I saw friends in the administration, and one evening Arthur Schlesinger startled me by asking, "How'd you like to be ambassador to Switzerland?"

I told him I didn't know anything about being an ambassador nor did I know anything about Switzerland, though I had the impression it was a rather dull place. He asked, "How about Morocco?" but it turned out that the king of Morocco still cut off the hands of thieves, not a pleasant prospect. Arthur said, however, that it was not easy to find capable people to staff the new administration and that I ought to think about it.

It was, as I have said, something I never had thought of during the three presidential campaigns I had worked in. But Washington was always a lovely city, never lovelier than that first spring of the Kennedy administration, for it was suffused with an atmosphere of youth, of vigor, of hope. The man who made it so was the new young president. And my friends were now at his side, dealing every day with high policy, at the very center of power in the most powerful nation on earth. But here was I, applying to television executives for information about their grubby businesses and peddling it to the *Post.* But there was more than that wrong. Recently I had done a four-part *Post* series on changes wrought in the Midwest since World War II. It was a good enough story. But it troubled me. I was repeating myself. Was doing all over again what I had done so long ago in Muncie for *Harper's.* It was getting too easy, too expectable. I have always worked best when I worked against a resistance, writing something new, something hard. And recently too I had written a piece for *Look* about a young man in New Jersey who had given ample warning that there was something wrong with him but had got no help from his schools and a state hospital and had killed. It was a good story, and *Look* loved it. But I knew I was repeating myself. I was restless, wondering if I ought not to change course, try something new, take a risk.

Three New Frontiersmen asked me to write a speech that spring—Bobby Kennedy, Newt Minow, and Bill Blair, the last off to Denmark as ambassador. I did. Of the three speeches, Newt Minow's had the most impact. It was his first speech as chairman of the FCC to the National Association of Broadcasters, the powerful organization of broadcasters. It was for Newt an important speech,

perhaps the most important he would ever make, for he intended to try to reform television and the FCC alone had the power to do it. At that same time, I was starting to write my series on TV for the *Post,* and I began that series by describing the day I had put in watching Channel 5 for twenty hours straight, concluding that it had presented "a vast wasteland of junk." Now in writing Minow's speech I suggested he say to the broadcasters, "I invite you to sit down in front of your television set when your station goes on the air and stay there ... and keep your eyes glued to that set until the station goes off. I can assure you that you will observe a vast wasteland of junk." In editing the speech himself, Newt had the wit to cut "of junk." He delivered the speech in May 1961, in the old Wardman Park Hotel. Riding there with President Kennedy, he told the president that what he intended to say was pretty tough on the broadcasters, and the president told him to go ahead. He stunned the broadcasters. More, he became something of a symbol of the newness and boldness of the Kennedy administration. And the phrase "vast wasteland" made his reputation and clings to him yet. As for me, in writing my *Post* series, I stuck to my lead on my twenty-hour day but I was obliged to change the ending of the passage, offering "vast wasteland" not as my own summary of what I had seen but, instead, writing, "This is what Newton N. Minow, the beleaguered new chairman of the Federal Communications Commission, has called a "vast wasteland." I had approached in my work a conflict of interest. It didn't bother me.*

The newspaper headline on May 31 that year, 1961, said that Generalissimo Trujillo, dictator of the Dominican Republic, had been assassinated, and all of a sudden, having a drink with Fran on the back porch, I asked, "How would you like to be the wife of the ambassador to the Dominican Republic?" I had not previously thought much about what Arthur had said about my becoming an ambassador. But the Dominican Republic and its people—if, after

---

* To say that I originated the "vast wasteland" phrase takes nothing away from Newt Minow. This sort of thing happens all the time. Louis McHenry Howe put "... the only thing we have to fear is fear itself" into Franklin D. Roosevelt's first inaugural; Dick Goodwin named President Johnson's "Great Society"; Ernesto Betancourt coined President Kennedy's "Alliance for Progress" and passed it on to Goodwin via Karl Meyer. It is the business of holders of high public office to broker ideas to the public; Newt Minow had the wit to recognize a good phrase and the courage to throw it in the teeth of the broadcasters and thus show the public the need for reform.

Trujillo's thirty-one years of bloody tyranny, now under President Kennedy's Alliance for Progress I could help establish freedom and democracy there: That was worth trying.

I called Arthur. He was enthusiastic and said he would see what he could do. Almost immediately it became clear that nothing would happen soon. The first question to be decided by the administration was whether to send any U.S. ambassador at all—the Organization of American States economic and diplomatic sanctions against the Republic were still in force. The OAS was preparing to send a delegation there to investigate conditions and determine whether to lift the sanctions. Reports were coming out of the Republic that Trujillo's secret police and his heirs were making a bloodbath to avenge his assassination. Arthur thought I might go down with the OAS commission, but Bobby Kennedy thought I should stay clear of it. Arthur persevered, however—at lunch with President Kennedy and Ambassador Stevenson at the UN, he asked Stevenson if he didn't think I'd be a good choice for ambassador to the Dominican Republic. To Arthur's surprise, Stevenson raised his eyebrows and said something like "John? I don't know. I'd have to think about it." I hasten to add, however, that subsequently Stevenson did write a letter to Secretary of State Dean Rusk, recommending me for the job.

But now things dragged, and early in August Fran and the boys and I went up to our Michigan place at Three Lakes. Toward the end of the day on September 1, a Friday, when we came out of the woods in the Jeep, Earl Numinen and Maurice Ball at Michigamme told me President Kennedy had been trying to call me all over town and wanted me to call back. By the time I got my call through, President Kennedy had left Washington for the long Labor Day weekend, and I talked instead to his brother-in-law, Stephen Smith. He said the president wanted me to come to Washington at once about the Dominican Republic.

There, I saw Bobby Kennedy, increasingly involved in foreign affairs since the Bay of Pigs, and Steve Smith, running a "crisis center" in the State Department because President Kennedy was impatient with the Department. They told me that at a meeting on August 28 the State Department had asked President Kennedy for some policy decisions on the Dominican Republic. The central question was: Should we urge the OAS to lift its sanctions against

the Republic? This, in effect, would mean that, with Trujillo himself gone, we accepted his heirs as rulers of the Republic. President Kennedy felt he lacked sufficient facts to base policy on. He wanted me to go to the Republic, investigate, and report to him. I asked when he wanted me to go. Steve Smith said, "Yesterday." He gave me a huge file of cables to study. The cables were classified, and of course I had no security clearance and no time to get one, but Steve told me, "You've got a Smith clearance—take them."

I was in the Dominican Republic three weeks. I did my work in the capital and in the second city, Santiago, and I did what I had always done in magazine legwork—talked to people of all sorts: businessmen, workingmen, doctors and lawyers, widows whose husbands had been murdered by the secret police only days ago, militant university students, a frightened Negro dock worker who wanted to organize a labor union, Trujillo's puppet president, cabinet officers, the boss of Trujillo's old political party—the only party he allowed—and leaders of the powerful but enlightened oligarchy in Santiago. I talked to leaders of the government, to Army officers cradling submachine guns in their arms, to leaders of the underground opposition parties.

José G. Fandino, a chubby young State Department career officer, bilingual, born and educated in the United States but of Cuban and Puerto Rican inheritance, went with me everywhere to interpret. Shapshots of that mission remain in my mind—

—inching forward in a car on a narrow downtown street with our political officer and a CIA man through a mob of thousands of demonstrators, the mob pressing against our car so that it could not move, banging on it, screaming, their faces contorted with rage, till the tanks came;

—from a balcony overlooking a plaza by the sea, watching delegations of the opposition bold enough to come to hear a civic leader speak, demanding that the OAS keep the sanctions on till the last Trujillos left;

—trying to talk to a young Marxist, evasive, smiling, rigid, clearly under Communist party discipline, impossible to communicate with;

—talking to a young lawyer who wanted to form a political party; neither Trujillista nor Marxist but ignorant of politics, he asked me for copies of the U.S. constitution and political party platforms, and

when I suggested he get them at the library, he looked at me as though I'd lost my mind—didn't I know Trujillo hadn't allowed such subversive literature into the Republic?

—dinner on the terrace at his villa by the sea with the handsome young dandy Ramfis Trujillo, son of the murdered dictator and his heir apparent, listening to him talk about the future of this shattered republic, the difficulty the OAS sanctions caused the national economy (which to a considerable extent meant his private economy), the danger of communism, the restlessness of his own military, his contempt for the opposition, the difficulty of his own position and his desire to "retire" after he had ensured "stability," the magic phrase. (I began to think we might be able to negotiate him out of power);

—and being driven by men of the underground by a circuitous route to a little house where I met the wife of a young oligarch, Yale educated, in whose tile factory two of Trujillo's assassins had hidden; he was still in prison, his wife unable to see him. She told me Ramfis Trujillo was making a great show of "democratizing the country," but "nothing is changed. There's been thirty-one years of murder. People now don't want any more Trujillo. There's a feeling that if you don't help us, we'll let anyone else do it. But we don't want to. We go to vacations in the United States, we send our children there to school, not to Czechoslovakia. Those sanctions— please don't lift them."

Everybody said the same thing, even businessmen whose businesses were badly hurt by the sanctions, everybody that is except Ramfis Trujillo.

During these three weeks I seemed extraordinarily sensitive to the sights, the sounds, the mood of this island, sensitive as I had been in the early years of my magazine work—sensitive to the clank of the tank treads on the capital streets, to the sinister whine of the Volkswagens used by the secret police, to the awful stillness of the city by night, its deserted streets and shuttered restaurants, all waiting for God knew what. These, and the bewilderment on the faces of everybody, a disoriented people, made impressions still fresh twenty-five years later. One evening I sat on the little balcony outside my hotel room, gazing out at the sudden black tropical night where lay the sea, and I asked Joe Fandino what life was like for an

ambassador in a small country, and he said, "Why, an ambassador is just like a king." King in a doomed country.

Back in Washington, I wrote a hundred-page report to President Kennedy. I thought the Republic was a sick, destroyed nation, to be viewed as one ravaged by a thirty-year war. I thought Ramfis was beginning to like the feeling of power; his puppet president Balaguer's "democratization" was window dressing. The military and Trujillo right, not the Communist left, was the danger to Dominican democracy. The democratic center, the opposition, was divided, its young leaders patriotic but childlike and of doubtful ability to govern, and I saw none we could wholeheartedly support. There was, really, no political structure; Trujillo had permitted none and bequeathed none. Now we faced the critical question of the OAS sanctions. We must adopt a policy.

Three choices were open, all bad.

First, we could do nothing. Dominicans kept saying, "If you don't help us, we'll kill each other," and one might be tempted to reply, "Go ahead," but we could not. Doing nothing was, really, a policy, for it would create a vacuum, and what filled the vacuum might or might not be in our own interests.

Second, support the Ramfis Trujillo regime—work with it, vote to lift the sanctions, and send an ambassador. That would, in my view, be wrong; we would be turning our backs on the people.

Third, try to help establish a broad-based provisional government until free elections could be held with OAS help; negotiate Ramfis out of his economic power at once by buying him out and later negotiate him out of the country; force Trujillo's brothers to leave the Republic immediately; disband the secret police, end the terror; establish political freedom, break the power of Trujillo's own party; help the Republic borrow money to get the economy moving; and lift sanctions gradually. It amounted to negotiating the Trujillos out if possible or, if that was not possible, throwing them out. I recommended sending a high-level negotiator immediately and sending the fleet to the horizon to back him up.

I gave the report to the Department but I also sent a copy direct to President Kennedy. Upon learning this, George Ball's assistant was highly indignant—I should have gone through channels; what did I

mean, going around Undersecretary Ball; he should have approved the report before it went to the president. George himself did not appear bothered when I saw him.

We were to see President Kennedy on Thursday, October 5, almost exactly five weeks after he had telephoned me in Michigamme. The political risks facing President Kennedy were grave. If he supported a Trujillo restoration, he would make mockery of all the brave words about democracy in the Alliance for Progress. But if he tried to help establish a democracy, and if it failed, that might result in "another Castro in the Caribbean." And so might doing nothing. Thinking of domestic politics, the worst thing that could happen to him would be a Communist takeover, the next worst a Trujillo restoration. The best was a successful democracy—but that last was by far the hardest. It was, however, the policy I advocated.

In the morning several high Department officials and I met in George Ball's office, a big suite on the seventh floor of the State Department, the power center of American foreign policy. Some of the others thought my recommendations too risky, I argued for them, and, in the car going to the White House, George said to me, "Look, John, we don't want to get in a row in front of the president," and I said I didn't want to get into a row but he and the president knew what I favored and I would argue for it if necessary.

At the White House, we were joined by others, including, as I recall it, Secretary Rusk; Undersecretary Ball; Undersecretary George McGhee; then Assistant Secretary for Latin America Robert Woodward; Wymberley Coerr of State; the director or a deputy director of the CIA; Teodoro Moscoso and Arturo Morales-Carrión of the Alliance for Progress; McGeorge Bundy, the president's national security adviser; and Arthur Schlesinger and Dick Goodwin of his staff. In the West Wing we waited in the Fish Room, where in FDR's time, Arthur had told me, Harry Hopkins, Ben Cohen, Robert Sherwood, and Adolf Berle had worked on the Four Freedoms speech. Soon, bidden, we went across the corridor into the Cabinet Room, large and white and quiet, with sunlight streaming in through high windows overlooking the Rose Garden, and we ranged ourselves around the long gleaming six-sided cabinet table. Presently Dave Powers, President Kennedy's personal aide, a constant companion and confidant, came in from the Oval Office and said, "Gentlemen, the president," and we all rose and President

Kennedy came in, not striding but moving as if he knew where he was going, to the center of the table; and as he sat, gesturing to us to be seated, he said to me across the table, "I've been reading your novel, John." He had it with him, my long memo; a speed reader, he had read it at lunch. He began by saying the alternatives didn't look attractive, and one by one the others joined in, and often he interjected questions; he was clearly in command of the subject. He asked how we could negotiate the Trujillos out. George Ball and George McGhee had worked out a plan for the Trujillos to deed their vast holdings to the Republic in return for money we would help the Republic raise. I thought it was going my way. It was—in the end the president adopted approximately the recommendations I had made and told George McGhee to go to the Republic the same day. As I was leaving, he said, "Thanks, John." I went home to Highland Park that afternoon. Seeing President Kennedy made you feel good all the rest of the day and for several days thereafter. There *was* hope. If ever a man was a leader, John F. Kennedy was. President Roosevelt must have been like that. They say that every man in his whole life has his president, and only one. Mine was President Kennedy (as Roosevelt had been my father's).

I told Fran about my trip and told her I had decided I wanted that embassy. She said, "I've never been married to a king before." I explained that my recommendations meant we wouldn't send any ambassador to the Republic soon.

That fall and early winter I talked to my friends in the Department and the White House. McGhee and Ramfis Trujillo reached agreement in principle at their first meeting, and Trujillo's brothers left the country. But the political parties could not get together, sporadic rioting began, a general began to emerge as a strongman, and the Trujillo brothers returned. We made it clear we would not recognize the regime or lift sanctions, they defied, us, and we sent the fleet to the horizon; and the brothers left again and this time Ramfis left too, taking his father's body with him. The day we sent the fleet is the only time in our recent history, so far as I can recall, when we threw our weight, including the threat of force, solidly against a rightist dictatorship.

But events stalled. I waited at home, pacing the floor. A presidential appointment—most of us read in the paper that the president

has appointed So-and-so to Such-and-such, and we nod and think, "Of course—the president needed a man for that job and he looked around and found the best one for it." Reality is otherwise. In appointive politics, as in elective politics, nearly always the man seeks the job, not the other way around. A man who wants an appointment campaigns for it, but quietly, inside the administration. And in many ways appointive politics is more difficult, more mysterious, and more cruel than elective politics. Few people in government, sometimes not even the president, know all about how decisions finally get made. In a sense, government is the perfect reflection of life itself, vast, fumbling, capricious, sometimes benign, more often malevolent, always inscrutable. Finally George Ball told me the Department had a candidate of its own for ambassador, a career officer, but George had an interesting ambassadorship to offer me instead, Tanganyika, newly independent (and now called Tanzania). I said I wanted the Dominican embassy and I would come to Washington.

There, he was quite discouraging. At breakfast next day, I talked to Newt Minow. He said I should go see Bobby Kennedy—earlier Newt had told Bobby I wanted the embassy badly, and Bobby, looking surprised, had said, "But John knows he can have any job in this administration he wants." I went to Bobby's office. I told his secretary, Angie Novello, whom I knew well from the Rackets Committee days, that I had to see him right now, on a personal matter. She said he was booked solidly but she'd squeeze me in somehow. She did, and I told him, "I've never asked you for anything in my life, Bobby, but I want the ambassadorship to the Dominican Republic and they're about to give it to the Department's candidate." He looked at me a long time. Then he said, "I'll speak to my brother." I left.

And waited again, this time in Washington in the apartment of a friend, Congressman Sidney Yates of Chicago. After six days, the crusty old deputy undersecretary of state for administration called: I was being appointed and should report to his office to start the paperwork.

This, and official briefings, took forever. I paid courtesy calls on my two Illinois senators: Paul Douglas, my old Democratic friend, who of course was delighted, and Everett Dirksen, a Republican leader of the Old Guard, anathema to liberal Democrats, who could

not have treated me more courteously. Fran and Dan and Fred came to Washington. She went to several briefings for ambassadors' wives but the most useful advice was given to her by Senator Douglas: "Foreign Service wives are terrible. Be on guard against them. Never meet them on their own ground—government, appointments, promotions, that sort of thing. Always keep them off balance—talk to them about books, art, things they don't know anything about."

After the Senate confirmed me, George McGhee swore me in, and I paid my courtesy call on President Kennedy. He had said publicly, "The Dominican people and their leaders confront a great and seldom given opportunity: the construction of a democratic society on the ruins of tyranny. It is a noble task, but it is not an easy one. We wish them well, and we assure them of our desire to assist them in their efforts." Now alone with me he said, "This one isn't going to be easy," and we talked a little about the Republic's problems. He said he intended to send Vice-President Johnson down about mid-April and "we don't want any riots." He asked if I'd seen Jacqueline's tour of the White House on television the other night; I hadn't, and he described it: "She was terrific." He talked a little about rumors around Washington that he himself was a skirt chaser—"You've heard them; they always do that." Twice he said, "Let me know direct if there's anything you want," and, seeing me to the door when I left, "If you blow this, you'd better not come home."

Fran and the boys and I took a plane to New York, spent the evening with Adlai Stevenson in his embassy residence, and next morning, March 4, 1962, took a plane from New York to the capital of the Dominican Republic, its rightful name now restored, Santo Domingo. As we flew high over the sandy islets and reefs of the Bahamas, I was thinking of the strange chain of circumstances that had led me here. Entirely by chance, many years ago in 1937 with Barbara, I had come to the Dominican Republic and en route home I had met a detective story writer, and that had led me to Chicago. Then the chain of chance led through John Voelker, the Upper Michigan writer, to his friend in a big Chicago law firm, and thence to Lou Kohn, who had introduced me to Adlai Stevenson. Because of the Stevenson campaigns and because of my writing about Hoffa, I had met the Kennedys. Because of that, I had joined the Kennedy presidential campaign. And by chance, not long after President

Kennedy had been inaugurated and I had begun thinking about joining his administration, Trujillo had been assassinated. And so now to the embassy. It was all chance, blind chance.

I thought of other trips I had made, traveling the United States and writing about it, finding much that was wrong and trying to make it better and never doubting it could be made better, and so into politics with zest and hope and dreams, traveling the nation with Adlai Stevenson and John F. Kennedy. In a sense, I was going to the Dominican Republic to test the dream, going with the same zest and zeal and hope. President Kennedy, I thought, must dream and hope for the world what I dreamed for the Republic. I remembered President Kennedy's speech to the Latin American ambassadors setting forth his Alliance for Progress, and his inaugural address presaging it: "To those peoples in the huts and villages of half the globe struggling to break the bonds of mass misery, we pledge our best efforts to help them help themselves, for whatever period is required, not because the Communists may be doing it, not because we seek their votes, but because it is right. If a free society cannot help the many who are poor, it cannot save the few who are rich."

Well, now I would try it. Now I really was on the other side—was no longer a journalist, was in government; was not on the outside looking in, was on the inside looking out; was not writing about policy but making it. This was, I thought, the end of a part of my life. And the beginning of a new part. I told myself that if it didn't work out, I could always go back to writing heavy fact for magazines, anyway I would after this was over (or would I?). The plane crossed the northern coast of the Republic and began letting down but not too steeply—we had yet to cross over the central mountain range, dun brown below, a narrow trail winding back from the coast into the mountains; then in a few minutes we swept in low over the Caribbean, turned, and landed at Aeropuerto Punto Caucedo, the Santo Domingo airport, concrete blazing blinding white in the sun. Fred, nine and round-faced and solemn in his best blue suit, led us off the plane and down the stairs, then Dan grinning and not quite eleven, then Fran smiling and pretty in a flowered dress, then I, carrying incongruously a heavy overcoat in the hot tropical sun.

PART FOUR

WATERSHED

ELEVEN

AMBASSADOR TO THE DOMINICAN REPUBLIC

1.

Four days after I arrived in Santo Domingo, anti-American mobs took to the streets. They burned my car, they stoned our consulate, and they invaded the Dominican-American school and were finally driven away by soldiers with submachine guns, while Dan and Fred watched from an upstairs classroom window. In the midst of this, I ceremoniously presented my credentials as ambassador to the Council of State at the National Palace.

After President Kennedy sent the fleet, we had helped patch together a provisional Council of State to govern for a year and hold free elections. The seven members of the council were a lawyer, two heart specialists, a businessman, a priest, and two assassins, the only two survivors of the twenty-odd men who had assassinated Trujillo.* Only one or two of the seven councillors had had any experience in politics and government.

---

* During the 1970s, in the United States, some U.S. government officials and the press indicated that we, the United States, had assassinated or assisted or procured the assassination of Trujillo, and an author who interviewed President Lyndon Johnson quoted him as saying, "We killed Trujillo." President Johnson probably believed it. I don't. As ambassador I read many classified documents written by Americans and Dominicans who had investigated the assassination; Antonio Imbert Barreras, one of the two surviving assassins, told me its story in great detail; I talked about it with many other Dominicans and later I studied the transcript of testimony before the Church Com-

The president of the council and of the Republic was Rafael F. Bonnelly, a lawyer, fifty-eight years old, light-brown-skinned, with graying hair, soft brown liquid eyes, a kind smile, and a fast skillful lawyer's mind. He was a sentimental man, and often when Dan and Fred walked past his house on their way to school he stopped them to talk and to give them Indian arrowheads. In a normal situation, an ambassador requests an appointment with a chief of state formally, through the Foreign Office. But this was not a normal situation, and if I wanted to see President Bonnelly, I did not call on him at the palace, I simply walked down the street to his house. Thus we avoided the public impression that the United States was exerting undue influence on the Dominican government. Bonnelly was no revolutionary—he was tied by birth and marriage to the landed oligarchy. Nor was he a demagogue or a charismatic popular leader. Early on when I saw him privately, I told him, "I've never been an ambassador before." He said, "That's all right, I've never been a president before." He was an effective one.

2.

We, the United States, had three major policy objectives: to help keep the shaky council in power for its year, to help it hold free elections, and to persuade the losers to accept the winner's victory.

To promote that policy, my jobs were two—to work with the Council of State and to work with the twenty-six political parties that had sprung up since Trujillo.*

As to the council, I had to adjust U.S. policy to help it (e.g., per-

---

mittee of the U.S. Senate. I lived with this for several years. In all that mass of evidence there is none that the U.S. government or any of its agents perpetrated, assisted, or procured the assassination of Trujillo. During the spring when he was killed, many plots were afoot in the Dominican Republic to kill him, and evidence indicates that the special group that passed on CIA covert actions did authorize the CIA to smuggle several guns into the Republic, but these guns were never passed on to any of the numerous dissident groups. Moreover, the men who actually killed Trujillo had no need of U.S. guns—they had access to the guns of the Dominican Army, for one of the plotters was head of the armed forces, drawn into the plot by Luís Amiama Tío, the other surviving assassin. But to my mind the best evidence that we did not kill Trujillo is that President Kennedy never told me we did. He sent me to the Republic on a fact-finding mission shortly after Trujillo's death, he sent me as his ambassador, he knew me well, he confided many things in me, and never, either in our meetings with other U.S. government officials or in our private meetings alone, did he so much as indicate that we were involved in Trujillo's assassination.

* As ambassador, I spent nearly all my time working on Dominican politics. A full account of that appears in my book *Overtaken by Events.*

suade the Kennedy administration to amend its worldwide sugar quota bill); to suggest programs to the council, such as public works programs to soak up unemployment, financed by loans from us; to suggest when to placate the military by cracking down on the extremist left. I worked on our Agency for International Development program with the council and our AID officers, devising AID programs to provide schoolbooks, school uniforms, and housing for the poor as well as money for big AID projects; and I lobbied with Washington ceaselessly for money for the council—in its one year, I believe, we gave or loaned the Republic more money than we had sent Trujillo in his thirty-one years as dictator. We supported the council publicly and privately. I not only made public speeches praising it but also in private talks in receptions at the embassy residence I made our aims clear to the nervous military inherited from Trujillo and to leaders of the church, oligarchy, business middle class, press, and political parties.

When people began to call the council a do-nothing government, we devised a program of reforms, including agrarian reform, and I urged it on the council. But President Bonnelly told me he didn't have the votes to pass it. Probing, I discovered which of the seven councillors was blocking it. By chance, Pierre Salinger, my old friend, now President Kennedy's press secretary, came to the Republic on vacation. I gave a reception for him, briefed him in advance, and during it he took the balky councillor aside and told him President Kennedy was greatly interested in the council's progress, particularly agrarian reform. The council passed it. Thus agrarian reform came to the Dominican Republic.

The military was the real danger to the council. Under Trujillo, the military had had absolute power; now they wanted it back (under the guise of anticommunism). Scarcely a week passed that rumors did not sweep the capital that the military was plotting a coup. Then I would call my three military attachés and my political and CIA chiefs to the embassy residence and send them around the city to talk to military men and politicians, while I hurried to see the councillors of state and President Bonnelly, all of us up half the night. I lost no chance to make it clear to the Dominican military that we supported the civilian council—Fran and I gave receptions for them at the residence, and when they seemed restive, we would

bring in the aircraft carrier *Boxer,* it would anchor offshore, and Fran and I would take the Council of State and the military high command aboard for lunch with full honors for President Bonnelly and the other councillors. It reminded the military that our fleet was never far over the horizon. President Kennedy authorized me directly to tell the military, "The United States would find it extremely difficult to recognize and almost impossible to assist any regime which took power by force or threats of force." A Dominican colonel, after several drinks at an embassy reception, sneered at me, "You and your little bow tie—we'll show you and your democracy." One of his civilian rightist friends told my political officer what he and the military would do to "all these Communists": "You know why there are no Protestants in Spain? Because we boiled them all in oil." Nice group.

My second job was to work with the twenty-six political parties ranging from extremist left to extremist right. To the leaders of all I insisted on elections on schedule, encouraged them to participate fully, and discouraged extremism. We could live with any of them, at least any that had a chance of winning. My political officers helped handle them. The favored party represented the middle class; the underdog was the Revolutionary party, led by Juan Bosch, with mass support among *campesinos* and the urban workers and poor. As for the far left, it was split into four parties, and some of its leaders received training, guns, and money from Moscow, Prague, and Havana. Taken together these leftists extremist parties could not have cast fifty thousand votes. But with their constant agitation they kept the Dominican military nervous and kept the Council of State off balance, they tried to disrupt elections, they generated anti-Americanism, and they paid unemployed young men fifty cents a day to riot at our embassy. Our CIA arranged counterriots. (As disorder increased, embassy people urged me to travel with a bodyguard. I declined. Those days were different from today.)

Soon I found myself urging the Council of State to deport some Communist leaders and to harass others as Emil Smicklas and his Chicago robbery squad did. It was illegal detention, perhaps even police brutality, an invasion of constitutional rights previously denounced by the ACLU and me. Now, trying to save a tottering democratic government, I found myself favoring it.

Trujillo had trained the Dominican police, when faced with rioters, only to shoot to kill. Now the council forbade this. So they stood by helpless. Home briefly for consultation, I told President Kennedy at a meeting in the Cabinet Room that the council was losing control of the capital streets; so far I couldn't get an AID public safety mission to train the Dominican police, and I didn't see why we couldn't get a couple of cops from Chief Parker's Mexican Squad— W. H. Parker was chief of police in Los Angeles. The president turned to Ralph Dungan, who handled Latin America for him, and said, "Ask Bobby if he can get him some help." Shortly, two excellent Spanish-speaking Los Angeles detectives arrived in Santo Domingo, and in a few weeks the council rewon the streets.

Intervention, all this? Of course. But the Dominicans, except for the left and right extremists, welcomed it, or at least recognized the need for it.

Everything we did, we did under President Kennedy's Alliance for Progress. This was crucial, both atmospherically and materially, for the Alliance provided both ideals and practical objectives understood throughout the Republic and the hemisphere. One of the seven councillors told me that while he was in Trujillo's prison, "One thing gave me hope—someone smuggled in a translation of President Kennedy's speech about the Alianza. At last the United States was going to pay some attention to Latin America." President Kennedy is indeed the only president since FDR to really care about Latin America. And to this day, in thatch-roofed huts in the Republic, families tend small shrines to President Kennedy.

3.

Fran and the boys and I lived in the embassy residence, a big blocky stucco structure that resembled a library and stood on spacious grounds, royal palms plumed on high, in a garden an enormous tree like a banyan tree sending limbs and roots down into the ground, a swimming pool, an acacia festooned with great split-leaf philodendron vines, the whole sloping down to the little chancery, a cramped building where the embassy staffers had their offices and the code clerks their equipment. The residence was well suited for official functions but unadorned and bleak; Fran put up pictures we had brought and a revolving show of paintings by Dominican artists.

Fran and I frequently gave "receptions," or cocktail parties, for 250 or 300 guests—the Dominican government, Dominican military, foreign diplomatic corps, American business community. Had a stranger dropped in, he would have thought it nothing more than a party. Actually, we were working. I always had my senior staff attend, and before the guests arrived we would meet in my study and divide up the guests—who would talk to whom, what we were trying to find out, whom we were trying to influence.

I did most of my work in my little study at the residence, not in my office at the chancery—talked privately with Dominicans, wrote cables. I also wrote, about every six weeks, a summary of the situation for the State Department and for the White House, where it was read by Ralph Dungan and Arthur Schlesinger and, sometimes, President Kennedy. I believe they sometimes passed the summaries along to Senator J. William Fulbright, chairman of the Foreign Relations Committee. In all this, I was, really, doing what I had done for *The Saturday Evening Post:* doing legwork and presenting facts and conclusions. But now I was writing for a smaller audience than the *Post's:* the president and the secretary of state and their aides.

Our mission contained about 200 people (plus some 160 Peace Corps volunteers) and I was responsible for everything all of them said or did—the political and economic and administrative officers and the three military attachés of the embassy proper, the CIA, the consulate, the Agency for International Development, the U.S. Information Service, and the Military Assistance and Advisory Group. Some of my Foreign Service career officers were terrible—one was fond of saying of all Dominicans, "If we go home, they'd all climb back up in the trees." On the other hand some were first-rate. Harry Schlaudeman, for example, head of the political section, was one of the best Foreign Service officers I ever knew. He was imaginative, analytical, precise, yet he had kept a young man's passion. He was an activist and a student of Marxism-Leninism and of Dominican history. (More recently, now an ambassador himself, he has been our envoy negotiating with the Nicaraguan Sandinista government.) Schlaudeman wrote well. Though I had little time to improve the staff's prose, I did ban from our cables two words then fashionable in the State Department, "viable" and "counterproductive." As

chief of mission, I had to sign all outgoing cables and I wouldn't sign gibberish.

The functions of the CIA station chief were two—collecting information and conducting covert operations. Some ambassadors wanted nothing to do with the CIA, holding that CIA men were all a bunch of dirty spies; they could do as they pleased as long as the ambassador didn't know about it. But I wanted to know everything the CIA was doing—I had to in the supercharged Dominican political atmosphere. My first CIA station chief was fine; he reminded me of Emil Smicklas. But he was replaced by an older man who, near retirement, played it safe. Any station chief when he sent a piece of information to Washington was required to rate it on a sliding scale as to probable truth and as to the past reliability of its source. This man rated everything right in the middle, may be true, source may be reliable, when I knew better; I protested and won only after carrying my protest to the White House.

I strove to get the Peace Corps to do practical down-to-earth things close to the people but it was hard—too many of them had studied philosophy in college, not enough carpentry and plumbing in vocational school. Nonetheless, the Dominicans understood immediately their young eager faces and their eagerness to help.

AID presented awful problems and I never really got hold of it. When I saw the hovels in the slums and the men without work, I wanted to plunge in with massive work-relief and housing programs—a New Deal. But it wouldn't work and even if it did it would simply accelerate the rush to the cities. I managed to do a few things—stopped AID from building expensive concrete houses that the people refused to use, established a school for diesel mechanics—the Dominican educational system produced thousands of poets and philosophers but few mechanics—helped establish an agricultural school, got money to build little farm-to-market roads to help the *campesinos* get their coffee and cacao down out of the mountains. Some of these projects still flourish, more than twenty years later. But there was never enough time, or enough peace, really to do it right.

I fear I slighted the other ambassadors in the Republic, though I liked several of them; I simply had no time, and many of them were in a different business from mine. Some played golf most of the

time, some were promoting trade, few if any involved themselves in Dominican affairs as we did. Their receptions were almost purely social. Nonetheless, I learned to respect one thing by which they set great store: protocol. The diplomatic corps had to attend certain Dominican public functions, and had it not been for protocol, confusion would surely have reigned when we entered—there might even have been unseemly scrambling for front-row (or back-row) seats—but with the Dominican chief of protocol assigning each of us his rightful place according to his seniority in the corps, all went smoothly; we looked as though we knew what we were doing, which set a good example for the common folk.

I fear I slighted too the American community. My predecessors had belonged to the country club and their personal friends had been U.S. businessmen; I spent my time with Dominicans. Some U.S. businessmen understood. But others, I fear, did not, such as some at La Romana sugar plantation, the biggest U.S. enterprise in the Republic, with several thousand workers (its overseers rode horseback through the canefields and wore pith helmets). And once I had trouble with the United Fruit Company. Striking workers shut off the lights and water at its headquarters town in the interior, the strike sounded nasty, and to make sure that the company's property and employees were in no danger I interceded with President Bonnelly and several other Dominican officials and labor leaders and sent my own staff officers there to check. For several days and nights I followed it closely. But in the United States, the president of United Fruit wrote to Secretary Rusk, complaining that American lives and property were gravely endangered and I had done little or nothing about it; a local fruit company representative called on me to show me the letter. Angered, I told him step by step what I had done; he apologized; I told him I wanted his president to apologize to Secretary Rusk; he said he himself intended to go to President Bonnelly; I told him to go ahead if he wished but I had been assured his people and property were in no danger at present, and if he ever had reason to think they were he would do better to come to me than to Secretary Rusk, who was too far away to do much about it. Rusk reassured the company. In the end, through my political intervention, the strike was settled.

My relations with the U.S. community probably hit rock bottom

on the Fourth of July in 1962. In the past, they had become accustomed to coming to the embassy on the Fourth for a day-long champagne celebration. And the embassy staff always had come too. I decided otherwise—such a celebration would seem almost obscene in the midst of Dominican privation. Instead, I arranged to have several hundred Dominican orphans brought in buses to the embassy to swim in the pool, eat hot dogs, drink Coke, and be entertained. Many embassy staffers and members of the U.S. community bitterly resented it. The Dominican kids loved it. (I also asked Louis Armstrong, the great jazz musician who celebrated his own birthday on the Fourth of July, to bring his band down and give a public concert for young people in Independence Park. He agreed enthusiastically and would charge only traveling expenses and minimum union wage. But I could not get the six thousand dollars out of the State Department.)

As a former journalist, I had good relations with most U.S. reporters. No U.S. paper or wire service kept a man full-time in the Republic. Instead, they all flocked there when something went spectacularly wrong. For this reason, lacking background, they sometimes got things a little out of focus. Few of them spoke Spanish, and so they had to rely on Dominican sources who spoke English—mostly upper-class Dominicans. Furthermore, they could not know fully what we, the U.S. government, were up to because I would not tell them. I never lied to a reporter. But several times, during crises, when their questions pressed too hard on policy, I had to simply say, "I'm sorry, no more questions." The task of a U.S. reporter abroad is hard. He is a reporter but he is also an American, and sometimes that makes him uncomfortable. I understood the problem. But I could never forget that I was now firmly seated on the opposite side of the table from the press, and *that* made *me* uncomfortable.

Every morning Fran and I were awakened by the military band at police headquarters across the street playing "The monkey wraps his tail around the flagpole," then the stirring Dominican national anthem. Listening, we drank our morning coffee on the upstairs porch outside our bedroom. Before going to bed at night we had a drink there too, talking about what this country could be if we could only get it to work. We had Dominican friends, but our life was in a sense a lonely one, I could never open my mouth without speaking

for President Kennedy. And so I could never relax and speak freely with Dominicans. Nor could Fran.

My mother and my aunt Verl came down to visit. How I wished my father could have lived to come. Our daughter Cindy came down, met a young Englishman who worked for Shell, Anthony Campbell, and dropped out of Sarah Lawrence and was married in the embassy garden. Fran and I managed to spend some time with Dan and Fred. I sometimes swam with them in the pool before lunch, and on official trips to the interior I was able to steal a half day to take them fishing or hunting. On a Sunday evening, I sometimes took Fran and the boys down to Columbus Park beside the great gray cathedral to sit on a stone bench with Dominicans and listen to the band concert and watch young couples promenade. Many times at dusk, during the lull between embassy activity and the evening's reception, Fran and I drove out the highway by the sea to the place where Trujillo had been assassinated: scrubby palms and a rusty wire fence, a fading monument erected in honor of the deed, the sun setting fast over the purple sea beyond the palms. I do not know why we did it; now it seems a little macabre.

I wanted to do some legwork of my own to find out what ordinary Dominicans were thinking and to tell them what we were up to, and so I made a series of trips into the interior, taking Fran and Dan and Fred. We went to towns that had never before seen an ambassador. I was whistlestopping, campaigning to promote Dominican-American relations and our policies. At each provincial capital I called on the governor and other provincial officials, inviting them to tell me their problems, then, in the evening, held a town meeting to which everybody was invited, several hundred people in the government hall or a thatch-roofed restaurant. I made a short speech then invited questions. They asked about slums, housing, jobs, the broken highway to the capital, squatters, exploration for oil, agrarian reform, no electricity, no drinking water. Later I took their complaints to President Bonnelly or our AID director, and now and then was able to get something done. Sometimes the crowd listened in friendly spirit; sometimes some of them sneered openly. Often heavily armed soldiers guarded the meeting. One morning in a provincial capital while Fran and I and the boys were with the governor, I heard the noise of a crowd in the street outside shouting,

"Yankees go home," and Dan and Fred stood in the window and called back, *"Viva los Domincanos,"* and high school kids in the crowd laughed, it seemed good-natured, but it made the governor nervous; and sure enough, when we came to leave, the crowd turned ugly; by now it was no longer just kids, it was grown men, some carrying sticks and rocks. A police line formed to cordon it off. Our car was at the curb. Just as we scrambled into it, the crowd broke the police line, beat on the car with their fists, shoved it, threw things at it, and two peach stones whizzed into the front seat where our boys were. That evening at our hotel, by prearrangement, the local leaders of political parties came to see me, including the leftist party that had organized the demonstration. (Its handbills had taken the standard Communist line on issues those kids knew nothing about.) Its two young leaders didn't know much either—they told me they wanted U.S. financial help to carry out social reform in the Republic but "it must come without interference—we are very nationalistic." I asked what kind of help. "Economic aid in the form of developing ways of eliminating unemployment," one said. I asked for specifics. They had none. Then I asked them what the hell they thought they were doing throwing rocks at my kids. They grinned foolishly. I told them that anyone teaching teen-age children to go into the streets and throw rocks at other children was doing his country no service. They were untroubled. They seemed brainless, posing as intellectuals but only mouthing canned slogans and speeches. One of their slogans was "Culture or death." I could not talk to them.

On one of these trips, in the arid southwest, the poorest section of the Republic, out in the country on a road so deep with dust we were in danger of getting stuck, we came suddenly upon a foreign plantation with a thick, lush grove of banana trees. Irrigation. The water had come from the Yaque del Sur River. We forded it and came to the village of Vicente Noble—mud huts set stark on a dusty plain, women in black with cans lined up at a trickle of water from a rusty pipe; nothing green, nothing growing, the whole place a gray, baked plain, gray earth, gray dust, gray and silent people. "Every night one third of mankind goes to bed hungry"—I'd always heard it; now I was seeing it. These people scarcely gazed up at us, imprisoned by the heat, the grayness, the dust, the hunger, as inert and dull-eyed as patients in a mental hospital. Here, I thought, was our opportunity:

to change this place. Dig wells, even dam the river. Put water on the land. If you did, you could grow anything, including healthy people. I resolved to do it. When I got back to the capital I talked to President Bonnelly about it; he would work with us. I got help from our Peace Corps and AID. But the project got lost in the Dominican bureaucracy; our Peace Corps did little; local people wouldn't work on the wells without pay, why bother, their wives had always carried water in cans from the river. The project failed.

I tried a different approach. The Dominican government had proposed to build a dam on a big river in the Cibao Valley up north near Santiago. They needed money from us. But the Cibao was already the richest part of the Republic, lush and green; dams there would benefit chiefly the oligarchy that owned the land; and development there would only lure Dominicans from elsewhere to the Cibao, already overpopulated. Rather, I thought, we should dam the Yaque del sur in the southwest desert near Vicente Noble—dam it not only for irrigation but also for hydroelectric power. For in all our travels in the interior I had become keenly aware of the need for electricity, and I envisioned a vast electrification program like Roosevelt's Rural Electrification Administration. That, together with irrigation, could truly change the lives of the *campesinos*. I set to work, talking first to Bonnelly and the Council of State, then, after the election, to the new president; writing and cabling to the State Department; talking to AID in Santo Domingo and Washington. And I realized that we, the United States, possessed precisely the agency that could make it work. The TVA. If we could transform the Dominican Republic as the Tennessee Valley Authority had transformed the Middle South of the United States, we would have gone a long way toward making President Kennedy's dream of an Alliance for Progress come true. Finally I got some money from AID and got a commitment out of the TVA chairman to himself bring technicians down to undertake preliminary studies on September 28, 1963.

Something else came out of our whistlestop trips. During them, Fran had been shocked by what she learned about the health of infants in the interior. Babies were dying simply because their mothers knew nothing about hygiene and nutrition. Fran decided to establish a baby clinic in Higüey, a small remote provincial capital with

no public medical facilities. Fran called on the bishop there, on the governor and mayor and city councilmen, on the local police and military commanders, on the doctors and on the wives of leading citizens. To all she explained she wanted to help them set up a clinic that they themselves could run, not an American clinic but a Dominican clinic. In a muddy square behind the market, two Peace Corps boys poured a slab of concrete, the Dominican Army gave her a big tent, people in town gave lumber to make tables and chairs. A friend of ours from Highland Park, visiting, gave her five hundred dollars to buy medicines. The wife of a staffer made brightly colored signs like WASH YOUR HANDS BEFORE EATING to hang in the tent clinic. Five local doctors agreed to donate one afternoon a week of their time. So did ten or twelve Higüey housewives. Fran taught them to keep a card index recording each baby's length, weight, age, condition, treatment. Since this was a "well-baby" clinic, it would treat only babies with minor ailments. The key was the card-indexed weight chart.

When the clinic opened, the papal nuncio came from the capital to bless it, and it was christened, in Spanish, "The Little Clinic of Higüey." Thirty or forty mothers came on the first day; soon more than sixty were coming each day, mothers and often fathers bringing their babies on horseback or carrying them miles afoot, waiting patiently for hours to see the doctor. Medicines ran short; doctors or volunteers didn't show up; when it rained the Little Clinic flooded; once the tent blew down. Fran persevered. The Little Clinic became a passion for her. Something, at least, that one North American could do to help these people. She badgered CARE, the Peace Corps, the minister of health, politicians and fund-raisers for help; friends of ours in Highland Park sent contributions and set up a tax-exempt foundation there to receive funds. When Fran explained the clinic to Lloyd Cutler, a Washington lawyer who came down on a business trip with Edgar Kaiser, the industrialist, he said he represented an organization of pharmaceutical firms—soon they sent so many drugs they filled the embassy residence.

Fran saw everything—babies with swollen bellies and copper-colored hair and skin shredding off tiny legs, all signs of malnutrition; babies with acute and often fatal diarrhea; babies so tiny that when she unwrapped the scrap of torn bath towel in which they were

swaddled she found little sticks of hands and feet that resembled more a bag of chicken bones than a human life. Almost without exception it was disease resulting from the mothers' ignorance—not contagion, not neglect, not lack of concern, but simple ignorance. Indeed, concern was strong in the mothers, and in the fathers too. Once Fran weighed a baby and found it had gained two ounces in the week since it had been there; the mother watched tensely during the weighing and then, in a burst of emotion, snatched up the baby off the scale and smothered Fran in her embrace.

Going to Higüey once or twice a week, staying in the miserable hotel there or in the Peace Corps house, Fran learned, I think, more about daily Dominican life than any of us. And she learned the real difficulties of improving things—poor Dominicans saw her simply as the nice North American lady with the big basket of goodies; provincial officials thought they might hurt their political fortunes by cooperating with the Yankees; local doctors saw their private practice and their siesta hour threatened; some of our own embassy staff looked upon this as the meddlesome pet charity of the ambassador's wife whom, God save them, they must indulge. She was, in fact, attempting the most difficult venture of all—a joint enterprise between North Americans and Dominicans, a sort of Alliance for Progress in miniature, with all its promise and difficulties. Her hardest task was to make clear the idea of self-help. Dominicans understood well the idea of charitable works and government largess. Trujillo had taught them. But he did not teach them self-help and community projects. No wonder—those are potentially revolutionary weapons. Fran learned too that Dominicans were unwilling to accept responsibility. Worse, she discovered, when the card index languished, that it languished because the white-uniformed housewife volunteers were as illiterate as their patients' mothers. They couldn't keep a card index because they didn't know the alphabet. Fran kept trying. Once a big black-skinned mother told her, "You have come down from your white heaven to help us." This idea of charity was, of course, exactly what she sought to oppose by teaching Dominicans to help themselves.*

* In later years, having seen what Fran could do with the Little Clinic of Higüey, which cost almost no money, I was struck with wonderment when I read from time to time that the U.S. government or some multilateral bank had allocated millions of

4.

Every now and then, a young reporter new to Washington, bemused by instant satellite communications and computers and other high-technology miracles, "discovers" that "old-fashioned" diplomacy is no longer of use. In the nineteenth century, the story usually goes, when it took weeks for an ambassador's dispatches to reach Washington by boat mail, an ambassador had considerable freedom of movement and, so, considerable personal influence. But today, so it runs, he is on a tight hot-line tether, and personal diplomacy is outmoded. I don't believe a word of it. True, the U.S. ambassador to Moscow can scarcely open a window in the embassy without instructions from Washington, but most of our ambassadors have considerable leeway (which is one reason it's more fun to be an ambassador to a place like Santo Domingo than to Moscow). Even the ambassador to Moscow's effectiveness depends in part upon his personal relationship with the Soviet leaders. In smaller places, everything may depend on it. Several times, upon my personal relationship with President Bonnelly depended the Dominican Republic's fragile experiment in democracy. Nor can anyone convince me that my own whistlestopping and Fran's clinic at Higüey did not in some small way advance the interests of the United States. Nor

---

dollars for a "small project" loan to some underdeveloped country for a health facility. And, having seen the crowds of mothers with their children in the tent at Higüey while the big fancy maternity hospital in Santo Domingo stood almost empty, its expensive infant incubators, gifts from the United States, dusty and unused, I was saddened by such big showy medical projects launched in poor countries by well-intentioned people of rich countries. So much more could be done modestly, it seemed to me. I was heartened to find agreement when I came across an article in *Foreign Affairs* by no less an authority than Dr. Lewis Thomas, M.D., chancellor of the Memorial Sloan-Kettering Cancer Center in New York. Dr. Thomas said that our own complex expensive system of medical care was designed primarily to cope with the medical concerns of people middle-aged or older, focusing on such diseases as cancer, heart disease, and stroke; whereas what is killing children in the Third World is diarrheal disease caused by contaminated water and faulty hygiene, especially dangerous to children fed inadequate or ignorantly chosen food, and, beyond infant and childhood mortality, parasitic disease. Replicating our own system, including, say, Sloan-Kettering, Massachusetts General Hospital, and a top-drawer U.S. medical school, would not benefit, might even harm, the people living in city slums or rural parts of poor countries. Instead (as Lewis Thomas has recently said), what they needed were plumbers and sanitary engineers, nutritionists and hygienists, antibiotics and vaccines, and, above all, nurses to run the program and a distribution system to bring it to everyone, probably through some equivalent of our old-fashioned local boards of health. Not high technology, just basic public health. What the people of poor countries want is not a comfortable old age but a better chance at life itself.

my cables and six-week summaries; for one of the really important things an ambassador can do is influence the policy of his own government toward the country he is accredited to. Especially can he do this if he has a personal relationship with the president, members of Congress, and the press. Above all the president.

When I went to Washington for consultations, I took with me a long list of the Republic's problems and a shopping list of things I wanted from the State Department and AID, then, with the other principals, met in the Cabinet Room with President Kennedy. I summarized the policy we intended to pursue from now till next February 27, when the Council of State was due to leave office and the new elected president to take over. President Kennedy asked questions incisively. Wasn't there a danger that so many political parties and so complicated an election law might produce a splintering election, with no one able to govern? How clearly could Radio Havana be heard in the Republic? Should we jam it? Was our military advisory group any good? Did I want more? What about coastal patrol boats? What about counterinsurgency training? What about the Social Christians—any hope there? What was the chance of Juan Bosch's party—Partido Revolucionario Dominicano (PRD)—winning? I answered his questions as rapidly and crisply as I could; I knew he was impatient with discursive replies, it was one thing about Stevenson that put him off.

I shocked the State Department by telling him Juan Bosch's proletarian PRD was now about even with the middle-class party. I said the Dominican military was getting more restless, and he told me carefully how far I could go in stopping a military coup. As the meeting broke up and he headed back to the Oval Office, he stopped for a moment with me and said, "I saw you last night," and then, "Good luck—and let me know if you need anything."

The previous night I had attended the annual White House correspondents' dinner, and President Kennedy, in top form, had done a takeoff on himself, one of the funniest speeches I ever heard. At that time, Washington was gay and hopeful. I was staying with the Arthur Schlesingers in their little rented house in Georgetown. Bobby Kennedy, I discovered, like me felt he had wasted a good deal of his time in college and had not received a good education, and so now he had organized what came to be called the Hickory

Hill Seminar, gatherings of cabinet members and other New Frontiersmen in Bobby's house, Hickory Hill, or another of their homes, to listen to a lecture by whatever leading intellectual was visiting Washington and to ask him questions. Arthur arranged the programs. One night while I was there the seminar met at Arthur's house, and the speaker was Sir Alfred Ayer, a visiting British philosopher (a logical positivist, Arthur helpfully informs me); and when he had finished, Bobby's wife, Ethel, an extremely devout Catholic, who was sitting up front with me, said she thought she had understood him to say he didn't believe in God and she wondered if this was possible. From the back of the room Bobby called out, "Shut up, Ethel." It brought down the house. And may have saved the positivist.

President Kennedy was planning to entertain all the Nobel Prize winners from the Western Hemisphere at the White House and he had to make a few remarks, so Arthur and I produced a draft, writing a line that went, "I think this is the most extraordinary collection of talent, of human knowledge, that has ever been gathered together at the White House." Delivering it, the president added "with the possible exception of when Thomas Jefferson dined alone." It was the Kennedy touch.

5.

On December 20, 1962, the Dominican people voted freely for a president for the first time in thirty-eight years. It was a day everyone had dreaded, a day everyone had predicted would result in riots, gunfights, God knows what. It passed calmly, cleaner than most elections in Chicago. The vote was huge. Juan Bosch and his PRD won by a landslide. Now we had a rarity in the Caribbean, a freely elected government of the non-Communist left. Could it endure? Could Bosch make his peaceful revolution? Could we help him? Would he let us?

Juan Bosch was a short-story writer and, by Dominican standards, an intellectual, a man of striking appearance, high cheekbones and curly snow-white hair and bright blue eyes. Even before he was inaugurated, he got in trouble. When a draft of his new Dominican constitution was published, President Bonnelly and other councillors took me aside at a private party to denounce it—said it

was "a Communist Constitution," did not protect private property, legalized concubinage and made divorce easy, did not guarantee civil liberties, did not consecrate the Vatican Concordat. This was the first outcry of the propertied class against Bosch and his revolution, real venom. Bosch went on the radio with a long foolish rambling speech, viciously—and pointlessly—attacking the Council of State and the business middle class. The reaction of the power structure was almost instantaneous. Important Dominican and U.S. businessmen thought him anti-American; press and politicians attacked the draft Constitution; churchmen thought their worst fears confirmed; the military stirred—the Air Force commander told my attaché that Bosch was "at least" beholden to Communists and that "it's easier now than later." My commercial attaché was flooded with phone calls; business came to a standstill.

Vice-President Johnson would lead the U.S. delegation to Bosch's inauguration. The day before he was to arrive, the CIA told me that U.S. immigration authorities had stopped two Communist terrorists from leaving New York for Santo Domingo. An American businessman who was always messing around in Dominican politics was demanding to know what our attitude would be if the Communist Bosch was overthrown before he could be inaugurated. A plot was afoot to assassinate President Romulo Betancourt of Venezuela, who was also coming to the inauguration. I wondered if we really should bring Vice-President Johnson into this mess.

We did, with the *Boxer* offshore and its helicopters flying air cover over him, and all went well. In the middle of the festivities, Dan's burro threw him, breaking his arm, and a Dominican doctor set it and cast it, but I wanted it X-rayed next day by a U.S. doctor aboard the *Boxer;* and I had to tell Vice-President Johnson about it, saying that unfortunately it meant that my wife could not accompany his wife to the Dominican School for the Blind next morning, as scheduled. Instantly the vice-president said, "Why don't you let me take the boy, and his mother too, up to Washington with me Thursday? They can take better care of him at Bethesda [Naval Hospital] than here." He said it absolutely spontaneously, purely a human gesture. Ever since, when people ask what I think of Lyndon Johnson, I think first of Dan's arm. Johnson saved it—it was broken near the growth center at the elbow, and if it had not been reset properly it would not have grown.

6.

I never developed the close comfortable relationship with President Bosch that I had had with President Bonnelly. One might have expected otherwise—after all, Bonnelly was quite conservative and he belonged to the oligarchy, while Bosch, was, like me, a writer, a liberal, and the accepted spokesman for the underdog. Bosch had spent twenty-five years in the underworld of Caribbean exile politics, which ill equips a man to govern. His was a dark and conspiratorial mind. To him, everything had to be a plot. He was brilliant and intuitive, but unstable and reckless. He was moody and unpredictable, arrogant and vain and streaked with martyrdom. As a child, he told me, he had become anti-American and now he was determined to pursue a course independent of the United States.

I sometimes thought I judged him too harshly. He was a wandering writer and teacher. It was unfair to compare him to the only other presidents I had known—to Kennedy, born to wealth and influence in Massachusetts, to Bonnelly, nourished in the Santiago oligarchy. At times I felt deep sympathy for Bosch. Both his mother and father died shortly after he took office as president. When his father died, I went impulsively to his house and told him I wanted to offer my sympathy. His face showed surprise, then set tight. He motioned me to a chair, and we sat down, and I told him my own father had died only two years before, I thought I knew something of how he must feel, and it might help him if he remembered that his father had lived to see him elected president, and so had his mother—he had made them very proud, and that was all a son could do. He said nothing for a moment, nothing at all. Then he asked, "How is Mrs. Martin?" Fine, I said. "And the boys?" We sat another moment, then I got up and said I did not want to keep him longer. Standing, he asked, "May I embrace you?" He was a strange man.

Personality aside, Bosch faced grave problems. The awful history of the Republic gave him little democratic tradition to build on. The economy was a mess. Politically, he was caught between the left and right. He owed political debts to the left. On the right, he was unalterably opposed by much of the oligarchy and the rising business middle class; he was viewed with grave suspicion by elements of the armed forces and the Church. In short, most of the real power structure of the Republic was arrayed against him. His overwhelm-

ing six hundred thousand votes (60%) meant everything on election day—but between elections they meant nothing, an inert mass. But his single greatest handicap was that he had almost no one to help him run his government. His election had been truly revolutionary: It had brought to power a whole class of people who had never before entered the mainstream of Dominican national life—the *campesino,* the small shopkeeper in the roadside store, the workingman, the poor. I knew a governor swept into power with Bosch who could not sign his name, a mayor who had never before worn shoes. True, it was time these people took their rightful place in Dominican life, but the fact remained that they were unqualified to govern.

The foreign aid policies of our own U.S. government had suddenly become restrictive. AID had no money. The World Bank was talking big projects but they were years away. Meanwhile, where was Bosch's revolution? What about unemployment, high as ever? When would he launch programs for the poor?

Justice William O. Douglas of the U.S. Supreme Court came down to the Republic, drawn, I suppose, by Bosch's reputation and opportunity. Justice Douglas was one of those rare men whom I had long admired from afar and, upon meeting, found even better than I had expected—not only courageous and liberal but also warm, sensitive, and very funny. At lunch and dinner, I told him about the Republic's problems. Believing we should promote education in democracy after Trujillo, Justice Douglas thought he might establish an institute here and bring in such lecturers as Robert Oppenheimer and Rexford Tugwell. Or send promising young Dominicans to Princeton for a few weeks' intensive training in government. The foundation of his friend Albert Parvin would commit its resources to the Dominican Republic this year, and he was open to suggestions.

I thought that Bosch could not spare any promising young Dominicans, not even for a few weeks' training. (Ralph Dungan and I had already discussed it.) As for lecturers, at first I had had the same idea but soon had realized that such a project was hopelessly too sophisticated. What was needed was to reach and teach the Dominican people themselves simply and directly. I had thought of a way: by television. The idea had developed out of my larger idea of rural electrification and the damming of the Yaque River. And out of

AID's experiences with education and the diesel and agricultural schools. Over television, we could teach the people not only about democracy, we could teach them mechanics, carpentry, plumbing; we could even teach them to read.

Justice Douglas was enthusiastic. He thought he could get American manufacturers to contribute the TV sets. I would ask President Bosch to give us time on the government television station and to permit us to put a television set in every town hall or in every abandoned local headquarters of Trujillo's old party.

For a holiday, Fran and the boys and I took Douglas to the mountains. We arrived at Constanza as dark dropped fast over the high valley. The bartender in the deserted hotel confided to me that local leftists were plotting guerrilla activity; they had been here last week, whispering together, and after they left he had picked up bits of paper on which they had scribbled battle plans. At dinner Justice Douglas and I amused ourselves by whispering conspiratorially and scribbling on scraps of paper in Spanish, Justice Douglas adding a few words in Persian. Next morning at dawn we crossed the backbone of the Central Mountain Range, ten thousand feet, I driving my Jeep, Douglas sitting beside me, the cold wind blowing his white hair.

I got Bosch's cooperation with our TV project, and in ensuing months Justice Douglas sent technicians down and they began taping a hundred programs to teach the Dominican people to read and write. Local teachers would have to be found, lesson books written. It was a formidable project. By late summer the first tapes were finished and the television sets were promised. We thought we could reclaim the generation Trujillo had wasted.

Bosch had begun badly; it got worse. The splintered political parties issued an anti-Bosch manifesto, uneasy businessmen muttered about communism, lines of unemployed people formed each morning at the Palace gate. Bosch tried to counterattack—senseless attacks on red-baiters and the defunct Council of State. I tried to help him quietly—offered several public gestures to demonstrate his ties to the United States, including lunch aboard a flagship of our Atlantic Fleet, coastal patrol boats, private mediation with the editor of the leading opposition newspaper, support if he would restrict

travel to Cuba, a dinner party for him and suspicious businessmen. Bosch accepted all this.

But at the same time he almost went to war with Haiti. I tried to restrain him, urged him to take his complaint against Haiti (which was legitimate) to the OAS. His military commanders suspected he wanted to destroy their forces in a Haitian adventure. In the end, Bosch did not get OAS help, he realized his armed forces were incapable of invading Haiti, and he himself felt defeated and betrayed and alone.

Harry Shlaudeman told me Bosch was losing his own political party supporters. Wherever I went, I myself heard poor people saying, "Juan Bosch is good for nothing." And my AID director told me quite casually, "Moscoso and Betancourt and Harriman have agreed that Bosch is gone and so hands off." I thought I too had noticed a certain reserve in Washington. Hal Hendrix of the *Miami News* wrote a series of articles attacking Bosch hard, and me too— the specter of communism. Other U.S. reporters were attacking. These correspondents would come to the Republic, talk to the Dominicans who spoke English and who were mostly businessmen opposed to Bosch, be told that he was a Communist or was handing the country over to Communists, would file their stories to their papers in the United States, and there the stories would be published in English then translated into Spanish and sent down to the Republic and printed in the Dominican newspapers—and the same businessmen who had inspired them in the first place would show them to the military and say "You see? Even the impartial United States press considers Juan Bosch dangerous and soft on communism." (No doubt most of the U.S. journalists believed what they wrote. I considered the Hendrix articles a vicious hatchet job, however, and told Hendrix so.) These stories also fed the fires in Washington. Congressman Armistead Selden of Alabama, chairman of the House Subcommittee on Inter-American Affairs, made a speech on the House floor denouncing "the advancing communist offensive of subversive penetration in the Dominican Republic." Bosch publicly denounced Congressman Selden. Senator Hubert Humphrey on the Senate floor defended Bosch. The lines were hardening. It was early June; Bosch's first hundred days were over. He had squandered them. I went to Washington to try to save him.

Coming into Kennedy Airport in New York was breathtaking: It was so big, so organized, everything worked, the young businessmen hurrying through the corridors exuded confidence; everyone knew what he was doing and how to do it. This was power, these educated, trained, competent people. This was a great nation. The poor Republic.

In Washington, I went all out to rally support for Bosch. I explained the Dominican political situation. Soon Bosch would have to move left, might even expropriate land without compensation. This would alarm the United States. To make it unnecessary, I wanted us to help him now. I asked for a $15 million loan for agricultural development; Moscoso of AID thought my AID director hadn't made a good case for it. The assistant secretary of state for Latin America, Ed Martin, denied there'd been a change in the Department's attitude toward Bosch and said if Bosch wanted financial help he'd have to come up with sensible projects, and he'd better not expropriate land without compensation as he'd threatened. I went over to the Pentagon, trying to get Bosch's patrol boats. I asked Abram Chayes, the Department's legal counselor, to work out an acceptable method of land expropriation. John Steele of *Time* arranged a dinner with fifteen or twenty leading writers and editors.

On Capitol Hill, I appeared in executive session before Senator Wayne Morse's Latin American subcommittee and Congressman Selden's House subcommittee. At lunch privately, Senator Humphrey told me Bosch couldn't expropriate U.S. land and he'd better give Dominican landowners fifty-year bonds. Congressman Selden received me courteously and sympathetically, and I tried to disabuse him of some of Hal Hendrix's notions, while he tried to disabuse me of any notion that he didn't want Bosch to succeed.

Over the Fourth of July weekend, I went to our camp in Upper Michigan. As soon as I saw the pine and lakes and deep blue sky, I knew they still held me. One day Earl Numinen and I walked in to Smith Lake, far out in the woods to the north, where I still hoped to buy land. And evenings sitting alone in front of the fire, I thought the long thoughts that always seemed to come in Michigan. It is still the most healing place on earth for me. Years ago I had first come here to fish, or thought I had, but as time passed I was less interested

in fishing, more in merely being in the woods, driving the Jeep or walking, watching for deer and coyote, partridge and bear. Once I had seen a timber wolf.

I stopped briefly in Highland Park, and when I tried to explain Dominican politics to our friends there, they simply looked bewildered. And went back to small talk—their children's summer camp, the racetrack, the musical season at Ravinia, golf and travel, whose daughter got into what college—the people and things they had made their place among. To me, thinking of Juan Bosch and Dominican democracy, my friends' lives seemed empty. But were they really? Living was nothing but personal relationship, private relationship. While I had been writing professionally, I had thought writing was what mattered—trying to help improve an American society that did not always work so well as it should. And I had felt that way too in the political campaigns. Then toward the end of that period I'd thought that those things mattered less than personal life, private life and inner life. Now in the Republic and in Washington I was involved with large public issues; I thought they were what mattered. Were they? It was an unsettling trip. Well, howsoever all that might be, the Michigan woods abided.

Back in Washington I wanted to be photographed with President Kennedy and have the photograph published in the Republic, and to return there with a public statement using President Kennedy's name and reiterating our firm support for Bosch. But I did not want to put President Kennedy out on a limb unless I was sure the Communists could indeed be contained, and so I asked for help in training an effective antisubversive force for Bosch—and, as a double check, I wanted a greatly stepped-up CIA covert operation of our own, one capable, if necessary, of keeping several people inside and outside the Bosch government under close surveillance.

When I saw President Kennedy in the Oval Office, accompanied by Ed Martin and Ralph Dungan, I told him about our Dominican problems, including Washington's cooling off on Bosch. We were gambling, I said, in supporting Bosch, but the alternatives were worse—a rightist coup, or a leftist takeover, "another Castro in the Caribbean."

The President listened carefully then asked hard questions. He

thought expropriation would create problems no matter how Bosch did it. He approved getting some AID projects ready to go. He liked my talking to members of Congress and the press. Once he got up from his rocking chair and, walking to a blue-green naval painting on the wall, asked if I was coming back to help him in the campaign next year, that is, 1964. I said I was at his disposition. He thought a minute, said, "Maybe you can do more for us holding that place together. Well, we'll see." He approved the statement I proposed to issue. A photographer came in and made the picture I wanted. As I walked out, past the desk of Kenny O'Donnell, the president pointed his finger at me and said loudly, "There he goes—the Earl E. T. Smith of this administration." They roared—Smith had been Eisenhower's ambassador to Cuba when Castro came to power. I was so startled I could only say to him, "What a thing to say," and he grinned and waved, and I left. Going back to Santo Domingo, after seeing him, almost anything seemed possible, even Juan Bosch's success.

But from then on, it was just a hopeless holding operation. The Dominican military, egged on by the businessmen, was hell-bent on exterminating communism. Fran and I gave dinner parties trying to bring Bosch together with the Santiago oligarchy, with Dominican businessmen, and with his own military. Strained parties. His opponents began pretending that the Church was against Bosch; I saw the papal nuncio. I cooked up a new AID program for Bosch; Washington was cool. Even Ralph Dungan was beginning to give thought to what we should do after Bosch fell.

Increasingly Bosch seemed resigned to his own failure. Talking to me he shook his head sadly and said, "There can be no revolution—there is no money." He talked of resigning. Fantastic rumors swept the streets, including one that the Pentagon had broken with me and President Kennedy and was conspiring to overthrow Bosch. We could do little but tell everybody we supported the elected president. Like Bosch, we ourselves were becoming increasingly isolated. In the end, Bosch had the support of only a minuscule Communist party, some of the Santiago oligarchy, and the U.S. embassy, mainly I myself.

On September 20, 1963, businessmen, provoked by Bosch's un-

wise proposal of another tax and land reform, closed their businesses—a-"general strike" against Bosch. Over the weekend violence began in the streets, the military came in, and on Tuesday Bosch sent an aide to take me to a villa where he was hiding out. In a little bedroom with a noisy air conditioner, drinking a Coke, Bosch told me, "There is a *golpe,* a coup. Yes. They are going to kill me or overthrow me. Today."

That night they did: The military overthrew him without bloodshed, despite all our efforts throughout the night. He seemed almost to invite the coup. At dawn I went to the Palace, talked briefly to Bosch, who was confined in his office under military guard, and asked the military to guarantee his physical safety then went back to the residence and called Ed Martin.

In all their history, the Dominican people had enjoyed eleven years of freely elected government. To this total Juan Bosch had been able to add just seven months minus two days. After obtaining the department's approval, I left for Washington, taking my AID director and military group chief with me. Fran and the boys stayed. The day I left was the day the TVA mission had been due to arrive. Police raided the office where we had stored the literacy tapes from Justice Douglas; we rescued them and locked them in my safe. At times in the Republic I had felt that everything in my past life had prepared me for this job—my reporting, my writing, my work in politics. Now all that, along with Bosch, had failed.

7

The military appointed a triumvirate, three unexceptionable civilians, to run the government, but the military remained the real power. In Washington I went to work to persuade my government to set its face against the new regime, to refuse to recognize it, and thus, I hoped, to bring it down or at least force it to return to constitutionality. Reaction on Capitol Hill was strong. Senator Humphrey encouraged me. No senator condoned the coup; one demanded that we rescue Bosch from the ship taking him to exile and put him back in the Palace, by force if necessary. In the House, Congressman Selden, while not applauding the coup, said he preferred a dictatorship that sought our friendship to a Communist dictatorship. I testified before House and Senate committees. Most of the press seemed to

believe we ought not to recognize the new regime. Sentiment in the Senate was moving that way. The House was less clear. The president would decide.

In the department we drafted policy recommendations for him: as our ultimate objective, a return to constitutional representative democracy; meanwhile, effective government and neither harsh military dictatorship nor Communist growth. What we wanted in exchange for recognition: free political activity for non-Communist parties, restoration of a semblance of constitutionality, a presidential election in one year, and more. We also drafted a public statement for Secretary Rusk.

When we saw President Kennedy, he looked at me and said, "I take it we don't want Bosch back."

"No, Mr. President."

"Why not?"

"Because he isn't a president."

He began discussing the paper point by pont. I said I wanted something in the secretary's statement specifically about nonrecognition. The president didn't want to use the word. Averell Harriman suggested "normalization of relations." The president rewrote the statement, asked what time it was, said, "We've got to get it out right now if we want to catch the bulldog," the early editions of tomorrow morning's papers, and picked up a phone, got no answer, jiggled the receiver impatiently, and still got no answer. Ralph Dungan took the statement and hurried out to release it. It was a tough statement, the kind I'd wanted.

After the meeting broke up, I wished I'd had an opportunity to explain to President Kennedy how Bosch had fallen, and later I asked Ralph Dungan if I could, privately. Dungan said, "If you're worried that the president has lost confidence in you, forget it—he hasn't." I was grateful, but it wasn't that. It was a guilty need to give him an accounting of my failure. I never got the chance.

During the ensuing weeks we struggled with the Dominican regime. We saw President Kennedy frequently. At first we labored urgently. When we went to see the president we sometimes met the officers concerned with Vietnam coming out of the Cabinet Room after meeting with him. But after a time the urgency wore off; other

issues, such as Vietnam, claimed his attention; and we were left in the Department to draft new instructions to the chargé. I had a little office on the third floor. We fell back from one position to another, dropping one by one our demands on the Triumvirate. It rebuffed our every move. We were under pressure—we feared a bloody Communist guerrilla rising, we feared the collapse of the Triumvirate and a naked military dictatorship, and we faced pressures from other governments, including Great Britain, to recognize.

Fran and the boys came up to Washington. After a week, they went weeping home to Highland Park. Our house there was rented, as it had been since we went to the Republic, and they stayed with neighbors. I stayed in Washington with the John Steeles. Every day I went down to the antiseptic Department—with its clean desks and locked files it always looked deserted. I came to hate it. It was always cold and wet in Washington that fall.

Bobby Kennedy's wife Ethel called to invite me to a surprise birthday party for Bobby at their home, Hickory Hill, on November 20. The party was big and gay and noisy. Old friends from the campaign were there, Kenny O'Donnell and Steve Smith and others, and while most of the guests danced the twist, we talked about the coming 1964 campaign.

Two months had passed since Bosch was overthrown. Now I had cooked up an elaborate plan to meet secretly with the former president, Bonnelly. It was almost our last plan. On Friday morning, November 22, Bonnelly said he wanted first to consult the Triumvirate. We told him to go ahead. Ethel Kennedy sent my topcoat to the Department—I'd left it at her party. I didn't go out to lunch, was waiting for word from Bonnelly. Restless, I began pacing in the outer office where the typists worked. A young Foreign Service officer came up to me and said, "Mr. Ambassador, the president was shot in Dallas."

That afternoon when the radio said he was dead I called Fran. She knew. She would stay with the kids. I'd be home as soon as I could. Outside my window in the Department, the flags were coming down to half-staff. I wrote a telegram telling the chargé to meet with Bonnelly for me. I left. It was dark, raining hard. At Arthur Schlesinger's house, I found a note on the door: "This is an upset

household, forgive us if we'd rather be alone." I went home to the Steeles. We sat. After a while I went up to bed in the attic. Sirens screamed all night. Next day I went as instructed to the White House, walking across Lafayette Park in the rain, seeing the terrible long black limousines pulling up at the portico; and went wet and alone into the East Room where the president's body lay in state with an honor guard. An old man and his wife were ahead of me; I waited till they passed, then went in and stood by the flag-draped casket alone, and said silently to President Kennedy I was sorry and thanked him, as many years ago when Fran's mother died I had silently thanked her for having given me Fran, and felt some vague stirring to ask God to help him and us all, but didn't, then went out of the room, the honor guard changing slowly too.

Downstairs on my way out I saw Clayton Fritchey, my old friend from the second Stevenson campaign, now Stevenson's press secretary at the UN. He was waiting for the Harrimans. They offered me a ride. Mrs. Harriman was crying and, because I was sitting next to her, I held her hand. Harriman asked Fritchey to get Ted Sorensen to work on President Johnson's eulogy for President Kennedy and asked me to work on one that Stevenson would deliver. At the Department, Harriman asked me to go up to his office with him, lonely too, I suppose, and we went and talked a long time, mostly about the Dominican Republic and the Alliance. Harriman felt he should be paying more attention to Latin America, he wanted me to help him think about it when I went back to the Dominican Republic. I told him I didn't think I'd be going back. He said I must, it was my duty, I knew more about it than anybody else, and we should have "rammed you down that bunch's throats" right after the coup.

Leaving, I ran into Ed Martin and said I intended to resign that day. He said I couldn't, President Johnson had asked that no ambassadors resign. I said I'd stay a few days then I'd like to go home for Thanksgiving. I went to Harriman's house in Georgetown and worked with Fritchey on a draft for Stevenson's speech.

Sunday I slept late at the Steeles', and was told of a sudden that the man who assassinated President Kennedy had himself been killed. The television screen was becoming a mirror of our national madness. On Monday the president was buried, and I walked down in the brilliant sun from the Department to Constitution Avenue

and watched the procession come slowly past, the awful black and muffled drums. Millions of Americans watched it on television and felt the same agony, the sense that all was lost. I went home to Highland Park. Fran had temporarily retrieved our house. Dan had lettered a sign and put it on my desk: ASK NOT WHAT YOUR COUNTRY CAN DO FOR YOU—ASK WHAT YOU CAN DO FOR YOUR COUNTRY. Dan had decided he wanted to become president. I tried to explain to Fran and Dan and Fred why we were not going back to the Dominican Republic, which they loved. Maybe some day, as private citizens. Right now I wanted to get out of government, to think, to write, to be with them and live privately and quietly. I would go back to Washington, see things through to recognition, then resign and come home. Maybe we would go up to Michigan. But the Dominican Republic, what we had tried to do there for the Dominicans, for our own country, for President Kennedy—that was all over, ended. The world was a different place.

It was hard for them. And Fran thought I should go back to help the Dominicans, and the United States, and our faith in what Stevenson and Kennedy had stood for in the campaigns, for if all who so believed departed, what then? Fran was worried too about the Little Clinic of Higüey. Dreams die hard. And maybe she was right.

On my way back to Washington, I stopped at the Chicago City Hall to pay a courtesy call on Mayor Daley. He too had been President Kennedy's friend and he was as shattered as the rest of us. I asked him if the new president, Lyndon Johnson, would be all right, and he said, "He will if he goes down the line for the program," that is, for President Kennedy's civil rights program. "He won't get his wheat and cotton bill if he doesn't go down the line for the program."

In Washington, President Johnson met privately in Secretary Rusk's office with the half dozen or so of us ambassadors who happened to be in town. Seated, he talked to us quietly, kneading his big hands, talking about himself, his boyhood on a poor Texas farm, now president of the United States.

Two weeks ensued. Guerrillas took to the Dominican hills, and government troops hunted them down. The Republic was polarizing. I told Dungan we could delay recognition no longer. He agreed and so did George Ball and Ed Martin. Ed Martin told me privately that, if I agreed, he also would recommend that the president accept

my resignation before we recognized, so I would not appear to resign in protest against recognition. I agreed. On Saturday he and I met the press and announced recognition. President Johnson accepted my resignation effective February 15, 1964.

I spent a few days saying goodbye to my friends in the administration, Bobby Kennedy hardest of all. How his face had aged in the years since I'd known him at the Rackets Committee. Well, whose hadn't? I stayed only a minute or two, telling him I'd do anything for him, thanking him, telling him I was going home to write a book. With that odd tentative half-smile, so little known to strangers, he said, "Everybody's writing a book," and "All right, John." And then, "Well, three years is better than nothing."

I took a train home as I had so many times in years past. That night I could not sleep and dozed, wakened, dozed, wakened, as the train rolled and pitched and shuddered, stopping a long time beside a black river near Pittsburgh; and I kept thinking: "Why did they kill him? Why him?" In the morning the train rolled across the flat land of Ohio, where I'd been born, and Indiana, where I'd been raised, that flat endless plain, white houses, red barns, two pheasants standing in a snowy cornfield, a woodlot, the neat rectangles of earth scattered complacent. So many years ago, twenty-six years, just out of college, I had crossed the plain, headed for the Caribbean, suffocated by the flat land, eager for the great world; and had sailed the Gulf of Mexico and the Carribean, Puerto Rico, Cuba, and, finally, by pure chance, Santo Domingo. How long ago. Then the flat fields of Indiana had seemed drab, dispiriting, the blue Caribbean with flying fish scattering before the prow exciting, miraculous.

Now the Midwest looked different. Here I'd spent most of my adult life, working, crisscrossing it, talking to its people and writing about them, I knew it, all of it, knew it in my bones. The scattered houses, the big town lots, a cord of stovewood in a backyard, here and there a rivulet, a gully—my father and I used to hunt rabbits on cold days like this in the gullies, though he always said we'd find more in the corn and wheat stubble, and he was right but it was less fun, the gullies were shadowy and mysterious. Now it all looked comforting, and I needed, the nation needed, comfort. I was going home.

We got a tall Christmas tree, and Cindy came home from Guate-

mala with her husband, and my mother and Aunt Verl came up from Indianapolis on the train called the *James Whitcomb Riley*, and after Christmas all of us except my mother and my aunt went up to Michigan. We stayed in our camp at Three Lakes, 25 degrees below zero, and went snowshoeing and rode the toboggan and took a Jeep ride in the woods, seeing a herd of deer black against the snow in a frozen swamp. I had written to the logger who owned the land at Smith Lake, the lake far out in the woods, and he had said it was for sale; now I met him and bought it, about 160 acres, nearly all the shoreline on the big end of Smith Lake in the rough, rocky, uninhabited—and in winter unreachable—country out north. After New Year's the others went home but I stayed alone, dreaming about building a camp at Smith Lake next summer, thinking about the book I wanted to write on my work in the Dominican Republic, at night alone in camp in front of the fire. All my life when hurt or healing, I had wanted to be alone.

TWELVE

LYNDON B. JOHNSON AND ROBERT F. KENNEDY

1.

In the embassy I had dedicated myself wholeheartedly to my work and disdained the trappings of powers. Nevertheless, anybody who leaves high public office and returns to private life has a reentry problem and will, if he is honest, admit he misses some of the perquisites of power. He will not be driven to his office along a tropical boulevard by a chauffeur in a limousine; he will stand in the January slush with the rest of the commuters waiting for the 8:08. At the office no Marine guard will snap to attention when he arrives, all will not rise when he enters. More than one former ambassador has bought a set of official china, bearing the seal of the United States, to use in his private home; but he himself must help his wife scrape the garbage from the plates in the kitchen. In the embassy, he had a sense of history, a sense of serious purpose, of doing something important for his country. On his judgment turned the decision whether to develop the northern valley or the southwest desert; a word from him might topple a government. Looking back, he can see he made mistakes. Reading the morning paper, he cries out to say, "Don't take that road; we almost took it, and it leads to the precipice." Whether he was right or wrong, he cared. He helped

make the foreign policy of the United States. What worthwhile can he do now? What—the ultimate question—will he do with the rest of his life?

Actually, there were times during the next four years when I didn't know what I was going to do with the rest of my life. We spent the four years between 1964 and 1968 somewhat adrift, summers up in Michigan, the rest of the year on the east coast at a university or in New York or Washington, often traveling abroad, dragging Dan and Fred to and fro with us.

Of one thing I felt sure: I would not return to writing heavy fact for magazines. I would write—it was all I knew how to do—but not what I formerly had. I could no longer imagine writing a John Simon story, or a Jackson Prison story. Now my interests lay in national politics and in foreign policy. One doesn't go back.

The fact is, I could not have gone back even if I had wanted to. While I'd been away, magazines had fallen on evil times. Television had taken their advertising. When I had written for the *Post,* its issues often had run to more than two hundred fat pages. Now the *Post* had become thin and wizened and had started to lose money, its owners had replaced Ben Hibbs, Stuart Rose, and the others, and the new editors had made changes—tried to jazz it up, to publish sensational exposés. It was no longer a natural market for me. In a few more months the *Post* folded. (Later its name was sold to another publishing company and it resumed publication, but it was an entirely different magazine.)

I had some loose ends to clean up. At the behest of Arthur Schlesinger, I worked in the White House with Bill D. Moyers, President Johnson's young chief of staff, and others, writing a fund-raising book for the Democratic National Convention of 1964. I made several television appearances on foreign affairs. Bits and pieces of Dominican affairs came my way. Fran and I bought a little beach house at Sosúa on the north coast of the Dominican Republic. More importantly, at Bobby Kennedy's request, I helped him set up an oral history project on his brother's presidency, and I interviewed him for it, long sessions in Washington and New York. It was excruciatingly hard work for both of us. He both wanted and feared to have me ask hard questions about his brother, and I felt much the same

way, not boring in as I would have in a different sort of interview, but at the same time conscious that I could not escape an obligation to history. We worked all through that spring, a time when he was becoming increasingly estranged from President Johnson, though still in his cabinet. I felt the interviews had been disappointing, even somewhat superficial. But people who since have used them, such as Arthur Schlesinger in writing his biography of Bobby, have told me they are valuable.

Several times during these years I thought to go back into government. Sarge Shriver was expanding the Peace Corps in Brazil to five hundred or seven hundred and asked me to head it. I declined. Several times I thought I wanted another embassy, and the Department once offered me Jamaica, but I declined that too; it didn't sound interesting or important after the Dominican Republic. Once, after I had performed several missions for President Johnson, I saw him alone in his office, and he proposed I come to Washington permanently as a consultant to him and the State Department. I didn't want to do it and made some noncommittal response, and we talked on, then he asked if there was anything else I wanted to say to him. I told him I'd be interested in another embassy but not a sinecure like Jamaica, an important one and one where we had a chance of success. The president said, "You're entitled to it. You've gone everywhere and done everything we asked. I'd like to see you have it,"and he asked where I wanted to go. I told him some place like Venezuela. As I left, he said, "We'll be in touch with you." Bill Moyers pushed the consultant job, saying I'd only nominally be consulting with the State Department, actually I'd be the president's principal speechwriter and one of his principal advisers, and he indicated it might well lead to a very good embassy.

Not until later, after talking to Fran, did I realize how carefully President Johnson had phrased his response. He'd said I deserved an embassy but he hadn't said he'd see that I got one, he'd said he'd like to see me have it. Presumably he never appointed me an ambassador because I declined to join his staff. He punished others more severely for less serious offenses.

Well, if not government, how should I go back to writing? *Reader's Digest* asked me to become its Latin American correspondent. Mike Bessie at Harper had an idea for a book, George Roy

Hill had one for a film. But what I wanted to write, and did write, was a book that was at once an account of my work in the Dominican Republic and a sort of memorial to President Kennedy and his Alliance for Progress. I called it *Overtaken by Events* (one of the few good phrases to come out of the State Department bureaucracy). And I wrote it at the Center for Advanced Studies at Wesleyan University in Middletown, Connecticut.

Fran and Dan and Fred and I lived there for a year and a half. The university gave us a small two-story shingled house converted from an old mill, standing on a high rock ledge above a creek that flowed over a waterfall, a secluded wooded place of winding roads and ravines and hills across the Connecticut River from Middletown and the campus. In addition to the house, I had the rank and salary of a full professor but with no teaching responsibilities unless I chose to give an occasional lecture or seminar, which I did. Only two things were expected of me—to be engaged on a serious piece of work of my own, which I was, writing *Overtaken by Events,* and to have drinks and dinner every Monday night at the center on the campus with the other fellows of the center and its director, Paul Horgan, the writer, and listen to a paper read after dinner by one of the fellows or a Wesleyan faculty member. Paul Horgan was one of the gentlest, most courteous men I ever knew, as well as a good writer, and he presided over the fellows with grace and elegance. Fran and I came to know well a number of the other fellows—Edmund Wilson, the critic, and his wife, Elena; Jean Stafford, the *New Yorker* writer and widow of A. J. Liebling; Sir Herbert Read, the British critic, and his wife. Edmund Wilson usually drank martinis before dinner and wine with dinner and slept through the paper. He was great fun and once, after a young university psychologist had read a dreadful paper on the psychology of mice—he had given mice alcohol experimentally and he seemed to think that rats were the parents of mice—I found in my letter box what purported to be a long complaint by a mother mouse against the professor, especially the difficulty she had in pushing a full bottle of gin across his laboratory in order for him to feed it to her. I guessed its author was Jean Stafford but it turned out to be Edmund Wilson; for several weeks the three of us composed epistles to one another written by mice and rats.

I spent one memorable Monday evening talking to a nuclear physicist who was a protégé of Niels Bohr, and he undertook to explain quantum physics to me, and it all seemed perfectly clear, but next morning I couldn't remember a word he said. On other evenings Fran and I would entertain several of the fellows and Paul Horgan and Victor Butterfield, Wesleyan's president, at dinner, or go to one of their houses for dinner. The atmosphere at the center was what one had always hoped a university atmosphere would be—a civilized community of serious scholars who could be fun. It was a pleasant life, and our millhouse was a good place to work. And I'm sure that by talking to the other fellows about *Overtaken by Events,* and by reading things they suggested, I made it a better book than I would have in Highland Park. I was writing the rough draft at a furious pace, eighty-five pages a day.

We were within easy driving distance of New York and several times took the boys to the theater there, took them too up to Massachusetts and Vermont, New Hampshire and Maine, where we visited my favorite store whence by mail I had bought sporting goods for years, L. L. Bean. Now and then Fran and I went to Washington. Arthur Schlesinger was leaving President Johnson's White House staff to write his book about the Kennedy administration, *A Thousand Days,* and his friends gave him a farewell party, renting a Georgetown bar for a night and putting up funny signs, one of which read, COME AS YOU WERE, and when Arthur stepped onto the dance floor to deliver his farewell speech, a spotlight focused on him and the band played "The Eyes of Texas Are upon You." The hour being late, his speech made little sense but no matter—by then few of us in his audience were making much sense either.

Friends of ours visited us—Harry and Carol Shlaudeman, now back in the Department in Washington, Gustavo Tavares from the Dominican Republic, Dick Goodwin, who had joined the White House staff and was writing speeches for President Johnson. Ben Shahn was lecturing at Harvard, and we went to visit him and Bernarda. We went too to spend long weekends with Dick and Eleanor Rovere at their house in Rhinebeck, New York, on the Hudson. Oddly, Dick and I rarely talked about writing, though we had spent our lives at it, and we knew each other a long time before we discovered that both of us had started out by writing fact detective stories.

Sometimes we talked politics; usually we talked about real estate and money. (Dick once wrote that he had the mind and soul of an accountant; so have I.)

2.

On April 24, 1965, a Saturday, the Dominican Republic blew up in what quickly became civil war. Juan Bosch was in exile in Puerto Rico, but supporters of his, including elements of the armed forces, attacked the Palace, overthrew the Triumvirate government, and passed out arms to the people; General Wessin y Wessin's loyalist tanks and troops began fighting them in the capital's streets. A bloodbath began, perhaps a thousand killed. The following Wednesday, April 28, President Johnson sent the Marines and part of the 82nd Airborne Division, some twenty-one thousand troops, about as many as we then had in Vietnam. That night on national television he said that Americans in the Republic were in danger, Dominican authorities could not protect them, he had sent troops to evacuate them. I was disheartened. I feared that once more we had ranged ourselves on the wrong side—*for* an unpopular regime, *against* the people.

George Ball and Bill Moyers called me at Wesleyan next day and asked me to come to Washington. They sent an Air Force Jet Star for me and I was in Washington on Friday by 6:30 A.M. In the Cabinet Room of the White House I met with President Johnson and the leaders of his administration, including Secretary Rusk and Secretary McNamara, Undersecretary Ball, the head of CIA, and the chairman of the Joint Chiefs of Staff. Until now, U.S. troops were under orders not to join Wessin's loyalist troops in aggressive action against the rebels but only to establish an international zone under an OAS resolution to protect embassies and foreign citizens. Reporting from the embassy was confused. General Wessin's loyalist forces might collapse today. If that happened, would we order U.S. troops to shoot Dominican rebels? Secretary Rusk said he wanted to point out to the president that sending troops into combat in a foreign capital was a very serious business. I said quickly, "Yes, Mr. President, that's the last thing we want to happen." President Johnson looked across the table at me with his hooded eyes and said, "No it isn't. The last thing we want is another Castro in the Carib-

bean." He foresaw two dangers—very soon we would see a Communist-dominated government in the Dominican Republic, or we would find ourselves alone with our troops in the Republic without any support in the hemisphere. He didn't want either one. He told Rusk and Ball to get to work with the OAS, told McNamara and the Joint Chiefs to get ready to do whatever might have to be done, and told me to go to the Republic at once and open up contact with the rebels—Ambassador W. Tapley Bennett, a conservative career officer who had replaced me, had few contacts among Bosch people—help the papal nuncio get a cease-fire (as the OAS had requested), and find out what the facts were and report to him. Already the press was criticizing him for having sent troops, President Johnson said, and he was willing to work for peace through the OAS or anybody else but he did not intend "to sit here with my hands tied and let Castro take that island. What can we do in Vietnam if we can't clean up the Dominican Republic?"

I went to Santo Domingo immediately on a Jet Star, taking Harry Shlaudeman as my aide. Santo Domingo was all shot up, parts of it burning, the Palace a wreck in no-man's land, gunfire heavy and close to our blacked-out embassy. Seeing thus this city I loved was painful. We got the cease-fire—I persuaded General Wessin, whom I detested and had not seen since the dawn he overthrew Bosch, to walk across the room in his headquarters to the nuncio and sign the cease-fire; then the nuncio and I went into the rebel zone, riding in his car with the gold and white Vatican flag draped over the hood, he in his billowing long white cassock, and persuaded the rebel commander to sign. Come to think of it, I suppose the instruments of U.S. policy, the nuncio and the Marines, were the same as the Spaniards' four hundred years before—subduing and pacifying the natives by using both the cross and the sword.

One night I flew to Puerto Rico to see Juan Bosch. Another night I went to see my friend Antonio Imbert Barreras, Trujillo's assassin and a former member of the Council of State. As we pulled up in front of his house, I was sitting in the front seat beside the driver with two young Marines in the back seat, and one of my young guards let his finger slip on the safety of his rifle and let off a string of shots behind my right ear. I dived for the floor, knowing Imbert's bodyguards would be hidden behind the hedge a few feet away, and began call-

ing out to them not to shoot, it was an accident, I was Ambassador Martin, and waited, expecting them to open up with their machine guns. They did not; they were well trained and they knew me. Had they been any other Dominican troops they'd have killed me.

Often I telephoned President Johnson, once about 3:30 A.M.; he was running this operation like a desk officer. Shlaudeman and I talked to many Dominicans, and I became convinced that political leadership of the rebellion had passed to Communists and other extremists and I said so at a press conference, thereby putting my reputation as a fact finder and a liberal on the line.

The danger to the United States was that we would range our own troops against the rebels; we needed a third force. Tony Imbert undertook to form a provisional government, and I wrote his inaugural speech, and he led Dominican troops in an assault. At my suggestion, we interposed our troops between his force and the rebels and kept the peace. Imbert's government prospered briefly; but liberals in the U.S. press attacked President Johnson for installing an assassin as his proxy, and Undersecretary of State Tom Mann, McGeorge Bundy, and Undersecretary of Defense Cyrus Vance came down and cut the ground out from under Imbert and tried to install a president of more liberal coloration.

I went back to Washington on May 18 and next day met with President Johnson and the other principals—Vice-President Humphrey, Secretaries Rusk and McNamara, and others. President Johnson felt himself at bay, pressed hard by liberal journalists, many of them my friends. His eyes were almost slits. He went around the table and polled us one by one on whether we favored Imbert or the tame liberal. He would brook no equivocation, no suggestion that this was not a matter of either-or; and if one of us balked—as I did—he read aloud a transcript of a recording he had made of a long telephone conversation we had had with him from Santo Domingo, when he had asked our views on the same question. He told us that no American president since George Washington had been subpoenaed by the Congress but that he might be, and if he was he would take all of us with him and the transcript as well. After the meeting had been going on more than three hours, it began to relax simply because of the passage of time, and some of us caught ourselves forgetting we were addressing the president of the

United States, he seemed more like a county board chairman running a courthouse meeting on a sewer bond issue. Throughout, President Johnson kept needling the State Department, and Secretary Rusk did not like it and he did not smile. When the president did this, Vice-President Humphrey would nudge me, sitting beside him, and wink at me. Then the president would turn to Secretary McNamara and, calling him Bob, say something comradely. All this—pressure and camaraderie—was President Johnson's way of getting what he called a consensus. He operated so differently from President Kennedy. President Kennedy's meetings rarely lasted more than an hour, usually less, he never allowed any doubt that he was President, he never used pressure, if he was displeased he simply disposed of the question by hardening his voice, he never descended to our level. I remembered Bobby Kennedy's telling me once that President Johnson despoiled everything he touched by his crudity, his ignorance, his refusal to learn. And yet this was the same man who had saved our son Dan's broken arm.

Life and *Reader's Digest* asked me to write a piece about our intervention, and I did. I spent a good deal of time, with the president's encouragement, talking to reporters and editorial writers. Some had been criticizing me for supporting our intervention. Several, however, defended me, Jack Fischer of *Harper's* writing that if John Bartlow Martin said there were Communists in the rebel movement, there were Communists in the rebel movement. Some of my liberal friends, like Arthur Schlesinger, refrained from public criticism but plainly thought me wrong. (Averell Harriman had loyally gone to South America to explain and defend President Johnson's intervention but Arthur refused to do the same in Central America.) Over the years, vice-President Humphrey and I had manned the barricades together in many a liberal cause, and I explained to him what we'd been doing in the Dominican Republic, especially the Imbert gambit. He shook his head and said, "And now I've got a delegation of neo-Nazi politicians from West Germany waiting for me. You sure get mixed up with some funny people if you hang around long enough." One day Fran and I had lunch at Kay Graham's house with her and Adlai Stevenson, come down from the United Nations where, bewildered, he had been trying to explain our intervention. He and I had a swim in the pool before lunch—Fran said

we made a spectacular pair, he so fat, I so thin, which said something about the ways we had been spending our time—and after lunch Stevenson and I went to another room to talk. For an hour or more. At the UN, despite our liberal friends' criticism, he had loyally if uncomprehendingly defended our intervention, and now he asked me what the hell we'd been up to. I explained it, and he seemed satisfied. He also asked me to come to New York to talk to him about a major writing project he had in mind. I got the impression he wanted me to help him write his autobiography. I never saw him again; he died a few weeks later.

With considerable difficulty, we persuaded the OAS to join our peace-keeping efforts. Eventually Ellsworth Bunker, our ambassador to the OAS, aided by Shlaudeman, managed to install a provisional president who would hold free elections. He did, and since then the Dominican Republic has held five more free elections at scheduled intervals. These days, when I think of my Dominican experiences, including my efforts to help Juan Bosch succeed as president, I tend to think of them as a failure. But actually, through all the twenty-four years that have passed from the assassination of Trujillo to this writing, except for the brief civil war in 1965, the Dominican people have lived in peace and freedom, the longest period of peace and freedom in all Dominican history. Our military intervention turned out far better than we had any right to expect.

3.

"Intervention"* has become a dirty word. It is used somewhat indiscriminately. For the United States, intervention has usually taken two forms—trying to influence and even control the internal politics of a smaller country by political means and, usually after that has failed, by military means. (In recent years, perhaps emulating the Soviets, we have tried a third method—using a proxy native military force. This has not led to happy results to date in Nicaragua any more than it did in Vietnam.)

We have intervened most frequently in Central America and the Caribbean. Usually our intervention there has been a corollary of our global policy (and our presidents' domestic political con-

---

*Talleyrand once said, "Non-intervention is a political and metaphysical term and means about the same as intervention."

cerns)—we intervened in the Caribbean basin under Theodore Roosevelt and Woodrow Wilson in the name of "antikaiserism"; we intervened there under Presidents Kennedy and Johnson and Reagan in the name of "anticommunism." Debate about military intervention is usually sharp and clear, debate about peaceful political intervention more muffled and confused.

We are bound by international law not to intervene in the domestic politics of other sovereign nations. But we do, constantly (and so do other powers, and not only the Soviet Union). Whether we ought to is the subject of intense quiet debate among our policy makers. Viewpoints change. Early in his career, in 1923, Sumner Welles, who later became undersecretary of state, while he was our chief representative to the Dominican Republic brought together the quarreling Dominican political party leaders and virtually dictated a settlement that resulted in a peaceful election and returned the Republic to constitutional rule after years of dictatorship and U.S. military occupation; and later as our man in Havana he virtually engineered one dictator's overthrow and ended by supporting another, Fulgencio Batista. Yet in his later years, as undersecretary, Welles came to oppose any intervention whatsoever, he explicitly forbade U.S. representatives to offer any advice on a domestic political question even if asked, and he went so far shortly before Pearl Harbor as to declare that the United States should not intervene in any Latin American country even though its government was under the influence of the Axis, as Peron's clearly was.

As ambassador to the Dominican Republic, I myself had felt that if we did not support the provisional government and influence the contending opposition parties, the provisional government would likely fall, elections could not be held, and democracy would fail— the democracy that we and all Dominican elements except the extreme left and the extreme right were trying to build. In this policy we succeeded, but only through heavy political intervention. Arguments against intervention were many and powerful—that Dominicans must do it for themselves, that if we continually propped up the provisional government it would never learn to govern, and that after the election no government elected only because of our stabilizing influence could by itself succeed.

As it turned out, Bosch, once elected, refused our help until it was

too late; whether he might have succeeded with it we shall never know. After his fall, I was not there, but I have the impression that we pursued a hands-off policy, that we did not intervene politically, and that the pro-Bosch rebellion resulted, obliging President Johnson to intervene militarily. Again we shall never know whether our political intervention would have averted the rebellion.

It may be unfortunate but it is true that we do not yet live in a world of enforceable world order, where individual nations are willing to subordinate their own interests to the good of all. We live, instead, in a world of nation-states. In this world, the big powers, especially the United States and the Soviet Union, each has its sphere of influence. We do not declare war on the Soviet Union because it imposes its will forcibly upon its near neighbor Afghanistan; the Soviet Union does not declare war on us because we send some twenty thousand troops to Santo Domigo. This may be far from ideal. But it is a fact of international life today. This being so, the wisest course for us would seem to be to exert political influence in order to avoid using military force; for as the world stands we will always intervene to the extent necessary in our own sphere of influence to protect American lives, property, and other vital interests. What is a "vital interest"? Anything we say it is—that is, anything we would go to war to protect, above all any clear and generally agreed threat to our own national security (the Russian missiles in Cuba were deemed so in 1962).

(To my mind, none of this by any means excuses such harebrained adventures as our invasion of Grenada or our recent dangerous assaults on Nicaragua. Indeed, all this is to denounce those military interventions, for they were undertaken while we ignored or rejected political settlements that might have made the last resort to force unnecessary.)

Even activist political intervention is by no means universally favored. Often it will take us deep into the internal affairs of other countries. It casts us in the unwanted role of judge and court of last resort, it sometimes involves matters beyond our strength or wisdom, and it is certainly not a policy popular among my liberal friends. Nevertheless, in the present state of the world, I see no other course, at least in this hemisphere.

* * *

But intervention, of itself, is only a part of a wider question: America's place in the world. Perhaps there too we can learn some lessons from our Dominican experience.

In our times, when a dictator falls, he seems to be followed by, first, political chaos and then by an extremist regime, often anti-American—Batista was followed by Castro, the shah of Iran by the ayatollah, Somoza by the Sandinistas.

But Trujillo was followed by democracy. How so? We, the United States, had a good deal to do with it.

When Trujillo fell, as we have seen, President Kennedy sent the fleet to throw the Trujillo dynasty out of the Republic. Then he sent me to support strongly and openly the shaky Council of State for a year, to help it hold free elections, and to support the elected president. True, Dominican democracy stumbled—President Bosch was overthrown. But after we stopped the brief civil war, a new president was freely elected and since then, as I have said, democracy has prevailed for nearly a quarter century.

As we all know, democracy in that part of the world is fragile. Even in Chile, with a long tradition of peaceful civilian government, the military overthrew as a Communist Allende. And to be sure Dominican democracy might collapse again the day after tomorrow. But so far it has worked.

If we had followed the same policy in Nicaragua, we might have avoided much trouble. But we did not. Even with the Sandinistas in the field against Somoza, our ambassador supported him at least as publicly and as fervently as I supported the Dominican Council of State. When it became clear that Somoza was going down, President Carter could have sent the fleet to throw him out, as President Kennedy sent the fleet against the Trujillos. But he did not. (I am told President Carter considered doing it but at the last minute he and Secretary of State Vance lost their nerve.) And after the Sandinistas came to power, we could have supported them wholeheartedly, as President Kennedy instructed me to support the council and Bosch. We did not. True, early on President Carter sent them money and a sympathetic ambassador. But soon he cooled off, and in any case he had only a few months left in office and he had to spend them campaigning for reelection. And after that, under President Reagan, we drifted from "cool but correct" relations with the Sandinistas into

outright hostility. We did so for ideological reasons, concern about the wider Central American crisis, and fear of "another Castro in the Caribbean."

If we had thrown Somoza out and wholeheartedly helped the Sandinistas, we might have no better friends in the Caribbean than they. Now we have no more bitter enemies.

But all this is true not only in the Caribbean and not only today. Time and again, around the world, and ever since the end of World War II, we have followed the same misguided policy. As after the war the old colonial empires broke up and rebel forces demanded independence, over and over we tried futilely to prop up the status quo. Why?

Every president from Harry Truman on has known that to be in the White House when any country in the world "goes under to communism" is not politically healthy. With his grand inquisitor's cry of "Who Lost China?" Senator Joe McCarthy made it so. Incredibly, McCarthyism has distorted American foreign policy for at least thirty-five years. It has seized George Kennan's sensible and successful containment policy, which was designed for the heart of Europe, and applied it everywhere, to backward agricultural societies anywhere in the world that communism threatens—to, among others, Korea and Vietnam. And has emphasized almost exclusively its military aspects.

After Vietnam, for a time the United States seemed headed back toward a sort of neo-isolationism—"no more Vietnams." Vietnam, it appeared, would be the high-water mark of military containment. But then President Reagan, with his patriotic chest thumping, seemed bent on taking us back toward worldwide containment or even toward a worldwide "rollback" of communism, a policy of driving the Soviets back to the gates of the Kremlin. One of President Reagan's proudest boasts was that during his first term, no country anywhere was "lost to communism."

At this writing, it is uncertain whether we will intervene everywhere. But it seems certain we will continue to intervene at least in the Caribbean basin.

If so, intervene on which side? On the side of the status quo? Or on the side of change?

It may be wiser to support change, even revolutionary change. Revolutions begin because of local repression, poverty, injustice; as

they are about to win, communism from afar may take over. We might consider beating communism to it—consider whether, in prerevolutionary countries (like, say, South Korea today), it might not be better and cheaper to "contain" the revolution by joining it before it wins—by throwing out Somozas before they fall, by throwing out the Trujillos and helping the new government.

This is not an easy course. The future may belong to the young students and labor and *campesino* leaders who oppose the dictator, but they are not easy to work with. Immediately after Trujillo fell, there or four of them came to Washington to talk to Bobby Kennedy. He was probably the most radical of the New Frontiersman but even he told his brother, "They're lunatics—we can't work with them." And indeed on my own mission to the Republic a few weeks later, I found them so. Idealistic and patriotic, yes, but also young and wild and reckless; certainly not set in concrete for Russia but equally suspicious of the United States; rudderless and malleable but unstable; more interested in dignity and honor than in ways and means; more given to heroic gestures than to the hard work of governing; hopelessly naïve and wholly inexperienced. I told President Kennedy so, and we turned away from them as from the stable but despicable Trujillo right, and sought the center. After I became ambassador, these young idealists went into Dominican politics, and often I saw them behave in the same lunatic way. They were forever threatening to throw themselves over the cliff. Time and again, even councillors of state threatened to resign, candidates for president to withdraw from the election. Once the Social Christian candidate and his followers had gone armed to another town and, when opponents tried to break up their meeting, had started shooting; and a bystander had been killed. When I pointed out that this was against the law, he struck a dramatic pose and said, "We obey the law of God." Just so, the kids in Nicaragua who ran the Sandinista government declared with equal passion to one of our negotiators they were Marxist revolutionaries and would gladly die rather than have anything to do with us and our democracy. They knew little of either democracy or Marxism. How could they? The president of Nicaragua had as a schoolboy joined the opposition to Somoza, been jailed by Somoza, been released, and gone to risk his life with the Sandinista guerrillas—he went from teen-age dropout to president. Heroic, yes; but qualified for president? Is it possible to really

imagine, as President Reagan seemed to, that such a man could rule an efficient "totalitarian" state that functioned smoothly as an arm of an "evil empire"? The Sandinistas would not have known how to do it even if they wanted to. Far easier to imagine them making the same mistakes President Bosch made. It is no accident that *Don Quixote* is a Spanish novel and that it is set in the same lovely part of Spain, Andalusia, that both the Dominicans and Nicaraguans originally came from. (Nicaraguans are more like Dominicans than any others in the Caribbean.)

We cannot expect that it would be easy to work with such revolutionaries. Far easier to work with the dictator. But since most of modern history shows the dictators on the losing side, and since they are unjust, let us work with the people against them. Even at the risk of "another Castro in the Caribbean."

If we look at what followed Batista and the shah and Somoza, and if what happened after Trujillo was indeed unique in our time, then perhaps President Kennedy's policy and my efforts to make it work amounted to more than we thought.

4.

When, on July 14, 1965, Adlai Stevenson died suddenly of a heart attack in England, Fran and I helped with funeral arrangements, then with Newt Minow and other of Stevenson's friends and relatives went to the services in Washington in the National Cathedral (where President Johnson, offering condolences, said to me, "He showed us the way"), and with other Democratic friends went aboard the president's plane, which took Stevenson's body home to Illinois. En route, Arthur Schlesinger told me I should write Stevenson's biography. In Springfield at a wake in the judges' chambers in the Illinois Supreme Court, the talk turned to a memorial for Stevenson, and I told his three sons I hoped they would not merely name an expressway after him but would do something like establish an institute, perhaps at a university, that could train promising young leaders from the Third World, the Third World whose importance Stevenson had been early to realize. Stevenson's sons and his old friends did establish such an institute, and though it was not precisely what I had had in mind, it did bring together scholars and leaders from around the world.

Stevenson's oldest son, Adlai III, was looking for someone to write his father's biography and asked my advice. Adlai hoped to get some money out of the biography for the Stevenson Institute and asked if I thought a writer would share his royalties, perhaps divide them equally. I told him that I myself had never split royalties but that in these circumstances, to help the institute and because of my feeling for his father, I probably would. I recommended several writers. They didn't work out. After a time Adlai asked me to do it. Fran was against it. She thought it was "going back." She didn't want me to relive the past but to move ahead. She thought Stevenson's family could be difficult. And it would take a long time. But I decided to do it and Doubleday, which was publishing *Overtaken by Events,* agreed to publish it. Being already committed in principle, I agreed to split my royalties equally with Adlai and his two brothers and also to give Adlai, acting for the family, the right to review the manuscript before publication. (If it contained things he objected to and he and I could not agree on changes, the issue would go for binding arbitration to Carl McGowan, Stevenson's former chief of staff and now a U.S. appellate judge in Washington, or, if McGowan was unable or unwilling to serve, to Newt Minow.)

The Life of Adlai E. Stevenson—I thought it would take three years to write. It took ten. I was fifty years old when I started. Your fifties are supposed to be the years when you make the most money and do your most important work. I spent mine writing the biography of Stevenson and I have never regretted it. I've heard it said that some writers who spend so long on a biography become bored with their subject or, worse, come to resent him for taking so much of their lives to write his. Luckily I escaped both infections.

Since my biography of Adlai Stevenson contains a full account of his life, here I will only describe briefly how I researched it and wrote it. Stevenson was a string-saver. He almost literally never threw anything away. Among his papers I found not only longhand first drafts of famous speeches but also Princeton football-game ticket stubs and old dance programs. His archive was enormous. His papers existed, for the most part, in four locations. Most of the papers relating to his governorship, and some early family letters, were at Springfield in the Illinois State Historical Library. Those relating to his ambassadorship to the United Nations were in the State

Department in Washington and in the U.S. Mission to the UN in New York. The rest were at Princeton. In addition, his family and friends had a few of his private papers.

At the outset I persuaded my old friend Francis Nipp to act as research director of my project. He worked at it for two years then gave up, why I never understood. Roxane Eberlein, who had been Stevenson's private secretary and assistant at the United Nations, took over the research. We made Xerox copies of several hundred thousand pages of his papers. We put the copies into several hundred looseleaf binders, each numbered and given a symbol designating whether it contained correspondence, speeches, or whatever. We indexed the copies, making an average of perhaps a thousand 5-by-8-inch cards on each of the sixty-five years of his life, and arranged them chronologically. To fill in the gaps, I interviewed about a hundred people who had been close to him, dictated my interview notes, and indexed them too in binders.

We started out at the beginning of 1966 by renting the house that he had loved in Libertyville. But I realized that if I wanted access to his UN files, many of them classified, I had better get to them right away, while my friends and his were still in power in Washington; so we moved on to Washington and rented a little house in Georgetown. George Ball, still undersecretary of state, arranged for me to have access to all of State's files. I spent the spring researching them and interviewing people who had worked with him there.

I spent that summer back in Illinois interviewing Stevenson's family and friends, especially those in Bloomington, his downstate hometown, for you could never understand Stevenson unless you understood the small town where he grew up. It was there that I discovered that Stevenson's childhood, far from the happy time usually pictured, had been a horror. And from my interviewing in Chicago and Lake Forest I learned that his private life as a Chicago lawyer had been almost equally unhappy.

In the fall we moved to Princeton. By then it was clear that my half of Doubleday's generous royalty advance and research grant would not support me to the book's completion; I needed supplementary income. I could do an occasional magazine piece, not enough. That fall I was given a one-year appointment as visiting fellow in public affairs at the Woodrow Wilson School of Princeton University. After that, Arthur Schlesinger had me appointed visiting

professor at the Graduate Center of the City University of New York, where he himself now taught, and I commuted to it one day a week from Princeton to teach a seminar.

The seminar dealt with the limits of American power in foreign policy. Each student was required to write a paper on a single foreign policy crisis, such as the Cuban missile crisis or the Korean War, laying out the policy alternatives among which our policy makers had been obliged to choose and identifying the factors that had limited American power and thus helped force the policy choice. I had been obliged to think about this while writing *Overtaken by Events,* while researching Stevenson's UN work, and while watching those limits operate as an ambassador. Despite all our power, we cannot always do everything we want to do everywhere.

I had been making a number of policy speeches, especially on our Dominican intervention, to universities and the National War College and to several political groups, such as the national Women's Democratic Club in Washington. These speeches cast me in the role of defending President Johnson's Dominican intervention, which I did not mind, since I thought he had had no choice but to intervene. At this time, however, protest was rising against his escalation of the war in Vietnam, and many people tended to link our Dominican intervention with Vietnam. I was careful to explain our Dominican policy but stay clear of the Vietnam War. Nearly all my friends, such as Arthur Schlesinger, opposed that war vigorously. I knew little about it and was slow to pay attention, perhaps because I was preoccupied in 1964 with President Johnson's reelection campaign and in 1965–1967 with the Dominican civil war. By late 1966 or 1967 I was as much opposed as everyone else. Both Stevenson and I had been burned by this—his friends had begged him to resign as ambassador to the UN to protest our involvement in Vietnam, just as my friends had deplored my defense of Johnson's Dominican intervention.

5.

Politics again—in 1964 I helped President Johnson run for reelection. (This was before our Dominican intervention, before Stevenson's death, less than a year after President Kennedy's assassination.) When at his request I went to see President Johnson,

he ruminated about politics: "It's going to be Goldwater. He's underrated. He thinks he can take the South, add Indiana and Illinois and Iowa, the conservative Midwest, add New Mexico, Colorado, and the mountain states—and do it. And he might." I told him I'd spent most of my life in the Midwest, and he was right—this year its conservatism would come out as white backlash against Negroes.

He asked, "Is the peace issue important?"

I said, "Very. People are scared to death."

At that time, June of 1964, we were rather lightly involved in Vietnam. President Johnson said, "We need you. You write it and tell me what to say and I'll say it."

He was, in that sense, an easy man to work for—easier than John F. Kennedy, far easier than Adlai Stevenson. As I left, he called, "Get some new ideas, John," as all candidates do, and I said I would, as all writers do.

That fall, I had an office in the Executive Office Building next door to the White House. So did Dick Goodwin and Bill Wirtz, by now secretary of labor but writing speeches in the campaign. In overall charge of speeches was Bill Moyers. I did not travel with President Johnson; I saw him occasionally in the White House but for the most part I worked with the other writers in the White House and I traveled alone to various parts of the country doing editorial advance. For example, I made a swing through Indiana and Illinois, and after talking to politicians and labor and business people and ringing housewives' doorbells, I wrote a memo to the president telling him that people in the Midwest were saying the election was a choice between "a kook and a crook," President Johnson being the crook and his Republican opponent, Barry Goldwater, the kook. (I know this disputes various testimony that staffers dared not bring distasteful news to Johnson, but I never found that true.) Throughout the campaign, we endeavored to picture President Johnson as trying to unite the country, to restore and heal it after President Kennedy's murder, and to picture him as promising peace and, in Vietnam, moderation, while picturing Senator Goldwater as a bloodthirsty mad bomber.* Our advertising agency prepared a tele-

---

*The Pentagon Papers made public several years later indicated that President Johnson was secretly planning to send warplanes and combat troops to Vietnam even at this time, while campaigning as the candidate of military restraint. I can say that, al-

vision commercial showing a little girl plucking a daisy, while a voice-over intoned a countdown, "Ten, nine, eight, seven, six, five, four, three, two, one," whereupon the screen exploded in a mushroom nuclear cloud; and before we were obliged to take the commercial off the air as unfair, the message had come through: Goldwater was the mad bomber. (Goldwater had let slip in a press conference, when asked about ex-President Eisenhower's opinion that our six NATO divisions in Europe could be cut to one, his own view that they "probably"could be cut by "at least one-third" if NATO "commanders" in Europe were given power to fire tactical weapons in an emergency. Even blowing up a bridge can in combat be an emergency. We immediately interpreted this as empowering any second lieutenant in NATO, despite his staff's frantic explanations that he meant the succession of NATO supreme commanders). Another commercial showed a pair of hands tearing up a Social Security card (Goldwater had "ruminated about," as Teddy White puts it, making Social Security voluntary, a silly idea.) President Johnson had decreed that no speech of his could be longer than seven hundred words. With commercials like that to explain complicated issues, who needed long speeches?

Fran came down for election night, and with Clark Clifford and his wife and others we watched returns in Bill Moyers's office. President Johnson won the biggest landslide till then in American history, with 61 percent of the vote. He himself spent election night at his ranch in Texas, and several of us talked to him during the evening, and I did a draft of his victory statement that sounded Stevensonian. He liked it.

For Fran and me, the 1965 inauguration of President Johnson should have been a more satisfactory celebration than that of President Kennedy—the weather was better; we knew our way around official Washington better. We even got to Kay Graham's party. And we happened to arrive at the inaugural ball at the old Wardman Park Hotel just as President Johnson and his party arrived and so found ourselves propelled with them down the roped-off aisle through the crowded ballroom, and saw Dick Daley waving and calling to us from the throng on the wrong side of the ropes. (The

though I met frequently with Clark Clifford and Abe Fortas, the president's senior advisers, and although I saw the president occasionally and Moyers, Goodwin, and Wirtz daily, I had no inkling of any such a move and I doubt that my colleagues did either.

president's box itself was full; Adlai Stevenson had entered with us, and Bill Moyers found a seat for him in the president's box; Stevenson had brought the bright beautiful Marietta Tree, who worked with him at the United Nations, and, seeing there was space only for himself, he promptly abandoned her; Fran and I rescued her, found places for her and ourselves in the box of Governor and Mrs. Pat Brown of California. The first rule of the "A Party–B Party" game: Sacrifice your buddy. Loyalty, as I have suggested, was never one of Stevenson's strongest qualities.) All in all, the inaugural was, for us, as joyless as the campaign.

Two years later, in the fall of 1966, out in Illinois, my own senator, Paul H. Douglas, was running for reelection, and during the last weeks of the campaign I went to Chicago to help him. He was an old friend, and that spring in Washington he had let Fred work in his office on Capitol Hill, carrying his briefcase, helping him sign letters, and ushering visiting constituents around. Paul Douglas was, I thought, one of the ablest—and noblest—men in the Senate. But now he was seventy-four years old and a strong young Republican was running against him, Charles H. Percy. At lunch in Washington, when Paul first asked me to help him, I had asked what his position was on Vietnam, and he'd said, "I support the president." I tried to suggest that perhaps he should develop a Douglas position on Vietnam rather than endorse everything President Johnson had said and done. But Paul was adamant—he had supported the policy all along because he thought it right and he was not going to waver now because public opinion was shifting.

His campaign that fall was all uphill. In his headquarters I worked with his son, John, a Washington lawyer close to the Kennedys, and Richard Wade, a young University of Chicago history professor and friend of Arthur Schlesinger. I wrote speeches, as usual, and it also fell to me to appear in public several times on Paul's behalf, including once at an anti–Vietnam War student protest rally, where I had the task of explaining both President Johnson's Dominican intervention and his Vietnam policy, while the students asked questions and a fat girl in a long fuzzy sweater played a guitar and sang protest songs. Election night in Paul's hotel suite I watched the early returns. It was clear we were losing big, and

I thought Paul should concede and end his career gracefully. I went into the bedroom where he and his wife were. He was stretched out on the bed, exhausted—he'd been campaigning on the streets up to the end. I told him what returns we had and advised him to concede. He said he'd have to clear it with Mayor Daley. He called the mayor and spoke to him briefly. When he finished he threw himself on the bed on his back and burst out laughing. I asked what the mayor had said that was so funny. Paul, scarcely able to speak, said, "He doesn't want me to concede yet—he's got some paper wards he wants to hold out," that is, some wards that voted by paper ballot that Daley wanted to hold until he knew how many votes he needed from them to save the county ticket. Paul said, "So after all these years the truth finally comes out."

6

One night that summer up in Michigan, while Earl Numinen and I were taking a sauna, he and I decided to go to Finland. Born there, he had been brought to America when he was nine; now he was nearly fifty-nine but he had never been back. When we left on June 6, 1967, New York was hot and humid, but the minute we stepped off the plane in Helsinki we felt as if we had come home to Upper Michigan—the airport was ringed by pine and the air had the Michigan tang.

The Upper Peninsula of Michigan contains the largest Finnish colony in the United States. The Finns are a lost people. Where they originated, history does not know. Their language resembles no other except Hungarian. Some authorities believe the Finns originated in Mongolia, and I remember that Earl Numinen's father, who lived to a great age, resembled, in his last years, a Mongol. His father, Earl told me, had been a serf in Finland. Earl had always wondered if his father had been the illegitimate son of a nobleman; on this trip he hoped to find out.

We left Helsinki in a rented car and drove to the gentle farmland of south-central Finland whence Earl's people had come. For a week we visited Earl's relatives and childhood friends, a reunion after half a century, and they told us how life had been in Finland during those years. Especially they talked proudly about the Winter War, when tiny Finland had held Russia at bay. Earl uncovered

family roots he had forgotten or never known; in old church records he traced out his mother's genealogy but he was unable to untangle his father's (at least so far as I know—after a time he stopped talking about it). He was grandly received by the country folk. Some were landowners, of the class that had held his father in thrall. They served us milk in cut glass, cookies on their best china. On a sloping hillside, we found the ruins of the house where Earl was born; in the dump we found smashed pieces of heavy brown glazed pottery. Earl thought he remembered its pattern from childhood—yes, it was the remains of the kitchen stove. Each of us took a piece, and when Fran and I built the fireplace in our new camp at Smith Lake, I put the shard of pottery into its face.

We left the farming country and spent a glorious day on a boat on the Finnish inland waterway, sitting on the upper deck in the sun, drinking a bottle of gin with lemon and ice; that night we took a sauna at Aulunko, Sibelius's home. We toured a good deal of Finland. But I think what Earl enjoyed most was being invited—the son of a serf—to lunch with the American ambassador. Afterward, on our last night in Helsinki, looking out at the clear blue sky and the blue water of the harbor, Earl said, "This has been a wonderful trip. I'd never have come but for you." Surprised, I asked why not. "Because I didn't think there was anything here I'd care to see. Because I always associated Finland with hunger and want. And being unequal—that was driven into me in school. There was nobody I was equal to." He leaned back, smiling a little. "And now to see Finland so friendly, and the people supposed to be superior treating me as their equals—never in my wildest dreams. Don't you see?"

We went to the Soviet Union for a week—to Leningrad, where we visited the shrines of the Revolution, and then to Moscow. The hotels didn't work, and the police state atmosphere was oppressive—a couple of incidents convinced me we were under the surveillance of the secret police, perhaps because I had been a U.S. government official, perhaps because Earl was Finnish: A Russian girl accosted me on a Leningrad street and gave me her photograph and passport number and asked me to help her escape Russia to find her British boyfriend, and I threw the evidence into a potted plant and a little later returned to find it gone; and in Moscow after we had been in our hotel a few days, the bar we frequented suddenly

filled up with good-looking young Finnish girls, students, they said, and in the near-empty dining room the headwaiter seated us next to two of the pretty students and suggested we dance with them once then take them to bed. Trujillo had used such entrapments with visiting American congressmen. But aside from all that, I thought Moscow, with its sweeping streets and onion-shaped domes and yellow walls, exciting, and above all I thought the Russian people admirable—they had accomplished so much with so little; everything was so hard but they did it without complaint. One day, driving about the city with a young U.S. embassy officer, we ran low on gasoline, and our friend pulled into a filling station. It was out of gas; we would have to wait. Presently the tank truck arrived. The driver's helper got out and shoved a small triangular steel platform in front of one front wheel, the driver drove up onto it, and they unloaded gasoline not by pumping but by gravity. One has to be impressed by a people that puts up with such primitive devices and yet finds the resources to send men to the moon.

Earl went back to the States and I went to Italy, picking up a new Mercedes in Germany and stopping overnight in a small hotel in a small German town. There, after supper, I went for a walk but though it was still daylight the streets were deserted, everything closed. I went back to the little hotel. In its bar four or five middle-aged and elderly men were sitting at a table saying nothing, staring into the beers in front of them. The place was dead silent; you could hear the floor creak as the waitress crossed it. Of a sudden the door burst open and in bounded a strapping blond young man in jackboots and a leather jacket, a motorcycle rider. The men at the table looked up, smiled broadly, asked him for news, bade him sit down, and he straddled a chair and declaimed the news from the outside world. He electrified the room; he was life itself. I suddenly thought I understood at last how Adolf Hitler had come to power in Germany and how the Ku Klux Klan had come to power in Indiana— through the hearts of the men in the small towns who were downtrodden and defeated but above all bored.

To support the Stevenson biography, the Rockefeller Foundation had invited us to its Villa Serbelloni on Lake Como in Italy, a villa to which it invited scholars and men leaving high public office in

need of time for decompression. Fran and Fred had arrived a day or two earlier, bringing with them some seventeen footlockers of Stevenson research material. Presently Roxane Eberlein and her sister joined us and we dug in on the Stevenson book. Villa Serbelloni was a huge villa built on a hill overlooking Lake Como by Pliny, whether the elder or the younger I forget. Here we caught a glimpse of the elegant life that Adlai Stevenson had savored both as a young man and in his last years. We had an apartment in an ancient yellow monastery close to the lake. We went up the high hill to have lunch or dinner with the dozen other Fellows. Over us presided John Marshall and his wife, Catherine, an elegant couple who had become expert on the villa and on Italian wine and food, and behind each guest's chair stood a footman. At five o'clock Fran and Fred and I took a thermos of martinis down to the Roman bath at the edge of the lake below our monastery and sat in the bath watching the clouds roll in over the Alps beyond. We discovered that if we caught a minnow in a paper cup and poured a little martini onto him, he stiffened dead instantaneously. The foundation had allowed Fred to accompany us with misgivings—it had never had a child guest, and Fred was only fourteen that summer, they didn't know what he'd do with himself; but he soon allayed their misgivings by defeating John Marshall at chess and playing a piano duet with Otto Luening.

Dan was attending the Putney School in Vermont and that summer he went on a school trip through Scandinavia—they hiked across Lapland at the top of Europe and before the altar of an empty stave church sang, spontaneously and *a cappella,* a Bach chorale. This done, he came to Como, and we all went driving through Spain, and Spain was glorious—the Prado and Goya's blinding *Tres de Mayo,* the great hotels of Madrid and Seville, the awesome plain of La Mancha, a dusty white mountain town jammed with people come to see El Cordobés fight a bull (El Cordobés was a daring young man who looked remarkably like Bobby Kennedy), a picnic with Tad Szulc of *The New York Times* at the little bridge above Madrid where Hemingway had set the climax to *For Whom the Bell Tolls.* (During the Dominican intervention, Tad had written quite critically of President Johnson's policy and of me. Now we put our differences behind us.)

In September, Dan flew back to Putney from Rome, and some weeks later Fred flew to New York alone and went on up to New Hampshire to enroll himself at Exeter. (The Italian police insisted that in the case of a traveler so young they be given the name of someone who would meet him at New York, so we gave them the name of the manager of the Algonquin Hotel, and indeed as it turned out the head bellman at the Algonquin, Earl, a friend for many years, telephoned Exeter for Fred and saw to it that he made the right train and bus connections to New Hampshire.)

Fran and I and Roxane and her sister proposed to leave Italy on a Spanish freighter for the Dominican Republic to spend the winter working on the book in the beach house we'd bought at Sosúa. We were to sail on October 16. Six days before that two young vice-consuls from our embassy in Rome came to Serbelloni with a cable from John Crimmins, our new ambassador to the Dominican Republic, whose appointment I had recommended to President Johnson. Crimmins thought that, because of *Overtaken by Events,* my presence in the Republic now would be politically unsettling and against the interests of the United States. He apparently felt I was hated by both the Dominican right and left; it might not even be safe for me personally. I disagreed with all this and protested by cable to Secretary Rusk. Rusk replied supporting Crimmins. There was, of course, no way the Department could have prevented me from going; on the other hand, one does not like to go somewhere if one's government thinks it against the national interest. I agreed to get off the boat before it reached the Dominican Republic. Aboard a rusty Spanish freighter, the *Ruiseñada,* the voyage took a month. There were ten passengers aboard, counting us four. One was an aging Dominican who, when the Trujillo government fell, had been given his choice of going to prison, where he might find a firing squad, or going abroad as a Dominican consul in Italy. He had found the choice easy. One night I sat up late talking with the ship's first mate, a Spaniard born the year Franco took power and educated in Franco's schools; he was convinced that the United States was at war in Vietnam only because of the influence of "the Jewish bankers." He soon dropped out of our nightly poker game (played in Spanish) when the Dominican consul denounced him, not because of his politics but because he insisted on dealing cards three at

a time. At about that point in our voyage, flying fish appeared, for we were crossing the Tropic of Cancer into the third of the world between it and the Tropic of Capricorn; and I dragged a chair to the tiny deck outside our cabin and sat in the sun, holding a clipboard full of Stevenson manuscript and watching the flying fish above the turquoise sea. Our course approximated Columbus's, Roxane informed us after research, and our food was the same greasy chickpea and fish soup served to Columbus's sailors. By now, Roxane had become a member of our family. I was beginning to think about politics again, had written to Bobby Kennedy from Como saying I suspected President Johnson might not be reelectable and suggesting Bobby line up second-choice convention delegates for next year, 1968, for himself. Yet the thought of his running made me uneasy, I had vague stirrings of the fear he might be assassinated.

7.

Every June during these years at eastern universities, Fran and the boys and I went to the Upper Peninsula of Michigan and stayed till Labor Day. Though we didn't think of it this way, we were pioneering—we had bought our remote new land far out in the woods at Smith Lake in 1964 and that summer we set out to explore it. Starting from the logging town of L'Anse on Lake Superior in our Jeep, on one of those great Michigan days, puffs of clouds sailing across a deep blue sky, we needed an hour and a half to drive by logging road to within a mile of Smith Lake, and it took us the rest of the day to carry our tents and boat and outfit the last mile through the woods. We climbed the steep hill to the high granite cliff that I had shown Fran years earlier, rising 60 feet above the lake, covered with a grove of majestic hemlocks. No brush here— only cool shade and a forest floor of leaves and needles. Below the cliff, from water's edge on a narrow bench of land, rose enormous white pines, so tall they soared above the tops of the cliff-borne hemlocks—they must be at least 150 feet tall, and they grow there yet. A beautiful campsite. Here we would build our camp. From here we crossed the bay and found a sand beach. The shores of most lakes hereabouts were either rock or bog; our sand beach was a rarity. Not far from the water's edge, hidden in balsam, stood the ruin of a trapper's shack, the roof gone, the log walls sagging, ferns

growing through the rotted floor. This, we decided, we would rebuild into a temporary camp. We pitched our tents at the beach beneath two ancient white pines, and it was past dark when we cooked our dinner. The mosquitoes were not too bad, and we sat awhile on logs in front of the tents, watching the fire die and the stars wheel up. In Chicago, you can scarcely see the stars at all. Here at Smith Lake, the Milky Way looks like a white river, and every star is blazing, and we watched man's satellites slowly tracking across the firmament. In the pale afterglow before dark, we heard a mad laughing cry, a loon, no, a pair of loons. So we had loons on our new lake. And after we went to bed in our tents and the fire died, we heard coyotes barking up on our cliff campsite. So we had coyotes too. And a few nights later we heard the commanding howl of a timber wolf.

We stayed several days, mapping our lake and land. Smith Lake lies about 47 degrees north latitude, as does Quebec (and Ulan Bator). The primeval forest in the Upper Peninsula had been white pine; loggers had long ago cut nearly all of it, but Smith Lake was still ringed with it. Smith Lake was shaped like a lopsided hourglass. It was divided into two unequal parts, the west part, ours, much the larger and deeper, the two parts joined by a narrows near the sand beach. On some old maps it is called Cliff Lake, and I like to think that the name got changed when some political hack in the courthouse, drawing a map, called to another, "What's this lake, hey?" and his colleague replied, "Cliff Lake," but the draftsman misunderstood him to say, "Smith Lake."

Fishing, we caught nothing but chub and stunted sunfish and perch. One day fishing, we came upon a deer swimming the narrows; we stayed away so as not to disturb him. Game trails were everywhere. On another day I brought out Earl Numinen, the highway engineer, and he and I laid out a route for a mile of road to our clifftop campsite, climbing steep rock ridges, skirting deep tag alder and cedar swamps. We did not want a good road passable by passenger cars—that would encourage curious visitors, and one reason we had come to Smith Lake was to be alone. What we wanted was a Jeep road. On Earl's advice, I went to Herman, a dying Finnish farm hamlet of about eighty people twelve and a half miles from Smith Lake, where the paved road from outside ends, and talked to

Charley Dantes, an elderly man and a remarkable one, well read, once the sheriff, now town leader, Democrat, and when he discovered I had been a friend of Adlai Stevenson, he could not do enough to help us. His son Charley ran a little sawmill at Herman, and at his father's behest he bulldozed our Jeep road to our new campsite.

Originally we had intended to build only a one-room shack at Smith Lake that we could use on weekends, continuing to spend most of the summer at Three Lakes. But Fran had come to dislike Three Lakes, too filled with tourists, and she too had fallen in love with Smith Lake—she wanted to try to live there instead. I told her how hard it would be—hard to build and make comfortable, hard to get to. Equipment, indeed every board and every nail, would have to be carried in by Jeep and by hand. And it would be hard to persuade workmen to come all the way out here. More, it would be lonely living here, with no neighbors for many miles. She wanted to try anyway. We were, however, unwilling to put up with an outhouse and a hand pump. We had started out that way twenty-five years ago at Three Lakes and now we were, as a Hollywood director confronted with Marilyn Monroe's idiosyncrasies told her, "Miss Monroe, I am too old, too rich, and too famous to put up with your temperament." So we decided to try to install conveniences at Smith Lake. But how? There was, of course, no electricity closer than Herman. Instead, we would use bottled gas—propane—for our basic source of power. We would install a thousand-gallon tank (if a truck could bring it in over our terrible Jeep road). We would use gas to cook with, to run a refrigerator, to run a hot-water heater, to light the camp, and, most importantly, to run a generator that in turn would make enough electricity to run an electric water pump—and thus we would have running water in the kitchen and bathroom. This also meant, of course, digging deep enough in this rocky earth to install a septic tank and a drain field. And so on—the project became increasingly formidable. As I made sketches, the camp grew to thirty by thirty feet. It would be built entirely of logs. It would be divided into three main rooms—a big living room, a kitchen, and a bedroom (plus bathroom). There would be an enormous fireplace, or rather three fireplaces, one in each room, with the three separate flues all enclosed in a common chimney, the whole built of some fifty tons of native rock. We would perch the camp amid the hemlock at the very edge of the high cliff overlooking the lake.

The project took four years. Initially Dan and Fred and I, living in tents, rebuilt the crude little one-room trapper's shack at the sand beach ourselves. Then two Finnish log carpenters used it as a temporary camp—lived in it while they built the big camp up on the cliff, built it slowly, painfully, log by chipped and fitted log, a beauty. Dan and Fred and I worked with them, summer-long work. We learned a good deal about carpentry and plumbing, building Smith Lake. Not until 1968 were Fran and I able to use the big camp, and work on its interior and its outbuildings continued for several years. But we succeeded.

It was during these years when we were building at Smith Lake that Dan and Fred passed through that unnoticed transition from the time when I took care of them to the time when they took care of me. It is a subtle shift we all go through. The first year at Smith Lake, they performed only assigned chores—washed dishes, hauled water, made kindling, did what I told them on rebuilding the trapper's shack. In a few years, they were taking initiatives—had learned what needed doing and did it, without being told. It became they who staked out the tent, who rowed the boat, who made the campfire. By the time we had finished building at Smith Lake, they were not only doing the heavy work but were participating in important decisions, such as where to fish on a given day. I do not know precisely at what moment it happened. I only know that one day when we got out of the Jeep at a remote lake in the woods, it was Dan who, without a word shouldered the boat I had carried for so many years, and it was Fred who picked up the pack and oars and tackle box, saying only, "Can you bring the rods, Dad?" I was grateful but never felt older.

8.

Robert F. Kennedy's Indiana primary campaign for the 1968 Democratic presidential nomination was in many ways the climactic event of my life, bringing together writing, politics, and Indiana. Yet it rather sneaked up on me.

We began the year in a rented house in Princeton where I was writing the Stevenson rough draft and commuting once a week to New York to teach my seminar at City University. (After it, I usually went to dinner at the Century Association. I had been admitted to the Century while at Wesleyan and ever since have found

it one of the most agreeable places on earth, an ornament of American civilization, as, I believe, Dick Rovere once called it). A search committee looking for a new president of a small college in Illinois approached me; people from Gulf and Western, the conglomerate, told me they were buying the big La Romana sugar plantations in the Dominican Republic and asked me to become their consultant; nothing came of either. (I told the Gulf and Western executives they could either run the plantations the way the former American owner had—authoritarian, colonialist, squeezing out fast every dime of profits even though their cane-cutters were sullen and hostile—or they could plough some of their profits back into workers' schools and housing and look forward to a long future. That ended my consultation.)

All during this period, the presidential politics of 1968 had been moving to the fore. At the end of November, Senator Eugene McCarthy of Minnesota, an opponent of the war in Vietnam, had announced his candidacy against President Johnson in the Democratic primaries in New Hampshire and other states. At the end of January and early February, the North Vietnamese launched the massive Tet offensive. Many people had been urging Bobby Kennedy to announce his own candidacy—as I've said, I myself from Lake Como had suggested the preceding fall that he start rounding up convention delegates. But he had hung back for fear that people would think he was opposing Johnson's reelection not on principle but out of personal animosity.

Bobby Kennedy and Lyndon Johnson had long disliked each other. Even before President Kennedy's assassination, Vice-President Johnson felt that Bobby had usurped his rightful place as number two man in the government. President Johnson believed Bobby had tried in 1960 to deny him the vice-presidential nomination. Bobby considered Lyndon Johnson a liar—"He lies even when he doesn't have to lie," he told me. While I was interviewing Bobby for the oral history project after President Kennedy's assassination, he said, "Four or five matters arose during the period of November 22 [when President Kennedy was killed] and November 27 . . . which made me bitterer, unhappy at least, with Lyndon Johnson." He seemed bothered by the clumsy handling of matters aboard Air Force One as it returned from Dallas and by how rapidly and un-

feelingly Lyndon Johnson had moved into the president's office. Bobby went there the day after the assassination—"I wanted to make sure the desk was gotten out of there, and I wanted to make sure all his papers were out." The desk especially seemed to upset him. Johnson had told him at that time, "I need you more than the president needed you." Bobby resented it. In another oral history interview, he told William Manchester, "I said I don't want to discuss it and . . . that it was going to take us a period of time to move out of here, and I think, maybe, can't you wait?" But Johnson said that Secretary Rusk and Secretary McNamara had told him he must move in at once. Soon President Johnson was denouncing Bobby openly to the White House staff, including some who had been closest to the Kennedys. As the presidential politics of 1964 had begun, Bobby had been proposed for vice-president. He told me that spring that the last thing President Johnson wanted was Bobby as vice-president. "I think he's hysterical about how he's going to try to avoid having me." Bobby said that Johnson wanted an "all-American" party, not the Democratic party, and, Bobby said, businessmen and everybody else who had opposed President Kennedy loved it—but he himself didn't like it. I wanted Bobby to become vice-president and suggested that Bobby, with his own constituency, would be different from other vice-presidents. He replied, "I don't think you can have any influence. Lyndon Johnson didn't have any influence." He said Johnson was doing nothing for the Alliance for Progress and not paying proper attention to Panama and Brazil; if Bobby were in the Senate, he could do something about it, but not as vice-president. His running for senator from New York was also being discussed that spring. I said there were a hundred senators. He said, "Yeah, but I'm not just a senator. I'm senator from New York and I'm head of the Kennedy wing of the Democratic party." Finally as the convention neared, President Johnson announced that he would not consider for the vice-presidency any cabinet member or anybody who met regularly with the cabinet. This excluded both Bobby Kennedy and Adlai Stevenson. Bobby told the press, "I am sorry that I had to take so many nice fellows down with me," and soon announced his own candidacy for senator from New York; that fall he was elected.

All this, then, was the background of the Bobby Kennedy-

Lyndon Johnson relationship four years later as the 1968 presidential primaries began. In the New Hampshire primary on March 12, Senator Eugene McCarthy did not win but his supporters justifiably claimed a "moral victory," since his "children's crusade" against the Vietnam War—he had mobilized students at New England colleges and boarding schools—got him 42 percent of the vote to President Johnson's 49 percent. The day New Hampshire voted, Bobby Kennedy called me in Princeton and said he was going to announce his own candidacy on Saturday, asked me to give him a draft of an announcement statement, and said he hoped I could help him in other ways. I drafted the statement and telephoned it to his secretary, Angie Novello, and on March 16 he announced his candidacy for president in the Senate caucus room where he had held the Hoffa hearings so long ago.

Often during the next two weeks I saw Arthur and others interested in Bobby's campaign. Ted Sorensen, who was Bobby's campaign director in Washington, called several times—Bobby was going into the Indiana primary, and he and Ted Sorensen knew I was from Indiana. Such friends from Illinois as Marshall Holleb and Newt Minow called me, asking what they could do to help. I wrote a speech for Bobby for Indiana and one on foreign policy. His announcement generated tremendous excitement, and everywhere he went he attracted huge crowds, especially on college campuses, where students mobbed him, trying to get close enough to touch him. He was the most exciting candidate since his brother had run in 1960. On March 31, President Johnson on national TV stunned the country by announcing he himself would not be a candidate for reelection. He also announced a suspension—later modified to a limitation—of the bombing of North Vietnam. Thus Bobby had lost two of his best issues—the unpopular president and the unpopular war. Three days later, on Wednesday, April 3, at the University in New York as I came out of my seminar, Ted Sorensen called and said Bobby wondered if I could go out to Indiana with him tomorrow. I said yes, went to the Century, called Roxane in Princeton and asked her to pack a briefcase and suitcase and bring them to the Algonquin, got a room at the Algonquin, and early next morning met Bobby and his wife, Ethel, at Washington National Airport.

We had a chartered Electra, a prop-jet plane, crowded with about

forty-three press and twenty staff. Bobby's writers aboard were Adam Walinsky and Jeff Greenfield. Walinsky was young, a little abrasive, sure he was right, reminding me of the early Dick Goodwin. Jeff Greenfield, Arthur had told me, was "about eleven years old" (actually, I think twenty-four); he was blond, bright, friendlier than Walinsky. Neither wanted me around, which was natural, of course—permanent staff people are always possessive of a candidate. They had a guitar and played and sang what were, I think, war protest songs. Bobby sometimes said in annoyance, "Where are my writers? Playing the guitar, I suppose." Frank Mankiewicz was aboard as press secretary. Fred Dutton was always at Bobby's side.

Bobby looked fine and relaxed. He was wearing, as usual, a gray plaid suit. He always looked slight, slender, even thin, with a wry grin. But he no longer looked boyish. His hair was turning gray, his face deeply lined. He had aged a great deal since his brother's murder five years ago. He aged even more as this spring campaign wore on. On the plane going to Indiana he came and sat beside me and asked, "Do you think it can be done?" I said I did. He told me about writing speeches for him—said they couldn't be Stevensonian, had to be simpler. He wanted to talk about improving the quality of American life. He suggested I travel the whistle-stops with him for a few days and listen, "to get the rhythm." He wanted me to stay with him on this trip, which included Indiana, Ohio, Louisiana, West Virginia, Kentucky, Michigan, Alaska, and South Dakota. We'd be gone a week. He wanted me to do a foreign policy speech for Thursday for Louisiana State University, a serious substantive speech "for once." He said Walinsky was good but "he's more radical than I am." I proposed a speech about the creative foreign policy of President Truman, rigidity under Eisenhower-Nixon-Dulles, new flexibility and hope under President Kennedy, Johnson's return to Dulles-Nixon rigidity, the need for flexibility now. He said this was fine. I showed him a draft I'd sent him earlier saying the question was whether we would have one nation or two or none. He said he'd liked it and used it but hadn't known where it came from. He especially liked three or four sentences in it, one quoting Adlai Stevenson as saying that self-criticism is the secret weapon of democracy; he now asked me to give those lines to Jeff and have him put them

into his speech for today, which was being put on the speech type-writer in the front of the plane. I didn't yet know who Jeff Green-field was so gave it to Walinsky. He couldn't believe Bobby wanted to quote Stevenson and refused to put it in. After the speech Bobby was angry because Walinsky and Greenfield had cut part of his speech without telling him. This campaign promised to be like others I'd been through.

First stop: South Bend, Indiana—a crowd of kids at the airport mobbed him, and he gave his standard speech from the airplane ramp, asking, "Will you give me your hand?" and "Will you ring doorbells?" and "Will you give me your help in this election?" and "If you do, I think we can turn this country around." We motor-caded through the Negro district, kids running alongside his car, to Notre Dame and a packed indoor college crowd, a hot crowd. His jokes were good, he used little of his prepared text, gave them an ad-libbed whistlestop speech, while I made notes on applause break-ins. In the question period after the speech, a student asked what he thought of the draft law. "Unjust and inequitable," he de-clared, to great applause. Then, "And I'll tell you why—we should abolish college deferments." Loud boos, and he waved his arms and cried, "Let me explain," and argued his case that college deferments discriminated against those who could not afford college, and in the end they cheered him. He was nearly always at his best when trying to convince people who disagreed with him.

He left South Bend in a small plane to make another college stop, this one at Muncie. I went with most of the staff in the Electra to In-dianapolis. At the Marott Hotel up on North Meridian Street, I went to Walinsky and Greenfield and proposed dinner. I had learned that in a campaign you always eat and sleep at every oppor-tunity, since opportunities are few. But Walinsky wanted to talk first, and I outlined the foreign policy speech I'd suggested to Bobby, and Walinsky argued against it, saying it was unfair to Presi-dent Johnson and, moreover, he didn't think our foreign policy had been good under President Truman and President Kennedy. A sec-retary came in with a report that Martin Luther King had just been shot. I said we'd better go down to dinner because if it was true we might not get another chance to eat, and we went down to eat and continued our argument—Walinsky was against foreign aid, he thought President Truman and President Kennedy by their loose

promises to defend freedom everywhere had got us into the mess we were in now in Vietnam. He was a revisionist and apparently believed that we had started the cold war and that our containment policy was an aggressive act. Some years later, I've been told, Walinsky, like George Leighton of old and others, switched 180 degrees from Democratic liberalism and in 1982, in Ronald Reagan's time, became an important member of the staff of the right-wing Republican, Lew Lehrman, who ran against Mario Cuomo for governor of New York.

Walinsky got a call—Martin Luther King was dead, murdered. Bobby was due to land in Indianapolis at about this time. I said we had to make sure he knew King was dead. He had been scheduled to go to the opening of his Indiana headquarters, then to an outdoor Negro rally. I thought he ought to skip the first and go to the second, announce King was dead, ask them to pray, and then ask them to go home. In a squad car at the curb, I found an Indianapolis police inspector and asked if Bobby should appear at the Negro rally. He said, with a fervor I imagine was rare in him, "I sure hope he does. If he doesn't, there'll be hell to pay. He's the only one can do it." Reports were coming in that Negroes across the country were in revolt. He feared they would riot here. I suggested he call headquarters. He did—Bobby was on his way to the Negro rally. The inspector said he'd go there. Walinsky went with him to be sure Bobby knew. Greenfield and I went to our rooms to draft a statement on King's death for Bobby.

When Bobby and the others came to the hotel, we gathered in his rooms, and Fred Dutton told us what Bobby had said at the Negro rally, and it was so good we threw our drafts away. He had spoken extemporaneously, a short speech, little more than a few words really, eloquent, quoting Aeschylus (something he had learned at a Hickory Hill seminar):

> *In our sleep, pain which cannot*
> *forget falls drop by drop upon the*
> *heart until, in our own despair,*
> *against our will, comes wisdom*
> *through the awful grace of God . . .*

and going on: ". . . to tame the savageness of man and to make gentle the life of this world. Let us . . . say a prayer for our country and

for our people." The Negroes did not riot in Indianapolis. They rioted, however, nearly everywhere else.

Bobby put in a call for Mrs. King, to offer his airplane to go to Memphis to get the body. When the call came in, he asked, "What should I say to her?" Since no one else answered, I said, "Just tell her how you feel. It has to come from you."

While he was talking, we had the television set on. It was showing film clips of King's speeches. Watching, I realized I didn't care about King as much as the young writers. I'd done all my weeping in 1963, when President Kennedy was killed. But now Walinsky and Greenfield were extremely upset, convinced that "some cop" had shot him. The big civil rights march in Washington in 1963, when King had made his "I have a dream" speech at the Lincoln Memorial, had been a high point of their lives. Not of mine. Watching the film clips, I thought King a demagogue, as I always had, and I also remembered that he had not always been worthy of trust, as when he had met privately with Mayor Daley and they had agreed to say nothing publicly about their talk but King, almost immediately on leaving the mayor's office, had told the press everything they'd said.

Bobby came back and we discussed the rest of the schedule. I favored canceling everything till after the funeral. Dutton was reluctant. He thought this would blow over, it wasn't all that big, people forget, life goes on, let's not get excited and cancel everything; and Bobby said, "There are a lot of people who just don't care." He said it flatly, without emotion. I felt the same way, though still favored canceling. The kids thought King's murder would tear the country apart. It turned out they were closer to right than the rest of us. In the end we canceled the rest of the trip except for Cleveland and next day went back to Washington. As our plane came in low we could see smoke rising: Washington was burning. Before our eyes, the American civil rights movement was turning into the Negro revolution. On the ground Bobby and several of us stayed aboard because he wanted to go into the streets of Washington to try to quiet the crowds—"I think I can do something with these people." I told him he couldn't if they were rioting in the streets. Fred Dutton said he couldn't go into the streets without checking with the mayor. I suggested we get more facts and call the mayor. Several went to do it. I argued that going into the streets would look like grandstanding. Reluctantly he went home.

I spent Saturday and Sunday in Washington writing two speeches and went to a meeting at Hickory Hill that lasted from 4 to 10 P.M.—with Bobby, Ted Sorensen, Fred Dutton, Dick Goodwin; two television producers I knew, Charles Guggenheim, from earlier campaigns, and John Frankenheimer, from *Playhouse 90* at CBS; plus people from an advertising agency. The advertising people did most of the talking, much of what they said made little sense, the meeting dragged on, Bobby became impatient, an advertising time buyer said he had "people" out in Indiana, and Bobby, exasperated, said he didn't want those faceless people out there, he wanted *him.* I said everybody should go to Indiana. He agreed. In such a meeting, Bobby would sit and listen for a long time and watch each person who spoke, saying nothing himself, and it was impossible to tell what he thought of what was being said, though usually he looked skeptical or worse, then he would decide. He ran a meeting hard.

The advertising and TV people left, and Bobby, Sorensen, Dutton, Goodwin, and I talked speeches. I gave him my two drafts. They seemed suitable. Bobby said he must start giving substantive speeches, not just motorcading wildly with huge crowds—"I've got to stop looking like Frank Sinatra running for president." I warned against his becoming the candidate of only students and Negroes. He agreed—he had the Negroes in Gary, now he wanted to do something in the Polish backlash suburbs of Gary.

Everybody believed that, of all the primaries, Indiana was the big one—it was the first contest between him and McCarthy and, moreover, everybody in the press was saying it was the big one. Bobby said, "Indiana is the ballgame. This is my West Virginia." In 1960 West Virginia had been the critical primary for his brother in his contest with Hubert Humphrey. He wanted to say this in his speeches. I opposed it. The Indiana primary this year was a three-way race among him, McCarthy, and Indiana's incumbent governor, Roger Branigin. Branigin had a machine that took 2 percent off the state employees' payroll; he had the dominant Pulliam papers in Indianapolis; he was widely considered Johnson's stand-in for Vice-President Humphrey. I thought Branigin might very well win the primary (I didn't say so but at that time thought Bobby's best chance was to come in second, behind Branigin but ahead of McCarthy), and for Bobby to say "Indiana is my West Virginia" risked too much on a doubtful state. Bobby demurred—the press

would say it anyway. He argued that the people of Indiana should be reminded that his brother had never forgotten that West Virginia helped him mightily, and after he became president he gave West Virginia all kinds of preferments. I said he could say this privately to politicians but not publicly. Ted Sorensen thought Bobby should say that Indiana can pick a president. I liked this—Indiana's presidential primary had never before been important. He began saying in almost every speech, "Indiana can help choose a president."

Bobby wanted me to go to Indiana and do the same thing for him that I'd done for his brother in California in 1960—editorial advance. I went, for the duration. Soon Fran joined me—she and Marian Schlesinger went to college campuses to speak on Bobby's behalf to little groups of faculty wives whose husbands were bemused by McCarthy. En route to Indianapolis, I stopped over in Chicago to have lunch with Adlai Stevenson III. He was by then state treasurer of Illinois and had been considered for senator or governor but the machine had refused to slate him. I had tried to persuade Adlai not to come out for McCarthy; now I found him leaning toward Hubert Humphrey, who seemed about to announce. He said Daley had called him in recently, told him he himself would stay neutral right down to the convention, and said he didn't see how anybody (meaning Adlai) could do otherwise. Adlai, however, told me he wanted to endorse somebody before Daley did in order to establish a leadership position for himself. But he promised not to endorse anybody before talking to me. In coming weeks, I kept in touch with him but he was independent and soon he did come out for Humphrey—and he did it without telling me in advance, which I didn't like.

In Indianapolis, Fran and I lived with my mother and Aunt Verl in the house on Kessler Boulevard. I worked in the Kennedy headquarters in a loft upstairs over the old Indiana Theater downtown, surely one of the dreariest places in dreary Indianapolis. Milton Gwirtzman and P. J. Mode, two Kennedy staff writers, and Joe Dolan, the scheduler, and I were able to bring together scheduling and editorial advance, able to shape the campaign. Everybody thought the name Bobby unbecoming to a candidate for president, though that was what we had always called him, and they began calling him Robert. This was too much for me; I called him Bob.

I thought that so far in Indiana, Bob had gone to too many universities and had had too many mob scenes with youngsters screaming and tearing his clothes off. For Indiana, this was wrong. I
thought that the ordinary Hoosier at home watching TV was sick of
scenes of violence in Vietnam, of Negroes rioting in the cities after
King was killed, of kids pulling Kennedy's clothes off. Eugene
McCarthy, on the other hand, was running a low-keyed soft-spoken
campaign, which might be effective by contrast with Bob's.
McCarthy was a single-issue candidate—Vietnam—and his main
appeal was to students. Bob should be broader-based both as to
issues and as to constituency—Johnson had partly neutralized Vietnam for the time being, the Negro revolution was suddenly in full
swing, and Bob ought not to compete with McCarthy for students
but should also appeal to blue-collar factory workers and many
others. So far, Bob was too exciting. The people, I thought, did not
want to be excited. This year, 1968, resembled 1952, the year of Stevenson's first campaign, more than 1960, the year Jack Kennedy
had won. In 1952 the people had been weary after twenty years of
New Deal and two wars; they had turned to Eisenhower for change
and calm. In 1960, after eight years of Eisenhower's do-nothingism,
they had been willing to follow a new exciting young leader, Jack
Kennedy. Not in 1968—once more they wanted change, change
from Vietnam and from riots, but change and calm, not a summons
to great adventures. So far, I thought, Bob's campaign had had too
much razzle-dazzle. The razzle-dazzle had been necessary after New
Hampshire, to catch up with McCarthy. But now it was time to cool
it, to reassure people, and once in a while make a substantive
speech. One way to get away from razzle-dazzle was to identify with
Indiana's past greatness by paying quiet visits to the shrines of its
heroes, people like Abraham Lincoln and James Whitcomb Riley.
Another was to evoke Hoosier nostalgia, and I wanted a railroad
whistle-stop trip, and at P. J. Mode's suggestion we picked a train
called the *Wabash Cannonball,* a traditional train on the old Wabash railroad recently discontinued. And I wanted to get Bob into
some of the red-neck backlash factory cities. All this, of course,
meant changing the schedule radically.

Bob was campaigning in other states, coming in and out of Indiana for a day or two. I spent several days promoting these ideas with

Senator Ted Kennedy, Dick Goodwin, Larry O'Brien (who had left the Johnson cabinet to join Bob), and others, working with Joe Dolan to schedule the events I wanted, doing research and editorial advance on the new stops, and writing a memo to Bob on our plans. We worked out a quiet history day in southern Indiana for next Monday, April 22, Bob's next visit to Indiana—the George Rogers Clark and William Henry Harrison memorials at Vincennes, then through several small towns following the Lincoln family's trail through Indiana, then a visit to the grave of Lincoln's mother, Nancy Hanks, in Spencer County down near the Ohio River, actually the Lincoln trip I'd made with Fran and Cindy in 1952 for the *Post*. For Tuesday we scheduled a string of stops in backlash factory cities to the north—Elwood, Marion, Kokomo, and others—and a ride on the *Wabash Cannonball* through northern cities ending with an evening speech at Fort Wayne. I had known every one of those places for many years. By Sunday afternoon we had finished the schedule and the briefing sheets for each stop and I took them to Washington and gave them to Bob at Hickory Hill.

The house filled up—Ted Sorensen, Fred Dutton, Dick Goodwin, George Stevens, others At dinner Bob read my memo about Indiana and I told him about his Monday-Tuesday schedule. He thought he'd be wasting a lot of time at historical markers on Monday and he balked when I suggested he take a couple of his children along on that trip. With Fred Dutton's help, I persuaded him that every Hoosier takes his wife and kids to visit the Lincoln shrines. He did not like Tuesday at all. I explained that the white backlash vote in such factory cities as Kokomo differed from that of the Poles around Gary—it consisted of workers who had come to Indiana from Kentucky and Tennessee to work in war industry and stayed on, red-necks and Klansmen. "Why am I going there then?" he asked. I said, "Because there are a lot of Democratic votes there and you've got to convince them." He asked how. I told him he should change his pitch—should speak strongly against rioting and violence, using his experience as attorney general, but he should not omit a plea too for justice—should say that violence and rioting cannot be tolerated; neither can racial injustice in the big cities be tolerated (big cities far away). Milt Gwirtzman had suggested that he refer to himself as "the former chief law-enforcement officer of

the United States" rather than as "former attorney general." Bob nodded, saying, "I can go pretty far in that direction. That doesn't bother me." I also urged him to praise private enterprise in speeches to Rotary clubs; he said he didn't mind and started talking about his Bedford-Stuyvesant project in New York City. As we talked, he seemed to come around to accepting my advice. Dinner finished, he slumped down on a sofa and started reading a speech I'd written for his historical day. He stopped at the first sentence, snorted, read it aloud to everybody, and asked, "What the hell does that mean?" I said it meant just what it said. He went on reading. He didn't like it. We'd already released it to the press—that was unusual but we'd done it because Milt Gwirtzman wanted to mail it out to small papers all over Indiana. He didn't like that either, wanted every statement cleared by Dutton and himself. (It did, however, get widely published.)

He started looking through my briefing sheets, one for each stop he'd make. He read aloud, "Setting," mockingly. He had a wry mocking humor, almost bitter. Nobody said anything. He read on and got interested, he read straight through the Monday historical book without comment. After that the meeting turned back to television, and I went home to the Hay-Adams.

Next morning we flew to Vincennes. I was somewhat surprised to see two or three of his children aboard the plane. At Vincennes, when Bob and his family went into the historic church, his dog Freckles was ahead of him to the altar. Fred Dutton picked him up and handed him to me and we got him out, and Fred or Dick Tuck told a reporter, "This may look like a dog to you but it looks like an embassy to me." Bob walked around several historic shrines in Vincennes, Fred Dutton close by him and I a few feet away, and once or twice Bob said to me, "This is nice," or "It's good, isn't it?" He spoke at lunch to businessmen on private enterprise. Then we motorcaded through a string of little southern Indiana towns like Oolitic, the country my father and I used to hunt rabbits in. I rode in Bob's convertible, he and I and Ethel and the kids and the dog and Dick Goodwin all scrambled together, Fred Dutton lying on the trunk and hanging on for dear life as the motorcade drove fast across the countryside, a police car ahead, the photographers' car behind, then a couple of cars with local politicians and Bob's body-

guard, Bill Barry, then two press buses. At each town the motorcade would stop in the main street and Bob, who had risen to the tonneau of the convertible as we approached town, would climb out onto the trunk and speak. Previously he had been using a bullhorn; I objected that the bullhorn had become a symbol of southern sheriffs during the civil right troubles and of Lyndon Johnson, and a small microphone was substituted. I would hand him the microphone; when he finished he would toss it to me. While he spoke I kept a hand out so he could grab it if the crowds pulled him off the trunk. (Once they did, and when he fell on his face on the street he broke a tooth.) Though the towns were small, the crowds were big. They screamed and tore at him. They were savage. Once or twice we stopped to make a courthouse steps speech, and I had to help get the Kennedy children through the crowds, a bruising business—Fred Dutton, Bill Barry, and I did the blocking. The crowds delayed us, and as I had feared we got to Lincoln's mother's grave too late to have enough light for television. But Bob seemed to enjoy it, the place was quiet, and as he walked around he said to me, "It's a nice place, isn't it?"

Next day we motorcaded all morning through the north-central factory towns. At the courthouse stops I hung around the edge of the crowds. Indiana people just stand there, hands in pockets, listening, as though to say, "Go on—I dare you to make me clap." Bob followed the line I'd given him. When he emphasized that violence could not be tolerated, he got big applause; when he went on to say injustice could not be tolerated either, everybody was entitled to jobs and schools, they didn't applaud but they didn't mind—they'd heard what they wanted to hear, that he was against violence in the streets, and that was enough. It worked.

That afternoon we boarded the *Wabash Cannonball* and whistle-stopped from Logansport to Fort Wayne, and it was terrific—a hillbilly guitar band aboard playing an old song called "The Wabash Cannonball" and a Kennedy song Ted Sorensen had written to the tune of "This Land Is Your Land," big friendly crowds, good back-platform speeches pitched at each town, great TV, and a mood aboard the train among press and staff that was happy. After each stop Bob would sit down beside Fred Dutton or me, bend his head forward a little, and look up from beneath the lock of hair, a quizzi-

cal mocking smile on his face. The *Cannonball* made good network evening news. As we rode, Milt Gwirtzman gave me the evening speech for Fort Wayne and said Bob wanted me to touch it up and give it some class. I put in a quotation from Pericles and sharpened some of the applause lines.

He delivered it in a college gym to a friendly audience of towns-folk. He came upon the Pericles passage unexpectedly and stumbled through it—it *was* hard to read—and while he was stumbling a baby started to cry in the audience. Its parents tried to hush it but couldn't. Bob involuntarily looked at it in annoyance, and then went back to his speech, and its parents took it out. He turned toward them and put out his arms and pleaded, "Please don't leave," then turned back to the crowd and made a face, then back to the parents with another plea, then to the audience, "You see how ruthless I am—I've just thrown a baby out of the hall." Often during the campaign he kidded himself about being ruthless, as he had at the end of his 1964 campaign for senator when he said, "I'm glad this campaign is almost over, because then I can go back to being ruthless." He just about killed the ruthlessness issue in the 1968 spring primaries. After his formal speech on education at Fort Wayne, which he plowed through and which was listened to quietly, he took questions on all subjects for at least a half hour, and he was at his very best. He finally announced he would take only one more question, and did, and the crowd stood and clapped, thinking it was all over, as did I; but Bob hesitated, then motioned for silence, then said quietly, "Camus once said there will always be suffering children in this world but perhaps we can make it a little less suffering and if you and I don't help them, who will?" Then he added very quietly, "Help us," amid dead silence and walked off. It was, like Stevenson's welcoming speech to the 1952 convention, one of the most moving political moments of my life.

Later, looking back, I thought those two days, the history day on Monday and the factory towns and the *Cannonball* on Tuesday, were the days when Bob Kennedy turned the corner in Indiana (though perhaps I'm biased). Before then, his campaign had not been in tune with the Indiana voters. On those days, it was—he felt at home with them, and they with him. He knew it, and so did

the newspapermen. His brother Ted and Larry O'Brien thought we were doing it just right. Bob told me the briefing sheets were a life-saver. Fred Dutton did too—they gave Bob a sense of security coming before a strange audience.

Not everybody was pleased with the new Bob Kennedy. Bob himself had misgivings—once he asked plaintively when he could have a liberal day. Fred Dutton and I told him we would get him a labor audience for that purpose but he'd have to remember they were red-necks and nigger haters as well as workingmen. Once he asked why he had ever entered the Indiana primary in the first place. I said nothing but the fact is that had I been consulted I would have advised him against it—Indiana is just not Kennedy country. Once when I wrote something conservative, Fred Dutton vetoed it, laughing, saying, "I understand what you're trying to do, turn him around, and that's okay, but don't turn him around too fast." *The New York Times* said that Dick Goodwin and I had turned Kennedy around and made his speeches sound like old George Romney speeches on free enterprise. (Dick Goodwin was innocent; I did it.) Arthur Schlesinger called me from New York and asked what the hell we were up to, and I told him, and he said, "Well, maybe, but it makes very curious reading in the East." No doubt it did, But Bob Kennedy couldn't have won in Indiana by making speeches that pleased eastern liberals (which Arthur understood better than many). Adam Walinsky and Jeff Greenfield were hurt—they, especially Walinsky, thought they had turned Bob into a liberal and now I was turning him back into a conservative. They conceived all this as a struggle for the soul of Bob Kennedy. I conceived of it as an effort to win the Indiana election. They were quite funny about it. One night I found them making up limericks about how Robert Kennedy came to Indiana and joined the Ku Klux Klan. By this time they had all but abandoned the Indiana campaign.

Actually, Bob had been a liberal when they were children, and indeed he was by instinct and conviction a good deal more liberal than his brother Jack had been—he had a real passion for the disadvantaged, the Negroes and poor Appalachian whites, the starving American Indians and Mexican migrant workers, for *los de abajo*. These people knew he cared. He was the only white man in America that Negroes trusted. They didn't care if he talked backlash to the

Kokomo autoworkers. They knew that in his heart he was for them. Once during the Indiana primary he went into black Gary and white-backlash Hammond and Whiting all on the same day, something no other candidate in America would have dared to do that terrible spring. But never in Indiana did he simply declare that violence and rioting cannot be tolerated and let it go at that; always he followed it by saying that neither can injustice be tolerated. At least, that was true every time I heard him speak, and I was watching him closely and would have picked him up quickly if he had missed a beat, because I knew the press would crucify him. This may be viewed as a cynical effort to have it both ways; it may also be viewed as an effort to heal the country's wounds, to bring us together again. God knows we needed it, after Vietnam and the murder of Martin Luther King. And no one would maintain, indeed, that Negroes could go on tearing the cities to pieces—or be expected to endure forever the injustice of poverty and second-class citizenship. Bob said nothing in Indiana he would have to take back if elected, nothing he would have to disavow in other states.

I spent a good deal of time briefing newspapermen and TV people on Indiana, explaining why this was not Kennedy country—redneck conservative voters who supported Governor George Wallace of Georgia, Governor Branigin's machine, business against Bob, labor too, and the growing suburbs, all the other reasons he would do badly. I could do this better than Bob's press secretaries, Frank Mankiewicz and Pierre Salinger, because I knew Indiana, I myself was a journalist known to the national press, and, furthermore, I believed what I was saying. I told the reporters where to check what I was saying. For example, I steered John Steele of *Time* to Kokomo, and he came back with a briefcase full of Ku Klux Klan literature.

Bob got along well with the press. He usually ended a whistlestop speech with a quotation from George Bernard Shaw, "Some people see things as they are and ask why? I dream things that never were and say why not." (I doubt that half his crowd understood it, but he delivered it well and it always worked.) When he came to the start of that line, the words "George Bernard Shaw," the newspapermen traveling with us started moving to the buses. Once, for a joke, he omitted it and left quickly, almost stranding them. Aboard the

plane, at the end of a day, he would leave the back of the Electra where Ethel and we staffers rode with him and go mingle with the press. The effect was curious. They liked him. But some of them wrote nasty stories—they were afraid they were being taken in by him and bent over backward to be "objective." (His brother Jack had been far less free with them.) Roger Mudd, the television broadcaster, was given all kinds of breaks to do a special show on Bob, but it turned out to be just short of a hatchet job. Bob got even: In California, Mudd interviewed him, and Bob kept telling him to watch his language, throwing him off balance.

Once I told Bob he was weak with suburbanites and businessmen; he ought to quit talking to Negroes and students. He said, "But those are the audiences I like to talk to. I feel at home with them." It was true. He had no feel for the petite bourgeoisie, the suburbanites. It would have been his gravest weakness as a national candidate, particularly in such states as Illinois and California. In Indiana he simply did nothing about it. In California, he had to try, though he hated it. It probably cost him Oregon, a state of petite bourgeoisie, pseudointellectual college professors, righteous good-government people. Once Bob said to me, "Who else could have put together the combination against me—business, labor, and the South?" I added, "And the Jews." It was true. Big business feared him; President Johnson had told big labor to oppose him; the South hated him for implementing desegregation. (Why Jews opposed him I never clearly understood.*)

*Various writers, including Arthur Schlesinger, Adam Yarmolinsky, William Vanden Heuvel and Milt Gwirtzman, V. O. Key, and Richard Dawson Kahlenberg, in pieces published and unpublished, have referred to Jews' unfavorable opinion of Bob. As its sources, they have suggested his father's reputation, his own Catholicism, his tough shanty-Irish demeanor, his six months as assistant counsel to Senator Joe McCarthy's witch-hunting committee, his "ruthless" pursuit of Jimmy Hoffa and other witnesses later before his Rackets Committee, his very 1968 campaign style—mingling with the sweaty crowds, while Eugene McCarthy campaigned in television studios and suburban ladies' teas, both elements more congenial to suburban Jewish voters. Schlesinger has written, "Labor, the party regulars and the south brought [Hubert] Humphrey great strength. [Humphrey] also had a long record of service to Jewish causes.... McCarthy too had strong Jewish support. The Jewish community saw him, said Adam Yarmolinsky, as 'the professor who gave your bright son an A, and Bobby Kennedy was the tough kid on the block who beat up your son on his way to school.' When Kennedy came to New York the day after Indiana [Vanden Heuvel and Gwirtzman reported], a group of rabbis waited on him. 'Why do I have so much trouble with the Jews?' he asked. 'I don't understand it. Nobody has been more outspoken than I have.... Is it because of my father when he was in England? *That was thirty years ago.*' One of his visitors said that, after the Six Days' War, American Jews needed 'continual

When Bob had decided to enter the primaries, his brother-in-law Steve Smith, who managed the Kennedy family money, said, "This is going to cost us four million dollars and we're not going to get a damn thing for it." In every state the opposition constantly accused the Kennedys of buying the election. Actually, in Indiana, Eugene McCarthy and the Kennedys spent about the same amount of money; in Oregon, McCarthy spent more; in California, the Kennedys more. McCarthy's main sources, Steve Smith said to me in California, were the AFL-CIO's COPE and the Teamsters union. Smith said, "What the hell do Robert Kennedy's relatives want of him for their money except that he be a good president? What do George Meany and Jimmy Hoffa want from McCarthy?" This rankled all the more because McCarthy was so sanctimonious about his ineffable children's crusade. Walt Sheridan, the investigator from the old Rackets Committee who was now on Bob's staff, told me that the Hoffa money was being channeled through a man in Chicago.* I offered to ask Emil Smicklas to investigate it if Steve Smith and Sheridan thought it important. They did. I would move on it right after California.

Bob wanted to do sidewalk campaigning in an Indianapolis blue-collar white neighborhood. I remember East Tenth Street not far from my old home on Brookside Avenue, with a movie house where I used to watch my aunt play the piano on Saturdays as a kid. Bob motorcaded it with several stops. He toured factories, shaking hands; and watching, I thought him, surprisingly, not so good at it as Stevenson. Stevenson had liked to stop and talk for a long time with two or three men. Kennedy shook more hands, but it was more

---

reassurance' about Israel; Kennedy wearily said he would make his position clear again on the west coast."

My own Jewish friends supported Bob. But they were sophisticated political people; perhaps other Jews were put off by things like Irish toughness. The problem must have been more atmospheric than substantive. Certainly Bob was aware of it the day he and I discussed it.

*Allen Dorfman, an insurance man. Earlier Bob's Senate Rackets Committee had investigated whether Dorfman and his father had loaned Teamsters pension money, which they handled, to leaders of organized crime. Years later, in 1982, Dorfman was convicted, together with the new head of the Teamsters and a gangster and two others, of conspiring to bribe a U.S. senator from Nevada. While Dorfman was out on bond awaiting sentencing, a sentence that seemed likely to be long, the Syndicate became suspicious that he might talk freely to the FBI about organized crime in return for a lighter sentence, and one day in 1983, in a suburban shopping-mall parking lot, he was assassinated in the manner favored by gangsters.

mechanical, and he did not give the impression he was genuinely interested in the men, as Stevenson had. As part of my Indiana's-past-greatness notion, I wanted him to visit the old home of James Whitcomb Riley, the poet, in Indianapolis. Fran and I visited it—we had once taken our kids there—and near it we found a day nursery. Bob resisted going but, on my urging, went, and at the nursery, while he was speaking briefly, two little Negro children laid their heads in his lap, and he patted them and went on speaking. A photograph of it was printed in *The Saturday Evening Post* with some such caption as "How could anybody hate Robert Kennedy?"

The problem of most politicians is how to get crowds. Bob's that spring was how to avoid them. Eugene McCarthy, and even Governor Branigin, with his machine, spoke to half-empty halls. Not Bob—he could not even stroll along a sidewalk quietly without getting mobbed. He was kinetic. Once he ventured into Monument Circle, the heart of Indianapolis, and his crowd was the biggest I ever saw there; he could not speak, and I got separated from him somehow and had to climb over three or four cars to get back to him. The crowds in the cities were almost frightening. Few things anywhere contain the frenzy, the drama, the unbelievable tensions and pressures of an American presidential campaign. Often, exhausted, Bob would say, "There must be some better way to pick a president." It was worse than that, though. It was a cruel, bloody, and bloodthirsty spectacle. Yet there was a fascination and an exhilaration in it too. And we were winning. We were beating the terrible local press, the suspicious national press, the sanctimonious McCarthy, the dull governor, the skeptical parochial narrow-minded Hoosiers themselves. Were beating them all. Or, rather, Bob Kennedy was. More than most candidates, despite his big staff, he seemed alone. He took advice but he would turn a speech line and make it his own. He went yammering around Indiana about the poor whites of Appalachia and the starving Indians who committed suicide on the reservations and the jobless Negroes in the distant great cities, and half the Hoosiers didn't have any idea what he was talking about; but he plodded ahead stubbornly, making them listen, maybe even making some of them care, by the sheer power of his own caring. Indiana people are not generous nor sympathetic; they are hardhearted, not warm and generous; but he must have touched something in them, pushed a button somewhere. He alone

did it. He always looked so alone too, standing up there by himself on the trunk of his convertible—so alone, so vulnerable, so fragile, you feared he might break. He was thin. He did not chop the air with his hands as his brother Jack had; instead he had a little gesture with his right hand, the fist closed, the thumb sticking up a little, and he would jab with it to make a point. When he got applause, he did not smile at the crowd, pleased; instead he looked down, down at the ground or at his speech, and waited till they had finished, then went on. He could take a bland generality and deliver it with such depth of feeling that it cut like a knife.

Eugene McCarthy, by contrast, could say startling things and nobody noticed. He had a low-keyed easygoing manner that suggested a professor—or a preacher without conviction. He never cut, except when he campaigned in New Hampshire against Vietnam, and even then it was the issue, not the candidate, that cut. Bob always cut. He pushed buttons no one else pushed; he aroused wild enthusiasm and love and equally wild hate. Nobody hated McCarthy. Nobody hated Humphrey. But a lot of people in this country hated Kennedys. Bob Kennedy was no more comfortable with professional politicians than with small businessmen. His people were the disadvantaged. Somehow, all this came through, to both his followers and his enemies. For a politician, Bob had an off-trail personality. There seems to be something in the American electorate that cuts down the off trail, the best, the truly good—Stevenson, Jack and Bob Kennedy— and turns instead to the ordinary, the second rate, the Johnsons and Nixons, Carters and Reagans. Maybe the country deserves a hollow man like Nixon.

Before Bob entered the primaries, Jacqueline Kennedy, the president's widow, had told Arthur Schlesinger, "If he gets in, they'll kill him, just as they did Jack." All this spring he rode in motorcades on the back of a convertible, completely exposed. I never rode in a motorcade or went into a crowd with him that I did not watch the windows of surrounding buildings and watch people in the crowds. Once in a town in California a few days before he was shot, while we were whistlestopping the Central Valley, I saw a man close to the train's rear platform ask a hostile question with a look of sheer hate on his face; and all through Bob's speech, I stood close behind Bob and I watched the man, and if he had made any move like reaching in his pocket I would have knocked Bob down. This was on all our

minds all spring. He had only one bodyguard, Bill Barry. I talked to Barry and Fred Dutton, but it was no use—Bob had a fatalistic view that if he was going to get killed he was going to get killed and there was nothing to be done about it. I still told Barry and Dutton that you could at least cut the odds—put him in a closed car in motorcades, get more police out to precede the motorcades and search the buildings, not publicize the motorcade route in advance. It was no use. They were for it but they knew he wasn't, so nothing was done.

It was partly for this reason that I came to despise McCarthy. The weekend before the Oregon primary, with California another week away, McCarthy said publicly that rumors would undoubtedly be spread the final weekend that an attempt would be made to assassinate Robert Kennedy. It was a terrible thing to say.

Fran compared Bob with Manolete, the bullfighter. Monument Circle and the other mob scenes were a little like a bullfight. The populace came to see people tearing Bob Kennedy to pieces. They pulled his clothes off him, tore his suits, ripped off his cuff links and necktie. A book about Manolete said that the crowd kept demanding more and more of him, and he kept giving it, until there was nothing left to give but his life, and he gave them that.

The Indiana primary was May 7. On Monday and Tuesday I tried to educate the TV people on Indiana. They weren't listening. One of them showed Larry O'Brien and me his network's tabulation of delegate strength state by state—*including Indiana*—and said they were going on the air with it twenty minutes after the polls closed in Indiana. I wondered why we bothered to have elections at all. Fran and I watched the returns on television with Bob and the others in his suite. It soon became clear we were winning and pretty big. After a while McCarthy went on TV and said he didn't think it made much difference if one came in first or second or third. Bob grinned and said, "That's not what I was taught." He came in first, Branigin second, McCarthy third. He had not only beaten McCarthy; he had beaten an incumbent governor in his home state. That was a great night. Going home to my mother's house, Fran and I said it was nice to win one. It seemed so long since we had. Indeed, the five years since Jack Kennedy's death had been dreary and bleak ones for the

country. Now for the first time since 1963, during these weeks of the Indiana spring primary of 1968, Fran and I had felt hope. We had been doing something we thought important, doing it together, and it had worked and we'd won; we were on our way now, for the first time in five years. This was, really, what Robert Kennedy had to offer the people—hope.

I went out to California for Bob. I wasn't sure I needed to, Fred Dutton knew it well, but he and Bob thought I should do the briefing sheets for his stops. Fran and Marian Schlesinger went to Oregon to do their sister act with faculty wives.

Bob won the Nebraska primary. I thought that after Indiana, McCarthy had decided to let Nebraska go, to put everything he had into winning Oregon, and to hope that a victory there might propel him to a victory in California. Bob had to win California. The press was discounting Indiana because it was small, atypical, and full of Negroes. California was a truer test, big and diverse, a nation and an empire in itself. And early polls had shown Bob in trouble there. California is, probably, the hardest state in the nation to campaign in. The suburbs around Los Angeles reach for unbelievable miles and miles and miles. It is a scheduler's and an advance man's nightmare. I'd been through it all before, but the others hadn't, and it floored them.

The reports from Oregon were bad. Fran told me she and Marian couldn't move votes, the campaign was disorganized, scheduling and advance were poor, nobody seemed to know Oregon, she was uneasy. On my way back west from my weekly trip to teach my seminar in New York, I stopped in Portland, and from Fran's room at the Benson Hotel looked down on Bob, walking back to the hotel from a street rally. Somebody said it'd been a good rally but it didn't look good to me; he shouldn't be able to walk down a street in the center of town without anybody paying attention. In his room he asked if I'd been doing the briefing sheets. He liked them. He wished I'd write major speeches too because "I haven't really had a speech since Bloomington." He said it almost plaintively. He really was pulling these campaigns out of his guts, and he looked it, drawn, nervous. I asked if he wanted me to stay with him in Oregon or go back to California. He thought about it a long time. Finally he said,

"I don't know. I guess it's too late in Oregon. But I'll leave it to you." It wasn't like him. I went back to California.

I asked Arthur Schlesinger to come out and help with speeches. The day before he arrived, Bob lost Oregon to McCarthy. Bob took it very hard. We saw him for a long time that Wednesday night in Los Angeles at the Ambassador Hotel and urged him strongly not to say—as he had intimated—that he would drop out of the race entirely if he lost California. Only a week to go. Next day, Thursday, May 30, Arthur and I went with him to Fresno. On the plane I got Bob to do his homework—read his day's briefing sheets. He was distracted. We began talking about making news. Bob asked why he didn't send a telegram to Hubert Humphrey challenging him to join his debate Saturday night with McCarthy, and Arthur drafted one. At the Fresno airport he read his Humphrey telegram, then began kidding the crowd. The crowd was small and unresponsive, and Bob wasn't good. I noticed his legs were trembling. We went whistle-stopping up the San Joaquin Valley, and I told him to turn the speech around—kid the crowd first, then go into the issues, including the telegram. He used the telegram all day. He kept losing it, several times started to read it, couldn't find it, turned to me and asked for it, once saying to me, "Where's that damn telegram?" but saying it into the microphone so the crowd heard it. The next time I gave him a copy as he went to speak; I told him it was the last I had and if he lost it this time he was on his own. He kept losing his briefing sheets too, so didn't know what crop was grown at each stop, and Fred Dutton or I had to write it out in big block letters at the last minute. I had dug up a good story for him about Mexican migrant workers but he didn't use it. Indeed, he gave the Mexicans small comfort that day in the valley. Previously he had been identified with Caesar Chavez, the radical organizer of Mexican migrants. Now Fred Dutton was turning him around, as I had in Indiana, fearing he was becoming too closely identified with Mexicans and Negroes in California. As the day went on, the crowds got bigger and more responsive, and Bob got better. He knew how to work a crowd. At one stop he began:

"Has Senator McCarthy been here to Turlock?"

Crowd roar: "NO."

"He hasn't? I'm shocked. Well then, surely Vice-President Humphrey has been here?"

"NO."

"No? I can hardly believe it. You mean Senator McCarthy and the vice-president don't care about Turlock?"

"NO."

"Are you going to vote for somebody who doesn't care about Turlock?"

"NO."

"Who are you going to vote for?"

"KENNEDY."

"I don't believe it. On election day, you'll forget how to spell my name."

"NO."

"You'll forget all about me."

"NO."

"Do you promise?"

"YES."

"Do you know what my family and I had for breakfast this morning?"

"NO."

"Turlock turkey. [Turlock called itself the Turkey Capital of the World.] We have Turlock turkey every day for breakfast. Do you believe that?"

That was the way he used the crops from the briefing sheets. He had another routine:

"Are you going to help me?"

"YES."

"Are you going to vote for me?"

"YES."

"Have you read my book?"

"YES."

"You lie."

Earlier in his campaign he had used the rather strident closing that his brother Jack had used: Give me your heart, give me your hand, your help in this election; but by now he had shifted to kidding the audience, much more in character for him. They were very different men. John F. Kennedy was more the politician, saying things publicly that he privately scoffed at. Bobby Kennedy was himself. Campaigning, Jack gave the impression of decisive leadership, the man with all the answers. Bob seemed less sure he was

right, more tentative, more questioning, and completely honest about it. Leadership he showed; but it had a different quality, an off-trail unorthodox quality, to some extent a searching for answers to hard questions in company with his audience.

I do not mean to extend this into what the McCarthy people kept calling "the politics of participation" or "the new politics." There was a great deal of talk that spring—and later too—about "the new politics" and most of it was baloney. We campaigned the old-politics way—Negroes, blue collar, white collar, ethnic groups, Mexican-Americans, Catholics, pitching the speeches straight at his audiences. The idea of "new politics" arises periodically, as it did in 1952 when Stevenson attracted volunteers, including Lake Forest Republicans, or in 1968, when McCarthy's Vietnam stand attracted the kids, or, at its zenith, in 1972, when George McGovern attracted kids and homosexuals and "women's liberation" women and anti-political-boss people and all manner of zealots. All three—Stevenson, McCarthy, and McGovern—lost. And lost to the practitioners of the old politics. And the day after the voting, everybody forgot about "the new politics."

In Indiana, looking ahead, I had worried about the California crowds—the Indiana crowds were mobs, but I knew how volatile California crowds could be and was afraid Bob might get hurt. He found that if we used police in a California crowd the police shoved and the crowd shoved back. But if we just used Bill Barry and a couple of us, the crowd gave way. Nevertheless, we often wondered what would happen if one of those crowds turned hostile. In California, we ran into more zealous and hostile McCarthy hecklers than in Indiana—they sometimes drove their cars in and out of our motorcade on a Los Angeles freeway, trying to break up our motorcade, a dangerous business. John Siegenthaler asked my advice about scheduling Bob into Berkeley, the epicenter of student radicalism in America. I was for it provided he had security. I thought most Californians didn't like Berkeley, and if student radicals prevented him from speaking, it would help him with other Californians—he could afterward tell the press that if allowed to speak he would have told the students, "You remind me of the Hitler Youth movement." While we were discussing it, hecklers booed Bob down at another college, and he sent word: No more colleges in Califor-

nia. Watching his final TV debate with McCarthy in San Francisco, Fran and I thought Bob at least held his own. After the debate we went with Bob and the others to a fund-raising gala at the city auditorium where Hollywood stars performed and, since we arrived with the candidate, we wound up in the front row. One beautiful performer, Raquel Welch, announced she was for John F. Kennedy, meaning Bob. Jerry Lewis, the comedian, doing his heckling act, took the microphone to, of all people, Arthur Schlesinger and told him to sing "Shine On, Harvest Moon." I was probably the only person in the United States with a worse voice than Arthur and the only one more discomfited by such a spotlight. Arthur manfully croaked. Lewis stopped him. Lewis tried three or four others, including me. All either collapsed in laughter or screeched off key. Then he took the microphone to Fran, and she, who had a good voice, sang it perfectly, and the house cheered, five thousand people, she stopped the show. A good night.

On Sunday we all went to Los Angeles. I spent Monday and election day at the Ambassador Hotel working on a memo titled "Beyond California"—what Bob should do between the California election and the Democratic National Convention. I also wrote California election night victory and defeat statements for Bob. I thought if he won California, he had a pretty good chance of being nominated; if nominated, I felt sure he'd be elected president.

Election day was nervous. I'd thought we'd been ahead in California but that McCarthy was catching us during the last week. It depended now on whether our poor people voted. Fran and I went to Bob's suite in the Ambassador shortly before the polls closed, and it began to fill up. Bob wasn't there. The South Dakota primary was the same day, and Bob won. At about eight Bob stuck his head in the door and said to everybody. "You want me to tell you about the Indians? In one county in South Dakota, there were eight hundred sixty-eight votes and I got eight hundred sixty-six and Humphrey got two and McCarthy got none." Then he disappeared.

We were watching NBC, Huntley-Brinkley. They were not "projecting" a California winner. But their actual returns showed us losing. We couldn't find out where the votes came from or what they meant. On CBS, Cronkite was "projecting" Bob the big winner, but his returns were small and kept fluctuating wildly. Worried, I went

to try to persuade Bob not to withdraw if he lost. I found him in a small room across the hall with Fred Dutton, Ted Sorensen, Dick Goodwin, and Jesse Unruh of California. Bob seemed out of sorts, distant, withdrawn within himself. Goodwin was urging him to go on TV and claim victory on the basis of the CBS projection. Unruh opposed it. Bob told Steve Smith to do it. We tried to talk to Bob about what he would say; I drifted back and forth between the little room and the suite, Fran with me, and gave him my "Beyond California" memo and he started to read it but I told him to put it in his pocket and read it tomorrow; and Fran gave him a memo he'd asked for analyzing the Oregon defeat, and he put that in his pocket too. Pressures mounted from reporters and TV directors for him to go down to the Ambassador ballroom and speak. Finally he did, followed by the photographers and reporters, one of whom asked if I wasn't going down with him "into the burning pit," or something like that, and I said no, I'd been there before, I'd wait here. We watched TV in the little room. He came on and was very good, bantering with the audience. I must have quit watching and wandered out into the hall to get some air. Jeff Greenfield came running by, saying something that ended with "shot," and I ran after him, saying, "What did you say?" and he said angrily, "You heard me," and kept running and I followed saying, "No I didn't," and he said, "There's a rumor Kennedy has been shot." I went back to the little room. Sorensen, Goodwin, and somebody else were watching television. On TV the ballroom downstairs was a madhouse. Steve Smith was asking people to leave, somebody was asking for a doctor in the house, the announcer was saying that nobody knew for sure but it was thought that several people had been shot and one of them was Bob. But he thought Bob had been shot in the hip. Fran put her arm around Ted Sorensen. We kept watching the horror. Then the announcer said it was said that Bob had been shot and in the head. Every one of us said, "Oh no." Ted got up and walked to a window, and Fran went with him. Then somehow Fran disappeared, one or two young staffers came in, then somehow all the staffers, young and old, began to hurry to the elevator—outside we could hear sirens, they were taking him to the hospital—and I started running with them, it was a natural impulse to go where your candidate was, but as we turned a corner I stopped and thought, What the hell am I

going there for? He needs a doctor, not a writer. If I can do anything for anybody it's for Fran. I remembered that when President Kennedy had been shot I'd stayed alone in Washington and not had Fran come to me, and later this had hurt us both; so I let the others go and went back to Fran and we sat watching television and grieving. About 4 A.M. we went to bed. I kept wondering if I could have helped if I'd gone down with him.

Next morning we had thought to go to New York but instead we watched television and missed our plane. We went to get something to eat. The hotel seemed empty. Fran wanted to see Ethel, she said she couldn't leave without seeing her or getting word to her. I felt helpless. A *Look* photographer who'd been with us throughout Indiana helped us make calls to find out how to get into the hospital. We went there, to the intensive care unit. We talked a little to John McCone and his wife; from California himself, he had been President Kennedy's director of the CIA and was a close friend of Bob's. Ted Kennedy came in and we talked to him a few minutes and I scribbled out a note to Ethel and gave it to him, something like "Dear Ethel, we are praying. God bless you and yours. Fran and John," and asked if Ted would give it to Ethel, and he read it and said, "I sure will." The McCones took us back to the hotel. The rest of the day we watched TV and made plans, called Dan and Fred and my mother. (Dan had been dating one of Bob's daughters at Putney.) Adlai Stevenson III called, as did Newt Minow and others from Chicago. When we went to bed past midnight Bob was still alive. We thought if he could just make it through the night he might be all right. Early in the morning Newt Minow called and wakened me: Bob had died in the night.

We walked around the hotel, looking for somebody or something. I bought a black necktie. We found Walt Sheridan making lists of people to go on Air Force One, which President Johnson was sending, to take Bob's body back to New York for the funeral, and they had us on the list, but we decided not to go—we had to get to our children. Fran and I took a plane to Boston, rented a car, picked up Fred at Exeter and Dan at Putney, both crying, then went to New York and rejoined the campaign party at the Commodore. Ed Guthman asked me to stand vigil, and Fran and I walked to St. Patrick's Cathedral, and I stood vigil from 12:30 to 12:45 beside the

casket in the cathedral with Burke Marshall and Jacqueline Kennedy and Dick Goodwin and others. Late as it was, there must have been a million people on the streets just standing and staring toward the cathedral. In the morning we took the boys and went to the funeral service in the cathedral, where Bob's brother Ted so bravely spoke, then we got on one of the buses and went to the train. The locomotive was freshly painted black. The train ride to Washington took forever. The train was at once terrible and great. He had loved whistlestopping by train. The crowds were astonishing. They lined the railroad right-of-way. Trains run through poor parts of town. Negroes and factory workers. They were his people. The disadvantaged. Old men stood with their hats over their hearts. Young women held babies. Factory workers stopped work and leaned out of windows and climbed up on roofs. Aboard the train, people, Bob's family, the staff, press, kept moving around, people we'd been with all spring. Fred told Paul Douglas, who had recommended him for Exeter, about the project he started after Martin Luther King had been killed to get Exeter boys to help paint apartments of Negroes in the Boston slums. We reached Washington in dark and rain and went in buses to Arlington National Cemetery. So it really was all over. Fran and I took Dan and Fred and fled to Michigan.

THIRTEEN

AS TIME GOES BY

1.

Up in Michigan, I seemed able to accomplish little. I did manage to say no to George Ball, who called to ask me to help Hubert Humphrey, the probable Democratic candidate for president. I had said after Bob Kennedy's death I was through with politics. Fran had said the same thing and to this day she has shunned all public deeds. I took up the Stevenson manuscript, put it down, tried to read left-over student papers, put them down. I could think of little but Bob. Finally, to exorcise it, for writing has always been my salvation, I began writing a journal of the Indiana and California campaigns, writing about him, the Bobby Kennedy I had loved.

Early in August the Republican National Convention nominated Richard Nixon for president, and that galvanized Democrats. I began getting more calls asking me to help Hubert Humphrey and to go to the Democratic National Convention in Chicago. Adlai Stevenson III was a delegate and thought I would be. There would be a ceremony honoring his father.

The Democratic National Convention of 1968—God help us! Lyndon Johnson was in many ways an admirable president who pushed through Congress more progressive social legislation than

any other president since FDR. Mayor Richard J. Daley was, as I have suggested, almost surely the best mayor Chicago ever had. Both understood power better than anyone else. Their behavior at the 1968 convention was therefore inexplicable. As Daley's police beat the kids in the streets, and as Johnson's political operatives smothered the convention, one could only feel that two stubborn old men were destroying any chance the Democratic party had to keep the unspeakable Richard Nixon out of the White House. The real victim of the convention was Vice-President Humphrey, now help-less heir to Johnson's Vietnam War. One day as I was walking down Michigan Avenue, a limousine pulled to the curb, and the vice-president stuck his head out and called, "John!" We shook hands, and he said, grinning but his jaw thrust out at the same time (some-thing no other man can do), "I'm going to get it and I want you to help me in the fall." I said I would. He was always direct, he never hesitated to ask help.

The rest of the convention was far less cheerful. One night I sat in a room at the Chicago Club with Ralph Bellamy, the actor—he and Dore Schary had taken part in the memorial to Adlai Stevenson— looking out the window at Michigan Avenue, where a wave of young Vietnam War protesters pursued by police swept down the street, tear gas bombs smoking among them. Disheartened, we called Fran up at Three Lakes. She reported that she had just re-turned from Smith Lake and that, as she was driving the Jeep out of the turnaround at Smith Lake, she had seen a black fox. Bellamy could hardly believe that anywhere in the United States one could still see a black fox in one's own driveway.

I went to Washington September 29 to help Hubert Humphrey. Hubert Humphrey ran for president on courage alone. His party, torn by the primaries and convention, was shattered by the revolt of the black and young against Vietnam and racial injustice, by the counterrevolt of blue-collar workers. His campaign was floundering. He had little staff, few good writers, no position papers; no direction. My first weekend in Washington I met with him and his other ad-visers in his apartment. They began to show him advertising materi-als they had prepared but he interrupted, "Wait a minute. I want to ask some questions." He said he had spent last week in the West and South, and the crowds had been good, but when people asked for

bumper stickers and buttons, there were none. Nor any TV or radio spots. He said, "Where the hell is the campaign?" The others tried to evade. Finally Larry O'Brien told him the truth: The Democratic National Committee was broke. Contributors thought this a lost cause. The people who make buttons and bumper stickers had shut off the national committee's credit. The committee could not pay the fuel bill for the vice-president's airplane—it might not take off Monday.

Humphrey sat silent a moment. Then, thrusting out his jaw, "All right. I see. Well, I can raise money," and all fall he did, seeing people he shouldn't, and never complained. His was a brave campaign.

I had no great heart for it but I admired Humphrey and I did not want to have in the White House Richard Nixon. I thought Nixon a thoroughgoing scoundrel, a hollow man, a master of deceit, and, considering his and Joe McCarthy's campaign against Stevenson in 1952, a real menace to civil liberties. When my liberal friends like Arthur Schlesinger refused to help Humphrey, considering him an apologist for Johnson's war, I told them, "All right—you can abstain if you want to, but you're going to help elect Richard Nixon." Similarly, on an October afternoon when Humphrey mounted a loading platform at a factory and took off his coat and harangued the workingmen, some of whom heckled him and held up George Wallace signs, Humphrey leaned forward and told them, "All right, vote for Wallace if you want to—you'll get Richard Nixon for president and you'll get a recession and you'll lose your jobs." I was proud of him.

I spent two weeks in the Washington headquarters, writing speeches, then went to California to find out what we ought to do there. But in San Francisco I ran into Ted Sorensen's brother, also working for Humphrey, and, talking, we realized that California issues didn't matter, the only thing that mattered was Vietnam: Humphrey had to break at last with President Johnson on the war. We did not think he could repudiate the administration wholly—he had been its vice-president for four years—but we devised a formula, details of which I now forget, that would avoid an open break yet free him from the fatal Johnson embrace. The election was only about two weeks away. I flew all night from San Francisco to Hartford, Connecticut, where Humphrey was campaigning, missed him

there, chased his motorcade all day through whistlestops, and finally that night on his plane to New York made my presentation. He said he would think about it. I kept other people away so he could. As the plane was descending, he said, "I'll do it. But I'll have to see him first."

His chief aide, Ted Van Dyk, arranged for Humphrey to see President Johnson privately the next day, a Sunday. But when Humphrey got to the White House, a presidential aide told him the appointment was canceled. (News of the appointment had leaked to the press; Johnson would never do what the press predicted.) Humphrey, for once, was speechless. The aide said, "Maybe you can see him Monday." Humphrey told him to tell the president where he could shove the appointment.

During the last week Humphrey did move some distance away from Johnson on the war—not so far as we had hoped, but far enough to help. I went with him around the country—Los Angeles, Ohio, Pennsylvania, New York, Baltimore, Michigan, Illinois, Ohio again, Texas, Los Angeles again, a frantic campaign, big speeches and a murderous schedule everywhere. Despite everything, he never lost his boyish bubbly enthusiasm. Once on the plane, reading a speech I had drafted for him, he looked up and said, "God—he makes me sound like Stevenson." Kidding himself—he always did. We knew Humphrey was closing the gap. Fast enough? The poll takers and TV anchormen kept predicting a Nixon landslide. Right up to the end, Walter Cronkite on CBS kept "projecting" that Humphrey would carry only two states and the District of Columbia. (How would you like to raise money for such a candidacy?) We knew it would be far closer than that and after all, we had been in national politics before, Ted Van Dyk and I and Jim Rowe, who campaigned with us. It turned out to be one of the closest elections in American history. I have always thought that if the terrible Chicago convention had not torn the party to pieces, Hubert Humphrey would have been president of the United States and Richard Nixon never would have. What that would have saved the country!

On November 20 that year, 1968, Fran and I went home to Highland Park and, after six years, dating from the time we had gone to the Dominican Republic, we retrieved from tenants our old Victorian house on Maple Avenue. That day was her birthday, and it was

also Bob Kennedy's birthday, and when we arrived we found, too late, a telegram from Ethel asking us to come to a memorial service that day.

2.

On Maple Avenue, we dug in to finish the Stevenson book. On June 5, 1970, three and a half years after I had begun writing, I finished the rough draft—more than sixteen thousand pages, some two and a half million words. I spent another year and a half cutting and re-writing it into a semifinal draft, still enormous, then I began clearing it with young Adlai, a difficult sometimes almost painful process that stretched over three more years. He raised numerous objections, but we never were forced to arbitration. Most of his objections related to my account of his father's relations with his lady friends, his remarks about Jews, and his feelings toward Negroes. I must say I thought young Adlai behaved well; I am not sure I would want to read a candid biography of my own father. In any case, he did not gut the book, nor did I falsify it. I also now think, upon reflection, that when I wrote the first draft I had been too keenly aware that I was a partisan of Stevenson and so, trying to be "objective," had been hypercritical of him; young Adlai's objections helped restore balance.

I had also promised to show parts of the book to various people in return for their cooperation, such as George Ball, who had given me access to State Department files. And I had to get permission to quote from letters other people had written to Stevenson. (If you write a letter to me, I own the leter and I can sell it, burn it, do anything except publish it—you have a common-law copyright in it.) Most biographers, I am told, paraphrase letters written to their subject—too much trouble to seek permissions. But I wanted to quote from many verbatim, especially those from his lady friends, in order to preserve the flavor of his friendships. In certain cases, obtaining permission resembled diplomacy far more than literary endeavor. Nearly every one of his friends was extremely generous, not to say courageous, in giving permission even when their letters did not show them at their best. All this stretched on through 1976. And so did final editing—Sam Vaughan at Doubleday was, rightly, determined to publish the book as one volume. But we could not cut it

enough, and it had to be published as two volumes, each eight hundred or nine hundred pages. The two taken together were entitled *The Life of Adlai E. Stevenson.* The first, covering his life through his first presidential campaign, was called *Adlai Stevenson of Illinois.* The second was called *Adlai Stevenson and the World.* Doubleday launched the first in 1976 with fanfare in Chicago, the second a year later in New York at the United Nations. More than ever before, I made speeches and television appearances around the country, that dubious effort to publicize a book that has become so much a part of publishing. The book was widely and favorably reviewed. It sold only moderately well. Perhaps most disappointing to Fran and me, it won neither a Pulitzer Prize nor a National Book Award. I came to feel that if I had written it fast and published it as only one volume soon after his death, it would probably have been best-seller and won a major award. On the other hand, it would have been a very different book. The enormous amount of documentation made it so long. The material did not overwhelm me. But I was always conscious that I alone had free access to all of Stevenson's papers and I felt an obligation to history. In any case, for better or worse, the biography of Stevenson is done, it exists, and nobody needs do it again.

After it was published, I was often asked three things: What will Stevenson's place in history be? And did I admire him as much when I finished as when I began? And would he have made a good president? As to the first, his place in history probably depends upon what direction history takes. If it moves in the direction he hoped, toward world order through international organization, he probably will rank high, but if it goes as it has seemed to be going, toward a world of competing or even warring nation-states, he may be seen as nothing but a failed prophet. The last is really unanswerable—we never know what kind of president a man will make until he becomes president, during the election of 1860 few people would have predicted that the plain lanky man from rustic Illinois would make our greatest president, nor would many have said in 1945 that the failed haberdasher from Missouri would also make a great president. That was the answer I usually made in public. Actually, I think from his record, we can conclude that the prognosis for Stevenson's presidency was good. When he was governor, nearly all his appointments were good, he was able to get his program through the balky legisla-

ture, and he elevated the tone of Illinois government and led the people. As a presidential candidate, he attracted some of the ablest people in the country to help him and he could have put them into his administration. In domestic policy, he was a centrist, often less liberal than I myself might have preferred but perhaps that was apposite to his times, and in any case, his real interest lay not in domestic affairs but in foreign policy, a trait that in a president is not bad. At the United Nations he made little policy—policy was made in Washington, not in New York—but he was an able advocate of America's cause and, moreover, by his own prestige he enhanced the UN's prestige: Never since he was there, nor for that matter before, has the UN stood so high with the American people. He was in a sense the ambassador of the UN to the United States, not the other way around, and as president one could expect he would have used the UN well. And finally as president he would have understood the power of the presidency and coupled it with his own eloquence to rally the people to his purposes. As to whether I admired him as much when I finished writing his life as I had when I began, the answer is clearly that I admired him even more. I had always known he possessed great political courage, as when he stood almost alone against Senator Joe McCarthy. But what I had not been fully aware of was his personal courage. For I had not realized what a horror his private life had been. He had an unhappy and on one occasion traumatic, childhood, a foolish father, a pretentious and suffocating mother, a domineering older sister, a disastrous marriage, and, despite all the friends and comings and goings, an essentially lonely life. He never complained about it; it was as though he simply assumed that one's private life was torture.

Adlai Stevenson was one of the most important figures in my life. In life, he gave me a great deal, and I like to think I helped him. After he died, he remained important to me because of the biography. Its second volume was published just twenty-five years after I first met him.

3.

In 1969, to help support us while I finished the Stevenson book, I resumed teaching, this time at the Medill School of Journalism at Northwestern University in Evanston, just a thirty-five minute drive from our house. For a year I was a visiting lecturer, then Dean I. W.

Cole appointed me a full professor, complete with tenure and Blue Cross. I taught there ten years. In the main, I taught two graduate seminars, one the seminar on the limits of American power that I'd previously taught in the East, the other a seminar on magazine writing.

Writing cannot be taught (and I told my students so). If, however, they could write a decent English sentence, I could perhaps teach them to write a better one, with help from Strunk and White and from Fowler, and I could also perhaps teach them something about how to do legwork for a magazine article, how to structure their material in a way suitable for magazines, and how to cut and shape a rewrite—what I'd learned. Most of them had had no experience at anything but a spot news story. Each was required to submit an outline of a proposed piece, then to report and write and rewrite a story of from fourteen to eighteen and a half pages. They wrote on all sorts of subjects—Alcoholics Anonymous, a plane crash, a solar-heated house, a Chicago slum, the American Nazi party, a murder case (but I soon learned that a murder case was beyond most of them). The class rarely met as a group. Instead, I met individually with each student at various stages of his project. Wearying of marking up their drafts in longhand, I devised a set of rubber stamps saying such things as "awkward," "loose, wordy," "not entirely clear," "says little," "what mean?" On some pages I stamped as many words as they had written. I also wrote critical memos to each student. And I tried to discourage them from certain fashionable but erroneous usages, such as "media" for "television" and "image" for "reputation," as well as "impact" as a verb for "affect" and "input" for "suggestion."

When I started teaching, I was, by and large, on the students' side. But after a few years, after all the unmet deadlines and broken appointments, after all the superficial interviews and sloppy drafts dashed off at the last minute, I found myself approaching each new student somewhat warily. The Northwestern students seemed to be of about the same caliber as those I'd known in the East. Some found magazine writing all but impossible. Some could not do penetrating interviewing, many had trouble conceptualizing the story, nearly all had trouble organizing their material. Most of their writing was disappointing. Grade schools and high schools, ap-

parently, no longer teach English. I taught my course to fifty-four students each year; if I found one or two who had a chance of making it as a writer, I counted it a good year. And a few of them did—I still occasionally hear from one.

I was troubled by Northwestern's "affirmative action" program. Under it, admissions officers were obliged to give preference to Negro applicants. Since many of them came from slums with terrible public schools, they were simply not equipped to do college work. It was not their fault—they had been short-changed in the lower grades. I thought it laudable that we try to redress the injustice done for so many years to Negroes by giving them preference for higher education but it did create problems for us teachers and sometimes for them too. I had one Negro student in his late twenties who had been working as a television reporter and who came to us on a scholarship provided by his employer. He simply could not do what my course required, and I had to give him a C. That same term he received Cs in his other two writing courses. So he was obliged to leave us (he needed a yearlong B average to graduate). We had done him no favor by accepting him and then sending him home a failure to the employer who had thought him so promising. And yet on principle I see no alternative to affirmative action.

What I found most disheartening about my students, however, was that so many were careerist. They—mistakenly—regarded a graduate diploma from Medill as a union card that would guarantee them a job on a newspaper. They were not interested in the pursuit of knowledge or of excellence. They wanted a degree and a job. (But, then, so had I when I was their age.)

When I began teaching, American campuses, even conservative Northwestern, were aflame with the Negro revolution and antiwar protest. More than once our campus was closed by student strikes and demonstrations. Students wore long hair and beards, sandals and chains. "Wow," they said, and they would "trash" something and "get stoned" on narcotics. Some insulted and harassed their professors, though for some reason not me. Those were the years of the Kent State massacre, of President Nixon calling young people "bums," of the Weathermen and the Black Panthers, of what in Chicago were called the Days of Rage—Fran and I happened to be in the Loop just a couple of blocks away the day the violent young

men and women fought the police on the street and broke a city official's neck. It was a hard time to be a student, a hard time to be a parent, and even a rather hard time to be a teacher. Yet I preferred all that to the inertia and careerism that replaced it. Students were at least alive.

Teaching made me reflect on my own work. What does a writer need? Well, he needs to read good writing. He needs to write. And he needs to rewrite, and rewrite, and rewrite his own sentences until they say as precisely and as economically as he can make them what he intends them to say. He needs to acquire respect, even reverence, for the English language. And while he is working, he cannot be conscious of any of this. I myself write all the time. For example, I don't know what my hunting and fishing partners think about during the long hours of silence while we're together, waiting for the fish or the game to appear, but I know what I do: I write. Almost automatically, in my mind I form sentences, an idea or a snatch of description; then rearrange the words, then revise them inside my head again and again.

What does a good reporter need? Well, he needs first of all an inquiring mind. He needs skepticism but he also needs humility—when his probing shows him that his initial skepticism was wrong, he needs enough humility to admit it and report what he originally doubted. He must be fair. He needs a deep sense of responsibility, responsibility not only to his readers and to society in general but also to the people he is writing about. He must not become so bemused by "scoring a scoop" or publishing a sensational exposé that he does irreparable damage to human beings. Always he must have doubts, not certitudes, about his own impressions. He needs, of course, to see all—not just "both"—sides of every question. He must realize that the hardest thing of all is to discover the truth and that many men do not want to hear the truth—they kill the messenger that brings it. (How many times in my own writing have I been denounced for bringing it.) And of course at bottom he needs to be able to inspire trust, for without that nobody will confide in him, and he will get no story.

Early in my career, it took me three weeks to do a story—one week to get it, a week to write the rough draft, and another week to

and McCarthy's so-called patriotic anti-Communist crusade. "Patri-otism [is sometimes] the last refuge of scoundrels. . . . Patriotism with us is not the hatred of Russia; it is the love of this Republic and of the ideal of liberty of man and mind in which it was born." I did it for Hubert Humphrey in 1968, when I thought he needed to do something courageous—I conceived a speech in the South attacking the South's racist hero, George Wallace. These are both creative ideas. And often within a speech is a small creative bit. When in 1960 Kennedy agreed to address the Greater Houston Ministerial Conference on the subject of his Catholicism, Ted Sorensen knew the speech could not deal only with Kennedy's religious beliefs; it must at least include local references. I suspect his thinking went like this: Where is the candidate going? To Texas. What happened in Texas? The Alamo. Did any Catholics fight at the Alamo? He called our researcher, Myer Feldman; Feldman came up with a string of Irish names of men who had fought at the Alamo but he could not find out whether they were actually Catholic; and so Sorensen wrote, "Side by side with Bowie and Crockett died McCafferty and Bailey and Carey, but no one knows whether they were Catholics or not. For there was no religious test at the Alamo." Politics? Yes. But creative thinking too. In my own magazine and book writing, I often similarly conceptualized a story. The Centralia mine disaster story, as I have suggested, wasn't there till I conceived it. So with "Why Did They Kill?" about the three boys in Ann Arbor who murdered the nurse. So with others. Over the years, I must have poured a good deal of creative energy into political speeches for candidates. Who know what novels, what *War and Peace*, I might have written? (And might not have.) But then I would not have been an ambassador nor would I have learned to care so deeply about certain public issues nor come to understand so fully the importance of serious politics to the life of our democracy. No regrets. (But I warned Fred.)

4.

Odds and ends—in these years, I was making an occasional speech and writing an occasional opinion piece for a magazine or newspa-per, *The New York Times, Washington Post, Chicago Tribune, Phila-delphia Inquirer, USA Today,* often on politics or on U.S. policy in

the Caribbean. Magazine editors and book publishers wanted me to go back to doing heavy fact, crime in its social context. But I'd be repeating myself. I received honorary degrees from Indiana University and Knox College, gave my papers to the Library of Congress, four and a half tons of them. For several months I wrote a column for *Life*, and the editors began to negotiate a contract, through Dorothy Olding, making me a permanent contributor. At that point, however, the editors were fired; my career at *Life* ended (and so, for a time, did *Life*). The editors of *Look* asked me to do a piece, but about the time I finished it, those editors were fired; soon *Look* too folded. In the '70s and '80s, the magazine market was hardly the stable haven it had been in the 1950s.

Newt Minow was chairman of a task force established by the Twentieth Century Fund on political campaign television and asked me to write the final report. This led to a new project—he and I, together with Lee M. Mitchell, a young Washington lawyer, wrote a book for the fund, *Presidential Television*, discussing the problems raised by the awesome power of the president to simultaneously command the attention of virtually the entire nation.

I next did a book for the Twentieth Century Fund, *U.S. Policy in the Caribbean*. It seemed to me that the United States had had no real policy toward the Caribbean since President Kennedy's Alliance for Progress. Roxane Eberlein did the historical research; I did interviewing in Washington, New York, and the Caribbean basin. In the book, I discussed recent revolutionary changes that had caused the Caribbean nations to drift away from us. I argued that the United States had important strategic, economic, and political interests in the Caribbean. But we remained indifferent to it. We were the only great power that did not take its near neighbors seriously. We should, I argued, take a national decision that the development of the Caribbean societies was in the vital interest of the United States and we should place that interest high on our list of priorities, perhaps in fourth or fifth place, or right after the survival of Israel. I offered some twenty-nine specific recommendations, such as normalizing relations with Cuba. The book was respectfully received but it had only marginal effects on policy. We will no doubt see little real change until we elect a president with a real interest in the Caribbean. We have not had one since President Kennedy.

5.

To succeed, a politician needs not only to be articulate, attractive, and a leader, he needs even more to be lucky. Adlai Stevenson had been lucky for a time, had hit a rising curve that carried him to the Governor's Mansion and propelled him toward the White House. But then his luck went bad—he was obliged to run against Eisenhower, was overtaken by Kennedy. His son, Adlai III, had the good luck to run in Illinois for state representative in a year when he could run at large and could lead the ticket statewide; he was handy when Dick Daley's Democratic machine needed a clean candidate for state treasurer; and then one September day in 1969 lightning struck: In the midst of a political rally at his father's old house in Libertyville, word came that the incumbent U.S. senator from Illinois had just died. Instantly young Adlai, at thirty-nine, became the leading candidate for the Democratic nomination for the Senate the next year, 1970. Throughout that fall and winter, I went down to the Loop nearly every Saturday to meet with him and a small group of advisers as he maneuvered, like his father, to win the support of the Daley machine yet to maintain too an independent stance. Nominated, he went to call on Mayor Daley and asked, as he was leaving, "Do you have any final advice for me?" The mayor pondered a moment then said, "Yes. Don't change your name." "Name recognition"—the Stevenson name was indeed known all over Illinois. In the fall campaign of 1970, I wrote speeches in his Loop headquarters. Since it was a small staff and since he was accessible, I was able once more to coordinate speeches, scheduling, and campaign strategy. Young Adlai campaigned well and was again in luck: His opponent was a downstate courthouse politician who made nearly every mistake possible. To try to save the hapless Republican candidate, President Nixon and Vice-President Agnew—remember Agnew?—came repeatedly into Illinois; every time they did they handed us about six thousand dollars worth of television time free, for the stations felt obliged to give Adlai free time equal to theirs. (How all-absorbing are such tactics during a campaign—and how quickly forgotten.) Young Adlai was less eloquent and less dazzling than his father, but he gave the impression of great solidity, of trustworthiness, and the time was right for that too. It was one of those rare

campaigns where we did everything right. He won big. He was later reelected and in the Senate he worked hard. But he was not happy there, for reasons I never fully understood, and when his second term expired, did not run for reelection.*

While he was in the Senate, I saw young Adlai frequently and from time to time sent him memos or speech drafts on issues I felt strongly about. I did the same with Ted Kennedy. I regarded those small private contributions to public policy as more important than the writing I was doing.

In 1972, I became involved in a presidential campaign for the last time. Before the early primaries, I tried to help Senator Edmund Muskie, whom I had long admired and who, in the beginning, was the front runner for the nomination. I traveled with him a little and I went a good many times to Washington to meet in Clark Clifford's quiet office with Clifford and Muskie's other senior advisers, Senator Albert Gore, Sol Linowitz, and Jim Rowe—a useful exercise.† Muskie, however, proved to be a surprisingly weak candidate, and he was overwhelmed by the sudden surge of revolt and fragmentation that swept the Democratic party. The unthinkable climax came when the young rebels actually threw Dick Daley and his delegates out of the national convention. And nominated Senator George McGovern, a thoroughly nice man, but surely not a president.

Nonetheless, that fall I went to live at the Hay-Adams in Washington and to write speeches for McGovern. A number of people asked me to, and he was after all running against Richard Nixon. I could do little for him. His cocksure young staff, Gary Hart and the others aboard his plane, guarded him too jealously. Some of them were given to noisily and publicly resigning every few days and to

---

*Instead, he ran in 1982 for governor. Here his luck ran out. Given the circumstances of that time, he should have won rather easily. Instead, he lost (by about five thousand votes out of about three and a half million cast). His excellent political sense seemed to desert him. He beat himself. And he lost many of his and his father's old friends.

†Clifford had played a similar role in Jack Kennedy's 1960 campaign and now, since he had served quietly on intelligence panels and had been for a time President Johnson's secretary of defense, was considered not only one of Washington's most powerful lawyers, but also an elder statesman. He was also an expensive lawyer—a story, probably apocryphal, was told that he once conferred at some length with a voluble client, then sent him his advice in a one-sentence letter, "Do and say nothing," along with a bill for five thousand dollars, then huge, and when the client expostulated and at some length demanded to know precisely why he should do and say nothing, sent him a second one-sentence letter, "Because I said so," together with a bill for another five thousand dollars.

talking freely to the press, bewildering to anyone who had known the anonymous staffs of FDR and Truman and Stevenson. I worked at the Washington headquarters. I had written speeches and done editorial advance work in the fall campaign of every Democratic candidate for president in the last twenty years, starting with Stevenson in 1952, and in presidential primaries and senatorial campaigns as well, but I had never seen any campaign so poor as the McGovern campaign. Ted Van Dyk and Milt Gwirtzman, whom I had worked with before, now nominally in charge of issues for McGovern, were able professionals; but nobody else on McGovern's staff seemed ever to have worked in a national campaign before. I told Fran my arrival had raised the average age of the staff to thirteen and a half. The headquarters had the uproarious atmosphere of a college dormitory—scores of barefoot girls in blue jeans and boys in long hair and beads racing about mindlessly, taping up funny signs in the corridors. Over the door to one office hung a sign WAR ROOM, and inside, a half-dozen youngsters were always lounging about in broken chairs, playing with maps, and denouncing the Vietnam War—to each other. The chief fund-raiser was named Kimmelman; a woman's liberationist changed his name on the door to KIMMELPERSON. I should have realized that this campaign was not for me when I found that one of my speechwriter colleagues was Stephen Schlesinger, the son of Arthur. (Stephen, I should add, was a serious and effective young writer, as uncomfortable as I with the silly children surrounding us.) If you left your desk unguarded to get a cup of coffee, when you returned your pens and paper and sometimes even your typewriter would be gone. I was grateful when I was assigned to write the major speech of the campaign, the one on Vietnam, and could withdraw to Clark Clifford's quiet law office to discuss and write it with him. We produced a passable speech that was at least carefully drafted, but the staff on the plane rewrote and fussed over it so long and amid such frenzy that sloppy drafting crept in, with the result that the press, not unjustly, accused McGovern of shifting his position.

McGovern himself made mistake after foolish mistake. A friend of mine who had investigated Jimmy Hoffa for Bob Kennedy was investigating the Watergate burglary, new that fall, and when from time to time I ran into him he told me he was sure Watergate led straight to the White House and was deadly serious; but McGovern

persisted in referring to it, in the cant of that strange time, as "the Watergate caper." He, who was supposed to be a plain man of integrity, anything but slick, fell into the trap of performing for the television cameras, as when he journeyed all the way to Superior, Wisconsin, in order to read a statement on wheat while standing in front of a grain elevator for the benefit of television cameras—a "television event," his youthful staff called it; a stunt. On Columbus Day, he made a speech praising Americans of Italian descent as the most law-abiding of all Americans—doing clumsily what Dick Daley had done skillfully for years: ethnic politics. I used to dread the morning paper; it was almost sure to recount another blunder. Near the end, Ted Van Dyk said, "John, if he wins we're going to have to work harder than we ever worked in our lives." None of us thought he would. Never before had I worked for a candidate I didn't believe in. I was pleased, however, when in later years he became a sort of elder statesman of the Democratic party.

In 1976, the mad proliferating primaries gave us Democrats a presidential candidate who was a caucus politician from a southern state, with no national experience. Fran and I watched the convention on television with dismay. For us, it hit a maudlin low point when the father of Martin Luther King, Jr., shouted to the convention that he had "talked to all three of them up there" (President Kennedy, Robert F. Kennedy, and Martin Luther King, Jr., presumably in heaven). After the convention I composed a song lyric to be sung to the tune of "Rock of Ages":

> *Jimmy Carter is our boy*
> *He will bring eternal joy.*
> *Never lies, oh never sins,*
> *Never loses, always wins.*
>
> *Take the even, take the odd,*
> *He will lead us back to God.*
> *No more whiskey, no more gin,*
> *He will save us all from sin.*
>
> *Jimmy Carter and his sis,*
> *They will bring eternal bliss.*
> *He the master, I the clod,*
> *On my stumbling way to God.*

Smite the heathen, praise the Lord,
Cleanse the evil Gerald Ford.
Send us manna, send us joy.
Give us peanuts, Jimmy boy.

Peanuts, popcorn, Cracker Jack,
Jesus Christ—our Jimmy's back.

It may seem unfair to poke fun at a man's religion, but when a man uses his religion to win public office, it is fair game.

For the first time in twenty-four years, I had no part in the campaign. Not to be part of a presidential campaign is liberating. If you're on the plane and the candidate blunders, you forgive it, he's *your* candidate, sitting only a few seats away; but if you're on the outside, you see him for what he is, a blunderer. I couldn't bring myself to vote for either Carter or Ford; I wrote in Ted Kennedy. In the fall of 1979, I thought Carter could not be reelected and suggested, as did others, that Ted Kennedy consider running against him in the 1980 primaries, and he did, but Iran and Afghanistan saved Carter, and Ted failed. And we got Ronald Reagan, an amiable actor who after a short while stopped seeming to me even amiable. Adlai Stevenson and President Kennedy—oh to live in such a time again!

My malaise during the McGovern campaign was not, of course, all his fault. In part it was my own. The country was changing, and I wasn't. After President Kennedy's death, President Johnson had pressed forward in the FDR-Truman-Stevenson-Kennedy tradition; but all the while, the ground was shifting beneath his feet, and it collapsed in 1968—the year of the Tet offensive, the Bob Kennedy and Eugene McCarthy primaries, campus revolt, and the Chicago convention. Out of all this came somehow a new style in politics. The "New Liberalism" and the "New Politics" arose, as I have said. Young people were in revolt. They declared they wanted to "open up" the party—no more boss-controlled conventions, let the people through the primaries decide. What they did not realize was that they were handing control of politics over not to the people but to the poll takers and the television anchormen. And control through a handful of small unrepresentative states—it is absurd that a few farmers in Iowa and New Hampshire should choose the leader of

the Western world. When in 1972 the press and television announced that Ed Muskie should get 50 percent of the vote in New Hampshire, and when he got 46 percent, far more than any other candidate, they announced he'd lost. Later they discovered he'd actually gotten 49.9 percent—but that was long after they'd driven him out of the primaries. As for issues, forget unemployment and inflation, nuclear arms control—what mattered to these young people were such issues as "women's liberation," "gay liberation," abortion, legalization of marijuana. *Those* were, to them, the questions by which the Republic would live or die. The rebels demanded proportionate representation among convention delegates for women, Negroes, and Hispanic Americans, which, of course, could only lead to the odious quota system long ago abandoned as racist. Even Richard Nixon—he of the Watergate cover-up—talked about an "open" government. New leaders arose who spoke in the idiom of populism and seemed bent on dismantling the government. All these changes were said to be destroying big-city machines, making national conventions obsolete, and creating something on the order of a New National Democracy. It struck me, however, that if we want a New National Democracy, more than the usual 20 percent of us will have to vote in the primaries; and the press, especially television, will have to stop covering the primaries like a series of baseball games—will have to stop predicting who will win and start telling us what we may expect the candidates to do if they do win. Time was when reporters told us what the candidates thought about issues—Lincoln on slavery, Bryan on silver, Stevenson on Korea. Nowadays each night during the primaries they tell us who will win by what percentage next Tuesday and why they were wrong last Tuesday about who would win by what percentage. At least since ancient Athens, men have heeded soothsayers' predictions. Yet *who will win* is a question of no importance whatsoever to the voter (he will know anyway on election day), though it may help the gambler place his bet and the candidate plan his strategy and raise money. ("When the polls go good for me," Richard Nixon once said, "the cash register really rings.") And what if we awake some morning to learn that a member of the press—not, probably, a leading television commentator, but one of his anonymous writers—or a poll taker has been corrupted by a politician? What if the Watergate conspirators, in-

stead of merely hating the members of the press, had bought a few?

Some advocates of the "New Politics" maintained it was new because it brought mass popular protest movements, such as the civil rights and anti–Vietnam War movements, into the mainstream of politics. But this is precisely what the old politics has always done. The farmers' protest movement beginning in the 1870s, for example, was taken up by the Populist party, and that in turn was absorbed into the Democratic party and remained for many years a powerful force in the Democratic Party. It is the genius of the American political system that the two parties have historically acted as sponges, soaking up conflicting pressures in society by the very process of bringing them into the mainstream and making them heard. The only time the system broke down, the Civil War resulted.

In taking our politics away from the professional politicians, we have handed it over to television and poll taking and advertising. So powerful is television that it takes over whatever it becomes involved in. When it covers a professional football game, not the weariness of the players decides when time out will be called; instead, television decides. A little man with a little red hat stands down on the sidelines; he works for television, and when he lifts his little red hat, time is called, for that signals it is time for a television commercial. Even baseball, virtually our only remaining national innocence, plays most of the World Series not on golden afternoons but at night, "in prime time." During political campaigns, hired "television consultants" not only school their candidates in words and gestures; they chart strategy and select issues. They are prima donnas and behave during campaigns as if *their* fate were being decided. And indeed it is—a television consultant with a string of losing candidates will not find his services in demand. The star system; once again, winning, not governing, is the object. Having schooled their candidate in words and gestures and issues, they put him on TV display then send forth their poll takers and await the verdict; and if the poll takers' computer spits out an unfavorable verdict, they change the words and gestures and issues. Television converts serious political questions into theater; thirty-second spot commercials may take over entirely. Television killed magazines; it has also killed serious political speeches.

During the 1976 campaign, President Ford's staff offered him up

to a live TV interview in Chicago provided the questions were easy. The interviewers, whom television likes to call "electronic journalists," asked him only whether winning Illinois was important, what kind of weather he would like on election day, and his views on the Michigan–Ohio State football game. This is journalism? The Ford campaign bought television time to broadcast half-hour "documentaries." The broadcasts showed Ford appearing at rallies during the day, reproduced the crowd's roar—or some other crowd's roar dubbed in at the studio—and showed a running commentary by a sports announcer who supported Ford. They showed Ford speaking, but one did not hear a word he said. Instead, one saw and heard the sports announcer comment, "The response from the people was tremendous, overwhelming." The sports announcer then "interviewed" Ford, asking, "How many leaders have you dealt with, Mr. President?" "One hundred and twenty-four leaders of countries around the world, Joe."

TV news broadcasters themselves often undermine our political system. Some local anchormen, straining to attract attention to themselves in order to raise their ratings, affect to hold in contempt all politicians and parties. They cover serious politics as gossip columnists cover divorce rumors. They degrade politics. Some anchormen, both network and local, who become well known pretend modestly to be simple reporters while presenting what is actually nothing but their own opinions. Some become oracular, presenting their opinions as final judgments; people see it and believe it.

As is well known, broadcasters and their partners, the poll takers, devised a technique called exit polling—asking voters leaving the polls how they voted—and early on election night they use those polls to "project" who is winning, often doing so with east coast results hours before the polls have closed in California, thus, probably, causing some west coast voters to stay home—why bother to vote for someone who's already lost? Moreover, serious students of politics tend to take exit polls as definitive. But they are no more reliable than any other poll.

In 1984, virtually every work and every act of both the Republican and Democratic candidates was aimed at nothing but the evening TV news. Their staff poll takers and TV writers strove single-mindedly for, in their strange vocabulary, "the sound bite"—

the fragment of a candidate's speech that gets on the network evening news. Issues, smissues. Reduce the complexity to bumper stickers. Mondale's poll taker, who virtually took over his campaign, in preparing him for his first "debate" with President Reagan instructed him not to come out fighting, as the president's staff expected, but to treat the president with respect, to praise him for his good intentions, to appear to regret that such a kindly nice old man could not seem to remember the facts of the issues—what reporters called the gold watch speech, one given at the dinner honoring a faithful, grandfatherly employee upon his retirement. Along with a pat on the head. Nevertheless, the poll taker, worried by the movement in his polls of young white men toward Reagan, and fearing it might be reinforced by Reagan's height and actor's dominance of the platform, instructed Mondale to assert his own manhood—to turn to face Reagan, to take one step toward him, and only then to return to his lectern and speak to the people. Mondale did it, and with considerable help from the befuddled president, "won" the debate. (Mondale did not, however, as the poll taker also suggested, plant the idea that the president's hearing was poor by lowering his own voice or turning away from Reagan while speaking.)

Newspapers and TV networks alike covered the two debates as though nothing else happened during the campaign. Indeed, nothing else did, for those two debates were nationally broadcast live on all three networks. Yet debating is one of the few things a sitting president is never called upon to do.

It may well be that by now the evening TV news has acquired more influence over the electorate than the president or Congress. But nobody elected these anchormen to anything, and they are responsible for nothing and accountable to no one. Political parties are responsible and they are accountable; they have to listen; if they don't, their candidates will be voted out. They meet the people's needs through negotiation and compromise; they determine who gets what. Who weakens the party system weakens democracy. TV is no substitute at all.

When television and poll taking were new, candidates and their staffs relied on George Gallup's periodic poll and paid little more than passing attention even to it. Today every candidate has his own poll taker. In 1984, each actually took a poll every day. "Tracking

polls," they called them, and they decided the candidates' policy positions, his campaign strategy, his travels, his speeches, his money raising, his mannerisms and dress and gestures. And in a sense, our future.

Yet polling is notoriously unreliable. As I discovered years ago, while reporting on opinion in Muncie, people often will not tell even a reporter what they really think, as I have said, though they may tell him what they "hear people saying." And polling is not done by experienced reporters with plenty of time; it is done by young clerks holding a clipboard. Or even done by telephone. People lie to poll takers. Or they refuse to talk to them. (I myself have been approached by three poll takers, one face to face, two by telephone; I refused to say anything except that I don't like polling.) In constructing their "voter profiles," poll takers can be reasonably sure of some things—they can, for example, verify by objective fact that a man is a Negro, either by checking his address (in most cases) or visually (in most cases). But other data they cannot verify—his income bracket, for example, or how long he went to school, or his age, or his religion, or, except in some primaries, whether he is a Democrat, Republican, or "independent." For these and other "facts" they have only his word. How do they know he is telling the truth?

How good is "scientific random sampling"? I am not statistician enough—or numerologist enough—to know. But I do know there is no magic in numbers. Yet numbers seem to increasingly run our lives. Figures on population, the economy, money, unemployment, arms control, politics, the numbers of poll takers, the numbers of TV ratings—it is not really things but numbers that are in the saddle. People believe numbers, believe them just because they are numbers. This is a mistake. "I still think," Joseph Wood Krutch wrote, "that a familiarity with the best that has been thought and said by men of letters is more helpful than all the sociologists' statistics."

When I worked on presidential campaign staffs, my colleagues included such men as Carl McGowen, Ken Galbraith, Arthur Schlesinger, Bob Tufts, Dave Bell, Bill Wirtz, Bill Blair, Ted Sorensen, Kenny O'Donnell, Fred Dutton, Larry O'Brien, Jerry Bruno, Ted Van Dyk, Milt Gwirtzman. Not one of them ever imagined that he was "molding the candidate's image"; not one talked to the press much or leaked anything to the press that harmed the candidate; not

one ever imagined that he was himself the candidate. One of them, the late Jim Rowe, liked to relate how, when he was on President Roosevelt's White House staff and insisted that FDR do something his way, the president ended the discussion: "I do not have to do it your way," the president said, "and I will tell you the reason why. The reason is that, although they may have made a mistake, the people of the United States elected me president, not you."*

Today, young poll takers for hire and young television consultants for hire infest Washington. They are paid and well paid. They completely dominate campaigns. Some intend to remain in their profession; others see a campaign as a step up to an even higher paying job. They advance their own cause, not their candidates', by talking freely to the press. Sometimes they favor correspondents with their unfavorable opinions of their candidates. They feud endlessly among themselves; they go public with their feuds. Every now and then they resign, publicly and noisily. To me, they seem to be monsters. Some seem hysterical, even heartless. Mondale's own manager, two weeks before the election, flew from the cool computerized Washington office to the sweaty campaign plane in Milwaukee to tell Mondale that their polls and other "evidence" showed a Reagan landslide. Mondale had just come in from a triumphal bus trip through his own Mississippi Valley heartland, ablaze in golden October glory, and his crowds had been big and warm, even hot. He was campaigning his heart out; he'd felt that maybe at last he was turning it around. To his manager he protested piteously that he'd thought his crowds had been good lately. No matter—he was twenty points down in their polls. After that they left him alone, and for the first time he came alive. He did it all alone.

We have always been a wasteful people, never more than in the late 1960s and 1970s and 1980s, when we wasted all our politics on appearance. While our "young activities" were loudly debating their nonissues, the rest of the world was facing issues of a wholly new order. Nearly half the two billion people living in poor countries are starving. The poor countries no longer look to us or to Moscow— they are on to both of us; that game is over—they look to themselves

---

* Arthur related this in his fond memorial to Jim Rowe in the annual report of the Twentieth Century Fund, of which Jim had long been a director.

and to each other. And in each poor country, the poor eye the rich hungrily, the rich the poor warily. The Law of the Sea goes unsigned by us, yet the deep seabed may shape our future more than the moon and Mars. Energy is an issue containing all others; we have not begun to face it. Such issues are of a wholly new magnitude, for they are planetary. Almost nobody talks about them. The arms race is all but out of control. Nuclear proliferation is not a threat, it is a fact: The bomb will reach desperate hands. We know now that nuclear war will likely mean the end of man.

One of the books that impressed me most when I was in college was written by another Indiana author (and ambassador), Claude Bowers. *The Tragic Era* recounted the history of the period of Reconstruction after the Civil War. It seems to me, unhappily, that our country has during the twenty-odd years since the death of President Kennedy passed through another tragic era. Since then, it has been all downhill. My privilege was to live during the time when Roosevelt, Truman, and Kennedy were president—times when the United States under their leadership was behaving like a great nation. Since President Kennedy we have had a succession of failed presidents. And it is almost as if the country itself, buffeted by assassination and Vietnam and Watergate, became unhinged. Dismayed as I have been for these past twenty years, I cannot believe that the country, given a true leader, will not pull itself together and once more regain its rightful place as the leader of the Western world and the model of a good society that cares for its own disadvantaged. I have no patent on patriotism. But anybody who has written about this country all his life and ached to see it better cannot help but thrill when it does something right; anybody who has occupied high public office cannot watch without emotion as the flag goes by. My faith in this country is unashamed.

6.

Of late, young senators have been declaring that the "old liberalism" of the 1950s and 1960s (and earlier) will not do in the '80s (and beyond)—we need, they say, "neoliberalism" (though I have yet to see a clear explanation of what "neoliberalism" means). Nonsense. True, the economy must be adjusted from smokestack industry to high-technology industry, as the young senators keep saying.

But the human needs are the same for a man on a computer assembly line as for a man on an auto assembly line—his wife gets sick, he is laid off, his kids get in trouble, and he gets old. A generation of conservative yammering about "big spenders," plus the yelping of George Wallace *et al.* about sending a message and getting the government off somebody's back, plus pseudosociological notions about a combined blue-collar and white-collar middle-class new majority, have scared some liberals. The 1980 election of Ronald Reagan was called a basic political realignment, and after his reelection landslide in 1984, it was said that the Democratic party's old coalition had fallen apart and the party was intellectually bankrupt, devoid of new ideas. But the truth was that the party's problem was not ideas, it was leadership. We Democrats had not had a truly presidential leader since Robert Kennedy and Hubert Humphrey. In 1972 not McGovern, in 1976 and 1980 not Carter, in 1984 not Mondale—as national leader, not one measured up to FDR or Harry Truman or John F. Kennedy. Or, for that matter, to Dwight Eisenhower.

After the Reagan victories too the notion arose that the country was "turning conservative," and many Democrats thought their party ought to follow that trend, at least tactically. To my mind, it would be as suicidal for the Democratic party to abandon its traditional liberalism in 1988 as it was in 1972 to surrender to the then-fashionable young people's New Politics. The Democratic party, as Dean Acheson once said of it, is my party because it has always been the party not of one interest alone, the business interest, but of the many interests.

The conservatives crusaded against "Big Government" and swore to "get the government off the back" of their beloved free enterprise. Deregulation. How did that turn out? In Arizona and a dozen other states, the legislatue deregulated interest rates on consumer loans. According to *The Wall Street Journal,* an elderly Navajo woman in Arizona with a family of twelve, who had won a land dispute and been given a house in town by the government, left the reservation and moved to town, though she knew little English and knew little of the ways of town. She earned five hundred dollars a month. Soon her son needed money for clothes, and she borrowed seven hundred dollars from a loan company; she put up her new house as collateral.

The loan company charged her 127 percent in interest and "points." (Often the interest rate itself was advertised as "only" 28 percent; points—one point equals 1 percent—for administrative costs and so on ran the bill up. Borrowers don't read the fine print.) A South Carolina used-car dealer claimed the right to charge 500 percent. Some of these lenders were huge national finance companies.

But they were not alone. In the new atmosphere of deregulated free enterprise—and unrestrained greed—not only loan sharks but also executives of some of the nation's big banks and other financial institutions were caught conniving against the rest of us for profit, and so were mighty defense contractors as well as the manufacturers of defective and dangerous automobiles. These were not fly-by-night loan sharks; these were big, respected, famous corporations. How did they get so famous? By advertising their respectability on TV. How so respected? By getting big. How did they get so big? By screwing the little guy. And who was to protect the little guy if not the government? Nobody. And who chooses the government? The political parties. The Navajo woman can survive in such an unregulated jungle only if some political party looks after her "special interest" in her house.

None of this is a "new idea." Farmers in the last century restrained the railroad's greed only through the new government regulatory agency, the Interstate Commerce Commission. Theodore Roosevelt carried on with his trust-busting, and so did Woodrow Wilson, and the whole reform movement came to a thundering climax under Franklin D. Roosevelt. "A new deal for the American people" and "malefactors of great wealth," "one-third of a nation ill-housed and ill-clothed and ill-fed" and "the forgotten man" were far more than slogans; they were the pledges and the protests of a leader of a people that had had enough of greed and injustice. Any young senator worrying today about "population transfers" and "structural unemployment" during the transition to "high tech" would do well to worry instead about injustice—the wrongs of our society today and tomorrow. That, not electronic chips, is still the test of our society. Things may be in the saddle but they cannot ride mankind. Our Democratic party need not worry about new ideas if it keeps its eye on the old idea, the idea of a just society. That requires a leader.

The period of our failed Democratic maximum leaders, both elected and defeated, spans four consecutive presidental elections, 1972–1984. But even so many years are transitory. What, in the liberal faith, is not transitory? From all the tumult over my lifetime and more, what abides? Let me try to restate it.

First Principles: We liberals start with (but pretend no patent on) the great charter, the U.S. Constitution. We resist frivolous efforts to tinker with it for transitory purposes, whether to prohibit liquor or abortion. We regard any assault on the Bill of Rights as a dangerous attack on our most fundamental liberties. Citizens free to worship or not to worship, free to say or publish what they think, secure in their persons and homes against unreasonable search and seizure, assured of due process of law and trial by an impartial jury, safe from self-incrimination—those are *American* citizens. Everybody, of course, says he supports the Constitution. But when we say it, we mean not only the separation of powers and civilian supremacy over the military and other vital underpinnings but also certain quite specific rights, some embodied in judicial decisions grown out of those amendments that guarantee our rights. We oppose, for example, any effort to abrogate or weaken the rights of defendants in the criminal justice process—sometimes dismissed as "mere procedure"—including the exclusionary rule, right to counsel, total protection against illegal detention and search and seizure, against coerced confession and self-incrimination for even the most despicable defendants, indeed, especially for the most despicable—efforts all too often undertaken in the name of "law and order" or "taking the handcuffs off the police." In my writing, I saw enough victims of criminal *in*justice to convince me of the importance of "mere procedure"—feebleminded John Simon wrongfully in prison in Pittsbugh, Álvaro Alcorta of San Antonio unfairly awaiting the electric chair, a suspect vomiting blood on the police station floor in Chicago, many more.

Domestic Policy: Apart from the Constitution, we liberals believe the government should do for its citizens things they cannot do for themselves. It should protect them against disaster, whether economic or medical, not of their own making. How big should government be? Big enough to do what needs doing. Government, we believe, should not be afraid to plan, however unfashionable plan-

ning has become; we cannot leave matters to a mythical free marketplace. Government should enforce equal opportunity for all citizens and liberate their fullest potentialities. We believe fervently that the will of the majority must prevail; we believe equally fervently that the rights of the minority must be protected. From time to time we liberals have discerned enemies—in Jackson's time the Bank, in Bryan's the cross of gold, in TR's the trusts, in FDR's the malefactors of great wealth. So here is another liberal thread—one enemy is the money power. We do not seek to create an egalitarian society; we seek to curb the excessive power of money and its abuse to exploit the weak; we seek to curb greed. We support the labor movement, not those of its leaders who are racketeers or dictators and not all its political program. But we believe that a strong and free and democratic labor movement in an adversary position to management is not only the workingman's best protection against predatory big business but also one of the most important bulwarks of our general society.

When a liberal goes to Vicente Noble in the Dominican Republic, as I did, and sees the gray-haired women carrying water in pails on their heads through the deep dust to their huts, and sees the children with bloated bellies eating dirt, he says, "Let's dam the river and irrigate and make the desert bloom as it does ten kilometers away on the fruit company plantation." When he watches the electrocution of a slum boy for murder, he says, "Next time, let's do better." The liberal does not believe that man is perfectible; that is too much. But he believes we can make things better. Life, as President Kennedy said, is unfair. But perhaps we can make it less unfair for some. The machinery that runs our lives, of which I spoke in the Centralia story—to make it work better, more fairly for all, that is the liberal mission. No liberal believes that all Soviet leaders are magnanimous and trustworthy. No liberal believes that all the American poor are industrious and noble. No liberal believes that the state can cure all the afflictions of old age. But all liberals believe that we can try. The American people may or may not be a liberal people, but they are a compassionate people. It is to this compassion that liberalism speaks. Of the disadvantaged, we say: Send them to us. This is not softheaded hearts and flowers. This is only good sense. A society's greatness is not measured only by its military might, or by its gross

national product. It is, at bottom, measured by the well-being of its citizens, especially its lowliest citizens. When they dwell in misery, the whole society rots. The well-being, the very security, of the highest depends upon the well-being of the lowest. Political stability and national security come from all, not from a few. From the improvement of the condition of the weakest comes the nation's strength.

Foreign Policy: Here I lack both the information and the wisdom to state the liberals' view (if there is one) of America's proper role in the world, much less to discuss the budgetary implications of foreign policy alternatives or to recommend one of those apocalypic revisions of our role, such as disengaging from NATO or declaring "no first use" of nuclear weapons, which appear, fortunately, in learned journals. I simply don't know enough. Rather I will merely put forward a few ideas in areas I have studied or had some firsthand experience in.

We liberals would hope that other nations establish elected democratic governments, since we believe that their peoples will fare best under that system; but we think it is really none of our business how they choose to organize their societies, and if one of them goes under to a dictatorship of the left or right, we pity its people but we will not intervene so long as that dictatorship's policy does not threaten our own vital interests. This does not mean that we should shut our eyes to repression. We should make it clear by our words, but even clearer by our diplomatic deeds, that we prefer freedom to repression. Small things count—we can invite the representative of, say, democratic Costa Rica, but not the representative of a dictator, to White House receptions; we can send the vice-president to ceremonies in the democracies; more tangibly, we can give the representatives of democracies access to high levels of the State Department. And even more, we can deal promptly and sympathetically with whatever problems they wish to take up with us, including their loan applications and the terms of their trade. Yet we liberals resist those who would put our policies into an ideological straitjacket—we oppose a mindless anti-Communist crusade, for example, or, for another example, human rights as a rigid policy, for while we think we Americans should always stoutly uphold the principle of human rights as we conceive them, to attach the word "policy" to them may

be dangerous, since to do so might lead to a crusade to impose our view on other nations—some of which have different views, such as the Soviets' view that the right to a job is a basic human right—and might ultimately lead us to try to police the world. What we favor instead might be called a policy of live and let live. Or, as President Kennedy said, "make the world safe for diversity."

We liberals believe the United States should develop a truly special relationship with Mexico, Canada, and the nations of the Caribbean basin. We would strengthen the OAS, and we would revive the principles of the Alliance for Progress throughout the Americas. We believe that, worldwide, we and the other developed nations should work for North-South accommodations. We wish to promote the development of underdeveloped nations and underdeveloped peoples, not only because it is just but because it is in our own interest. We would stop or virtually stop selling arms, especially to poor countries, sales that are an obscenity; arms do not develop, arms kill. We favor an all-out effort at arms control and, ultimately, at disarmament, especially nuclear arms control and if ever possible nuclear disarmament by the United States and the USSR. We know that every arms race in history has led but to war.

Finally, we would work to strengthen the peacekeeping ability of the United Nations and to use the UN more. In recent years, as small new nations have flooded the United Nations and swamped the United States in vote after vote in the General Assembly, U.S. presidents have tended to bypass the UN and our ambassadors there have even publicly denounced it. But before we adopt that long-ago slogan of Barry Goldwater, "Get the UN out of the U.S., and get the U.S. out of the UN," we should pause and ask ourselves: Do we really want to go back to the world we had before the UN existed? After World War I, we did indeed keep the League of Nations out of the U.S. and the U.S. out of the League. The League collapsed; we and the rest of the world lived in a jungle and ended up in World War II. Out of that came the determination "Never again," and we built the UN. Its flaws are all too apparent. In the General Assembly, often the Third World countries are indeed exasperating, irresponsible, and ridiculous. The Security Council is impotent in big-power confrontations. Yet it has dealt successfully with other disputes. Time and again the UN has served as a fireman to put out

a brushfire. Had it not been there, the brushfire might have suddenly become a major conflagration. And today, general war is more likely to result from some suddenly escalating rimland dispute than from ignition at the European–North American heartland. If the UN did nothing more than put out brushfires, we liberals believe it would be worth all the millions of dollars it costs us. For we don't believe that we—or the Third World either—really want to go back to the ancient Greek world, when, as we learn from Thucydides, the powerful Grecian ambassadors said to the Melian ambassadors: "You know and we know, as practical men, that the question of justice arises only between parties equal in strength, and that the strong do what they can, and the weak submit."

Eight American presidents have died in office. The deaths of three changed history—Lincoln, Roosevelt, Kennedy. With Lincoln, we would not have had the agony of radical Reconstruction; with Roosevelt, we might not have had the cold war; with Kennedy, no Vietnam or Watergate. Men are both the creatures and the creators of history, some more the one, some more the other; those three were clearly creators. As to Kennedy, and Vietnam, we shall never know, since history does not reveal its alternatives, but to me and others who worked with him, it is inconceivable that President Kennedy would have allowed himself to be dragged so deeply into Vietnam as President Johnson did. He had learned at the Bay of Pigs to be skeptical of the intelligence experts and military experts; he would have given due weight to the other issues involved; and in the end he would have asked, when the Joint Chiefs wanted another fifty thousand troops. "Hey, wait a minute—what's in it for me?" A few weeks before his death, when he and I were discussing our failure to prevent the overthrow of the Dominican president, he said quietly, "There are some things we simply cannot do." Already he had learned that there are limits to American power. As to the blacks and the young, they would never have revolted against Kennedy. And Watergate is inconceivable for him or his staff.

Surprisingly, in the 1970s, nostalgia arose for the 1930s and 1940s. Surprisingly, because the 1930s found us in the worst depression in history and the 1940s found us in the worst war in history. I suspect we look back on those years less, really, with fondness than with

pride. For during those two decades we behaved as a great nation. In the 1930s our government declared its compassion for the unable; in the 1940s we showed the world what we were willing to fight for. We have reason to be proud of those decades. Perhaps nations like individuals need luck; perhaps they too hit rising and descending curves. The United States hit a rising curve in the early 1930s that carried it through the 1940s; since the awful November of 1963 it has been on a downward curve. I myself hit a rising curve about 1948 and it continued in writing and politics until 1963. (How incredibly lucky, really—to hit the great days of both magazines and quality television, to have Stevenson and Kennedy for my candidates!) I think I realized it was all over the morning in 1968 after Robert Kennedy was shot; Fran and I left our room in the Ambassador Hotel in Los Angeles to go to the hospital and found in the hotel driveway automobiles already bearing bumper stickers: PRAY FOR BOBBY. Pray—a lot of good that did.

A lad eighteen today was born that year. He can have not the slightest idea of how different our country would be today if Jack Kennedy and Bobby Kennedy had not been murdered. There would have been no Vietnam and no Watergate; no President Nixon and no President Reagan; no president calling our children "bums," as Nixon did, or our adversaries "an evil empire," as Reagan did; no elevation of the Bible-bangers' pet issues, such as abortion and school prayer, to the solemn deliberations of our most exalted wise men (and it was Carter, not Reagan, who first lusted after the fundamentalist vote); and, finally, perhaps even no uncontrolled arms race to Armageddon. Poor eighteen-year-old—at least we elderly know the United States was not always so, and need not have been but for one lunatic assassin in Dallas and another in Los Angeles.

Let us all hope, however, that he does understand one thing better than we do—that the nuclear issue, nuclear arms control, is like no other ever. And this issue will arise only this once. If we make one mistake, if we unleash the nuclear weapon, we will get no second chance. This is something new on earth.

7.

During these years of politics and writing and teaching, our kids were growing up and finding careers. (Kids! Cindy is past forty; even the youngest, Fred, is past thirty.) All three ended up in the

public sector and in Washington. Cindy, trained as a social worker, settled into working with Cambodian refugees. Dan, after succumbing briefly to the upheavals of the late 1960s, graduated from college, worked as an advance man in a couple of Illinois campaigns and for Ted Kennedy, then went to work for the Inter-American Development Bank. Fred did well at Exeter and Harvard—at commencement Fran and I sat in the sunlit Harvard Yard and watched him deliver the student speech—and, after his graduate work in history led to a book on Democratic party liberalism, went to work for Mondale, as I have said, and for Geraldine Ferraro and then for New York Governor Mario Cuomo. All three kids have been a great satisfaction to us. When they were growing up, the times were difficult and we were lucky. They avoided the shattering disasters I'd done so much writing about—no violence, no prisons, no real problems. We have friends who to this day don't know where their children are, for in the 1960s they went underground, as the saying went, with some radical student movement.

Fran and I were traveling a good deal during these years. For several years we took to going south in the winter. One year we went to Puerto Rico, another to Key West (mainly to visit the Dick Roveres). And we finally went back to the Dominican Republic. We had long since sold our beach house there—Sosúa was filling up with tourists—and so we rented a house in Cabarete, a remote coastal hamlet. We saw old Dominican friends from Santiago; to avoid Dominican politics we kept out of Santo Domingo. We stayed three or four months, taking with us our cat, named Miss Prettyface, and making her plane reservations when we made our own. (She got us through customs rapidly; everyone was too busy admiring her to pay heed to us. Fran said what a wonderful cover for a CIA agent—to arrive in a country elderly and carrying a cat in a cage.)

But after several years of winters in a Dominican hamlet and long summers at Smith Lake, we realized we had too little time, only two months in the spring and two in the fall, in our old house in Highland Park, with its spacious lawn and its lilacs and honeysuckle, with our books and records, pictures and Ben Shahn drawings, and *things,* familiar things we had accumulated over more than forty years together; and so we took to staying home winters, harsh as the climate is. The climate bothered us little; we simply stayed in the house, arguing with the cat and watching old movies on television,

especially W. C. Fields, Laurel and Hardy, and *Casablanca.* And it was nice to live in the Chicago milieu. I was heartened to observe that Chicagoans had lost none of their side-of-the-mouth humor. When jogging became a national craze, the Chicago saying was "The only trouble with jogging is, you can't hit anybody." And when the Cubs, playing on the distant shores of San Diego in 1984, seemed—and were—on the verge of kicking away their first chance in nearly forty years at winning the National League championship, one of their loyal long-suffering fans said, watching it on TV in a bar across the street from Wrigley Field, "The goddam Cubs—they oughta name a disease after 'um."

Smith Lake became increasingly important to us. After we had spent several full summers there and found that the place worked, we sold the old camp at Three Lakes and moved to Smith Lake for good. For several months a year, we'd rather be there than any other place on earth. No television, no telephone, once a week to town for mail. We made improvements—built a big screened porch onto the camp, built a log sauna, built a separate guest house that also contained a carpentry shop for me and a room for me to write in. The great addition was the porch. We cantilevered it out over the cliff beyond the camp among the high pines, almost overhanging the lake, and there, when I am not fishing or writing, we sit together and stare out at the loons on the lake. One day we watched a moose swim the length of the lake. Once a doe with two fawns came and nuzzled against the screen wire. A fierce mink chased our cat. Once a bear came to the porch; Fran and Dan chased it away; it returned; they chased it again; and when it came back a third time Dan shot it. Fran kept saying, "If I sit here on this porch long enough and stare at the lake and the trees, some day I'm going to see an eagle in the tallest pine near camp," and one day she did.

8.

Once more the little personal things mattered, not great affairs of state or writing to improve society. Things like sitting on the porch and seeing an eagle, an unexpected call from an old friend, Miss Pretyface's digestion, her devotion too, and the scilla suddenly ablaze in spring. Too bad, though, how many of the little things are irritating—unctuous doctors and imperious nurses, "new improved"

plastic packaging that cannot be opened, incomprehensible Medicare forms, putting up with a cowboy taxi driver because you can no longer see well enough to drive, forgetting. You resist too allowing nothing to matter but health and money. And the magnification of disaster—what would not long ago have been only a serious concern, like your wife's surgery, becomes a consuming, paralyzing nightmare.

I have always been greatly bothered by Leon Trotsky's death. Not that he was murdered but the manner in which he was murdered—a man crept up behind him while he was writing at his desk and drove an ice pick into his brain. That brain—it had learned so much, remembered so much. Shattered, destroyed, in one instant. Now somebody would have to learn all that over again. I've said earlier that any elderly man retired from public life, observing his young successor's moves, wants to shout out, "Don't take that road; we almost took it, and it leads to the precipice." Yet if all the old men lived forever they would go on making the same mistakes that have produced the muddle we're in now. Well, so far I've been lucky: I can read. And so I've been writing, and, chance permitting, I intend to write till I drop.

My writing, however, has taken a perilous course. Many years ago, when I began my freelance career, I wrote on speculation; but I quickly learned to write magazine pieces only on assignment and books only on contract. When you write for a living, you cannot afford to write on speculation. But now, blessed with an income first from teaching then from retirement, I was ending as I had begun—I wrote on speculation. It is liberating—you can write whatever you wish. But it is dangerous—the writing itself can become undisciplined and even self-indulgent.

I first wrote a book about Smith Lake and called it *Sometimes in the Summer*. (The title comes from a line out of an early book by my Michigan writer friend John Voelker, one of the loveliest English sentences I ever read: "Sometimes in the Summer in the nighttime, when there was a moon there was a mist, so that the fields looked like a lake.") Never have I rewritten a manuscript so many times, changing not mere sentences but the whole concept. Having nearly always avoided writing in the first person, I found doing so ex-

tremely difficult, the hardest writing I ever did (till now). When I finally got it the way I wanted it, I loved it. Publishers hated it, and it remains unpublished. I still think it one of the best pieces of writing I have ever done. But, then, ever since my first book, I've had trouble writing about, or getting people to read about, Upper Michigan. In that respect, it resembles the old saying about Latin America—the people of the United States will do anything for Latin America except read about it.

Having finished *Sometimes in the Summer,* I turned next to something I had secretly wanted to do all my life: write a novel. I had never been able to afford the luxury of trying. Now I did. For some years I had been bothered by political television and poll taking. But I didn't see a factual piece in it—once you've said, "Television and poll taking are corrupting American democracy," there is little more to say. (John Voelker once conceived a short story entitled "Lost All Night Alone in a Swamp with a Bear," then realized he'd told the whole story in the title.) It occurred to me, however, that one could take the television-polling theme and elaborate it through the characters of a novel. So I wrote a novel. To feel comfortable in attempting it, I made the work as close as possible to writing heavy fact (as, earlier, I had done in writing a screen treatment for a movie). I wrote an outline of the plot—a U.S. senator from Illinois running for reelection sees his campaign faltering and brings in a Washington television consultant, and the television consultant, taking over the campaign, bribes the leading TV poll taker to predict a landslide victory for the senator, thereby shutting off his opponent's campaign contributions; exposure of the bribery causes the senator's downfall. I invented characters—the senator, his frigid wife, his loyal chief of staff who hates television, the chief of staff's wife and a beautiful girl TV reporter with whom he has an affair, the TV consultant as villain, the professional poll taker. I sketched a biography of each. I constructed a detailed campaign schedule and wrote notes about places—the uproarious campaign headquarters, rallies, a TV studio, the campaign plane, and so on. Only then did I start writing the rough draft.

I had always known that magazines like the *Post* used up a great amount of material—about eight pieces of heavy fact a week, fifty-two weeks a year. And that television chewed up even more. What I

had not known was how much material a novel chews up. Into this novel I put pieces of a score of people I'd known plus more that I invented in order to make a handful of characters. Into it I put a dozen political campaigns. Into it I put a lifetime of living. It was all packed down—a novel deals in essences. When I finished, I thought I could never write another novel—I'd put into this one everything I knew.

Doubleday published it with a terrible title, *The Televising of Heller.* Arthur Schlesinger and Ken Galbraith liked it and gave it great jacket blurbs. (Ken told me privately as a joke that Arthur was miffed because both Ken and I had now written novels but Arthur hadn't.) John Houseman took it to CBS and proposed a movie, and CBS concurred, and Houseman bought an option on the screen rights and was ready to go into production. CBS at that time fed scripts it was considering into a computer, and if the computer declared that the show would get a low audience rating, CBS turned it down. The computer hated *Heller;* CBS dropped it. The final irony—a computer bars from TV a novel denouncing poll taking and TV.

Thus encouraged, I started another novel, an autobiographical one called *Farewell to Indianapolis;* but it kept sounding like Eugene O'Neill's *Long Day's Journey into Night* or Thomas Wolfe's *Look Homeward, Angel,* and after a time I put it aside and started a third novel. This one, it will come as no surprise, was about an ambassador to a small Caribbean country; I called it *Your Excellency,* and my agent Dorothy Olding submitted a rough draft, and publisher after publisher turned it down. But writing it and *Farewell to Indianapolis* made me realize what I really wanted to do: write my memoirs. And so I have. On speculation.

ACKNOWLEDGMENTS

As Maureen Stapleton said when she won an Academy Award, "I wish to thank everybody I have known in my entire life."